An Unfinished Woman

A Novel by
Michelle Horwitz

PublishAmerica
Baltimore

First printing

ISBN: 1-60610-496-9
PUBLISHED BY PUBLISHAMERICA, LLLP
www.publishamerica.com
Baltimore

Printed in the United States of America

Dedication

For my mother Susan and my grandma Sonia
in whose enduring memory and undeniable presence
I am convinced there is something *more*—
something profound and compelling that transcends the rational universe
and exists mysteriously *beyond* The Moment.

For my precious sister Carol
in whose treasured company The Moment has always been enough—
each one a gift more meaningful and sacred to me than the last.

And for Sherry, *especially* Sherry—my sustenance and my beloved—
in whose eyes and arms The Moment is all that has ever mattered
and all that ever will.

Acknowledgment

However compromised by personal inadequacies—
however diminished by quiet regrets—
if I have managed to live correctly
those to whom I am eternally grateful
have long been sure of their place on this page.
For the indelible impression each of your lives has had on mine,
your names, in my heart, are permanently inscribed.

Sadder than what will be lost in a woman's lifetime
is what will go unclaimed.

Chapter 1
Amherst, Massachusetts
June 28, 1985

Dreams die hard. In the romantic and vibrantly spirited version of herself—one she no longer recognized without painfully deep reflection—Beth Garrison would have sworn it was the fragrant dew and fervent chirping of summertime birds that drew her out of sleep into the translucent blue wash of early morning as it spread like liquid across the bedroom walls, furniture, between her fingers and deep into the creases of the cotton bed sheet that wound loosely around her body. It was a color so familiar she didn't have to check the alarm clock just beyond the rise of her husband's bare chest to know it was somewhere between five and six AM—the hour of nature's *own* reluctance when night turns in its own semi-conscious sleep—not quite ready to accept the responsibility of its own light—but resigned to the course of its faithful duty, goes forward anyway, giving the world yet another day. It was an hour the forty-six year old housewife knew well, having not managed to sleep past it—or her own denial—for longer than she cared to remember. And in matters of unquestioned loyalties it was a sense of reluctance she secretly shared. This morning, like all the others since her son Danny had died, Beth knew that it was neither sweet sounds nor deep fragrances—only the annoying sensation of a full bladder—that awakened her senses to this new day. It was just that inane and just that unenchanting. Certainly not the stuff poetry was made of and certainly not what the younger Beth Garrison would ever have imagined for herself years ago. The saddest part, she realized, was that she'd come to accept the terms of this hour and this day as the terms of her whole life. She tossed aside the bed sheet managing to free her legs—if not her disappointed heart. By now, accustomed to the burden of such a lackluster start, she rose and shuffled off to the bathroom. There she would once again perform the daily ritual of reconciling the *Beth that might have been* with the Beth that she'd become.

Not that the outside world would have guessed any of this. The Beth Garrison they all knew possessed the interchangeable persona of the Good Fairy and a good shrink—depending upon who needed what, when. In extreme cases, she'd actually managed to pull off being both at the same time. In a style all her own Beth offered all the security of 911, all the assistance of the American Red Cross and all the comfort of a perfectly timed Hallmark Card—the kind that always arrives just when you need it the most and always says just what you need it to say. At times there seemed to be no end to the lengths she would go. Someone only had to ask—and someone always did!

That's not to say that folks weren't aware of her pain. After all, it had only been three years since the tragic loss of her older son just days after his high school graduation. But after awhile—as short a while as possible—most simply preferred to ignore it. It was just a case of human nature at its shallow best—especially glaring if you made being insensitive as convenient for everyone to be as Beth did. No matter how she was feeling, she never gave you reason to think you might be imposing. Hers was the heart that always listened, the smile that always lifted and the touch that always lingered—safely apart from her own despair. Besides, it really didn't matter to others what the truth was… whether the *real* Beth was all of those wonderful things or none of them. It had no bearing whatsoever on their day whether or not she still rejoiced in the early morning concert of summertime birds or that most mornings she had to fight the dead weight of her own heart just to get herself out of bed. What mattered was that Beth was always Beth by the time everyone needed her to be, and somehow, she never failed anyone. Assuming of course, she never counted herself.

Like so many other mornings, Beth chose to linger in the bathroom. There, she'd sit staring at the same crack that for years had drawn her eye to one particular floor tile, and in a transcendental-like gaze, confess to it all the silent longings of her soul. In its quiet acceptance, that little ceramic square provided for Beth all the response she needed. She did wonder at times how many people would still rely on her like they did if they knew she confided in a one-inch floor tile each morning. Still, Beth would never really consider betraying the depth of her affection for her own quirkiness by trivializing it. Truth was, more than any other quality about herself, she treasured her quirkiness. She delighted in it and, in recent years, often clung to it in desperation. Intuitively Beth knew this odd eccentricity was actually the very core of her stability and sanity. It was, over and over again, the only thing she could really count on in herself to hold it all together. Like the last portion of an image that remained of an old tattered photo, it became for her a small piece of herself she could still recognize—a faded but tangible confirmation of her younger, more spirited self and she would fight to the death anyone who dared try and take it away.

Her husband, a considerably more straight-laced individual by nature as well as by choice, learned this about Beth early in their marriage. Despite his initial half-hearted attempts to change her, *the renowned Dr. Bennett P. Garrison*—as Beth would playfully call him whenever he took himself a bit too seriously—eventually came to accept much of his wife's idiosyncrasies and, on this particular morning, with only a few hours until his flight, found himself swollen with memories of their charm. Beth had no idea how long she'd been sitting there trying to hold the real and imagined consequences of all her thoughts at bay, when from their bed Ben's voice broke their charge and rescued her from the obscurity of their attack.

"Beth?"

"In here."

"It's so early. Are you okay?"

"I'm not sure I know what that means anymore."

Her response was laced with too many *issues* to wrestle with first thing in the morning—especially *this* morning. He chose to ignore it completely.

"What have you been doing in there all this time?"

Beth appeared in the doorway of the bathroom assuming the awkward pose of a child caught playing an embarrassingly silly game of make believe. Ben just shook his head and smiled.

"Let me guess. You've been talking to your friend Tyler."

Years ago he'd caught her in a one way conversation with the broken tile, and finding it surprisingly amusing, had asked to be formally introduced. Explaining that she had never given it a name, Beth recalled now, with deep affection, how Ben spontaneously got down on one knee and tapped the tile three times with the end of the toilet bowl plunger.

"Then I now dub thee 'Tyler Garrison The 1st'." Ben had paused, turned and looked up at her. "He is the 1st, isn't he? Or should I fear there've been others?"

"God," she thought, looking at him now and remembering that silly, tender moment, "why can't I just appreciate this man and let that be enough?" He was, after all, everyone else's idea of the perfect husband. It was no wonder that so often Beth felt ungrateful for still needing something more. It was a yearning so deep, so vague she couldn't explain it to herself, let alone to him. Understandably hurt, at times Ben took sweet pleasure in the pain of her unspoken guilt, but in his heart that truly loved her he could never bring himself to hate his wife for her unanswered longings.

Just a few feet apart, their eyes locked in a sadness Ben could read from a thousand miles away. Over the years he had grown quite sure of her affection—but equally sure that for her, that affection would never be enough. Against the weight of that sadness, he extended his arm.

"We've still got some time. Come back to bed so I can hold you."

Once more Beth crossed their room in the direction of this familiar sanctuary—a sanctuary that had for so many years made it too easy for her to hide from her unmet yearnings. Halfway to safety her eyes caught the stark reality of her husband's suitcases beside the door. Instantly the stabbing recognition of a summer apart slammed viciously against her chest, her head, her stomach like a cold steel pinball racking up points for each wave of panic it sent ripping through her body. Beth forced herself to turn and continued toward him, for the moment finding relief that even on this morning, Ben's warmth and affection still remained. Grateful, she crawled back into the welcoming fold of his arm, remembering a time when she would have let this comfort be enough. Guided by endearment and a silent coding that only comes with time, their arms and legs wound naturally around each other like a pair of old, familiar vines that long ago took root beside each other and began their climb against the same wall. Over the years, their touching drew further and further back from the edge of arousal so that these fragile moments of companionship could remain safe from the perils of a more demanding sexual intimacy—an intimacy they no longer shared. Resigned to these unspoken terms, they had both stopped asking for what the other found impossible to give. Each too wounded to risk seeing only more disappointment in the other's eyes, they came to lie in this agreeable position of easy warmth and mutual forgiveness—free of expectation or blame. Now content to be silent in each other's arms, Beth recalled how in the early years of their sexual withdrawal she'd persisted in engaging him in exhaustive examination and endless dialogue, hoping that their ability to communicate *verbally* would somehow alternatively validate their union. Ben had tried to accommodate her and for a while she felt relieved that their marriage would survive. But in their shift from making love to making words, something comfortable between them died. Where once in their coming together neither could have explained the essence of what they shared, thanks to the cruel rewards of 'a meaningful relationship', they could now discuss, in painful detail, all that was no longer theirs. It was one of life's true ironies; how empty and broken their accomplishment had left them, and on this morning especially, Beth had to hope that one day the odd pieces left between them would somehow fit together in a way that would make the pain of their wounded history worthwhile. With his cheek resting against her hair, Ben ran his hand up and down the length of his wife's bare arm as it lay draped across his chest.

"Beth… Beth… Beth…"

Each time he repeated her name she felt the thickness of his emotion. Feeling responsible, she accepted it willingly and completely—absorbing it through every pore until she sensed that he was relieved of his melancholy. Aching for him and with him, Beth eased herself out of his embrace and lifted herself onto one elbow so that she could look directly into his eyes. Her voice was soft and kind and full of apology.

"I think I love you most when your eyebrows are still creased from sleep."

Beth wet her finger and tried to smooth them out. She would have settled for a quiet smile in reply, but his eyes could only reflect a thousand unfinished conversations.

"Honey please, change your mind and come with me. Adam leaves for camp in a few days. You could meet me in London by the end of the week. You'll see, it'll be wonderful… just the two of us… a summer abroad, exploring the English countryside." He hesitated. "It'll be three years since Danny's gone. You need to get away from here Beth, can't you see that?"

Before he could go any further, she cut him off—her voice hardened out of necessity.

"Ben, please. Don't do this to me. Not this morning. We've been over this a thousand times. You said you understood."

Ben wavered between resentment and resignation.

"Well, I do… and I don't. Explain it to me again."

Beth pulled away slightly—a sign of gentle warning not to pursue this issue any further.

"Well, sorry. I can… and I can't."

"Very funny" Ben said, only half accepting of her answer.

"But very true!" she added deliberately, making the resolution final for both of them. Lately she'd been doing a lot of that. Not because she was any surer of those resolutions than he, but because it was *her* life that so desperately depended on them.

Ben knew when he'd hit a wall.

"Shower with me this morning."

His request caught her off guard. Was he initiating sex?

"We haven't showered together in years. Why now?"

He pulled her closer.

"I thought maybe if I lathered you up enough, that monkey you've been carrying around on your back might lose its grip and slip off."

Beth tried to keep things light.

"I get it! You want that monkey for yourself."

Ben took his wife's chin in his hand and turned it up toward him. His eyes were solemn.

"No Beth. I just want you."

For a moment, she was silent.

"I can't imagine why, anymore."

"*Why* is the easy part… because I love you. It's *how* that I wrestle with. *How* can I help you? *How* can I make it better for you?"

"It's not your problem to fix, Ben!"

"You're not a problem Beth… you're my wife… you're the mother of my children… you're so many things to so many people. For God's sake, how can you feel so lost… so alone?"

The veins of his neck pulled forward, straining against the limits of his patience and *real* understanding.

Beth stiffened, this time pulling away completely.

"Stop telling me who I am… to you… to Adam… to the whole goddamn world! You just don't get it, do you? I'm sorry if it hurts you, but that's just not enough anymore. I have no idea where I begin and end for myself!" Her anger wouldn't allow tears. "God, listen to me. I sound so pathetically trite." She shook her head with disgust. "Do you remember when I actually thought I was someone special…that my talent was special…that my dreams were special?"

"I still think you're special, Beth."

He reached for her hand, but she pulled it away.

"Well I don't! And I'm not sure if I ever will again! Right now I'd settle for just feeling alive." Beth stared straight ahead, avoiding the distraction of his eyes. "For years I've felt like I've been slipping away. Sometimes the fading was so gradual from one day to the next that when no one else ever seemed to notice, I thought maybe I was just going crazy." Aware that he was listening to all this with great discomfort, Beth chose not to meet his eyes. "But ever since we lost Danny, I feel like I've been breaking off and disappearing in bigger and bigger pieces. I'm scared to death that if I don't face the little that's still left of me, it won't be long before I don't exist at all." She turned and looked at him. "Do you know that some mornings I'm actually afraid to pass in front of a mirror? I'm terrified there won't be anyone there looking back. I feel like some sort of ghost that desperately needs to make peace with it's own death so it can move on. I feel haunted Ben, in a way I can't begin to explain..."

It was part frustration and part bitterness that propelled Ben up out of bed and intentionally away from her.

"Is that what you're going to be doing here all summer... roaming through these empty rooms alone... like some ghost?"

Beth chose to ignore the disapproving tone in her husband's voice.

"I'd like to think these rooms are not empty... that all the years and all the memories we've made in them count for something. And I won't be alone. I'll have BJ and, I'd like to hope, I'll have myself again... eventually. But yes, to answer your question, that's *exactly* what I'm going to be doing. Do you realize I haven't been alone with myself since we've been married? I don't mean for an afternoon or a weekend! I mean *really* alone—for a long enough time to know what it's like before it's over. I can't imagine how I'll get through the days... or the nights... but I'm determined to find out. I have my volunteer work at the nursing home. Maybe I'll take a summer course at the university. I'm almost afraid to believe I might sit down at the piano and still be able to find middle C." Beth walked over to where her husband had positioned himself, hoping that her touch would soften the isolation he felt. "I know you really don't understand any of this... why I *can't* go with you this summer... why I *won't*. But this is something I *have* to do. Something deep in my guts is telling me to stay here... that my life depends on it. It's that important... and that simple."

As Beth grew more reassured by her own words, Ben grew more upset.

"What exactly am I supposed to tell my parents? They're under the impression that when I accepted the invitation to lecture at Cambridge, naturally you'd be coming with me."

The elderly couple lived abroad. Beth couldn't believe her ears.

"Wait a minute! Are you telling me that you never explained to them that I wasn't coming with you?" She didn't wait for his answer. "No, of course you didn't! You were sure you'd get me to change my mind."

She glared at him in disbelief.

Ben's own eyes were vacant as he looked back at her.

Beth was incensed.

"Well I guess you'll have to explain it now, won't you?"

"I don't know what to tell them."

"How about the truth?"

"They won't understand."

"Why, because you don't?"

Ben's voice grew hostile under her attack.

"I'd tell them the God damned truth if I knew what the hell that was! And then whose truth would that be, Beth? Yours? Mine? The tile's? The ghosts?"

Even understanding his pain, Beth refused to accept the sting of his sarcasm.

"Well maybe I'll have that answer for you by the time you get back. God knows I can't go on like this!"

The sharp buzz of the alarm clock suddenly pierced their escalating tension. Ben leaned across the bed and slammed his fist against the button, grateful that it provided an immediate target for his frustration.

"Yeah, well I can't go on like this either!"

Reading his mind—and his heart—Beth sat down beside him. She placed her hand on his lap and stared at the clock.

"Don't you wish everything in life was so easy to turn off?"

Ben refused to look at her. It simply hurt too much.

"It's seven o'clock. We should get going. Do you want to shower first or should I?"

Beth did her part to help them move on.

"You go ahead. I'll get Adam up and flip on the coffee."

Deliberately avoiding Beth's eyes, Ben patted his wife's hand, then got up and headed for the bathroom. This day had barely begun and already Beth was emotionally drained. Eventually she stood up, slipped out of her nightgown and into an old tank top and shorts. For a split second Beth was tempted to undress and give into Ben's request—hopping in the shower to lighten his mood. But when she tried, she found she could only move in the direction of the bedroom door. This time she wasn't fighting her instincts. After all, they were the only things she could count on to get her through this summer. She might as well start now.

Beth stood in front of her son's door and knocked until she heard BJ's bark and Adam's predictable whine.

"Go away! This is child abuse."

"Sorry kid, rise and shine. We've got to get dad to the airport by ten. That's just a little more than an hour."

Adam moaned from his bed.

"Wake me in forty-five minutes and I'll still be ready before you."

"I want us all to have breakfast together."

Adam made a few more sounds of obligatory teenage angst before finally giving in.

"You owe me big time for this!"

Mocking his dramatics, Beth leaned against his door and clasped her hands against her chest.

"Oh thank you. Thank you for granting your impossible mother such a foolish and sentimental request."

Without waiting for his response, she continued down the hall smiling, knowing that under his blanket Adam was surely smiling too. It consoled her to know she still had that effect on *somebody*. In the glow of that small triumph, Beth returned to her own bedroom before going downstairs. Ben was still in the bathroom, out of the shower and shaving. She came closer and stood beside him. Neither of them ready for direct eye contact, they spoke to each other through the two people reflected in the mirror. Looking into it, Beth leaned her head against her husband's bare shoulder. For a moment he didn't react, testing her willingness to remain vulnerable in the face of his possible rejection. Still wounded, Ben couldn't resist hitting her with her own words. It was his last halfhearted blow before his own pain receded into kindness. He let himself smile back at her.

"Well, *I* see you. The question is do *you* see you?"

"Very funny Professor Garrison." Beth shoved him playfully in the arm. "When you get behind that podium this summer, stay away from comedy."

This time the couple smiled directly into each other's eyes. Beth took her finger and smeared some of his shaving cream across the tip of his nose.

"What can I make you for breakfast?"

"I'll have 'the good old days' on anything you've got."

She sighed.

"Will you settle for imitation butter?"

"Why not? Anything 'make believe' would be a lot easier to digest these days."

Beth understood all too well.

As she turned, he reached for her hand.

"Whatever you throw together will be fine. You never disappoint me."

She knew he meant well.

"God, if only that were true…"

Caught between wishing it was—and knowing it wasn't—he ignored the difference between the two.

"Beth, I really *do* love you. I'm sorry if that makes all this more complicated for you, but it's true."

"I'm fine with your truth, Ben... and oh how I wish our truths were transferable... but unfortunately they're not. So I'm stuck having to find my own."

He nodded reluctantly.

"I'll miss you these next two months."

"Dear, sweet Ben... you've been 'missing me' for years. We both have. I just hope I can do something about that... starting with this summer."

She was halfway down the hall when Ben called after her.

"For a ghost, you still have a pretty terrific ass."

Beth held up her index finger and twirled it around in the air.

"Whoopee! What a relief to know there's a part of me I won't have to work hard to get back."

Just as she passed Adam's door it flung open and BJ, the family's Golden Retriever came bounding out. His was much more a reception than she got from her son, who leaned against the frame of the doorway, his face expressing all the burdens of the world placed unfairly upon his young shoulders. Beth stroked the boy's cheek and mimicked his pout.

"What... only a lick from BJ this morning?"

"Don't push it mom."

"I wouldn't think of it. C'mon, you can escort me down to the kitchen for this momentous family occasion." Beth locked her arm around his, coercing a reluctant smile while the loyal animal followed close behind.

Once downstairs Beth was determined not to let on just how difficult this morning had already been. Though Adam sensed the real truth he chose to play along. If his mother wanted to pretend that this morning's breakfast was more a celebration than a distraction from the painful parting it was, he would let her. He'd even help her pull it off. Deep beneath his age appropriate rebellion, Adam felt a real closeness and protectiveness toward his mother—this unusual centerpiece of family tradition that he'd come to value on his own terms. Out of all of his friends, Adam knew of no other mother quite like his and when he wasn't too threatened or embarrassed by her unresolved passion for life, he actually appreciated that she was as unconventional in spirit as she was. That, and the fact that without her he knew he never would have gotten past his brother's death. But that was an appreciation so deep and so silent it would take years of manhood to repay. Manhood that had not yet ripened, but in the complex demands of this particular morning, grew quietly closer towards the fullness of its potential.

Adam collapsed at the kitchen table. Heavily invested in his pretense of exhaustion, only his eyes moved as he watched his mother. He was in awe of her fluid-like movement; maneuvering from one kitchen appliance to another—deftly orchestrating the juicer, the coffee maker, the toaster and the microwave into a symphony of mechanical sounds that, under her expert conduction, somehow became breakfast. All of this without once stepping on BJ who had managed to plant himself most inconveniently on a small patch of kitchen floor warmed by the morning sun. Beth was well unaware of her son's lazy scrutiny.

"Would it be asking too much for you to set the table?"

"Actually, it would."

Over the years, motherhood taught her the perfect balance between request and command.

"I'd appreciate it if you did it anyway."

Over the same years, her son had learned to interpret, unquestionably, when she meant which. In this case, her tone left little doubt. Adam lifted himself from the table and shuffled over to the closet. BJ rose and moved out of his way quickly, taking no chances that the boy's footwork would be as considerate as Beth's. Adam swung open the door to the pantry and stared into it blankly, like he'd never seen its contents before.

"What do we need?"

Beth's expression bordered on impatience.

"For heaven's sake Adam, is this your first breakfast here on earth? We need plates, juice glasses, mugs, utensils and napkins. And if it won't short circuit the wiring in your brain to tackle the fridge… that's the big white thing over there against the wall… we need the margarine, the jelly, the OJ and the milk."

Adam made a begrudging face.

"As you wish, Earth Mother."

Her son's impersonation of a robot amused Beth as he hammed it up with mechanically precise movements, exaggerating every bend and turn until everything was set out just as she ordered. When he'd finished, he froze into a mechanical-like smile and waited for her approval.

She obliged

"Good work my little alien . Now, would you care to join us for breakfast here on earth or do you have to return to your planet immediately?"

Before he could answer, they both burst out laughing. Beth relished these moments and Adam felt equally pleased that he could lead his mother to this place of playful safety. But this particular time his relief was short lived. Beth suddenly grew eerily still. Her smile faded into something threateningly distant. Her voice was now smaller.

"Dad should be down in a few minutes."

Her words seemed to lead nowhere. Adam stood cautiously by as his mother stared blankly at the table that just moments ago brought such giddy delight. Attempting to preserve what little remained of his mother's delicate balance and not knowing what else to say, he focused on where they'd left off—the table setting.

"Look's like the only things we're missing are party hats and blowers."

As if magically restored, Beth's eyes once again began to twinkle. It was a spark that Adam and his brother had learned early in their childhood to prepare for with equal amounts of misgiving and thrill. It usually meant that their mother was up to something wildly spontaneous.

"Oh Adam, thank you, honey. You just gave me the most wonderful idea!"

Without saying another word, she grabbed the stepladder and set it down in front of the cabinet above the refrigerator. She climbed up and began rifling through the shelves. With her head burrowed deep between the opened doors, Beth's muffled humming exuded unmistakable joy.

"Honey, take this from me, will you?"

Adam reluctantly held out his hands into which Beth placed an old cardboard box held together with pieced of yellowed Scotch tape on all four corners. The words 'misc. cake/party decorations' were written on one side. Adam moaned.

"Forget it! There's no way I'm wearing some stupid party hat while we eat breakfast."

Beth took his lack of enthusiasm in stride.

"Don't worry, sweetheart… that's not what I had in mind."

"I'm afraid to know what is."

"You'll see…"

Suddenly Adam began to feel the strain of 'guarding' his mother alone.

"What's taking Dad so long to get down here?"

Climbing down off the ladder, Beth ignored her son's uneasiness.

"Actually, I'm glad he's still upstairs. I want this to be a surprise."

She placed the box on the counter and carefully removed the lid as though exposing a sacred family heirloom. Adam couldn't help notice that for a moment his mother's breathing seemed to stop as her eyes fixed on its contents. Beth reached inside almost as if in slow motion. Everything she touched spun a kaleidoscope of memories. Colorful fragments of one celebration blended, bended and broke off into pieces of the next; Adam's first birthday, their tenth anniversary, a New Year's Eve get-together, Danny's graduation. It took all the willpower Beth had not to pick up and caress each and every plastic cake topper; a clown, a cowboy, an Easter bunny, a graduate. She stoically refrained from straightening the bent corners of each cardboard letter in a string of assorted banners. Guided by her sense of purpose, Beth fought back waves of sentimentality and managed to collect three wax candles and three plastic candle holders. She put them off to the side and replaced the lid as lovingly as she'd removed it, letting her hand rest upon it until her heart began to break beneath the crushing weight of its own restrain. Determined not to cry, she quickly turned and reached across to the other end of the counter, picking up the plate of assorted muffins. She held them out to her son and forced a smile.

"Pick one."

Adam knew better than to try and wrestle down her renewed enthusiasm, but he couldn't resist rolling his eyes as he chose. Beth approved his selection.

"Blueberry, good choice. Now dad should have the bran… traveling always constipates him"

Adam looked grossly put out.

Beth simply met his disgust with matter of fact wit.

"I know your generation is fond of saying 'shit happens', but trust me, when you reach a certain age sometimes it needs a little help. I'll have a corn muffin."

Adam watched as his mother lit a match and melted the base of each candle into a candleholder, then mounted each of the candleholders on top of the 3 muffins and placed each one on its respective plate. Beth had stepped back from the table to rejoice in the quiet glory of her inspiration when Ben appeared in the doorway behind her. BJ slapped his tail against the floor.

Adam's expression showed relief.

Ben winked at him from behind his wife's shoulder.

"Hmmm… coffee smells great."

For a split second the familiar texture of her husband's voice added to the joy Beth had managed to find in the pleasure of her special table setting, but when she turned around, the stark reality of his suitcases—one in each hand—immediately renewed her turmoil. Ben reacted quickly.

"I'll just put these in the car. Be right back."

He returned a moment later and caught his first glimpse of the unexpected breakfast setting.

"Adam gave me a great idea."

"Hey, don't put this on me" he insisted.

Beth grew quietly sentimental.

"Before we have our last breakfast together I thought it would be nice if we all closed our eyes and made a wish for whatever it is we're each hoping this summer will bring us."

Adam just remained expressionless until his father kicked him under the table. The sudden jolt evoked a cardboard smile that barely concealed the pain behind it. None the less, Beth accepted it graciously. Ben patted her shoulder.

"That's an awfully sweet idea, honey. Go get the matches son."

Ben read the quiet appreciation in Beth's smile. He took the matches from Adam and handed them to his wife with all the kindness she had grown to love him for.

"Here sweetheart, you deserve to do the honors."

Though his voice was considerate and reassuring, as Beth reached out to take the matches her hand began to tremble. Had Ben not been so quick to her rescue, in another moment she'd have fallen completely apart right there in front of both of them.

"Here, let me help you."

Ben picked up each of the three muffins his wife had so thoughtfully decorated and, one by one, held them out for her to light. He did this with all the compassion and tenderness of heart that one could bestow upon another, and for that she thanked him eternally with her eyes. Watching his parents in this sacred exchange, Adam himself grew genuinely solemn. Though at thirteen he had no real vocabulary yet to describe what he was seeing, somewhere deep inside he understood that he was witnessing one of life's most profound lessons: that loving may never be whole in its success, but in its quietest displays of affection, it is most perfectly complete. The only way he knew to honor the sanctity of this moment was to keep himself respectfully outside his parent's intimacy. He did this by remaining absolutely still while his mother lit each of the candles, after which his father kissed her gently on the cheek. Somewhat calmed, Beth smiled and suggested they close their eyes and join hands as each made a private wish. Whatever they were each thinking, father and son closed their eyes. Except for their breathing, the room became still. For Beth it was a stillness molded of shapeless uncertainty—in the moment—in the future—in the wish itself. As if reading her mind, Ben squeezed her hand just a little tighter hoping to reassure her that his love would always be constant—that he would somehow always be there—throughout this summer apart and throughout the rest of their lives—no matter what. Instead of soothing her, his silent gesture made Beth's heart ache all the more and she burst into sobs. Simultaneously, Adam and Ben opened their eyes. Beth's apology fit between her tears.

"I'm so sorry. I wanted this to be a happy celebration of summer. I asked you both to indulge me in this ridiculous little ceremony and then I went and ruined it."

Ben wouldn't let her continue.

"You haven't ruined anything, sweetheart. The ceremony is a great idea, so c'mon'... at the count of three, let's all blow out our candles. One, two, three!"

Too weakened to challenge her husband's initiative, Beth joined them in blowing and for a brief moment actually felt a bit of relief. But the distinct smell of extinguished wicks and melting wax brought on the stabbing recognition of all the family celebrations gone by. The rush of memories only added to Beth's already over-burdened heart. She dabbed her eyes with her napkin and stood up.

"I'm not very hungry after all. I'm going up to shower and get ready."

By now her pain had become so raw that even BJ, who until then seemed to be paying more attention to the path of a fly traveling across the screen door, instinctively rose to accompany her upstairs. With nothing more he could do to make her feel any better, Ben reached out and caught his wife's arm as she passed.

"Beth, I love you."

"*We* love you mom," Adam blurted out.

Beth was sure they really meant it.

"I know. I love you guys too."

Neither of them moved a muscle or spoke a word until they heard the shower running upstairs. With his mother safely out of earshot, Adam pushed his chair back from the table. Finally able to let his guard down, his body went limp.

"Man, what was that all about?"

Ben tried to conceal his own strain.

"This is an extremely hard day for your mother."

"Yeah, I kinda' got that part."

Ben realized his son's eyes reflected a much deeper confusion. He got up, poured himself a fresh cup of coffee and came back to the table.

"You know, staying home this summer wasn't an easy decision for her."

"But I thought that's what she wanted."

Ben took a labored breath.

"It was. It still is. Trust me, I tested it as recently as this morning. Caught hell for it too. But that doesn't mean it's gonna' be easy for her. It'll be quite an adjustment being here all by herself."

"Then why is she doing it?"

"I'm afraid you'd have to be able to break the code of your mother's private wish to know the answer to that one."

Ben weighed the appropriateness of sharing more. He said it anyway.

"Frankly, I think your mother feels safer being miserable than being happy. Ever since your brother died, happiness has become too fragile. Misery doesn't break."

Adam shook his head, his face registering a thorough mistrust of any logic having to do with life after 30. Ben quickly realized the futility in trying to make him understand. There was no point in burdening him with anything more.

"Look, there's no need for you to worry about any of this, but I do want you to make me a promise."

"For a price, anything!"

"I'm serious about this, Adam." Ben hesitated for a moment, listening to make sure he still heard the shower going. "Your mother would kill me if she heard me say this, but I want you to be more attentive than usual this summer. I know you'll be leaving for camp in a few days, but for God's sake, don't make her feel that once you get on that bus you've forgotten all about her. Drop her a few post cards… maybe even a letter. Call her… and not just when you *need* something. I'll do what I can from England, but you're going to be a lot closer."

"Oh man! A letter!"

Adam waited for his father's smile, but it didn't come. He was stone serious. In all of this 'father-son talk', that much the boy grasped with finite clarity.

"Look Adam, she's always been there for you… for your brother… for all of us. I'm counting on you to be there for her now. I don't want her to feel deserted. In a few weeks it'll be three years since Danny's accident." Ben shook his head. "God, three years!"

Adam looked hurt.

"Thanks a lot dad. Like I could forget. He was *my* brother, you know."

Ben didn't mean to be insensitive.

"I'm sorry, son. I know how much you miss him."

"Yeah well, life goes on. Isn't that what you grown-ups say?"

Ben struggled with his own sense of defeat.

"That's the rhetoric. We don't know how or why ourselves." He searched his son's eyes. "So, can I count on you?"

"Don't worry, I won't let you down."

"Thanks. That makes me feel a little better and the truth is not much does these days."

Adam noticed his dad hadn't touched his muffin yet. Now feeling responsible for his father's well being too, the boy camouflaged his own very real concern.

"You better eat that thing. Mom says you don't crap when you travel."

Ben smiled, laying the thinnest veil over his sadness. Reminded of the many levels of intimacy he shared with his wife throughout the years, now it was Ben's heart that again began to ache.

"I suppose that's true."

He picked up his muffin and slowly turned it around in the palm of his hand so he could study it from every angle. Adam looked at the clock. He took the muffin from his father's hand, removed the candle and set it back down on his plate.

"Eat… or I won't write those letters."

Ben noted the not so subtle role reversal. Adam waited until the muffin was half gone.

"What about you, dad? How are you feeling about this summer?"

Ben looked his son dead in the eye.

"My plane leaves in two hours… don't get me started!"

Surprisingly, Adam dug for more.

"Are you excited about lecturing at Cambridge?"

"When I think about it, I sure am. It was quite an honor to be asked."

"You must really be 'somebody', huh dad?"

Ben was amused at how nonchalant both his sons had always been about the extent of his professional accomplishments.

"Well, it's a good thing you're not standing up there and lecturing in your shorts 'cause you've got the nastiest pair of legs in the family!"

"Thanks for the reality check son. I'll be sure to keep my pants on."

Adam chomped on his muffin.

"Now mom on the other hand…"

The boy's remark caught Ben off-guard.

"Since when did you start admiring your mother's legs?"

"Not *me*! That would be really twisted. Let's just say the guys don't like hangin' out here in the warm weather for mom's cheese whiz and lemonade."

Ben appreciated his son's sense of humor.

"I see. Anybody in particular I should be worried about while I'm away?"

Adam folded his arms

"If ya' really want to know, the guy I'd watch out for is one of *your* buddies, not mine!"

Ben leaned forward, questioning his son more seriously with his eyes.

Adam responded matter-of-factly.

"Gimme' a break, dad. Don't tell me you've never seen Nick come on to mom?"

Ben relaxed.

"Ah, he's harmless. He's been flirting with your mother ever since we started at the university together… before you kids were born."

"Doesn't it bug you?"

"Not as long as it doesn't bother your mother. She just thinks he's insecure and always needs to prove himself. You know, immature stuff like that. I hate to admit it, 'cause I really like the guy, but your mother's got his number. I asked a long time ago if she wanted me to say something to him, you know, put him in his place. She was quite clear, that if it ever got to that point, she'd be the one to do it herself. Besides, Nick may be a jerk in that way but he's also been a damn good friend. He was really there for your mother and me after your brother died." He waited a moment to see if Adam had grasped his explanation. "Thanks for the tip though, you know, man to man."

The boy didn't seem entirely convinced that his father was reading the situation accurately.

"Whatever. The word around school is he's had lots of affairs… even one with Miriam's best friend. She found out and that's why their marriage broke up."

Ben didn't comment, but not for lack of the facts. He remembered all too well the consequences of his friend's serial indiscretions. Miriam too had been a close friend for years. She was devastated by the affair, even suicidal for a while. He and Beth were literally caught in the middle and often at odds with one another over issues of loyalty. To this day Beth still hadn't entirely forgiven Nick for Miriam's ongoing bouts of depression.

"What can I say, Adam? 'A friend should bear his friend's infirmities'… William Shakespeare."

Adam wasn't impressed.

"'There goes Nick the dick'... Billy sanders, 3rd period gym." Adam hesitated awkwardly. "The way you were with mom before... ya' know, helping her with the candles and stuff... that was nice. You're a really good guy dad. Not like *him*."

Ben reached across the table and rested his hand appreciatively on Adam's shoulder.

"Thanks. That means a lot... especially this morning. You know how much your mother and I love each other."

Adam nodded.

"I kinda' do." He stared down at the floor. "Dad, when you get back from England...," he struggled to say the words, "are you and mom getting divorced?"

Ben was startled by his young son's question. It was wrought with an insight and sad irony that he himself had only begun to grasp at forty-eight—that two people can actually grow closer and apart at the same time. He drew a deep breath and answered truthfully. Adam's sensitivity deserved that much.

"Not if *my* wish comes true, son. Not if *my* wish comes true."

For a painfully long moment, Adam sat perfectly still, taking in the meaning of his father's reply. Then he looked up and rescued them both from the grip of life's uncertainty.

"Wanna' know what I wished for?"

"Sure."

"That I'd meet a really hot babe at camp."

Ben laughed out loud, relieved to have this little father-son talk end on such a normal note.

"I hope so too, kiddo." Ben glanced at his watch. "I'd better get your mother moving if I'm going to make that plane."

He thought about going upstairs but knew that would be a mistake. The idea was to get closer to the front door and eventually into the car. Instead, Ben called up to his wife from the bottom of the hall stairs.

"Hon, how are you doing up there?"

His voice startled her.

"I'm almost ready."

Distancing herself from everything, somehow Beth managed to shower, wash and blow-dry her hair. She even succeeded in camouflaging the redness around her eyes with a little bit of makeup. She didn't remember doing any of it. It had become too dangerous to actually concentrate on anything. Not the past. Not the future. Not even what to wear. She pulled open a drawer, threw on the most accessible pair of shorts and t-shirt she could find, then checked herself quickly in the mirror. Nervously brushing her hair through one last time, she coached herself out loud.

"Deep breaths, Beth. Take deep breaths. You can do this." She glanced over at BJ who'd been keeping a watchful eye on her all along. "God, what must you be thinking after a morning like this. I'll bet you're not looking forward to being left behind with *me* all summer." She bent down closer, to reassure him. "Don't you worry. We'll get through this together, I promise."

Beth put out her hand. BJ immediately met it with his paw.

Ben called up again.

"Hon... c'mon it's getting late."

Beth straightened up like a soldier coming to attention. She grabbed her bag and turned back to take one last look at her bedroom. It was as though she was the one leaving this morning and, in a strange way, she was right. Beth knew everything familiar would no longer be so. Everyday routines would come undone and everything caged would be set free to come at her when she was least protected. But that was the way she wanted it—the way she knew it *had* to be. The eyes of her heart gravitated to the most sentimental things; her husband's pillow, their wedding picture, a porcelain music box they'd purchased on their honeymoon. She looked upon these things with hungry scrutiny, trying desperately to fill her senses with every detail of their past meaning. She knew when she returned home later to this very same room only the unknown would be there to greet her.

Beth entered the kitchen hesitantly, as if returning to the scene of a gruesome accident. Wincing in the direction of the table, she was relieved that not a trace remained of the collision that took place there earlier between her heart and her head. There was neither a crumb—nor a torn piece of flesh. She looked at her family sheepishly.

"Thanks guys, for cleaning up... *everything.*"

Ben pretended that the worst was behind them.

"We'd better get going. I assume we're taking 'the tank'."

That was the nickname Ben had given his wife's old beat up green Volvo station wagon. It had over fifteen years and 200,000 miles of family errands ground into the heart of its engine. Every time he would suggest buying her a new car she resisted, pledging unconditional loyalty to every dent and scratch on this old family workhorse. If he wanted a shiny, new 4-wheel-drive thing for himself, that was his choice. She and 'the tank' were inseparable.

"Yes, I'd prefer that car."

Ben was obliging.

"The luggage is already in the back… let's go."

Beth's stomach tightened into a nervous spasm. She stopped at the door and squinted, waiting for the next sign from her body. She didn't have to wait long.

"You guys wait in the car. I think I need the bathroom."

Sensing his son's growing reluctance to deal with much more of all this, Ben put his hand on Adam's shoulder and ushered him out toward the car. The boy slid into the back seat. Ben got in behind the wheel. Except for Ben's nervous tapping on the wheel the two sat in complete silence, alternating glances toward the screen door.

Eventually Beth appeared and hurried toward the car.

"I'm glad that didn't hit me after we left but I took two Imodium just in case." She looked at Ben behind the wheel. "I'm driving."

"You're not feeling well."

"I'm perfectly capable of getting you to the airport!"

Adam was a lot less subtle than his father.

"C'mon mom, face it. You've been a nervous wreck all morning! Why can't you just admit it and let dad drive?"

Beth responded with dry humor.

"Just buckle up and have a little faith."

"I *have* faith. But I'd like to have a *future* too!'

Beth took the boy's sarcasm in stride.

"Okay. I admit I was a little shaky back there, but I'm fine now."

Ben looked at his watch. He wasn't entirely convinced but there was no time to argue about it any more. He opened the door, got out and went around to the other side of the car.

Appreciative of Ben's concession, Beth slid in behind the wheel, buckled up and readjusted the mirrors. She turned to her husband.

"Have you got your ticket?"

"I have it Beth."

"And your wallet?"

"Got it."

"Your glasses?"

"Yes, both pairs."

"What about something to chew during take-off?"

Ben's jaw began to tighten.

"I'll pick something up at the airport."

Beth took a deep breath and tried to sound upbeat.

"Okay then. I guess we're off."

Fighting his own tightly managed anxiety, Ben reached over and gently squeezed his wife's shoulder, silently hoping to foster her courage. Beth smiled back appreciatively, then slipped on her sunglasses and turned on the ignition. Knowing his mother could see him clearly in the rear view mirror, Adam mockingly make the sign of the cross against his chest as she put the car in reverse and slowly began backing up. Beth pretended not to notice. Under the circumstances she figured it couldn't hurt to have some greater power along for this particular ride. She rolled to the end of the driveway, then backed out onto the street.

"Well, so far, so good," Beth thought to herself. She knew for sure how to get to the airport and she knew for sure how to get back. Beyond that, Beth Garrison was sure of absolutely nothing.

Chapter 2

As Beth backed out of her driveway, some 60 miles south on I-91 Joanna Cameron threw on her right directional, preparing to turn off at the next exit. In the hours since sunrise she'd managed to put over 150 miles between herself and New York City; each of them marking a painful and deliberate separation from everything in her life that once mattered. Uncertain her determination was enough to outrace her doubt, she had climbed past the speed limit for most of the way—cautiously on the lookout for state police and the slightest reason to turn back. But by some diabolical law of physics that forbade anyone to ever leave their past behind, the faster she sped, the faster came the images in a backward blur of memories and tears. When Joanna's mind finally cleared against the warm summer air, she was left with only a drier sorrow. Checking the rear view mirror, she crossed over the white lines that stretched along the open roadway as far back and ahead as the eye could see. They were like large white basting stitches that held together the seams of her life. Joanna needed desperately to believe that somehow those lines would connect her past with her future. She figured 150 miles was a safe enough distance away from her West Village loft to finally stop for a tank of gas and a place to pee. At least for the moment, both were much more pressing matters than anything else in her life.

Driving slower along the service road, Joanna felt the physical beauty of the area coming back to her. In spite of her stubborn resistance, her senses submitted to the intense natural power of the surroundings. In her gradual surrender, the knot in her neck and across her shoulders began to ease. She took it as a reassuring reminder why three years after her first visit she was returning to the small New England town of Amherst, Massachusetts. *This* time, by choice.

So much of Joanna Cameron's life seemed to have come undone since she'd been sent up there by her agency on a last minute production shoot. She recalled how fiercely she had protested having to change her weekend plans on such short notice. Looking back now, she'd swear it was more than just plain resentment; as if some primal voice deep inside was trying to warn her to protect the boundaries of her life at all costs—sensing that if even one tiny aspect was disrupted, all the other pieces of her well-coordinated existence would no longer fit together. Like an animal threatened, Joanna had fought hard to defend her life, but the promise of being made senior creative director by the end of that year somehow made the prospect of being devoured considerably less gruesome. She'd reasoned that after the promotion she'd just be one step away from becoming a partner and in the largeness of that scheme, her silly irrational fear seemed rather inconsequential. Within twenty-four hours she'd found herself on location: 'Campus Plaza', a typical strip mall with a mega-sized supermarket, a coffee shop and several other retail businesses extending out on either side. Shooting had begun immediately. But a grueling production schedule, killer humidity and a miserably temperamental crew weren't enough to distract her from an unusual and intense connection she felt with the surroundings, especially strange because she'd never been there before. It was not that she welcomed this mysteriously illuminating sense of familiarity. Quite the contrary. No matter how hard she tried she was unable to ignore it. It was nothing that made any sense, but it was enough for her to think that one day she might like to have more time to consider the powerful distraction of those surroundings for it awakened in her an eerie longing that once back in New York she could neither identify nor escape. That was when the reoccurring dream had started and when, in spite of the promotion that came through as promised, Joanna's whole life began to fall apart. Now with everything at stake and so much to sort out, the town of Amherst where it all started to unravel seemed like the necessary place to begin. The problem was, few people loathed *beginnings* as much as Joanna Cameron did.

Even as a child she couldn't wait to get on with things, always leaning forward—always pushing the wind. It was as if some great gun had been fired the moment she was born and from then on she raced everything in sight: neighborhood dogs, a throw to first, the moon, even 'time' itself. She was an extremely intense child who seemed to have come into this world knowing exactly what she wanted from life—like something had once been taken from her and she was determined, at any cost, to get it back. If bypassing childhood was the fastest route, then Joanna was going to take it. It never occurred to her to simply *play* at anything. She wondered why other kids would waste time playing make-believe when you could just set out and make it happen for real. So while others her age were crawling around on the floor ambushing each other with plastic cowboy action figures on horseback, she took herself over to the stables down the road and convinced the stable boy to teach her to ride. When other little girls were busy playing with dollhouses, she preferred to hang out at the construction site with her father, a local contractor, helping his next spec-house go up. And while her brother was spending his whole allowance on model car kits, Joanna was saving up hers to buy… and maybe even rebuild, the 'real thing'! It never mattered that she was years away from being old enough to drive or that girls weren't even supposed to be interested in cars. She had dreams! And age, gender or the limitations of reality had very little, if anything, to do with them. Despite an occasional warning about growing up too fast, her parents mostly just kept a close eye on things and stayed out of her way, letting her grow up according to the rules of her own very determined nature. While most kids needed herding from one activity to the next, free rein was never a problem for Joanna, who always possessed a natural control over the course of her own life. More often than not, she enjoyed being alone, preferring her own company to anyone else's. It was not at all unusual for her to spend days on end locked in her room, churning out elaborate drawings and diagrams, continually rethinking, reworking and reorganizing the master plan for her life. Whenever she did feel a need for some sort of social connection, she would invariably seek the company of people much older than herself. She had little interest in anyone who couldn't teach her something new, and grown-ups were generally better for that. Kids her own age almost always bored her and she was more or less indifferent to the whole immature lot of them. All except for Betsy McCullin who, one afternoon, offered to teach her how to tongue kiss a boy. Joanna had long been in awe of Betsy, a lovely young creature with flowing hair and full red lips—who at twelve, already wore a bra and somehow comprehended not just the mechanics of sex but the much more alluring mystery of it as well. Joanna imagined that everybody eventually got there in time, but that nature had a way of pushing girls like Betsy a little further along, a lot sooner. Joanna was never sure just how much of all this coaching she actually wanted to use on *boys*, but she was one hundred percent sure she wanted to learn as much as she could from Betsy. Often she would pretend to get it all wrong so that her 'teacher' would have to repeat the lesson over and over. If Betsy had caught on she never called her on it and that, for a smitten Joanna, made those sessions all the sweeter.

With a tenacity for digging in and exploiting the hell out of life, it was not at all surprising that by the time Joanna finished grade school she had all the important things figured out. What really pissed her off was that now, some thirty years later, she was virtually back to square one—forced to start at the beginning and rethink her whole God damned life. Her 'master plan' was no longer working. It was as if that creepy premonition she'd had about what would happen if she changed her weekend plans for that production shoot had actually come true. Joanna certainly wasn't about to gamble the future of a highly successful career and long term relationship without coming away with something of even greater value. With the balance of her life riding on it, this summer would have to be a major departure from the way Johanna had grown accustomed to living. For once in her life her plan was to not have a plan. These next two months were going to be an uncharted adventure into the unknown—a relinquishing of control—a dizzying ride of spontaneity. None of which Joanna had ever taken to well. All of which made her absolutely sick to her stomach. In a bold and desperate move she'd taken a leave of absence and perhaps a leave of her senses as well. She was determined to discover what the wisdom of those mountains meant for her to know and she was going to enjoy it even if it killed her! Her *mind*, if not her *heart*, was made up. She couldn't remember the last time the two agreed on anything, anyway.

What Johanna was looking for—at least in the immediate sense—was one of those modern self serve stations with a convenience store and sparkling clean restrooms. What she found instead was an old rundown gas station that looked like a Norman Rockwell cover for the Saturday Evening Post. It was hard to imagine that something so antiquated existed in the same world as the Internet. But technology wasn't what Joanna needed at this precise moment—a toilet of any kind was! She pulled in and waited along side one of two pumps—neither of which looked like it had been used in years. She waited about 30 seconds, which by New York City standards, was twenty-nine seconds too long. Straining hard to be 'mellow', she gave it another ten seconds before honking her horn—not once, but twice.

The only sign of life she drew with her impatience was an old dog that meandered out from behind a rusted Coke machine. Once again she leaned on her horn until finally a voice called back from inside the garage.

"Heard ya' the first time. Be right there."

Joanna imagined the usual old coot with greasy hair and a mouthful of crooked, yellow teeth. She was way off about the age but closer than she cared to be about the teeth. The young mechanic wipe his hands on a rag that appeared even dirtier.

He whistled lustfully as he came toward her.

"Man, would I love to get my hands on *you*!"

Joanna's blood began to boil until she realized that the object of his desire was the car she was driving.

The young man seemed in awe of the classic beauty.

"'57 T-Bird, right?"

She was impressed.

"You obviously know cars."

He walked around its body slowly, admiring every curve and detail.

"Man, she's in mint condition."

Joanna never warmed up to strangers quickly and over the years she'd acquired a demeanor that told them so. But if she had an immediate rapport with anyone, it was someone who shared her passion for vintage cars. Greasy hair and dirty fingernails aside, she found herself responding to the mechanic's enthusiasm, offering even more information than he'd asked for.

"I just picked it up last year. A friend of mine's a dealer. Had my eye on this model for years."

He stared at the car longingly, like a dream out of reach.

"Big bucks, huh?"

Joanna's tendency toward reflection hooked itself on the edge of his remark.

"Money was never really the issue. Sometimes we can afford to *buy* ourselves something but we just can't let ourselves *own* it. Know what I mean?"

For a split second, she was sure he registered the pained look of concentration. A second later his expression went blank, like the wiring just behind his eyes had suddenly burned out from a 'power surge'. Although he hadn't the slightest notion what she meant, the young man was too polite to ignore her question. He nodded vacantly, hoping that would do it.

Joanna took a sobering breath. What could she have been thinking? Here's a guy, not even 20, who probably spent half his life on top of his girlfriend and the other half under his car with just enough time going from one position to the other to grab a cold beer. Annoyed with herself for her lapse in judgment, she snapped back to reality.

"Do I need a key for the bathroom?"

"Nope, just a strong stomach."

He pointed to a beat up wooden door on the side of the building. Even from the distance it looked worthy of a warning to all womankind: Enter At Your Own Risk!

Having seen enough from the outside not to expect any toilet paper, Joanna shoved a fresh pack of tissues from the glove compartment into the pocket of her jeans. Careful to avoid touching anything she didn't have to, she pushed open the door with the side of her moccasin. The stench of urine and cigarettes hit her like a brick wall.

"Oh man!" she blurted out.

If she didn't have to go as badly as she did, she would have just backed out, hoping to escape whatever evil lurked deeper inside the God forsaken room. As she stood in the center of the grimy tomb Joanna caught herself feeling utterly repulsed by all men—even her father, her older brother and her 2 nephews, all of whom she ordinarily adored. She looked at the cigarette stained sink mounted haphazardly on the wall. Since the water was already running and she didn't have to touch the faucet, Joanna rinsed off her hands and dried them on her pants. Over the rusted sink a small cloudy mirror hung precariously on one nail. She looked at her reflection.

"Christ, I look like shit." She leaned in closer to scrutinize the lines that circled her eyes in a spiral of self-pity and frustration. "Pull yourself together, Cameron. Ordinary people whine. Great minds lament."

She slipped on her sunglasses, kicked the door open and stepped back out into the sunlight and fresh air, releasing no less than a dozen flies from captivity. At least another five minutes of the miserable summer were over.

The mechanic was just waving off a friend.

"See ya' 'round man. Hang loose and rash free."

Still disgusted she called out, "Yeah, guard those genitals. There's a whole world of bathroom walls out there waiting to be sprayed!"

The slow-moving man replaced the gas cap and scratched his head.

"It's pretty gross in there, huh? My girlfriend's always gettin' on me to clean the place up."

"Forget it! Just level the building and start over."

Oblivious to Joanna's change in mood the young man foolishly attempted to continue their conversation.

"Don't think I ever got your name. Mine's Pete. Where you headed?"

Joanna realized it was simply easier to answer succinctly than to ignore him.

"Amherst. How much do I owe you?"

"Twelve bucks oughta' do it."

She dug into her pocket for a $20 bill.

Young Pete reached into his for change.

"Got a cousin up there. Real pretty country. Like a picture book."

How profound, she thought. Perhaps his range of reading material actually exceeded Penthouse and Playboy.

Pete peeled some singles from a roll and handed them to her.

"So, where ya' from?"

"New York City."

He looked at the plates.

"I shoulda' known from the way you was leanin' on that horn before. That's one crazy town! Been there once. Gotta' tell ya, once was enough! Everybody's in The Big Hurry —just like you when you first drove in here."

Joanna got back in the car and slammed the door. His remark hit home. She felt particularly vulnerable.

"I suppose we're all racing around, searching for the meaning of life."

Pete dug his hands deep into his pockets.

"Well, sure hope you find it."

"Be nice if I just knew what '*it*' was."

"My grandma Bessie used to say, if you're not sure what you're lookin' for, try sittin' still for a bit and give it a chance to find you."

"What a lineage" Joanna mused as she turned the key in the ignition."

Without so much as a civil good-bye, she peeled away from the pump forcing Pete to jump back as he waved her off.

"Enjoy your vacation!"

You must be joking, she thought to herself repeating the phrase in her head, as her burdened heart spaced each of the words.

"Enjoy—Your—Vacation."

Suddenly she felt like a child condemned to her chair, pushing around a plate full of awful peas, waiting for her mother's urging: "Finish your vegetables!" It struck Joanna just how much energy we all spend tending to an endless string of three-word phrases that dominate our lives from the moment we're born: "Come to mommy—share your toys—clean your room—do your homework—wipe your nose—say your prayers—make me proud." For years we're told everything we should do, everything we shouldn't. Then one day, when we couldn't possibly be less prepared, we're handed the most demanding three little words of them all—the words of eternal human conflict, responsible for our greatest triumphs and most devastating defeats: "Follow your heart."

While his luggage was being tagged at the curbside check-in, Ben Garrison whispered those very words into his wife's ear. Beth could only hold him tighter, wondering how in the world she would ever begin. With her cheek pressed against his, she whispered back.

"I promise I'll try Ben, for *both* our sakes."

Luckily for Beth who couldn't imagine how, it was Ben who ended their embrace in order to take back his boarding pass and hand the man a tip. The skycap was appreciative.

For a long time, neither moved. Instinctively, Adam stepped closer to his mother assuming his father's place of protection, freeing him to leave. Ben smiled and took his son around.

"Have a great summer, kiddo. I hope that wish of yours comes true."

Adam was unusually receptive to his father's hug.

"Yours too dad."

His parents exchanged one last kiss. It was a kiss torn between trying to say everything and nothing.

"I'll call you as soon as I get settled."

"Send my love to your folks. Please do your best to explain."

Ben was sincere.

"I'll try, I really will."

Aware that her eyes were following after him, Ben turned back for one last reassuring smile. Everything had finally come down to this moment. Beth watched her husband push through the revolving door of the terminal and eventually disappear into the thickening crowd. She stood there, motionless, watching the interaction between strangers—some hugging each other hello, other hugging goodbye. Airports were a lot like embraces, Beth thought to herself. Sometimes they ended the longing. Sometimes they began it. Adam sensed his mother needed to be coaxed along.

"C'mon mom, let's go."

Dazed, Beth opened the door and got back in the car, responding to Adam's words more like a command under hypnosis than his actual voice. She felt bruised from the inside, out. Adam needed some assurance for the drive home.

"Are you okay mom?"

With the instincts of a mother protective of her young, Beth ignored her own apprehension in order to rescue him from his.

"I'm fine honey. You don't have to worry."

Beth pulled away from the curb, merging gradually into the traffic that moved in its usual flow, unaware of how extraordinarily unusual the events of the day were for her. It's amazing how everything just goes on, she thought, determined that *somehow*, she would too. In an attempt to normalize things for both of them, she turned on the radio and for much of the drive back each was happy to let the music hide a much deeper silence.

Now, just a few miles from home, Beth's heartbeat began to quicken, pumping a liquid panic through her body. She groped for anything that would postpone having to walk through that door and face her decision so soon. The light turned green. In a split-second decision, Beth made a spontaneous hairpin turn, swerving into the parking lot of Campus Plaza.

"Mom… watch out for that car!"

Adam closed his eyes and braced himself for the moment of impact.

Joanna Cameron slammed on her brakes. She leaned so far out of her window Beth was sure the woman intended to grab her by the neck.

"Are you fucking crazy, lady?"

Beth tried to apologize.

"I'm so sorry."

In disgust, Joanna pulled into the nearest space making sure that Beth heard her parting thought.

"Asshole!"

Shaken and embarrassed, Beth drove cautiously past the car she almost hit, making every attempt to avoid eye contact with the woman glaring at her. She began to hum in a feeble attempt at normalcy.

Adam wasn't about to let her off the hook.

"What are we doing here anyway?"

Not wanting to appear any more ridiculous than she already felt, Beth wasn't about to admit that she was simply afraid to go home.

"We need a few things. I just thought while we're out…"

"Mom, the refrigerator's packed and I'm leaving for camp on Monday. How much food can you eat by yourself?"

Beth was desperate to establish some credibility.

"I thought I'd make us a special dinner tonight. All your favorites. What do you say?"

Adam quickly realized this wasn't about dinner at all. His mother just needed something to fill up this day—something to distract her from all the things she was really feeling. He resigned himself to the promise he'd made to his father earlier.

"Fine… whatever."

She was instantly relieved.

"Why don't we rent a video too?"

Adam made a face and Beth decided not to push it. As it was, she was genuinely grateful.

"Thanks honey."

"For what?"

"I think you know."

His mother smiled shyly and leaned across the seat to kiss his cheek.

Adam pretended it was no big deal.

In exchange for his concession Beth agreed not to be long. Adam could check out the new roller blades in the sporting goods store while she shopped and they'd meet back at the car in fifteen minutes.

Just when Beth thought he was going to spare her any further humiliation, Adam brought up the accident she'd almost caused.

"Ya' know, you came real close to demolishing that car back there."

Beth shuddered at the thought.

"Just let it go, will you Adam. I don't even want to think about what that woman would have done if I'd actually hit her. God, she was awfully mad, wasn't she?"

"Can you blame her? What kind of car was that, anyway?"

"A very prized and expensive one I'm sure."

He reminded her of her promise.

"Don't forget, just fifteen minutes."

With that, Adam dashed off in the direction of the sporting goods store, leaving Beth at the entrance of the supermarket. Once inside, she glanced down at her watch. Ordinarily Beth would wander slowly through the supermarket, but this time she was on a mission. She whipped up and down aisles pulling things from their shelves with one hand while struggling to keep control of the cart with her other. In her haste, she'd grabbed one with a faulty front wheel; the kind that wobbled and pulled to one side like a misbehaved dog. Time was ticking. Fortunately for Beth, she knew the store like she knew her own pantry. She took all the shortcuts maneuvering her runaway cart down one aisle and up the next.

Joanna Cameron, on the other hand, knew where nothing was. The size of the supermarket alone was enough to rattle her nerves.

"Christ, I could get cross-town in less time than it takes to get from one end of these goddamn aisles to the other."

She had just spent the last ten minutes trying to find a lousy bag of chips, a can of soda, a box of Tampons and a bottle of Motrin; grumbling under her breath every step of the way. Her period was just what Joanna needed to round out her love of 'beginnings'. But like it or not, she was due today—any minute, in fact—judging from the degree of her cramps.

Beth got on the express line and checked her watch, thrilled she was going to make it back to the car on time. She was reveling in her first major accomplishment of the summer when she realized she'd forgotten the marshmallows for the sweet potato pie.

"Oh darn" she mumbled to herself, abruptly pulling back from the check out line.

In a frantic attempt to make up the time, she swirled the cart around at lightening speed, accidentally slamming into another customer. The few items in the shocked woman's arms went flying into the air. She dropped down, grabbed her bruised ankle and moaned in anguish.

"Shit, shit, shit!"

Beth felt awful.

"I'm so sorry. Are you alright?"

In obvious distress, the woman looked up in the direction of the apologetic voice. Instantly her eyes switched from pain to rage.

"It's you again!"

Once Beth realized her victim was the same woman whose car she had almost hit earlier, she wanted nothing more than to die as swiftly as possible. Beth didn't know which was more horrifying: the two-headed baby on the cover of the National Inquirer or the expression on Joanna's face, but if looks could kill, she would have gotten her wish.

"Oh my God," was all a mortified Beth could utter.

Joanna's face remained chiseled in anger.

"Christ! Can't you handle *anything* on wheels?"

Beth's first impulse was to abandon her wagon and run, but her sense of genuine concern for the woman's ankle wouldn't allow her to flee. She fought through her fear in order to speak.

"Do you think it's broken?"

"How the hell do I know?"

Beth nervously began gathering up the things Joanna dropped when she was rammed.

"If it broke the skin, I think I have a Band-Aid in my purse."

"Lady, I'd rather bleed to death! Just give me my stuff and let me get the hell out of here while I'm still alive."

She reached out, snatched the items from Beth's arms and limped off in a huff. Beth just stood there for a moment, watching her and imagining the pain in every step.

"I'm so sorry," she blurted out again.

Joanna turned and gave Beth the dirtiest look she'd ever seen in her life. Beth nervously gripped the handle of her wagon with both hands.

"God, what's the matter with me today?"

Joanna tossed her purchases into the car, sure that the still throbbing ankle was some cosmic punishment for ever leaving New York.

"Fuck it," she grumbled through her pain.

Nothing as insignificant as the forces of the universe could compete with Joanna's 'get in—get out—get on with it' style. She started the ignition and began to pull away when suddenly an overwhelming wave of melancholy swept over her. It was so powerful, it actually made her heart ache. By now it was obvious that today those cosmic forces were going to give Joanna a run for her money. First physical pain… now *this*. She didn't know what to call it. But whatever it was, it was damn near paralyzing. She put the car in park, reassuring herself it was nothing more than a little P.M.S. kicking ass. Joanna steadied herself and tried again. As soon as the car began to move, she was seized by a devastating sense of loss. This time, the pulling away felt like she was being torn from the core of her own life. It was a feeling much different than what she'd experienced earlier this morning when she left New York. It was much different than anything she'd ever known. Joanna pulled back into the parking space, turned off the motor and tried to calm herself down. She leaned forward toward the rear view mirror for a reality check. Her face was covered with perspiration, but she was relieved that at least it was still *her* face. She'd never felt anything this unsettling or unfamiliar. As she patted her skin dry, Joanna remembered the ice cream store just a few doors down from where they shot the commercial. A nice, thick shake might be just what the cosmic forces ordered. That, and a couple of those Motrin. She dug into the bag, found the bottle and ripped open the top with her teeth. Clutching her car keys in one hand and two pills in the other, Joanna opened the door, relieved to find the store empty and the air conditioner on full blast. The young boy behind the counter greeted her with a smile that showed a remarkably good nature, given the size zitz he was obviously battling on the side of his nose, just above the nostril.

"Hi, what'll it be?"

"A large chocolate shake."

Joanna had forgotten the last time making a decision was that easy.

"And some water to take a pill."

As the boy reached for a plastic cup, she tried not to think about his fingers that must have worked hard at trying to squeeze out some of that pus before he left his house this morning. She forced herself to focus on a tray of colored sprinkles while he prepared her malt.

"Will that be to stay or go?"

Joanna gulped down the pills and tossed the cup in the trash.

"To go."

She noticed the tables off to the side and remembered Grandma Bessie's advise about sitting still for a while. What did she have to lose?

"Forget the lid. I'll drink it here."

She paid the clerk and chose a seat deliberately facing away from his nose and that pimple.

"Okay Grandma," Joanna thought to herself while trying to ignore her throbbing ankle, "I'm sittin'... do your thing."

She had taken a few sips and was actually began to feel a little better, when the door to the shop swung open. Jo looked up and almost bit off the tip of her straw. She jumped to her feet, held her arms out in front of her and made the sign of the cross with two fingers, as if warding off a bloodsucking vampire.

"I'm warning you, lady, keep back or I'll drive a stake through your heart!"

Mortified at having to face this woman yet again, Beth noticed the confusion in the counter boy's eyes.

"She's only kidding. We know each other... sort of."

Beth turned to Joanna and smiled timidly.

"Don't worry, I won't come anywhere near you. I promise. I'll just get my ice cream and leave."

Joanna sat back tentatively and glared while Beth ordered a quart of Rocky Road. She could feel Joanna's eyes burning through her back while she waited. They were, without doubt, the longest few minutes of Beth's life. She paid the boy and slunk out as inconspicuously as possible, grateful that Joanna hadn't said another word or done her bodily harm.

Joanna tossed the empty container into the trash and pushed open the door.

"If Grandma Bessie shows up, tell her I think her advice sucks!"

The boy just nodded, not understanding any part of what had just happened, but greatly relieved that both women had left without a scene. Coping with acne was something he obviously had lots of experience with, but two crazy women was not.

Beth had already begun loading the groceries into the trunk when Adam approached.

"Wow, I'm impressed. I never though you'd beat me back to the car."

She slammed the door of the trunk.

"Just get in the car and let's get out of here!"

Adam didn't understand his mother's newfound urgency to get home, but it was more than fine with him. Beth put the car in reverse, taking extra care in backing out of the parking space. She was just beginning to feel a little relief knowing she was only a short distance from the safety of her driveway when a wasp unexpectedly shot out from behind her sun visor. The insect flew directly at her face, stinging her on the cheek just below her eye. Beth panicked and let go of the wheel, waving her hands frantically about her head trying to protect herself from another attack. Intending to step on the brake, she jammed her foot on the accelerator pedal instead, sending the car backward at an uncommon speed until the awful sound of metal crunching against metal brought it to a jolting stop. For a fraction of a second, all was silent except for the buzzing of the wasp as it flew casually out of the window. Though quite shaken up, fortunately neither she nor Adam was hurt by the impact. He leaned out of his window to see what damage his mother's infamous 'tank' had inflicted on the unlucky vehicle that happened to be driving past at the wrong time. Now seriously concerned for her safety, Adam quickly pulled his head back in and looked at his mother.

"Holy shit! You're not gonna' believe this, but you just rammed that same sports car you almost hit comin' in before."

Beth became frantic.

"Oh my god, Adam! What am I going to do? She's going to kill me!

Adam was no help.

"I hate to say this mom, but so would I." And he didn't even know about the incident in the supermarket.

Joanna sat in her cherished T-Bird, her eyes closed, her jaw clenched, replaying the last 30 seconds of her life and praying to God that what just happened wasn't *really* what just happened.

"If I don't move," she thought to herself, gripping the wheel with both hands, "this won't be real. I'll wake up from this fucking nightmare and everything will be fine."

It was only after Joanna opened her eyes and recognized whose car it was that just slammed into her, did she snap back into reality and then uncontrollable rage. She jumped out of her car and went around to the passenger side for a horrifying confirmation that indeed she was once again the victim of this bizarre woman's ineptitude. Only this time, it was not the mere flesh of her ankle. This time it was Joanna's most prized possession; the one thing in her life that still thrilled her completely—the only thing she had left that was pure, uncomplicated and perfect. Now that too had been destroyed, mangled, ruined by this ridiculous, insidious woman driving an old, beat up station wagon with Garfield the Cat suctioned to the side window.

With her cheek swollen from the sting and her knees literally shaking in anticipation of Joanna's wrath, Beth reluctantly got out of the car for a closer look at the damage she'd just caused. She barely took a step forward when Joanna lunged at her with a barrage of threats and epithets. Joanna's face was crimson with fury. She beat her fists on the hood of Beth's car and repeatedly kicked the tire with the back of her heel. Beth wondered how long the woman would take out her aggression on the car before turning it on *her*.

"You stupid fucking asshole!" Joanna ranted. "Now I have to kill you! Now you have to die!"

Beth actually considered letting herself be pummeled to the ground without putting up the slightest resistance. It was the least she could do, under the circumstances. Seriously concerned for his mother's safety, Adam leapt from the car and bravely stood in front of her, ready to fight Joanna off if he had to. A small crowd began to gather and Beth felt humiliated being at the center of such a loud public display. Trudy, a small, wiry woman with brassy red hair and large bangle earrings, came out of the luncheonette she owned to see what all the fuss was about. Not one to watch from the sidelines, she pushed her way through the crowd and was shocked to find Beth and Adam at the center of the commotion.

"Oh my! Honey, what happened? Are you both okay?

"We're fine Trudy, really. I just caused a little fender bender."

Beth was relieved to have a familiar and caring ally close by while Joanna continued to rant and rave, now even more incensed to hear Beth refer to her devastation as a mere 'fender bender'. Trudy turned to Joanna, calmly ignoring her irrational behavior.

"And how 'bout you, Missy... are *you* okay?"

For a brief moment Joanna fell silent, as if actually soothed by the stranger's concern. In reality it was more like the calm before the storm, while she tried to process the ludicrous question. A moment later, the small part of Joanna that was still restrained snapped completely and all hell broke loose.

"How the fuck can I be okay? Look what this idiot in this rusted piece of shit did to the side of my car!" The entire fender was bent into the wheel. "How the hell am I supposed to drive this now?" Joanna began to pace erratically. "Do you have any idea how hard it is to get parts for a car like this? And what the fuck am I supposed to do until then?"

Trudy interrupted only to point out that Adam was standing within earshot.

"Honey, maybe you can find a better way to express your feelings about this whole regrettable thing."

Joanna didn't know whether to laugh or cry at Trudy's suggestion. By now completely unnerved by Joanna's hostility, Beth was a total wreck. She knew she had to say something. She couldn't ask Trudy to protect her for the rest of her life, whatever little worth it still had.

"Please, I can explain..."

"You can explain? You can explain?"

Joanna's eyes flared and sparked with fire, each time repeating Beth's word in a more threatening tone. Each time leaning closer and closer into Beth's face, until she was close enough to inhale the scent of Beth's hair. For a split second Joanna's senses became confused and jumbled by it, but she was quick to renew her aggression.

Overwhelmed, Beth finally lost her battle to hold back tears. Adam, who up until then had been more embarrassed than anything else, stepped between the two women.

"Hey lady, my mother said she was sorry!"

Joanna was unrelenting.

"Oh yeah, well maybe you should consider those her last words before you watch me strangle her to death!"

Trudy had heard enough. With years of experience dealing with crowd control, she decided it was time to step in and calm everyone down. The first thing she did was disperse the crowd. She wisely waited for Joanna to vent the full course of her frustration, calling Beth everything from a simple-minded moron to a menace to society. Trudy waited patiently, then spoke in an even, no-nonsense tone.

"I hear what you're sayin' doll, but that's not the Beth Garrison I know. This here is one of the sweetest, most caring women around."

She took Beth around by the waist and pulled her close. Slightly reassured by Trudy's embrace, Beth wiped her eyes. Trudy continued her damage control.

"Let the cars be. Folks can drive around 'em. In the meantime the three of you come on inside. You can do the exchangin' of information while you have something to eat, on the house. That way I get to keep and eye on you and make sure nobody gets hurt." Trudy winked and bravely rested her hand on Joanna's shoulder. "As for you, doll... I think I can make gettin' that fancy car of yours fixed up a lot easier than you think. My Ruby runs the best auto body shop in town and it just happens his specialty is restorin' antique cars. Collectors from all over swear by him and he's got a reputation for gettin' parts faster than anyone else in the state of Massachusetts. So don't ya' go worrying that pretty little head off. You just gotta' know the right people and now you do. Call this your lucky day!"

Joanna was stunned into silence by the convoluted conclusion.

Under Trudy's watch, Beth found the courage to look at Joanna, hopeful for even the slightest sign of concession. Joanna held her eyes in a deadly grip. Finally she shook her head in resentful submission.

"Yeah, this is my fucking lucky day alright!"

Trudy quickly covered Adam's ears and herded the three of them into the luncheonette. She pointed to an empty booth. Adam eagerly slid across the seat, his focus already on the cheeseburger he'd be getting. Beth sat beside him and Joanna reluctantly slid in opposite them. The small booth hardly seemed like a sturdy enough structure to withstand the tension that was being forced into it. Smart enough not to leave them alone for too long, Trudy quickly returned with three settings and a poker face.

"Can I assume it's safe to put out knives on this table?"

Joanna didn't say a word. Beth's responded sheepishly.

"Well my weapon of choice seems to be wheels."

She looked coyly into Joanna's eyes for some kind of acknowledgement. Joanna remained deliberately expressionless, but behind her lack of outward recognition, she was surprised at Beth's quick sense humor. Trudy kept things rolling.

"I know Adam's gonna' have a cheeseburger and a large Coke. You gals wanna see menus?"

With no appetite, Beth's only need for one was to have something to hide behind—preferably one that was bulletproof.

"I'll just have a glass of ice tea."

Trudy nodded.

"Speaking of ice, I'll bring a few extra cubes for that swelling under your eye."

She turned to Joanna.

"What about you Toots?"

Reluctantly Joanna ordered a salad and Coke with no intention of touching either.

"Coming right up. Meantime, I'll call Ruby and get him over here to have a look at that car of yours."

Joanna just nodded, barely concealing her distrust that anything or anyone could actually make things better. Trudy picked up on her skepticism.

"Folks around here don't call me 'Sunshine' for nothin'."

At least that explained her ridiculous yellow circle earrings with orange points darting out in all directions. Joanna forced herself to be a bit more civil.

"Whatever you can do, I'd appreciate it."

As soon as Trudy walked away, Joanna's effort faded. She immediately took out her wallet and tore off a corner of the paper placemat.

"Alright, let's get this over with. Do you have a pen?"

Adam jumped on Joanna's question.

"Are you kidding? My mother's got everything in that bag."

"Well there's one thing she shouldn't be carrying… a driver's license!"

Beth fumbled around inside her bag until she indeed found a pen.

"I think it may skip."

"Naturally," Joanna mocked. "Why wouldn't there be a problem?"

Suddenly feeling the need to defend his mother, Adam launched into a litany of the morning's events.

"I told my dad she shouldn't be driving at all today. She's way too upset. He left for England this morning. He got this really great chance to lecture at Cambridge this summer. He teaches English Lit. at U Mass. Anyway, we were on our way back from dropping him off at the airport when mom decided she needed to cook this whole elaborate dinner tonight. That's when she turned into the mall at the last minute and almost hit you the first time."

Beth was horrified by the embarrassing details of Adam's purging. Poisoning his dinner tonight seemed a fitting revenge. She just wasn't sure she could wait that long to kill him. By now terrified her son would blurt out something about her earlier attack of diarrhea, Beth stopped him.

"Adam, please. I'm sure that…," she paused mid-sentence. "I'm sorry, I don't know your name."

Joanna responded by tossing Beth her registration. Accepting the coldness of her gesture, Beth picked it up, turned it around and read from the card.

"I'm sure that Joanna doesn't want to hear the story of our lives."

Beth handed Joanna back her registration.

"Keep it. You'll need to copy down the numbers."

Joanna's voice couldn't have sounded any flatter. Trudy returned, set down their plates and smiled at Joanna.

"Ruby's on his way. So just sit tight and enjoy your meal. Give a holler if you need anything else."

Joanna began to resent the mood of their cozy little meal.

"Can we get on with exchanging this information?"

Beth was quick to agree. She moved the ice tea aside, got out her wallet and began nervously looking through the compartments. Before she found her license and registration, Joanna was treated to an obscure view of at least a half dozen family snapshots. Despite her indifference, the photos were a curiosity. Annoyed with herself for this mental digression, Joanna's tone became even more matter of fact.

"I'll need the numbers off your insurance card too."

"It's in my glove compartment." Beth was relieved at the chance to get away from the table for a few minutes in order to compose herself. "I'll be right back."

Her body looked rigid enough to break as she stood up. Surprisingly, Joanna found herself experiencing a glimmer of concern over Beth's obvious strain. Her eyes followed the woman from the booth to the luncheonette door and then out into the parking lot. Suddenly aware that Adam was watching her as she watched his mother, Joanna confronted him directly.

"Is your mother always this much of a wreck?"

He poured more ketchup and answered her at the same time. "Are you always this tough on people?"

Joanna thought about ignoring his remark completely, but she had too much respect for his challenging comeback. It was just the kind of smart-ass response *she'd* have fired back as a kid. She didn't necessarily like the sound of the truth, but she answered him honestly.

"Yeah, I suppose most of the time I am."

Adam took another bite of his cheeseburger.

"My mom's just the opposite. She gives everyone the benefit of the doubt. My dad calls her Saint Beth... Patron Saint of Amherst." With his mother not there to stop him, Adam continued his account of the morning's events. "The accident wasn't really her fault. A wasp flew out from behind the sun visor and stung her right on her face. She just freaked out and lost control of the wheel. Sorry about the crash, though. You have a really cool lookin' car."

"It was... until your mother plowed into it."

For some reason, this time Joanna's recrimination didn't have the same sting to it. Adam took advantage of her slightly less hostile tone.

"You from around here?"

Jo remained guarded.

"No, New York City."

"Cool. I was there once when I was just a kid."

Joanna smiled inside, reminded of the kind of arrogance she felt at his age.

"It was over our Christmas vacation with my folks and Danny. He's my older brother…." Adam hesitated. "He died."

Joanna's eyes automatically shifted to the window. Watching Beth, her conscience formed a knot in the pit of her stomach. She looked back at the young boy sitting opposite her, really seeing him for the first time.

"I'm sorry to hear that."

"He died in a car accident three years ago. It was a rainy night. His car skidded off the road. He would have been twenty-one this year." Adam looked outside to make sure his mother was still at the car. "It's been really tough on her. My dad didn't want to leave her alone all summer, but he couldn't convince her to go with him to England. I'm leaving for camp in a few days, so she's pretty much gonna' be on her own. She says it's what she wants but my dad's really worried about her. She hasn't been the same since my brother died."

Joanna spoke in Beth's defense.

"Something like that changes you forever."

Adam glanced out through the window at his mother who was now walking back from the car. Her eyes copying his, Joanna let herself study the woman less harshly. Somehow in the calculations of Joanna's mind, having the courage to survive the death of a child cancelled out the sheer stupidity of having some ridiculous plush cat suctioned to the window of her car. As Beth approached the booth, Joanna felt a twinge of regret for having been so verbally cruel to her earlier.

Beth sat back down, unaware of all that Joanna's now knew.

"I copied down all the numbers you'll need to report the accident to your insurance company. I don't think I'll bother reporting it to mine. What're are a few more scratches on that old 'rusted out piece of shit', as you so aptly described it?" Whatever composure Beth had regained being away from that booth quickly faded now that she was once again sitting across from Joanna. She felt compelled to offer an apology. "I know it doesn't change anything, but I can't tell you how awful I feel about hitting your car."

Adam didn't look up from his plate. He was hoping his hunch about Joanna was right—that there was a kinder side to her after all, a side that would cut his mother some slack. He wasn't disappointed.

"Look, I'm sorry I lost it out there but that car means a lot to me."

Beth couldn't believe Joanna was apologizing to her. She noticed Adam smiling slightly and wondered what part in all this was *his* doing. She looked back at Joanna.

"You had every right to be furious. I would have reacted the same way if the situation was reversed."

"That's not what I've heard… from Trudy… or your son. Truth is, you're probably a lot nicer person than I am."

With no reason to think otherwise, Beth still came to Joanna's defense.

"I don't believe that."

"You should. My mother always said: "Believe what people tell you about themselves… especially in the beginning. That's when they're most likely to tell the truth."

Adam knew his own mother well enough to know she wasn't about to let this go. He was right.

"I'm not sure if I agree with that."

Joanna leveled her eyes.

"Well I hate to burst your bubble, but beneath the surface of some people's cold and aloof *exterior* is an equally cold and aloof *interior*."

"And I suppose you're one of those people?"

Joanna sat back and crossed her arms.

"I say if the armor fits, wear it."

Beth just smiled, accepting Joanna's warning at face value. It was a smile Joanna found as appealing as she did challenging.

After an uncomfortable silence, Adam sensed that this newfound rapport between his mother and Joanna was much too unstable to leave in either of their hands.

"Joanna's from New York City. I was telling her that we once spent our Christmas vacation there."

It was obvious to Beth that her son was trying to keep things on this much more pleasant keel. She hoped Joanna was willing to go along, if only for his sake.

"So, you're a long way from home."

Joanna's heart struggled for a reasonable definition of the word 'home'.

"Let's just say it started feeling like I was a long way from home way before I left."

Beth's own heart shook with instant recognition—the kind that transcends anything she could have conveyed with words. She tested Joanna's eyes, now seeing in them more pain than anger. Joanna suddenly became undone by Beth's perception. This time the silence between them was not awkwardly cold, but awkwardly intimate.

Adam was lost.

"So are you on vacation?"

Joanna considered her response carefully.

"I'm not sure what you'd call it. More like a journey, or a search."

Once again Adam felt defeated by the ambiguity of the woman's answer. Once again Beth felt overwhelmingly drawn in by it. Surprisingly, Joanna offered more.

"I took a leave of absence from work to spend the summer up here. I think they call it 'communing with nature' and 'getting in touch with one's inner self'. For me, that translates into a large can of insect repellant, an old pair of jeans and a thick sketch pad."

Adam was intrigued.

"Are you some famous artist or something?"

"Sorry to disappoint you, but no. I'm a creative director at an advertising agency."

Adam had never heard the term.

"What's a creative director?"

Joanna looked him straight in the eye.

"It's someone who gets paid a lot of money to manipulate people... people like you and your mother."

Adam looked hurt by the sharpness of her reply. Joanna was immediately sorry she'd put such a deliberately cruel spin on the truth.

"I create TV commercials and ad campaigns intended to get millions of people to buy millions of products they don't really need."

Adam's face changed.

"Wow, that sounds really cool... shooting commercials and stuff."

Beth played with her straw.

"That does sound like exciting work."

Joanna shrugged.

"I used to think so." She turned to Adam. "When I was your age, I swore that one day I would be that 'famous artist'." Her eyes became nostalgic, as though she were recalling the happiest years of her life. "I drew. I painted. I sculpted. I took photographs. I used whatever I could get my hands on. I told myself that the inspiration that moved the pen, the pencil and the brush was the same inspiration that moved the sun, the moon and the stars, and that whenever I was creating I was somehow controlling all the forces of the universe." Joanna's eyes unsealed the disappointment of an adult whose childhood visions had not come true. "I think our dreams are something we pursue by heart—our goals, by plan. One day I just stopped paying attention to the difference."

Beth couldn't believe she was listening to the same woman who, less that an hour ago, spew only profanities. For now, Adam had just about given up trying to get a simple conversation going. He wolfed down his last French fry and looked at the clock on the wall.

"Mom, if you're done with all this insurance stuff, can we get going? I promised Jeff I'd call before noon."

Beth was desperate for more time with Joanna. She handed Adam a quarter.

"Use the pay phone."

Beth ignored her son's impatience. She had no intention of leaving until she found out what happened to Joanna's dream, hoping that maybe somewhere in the stranger's answer there was a clue to what happened to her own.

Joanna was amused by Adam's response.

"Looks like your son lost interest in the story of my life. Not that I blame him. Somewhere along the line I seem to have lost interest in it too."

Beth leaned forward on her elbows.

"Well I haven't. So, how did the soul of an artist wind up in such a soulless career?"

Joanna became defensive.

"I never said it was soulless."

"You didn't have to."

Their eyes locked in a willful battle of truth or dare. Joanna was impressed with Beth's courage to go one on one and eventually admitted the truth.

"It's simple really. I traded a soulful life for a successful one." Joanna leaned back and looked at Beth with a curious scrutiny. "I like your questions."

Beth smiled.

"I'm not sure I like your answers. They hit a bit too close to home."

"Ah, home… there's that nasty little word again. Looks like we've come full circle."

Beth felt herself die a little inside.

"It does look like it."

This time their silence thickened as it set. With Adam away from the table, the two women were left to their own devices. Beth wrapped an ice cube in a napkin and pressed it to the swelling on her cheek.

"I'm really sorry about the accident."

Joanna collected her license and registration. She handed Beth back her pen, careful not to sound overly pleased.

"You're not who I thought you'd be."

Beth felt an ambiguous sense of pride.

"The surprise is mutual. Neither are you."

Once again the women fell awkwardly silent. However secretly grateful for their chance encounter, Beth felt terrible knowing that the woman's inconvenience was her fault. She hoped Joanna would permit their fragile rapport to continue.

"If you don't mind my asking, what were your plans before I… altered them?"

"You mean before you demolished my car?"

The redness in Beth's cheek spread across her face and neck. Her embarrassment gave Joanna enough satisfaction to remain civil.

"I was gonna' take a room over at the Mountain View Motel for the night. That's where the production crew stayed when we shot a commercial a few years back. It's still there, isn't it?"

"I'm afraid things in this town don't change very much. At least not on the outside."

Joanna found herself reading between the lines—and the longings—of Beth's answer. Though intrigued, she tried to ignore both.

"Anyway, I thought I'd spend the night there and if I didn't change my mind by morning, I was gonna' buy a paper and check out a few local real estate agents to see about renting a place for the summer."

"So you can commune with nature…"

Joanna smiled.

"Yeah, mostly my own."

"I see…."

Beth felt hesitant about asking any more questions.

Adam returned to the table, but wouldn't sit down.

"We got cut off. Can we pleeeeease go? At this rate, dad will be in England by the time we get home!"

Beth was obviously torn. There was so much more about Joanna she wanted to know.

"Sorry Adam, we're staying until everything gets straightened out here. It's the least I can do."

Beth hoped she sounded more decisive than desperate. Joanna was dismissive.

"Ruby and I will work something out. I'm sure he'll give me a lift to the motel. The insurance company can handle it from here."

Adam rallied on the strength of Joanna's insistence.

"C'mon mom, even *she* thinks we should go."

Whatever connection Beth felt they'd just made obviously meant nothing to the woman at all. Certainly if Joanna cared to continue their conversation, she might have suggested having dinner, or just meeting for a cup of coffee sometime. After all, she did say she was going to be in the area all summer, and it didn't sound like she knew anyone else in Amherst. Was the company of no one actually better then *hers*? Beth felt quietly humiliated. Here she was, thoroughly engaged by the most intriguing person she'd met in years, while Joanna, whose entire life Beth imagined was filled with fascinating people and stimulating conversation, couldn't wait to be rid of her. Besides, what could a woman like Joanna possibly want to know about a typical housewife that she couldn't just get from one of those market research studies her agency spit out every other week?

"Fine. Let's go."

The declaration left no room for Beth to change her mind. It was the only way she could leave with any dignity left at all. She began gathering up her things, purposely avoiding any last minute eye contact with Joanna.

"I'm terribly sorry about the accident. I hope it doesn't interfere with the rest of your plans… or should I say, 'Journey'." She tried to sound as casual as possible. "Who knows, if you're going to be in the area for the summer, maybe I'll run into you again."

Adam burst out laughing.

"God, I can't believe you said that mom!"

Flushed with embarrassment, Beth turned to Joanna.

"Well, I'm waiting, aren't you going to make fun of me too?"

For a moment Joanna remained thoughtfully silent, then stood up leaving them only inches apart. Her eyes were penetrating and sincere as she extended her hand.

"I'm glad we met…," she pulled out the folded piece of paper with the insurance information, "Mrs. Beth Garrison of 16 Elm Street, Amherst, Massachusetts."

Beyond that slip of paper and the information it held, the mystery felt endless. So too did the moments in which the women felt the warmth of each other's clasped hands. Once again Joanna had managed to disarm Beth, leaving her to have to say goodbye without the reinforcement of anger. Fortunately, Ruby's interruption served as the next best thing.

"Heard about your little mishap. Got here as soon as I could."

Beth greeted him with a kiss.

"Thanks for coming over like this."

"No problem. How's Ben?"

Her husband had been the furthest thing from Beth's mind.

"We just dropped him off at the airport. He's spending the summer in England, lecturing at Cambridge."

"Sounds mighty impressive. How come you didn't go with him?"

Joanna found herself much too interested in Beth's reason.

"Let's just say, wrong place… wrong time."

Adam watched Ruby struggle to make sense of his mother's answer. He already knew that simple questions were a big mistake today. Joanna, on the other hand, understood perfectly. Ruby didn't respond one way or the other.

"Well, send him my best when you speak to him."

He turned to Joanna, who was still considering the ambiguity of Beth's remark.

"Hi, my name's Ruby."

She extended her hand.

"Joanna Cameron."

Ruby wiped his hand on his pants before clasping hers .

"If you folks are finished here, why don't I have a look at that car of yours? Hear it's a beauty."

Joanna remembered her heartache.

Trudy came out from behind the counter.

"Honey, see if you can help this lady. She was lucky enough to meet Beth and Adam but not under the best of circumstances."

She hugged Beth and Adam goodbye, then grabbed hold of Joanna's arm.

"Once you get yourself settled, you be sure to stop back in. I wanna' be able to say I told you so once Ruby works his magic on that car of yours."

Joanna was careful not to make any promises she had no intention of keeping.

"Thanks for your help."

Trudy called out to her husband one last time.

"See ya' home sweet cakes. Leftovers okay?"

"Fine by me… just so long as you're sittin' on the other side of the table!"

As Adam bolted out the door Beth's stomach began to tighten, certain that the reality of the collision would send Joanna back into a rage. She was right.

"Oh Christ, I can't believe what you did to my car."

Ruby knew how to fix more than just cars.

"That's why they call these things 'accidents', ladies."

While Ruby got busy hooking up her car, Joanna walked over to Beth's window.

"I'm sorry I went off like that again."

Beth refused to look anywhere but straight ahead.

In the little time she had left, Joanna tried to leave things on a positive note.

"Looks like the swelling's gone down."

Beth put on her sunglasses in order to avoid Joanna's eye.

"With any luck, in a few hours it'll disappear completely and there'll be nothing left to remind me of this whole regrettable incident. Nothing at all!"

"Okay Beth," Ruby called out from his truck, "you're clear to pull out now."

Joanna walked alongside Beth's window of the car as it rolled backwards. She ducked down to get a last look at Adam through the window.

"Take it easy kid. Enjoy your summer."

"You too. If you stick around, watch out for mom in 'the tank'."

Beth gave her son a dirty look. Then she pulled alongside Ruby's truck for reassurance.

"Are you sure you can help her?"

"Sure enough not to worry yourself sick about it."

With her conscience relieved, now she wouldn't have to give Joanna Cameron another thought. She thanked Ruby again and pulled away, refusing herself even one last look through the rear view mirror.

Joanna was not as strong willed. Her eyes followed the old station wagon as Beth inched up behind the two cars at the stop sign waiting to pull out into the flow of traffic. Joanna struggled desperately with the urge to try to stop her—to explain what this summer *had* to be about. No friendships. No connections. No distractions. She could feel her heart fill with regret, one that felt much older than this incident or this day.

"Let it go, Cameron," she told herself. "The last thing you need in your life right now is a woman who's actually capable of surprising you."

Ruby dug through the cab of his truck for an estimate pad and a pen.

"Okay pretty lady, let's you and me talk miracles here."

Joanna was still watching to see which direction Beth would be going once she pulled out of the lot. Ruby couldn't help but notice her distraction.

"Hey there, ya' with me?"

Joanna turned away from the road, grateful for his voice that pulled her back from her unexplainable longing. She did everything she could to focus on her car.

A traffic light away, Beth did everything *she* could to refocus on the day's plans.

"Now where were we?"

She reached for the radio dial, but Adam turned it off. It was almost as if he was deliberately trying to make this harder for her.

"So what's her story?"

Beth foolishly tried to pretend that she'd already forgotten all about Joanna.

"What's *whose* story?"

"Joanna! Who do you think I mean? What's she gonna' do now that you demolished her car?"

Beth persisted in changing the subject.

"Oh God, the ice cream must be completely melted by now. Thank heavens it's in a plastic bag."

Adam was just as determined to get an answer as she was in avoiding one.

"She had a really great body, didn't she?"

"Ah, hence the reason for all your concern."

"Hey, I'm just a normal kid with raging hormones. Did you find out what she's gonna' be doing here all summer?"

"What difference does it make to you, Casanova? You're leaving for camp in two days."

"So what... I'd just have to work fast."

Adam wasn't sure himself whether or not he was kidding.

Either way, it didn't matter to Beth. The last thing she wanted to do was dwell on Joanna Cameron. What she really wanted to say, was what she really wanted to feel: 'I don't know and I don't care'. Instead, she reluctantly repeated to Adam what Joanna had told her.

"She said she'd get Ruby to give her a lift over to the Mountain View Motel, spend the night and if she hadn't changed her mind by morning, she'd rent a car and start looking for a place to stay."

In retaliation, Beth poked fun at her son's pubescent fantasies.

"If there's anything else you care to know, like her marital status or if she prefers younger men, let's say around thirteen, you'll have to find her and ask her yourself."

Adam became suspiciously silent. Beth could hear the wheels in her son's head cranking up to full speed as she stopped at the next light.

"Oh man, I don't believe it! This is perfect! Just perfect!" Adam spoke quickly, over the protest in his mother's eyes. "Look, renting a place for the summer is gonna' cost her at least a few thousand bucks. That's probably what it'll take to fix her car. If you let her stay in the carriage house for nothing, she can take the money she'd save by not having to rent a place and use it to pay

Ruby, instead. This way, she doesn't report it to the insurance company and dad won't have a shit fit when he hears you had an accident only an hour after he left." He waited for her response. "So, what do ya' think?"

Beth found merit in that last part, especially having assured Ben she was quite capable of driving safely. From a strictly practical point of view, she had to admit that Adam's plan made a lot of sense, assuming, of course, that Joanna would even consider it. In every other way, the whole idea shook her to the core. Adam's face glowed with the brilliance of his plan.

Beth kept her eyes on the road.

"It's completely out of the question!"

"Why? Give me one good reason."

All of Beth's feelings about the carriage house were far too complex and certainly not open for discussion. She focused instead on Joanna.

"I'm sure the woman has no desire to do her communing with nature in such close proximity to anyone least of all me, wouldn't you say?"

Adam persisted.

"There's only one way to find out. Let's ask her. You said Ruby was gonna' drop her off at the motel. Drive over and let's wait for her there."

Adam obviously had no idea of the emotional roller coaster Joanna had already put his mother on.

"Absolutely not!"

"Aw c'mon, we're gonna' pass the motel on the way home anyway. What have you got to lose?"

"Whatever dignity I have left," Beth thought to herself.

"Just *do* it, mom. *Do* it!"

"I swear to God Adam, if you don't go into sales when you grow up, you're going to miss your calling."

"You'll see, you're gonna' thank me for this one day."

"I'll thank you for letting me run my own life."

Adam ignored his mother's scowl.

"Great! Now all I have to do is convince Joanna."

Beth wouldn't admit how ambiguous she felt about him actually succeeding. The motel was coming up on the right. Against her better judgment, she put on her blinker, slowed down and turned off the road into the parking lot. She pulled up next to the office, turned off the ignition and folded her arms in protest.

"I swear, I don't know how I let you talk me into this. Now suppose you tell me what's in all this for you?"

"Well, for one thing, it'll give me two whole days to get her to fall in love with me."

Beth rolled her eyes at the absurdity of her son's notion.

Adam was a little less forthcoming in admitting his other reason.

"The thing is, I kinda' promised dad I'd look out for you while he was away, so I'm trying to get you a roommate for the summer."

Beth became more than a little annoyed. She was ready to set Adam straight when Ruby's tow truck came into view. Her heart began to race with apprehension as she began to chew mercilessly on the inside of her lip—something she only did when she was extremely anxious.

"I'm telling you now, Adam, she's going to think this whole idea is absolutely ridiculous. *I* certainly do!"

"Relax, will you mom? Just let me do the talking."

Ruby pulled up alongside Beth's window.

"Well, look who's here."

He turned to Joanna, whose sunglasses were hardly sufficient to conceal the extent of her own emotional turmoil at the sight of Beth's car. She opened the door and got out of the truck, as Ruby leaned through his window.

"What are you folks doin' here?"

Beth shook her head.

"Ask my son. He's got everybody's summer plans all figured out."

Before Adam could launch into his explanation, Ruby interrupted.

"Look, if this doesn't involve me, I'd just as soon get back to the shop with this car and set the wheels in motion, so to speak." He turned to Joanna. "Looks like they have the vacancy sign out, so I'm sure you're gonna' be all right here."

Joanna nodded. She checked her pocket to make sure she had his card.

"I'll call you in a few days to find out how long you think it'll be before I can have the car back."

Ruby reached across the back, handed her out her bags and waved a collective goodbye.

Joanna watched with a swirl of dread and relief as this part stranger, part savior drove off with her most prized possession. She dug her hands deep into her pockets, turned and walked over to the station wagon she thought she's never see again. She intentionally approached the passenger side and leaned in through Adam's window, respectful of the distance Beth had drawn with her eyes.

"Please tell me you're not here waiting to run me over and finish me off for good."

Beth forced herself to look squarely at Joanna, if only to be crystal clear. "I want you to know this wasn't my idea."

Joanna looked at Adam curiously. She let her voice and smile suggest a harmless flirtation.

"I love a man with ideas... especially one that's chaperoned by such a forgiving mother."

Her eyes searched hopefully for Beth to interpret her apology but Adam immediately launched into his pitch, leaving the terms of Beth's forgiveness entirely unclear.

"Okay Joanna, here's what I was thinking..."

"My friends call me Jo."

Adam felt greatly encouraged that she already considered him a friend. Maybe two days was all he'd need to become more. With an air of inflated male ego that made Joanna smile, he made sure to exercise his newfound status.

"So Jo, this is what I was thinking...."

Joanna leaned in a bit, deliberately bringing her face closer to his. Beth quietly rolled her eyes. She wasn't sure she liked the idea that Joanna was playing with her son's obvious attraction, but she certainly felt he had it coming. She knew the poor kid had absolutely no idea just how far out of his league he was as he took a deep breath and expounded on the details of his master plan.

"Mom told me you're looking for a place to crash for the summer."

Joanna scowled.

"I'd think twice about using that word if I were you."

Adam apologized then quickly regained his stride. Nearly hyperventilating with excitement, he repeated the plan he'd just described to his mother. By now his head swirled with fantasies of a long distance romance with this beautiful, older woman who he imagined would write him long, seductive letters.

"We have a pool too! You're not married, are you?"

Joanna managed to conceal her amusement and just shook her head. Adam was quite obviously relieved.

"Great, 'cause I thought that even though we'll only have a couple of days before I leave for camp, we could hang out and get to know each other a little better. Once I'm gone, we can write."

Joanna imagined his long, passionate letters. She had certainly sent a few of her own by the time she was his age. By then, Betsy had moved to another state, leaving poor Joanna on the cusp of her sexual awakening. For months she became consumed by the torment of separation until one afternoon, in the midst of her longing, Joanna discovered that her hand could be used in much more gratifying ways than pouring her heart out on paper. As her pleasuring deepened, her letters thinned. Eventually she stopped writing completely, which is not to say that those lessons or those lips of Betsy's were ever forgotten. For a moment, Joanna said nothing. The truth was she was not at all prepared to respond to Adam's proposition. She tried to catch his mother's eye for some help. After all, Beth had made it clear that she'd been railroaded into this but for some curious reason allowed Adam to propose it anyway. Joanna came right out and asked her.

"What do *you* think of the idea?"

Beth was cautious about her answer.

"I have lots of reservations about it."

"I see."

Adam saw his fantasies slowly slipping out of reach. He wished his mother had not been so honest.

"Aw, c'mon mom... name one."

"I'll name several. The place hasn't been used in over a year. It's musty and dirty."

"I'll clean it."

"I have to beg you to straighten your own room?"

Adam swore he'd do more than his share to help.

Beth continued matter-of-factly.

"I'm sure Joanna was intending to stay some place much more comfortable and modern."

Beth used Joanna's full name intentionally, letting her know that by no means did *she* consider a 'friendship' quite so easily established as it was with her son. She looked at Joanna for some confirmation that her assumption about the accommodations was right, but Jo refused to give her the slightest indication, one way or the other. Realizing she'd have to get through this without help, Beth ticked off a list of other practical considerations.

Adam challenged his mother on every point while Joanna stood by watching their conversation like a ping-pong game.

Beth was growing weary.

"There's no air conditioning."

"It has two ceiling fans and no one ever complained... not even grandma, and she complains about everything. And remember how comfortable she said the new sofa bed was the last time she came to visit?"

Beth was now straining to pull some credible objection out from thin air.

"The screens aren't up."

"So, we'll call Steve to hang them."

Adam quickly regretted this last suggestion. He certainly didn't need any competition, considering how very good-looking Steve was.

Beth began to feel each of her objections futile against the strength of Adam's determination. The deeper truth was, having someone—especially Joanna—use the carriage house was a lot more complicated an issue than Beth intended to ever reveal.

Joanna had been listening very carefully to everything Beth *did* and *didn't* say. It was time to put an end to the woman's obvious struggle and at the same time be honest about her own doubts. She was careful not to hurt the boy's feelings.

"Look Adam, as much as I'd like the chance to get to know you better, since you'd be leaving for camp in just a few days I really don't think it would be fair to your mom to subject her to...," Joanna struggled to find the word he'd best understand, "the kind of *stuff* I'd be going through this summer."

"You mean because I won't be here?"

Beth had to turn away. Joanna remained kind.

"Well, that certainly won't make it any easier, but remember I said this was going to be more like a 'journey'?"

Adam nodded.

"Well, they tend to be a lot less pleasant than your regular vacations. I don't think your mom needs to be around that all summer, do you?"

Adam's response was completely unexpected.

"Are you kidding? That makes it even better! Dad told me mom wouldn't go to England with him this summer so that she could stay home and be miserable. So you guys already have something in common! Misery loves company, right?"

Joanna saw the defeat on Beth's face.

"Is that what your father said?"

"Sorry mom, but those were pretty much his exact words."

Beth threw up her hands.

"God, I don't know why I bother to talk to anyone... except for that bathroom tile."

Joanna tried not to appear too amused by Beth's frustration, but it certainly was one that looked perversely charming. In the deadlock of the moment, Joanna offered one final compromise.

"I'll tell you what. Before I check in here I'd be willing to go back with you now and check out this carriage house of yours. If your mother's right, it won't be the kind of space that would work for me and we won't have to agonize over it any more. You'll just drive me back to the motel and we'll all go our separate ways, once and for all." She looked at Beth. "How does that sound to you?"

Adam rushed to answer for her.

"It sounds great!"

This time, Joanna was stern with him.

"I'm talking to your mother."

Beth removed her sunglasses and massaged the bridge of her nose, foolishly hoping to relieve the tension lodged there. Without saying a word, she abruptly removed the keys from the ignition, got out and walked around to the back of the car to open the truck.

"Toss your stuff in."

Before she would, Joanna checked one more time.

"You've got quite a persistent kid there."

"Yeah, he's a real charmer."

"So this is okay with you?"

Beth purposely avoided a direct answer.

"If you value whatever you have in those bags, don't put it anywhere near that container of ice cream. It must be *soup* by now. And by the way, I didn't appreciate the theatrics you pulled back there in the ice cream shop."

Amused by Beth's assertiveness, Joanna actually enjoyed apologizing this time.

"I'm sorry, maybe I overreacted. My ankle was still killing me."

Beth softened somewhat.

"How is it feeling now?"

Joanna removed her own sunglasses and stared straight into Beth's eyes.

"Let's just say, at this very moment it feels like the *least* of my worries."

Thrown off guard, Beth hesitated to consider Jo's meaning, then slammed the trunk shut.

"One more thing. Did you really mean what you said about your interior being as cold and aloof as your exterior?"

"Why do you doubt it?"

"Maybe because I'm not as easily misled as my son."

Joanna knew she was referring to Adam's obvious crush. Beth's eyes dared her to be truthful. Joanna just stared back at her, then deliberately replaced her sunglasses as if to underscore her avoidance.

"Maybe you'll get to find out for yourself."

Jo walked around to the side of the car, opened the back door and got in, leaving Beth standing there wondering if the remark was meant as an invitation or a threat.

Either notion was enough to get Beth started biting on the inside of her lip again. This time she actually broke the skin. Cursing under her breath, she didn't know if she was madder at Adam or herself. At this point, what did it matter? This ridiculous plan of his was already in motion. Beth got back in the car and turned on the ignition, her tongue secretly pressed against the raw spot to hold back the taste of blood—if not all her apprehensions.

Chapter 3

Just a few hundred miles from the dignity of her stylishly appointed loft, Joanna felt as if she'd already been swallowed up by the jaws of mediocrity; sitting now, for all the world to see, in the belly of this rusted monstrosity of a car. It seemed that the cosmic forces were certainly impatient to have their way with her. Her uncharted 'journey' had quite obviously begun with the most dangerous of chauffeurs behind the wheel and a thirteen year old Casanova casting her in his wild, pubescent fantasies.

Outwardly she forced herself to maintain an air of quiet dignity like a soldier who'd just been taken hostage by the enemy, determined not to have her fears known or spirit broken. At every intersection, Joanna's impulse was to stick her head out of the window and scream: "This is not what it looks like! I don't even know these people. My real life doesn't look anything like this. My loft's been featured in Architectural Digest and the car I was driving was a classic '57 T-Bird in showroom condition! I can show you pictures! Someone—anyone—please!" What felt like an eternity was only the distance of two traffic light's. At the third, Beth turned off the main road, leaving Jo slightly less horrified that someone might see her. She needed to know how much longer she would have to keep up this charade of composure before she could get out and make a run for it—back to the motel. Maybe, even all the way back to the West Village.

"How much further?"

"It's less that a mile. Don't worry, I promise no more accidents."

Joanna didn't say a word.

Adam attempted to rally her enthusiasm.

"You're gonna' love it. Did I mention the pool is heated?"

Jo's response couldn't have been any flatter.

"Swell."

By now, the idea of drowning herself in it seemed a viable option compared to facing the summer ahead regardless of where she spent it.

Beth glanced at her passenger through the rear view mirror, quickly sensing Jo's threshold.

"Adam I think we've both heard all the fast talk we care to for now. Just give it a rest."

Adam shrugged off his mother's remark.

"Okay, but you're both gonna' thank me for this one day, you'll see."

Beth gave her son a dirty look that didn't even pretend to be subtle and he wisely retreated into an accommodating silence.

Joanna appreciated Beth's running interference. At the very least, with freshly mowed lawns along the way, this was certainly a more fragrant environment than the hellhole of a bathroom she had endured back at the gas station earlier. In fact, in the quiet of the ride that remained, Joanna was surprised to find the surroundings much more appealing than she would have preferred. She had hoped that it would be hate at first sight. Instead, this was the kind of neighborhood you took in with your heart and not just your eyes.

"Damn it," she thought to herself, "what next?"

As her unpredictable cosmic ride continued, the streets seemed to wind like dark velvet ribbon through the predominantly lush and supple landscape of respectable lawns and lovingly kept gardens. They struck Joanna as the kind tended to by the gloved hands of gardening enthusiasts rather than routinely maintained by the services of a professional landscaper. She guessed that the flowers, whenever picked, were honorably chosen for that special vase on the mantelpiece or dining room table.

In contrast to the delicate miracle of perennial bloom, massive elms, easily hundreds of years old with trunks too wide for human arms to encircle, lined the sidewalks. Their roots, like powerful muscles, burst from the earth and concrete that could no longer contain them. In many places their branches stretched halfway across the street, effortlessly meeting the span of the trees on the other side. The mesh of the interwoven leaves formed a natural tunnel that offered large patches of shaded relief from the heat of the sun. As Beth drove through the contrast of these quiet streets, Joanna imagined the city's congested intersections caught in the unforgiving grip of midday traffic. With her every breath long sustained by the empowering rush of cosmopolitan life, Jo could still feel the vibration of large trucks rumbling like clumsy elephants over the treacherous terrain of potholes and around ruthless pedestrians too impatient to wait for lights to give them the right of way. For so many years, she had been one of them. Inhaling the sweetness of her immediate surroundings, she could still smell the unmistakable fumes of a city bus emptying it's exhaust as it pulled away from the curb; its mere size earning it a respectable place in the swarm of taxis that swept down across the avenues like angry yellow bees, each aggressively maneuvering for it's next sting. For so many years she had held out her arm as a willing target. But as much as it had all become a part of her and she a part of it, from the backseat of such an unlikely starship, this uncharted tour through these lazy streets seemed to be taking her further and further off course.

Adam tried to get a read on her impression.

"Nice neighborhood, huh?"

Alarmed to feel as if she had actually begun breathing on her own again for the first time in years, Joanna was secretly grateful for his interruption. She tried to sound detached rather than deeply moved.

"Yeah, it is. At least from what I can see around this ridiculous cat on the window."

She was counting on her own sarcasm to reinforce her softening skepticism about possibly spending the rest of the summer hiding out in such gentle surroundings. Assuming, of course, that her better judgment didn't save her from making such a foolish and dangerous mistake.

As Beth turned up one street and down the next, each house stood like one in a long and winding receiving line that seemed to welcome Joanna to a place suspended in time. With the exception of a few newer constructions, the homes themselves were as old and proud as the trees that shaded them. Each was properly set back from the sidewalk and spaced discreetly apart, granting one another a thoughtful privacy. Whether charmingly modest or majestic, every home was had been lovingly preserved or restored to its original turn-of-the-century splendor. Joanna found herself drawn deeper and deeper into that past, imagining the gratitude of the families who originally lived in them. This was a neighborhood assured of its own quiet page in history—a page in time turned slowly and respectfully enough from one generation of owners to the next so that nearly a century later, on this peaceful summer's day, an old weathered porch swing still maintained an easy dignity beside a recently installed television cable box and a great climbing tree commanding the focus of an entire front yard still coaxed neighborhood children away from their computer screens and into its outstretched arms.

Against the background of this timeless harmony, clusters of chirping birds provided the perfect accompaniment to the spray of a sprinkler system hitting its leafy target, the slam of a squeaky screen door and the force of a watering hose hitting against the side of a family car being washed in the driveway. Separately and together, they were the reassuring sounds of normalcy that provided all the false security quaint little neighborhoods like this one were famous for. They were the sounds real estate agents counted on to sell houses easily—the sounds that fooled the naïve into thinking that if you lived on a street like this, life would always play fair. No curve balls, no punches below the belt, no broken promises. All your prayers would be answered. All your dreams would come true. But even in the perfect light of this perfect place, the undeniably dark side of personal enlightenment no longer permitted Jo the luxury of being that easily fooled. Something without a name that she could curse at or a shape that she could kick had not allowed that innocence to remain. It was something ominously vague and powerful and all the resistance and bravado she could muster turned out to be of no use against it. Yet, for all her bitter resentment of its inconvenience, it was in her eventual surrender that Jo found herself more reflective than she'd ever been before. At the core of her insight, she knew that in neighborhoods like this, families were careful to suffer in private. Heartache learned to weep in its sleep so that life's unavoidable tragedies could maintain a tastefully low profile without disturbing the beauty of things around it. Joanna further suspected that unlocked front doors and welcome mats cleverly disguised closely guarded family secrets sealed beneath layers of pretty wallpaper and thick tapestry rugs. And in the hours before sunrise while properly covered bodies lie between properly tucked sheets, she imagined the spirits of restless souls crawled out of opened windows and danced naked on rooftops to be closer to the moon, each other and the madness of their own obsessions.

As the car moved slowly through the streets, Joanna cautiously fixed her eyes and instincts on the invisible line between reality and illusion. The obscurity of her own longings blended like a chameleon into the poetic deception of the surroundings and she suddenly caught herself feeling much more comfortable in its ambiguity than she cared to admit. She closed her eyes to block the rest of it out. Adam's voice shattered Jo's thoughts like a glass bottle hitting the ground.

"This is it. We're home!"

His body seemed to levitate in excitement.

Yanked back into reality, Joanna's eyes shot open as the station wagon turned into the Garrison's driveway. The moment of truth had arrived. Like a stoic prisoner of war, Joanna tried to remain undaunted. *Enemy camp* was a masterpiece of disguise; a two-story old Victorian, creamy white with dark green shutters and matching front door, all naturally faded to a story book perfection. The front porch, five steps up from the ground, wrapped all the way around from one side to the other. Wicker furniture with overstuffed cushions was thoughtfully placed for easy conversation or quiet reflection, whichever the hour inspired and 'inspiration' seemed everywhere. Beneath the extended pitch of its roof, budding pastel colored flowers swung ever so gently in their potted cradles. A mixture of vines and yellow roses grew wild against the lattice frame beneath the porch. Like all the others, the house itself was set back from the street, but the elevation of this particular piece of property set it slightly higher than its neighbors on either side, affording it a subtle air of grandeur. Predictably enough, none other than the quintessential white picket fence framed the entire piece of property. The shadow of each slat lay at an angle, crisp against the sidewalk. It was obvious from the moment Jo laid eyes on it that if this neighborhood was some kind of cosmic trap, then this house, in all its understated, captivating charm, was surely the bait itself. If the carriage house was only half as appealing, she knew she was in big trouble!

The driveway was to the left and ended just beyond the side of the house in a separate 2-car garage obviously built years later. Beth parked beside her husband's Jeep. The sight of it was her first reminder, in the calamity of these last few hours, that he was really gone. Beth could never have imagined that her panicked attempt to put this unsettling moment off would lead to something so much more threatening.

Adam jumped out and gallantly opened Joanna's door for her.

"C'mon, I'll carry your stuff!"

Beth must have read Jo's mind. She certainly knew her own and spoke sternly for both of them.

"Hold it right there Adam! Joanna hasn't even seen the place." Beth went around and opened the trunk. "The only thing you can help carry are these grocery bags."

She loaded her son up and marched him off into the house, his face flushed with embarrassment. Joanna was grateful, even if it was at the boy's expense.

"Something tells me you're gonna' catch hell for that when you get inside."

Beth shrugged.

"Let him add it to the long list of things a boy growing up hates his mother for. When he's a man, he can work it all out in therapy, at his *own* expense."

Joanna liked the flair of Beth's response, but her smile folded into itself against the chill of Beth's tone.

"The carriage house is out back. The door is unlocked. Have a look around. I'll keep Adam away, even if it means I have to sit on him." Juggling the remaining groceries, Beth anticipated Joanna's decision. "When you're ready, I'll drive you back to the motel."

In spite of Beth's refusal to ask for help, Joanna reached up and slammed the trunk for her.

"Sounds like you've made up my mind *for* me."

Beth was tired of dancing around the truth.

"Look, we both know this is not what you had in mind."

She assumed Joanna knew exactly what she meant.

"What about you?" Jo was careful to sound impersonal. "Do *you* really want anyone around all summer?"

"Anyone… or specifically *you*?" Without waiting for an answer, Beth turned and headed for the kitchen door, leaving Joanna and her question hanging. "Like I said, I'll be in the kitchen when you're ready."

Joanna studied Beth as she walked away, shifting a bag of groceries and, it seemed, the weight of the world in each arm. When the screen door slammed behind her, all the appealing contradictions about this woman exploded sending shrapnel throughout Joanna's body. Afraid that any movement might set off another round, Jo waited for the pieces to settle in the pit of her stomach before she dared steal her first look at the carriage house itself. She took a deep breath and looked up at the sky. There wasn't a single cloud on which to focus her eye or plea, leaving Joanna no choice but to address the humbling vastness. This was not her style but she was desperate.

"Please… I'll go anywhere… I'll pay anything… just don't make this impossible to walk away from."

Jo wasn't sure if she meant the carriage house or Beth. At this point, it didn't much matter. She knew it had come down to bargaining with those cosmic forces for her life—a life she foolishly once thought only she controlled.

Beth set the groceries down on the kitchen counter and immediately went for the bottle of Excedrin while Adam alternated between glaring at his mother and avoiding her eyes completely.

"Thanks a whole lot mom. I really appreciated being treated like a baby out there."

Despite the pounding in her own head Beth tried to allay his sense of defeat.

"Actually Adam, you should be thanking me."

"Oh yeah, for what?"

"For saving you from making a very big mistake out there."

Beth began to unpack the groceries.

"Honey, let me give you a few pointers about women. If you want to get anywhere with her, you've got to be more subtle. Back off. Give her room to come around. It'll let her know you've got enough confidence in yourself to wait things out. Older women like that in a man."

Beth's little game of psychology worked like a charm. Adam's anger subsided and he began to help her put some of the groceries away.

"Mom, how old would you say Jo is?"

"I'd guess, mid thirties."

Adam looked shocked.

"Really! Can someone that old look that good in a pair of jeans?"

Beth made sure not to face him until her smile faded completely.

"I guess she proves you can."

Still, the idea that he could be attracted to someone *that* old seemed to confuse him. Ms. Lawson, the English teacher he often fantasized about while masturbating, was only twenty-five. Maybe twenty-six, depending upon which reliable source you believed.

"Do you think she's interested in *me*?"

As ludicrous as his question sounded, Beth answered as honestly as she could without having to hurt her son's feelings.

"It's hard to say. She's a tough read."

Her answer made Adam noticeably restless. He moved toward the door.

"I really think I should get out there."

Beth replayed her promise to Joanna. She immediately moved to block the door. If Adam took another step she would sit on him if she had to.

"Hold it right here Adam! You don't want her thinking you're so desperate that you can't wait it out."

At this point, Beth didn't know how wise it was to continue to encourage her son's delusions. She was sure that soon enough Joanna would return from the carriage house and break his poor little heart. She had to say *something* to soften the inevitable.

"Listen honey, chances are she won't be staying."

Adam's face looked pained.

"Don't take it personally. There could be a million other reasons that have nothing to do with you. Let's just wait and see what she says. In the meantime, don't just sit around. Go on upstairs and call Jeff back."

Adam's steps were filled with reluctance, but he decided to take his mother's advice.

Now if only Beth could follow her own. For reasons much less clear, she was just as anxious for Joanna's decision as her son. She deliberately chose to rinse off the bags of fresh fruit, a task that would put her at the sink and directly in front of the window that faced the carriage house. How many times in the past twenty-three years had she stood at that sink looking out at its familiar frame, sensing that in some mysterious way, it validated her very existence? Now with this strange woman walking around inside, picking it apart, judging its worthiness, she felt as if the meaning of her entire life was somehow on trial. In all the years Beth had secretly cross-examined herself about the carriage house, Joanna had instantly become the first and only person whose verdict counted. She knew this obsession with Joanna was absolutely crazy, but nevertheless, absolutely so. Beth began to feel more and more foolish as the minutes ticked by. What could she possibly expect Joanna to 'see' standing there in a dusty room full of mismatched furniture, outdated kitchen appliances and window sills lined with dead bugs? After all, no one else had ever seemed to respond to the carriage house as Beth had herself. From the very first time she wandered off away from Ben and the real estate agent and set foot inside alone, she felt something profoundly compelling about the space—like something precious and sacred once existed within its walls. And yet in all the years they rented the place out for extra income, not a single person who lived there ever spoke of it. Although at times that made Beth think she was insane, she was actually grateful and relieved that no one else, including the members of her own family, had ever seemed to notice its ethereal quality. Like the deepest and most private parts of herself, the carriage house remained *her* secret and *her* mystery. Until now, she had lived in resigned certainty that would never change.

Beth continued to stare through the window. As hard as she tried, she could make out nothing of Joanna's movements inside. At the very least she would be able to see Jo coming out, which would give Beth just enough time to steady herself against the fate of the woman's decision by the time she crossed the yard and reached the kitchen door. For a brief moment, Beth glanced away from the window and down at the sink. She was shocked to find the colander spilling over with assorted berries and cubes of melon. Although the water was running and there was a paring knife in her hand, she had absolutely no recollection of preparing any of it. Her nervous energy may not have provided her with any relief, but it certainly produced an enormous bowl of fruit. Beth looked at the clock over the window, then fixed her eyes back on the door of the carriage house. Her waiting felt endless; as if she'd been waiting all her life. As if she's been waiting even before her life.

Set quietly against the far side of the property, woven in glorious sunlight and vines of ivy, the simple A-frame structure with large, gracious windows and flower boxes was certainly pleasing to the eye. But from the instant Joanna caught her first glimpse of the carriage house from across the backyard, something far deeper—something that felt nameless and wanting—caught hold of her and coiled itself around the walls of her chest, tightening its grip with her every breath.

Now inside, sucking in the thick musty air, Jo couldn't be sure how long she'd been leaning against the wall nearest the safety of the opened door, before her body gradually became hers again. It could have been a minute or a lifetime. The stillness of the room seemed to absorb her voice as she tried to talk herself down into a reasonable state of calm.

"Okay Cameron, you know damn well all this is nothing more than PMS kicking ass again."

Instinctively she put her hand to the pocket of her work shirt, relieved to feel that the small bottle of Motrin she'd dropped into it earlier was still there. Jo didn't bother to look at her watch. As far as she was concerned, her body had just sent out enough undisputable signals that it was time for two more pills. Now the only thing she needed to reclaim her sanity was a few gulps of water to wash them down. Wiping away the beads of perspiration that had collected across the back of her neck, Joanna leaned her face closer to the opened door and drew a few breaths of fresh air to steady herself, before attempting to take a step. She removed her sunglasses and scanned the large open room with exposed vaulted ceilings with glazed indifference. Her only objective at the moment was to get to some water as fast as she could. On the far left side of the room was a compact, L-shaped kitchen built into the corner. With the pills clutched in the palm of her hand, Jo moved toward it, ignoring virtually everything in between. Some of the wooden floorboards creaked under the purpose of her step. She turned on the cold water and waited a few seconds until it ran crystal clear. Too frayed to start guessing which cabinet contained the glasses, she tossed the pills into her mouth, cupped her hand under the faucet and collected enough water to swallow. She threw some on her face before shutting it off, not without noting the bluish ring and chipped porcelain around the drain. Joanna was obviously starting to feel more like herself and had already begun scrutinizing even the smallest details of her surroundings. Joanna looked down to find herself standing on an oval shaped hook rug. She'd always hated those things, but this one struck her as particularly offensive. "Oh God," she thought to herself, and quickly looked away. The kitchen itself seemed marginally functional. It consisted mainly of some painted wooden cabinets built into the corner of the room and bordered on both sides by its only two appliances—an unplugged refrigerator at one end, and a stove on the other. She estimated both to be at least twenty years old and bottom of the line models. Even by 1970 standards, this was definitely a no-frills remodeling job all the way around. By comparison to her own magnificently designed, stainless steel kitchen appointed with every state of the art convenience known to man, Jo noted that this one had no dishwasher, no garbage disposal, no microwave, no coffeemaker and no espresso machine. Not even an electric can opener. As she scanned the deep red Formica counter tops, their finish noticeably worn in several places, she spotted a toaster-oven off to one side and a small electric percolator way on the other. Next to it was a large tin breadbox. For the hell of it, she sauntered over and pulled open its door. The cord to the coffee pot was packed neatly inside. She rolled her eyes. If her idea of 'roughing it' was a run-down kitchen with dated appliances, then she'd found her wilderness. She took a closer look around. The cabinets were painted creamy white. Judging from the dried streaks running across the front of the doors, it was obvious that this was only the latest of several layers of paint applied to them over the years. Bakelite handles were the originals and probably worth more that anything else in that entire kitchen. Skeptically, Jo decided to poke deeper. One at a time, she opened each of the cabinet doors along the wall. Collectively, their contents offered a mismatched though thoughtful assortment of basic kitchen amenities like Tupperware containers, mixing bowls, serving platters, pitchers and drinking glasses. The dishes, a complete service for four, were the only things that actually matched, but everything about the pattern and quality screamed 'yard sale special'. For no particular reason, she randomly pulled out a glass here, a plate there, and examined them more closely. Although everything was thoroughly lacking in style, she was impressed that it was all sparkling clean. Something else caught her attention, instantly causing her heart to swell. Thumb tacked to the front of the shelves was a two-inch red pleated 'skirt' just like the yellow one she watched her mother put up one afternoon when she was just a child. Even at nine, the silly plastic piping struck Joanna as a ridiculous addition and she didn't hesitate to say so.

"Why bother?" she had asked. "It's so stupid. You don't even see it when the doors are closed."

"It's just a lovely, little touch" her mother had explained. "One day when you have a home of your own, you'll understand that sometimes these little things matter more to the heart than they do to the eye." She's promised her daughter when that day came Jo's life would be richer for it.

How deeply Joanna missed the comfort of her mother's voice and wisdom. Even as a precocious youngster, Jo's relentlessly challenging nature would instantly succumb to it. Even at a young age Joanna had the capacity to be humbled by that which was intrinsically profound. Today, despite her sophisticated arrogance that was still true. The trouble was that most people weren't nearly challenging enough to send her into such soul-searching reflection. For the most part Joanna had to do *that* work alone and for the most part that was okay with her, especially when the lessons came hard and when she saw in herself things she preferred no one else see. But now, standing face to face with this powerful reminder of her mother's quiet wisdom, Joanna suddenly felt very much alone. She ran her fingers gently along the ridge of the plastic pleats, feeling the ache of her mother's death more than twenty-two years later as though it happened just hours ago. With the same green eyes that were her mom's, Joanna continued to absorb the rest of the kitchen with a softer heart, this time judging it as much for what it *was* as for all it *wasn't*. Her mother would certainly have encouraged that.

The cabinets below held an assortment of pots, pans and baking trays; all of them apparently well used over the years—none of which Joanna would have much use for. For all the hours she had spent drawing at the kitchen table while her mother prepared family meals, a love of cooking was definitely not something Jo inherited. As an adult Joanna never objected to indulging in fine food, just as long as it wasn't up to her to prepare it. Whether they were for business or pleasure, her dinner parties were always lavishly sumptuous and always guaranteed to be catered. Left to her own devices, a grilled hot dog and fries smothered in ketchup would suit her cravings just as well.

Joanna tested the drawers. Slightly warped by the humidity, each one stuck a little as she tried pulling them open. Among other things she found were some pencils, a small plastic sewing kit, scissors, some used candles, a book of matches and an old spiral notebook with half the pages torn out. She flipped through looking for some cryptic memos but found only a deeply embedded circular scrawling made by someone trying to start the flow of a ballpoint pen. Jo searched through the remaining drawers, finding an assortment of general kitchen utensils including a wire whisk, some wooden spoons, a spatula, a corkscrew and an ice cream scoop, a manual can opener and an old egg-slicer.

The silverware itself was hardly what one would call a set. Although placed neatly in a divided plastic tray, it looked more the selection of a person who had reached blindfolded into a barrel of assorted cheap diner utensils and came out with half a dozen knives, forks and spoons. She drew an immediate comparison to her own set of flatware, having looked at literally hundreds of patterns until she'd found one that suited her uncompromising taste. After all, it had to go with the dinnerware, which had to go with the napkin rings, which had to go with the placemats, which had to go with the centerpiece, which had to go with the table, which had to go with the chairs, which had to go with the Italian marble floor, the walls, the window treatment, the lighting fixtures and, of course, the art, each piece hung with painstaking consideration. And yet, when all was said and done and everything looked perfect, her guts would quietly churn inside when the food being served, though always gloriously presented, would unavoidably clash with the chromatic scheme of the room. Aware of how extreme and ridiculous her obsession with her environment was, Joanna could never actually bring herself to discuss this troubling aspect of the menu with the caterer. Instead, she chose to suffer privately behind polite dinner conversation and shallow smiles until the table was cleared. So extreme was Joanna's reputation for needing to control the aesthetics of her environment, none of her friends would ever think to visit dressed in anything that might clash with its interior. No one except for Gayle, who from the very start of her friendship gave Joanna a run for her money. Gayle had actually accused her of choosing her lovers on the basis of their coloring in order to avoid the trauma of waking up in the morning beside someone whose hair did not coordinate well with her designer sheets and pillowcases. For a moment Jo felt her heart fall to a million pieces, helpless to stop the pain. Still aching, she picked up a soupspoon and held it inches from her face. As she turned it from side to side examining all its scratches and imperfections, the cheap utensil seemed to meet her harsh scrutiny with the grace of a Zen master whose purpose was simply to reflect back the truth. The more Jo twisted and turned the old spoon, the more it did its humble work; its convex angle casting a quietly distorted image back at her. For a moment, the part of Joanna still humbled by intrinsic truths forced herself to reflect on the symbolic distortion that had somehow become her life. That moment—and her bravery—was short lived. Joanna tossed the spoon haphazardly back into the tray and shoved the drawer closed. Her conscience pulled her back. She reopened the drawer and saw that the spoon had landed in with the forks. She picked it up and placed it where it belonged, then shut the drawer more gently this time. She whispered under her breath.

"That was for you, mom. Just in case you're watching."

There was a hall just off of the kitchen and despite her attempt to remain indifferent, Joanna was curious where it led. A few steps later she found it opened up into a small alcove. It contained the only closet space in the whole place. The bi-fold doors had all been left open and except for a few wire hangers that ran along the pole and some bedding packed neatly in plastic bags on the shelf above, the closet was empty. Up against the other wall was an old painted chest of drawers and a mirror with a large chip in the corner. For the third time that day, Joanna was treated to the rather frightening image of herself.

Sudden panic drove her to adjust the fallen collar of her shirt. Wearing her collar up had become a longstanding trademark that fostered an air of aloofness. So established was this look of self-assured composure, Gayle had warned everyone that if Joanna's collar were to ever fall it would be the first sign that Jo was having a nervous breakdown. What seemed like an amusing observation back then now sent a renewed wave of anxiety through her. Out of desperation Jo focused on the rest of the room. An upright vacuum cleaner leaned against an old bookcase with water stains on top. Its shelves contained a box of old tools, some extension cords, several gallons of paint, a can of turpentine and some old brushes. An iron and ironing board were set nearby. An old crate held several empty clay flowerpots of various sizes, along with a bag of potting soil and some gardening tools. Six wooden screen window frames leaned up against one another on the wall beside the bookcase. On closer inspection, except for cobwebs and a little mildew, each one seemed to be in worthy condition, ready for hanging. Joanna crossed the small alcove to the doorway of the bathroom.

If she wasn't interested in the amenities of a Jacuzzi, a double basin sink with stainless steel designer fixtures and recessed lighting, the bathroom seemed adequate enough. The toilet, bathtub and sink all conformed to your basic 1960-remodeling job. Even in its blandness, much like the kitchen, she was surprised by the room's overall cleanliness. Except for a thin layer of dust, everything stood prepared and ready for use—somehow even seeming eager for the weight of a towel across its bar, the running of a hot shower or the drop of a toothbrush into a now empty holder. She swung the medicine cabinet door open and imagined that the lone bottle of aspirin and box of Band-Aids might have been startled by the sudden intrusion of light. She assumed that the matching floral window and shower curtains attempted to compliment the flowers in the nondescript wallpaper pattern, but they failed miserably. Joanna just shook her head in condescending awe of what some people called 'decorating'. Jo peeked behind the shower curtain. A rubber bath mat hung over the towel bar. Despite its age and the bluish ring around the drain, the porcelain was impressively white. For the moment, a lone spider had the whole cavernous tub to itself. Jo parted the curtain over the small bathroom window and gazed out onto a secluded corner of the yard. An old wooden Adirondack chair sat quietly alone amid the bushes and vines of wild berries. A sudden loneliness overcame her. Having traveled to so many parts of the world, Joanna never felt so far from home as she stared out into the stillness only a few hours drive away. Her heart seemed to pull back from itself as she let the parted curtain drop. Jo told herself it was time to wrap up this grand tour and get the hell out of here.

She passed through the small alcove and once again stood in the kitchen area looking out at the rest of the large open room. Although it had been so all along, it was the first time Jo realized that the space was flooded with the most breathtaking sunlight as it came pouring through the two front windows. For a moment Joanna just stood beside the small round kitchen table, unconsciously rubbing her hand across the smooth back of one of the four wooden chairs. Across on the far side of the room some basic pieces of furniture were arranged on an area rug in the usual living room formation. The new sofa bed Adam had mentioned sat centered on the furthest wall with two nondescript end tables and lamps on either side. In front of the sofa was an equally innocuous coffee table, probably purchases at the same thrift shop. A wicker rocking chair was positioned caddy-corner to the couch. Opposite it, a *dated* wood grained TV set sat on a rolling portable stand; its plug pulled out and resting across the top. Joanna played with the prongs of the plug.

"So this is my media room" she mused to herself.

Suddenly aware of her choice of phrasing, Jo's sense of amusement abruptly ceased.

The room started feeling stuffy again. Fortunately she was standing close enough to the wall switch that worked one of the two large ceiling fans hanging overhead. Jo didn't hesitate to test Adam's claim that they were enough to cool the room. In less than a minute the spinning blades broke through the stagnant air to prove him right. Joanna found herself thinking that if only one fan managed to cool the place down this well in the heat of the day, then both fans going at night would make sleeping comfortable enough. Once again, the direction of her thoughts rattled her.

Joanna started pacing from one end of the room to the other, the soles of her shoes clicking against the hard pine wood floor like a sadistic metronome. She began talking to herself.

"For Christ's sake, look at this place! Before today, you wouldn't have been caught dead in a room like this. So what the hell is the problem? Walk out of here, slam the goddamn door and let this kid's mother take you back to the motel. You can figure the rest out from there—once you're safe."

Her rambling suddenly stopped short, as though in her blind pacing, the gauzy meaning of the word caught itself on the jagged edges of reality that seemed to be ripping her life in two.

"Safe from what?" Joanna thought to herself bitterly.

The notion of any kind of security had become a total farce. It certainly wasn't something that came with a high-powered job, an award winning home or even the committed relationship. There was nothing left that Joanna could count on. Nearly everything she had for so long invested herself in felt bankrupt. Her environment had become an ironic reflection of her whole world. Everything had *worked* until one day it just didn't. In the course of those last three years, uncharacteristic bouts of self-doubt made it just as useless for Joanna to look back for answers as it was for her to imagine what could lie ahead. Her heart ached with a grievous sense of doom and her once robust spirit now cowered in shadowy corners while fierce denial and the ugly truth duked it out ruthlessly with little regard for long-held illusions zealously guarded. An older friend had tried to calm Joanna with two little words: Midlife Crisis. Joanna recalled the pat on the back and rest of the sermon.

"Think of it as a macabre roller coaster ride and hang on tight. After the first few drops, you'll get used to it. You won't even bother to scream."

Could *that* be all it was—something as clichéd as a midlife crisis? Only the smallest part of Joanna found any challenge at all in mastering the art of free-fall. With no apparent end in sight, she clung nauseously to what was left of her reinforced life. The T-Bird was actually her one remaining possession that still managed to bring Joanna some pure and uncomplicated joy, and now this ridiculous woman had robbed her of even that. Jo's stomach twisted at the realization of what had happened. Reliving the gruesome moment, her anger, like smoldering embers, rose up and caught fire all over again. Struck with a renewed desire to wring Beth's neck, Joanna suddenly remembered learning about the recent death of Adam's older brother, making her feel guilty all over again about having dealt with his mother so harshly.

"Damn it, what's one thing got to do with another?" she challenged her conscience.

With her hands dug deep into her pockets, Jo walked back over to the other side of the room and stood resentfully in front of the old TV set. She kicked her foot against the stand.

"Shit, I'll bet it's not even color!"

Completely worn out with conflict, Jo looked at the sofa just a few feet away and couldn't resist collapsing into a corner of it. For the first time since she'd left New York, her body began to relax against the welcoming softness of its cushions. As she sank deeper and deeper into an uncharacteristic surrender, she looked around at all the mismatched pieces of furniture. It was Joanna's worst nightmare. At least it would have been at another point in her life. But today, sitting there in the room that assaulted her every aesthetic sensibility, rather than feel uncomfortable, Jo found herself surprisingly amused by it all. There was a kind of contagious relief being in a room that felt so at ease with itself. Its atmosphere of quiet imperfection made it okay that *she* wasn't perfect either. Nor would this room ever require her to pretend that she was. Joanna marveled at how such an unlikely setting could actually make her feel more relaxed than she'd felt for a long time in the comfort of her own home. Her breathing became calmer than it had been in years. She found herself gradually letting go—drawing further and further back from all the hard edges of her expectations and drifting closer and closer to a place of vague but peaceful uncertainty.

Mesmerized by the millions of dancing particles that swirled inside the ray of sunlight, Joanna's eyes were drawn to the large window through which it poured in. She got up and stood directly in front of it. It took a moment for her eyes to adjust to the intensity of the light. She closed them and let it warm her. Once again an odd sense of timelessness swept over her. Disoriented, Joanna opened her eyes to find herself staring down at a small, bluntly shaped heart etched into what appeared to be the original wood frame of the window. Inside the heart were the initials A and E. The carving seemed as old as the window frame itself, probably dating back generations ago when the carriage house was used for its original purpose. Joanna unconsciously moved her hand to the carved heart, letting her fingertips gently trace over its shape, then slowly across each of the initials scratched inside. Undoubtedly influenced by the uncertainty of her own, she wondered about their identity, the course of their lives and whether or not *their* love had survived. She wondered why the heart had been placed there, in such quiet seclusion and not etched boldly on the side of some grand old tree for all the world to see.

Like a camera lens that sharpens and blurs the images nearest and furthest away, Joanna's eyes shifted their focus away from the window frame to the yard outside. The view was as enchanting from this vantage point as it had been from the front as they drove up. The yard itself was made completely private by the natural fullness of the shrubs and bushes that surrounded the property on all sides. Against the rear of the main house, a set of French doors opened up onto a brick patio. A deep green canvas awning over the doors had been left open to shade an antique wrought iron table and chairs. Pastel colored geraniums in various size clay pots were set about the perimeter with a barbeque grill just off to the side. The patio area itself stepped down and extended out to meet the lawn that surrounded the pool. At the shallow end, four chaise lounges faced the midday sun. Joanna's thoughts drifted along with a yellow raft that bobbed lazily in the cross currents of the jets. In a moment of weakness, she wondered what it might be like to actually spend the summer here. It was becoming much too easy to imagine. Jo felt her eyes drawn to the window of the kitchen into which Beth had so abruptly disappeared, wrestling with her grocery bags and God knows what else. Joanna fought hard with herself not to wonder and not to care. The little she already knew was already too much. In the privacy of the carriage house she began chastising herself.

"The last thing I need right now is to get caught up in the mess of that woman's life." Jo corrected herself. "No, the last thing is to have her get caught up in the mess of mine."

It didn't bode well that Joanna had already found it a struggle to avoid the inquisition of Beth's eyes in the brief exchange they'd already had. Her intention for a summer of anonymity already felt much too threatened.

She abruptly turned away from the window and faced the room again, hoping this time the reality of its style-less interior would disturb her. But try as she did to find it unacceptable, a part of Joanna had already settled in. Against her better judgment, she began to assess just how much work it would take to get the place in shape and make it livable for the next eight weeks. Considering how much tension she'd built up in her body lately, the idea of losing herself in some real physical labor was actually appealing. Jo remembered her father's long-standing response whenever she would complain about how 'soft' corporate life had made her.

"Show me you can still swing a hammer better than any guy I know and there's a job waitin' for you on my crew anytime you want to chuck big city life."

Often when his offer seemed too tempting, Jo's only recourse was to remind him that he could never match the salary she'd grown accustomed to making. He'd always come back at her the same way.

"Movin' parts were meant to move. If they don't, it'll cost ya' in the end."

Joanna smiled just thinking about him. There was something about her father's simple, earnest philosophy that never failed to get to the heart of any matter, nor had she ever known his spirit to be broken. Losing her mother was the closest he'd ever come, and even then he was always careful to speak hopefully of the future in front of his children. He'd always looked for the meaning of their loss and somehow managed to turn a family tragedy into a family triumph. He had always been a wonderful husband and after the death of his wife, he grew even deeper into his role as a wonderful father. As recently as their last conversation before she left New York, Joanna recalled putting down the phone and thinking how important his love and support had remained in her life. She wasn't quite sure just how much she was able to make him understand about 'things', but she was absolutely certain that his thumbs-up optimism was behind her all the way. Haunted by his reminder about moving parts, Jo's shoulders felt even stiffer than usual. She tried to recall the last time she'd actually climbed a ladder, clutched a hammer, guided a jigsaw or felt the vibration of an electric sander course its way up her arm and down through her body. She looked down at her work-shirt, unable to remember the last time she'd worn it to actually work in. It all seemed so long ago. Then again, everything really satisfying about life seemed that way. Long ago and far away. Joanna fought to reign herself in. This time she was much more realistic. There was no way she could stay.

Jo turned off the fan and slammed the door behind her. Forcing herself not to look back, she walked around the pool toward the Garrison's house. As a matter of simple reinforcement, she rehearsed her decision, repeating over and over again under her breath, "I'm sorry, but it's not what I had in mind… it's not what I had in mind… it's not what I had in mind."

Beth's waiting had finally come to an end. Her position at the sink had paid off. Watching through the window, her heart began to pound as Joanna crossed the yard and approached the porch. Suddenly Beth felt as desperate to have Jo gone, as she was to have her stay. The sound of Joanna's footsteps against the floor of the porch warned Beth she had only another moment to pull herself together. Hoping to buy herself even a few more seconds, she yanked open the refrigerator door and stuck her head and shoulders as far in as possible. Joanna knocked on the screen door rather than assume she was welcome inside. Beth tried hard to sound nonchalant.

"Come in."

She shifted and reshifted the same two or three items until she felt the hot flush on her face sufficiently eased by the chilled air inside the refrigerator.

Joanna waited awkwardly with her hands in her pocket. She used the time to rehearse her lines and peruse the room in which she stood. She tried to ignore that the Garrison's kitchen felt wonderful; not necessarily for its style, but for its obvious warmth of heart. It was a room that felt central to a strong family life. The kind she herself had grown up in. It was filled with all the 'little touches' her mother had told her about. Joanna's eyes raced against time to absorb them all. With the limited knowledge she had about Victorian era houses, Jo knew that the kitchen staircase led up to the master bedroom. She would not permit her thoughts to lead her there too.

Beth finally found the courage to come out of her hiding place. She backed out of the refrigerator, stood up and slammed the door so hard that the impact sent all of the magnets flying about. Joanna smiled and intentionally looked away, trying to ignore yet another of the woman's bumbling mishaps. Cheap shots weren't Jo's style. Mortified, Beth scrambled to retrieve the magnets from the floor while Jo groped for someplace else to look. The overloaded colander of fruit sitting beside the sink seemed worthy enough of a distracting comment.

"Either you and Adam are big fruit lovers or you're hosting a convention here in a few hours."

Beth's eyes followed Joanna's.

"I may have cut up too much." She nervously picked up the kitchen towel and began wiping her hands, despite the fact that they were neither wet nor dirty. "Would you care for some?"

Joanna just shook her head. Both women seemed reluctant to get to the point. After a long, awkward pause, Jo dug down deep for her lines.

"Look, the place isn't what I had in mind…"

Trying to appear unaffected by Joanna's decision, Beth immediately cut her off.

"Fine. I'll drive you back to the motel."

Joanna took a deep breath while Beth began nervously searching through her bag for the car keys.

"You didn't let me finish. I'd like to try it anyway. That is, if that's okay with you."

Beth whirled around to find Joanna herself looking as shocked with her own decision as she was. Beth was struggling for a response when Adam came bounding down the rest of the stairs.

"I told ya' she'd like it! Now can I take her stuff out of the car?"

It was obvious Beth needed some time to fully process Joanna's decision.

Frankly, so did Joanna.

"Why don't you give me and your mom some time alone. We'll let you know when we're done talking things over."

Adam winked at his mother for her earlier advice.

"Take all the time you need. I'll be outside shootin' some hoops in the driveway."

Intrigued by this new person, BJ hovered.

"Let's go boy. Give the lady some space."

Adam held the screen door open and the dog followed him out.

Beth couldn't stop wringing her hands with the towel, Joanna couldn't help commenting.

"Keep that up and the friction's gonna' start a fire."

Embarrassed, Beth practically slammed the towel down on the counter.

"Look, it's pretty obvious you're not thrilled with my decision. Just drive me back to the motel like we agreed. It was a crazy idea anyway. So let's just forget it."

She was halfway out the kitchen door when Beth stopped her.

"Wait! It's not that. Frankly, I never imagined you'd consider staying, so I never really thought about what it would be like."

Joanna let the door close and stepped back inside.

"To be honest, neither did I. Let's face it, I came up here to be alone and supposedly you stayed behind to be alone. From the sound of things, neither one of us were planning to be very social this summer. The last thing either of us needs is to have someone around all the time."

She paused for a moment and searched Beth's eyes. They were filled with undeniable conflict. That was enough for Joanna.

"I'll tell Adam I changed my mind and wait for you in the car."

Before Beth could stop herself the words came rushing out.

"But it's not like we'd be living under the same roof..."

Joanna turned and faced her.

"And nothing says we have to have anything to do with each other, right?"

Beth was quick to agree.

"That's right."

"If we both want the same kind of summer, maybe it *could* work. Why don't we try it on a week-to-week basis? You stay out of my way and I'll stay out of yours."

"Fine."

Beneath her seemingly nonchalant response, Beth's heart had begun to race wildly. The same was true for Joanna's.

"The minute it becomes a problem for either of us, we just say so and I'm outa' here. No questions asked and no hard feelings."

Beth repeated Joanna's words as if to assure herself she could handle Joanna's leaving later, rather than sooner.

"No hard feelings."

Once again another awkward silence fell between them. Beth tried not to resume biting the inside of her lip. It had only recently stopped bleeding. She scrambled for something to say.

"Are you sure wouldn't care for some fruit?"

"I'm sure."

For fear of another lapse, Jo tried to keep their exchange rolling.

"Okay then, here's what I think…."

Beth pointed to the table and chairs, motioning that perhaps they should sit down while they had this discussion.

Joanna pulled out a chair.

"Except for the cobwebs and dust, the place is in decent shape." Jo refrained from expressing any value judgment about the décor itself. "It needs a good airing out, but obviously we can't open the windows until the screens are hung. I checked them out and they seem to be in pretty good condition, so the first thing I'll do is put 'em up."

Beth interrupted.

"It's out of the question. You shouldn't have to do anything."

Joanna began to panic at the thought of being idle. She decided to be honest.

"Look, the truth is I *need* something to do that'll keep me busy for a while. At least until I wind down. The physical labor will do me good. I can hang the screens with my eyes closed and while I'm at it I'd be happy to take a look at anything else that needs fixing."

Jo couldn't help but notice Beth's skepticism.

"I'll give you the number of my father's construction company. Call him. He'll tell you that when I was a kid I chucked my Barbie doll for a tool belt. During the summers, I worked my way through art school on his construction crew. As a woman and the boss' daughter, I had a lot to prove."

Beth tried to explain.

"It's just that we try to throw Steve as much work as we can. He was a student of my husband's a few years ago. Ben thinks he's a very promising writer and he's struggling to support himself through his first novel.

"Fine. I'm just saying, I don't mind pitching in."

"The more the merrier. I'm sure you'll like him"

Joanna's face froze.

"I'm not interested in being social, remember? So don't go making any finger sandwiches!"

Beth began biting on her lip.

"I understand."

She looked down like a child who'd just been scolded.

Joanna regretted sounding so harsh.

"I'm sorry. It's just that something tells me I'm gonna' have my hands full just trying to moderate your son's fantasies. When exactly does he leave for camp?"

"Day after tomorrow."

Beth smiled.

"You'd better pace yourself. That kid can be mighty demanding when he fixes himself on something, and I suppose it's pretty obvious that he's altogether fixed on you."

Joanna sat back and folded her arms.

"Well, he's met his match. And I intend to make sure he more than lives up to his promise of helping to get this place in shape. He'll regret he ever suggested it."

"Do you have any idea how I'd have to beg him for that much help?"

"That's because he's not interested in fondling your breasts."

The explicitness of Jo's remark caught Beth off guard and for a moment she felt herself blush. Unable to remember the last time her own breasts were fondled, her heart filled with a longing that luckily Joanna didn't notice.

"Is there anything else you'd like him to do while I still have him under my spell?"

"Get him to clean his room. That would be a miracle."

Joanna snapped her fingers.

"Consider it done. Now, what's in all this for me?"

Beth thought for a minute.

"How 'bout the keys to my husband's Jeep so you don't have to rent a car?"

"Deal!"

For the second time that morning, the women shook each other's hand. This time a tentative smile rounded out their touch.

Beth's eyes sparkled with conspiracy.

"If it's a man's world the least they can do is start paying their dues while they're young"

"Seems like fair payback to me. I'll tell Adam he can take my stuff out of the car."

As she turned to go, the sincerity of Beth's voice broke her stride.

"Jo, what was it that make you decide to stay?"

Joanna was hardly prepared to deal with the complexity of Beth's question. She skillfully worked to avoid it.

"You just called me 'Jo'."

Beth seemed a little surprised herself.

"I guess I did."

"So two women playfully manipulating the opposite sex makes us *friends*?"

Beth was quick to correct her.

"Hardly. I'd call that *sisterhood.*"

Joanna let her eyes soften into a smile.

"I see. Something told me that developing a friendship with you wouldn't be that simple."

Beth folded her arms across her chest.

"You're right, it isn't."

For a moment Joanna felt both challenged and intrigued. She narrowed her eyes and stared back sharply.

"Well that's good. I'm glad to know you're not that easy. I was expecting your standards to be at least as tough as mine."

Jo was sure that her comment would make Beth fold. She was wrong.

"You haven't answered me. What made you decide to stay?"

This time Beth's eyes, if not her question, were impossible for Joanna to ignore. She answered her truthfully, barely able to say the words.

"I honestly don't know."

There was utter exhaustion in her voice.

If Beth had known Joanna better, she would have known to let it go at that. But Beth's need to have her own feelings about the carriage house validated made her foolishly press for more.

"There must have been *something* about it... something you sensed... something you felt... something that..."

Joanna suddenly slammed her fist down on the table, stopping Beth mid-sentence and mid-breath.

"Damn you, lady! I said I don't know!" She was fuming. "Do you have any idea how hard it is for me to admit that? Do you have any idea how much I hate those words? *Me*—the person who once knew every goddamn thing about what I wanted and now doesn't know shit! But hey, I can take a joke. It's only my life!"

Beth was completely unprepared for Joanna's reaction.

"I'm so sorry. I didn't mean to upset you. I had no right to press you like that. God, How many more ways can I manage to upset you in one day?"

Beth was obviously wrought with guilt. Joanna felt responsible.

"Forget it. It's not your fault. I'm just a fucking mess lately, that's all."

Beth instinctively filled a glass with water and handed it to her. To Beth's surprise, Joanna continued speaking, not daring to look up from the half empty glass. Her voice sounded tentative, almost shy.

"I know you're gonna' think I'm crazy but I think it was the red pleated shelf piping."

Beth didn't say a word. She simply reached out and touched Joanna's arm. Her eyes filled with tenderness.

"I don't think you're crazy."

Joanna wouldn't look up from the glass. She couldn't believe she'd just made such a ridiculous confession.

"You don't?"

Beth's voice was soft and reassuring.

"Not at all. Do you know how many times over the years I've gone in there and tried to take that piping down?"

Joanna listened as Beth continued.

"Each time I started, I'd get only so far and then something would stop me. Whatever portion I managed to take down, I simply wound up re-tacking. This went on for years. Between tenants, I'd go back in there and try again, until one day I just gave up and decided to leave it just the way it was. I imagine the caretaker's wife put it up back in the 1950s. I understand the couple lived in the carriage house while they worked for the doctor that Ben and I bought the house from years later. It just seemed unkind somehow to destroy something that someone had obviously put so much love and care into. I though of all the silly little touches I've added to our house over the years that mean so much to me. Things I wouldn't expect anyone else to even notice."

Joanna was quietly unnerved at how close Beth had come to understanding.

"What is that, some kind of a *mother thing*?"

Beth looked confused. Joanna shrugged.

"Never mind."

This time Beth was wiser.

"Maybe the piping touched you the same way. If it did, I certainly wouldn't think you're crazy." She hesitated. "Just very special." Her smile hinted at a little playful revenge. "Maybe even special enough to earn my friendship... *if* I decided I wanted one."

Joanna took her lashing well. That is to say, she simply nodded in acknowledgment of Beth's well-delivered point. She finished the water and put the glass in the sink.

"I'll go find Adam."

However hopeless her son's silly little crush, Beth felt happy for him. For reasons much less clear, she even felt a little happy for herself.

"I'm sure he's been counting the minutes." Beth paused for a second. "By the way, thank you for not saying anything when I slammed the refrigerator door and all the magnets flew off. With my track record, you must have known how embarrassed I was."

Halfway through the screen door, Joanna didn't bother to turn around.

"You missed one… on the floor under the table."

She let the door slam as if to punctuate her observation. Beth was intrigued at how effortlessly Joanna had bounced back from despair to her smooth and arrogant self. She bent down and picked up the flower shaped magnet Jo had pointed out. Instead of replacing it on the refrigerator door, Beth unconsciously held it to her heart.

Chapter 4

Concentrating his aim at the hoop above the garage door, Adam didn't hear Joanna approach from behind.

"Can I take a shot?"

He spun around and tossed her the ball.

"You and my mom work things out?"

Jo bounced the basketball a few times just to get reacquainted with its feel. It had been years since the last time she took on her brother in the family driveway.

"Enough for you to get my stuff from the car and haul it over to the carriage house." She shot from the side and watched with relief as the ball dropped smoothly through the hoop. At least there was *something* she hadn't lost her knack for.

Adam was obviously impressed. He retrieved the ball and tossed it back to her.

"Nice shot. How 'bout a game of 21?"

"You haven't got the time."

"Sure I do. I've got all day."

"I don't think so. Remember that promise you made about doing whatever it took to get the place in shape? Well phase one is about to begin."

Adam began to see what little romantic time he'd imagined with Joanna quickly dissolving by the minute.

"How many phases are there ?"

Joanna eyed the Jeep and considered the terms of the bargain she'd just struck for the keys. Without even the slightest hint of conscience, she put her arm across the boy's shoulder and led him toward the trunk of Beth's car. She lowered her eyes into something unquestionably suggestive and counted on his imagination to fill in the rest.

"That depends on just how capable a guy you turn out to be."

In a voice obviously straining to be deeper than it actually was, Adam took the bait.

"No problem. I can handle anything you need done."

Joanna smiled—but only slightly—hoping to conceal her amusement. She figured it couldn't hurt to reinforce her game plan by throwing in the threat of a little competition.

"Your mom's calling that guy—what's his name—Steve. She thinks we'd hit it off."

Jo watched the distress spread across Adam's face as he struggled to pull her things from the trunk. Adam tried hard not to show the strain of their weight. She took pity on the boy.

"I figure the more of us working, the faster everything will get done and the more time you and I will have to get *closer* before you have to leave for camp." She could see his mind racing to decode the exact meaning of the word '*closer*'. She could also see him really struggling to maneuver her bags all by himself.

"Let me give you a hand."

Adam pushed out his chest in a gallant attempt to appear larger and stronger than he really was. Working against him was the ridiculously oversized t-shirt he had on that only accentuated his gangly, underdeveloped physique

"No thanks. I've got it ."

It was a long way across the yard. Genuinely concerned that Adam might hurt himself, she figured the least she could do was give his morale a little boost.

"You're much stronger than I thought. I'm impressed. Wait for me inside. I'll be back in a few minutes."

Though his back was towards her, Jo could sense Adam beaming as he lumbered off across the length of the back yard. She continued to watch as he struggled to maintain his footing and balance as each labored step met the irregularity of the grassy earth beneath it. "Poor little man," she mumbled under her breath, "Be careful what you wish for. By the time I get through putting you through the paces, you'll be too tired to even remember where it was you were dreaming of putting those sweaty little hands of yours."

Jo turned and headed toward the house, eager to report back to Adam's mother the status of their little deal. She pulled open the screen door and noticed that Beth was on the phone. Jo would have preferred to wait outside but Beth signaled for her to stay.

"I'm just holding while Steve checks his schedule for tomorrow. I explained the situation. " At least the parts she could explain.

Joanna sat down at the kitchen table watching as Beth played nervously with the telephone cord.

"How'd things go with Adam?"

"Take a look for yourself."

Beth peered through the window, her eyes following her son's last faltering steps across the yard before struggling with the screen door and disappearing inside.

Jo couldn't resist gloating.

"The keys to your husband's Jeep are virtually mine."

Beth held up a finger indicating that Steve had come back on the line. Her face registered an immediate sign of relief. Beth placed her hand over the mouth of the receiver, quite certain that Jo's response was not the first impression she wanted Steve to form of her.

"What kind of bagels do you like? He's offered to stop and pick some up for breakfast on the way over."

"Not interested."

"It's only a bagel. Not nearly a social commitment as, let's say, finger sandwiches."

Jo was reluctant to give Beth credit for her wonderfully wry sense of humor.

"Onion or poppy, I couldn't care less."

Beth removed her hand from the mouthpiece and repeated the choices. She thanked Steve for his thoughtful gesture and assured him there'd be a fresh pot of coffee brewing when he arrived. Now for the moment of reckoning. She hung up and turned to gauge the level of Jo's displeasure. The look on her face was every bit as sour as Beth expected it to be.

"Oh come on…you're going to have to eat this summer."

She studied Jo closely, hoping for even the slightest sign of non-verbal truce. When she got it Beth decided to live dangerously and risk everything.

"As long as we're on the subject of eating, what would you say to an invitation to supper tonight?"

Jo's body stiffened immediately, but before she could hastily decline, Beth quickly continued.

"I'm making a roast for Adam and myself and I'm sure there's going to be much too much food for just the two of us." She rushed to emphasize the *practical* rather than the *social* aspect of the invitation. "You won't have anything in the fridge until you go shopping, and a home cooked meal beats pizza or Chinese take-out."

When Jo showed no indication of accepting, Beth offered one more possibility.

"At the very least, let me bring a plate over to the carriage house." She smiled shyly. "Whether you believe this or not, I've never dropped a hot dish on anyone. That's the truth."

Jo rewarded Beth's self-defacing reference with a concession.

"Okay, I'll come to dinner but just this once and only because I don't want to test your record and possibly end this day in the burn unit of the local hospital."

Beth was genuinely pleased. Then for reasons much too confusing to sort out she became increasingly nervous, almost wishing she hadn't mentioned the idea in the first place. She tried to calm herself with a little lighthearted disclaimer.

"Hotplates not withstanding, the only thing I *can't* promise won't wind up in your lap tonight is my son."

"I can handle *him* easily enough. It's *you* I've gotta' worry about!"

As soon as she'd said the words, Jo realized she wasn't at all sure if she was referring to her property or to her life itself. Her ambivalence went undetected.

"Adam will be thrilled. I'm sure he'd much rather be flirting with you than babysitting me all night."

"If these next few hours go as planned, he'll be way too tired to eat out of my hand, let alone make it up onto my lap."

A sudden wave of maternal instinct interrupted Beth's laughter.

"Shame on us. How can we take such unfair advantage of an innocent young boy?"

"Let's remember whose idea this was in the first place. This whole arrangement may turn out to be a disaster for both of us and all because of that conniving kid of yours."

After careful consideration Beth gave the command.

"Take no prisoners! Leave no man standing… including my son!"

Jo pushed back her chair, rose to attention and mockingly saluted.

"Especially your son!"

For an uncharted moment, the two women shared a burst of commiserating laughter. Together they peeked out through the kitchen window in the direction of the carriage house. Adam was wrestling with BJ on the lawn just outside its front door. Joanna drew a long deep breath and shook her head. She tried to remember what it actually felt like to have that much energy to waste.

"I'd better get out there and redirect some of those pent-up hormones.

"Adam knows where all the cleaning supplies are… not that he's ever used them with any enthusiasm before today. Get him started and I'll be over to pitch in just as soon as I get the roast going in the oven?"

"On the contrary. Do us *both* a favor and stay out of the way. Nothing breaks sexual tension between a pubescent boy and the object of his desire like the sound of his mother's voice."

Overly sensitive to Joanna's rejection, Beth conceded to her strict instructions.

"Well, far be it from me to interfere with your plans."

Joanna pushed open the screen door and leveled her eyes directly at Beth's.

"I'd say you crossed *that* line a few hours ago, when you rammed my car." For the second time that afternoon, she let the door slam to punctuate her remark.

Curiously, though, this time the sting of her sarcasm seemed to have missed its mark. As Beth watched the woman stride across the familiarity of her own backyard, she couldn't help wonder if Joanna had stopped aiming to kill.

As soon as he saw Jo approaching, Adam tossed BJ off his chest and scrambled to his feet. He was obviously embarrassed that she caught him doing something as childish as wrestling with a dog. His voice cracked with nervous anticipation.

"Your stuff's inside. I didn't know where to put it, so I just left it by the door."

"That's fine."

A part of Jo wondered if she would be staying long enough to unpack. In spite of her doubts, she wasted no time picking up where she'd left off. The sticky heat of the day was the perfect excuse for Jo to casually undo another button of her work shirt, making it obvious she wasn't wearing a bra. Rubbing the back of her neck and spreading the collar, she made sure it fell open just enough to keep him mesmerized and entirely committed to the task at hand.

"It's hot as hell, isn't it? Guess we'll both be working up quite a sweat together once we get going."

Joanna let the deliberate phrasing of her words slowly arouse his imagination—along with whatever other parts of his body were paying attention. Standing closer than he'd ever been to a *real* woman's breasts, for a few brief moments, Adam considered himself to be the absolutely luckiest man alive until the woman of his dreams began running down a seemingly endless list of chores he was to get started on immediately. Sensing his conflicted enthusiasm, Jo casually dropped her arm around his shoulder, just enough so that his arm made contact with the side of her breast as it moved loosely behind the pocket of her shirt. Adam's heart beat wildly as she led him inside the carriage house, completely oblivious to his sealed fate. Jo held the door open for BJ but his loyalty only went so far. After a moment's consideration, he opted for a shady patch of lawn and a long afternoon nap instead. Comfortably sprawled out on his side, he thumped his tail on the grass a few times and trained his intelligent eyes directly on Jo's. She found his mind easy to read.

"Lady, the boy may be a sorry fool, but your little charade is obvious to *me*."

Joanna stared for a moment longer and winked. Canine or not, she was duly impressed with his powers of perception, and in that instant, considered him a worthy friend. She let the screen door slam behind her. Determined to get the most out of her unsuspecting admirer over the next several hours, she carefully monitored Adam's attention span, skillfully adding a potent blend of harmless flirtation and random hints of flesh to the otherwise unpleasant mix of cleansers, scrub brushes and vacuum cleaner attachments. The heady mix proved to be so intoxicating that when Beth appeared in the doorway with an armful of freshly folded linen, a plate of cookies balanced on top and a pitcher of ice cold lemonade, she could hardly believe the transformation. Her eyes darted from one end of the room to the other in utter amazement. Every surface sparkled. Every inch of the floor was spotless. Not a cobweb, dust ball or dead insect remained. Though a far cry from 'the kitchen of tomorrow', every appliance gleamed and looked as though it was new. Each of the windows, once cloudy and sealed, was now shining and opened wide. The spinning blades of the two overhead ceiling fans circulated the fragrantly fresh country air. The set of screens had been pulled out from the small alcove, vacuumed and awaited hanging. Beth was in shock. Everything appeared amazingly fresh and revitalized. In contrast, Adam appeared thoroughly exhausted and drained. His shoulders, and morale, hung pathetically low. His thin young fingers looked like wrinkled old prunes. When Jo wasn't looking, the boy managed to catch his mother's attention and silently rolled his eyes, implying that things were not going exactly as planned. That was, of course, dependant upon which set of plans were being assessed. In spite of her own delight, Beth took pity on her son and tried to sound encouraging.

"Honey, the place looks wonderful! You did the work of at least three grown men."

She chose her wording carefully, hoping it would boost his frail masculine ego in front of the woman he'd obviously worked so hard to impress. Jo picked up on Beth's intention.

"Your son is absolutely incredible. He's turned this place completely around, almost single handedly. He's got more stamina than most men I know twice his age."

Completely taken in by Joanna's compliment and intentionally seductive wink, Adam felt a renewed sense of prowess. Eager to pad his chivalrous image, he grabbed the pitcher and offered to pour.

Joanna was anxious to get Beth alone for a few minutes so they could share the success of their little scheme.

"While Adam's pouring, come check out the amazing job he did back here in the bathroom. He managed to get the tub so clean I can hardly wait to strip down and shower."

Jo was shamelessly deliberate in leaving him with the image of herself naked… dripping wet… and only a few hundred feet from his bedroom door. As soon as the two women were safely out of view, they muffled their laughter and shook each other's hands.

"Congratulations" Beth whispered under her breath. "Apparently you know what you're doing."

Beth's eyes dropped to Jo's open shirt.

"It's obvious you don't believe in playing fair."

Jo shrugged.

"I had a bargain to seal. I did what always works."

Flustered by Joanna's commanding sexuality, Beth withdrew her hand as if to avoid some greater danger.

"You sound pretty sure of yourself."

Jo intentionally crossed her arms—a move she knew would lift her breasts and reveal more cleavage.

"That's because I am."

Beth tried to sound clever.

"How many more buttons will it cost you?"

"As many as it takes."

Once again, something about Joanna's sexual confidence completely unnerved Beth. Fortunately her son's well-timed call pulled her back to safety.

"Doesn't anybody want the lemonade I poured?"

Beth struggled to think quickly.

"We'll just be another minute sweetie. I'm giving Joanna some tips about the temperamental plumbing in here."

Jeep or no Jeep, the accumulating toll of this seeming endless day was finally taking hold. Jo parted the front of her shirt, once again drawing Beth's attention to the unfair advantage she held over her son.

This time, Joanna got more than the *rise* she was looking for. Though conscious of keeping her voice down, Beth responded sharply.

"You can be as merciless with him as you please. As far as I'm concerned, he's even got it coming. But let's get something straight. That kid out there is still legally a minor, and I have every intention of sending him off to camp in a few days the virgin I know he is."

Joanna couldn't believe Beth's insinuation. Fuming with indignation she managed to keep her voice and scathing anger in check.

"Trust me, your little man isn't even remotely my type."

Beth was eager to dismiss her unsettling desire to know who *was*.

"Good! I'm relieved to hear that."

Neither woman was ready to back down. Prompted by Adam's second call, Beth turned to rejoin her son. Jo grabbed her arm and held her back.

"Wait a minute. This isn't over."

Beth looked at her coldly, then down to her arm.

"You're hurting me."

Though still offended, Jo loosened her grip. She was, after all, a stranger and a highly manipulative one at that.

"I'd never do anything to violate your son. You *do* know that, don't you?"

Joanna waited until Beth nodded.

"Of course I do." She shook her head. "I don't know what came over me just now. That remark was totally uncalled for. Please, forgive me."

Jo was willing to assume her share of responsibility.

"I'm sorry I came on so strong. I was intentionally trying to provoke you and obviously it worked."

Beth looked at her curiously.

"Why?"

By now Jo was just too tired to evade the truth.

"If I was willing to admit for the second time today that I don't know, do you think this time you could just leave it at that?"

Beth offered an accommodating smile.

"I can do that."

"Thanks."

Overcome by a combination of physical and emotional fatigue, Beth pressed her hand to the still swollen wasp sting on her cheek. She let her hand drop, reached behind her neck and rubbed as deeply as she could.

"God. What an unbelievable day this has been, and it's not even close to being over."

"Tell me about it. You didn't by any chance spike that lemonade with anything stronger?"

"No, unfortunately not."

"Too bad. I sure could use it."

Beth tried to smile, but it simply took too much effort.

"Me too."

For a fleeting moment the expression in Beth's eyes bordered on something haunting and empty. As certain as Jo was about what she saw, that's how uncertain she was about what to do. She frantically pieced together all the fragments of information she'd found out about Beth in so short an amount of time: that it was just three summers ago that she'd lost her older son in a tragic car accident—that just this morning her husband left to lecture in England for the summer and that, for reasons far too complicated for the likes of Trudy's husband to understand—Beth had chosen not to go with him. From her own experience, Jo knew that the woman who carelessly rammed into her ankle in the supermarket and then into her car out in the parking lot, was frantically scattered and dangerously preoccupied. But she also knew that the woman behind this haunted expression—the one who somehow understood instantly about the silly shelf piping inside the kitchen cabinets—was intuitive and dangerously perceptive. Burdened with this unwanted knowledge, Jo couldn't help but wonder how the hell she'd managed to wind up smack in the middle of all of it. Wasn't the pathetic shambles of her own life complicated enough? How could this unlikely arrangement turn out to be anything but a complete disaster for both of them? From somewhere deep inside came two curiously different warnings. Her head said, "Grab your stuff and run." Her heart said, "This time you've got to stay."

Conflicted as she was, she couldn't ignore the woman's pain. Joanna's gut reaction was to reach out and take Beth's arm, but something uncertain prevented her from extending such personal comfort. Instead, she awkwardly dug her hands deep inside her jeans pockets. Safe from the danger of contact, she offered a more measured dose of concern.

"Are you okay?"

From her trance-like state, Beth answered mechanically.

"No, not really." She was surprised how easy it was to admit the truth to a total stranger.

Jo wasn't at all sure about what to do with Beth's honesty. She began to feel herself panic under the weight of such unwelcome responsibility.

"Do you think you can go out there and at least fake it?"

Beth sensed Jo needed reassurance that she had no intention of falling apart right then and there.

"Don't worry. I've been faking it most of my life. What's another day?"

Without waiting for a response, Beth turned away. Jo followed her back out into the large room. Adam was slumped in one of the kitchen chairs, the pitcher of lemonade already half empty. Beth tended to his feelings immediately.

"Honey, you did an amazing job in there. I'm so impressed."

She leaned over and kissed him lovingly on the cheek. Even in front of Jo he was too tired to protest her maternal affection.

Joanna was in awe of how quickly Beth had managed to conceal her own struggle for the sake of her child. For all of Jo's finely tuned talents, 'mothering' was truly an art that had eluded her. Standing there watching from the sidelines, she found herself aching all over again for the distant comfort of her own.

Despite Beth's praise it was apparent Adam had grown far too weary to be revived. Sensing that he could use some time alone with his mother, Jo picked up her glass, grabbed a handful of cookies and announced that she was going outside to collapse on one of the lounges. Beth signaled with her eyes that it was probably a good idea.

Hoping to bolster Adam's spirits, Beth was eager to give him the good news.

"Guess what? You won't have to spend all night alone with me after all. Your new girlfriend's going to be joining us for dinner."

She waited for his response, truly surprised to find him less than enthusiastic.

"That's nice, I guess."

Beth leaned in close and stroked his arm.

"What's the matter sweetie? I thought for sure you'd be thrilled."

Adam took a sweeping look around the room and shook his head in vague defeat.

"Man, I just hope all this was worth it."

"What do you mean? I can't imagine Joanna's not impressed."

"Who knows? One minute I'd swear I was really getting somewhere with her, and then the next minute I'm not sure. Are *all* older women as complicated to figure out?"

Beth felt a sudden pang of guilt for her part in this unfair game of charade.

"I'm afraid so, honey. The older we get, the more complicated we get." She moved her chair closer to his and extended a reassuring hug. "It comes with the territory, but I'm sure she's worth it."

Adam wasn't. When the phone rang from inside their house, he saw it as his chance to finally escape. He practically leapt out of his seat.

"I'll get it! I'm sure it's Jeff. He had to get back to me about something really important."

He bolted out of the door, barely acknowledging Joanna as he ran past her.

Not without great effort, Jo managed to pull the weight of her body off the lounge, picked up her empty glass and wandered back into the carriage house.

Beth was still at the kitchen table, her chin resting wearily on one hand. Their eyes met, but neither spoke a word. Though each had her own reasons, both of their faces showed clear signs of extreme emotional fatigue. Jo pulled out another chair, sat down and refilled the two empty glasses. The fan overhead worked as best it could to lessen the heat and toll of the day while the women alternated between lifting and lowering their drinks in silence. It was a silence that came close to feeling comfortable, and since there was little enough to this day to be grateful for, neither wanted to be the one to disrupt it. For a while they just sat there, staring off into neutral space. Finally, Beth broke the bad news.

"I hate to say this, but I think your losing your admirer."

Jo mockingly held her hand over her heart.

"I'm crushed."

"No really, I think you might have worked the poor kid a little too hard. He's confessed to having grave doubts about the payoff."

Beth looked around the room, still amazed at its transformation.

"You certainly managed to get the most out of his infatuation… even if it only lasted a few hours. The place looks really terrific, don't you think?"

She waited tentatively as Jo slowly scrutinized the room. Her eyes hovered skeptically on the set of brightly colored floral bed sheets that Beth had placed on the rocking chair a few feet away. Beth read Joanna's mind.

"If the pattern offends you, I'm sure I can find something solid."

Joanna looked around at her new surroundings and recalled her reluctant surrender to the room's endless imperfections. Assuming she'd never last more than a few days at the most, she just shrugged.

"Don't bother."

Beth didn't insist. "I'll bring over a batch of fresh towels as soon as they come out of the laundry…which, by the way, you're more than welcome to use anytime you'd like. The machines are in the basement. It really would be ridiculous to take your stuff all the way over to the laundromat in town."

All this talk of daily routines made Jo feel a bit too settled in. She felt compelled to reestablish the tentative nature of their arrangement.

"If I'm here that long."

Beth's eyes drifted over to the yellow telephone hanging on the kitchen wall. She thought it wise not to ask Joanna if she might want it turned back on for the summer. This time it was Jo's turn to read *Beth's* mind.

"Does that old thing still work?"

"It's disconnected, but if you'd like, I can certainly call the phone company and have the service turned back on... for however long you might stay."

Jo recalled agonizing for days over whether or not to take her cell phone and pager along on this so-called uncharted journey. Despite her definite misgivings about being cut off from the world of distractions she'd come to rely on, she'd ultimately decided to leave them both behind, hoping it would force her to focus on her inner voice instead. As a compromise to those few people in her life she knew really cared about her, Jo agreed to keep in touch, but only on her own terms and only when the spirit moved her. She was tired of making promises she had little or no interest in keeping.

Jo wavered over Beth's offer. At the very least, she'd need a phone to call out for a pizza or order in some Chinese. Even a hotel room had phone service and nobody she knew would have this number, so what possible harm could it do?

"Okay. Have it turned back on. I'll pay the charges for as long as I'm here."

"I'll call the phone company first thing Monday morning." Beth smiled wearily "*If* you're still here."

Joanna extended a silent acknowledgement just as Adam came bounding through the screen door. The boy now seemed more uneasy than depressed.

"Mom, can I talk to you for a minute?"

He glanced awkwardly at Joanna.

"In private."

Joanna was more than happy to return to that lounge outside to give them time alone.

Beth immediately scolded her son for his poor manners.

Adam wanted to avoid a lecture.

"You're right, I'm sorry, but I've got this really big problem."

Adam tried to avoid direct eye contact with his mother, hoping it wouldn't temper his own excitement while lessening the guilt of disappointing her.

"Look, I know I promised I'd have dinner with you tonight but do you remember Jeff's cousin Lori, the really cute one from Boston? I met her last

Christmas when her family visited Jeff's for the holidays?

"How could I forget? It was Lori this and Lori that for months. Then one day, you stopped mentioning her, so I assumed she'd become just another woman from your past."

"No way! I think about her all the time. Jeff just found out that at the last minute she decided to go to the same camp we are this summer!"

Beth couldn't resist a teasing reference to her son's absurdly fickle heart.

"Shall I assume this means you won't be proposing to Joanna before you leave?"

Adam was in far too good a mood to be annoyed with her for not taking his love life more seriously.

"Very funny mom."

Beth crossed her arms and looked at him unapologetically.

"Forgive me for not being able to keep up with all the women in your life. It's been somewhat of a rough day, in case you hadn't noticed. Anyway, what's all this have to do with dinner tonight?"

Adam seemed unable to get the words out fast enough.

"She's here... at Jeff's... with her parents... for the weekend. He got me invited to supper tonight. His mom even said I could sleep over if I want. What do you say? Can I?"

When she didn't respond quickly enough, he began to fear that she didn't understand 'the big picture'.

"Don't you see? I get to hang out with her now before camp starts, she falls for me *before* she meets anyone else and she automatically becomes my girlfriend for the whole summer."

Adam nervously searched his mother's eyes, counting on her unconditional love to forgive him the rest.

"Pleeeese mom. I just *have* to get over there tonight. I *have* to! The fate of my summer... maybe even my entire life... depends on it."

He leaned over her chair and wrapped his arms around her affectionately. Beth just shook her head.

"Adam, what am I going to do with you?"

"Please mom, say you understand."

Of course she did. At least from his perspective. But there was no way in hell she was about to let him off the hook with just a few patronizing hugs and kisses, especially since she'd just spent the last several hours preparing all of his favorite foods not to mention that his absence would now leave her sitting alone through dinner with Joanna. For his part in this impending disaster, she seriously considered not letting him go. If it was *her* life on the line tonight or *his*, she was much more willing to sacrifice his. She decided to shift the responsibility back to him.

"What about *Joanna's* feelings? Did you ever stop to consider the only reason she said yes to dinner tonight was so she could spend the evening with *you*?"

Adam's conscience seemed to have kicked in, if only for the moment.

"I know. I don't want to hurt her feelings but I just can't miss this chance with Lori tonight. There's gonna' be dozens of guys after her this summer."

However ridiculous her son's latest obsession, Beth couldn't withhold her deeper investment in his happiness.

"Tonight certainly would give you a considerable advantage over the competition."

"I knew you'd understand. So now, what do I do about Jo?"

Beth pretended to give his dilemma some serious consideration.

"Under the circumstance, there's no reason for Joanna to know about Lori. I'm sure she'd only be jealous and that would be unnecessarily cruel. Just say that your buddy Jeff is going through a tough time right now and could use a good friend. She'll probably think even more of you for being such a loyal and dependable kind of guy. Older woman really appreciate that in a man. We want to know you're someone we can count on in our hour of need."

She winked as if to seal the exchange of top-secret information.

Adam looked at his mother in genuine amazement.

"You're a genius mom! And I'll tell her that I'll be back as soon as I can tomorrow, but only after I'm sure Jeff's okay. That should buy me most of the day."

"Don't push it kiddo. Let's not forget *I* know the truth, and *I* want you home right after breakfast. You still have a lot to do before you leave for camp on Monday, and I'd like to spend a little time with you before then. That is, if it's not asking too much?"

Adam would have agreed to anything.

"Okay, I promise."

Beth reminded him of his responsibility.

"Before you call Jeff back it would be nice if you went to Joanna and explained things."

Adam agreed, reminding his mother of how well things were working out for all of them.

"Now that I won't be around to distract her, you guys will have all night to get to know each other."

He didn't seem to notice that the color had drained from his mother's face.

"I'm sure she'll be absolutely delighted with the chance."

By the time Beth finished her sentence, Adam was already gone.

Beth stood at the door and watched her son race across the lawn to explain things to Joanna. How desperately she wished for that kind of enthusiasm in her own life. Now dreading the prospect of her own ill fated plans, she began gathering up all the cleaning supplies Adam had left scattered about. She was in the alcove putting away the vacuum cleaner when Joanna returned. Beth was not at all anxious to meet Joanna's eyes.

She sounded just as pleased as Beth expected her to be

"I suppose you know I've been stood up tonight?"

Beth stuck by her son's alibi.

"Jeff is Adam's best friend. I guess he just couldn't let him down."

"Bullshit. I smell competition."

Beth was not entirely surprised that Joanna wasn't one to be fooled that easily.

"What can I say? The truth is, you've been dumped for a younger woman. I'm sorry but that's what happens when you get involved with a 13 year old boy. If it's any consolation though, you still hold the keys to my husband's Jeep, even if you no longer hold the key to my son's heart. At least you won't have to work at keeping him off your lap all night."

"Right. Now I can put all my energy into making polite conversation."

"Look, don't feel like you have to struggle on my account. We can sit in silence for all I care or we can both eat alone if you prefer. It's your call."

Joanna regretted the sting of her remark.

"I'm not about to be dumped twice in one night. I'm sure we can find *something* safe to talk about."

Beth shrugged and turned toward the door.

"Sounds thoroughly enchanting when you put it that way. I can't wait. Adam's being picked up at 6, and I'm sure we can both use some time to ourselves. Why don't you come by around 8:00? If you can think of anything else you might need between now and then, just let me know." She couldn't resist dotting her hospitality with her own touch of sarcasm. "That is, of course, if you decide to stay 'til 8:00."

"Can I bring anything… that doesn't require me having a car?"

"Just a little civility… if it's not too much to ask."

"I think I can manage that." Jo accompanied her to the door and politely held it open. "Look, I'll even start now."

Beth just shook her head like an adult who had tired of dealing with an exasperating child.

As she walked around the pool and across the yard, Jo's eyes bore into Beth's back like a prizefighter desperate to get inside the mind of his opponent before the bell to the next round.

Back in the house, Beth checked the roast in the oven, readjusted the temperature and dragged herself upstairs. She kicked off her sandals and collapsed on the bed. A moment later, Adam appeared in her doorway holding up two t-shirts.

"Which one do you think she'll like better?"

It took all the strength Beth had left to lift herself up onto her elbows. Both choices were equally unappealing.

"If you're trying to make a good impression, did you ever consider wearing a real shirt… you remember those things with buttons down the front and an actual collar?"

Adam looked at his mother like she'd just suggested he put on a tux.

She was simply too tired to care.

"Wear the one with the bulldog. Its says everything you're trying to say."

Wishing *she* had something in her life that could do that, Beth couldn't believe she'd just said something so absurd with such conviction.

"Thanks mom."

"How about a kiss for your incredibly understanding mother?" Beth held out her arms figuring it a fair enough exchange for his freedom. His mother made sure to steal an extra long, extra tight hug.

"Hey, watch the hair mom!"

Adam broke away and charged over to the dresser mirror. Fortunately the styling gel was still a bit damp, enabling him to carefully reposition each strand of hair she thoughtlessly pushed out of place.

As tired as she was, Beth watched her son attentively. She realized how very anxious he was to look his best.

"You look exceptionally handsome this evening. I'm sure Lori will find you absolutely irresistible."

Adam paced nervously until Jeff's dad pulled into the driveway and honked his horn. He grabbed his backpack and flung it over his shoulder.

"That's my ride. Gotta' go!"

"Don't forget… I want you home right after breakfast."

"I promise."

As her son raced down the steps Beth called out one last warning.

"Don't you dare run off and elope tonight!" She giggled deliriously. "Joanna would be devastated."

There were times when Adam appreciated his mother's warped sense of humor more than others. This was not one of those times.

"Get some rest mom… you're loosin' it."

Beth listened for the door to slam and the car to back down out of the driveway. When she felt she could finally trust the long awaited quiet, she rolled over and buried her face in her pillow. Alternating between moans and heartfelt laughter, she repeated her son's advice out loud. "Get some rest mom… you're loosin' it."

BJ seemed intrigued with Beth's odd behavior. He licked her arm as it dangled loosely over the side. Happy for his loving reminder, she reached around to pull him closer.

"Well aren't you the brave one to stick around while I go out of my mind. If he thinks I'm loosing it now it's a good thing that boy won't be here the rest of the summer, 'cause baby I intend to lose it completely!"

Too tired to think about the consequences of her own prediction, Beth reached across the bed, set the alarm for 7:00, then passed out cold.

Joanna looked at her watch. A quick shower and change into a clean shirt would leave her almost two hours to kill before dinner. As exhausted as the day had left her, she was much too wired to take a nap. Instead, she looked at her bags leaning against the wall—small visually familiar pieces of her life in these totally unfamiliar surroundings. If she dared to unpack it would take her all of ten minutes and that included time to ponder which of the four available holes she should drop her lone toothbrush into. Then what? She could make a few trays of ice cubes—a shopping list—maybe even count the room's glaring design flaws, like on those silly placemats that ask you to find all the mistakes in the picture. Joanna stared at the yellow wall phone. Had it been working she could have used it to call a local car service and make her escape. She was sure that anyplace else on earth was a safer—and *saner*—place to be.

Resigned to her immediate fate, Jo sat down at the kitchen table and looked around at her accommodations. A sense of restlessness propelled her to her feet. She randomly opened all the cabinet doors, then sat back down and stared blankly at the plastic piping that ran along the edge of the shelves. Just like the first time she'd seen it, the silly decorative detail actually managed to sooth her in a way very few things could anymore. Calmer now, Joanna's thoughts drifted to her mother; probably the one person, if she were still alive, who would have truly appreciated the charm of this imperfect place and would have given her daughter's surprising decision to stay her full blessing. Joanna was equally sure her mother would really have liked Beth as well; this crazy, unpredictable woman who somehow managed to handle the complexity of Jo's nature while obviously struggling to deal with her own.

Suddenly, Jo felt awful in the same familiar way she did as a young child when her deliberately impetuous behavior disrupted her mother's day. Upset with herself for being such a brute, Jo would often go to her room, close the door and conjure up ways to gain her mother's forgiveness. What had always worked was to make something special for her. A silly looking mobile Jo had constructed with various size paper hearts dangling from a coat hanger on strings of colored yarn became one of her mother's most cherished possessions. It took Joanna hours to make, but only a second to win her mother's heart. It hung in the kitchen for years until the time of her mother's death. When the cancer had run its awful course and treatments were no longer an option, her mother called a tearful Joanna to her bedside. In one of their private conversations before she'd lost consciousness for the last time, her mother held her daughter's hand and made her promise to place the mobile in her casket so she could hang it in her new home. That was the only time in Joanna's life she ever needed to believe there actually was a place called Heaven. On the day of her mother's funeral, Jo honored her mother's wish. Over the years, it remained a memory so painful that she could never bring herself to fully remember or fully forget every emotional detail. To this day, in the empty spaces of her heart either choice still hurt too much. A few years after her mother's death, Joanna left for college and, in many ways, never returned.

One of the few things she'd taken with her was a letter from her mother, written on Joanna's sixteenth birthday, just a few weeks before she died. Jo had memorized portions of it and, at times like this when her own heart felt frozen solid with regret, she'd recite the warmth and words from her mother's heart:

"Go on with your life, my child, knowing I am happy for your happiness. Create and fulfill your every dream. You have been blessed with so many gifts. Until the day when I shall once again cradle you in my arms, use your wondrous talent to bring as much happiness to as many people as you can. By doing so, you will give meaning to your existence and come to know the deepest joys in life."

A lone tear traveled slowly down Joanna's cheek and collected in the crease of her smile. Maybe her mother was right. Certainly all the awards and promotions didn't do it. She found her thoughts drifting from her own mother to Adam's. "That's it" Jo thought to herself, "I'll make Beth a bouquet of flowers! She jumped to her feet. "You wanted a little civility lady. You've got it." With all the enthusiasm of her mother's child, Jo tossed her duffle bag up onto the table and began rifling through the miscellaneous art supplies she'd packed. She dug around until she found a box of pastels, tubes of water colors, some brushes and a pad. Remembering that she'd seen a pair of scissors and some tape in the kitchen drawer, she raced over to retrieve them. Jo checked her watch. Given her limited amount of time and supplies, she closed her eyes and began to consider the steps of the construction in her head. Visualizing a dozen yellow roses, she tore off the twelve sheets of paper she'd paint green and then roll into stems. She'd create and attach the leaves later. A stack of napkins, once crumpled, cut and carefully blended with shades of pastels, would become the heads of twelve glorious yellow roses.

Sparked with inspiration, Jo glanced across the room at the old clock radio on the table beside the couch. If she were back in her loft, she'd be enjoying some great jazz on an expensive, state-of-the-art sound system while she worked. Instead, she walked over to the radio and with surprisingly little resentment, played with the clumsy tuning knob until she found someplace on the dial that offered more sound than static. It was one of those oldies stations that played stuff dating all the way back to the 50s. Joanna smiled. Listening to "Tonight I Fell In Love" by the Tokens, she envisioned her brother's black and chrome Zenith portable blasting proudly from atop his dresser. Although she was just a kid of seven or eight when that sound was popular, she loved listening along with him, especially when he primped for a date with Stacy. She would convince him to squeeze a bit of his Brillcreme into her hands too, so she could slick back her short, raven black hair to look just like his. Jo made no bones about having a major crush on her brother's girlfriend and loved teasing him about stealing her away. Every once in awhile he would look at her skeptically and comment.

"I swear, sometimes I really don't know about you Jo. If you were just a little bit older…."

He never could bring himself to complete that thought, either out loud or in the back of his mind.

Real or imagined, she loved the idea that he saw her as competition.

"You're just jealous 'cause you know when I grow up I'm gonna' be a whole lot handsomer than you."

That's when he'd usually swat the back of his sister's head and tell her to go play with some dolls. Once he even demanded that she let her hair grow, so she'd look more like a girl.

"That was another lifetime ago" Joanna thought to herself. She ran her fingers through her now long and flowing head of hair, reveling in the fact that her brother's had already begun to thin and recede. He and Stacy had become a middle-aged couple, married for over twenty years, with two teenage boys of their own. Tickled by the irony, Joanna found herself unconsciously singing along to the radio, amazed how the words she hadn't heard in years came back to her as though it was just yesterday. How desperately she wished it were. In some small way, the music brought Jo a little bit closer to a place that felt like 'home'. No matter where she wound up staying this summer, she knew she'd be listening to this station much of the time.

Her mood lightened. Jo took one final minute to consider all the details of her masterpiece, then picked up the scissors and confidently began cutting. She experienced a level of joy she hadn't felt in years. The more deeply lost in the project she became, the stronger the feeling grew.

"Okay Mrs. Garrison. I know I can be a royal pain in the ass sometimes but I hope you're prepared to forgive me. The truth is, you don't have a choice... Mrs. Cameron's little girl is about to melt your heart!"

Chapter 5

The alarm went off at seven. Beth woke from a dead sleep. She could have easily slept straight through until the next morning—maybe even through the next several weeks. In short spurts of horrifying recollection, clear pieces of reality broke through the fog. The carriage house! Joanna! Dinner! Alone! A thickening sense of doom lodged itself deep in the back of her throat.

"Oh God," she moaned, "how did I get myself into this?"

Beth remembered Adam's part in all this. When he returned home she'd have to wring his neck. That was, of course, assuming she survived tonight. Beth made the satisfaction of strangling him her sole incentive to get through the ordeal that awaited her.

Resigned to her fate, Beth dragged herself out of bed, undressed and stepped back into the shower for the second time that day. As the welcomed steam rose up around her, she hung her head forward and let the hot water beat against the troubles knotted tightly in her shoulders and neck. With little hope of anything reaching any deeper, Beth closed her eyes, appreciative of even the slightest relief, and tried to reconcile actual time against all that had happened in the hours between early morning and now. So much of the day still felt so unreal. So unimaginable. A part of her actually expected to find Ben still lying in bed with his arm outstretched, inviting her back into the familiar and comforting fold. But when she stepped out of the shower and peeked into the bedroom for a reality check, he and his suitcases were gone. In his place, BJ lay faithfully across the foot of the bed. Without lifting his head, he raised his eyes up to hers and thumped his tail against the covers.

"Can you believe this day?"

Beth took his reassuring presence to heart, then disappeared into the bathroom to finish getting ready—as if being 'ready' for the likes of Joanna was ever possible. Beth stared vacantly into the mirror, then she picked up the hairdryer and held it to her temple as if aiming a gun at her head.

"Nah, that would be a coward's way out. Besides, I wouldn't want to deprive my guest of honor the pleasure. I'm sure she has a much slower and more sadistic death in mind for me tonight."

For the next several minutes while she worked at blow-drying her hair, Beth continued to imagine Joanna's plan of attack. "She's probably in the carriage house right now, rehearsing enough sharp little remarks to psychologically wound me in a thousand places. That would be her style," Beth convinced herself, "Death by decorum… certainly a much more subtle way to take your enemy out." Beth ran the brush through her hair a few extra times. Turning her head from side to side, she spoke reassuringly to her mirror image. "If we're going down in a blaze of sarcasm, we might as well do it with our hair in place."

Beth convinced herself it was more for the sake of morale, not vanity, that she march into battle wearing a hint of eye shadow and a touch of lipstick. When she finished applying both, she went to her closet to consider her 'camouflage' carefully. She knew that her only hope of concealing her inner turmoil was to go for maximum comfort. With that in mind Beth chose her favorite sandals, her most comfortable pair of leggings and her very softest cashmere v-neck sweater. Underneath, no bra or bulletproof vest. She was determined to leave her heart exposed this summer and nothing—not even the threat of annihilation—would rob her of that chance. Beth checked the time. It was already 7:30. By sheer habit she replaced her wedding band and for extra measure her lucky gold necklace. While she fiddled with the clasp, Beth eyed the bottle of perfume on her dresser. Rationalizing it was a tactical precaution—something to disguise the smell of her fear—Beth dabbed some lightly behind each ear. With nothing left to do but face the enemy, she took one final deep breath and signaled to BJ that it was nearing zero hour.

"C'mon boy, we've got our lives and our home to defend."

Much more inspired by the scent of roast beef than his sense of duty, he followed close behind. When she finished basting the roast, Beth removed the sweet potato pie, covered the top with a handful of tiny marshmallows and placed it back in the oven. If Adam were around, she'd have playfully popped a few marshmallows into his mouth before closing the bag. Now, though, all she could think of was the proverbial bag he'd left her holding tonight.

Next Beth checked the zucchini casserole. As usual, it looked and smelled sensational. The overall picture perfect results made Beth feel surprisingly in control for the moment. She actually found herself humming until she looked at the clock. The hour was closing in on eight with only ten minutes to go. Making a salad would have to wait. She'd have to set the table first. As Beth grabbed the dishtowel to wipe her hands, a barrage of conflicted choices began misfiring in her head: tablecloth or place mats—paper or linen napkins—

everyday dishes or china—soda or wine—chandelier lights high or dimmed—candles or not? Once again Beth swore revenge on her son. If Adam were there, none of this would've been an issue. She'd have asked him to set the table and he would have thrown out a few plates, glasses and silverware. Had she suggested anything a little more special, he'd have made a face that would have convinced Beth that she was crazy. After more than twenty years of serving routine family dinners, coasting through countless holiday gatherings and graciously hosting formal dinner parties in this very room, Beth now stood frozen at the foot of her dining room table. Suddenly she was sure about nothing. Though she couldn't say why, her deepest intuition suggested tonight was somehow *special*. Her defenses insisted it was not. Her impulses encouraged her to go all out. Her better judgment warned her to hold back. She felt completely overwhelmed and Joanna hadn't even arrived yet. Beth collapsed into one of the chairs to mull over her options.

"The woman's gonna' go ballistic on you. You go out of your way to play down the invitation and make it seem like it's no big deal, then you hit her with a whole formal production. If she objected to finger sandwiches and put up such a stink over a few lousy bagels, how do you think she's gonna' react to all this? If you value your life, think plastic cups and paper plates not crystal, china and candlelight." The voice in Beth's head went silent to allow its warning to sink in. Then it took one last shot. "Remember what happened this morning when you tried to make breakfast a little special? It was a total disaster! Do you really want to leave yourself that vulnerable sitting across from a total stranger... especially one as intimidating as Joanna? Besides, have you forgotten how much you're dreading this dinner...how sure you are it will be the scene of your demise? Why on earth would you want to see your china flung across the room or have your guts spilled all over your favorite lace tablecloth? Why would you even consider it?"

Beth went to the cupboard for the everyday plates when a second voice broke through and responded to the first. "You want to know why you'd consider it? I'll tell you why. Because deep down inside you know that even in death there's ceremony. So what if there's bloodshed. Even war has its own etiquette... its own display of honor and glory. If this dinner does turn out to be the death of you, wouldn't you rather it be something splendid and memorable? Wouldn't you rather perish in the presence of your true inner spirit? For God's sake, you've let your whole life slip into something pathetically safe and ordinary. Look at tonight as a chance to reclaim some small portion of yourself instead of just surrendering without so much as a fight!

So what if Adam would have laughed and Joanna might become furious? Screw them both! Tonight's dinner is *your* party… *your* celebration… *your* emancipation! That's reason enough to make it something special. Stop compromising! You've prepared it… now find the courage to serve the damn thing the way you want it served. Didn't you promise Ben that you'd try to follow your heart? Wasn't that what you insisted this summer had to be about? You said your very survival depended upon it. So what'll it be… ordinary or extraordinary?"

"Extraordinary!" she blurted out loud. Beth looked down at the everyday dishes in her hands and without another moment's hesitation she put them, along with any lingering doubts, back into the closet and slammed the door on both. In a flurry of excitement, out came the Venetian lace tablecloth, the linen napkins, the china, the crystal stemware and her wedding silver. Although the formal dining room table sat eight, she deliberately chose to set two places directly opposite each other. "Let's go for point blank range," she thought to herself, "and what the hell, let's do it by candlelight!" Beth dimmed the chandelier, lit the candles and stood back in delight.

"There!" she giggled to herself. "If nothing else, it'll soften the gory scene for the paramedics when they arrive later."

Beth checked her watch. It was exactly eight o'clock. She was sure she heard her heart pounding wildly. Fearing that Joanna would hear it too, she raced over to the stereo in the living room hoping to fill the otherwise quiet house with some music. She rifled nervously through the stack of cassettes.

"Oh God, classical or soft jazz?"

She'd narrowed down her selection to two possibilities when she heard the ominous sound of Joanna's footsteps on the porch. Joanna knocked on the kitchen door rather than assume she could just let herself in. Straining to remove the trace of fear from her voice, Beth called to her from the living room.

"Come in. I'm just putting on some music."

The slam of the screen door signaled that the enemy was closing in. Beth fumbled with the tapes, dropped one on the floor and shoved the one still remaining in her hand into the machine. It turned out to be Pachelbel's Canon in D Major and whatever Jo thought of it, it would have to do. In the precious little time she had left, Beth quietly bent down to whisper a last minute run through of strategy with BJ.

"Now don't forget, keep a steady eye on her all the time, but don't break skin unless she goes for me first."

With her four-legged ally at her side, Beth had gotten as far as the archway between the living room and dining room when Joanna appeared in the doorway of the kitchen on the other side. Now only the soft ambiance and a dining room table stood between them. Jo had on a pair of jeans and a sleeveless white shirt that appeared all the crisper against the tawny glow of a few hours of outdoor work in the afternoon sun. Beth couldn't help notice that Joanna obviously had little use for buttons in general. From her guarded position, Beth welcomed her guest with a trembling smile.

"Hi."

"What the hell's all this?"

Though she stood her ground, Beth had a mental image of herself cowering behind the dining room chair. Gripping its back instead, she nervously attempted to divert Joanna's attention.

"I hope you're hungry. There's an awful lot of food."

Jo continued to stare coldly at the elaborate setting. Beth was convinced she only had a few more seconds before the woman exploded.

"I know this wasn't what you were expecting. Frankly, neither was I, but at the last minute I decided I was celebrating tonight."

Beth's explanation drew no response. Up against Joanna's dead silence she managed to regain her sense of purpose.

"I hope you'll stay, but if you're too uncomfortable, please don't feel obligated. I'll be more than happy to fix a plate for you to take back to the carriage house."

Still focused on the formal table setting, Joanna's response was entirely reasonable.

"Mind telling me what it is you're celebrating?"

Expecting a tirade, Beth was momentarily thrown. As absurd as she was sure it would sound, she answered truthfully.

"I'm celebrating my right to celebrate."

Beth waited for Joanna to burst into ridiculing laughter. Instead, Jo looked up from the table and directly into her eyes.

"I see."

After a long and thoughtful pause, she made her decision.

"In that case I'll stay."

Joanna's response was not at all what Beth had imagined it would be.

"You will?"

Beth's heightened defenses eased just enough to notice Jo's suspicious posture.

"That wouldn't be a weapon you're concealing behind your back, would it?"

"I suppose I've given you enough reasons to suspect it might be, but you can relax, it's nothing like that."

Now feeling a bit self-conscious herself, Jo held out the bouquet of paper flowers.

"These are for you."

For a moment Beth stood there, dumbfounded and bewildered. She came around the table and took the bouquet gently from Jo's hand. Her expression transported Joanna back to a time when she could delight her own mother in much the same way she had obviously just done to Adam's. For the first time in too many years she was sure her talents were well used. Still speechless, Beth held the bouquet out in wonder, turning it ever so slowly in order to appreciate every leaf and petal without missing a single detail of it's splendor.

"How in the world did you do this?"

She looked up from the gift, into Joanna's eyes.

"And *why*?"

"With watercolors, pastels, paper, scotch tape and a pair of scissors is *how*. To say I'm sorry for behaving so obnoxiously for most of the day is *why*."

Her heart successfully melted by Mrs. Cameron's little girl, Beth's impulse was to hug Joanna as hard as she could. Unsure of how Jo would receive it, Beth refrained.

"They're absolutely exquisite!"

Although she fought them back as hard as she could, tears began to well up in Beth's eyes. She awkwardly wiped them away.

"You'll have to forgive me. I've been weepy all day." Beth was more honest. "Well, not just today, for quite some time now actually…" Self-conscious about saying too much, she stopped herself. "No one's ever done anything like this for me. I don't know what to say."

Joanne was sincere.

"I'm glad you like them."

"Oh, I more than like them. How in the world did you know that yellow roses are one of my favorites?" Beth bent down to show the bouquet to BJ. "Look what Joanna brought me! Aren't they lovely?"

He sniffed curiously at the cluster of paper, then sneezed.

"I think he's allergic to their fragrance," Joanna joked, "it's workable fixative."

Beth considered how best to display Joanna's gift.

"Oh, I have the perfect vase!"

Her whole body hummed with excitement as she opened the glass doors of the credenza and carefully removed an intricately cut crystal vase. She placed it down in the center of the dining room table between the two glowing candles. Their light danced off each delicate angle. Joanna stood to the side watching as Beth set the bouquet lovingly inside the vase, twisting and turning each and every stem until the arrangement looked just right. When she stepped back her eyes seemed to behold a reunion between two long lost friends.

"They look absolutely perfect together, don't you think?"

Jo agreed. Although not at all her taste, she was surprisingly drawn to the vase itself.

"That's a very unusual piece."

"It's quite beautiful, isn't it? Turn of the century… from Paris. It was a gift from a very special friend. I've never used it before. I've been saving it for a special occasion. Somehow this just feels right. Oh, Arthur will be so pleased. I can't wait to tell him."

"Who's Arthur?"

Beth smiled wistfully.

"It's a long and rather unusual story. I'll tell you about it over dinner if you like. Speaking of dinner, I'd better get in there and check on things. I can't afford any more disasters in one day."

Joanna followed Beth back into the kitchen, deliberately positioning herself against the far end of the counter. She watched as Beth pulled the roast from the oven and cut deep into the golden brown slab of meat. Taking advantage of Beth's distraction, Jo had time to notice everything: the simple jewelry and the touch of make-up, the soft golden highlight of Beth's hair and the easy lay of the cashmere sweater against her breasts as she moved with the rhythm of her tasks. Against the unglamorous setting of a family kitchen, Jo actually found Adam's mother quite sensual in a shy, quiet sort of way. She wondered how long it had been since Beth had heard the words, "You're beautiful." She wondered how long it had been since Beth felt it—truly felt it—for herself. Jo's guess was it had been much too long.

"Everything's coming along. I'll just finish making the salad. We should be eating shortly."

Beth stood up and removed the oven mitt from her hand. For some strange reason, she became oddly conscious of her wedding band. For the first time all day she found herself thinking of Ben. It had only been hours since she dropped him at the airport but it felt as though they'd been apart for years. Beth wondered how she would ever begin to explain the events of this most unusual day when he called. She wondered what he would think, what he would say. She wondered if she would care and what it all meant. In the same moment Beth was desperate to be near him and desperate to be free of him.

Standing around was not Joanna's style. With nothing to do and little to say she felt increasingly uncomfortable.

"Can I help?"

Lost somewhere in the conflicted thoughts of her husband, Joanna's still unfamiliar voice startled Beth.

"You've already *helped*... with those flowers... more than you can ever imagine."

The vulnerability in Beth's voice left Joanna feeling awkward and in need of some immediate distance.

"Mind if I wander around then?"

Even as a child, Joanna was intrigued with the contents of other people's homes, convinced that the truth of their lives lay hidden in the secret code of their belongings. Sensing Joanna's restlessness, Beth didn't want to test just how easily a bouquet of paper flowers could go up in flames.

"I don't mind at all. If you get lost, I'll come get you when dinner's ready."

Joanna wondered if Beth somehow knew that feeling 'lost' had become a rather constant state of mind lately.

"Okay, I will."

Taking the path from the kitchen back through the dining room, Jo was once again confronted with the elaborate, candle lit table setting that Beth had insisted on. She caught herself repeating Beth's quirky explanation in her own head: "I'm celebrating my right to celebrate." Jo drew a long reflective breath.

"God help me for staying and God help me for being intrigued."

The archway across from the dining room table opened into the center of the living room, a veritable treasure of hidden clues. Not wanting to miss any of them, Jo stood in the entrance, slowly investigating every corner with only her eyes. The room itself, painted in a soft ivory tone, extended out on both sides, across almost the full length of the house. Four large curtained windows ran along the front overlooking the tranquil porch. On the far end of the room, off to the right, a set of French doors separated the main entrance hall with a staircase up to the second floor. There seemed to be another room off the foot of the steps. Jo assumed it to be either a family room or a study. To her left, a built-in floor-to-ceiling bookcase with old leather books lined the wall, flanked by two windows on either end. Although tucked humbly in the far corner, a white lacquered Baby Grand piano was unquestionably the majestic centerpiece of the room. Joanna was drawn to it immediately but forced herself to take in everything else before she would allow herself a closer look. She only hoped she'd have enough time before dinner was ready.

In contrast to the open floor plan of the room, the furniture was arranged in small intimate clusters. On an old hooked rug, two camel colored sofas sat facing each other in front of the fireplace. Between them, a large wooden coffee table offered more than enough room for a pair of outstretched legs without encroaching on the stack of oversized books and wooden fruit bowl positioned off to the side. Despite her own preference for clean, straight line and sleek contemporary furnishing, Joanna found an irresistible appeal in the overstuffed sofas and plush, oversized pillows covered in a tasteful floral chintz. She imagined how easy it would be to become lost there in a good book or good conversation for hours on end. To whatever extent the furnishing of the carriage house seemed poorly chosen and hopelessly mismatched, each piece in *this* room felt entirely comfortable with the others -like members of a tight-knit family that grew closer in the natural course of time. It struck Joanna that this was a home created not by plan but rather one that evolved through love and a sense of 'belonging' in a way that defined itself. Nothing seemed merely for the sake of show, but rather for the sake of valued companionship. She knew that the things in this home were the things that really mattered. All the more reason, Jo told herself, to have a closer look. She stepped out from the archway and into the room itself. On her right, a carved oak mantelpiece framed the brick fireplace on the opposite side of the dining room wall. Like the top of the piano, it too was adorned with countless family photos. Joanna sensed that the collection of beautiful antique frames were as lovingly selected and deeply cherished as the images they contained. She fought her impulse to scrutinize every one for the story each picture surely told. Recalling the snapshots that spilled from Beth's wallet in the luncheonette booth, she realized there was so much she wanted to know and so little she was willing to ask simply because that would give Beth the same right and something told Joanna that Beth's questions would not be the kind she could easily answer or avoid. Jo knew this was her only chance to learn more than she was willing to tell.

Intent as she was on examining the photos, the small oil painting that hung above the mantel distracted her eye. The image in the ornate wooden frame was of an old abandoned structure. The upper portion of the canvas had been ripped and mended much more with love than professional restoration skills. The aged pigment was cracked and worn in many places. Though Joanna was certain she'd never seen the painting before that moment, the image felt oddly familiar. She moved closer for a better look at the small female figure standing in the doorway of the house. She was dressed in turn-of-the-century costume, cradling a small cluster of flowers in her arms. A bicycle lay nearby in a patch of wild flowers and high grass that grew up around the rundown structure. As Joanna studied the small details, another wave of lightheadedness suddenly swept over her. "Time for another two Motrin," she told herself.

Frustrated by her unexplainable recognition of the image, Joanna assumed it must have been among the thousands of slides she bleakly viewed in one of those tedious, required art history courses she took to earn her degree. She scrutinized the faded signature in the lower right corner. As best she could make out it read, A. Wyatt. Wishing she'd paid more attention in class, Jo racked her brain but the name didn't ring any kind of bell. Engrossed and still fighting her physical discomfort, she was startled by Beth's call from the kitchen.

"Just another five minutes."

"No problem."

Joanna was grateful to know how much time she had left to gather as much information as she could from the contents of the room.

For the moment the photographs would have to wait. From the instant she set eyes on it, Joanna was drawn to the white Baby Grand. It thoroughly captured her imagination—in part for its beauty, in part for its mystery. She wondered whom in the family it 'belonged' to. Who in the family possessed it and who in turn was undoubtedly possessed *by* it. Lots of homes have a piano in them, Jo thought to herself, but none quite so commanding as the one that sat so regally in the corner of this room. This was not an instrument you played Chopsticks on, but rather to express an all-consuming passion. A part of Jo hoped that the piano—and the passion—belonged to Beth. Another part of her prayed it did not. Joanna approached the instrument respectfully as if to acknowledge its dignity and power. The matching ivory bench was pulled out enough for her to sit down without having to move it. It was an invitation she couldn't resist. Joanna took careful note of the pencil and pages of hand written sheet music that lay one behind the other on the music stand above the keys. Obviously someone was in the middle of composing an original piece. She wished she could read music to get a flavor of the composition. Disheartened, she looked up and noticed that the angle of the piano faced the composer directly toward a second set of French doors at the other end of the long bookcased wall. The doors opened onto a screened-in section of the back patio. Just beyond the wicker furniture and hanging plants you could see the carriage house. It was as if the piano had been placed there intentionally for that view. Joanna suddenly felt as though she'd be living in a fishbowl—assuming of course that she decided to stay. But in this hour of summer twilight, the setting was nothing short of captivating and in the sheer splendor of it she reluctantly waived her paranoia.

Running out of precious time, Jo slid out from behind the piano and quickly skimmed the leather-bound volumes lining the wall behind her. The collection included virtually every literary classic of the 19th and 20th centuries that she'd ever heard of and many she hadn't. The same was true for the countless volumes of English and American poetry. Still another section boasted all the important works by major playwrights from Shakespeare to Arthur Miller. Displayed among the books was an antique pipe stand with several hand carved pipes and a framed photograph of a distinguished looking man standing at a podium. He was serious and thoughtful looking with a neatly trimmed beard and mustache. Joanna concluded that the photo was of Beth's husband—the English professor who'd gone off to lecture this summer in England—and that the extensive literary collection was his. She recalled the cryptic explanation Beth conveyed to Trudy's husband about why she hadn't accompanied him. Perhaps the clusters of family photos that adorned the top of the piano and mantel would help Joanna break the code. For the moment they remained Joanna's last hope of gathering whatever valuable clues to Beth's life she could. Focusing on the photograph in front of her, Jo ignored her own confusion as to why any of this was important to her at all. She was just hoping her curiosity would be satisfied and pass before she had to deal with it.

Since Jo wouldn't take the liberty of picking anything up, as each image attracted her she simply bent over and moved in for a closer look. Separately and together the photographs told the story of a family—in many ways typical—in many ways not. More than anything Jo was struck by the strong, unrehearsed intimacy that clearly existed between all of them. In picture after picture, arms draped comfortably around one another's shoulders or wrapped tightly around each other's waist as if to pull one another's lives even closer together than they already were. Hands clasped hands instinctively and eyes met eyes with deep affection. Joanna found herself smiling. She felt genuinely happy for them in the same way she was happy for herself and her own family, for they too shared the same warmth and closeness sadly missing in so many people's lives. Jo recalled specific snapshots of her own family history: the formal celebrations and the ordinary, everyday moments. Each one captured a timeless bond that would one day be tested against the impossible odds that life would ever stay that way forever. With a renewed sense of personal loss, Joanna's smile slowly faded. She studied the photographs in front of her even more closely. They now told another story—this one of a young couple who were intensely devoted to raising two happy sons when their lives were suddenly torn apart by tragedy. Joanna noticed that the images stopped chronologically at their son's high school graduation. From Adam's disclosure in the coffee shop, she knew his brother was killed in a car accident soon after. It was as if from that moment on, all their unborn smiles were torn from their lives as well. There wasn't a pose they could manage or a background unfamiliar enough that wouldn't remind the family of the inconsolable reality that one of them was forever missing. How well Joanna understood. It took many years after her mother's death for her own family to eventually reintroduce a camera into their lives. To this day their picture taking fell into two categories for her—those taken *before* her mother's death and those taken *after* it. All these years later Joanna never snapped or posed for a family picture without thinking of it that way.

Jo looked closely at the boy's graduation picture. He was an undeniably handsome combination of both his mother and father, but his smile reflected all the potential of his own budding manhood. It was eerie to look at it and know he would never have the chance to grow into the later years and deeper expressions of his own life. She found herself wondering if he had at least experienced falling in love—if he knew what it was like to possess someone's heart utterly and completely and to have surrendered his own in return. For his sake, she hoped he had. Joanna recalled her mother's words as the cancer spread and her death became more inevitable: "To have loved deeply and been loved deeply in return is the only true measure of a life well lived." Joanna could still feel the warmth and conviction of her mother's hand as it tightened around hers, pressing the words deep into her daughter's conscience. Jo looked down at her own hand and smiled reflectively. If these last three years proved nothing else, they proved that her mother was right.

In the precious little time she had left, Jo intensified her scrutiny of the remaining photographs. Her eyes darted from one image to the next when something subtle jumped out at her. Among the many pictures the family had taken together were also several individual portraits of each of them—all except for Beth. Nowhere in the entire collection was there a photograph of just her alone. It was almost as if each of *their* lives had an identity separate and apart from one another, but that Beth only existed as part of *their* world—that outside her role as wife and mother she didn't exist by, or for, herself.

So immersed in considering the meaning of what she'd found, Jo had no idea that the woman she was trying so hard to understand was standing in the archway watching her. Dinner was ready and Beth had come to get her. Taking advantage of the fact that Joanna was obviously unaware of her presence, Beth took the opportunity to study her quietly, trying to reconcile the woman who nearly beat her to a pulp in the parking lot with the woman who had made her a bouquet of paper flowers. She watched quietly as Joanna showed an unusually intense interest in what she was looking at. Her body was bent forward, her face just inches from the frames. Not wanting to interrupt Jo's concentration, Beth spoke in a thoughtfully soft tone.

"It's a funny thing about photographs... you never know when you take them which will become the ones you'll spend the rest of your life trying to crawl back into once that moment is gone."

Jo sensed permission in Beth's voice to keep looking. After she felt she'd collected all she could for now, Jo turned around, commenting only on the safest part of what was apparent.

"You have a very loving family."

Beth walked over to the piano and picked up their picture.

"I tell myself I still have so much to be grateful for."

Jo hesitated.

"Adam told me about his brother. I'm terribly sorry."

Beth acknowledged her sympathy with a quiet nod. She put the photo down and reached for one of just her son. She stared at it longingly as she spoke.

"It feels like ever since he died there have only been two times in my life... the times when I *can* hold back the tears and the times when I *can't*."

Joanna said nothing as Beth lovingly replaced the frame among the others. Long ago she'd learned not to disturb the great silence that connects each of us to our deepest pain and most devastating losses. Beth seemed to appreciate the quiet space in which to feel her grief. She patted the top of Danny's graduation picture, took a deep, steadying breath and bravely managed the faintest of smiles.

"Come on, let's eat."

Joanna followed her into the dimly lit dining room. Hot serving dishes had been set out on trivets around the vase with her paper bouquet. The wine had been poured and the bottle placed off to the side. Jo took a seat at one of the two places Beth had set for them. In contrast to the soft music and intimate glow of candlelight, the glaring boundaries of their indefinable connection felt all the more odd, especially since it was only hours ago the two sat opposite each other, hostile strangers in a small luncheonette booth. Beth awkwardly lifted her glass.

"This calls for a toast!"

Her declaration sounded a lot steadier than her hand that shook slightly as she held it in the air. For an uncomfortably long moment the unlikely dinner companions sat in dead silence while Beth groped for something appropriate to say. Not at all certain what might fall out of this unpredictable woman's head next, Joanna remained deadpan. Beth bravely continued.

"Since tonight I'm celebrating my right to celebrate… this is a toast to my right to make a toast!"

Once again amused by Beth's convoluted reasoning, Joanna reached for her own glass. This time Beth's voice softened into something more sincere than silly.

"And to the magic of some art supplies and a very tender heart."

After exchanging tentative smiles, they both took a much-needed gulp of wine and in a flurry of precise movements, Beth began loading each of their plates with food. Joanna was uncomfortable being served, but under the circumstances, found it impossible to object. She waited until Beth had finished.

"Everything looks great."

Behind the casualness of her compliment, Joanna was in awe of Beth's greater accomplishment. The woman's courage truly defied her imagination. Mystified, Jo looked at the table and watched as Beth performed the ordinary task of slicing her meat. How does a woman bury her child, Jo quietly wondered, and ever let herself care enough to bother melting marshmallows into the top of a sweet potato casserole? Beth sensed she was being watched. She looked up, leaving Jo no time to look away. For a few fleeting moments their eyes met in a strangely intimate smile that unnerved them both. Simultaneously they each looked down, reached for their forks and began eating. By now, the two women were equally starved, equally strained and equally desperate to just get through this meal.

For a few safe moments the women kept to the business of eating. Neither looked up from the security of her plate for fear of being the first to say the wrong thing. Eventually their silence became more threatening than the neutral space they hoped to preserve. Joanna finally commented on the food.

"Everything's delicious."

"What you really mean is: she's a pretty good cook for someone who's a complete klutz."

Jo deliberately kept eating.

"You have to stop doing that."

"Doing *what*?"

Jo tried to minimize her very real concern.

"Reading my mind."

"Despite my many obvious inadequacies, I do have my specialties."

The mischievous tone in Beth's voice was quickly swallowed up by Jo's reluctance to say anything more. It was painfully obvious neither of them knew where or how to extend the fragile beginnings of conversation. Beth decided to risk being totally honest.

"I guess this isn't going as smoothly as we'd like since neither one of us knows what's safe to talk about. Truthfully, *I'm* afraid if I say the wrong thing you'll blow up again and *you're* probably afraid if you say the wrong thing I'll break down again."

She was hoping Joanna would add something more than just a nod of agreement. After a few more awkward mouthfuls of food, Beth's face suddenly lit up.

"I know just what we need!"

Jo refilled her glass with more wine.

"Another couple of bottles of this stuff."

Beth pushed her chair back and jumped up from the table.

"No… Cheerios!"

Without further explanation she disappeared into the kitchen.

If Jo had any doubts at all before this moment, she was now totally convinced she'd been sucked through the eye of a needle into a world too bizarre to explain. Beth returned with two juice glasses filled with Cheerios in one hand, and an empty bowl in the other. She set one glass down in front of each of them and placed the bowl in the middle of the table. She sat back down and smiled at the small 'O' shaped puffs. Compared to their insignificant value and size, Beth seemed disproportionately relieved by their presence. Joanna attempted to attach some reasonable meaning to it all.

"I get it. Your idea is to pretend dinner's already over and move us right along to breakfast."

Beth laughed. She enjoyed Joanna's struggle to make sense of her behavior. It reminded her of Ben's affection and all the years he attempted to do the same. She gave Jo credit for trying, especially with no frame of reference.

"Unfortunately my powers of denial aren't that well honed. I'm afraid tonight's dinner is still very much a reality for both of us. But I think the Cheerios are our solution. If we're going to at least *attempt* some kind of dinner conversation, it's obvious we're going to need to some help avoiding the things that either of us don't want to talk about. That's where the Cheerios come in. Anytime one of us brings up a topic the other doesn't want to discuss, she takes one of them from her glass and tosses it into the bowl. The subject is closed and we just move on… no questions asked. As soon as one of our glasses is empty, we'll call it a night and consider ourselves lucky if we get there without shedding any blood… or tears… along the way."

Joanna shook her head, cautiously amused.

"You have a very novel approach to problem solving, lady."

"It's from 'The Art of Negotiating Family conflicts'. I wrote the book, you know… mostly as I went along."

Jo helped herself to a second portion of sweet potatoes.

"Are all the methods in your book 100% effective?"

"I guess you could say I've had my share of results… and resistance… over the years. I certainly had enough opportunities to test my methods… and my nerves… bringing up the boys."

Despite her playful response, Beth's heart suddenly stumbled over the word 'boys'. Joanna followed her eyes as Beth stared across at one of the empty chairs. She was certain it was where Danny sat—probably from the time his legs barely dangled over the edge of the seat. Even from across the table, she could feel the pain in Beth's chest as though it were in her own. Looking at the Cheerios, Joanna decided to put her faith in the rules of Beth's game.

"I know this is a ridiculous question, but are you okay?"

Much to Jo's surprise, Beth did not instantly reach for her first Cheerio to change the topic. Instead, she smiled faintly.

"I see I'm not the only one at this table who reads minds."

Beth paused, then continued—her smile now faded, her eyes once again fixed on the empty chair.

"July 7th will be three years since Danny's death. I still can't believe it. On those rare days when the pain actually subsides a bit, it terrifies me to think it's only because my heart is *closing,* not *healing*."

With tears in her eyes, Beth looked away from the empty chair and back at Jo.

"There's a big difference, you know."

Joanna didn't answer but indeed, how well she did. Beth put down her fork, unable to continue swallowing over the familiar lump that had thickened in the back of her throat. Joanna felt awful about bringing the whole thing up in the first place.

"I'm sorry. I didn't mean to upset you."

"You needn't be. You see, I'm celebrating *everything* tonight… including my sadness."

Beth wiped her eyes and once again raised her glass of wine.

"Another toast! This one to self pity."

She took another sip, put down her glass and offered much more about herself than Joanna expected.

"I realized that these last few years I've been consumed with monitoring Adam and Ben's loss. I suppose it was just safer to deal with theirs than my own. It seems impossible when I think about how much I've already suffered, but the truth is I don't think I've even begun to grieve for *myself*. That's why I so desperately needed to be alone and apart from both of them this summer… to force myself out from hiding in the shadows of their pain and finally face my own."

She hesitated.

"Ben thinks I'm just afraid to ever dare let myself be happy again."

Joanna waited until Beth was able to meet her eyes.

"Is that what *you* think?"

Apparently overwhelmed by the question, Beth struggled, then looked away. She took one of Cheerios from her glass and tossed it into the empty bowl. A moment later she reached over, grabbed it back up and clenched it in the palm of her hand.

"No!" she said defiantly, leaving herself no room to change her mind, "I want to answer that. I've held this inside much too long."

Beth bravely unfolded her fingers, forcing herself to confront this unlikely metaphor of her dark and painful truth. Fearing she might lose the courage, Beth was careful not to look up from the Cheerio.

"Ben is wrong. I know in my heart that what I'm much more afraid of is finding out that I was never really happy in the first place… even *before* Danny died. At least not in the way I remember…"

Beth expelled a long and painful breath.

"And yet I don't even know what it is I can't seem to forget."

In the flickering candlelight, the crystal vase that held Joanna's flowers caught Beth's eye. She smiled and hungrily closed them as if to lock in some vague and distant sense of peace. Whatever momentary glimpse of joy the image held quickly vanished. Once again, abandoned by the incomplete expression of her heart, Beth felt miserably confined to the boundaries of her own life. Her voice fell.

"God, if only…"

Jo struggled for a way to help her. Perhaps if she repeated Beth's own words back to her, the woman might find her place.

"If only *what*?"

Beth snapped at Joanna's prodding.

"I don't know! I don't know! If only a million things, okay?"

Jo immediately backed off. She remembered how exasperated she had felt earlier in the day when Beth pushed her to explain why she had decided to stay. Jo hoped if she just gave Beth some time, she'd regain her composure on her own. She pushed back her chair and stood up. Sure that Joanna had had enough and was getting up to leave, Beth became panic stricken. She lunged for Jo's arm. Her voice was wrought with desperation. Her eyes emptied of life.

"No! Please don't go! I can't lose you again!"

Beth slumped back into her chair as if resigned to yet another unbearable loss.

"I was just getting up to get you some water."

In the kitchen, Jo replayed Beth's desperate plea in her head. It made absolutely no sense. Attributing the outburst to a very long, emotionally charged day and maybe a little too much to drink, Jo returned with an ice-cold glass of water. Beth had calmed down considerably, but signs of exhaustion were everywhere on her face. Joanna's advice was as pointed as it was practical.

"That's it! No more wine. Anymore toasts you feel inspired to make, do with *this*."

Jo handed Beth the glass of water and stood protectively by as she took long, welcomed gulps. Reasonably certain Beth had collected enough of herself, Joanna sat back down. Unable to look up, Beth allowed her finger to play along the rim of her empty wine glass.

"What I said before about losing you again… I honestly don't know where that came from."

Jo was eager to dismiss the whole thing.

"Don't worry about it. It's been a long day. We've both said a lot of things we didn't mean."

"I feel so foolish. I wish I could explain."

"It's not necessary. And don't waste one of your Cheerios. We don't have to talk about it."

For as much as she could, Beth allowed herself to feel less obliged. She backtracked to the moments just preceding her outburst.

"I'm sorry I snapped at you when you asked 'if only what?'."

"Don't beat yourself up about it. I know what it feels like not to know."

Beth grew noticeably withdrawn. Her voice was weighted with regret.

"The truth is, I *do* know. I wasn't being honest when I said I didn't. It's not 'if only a *million* things'. It's just *one* thing. It's always been just *one* thing and it's always been the *same* thing."

Beth nervously played the corner of her napkin.

"If only I could find the place where the longing begins."

Beth fell silent, but the pain of her confession continued to speak through her eyes. She looked at Joanna, not expecting a response, just grateful there was someone there to listen to what she'd never been able to admit out loud before that moment. With all that she'd accomplished and accumulated, Joanna herself was no closer to the yearnings of her own heart.

"I'm beginning to think that life is mostly longings and if we're really lucky, a few brief moments of *having*."

Beth's smile was filled with appreciation. She couldn't have imagined a more thoughtful insight.

"How beautiful… and I'm afraid, how painfully true."

Beth felt a dark melancholy sweep over her, but her resilient sense of humor rescued them from the depths of it.

"Maybe it would have been simpler if you had just killed me when I hit your car and put me out of my misery. I think I've had just about all the longing I can take for one lifetime."

"From the photos in there, it looks like you've known more moments of *having* than most people ever will."

Beth was careful not to sound ungrateful.

"Of course you're right. I love my family dearly. They're my whole world."

"That's obvious from the pictures too."

Though intended to reassure her, Joanna's comments only troubled Beth more. Her voice dropped to something tentative and barely audible.

"The truth is I'm not sure if they *should* be my whole world… or even worse, if they ever *really* were. Maybe I just convinced myself they were supposed to be and talked myself into believing that was enough."

Beth looked over at Danny's empty chair.

"If that's so, I lost more than my son three years ago. I lost *myself* long before that."

Jo remembered her observation about Beth not appearing alone in any of the photographs. Maybe her hunch was right. Joanna considered the disturbing confession in relation to her own mother's life. During one of their late night talks when her mother was still strong enough to have them, Jo had once asked her if she ever regretted any of the choices she'd made for the sake of her family. Even at sixteen, Joanna wondered how anyone ever knows when they've given up too much of themselves. She remembered that her mother seemed glad for all of her questions, grateful for every chance to impart as much motherly wisdom as she could before having to leave her daughter with so many important questions still unformed in the young girl's heart.

"There's a fine line between compromise and sacrifice," Jo's mother explained against the quiet snowfall of a winter's night. "One asks that you *open* your heart. The other asks that you *betray* it."

"But how will I know the difference" Jo recalled asking?

Her mother had smiled reassuringly.

"Don't worry honey, you'll know. Deep down inside we all know. But only the bravest among us have the courage to admit it to themselves. That's the kind of person you want to become. Those are the kind of people who's laughter and tears you want mixed with your own."

With her mother's words echoing in the back of her mind, Joanna privately acknowledged the largeness of Beth's confession. It had to have been a nearly impossible thing to have to face. Mistaking the distance in Joanna's eyes for indifference, Beth apologized for boring her guest with the troubling details of her personal life. Beth looked at the lone Cheerio she'd been holding. Somewhere along the way she had put it down on the table beside her plate. Once again she picked it up and tossed it back into the bowl, as if dismissing the value of her own courage. The slight sound of the tiny puff of cereal hitting against the ceramic dish was absurdly magnified against the silence. Beth stared at the silly significance of it.

"I should never have taken the damn thing out of the bowl in the first place. If I'd just left it there I could have spared us both some rather unpleasant moments. I'm sorry. I never meant to go on like that."

Still guided by the affectionate warmth of her mother's presence, Joanna felt a smile form between a few more sips of wine.

"So tell me… how many boxes of Cheerios did you have to go through before you could finally admit something like that to yourself?"

Beth found some much needed relief in Joanna's humor.

"Unfortunately, they're not nearly as effective when it's your *own* voice you're trying to avoid."

Jo was glad to see Beth smile again.

"I'm sorry to hear that. I was hoping to use them the next time I struggled through one of those conversations myself."

Beth seemed pleased.

"So you have them too?"

Jo had come to rely on Beth to do all of the talking. Her impulse was to go for one of her Cheerios and change the subject, but her conscience told her that Beth deserved more. Joanna reflected on the last three years of her own life. They had been plagued with the voice of her own heart. Even the silence had become unsettling; continually echoing the vague possibility of more distant sounds—sounds she could not name, sounds she could not bring closer nor make go away, no matter how hard she tried. Jo knew Beth was still waiting for her answer.

"I guess you could say I've had my share of them lately."

Though Jo made every effort to sound nonchalant about it, Beth saw a much deeper vulnerability—the kind that often makes standing in the light more terrifying than being lost in the darkness. She wanted to let Joanna know that she was safe here or at the very least, understood. Once again she looked at Danny's chair.

"It's odd, isn't it, how intimate we become with ourselves through loss. Three years ago I'd have sworn I knew everything about myself, but when we lost Danny I touched an emptiness and despair I never even knew existed in me. I couldn't explain it then and I can't explain it any better now, but his death awakened a sense of devastation I knew in my heart belonged to something other than that tragic night."

Beth paused.

"Since then, I've lived with an unspeakable sadness that feels impossibly older than even myself."

Joanna found Beth's description deeply unsettling. Once again a sense of disorientation came over her. Her body stiffened. Though she tried to disguise her sudden distress Beth read her discomfort immediately.

"Are you alright?"

"It's just my period. Or maybe I'm just allergic to clean country air. If you've got a couple of Motrin, I'd appreciate it."

"There's a bottle in the medicine cabinet upstairs. I'll go get them."

Joanna was as anxious for a few minutes of privacy as she was for the pills.

"Thanks."

Joanna stared at the lone Cheerio Beth had thrown back into the bowl. She recalled how Beth held it in her hand while she struggled to disclose the painful secret she carried in her heart. Jo reached for the small souvenir of the woman's courage and placed it safely in the pocket of her shirt. Certain that Beth would notice it was missing, Joanna took one of the Cheerios from her own glass and slyly replaced the one she'd taken. It was not like her to behave so sentimentally, but for some reason the silly little symbol of Beth's courage was something she felt compelled to preserve. Jo looked at the dog who hadn't yet taken his eyes off her.

"One word about this and you're dead meat, Fido."

BJ yawned and lay back down, unimpressed by Joanna's threat. She couldn't fool him. He'd seen the flowers and was convinced her bark was worse than her bite.

Beth returned with the bottle of Motrin and a glass of water. As she watched, Joanna tossed two into her mouth. Beth was convinced that Joanna was trying to swallow much more than a couple of pills.

"I can put up a pot of coffee. Or if you're feeling a bit more decadent, there's a gallon of ice cream sitting in the freezer."

"I know. I was there when you bought it, remember?"

Beth blushed.

Joanna checked her watch. It was close to 11 o'clock.

"I think I'll pass. It's late and we're both exhausted."

Beth wasn't sure if she was relieved or disappointed.

"It has been quite a day, hasn't it?"

Jo rolled her eyes. She couldn't believe it was only hours ago that she'd left Manhattan. It felt like another lifetime ago.

Beth was apologetic about much of it.

"I'm sorry you got stuck with Adam's crazy mother tonight. I didn't mean to go on and on like that. I still don't know anything more about *you*." Beth caressed Jo's flowers with her eyes. "Then again, I did find out you're as remarkably talented as you are kind. There must be so much more to know."

Holding Beth with her eyes, Joanna took her glass of Cheerios, turned it over and dumped the whole bunch into the bowl.

Accepting the clever deflection, Beth conceded, but not without one last innuendo.

"Shall I take that to mean you'd like me to know everything... or nothing?"

"Take it to mean I'm using your rules to officially call it a night."

"Fair enough."

Jo stood up and rubbed the back of her neck.

Beth grasped for a light comment to offset the decidedly heavy toll of the day.

"Fortunately you don't have far to go."

"Especially since I don't have my car."

Beth squirmed enough for Jo to let her off the hook.

"Can I help you clean up?"

"Absolutely not. I'll have everything in the dishwasher in five minutes. After all these years, I've got it down to a science."

Joanna was much too tired to insist.

"Thanks for dinner."

"Thank you for staying."

Beth insisted Jo take the bottle of Motrin.

"Think you can find your way home?"

Jo tensed.

"I can find my way back to the carriage house. As for the place I call '*home*', I suppose that remains to be seen."

Preferring not to further complicate their parting by questioning the deeper meaning behind Jo's response, Beth walked her out onto the porch. A light breeze carried the intimacy of Beth's perfume much closer than Joanna would have preferred. As Beth gazed up into the dizzying, star-filled sky, her eyes sparkled with an almost childlike sense of wonder.

"Look! There's a full moon tonight."

"That would explain at least *some* part of the last 12 hours."

Beth's eyes lingered on the sky.

"Judging from all the stars, it looks like tomorrow's going to be another glorious day."

Another 'glorious day', Joanna thought to herself in amazement. *Horrendous* is more how she would have described today. If *glorious* was how Beth actually internalized it, then she was either truly remarkable or truly insane! Too tired to decide which, Jo knew that either could easily destroy what little remained of her own powers of reasoning.

The call of a thousand crickets filled the damp night air. Beth rubbed her hands up and down the length of her arms to warm herself against the evening's chill. Feeling a strong, sudden urge to shield her from the cold, Jo managed to reduce her impulse to a safe, passing remark.

"You should go in."

Surprised and touched by Joanna's concern, Beth smiled.

"There'll be a fresh pot of coffee on in the morning. I'm an early riser, so don't worry about waking me. Come by whenever you'd like."

Joanna considered her options and realized that with an empty refrigerator, she had none.

"Thanks, but just tomorrow, until I pick some stuff up at the supermarket."

Jo wanted to be extremely clear she had no intentions of making breakfast together a daily habit, and Beth wanted her to know she got her message.

"Of course, just for tomorrow. Steve should be here around 10 with some fresh bagels."

"I can hardly wait."

Jo couldn't resist taking one more shot.

"Before I actually step off this porch and onto the lawn, are there any land mines or bear traps I should know about out there?"

Beth took her remark good-naturedly.

"I don't suppose you'll ever feel entirely safe around me, will you?"

Jo was quite sure Beth was referring to a much different set of dangers than the one she was really most worried about.

"No, probably not."

She dug her hands into the pockets of her jeans and stepped down off the porch.

"Good night."

"Good night."

Beth would have watched Jo until she reached the carriage house, but she was certain that Joanna was aware of her eyes and was no doubt waiting to hear the sound of the kitchen door open and slam shut. Suddenly aching to close the distance Joanna's long strides had put between them, Beth called out to her across the lawn.

"I never did get to tell you about Arthur and the vase. Maybe next time."

Joanna didn't bother to turn around.

"Yeah, maybe."

If there is a next time, she thought to herself.

Beth called out again.

"Thank you again for the flowers. They meant so much."

Forcing herself to ignore the incomplete longing in her heart, she watched Jo for another moment, then finally went inside. BJ was hovering deliberately close to his empty food dish. Grateful for the immediate distraction of his one-track mind, Beth carried the platter of meat from the dinner table into the kitchen and sliced off a few generous slabs. It didn't matter that he was obviously much more interested in what was in his dish than what was in her heart. She engaged him anyway.

"That went pretty well, don't you think? Much better than I expected. And those flowers... can you imagine...after what I did to that poor woman's car? And that outburst! God, what was that all about? She must think I'm completely crazy. Maybe I am..."

Beth sliced off a few more pieces of meat, refilled BJ's water dish and began straightening up. She blew out what little remained of the candles, pleased and proud of herself for following her heart and making the setting special. After a few trips back and forth, everything on the dining room table had been cleared away—everything except for the vase with Joanna's flowers. Beth sighed and shook her head.

"Lady, you certainly are a bundle of contradictions."

Beth carefully picked up the vase, carried it into the living room and gently put it down on the top of the piano beside the notebook and sheet music. Maybe the magic and power of Joanna's creation would inspire her to resume working on her own. The piece lay unfinished for so long. It was a haunting melody that she'd begun soon after her son's death, but like the sadness it evoked, seemed to belong to the incomplete memory of something else. Perhaps she was meant to spend a part of this summer remembering. As Beth moved the sheets to stack them more neatly, an index card slipped out from between the pages. On it was a quote by the painter, Georgia O'Keeffe.

"Nobody sees a flower, really.
It's so small—we haven't the time.
And to see takes time,
Like to have a friend takes time."

Though she couldn't recall how the card had gotten there, the quote seemed perfect beside the gesture and beauty of Joanna's bouquet. She leaned the card against the vase and stepped back to revel in their compliment. The piano—the vase—the flowers—the sentiment. In the wisdom of Beth's heart they all seemed to belong to each other, and tonight was all about honoring that wisdom. She turned off the remaining downstairs lights and stood quietly at the foot of the steps, looking back across the room lit only by moonlight and truth. Unaffected by the running dishwasher, a sacred stillness, unlike anything she'd ever known, settled softly over the house. Soothed by the uncommon tranquility, Beth would have lingered there in its caress for the rest of her life except for BJ's yawn that reminded her just how badly she too needed some sleep. With her eyes still transfixed upon the moonlit piano, Beth spoke to his expectation.

"Just one more minute sweetie, I promise."

Longing to preserve the image in her heart, she took one last impressionable look, not expecting any of it to be there for her in the morning. After all, *tomorrow* had already broken so many of its promises. BJ waited patiently while Beth memorized the smallest details of this illusive gift and when she was finally ready they climbed the familiar staircase in silence—down a hall she knew by heart—to a place she'd never been. There, Beth Garrison would spend the first night of the summer her unclaimed longings had pleaded for.

Back inside the carriage house, Jo was grateful that the full moon provided enough natural light not to have to turn on the one overhead. The last thing she wanted was to reawaken herself to the stark reality of this day. Groggy and still unaccustomed to the space, she stumbled over the art supplies left scattered about from the labors of her peace offering. By now Joanna was so thoroughly exhausted even the barrage of unfamiliar scents and sounds of her new surroundings weren't enough to rile her dulled senses into rethinking her unlikely decision. Resigned to not seeing anything 'clearly' ever again, she seemed uncharacteristically content to grope around in the darkness of the room and her life.

For a time Joanna stared wearily at the pile of bedding that Beth had placed on the rocking chair. She had neither strength nor desire to pull out the sofa and make up the bed. Instead, Jo took a pillow and blanket and tossed them across the couch. Undressing was out of the question. She felt much too vulnerable to sleep in the nude, the way she preferred. Despite her reluctance to surrender any part of what she had on, Jo kicked off her shoes and peeled off her jeans. Now only a pair of bikini briefs and shirt were all that remained of her imagined armor. They would have to be enough.

Jo was considering the nearly impossible task of washing her face when she noticed the light go on in one of the second floor bedrooms of the house. The amber glow drew her over to the window. Concealed in the darkness, she parted the curtain slightly to steal a look at the silhouette moving about inside the small golden patch of light. She remembered the Cheerio she'd taken from the bowl and hidden in her shirt pocket. Careful not to break it, Joanna reached in and slowly pulled it out. With it secretly in her possession, she now had a piece of Beth's heart all to herself. The notion soothed and scared her. Holding it like a precious diamond, she turned the Cheerio to study it in the moonlight. For the second time that day she noticed the small heart and set of initials carved into the old wooden sill. Jo peered out into the mystery of the night, wondering if *their* lives were any more complete or equally filled with longings. But this was no time for corny reflection and certainly no time to let her guard down. Like a night watchman on duty, Joanna stood diligently and waited for the upstairs bedroom window to turn dark before she dared to move. She told herself that only when Beth had gone to sleep would it finally be safe for her to do the same. Barely convinced of her own logic, Joanna dragged herself over to the couch. She took off her Rolex and placed the band on the coffee table protectively around Beth's Cheerio, then lied down and rolled onto her side. As ridiculous as it seemed, Joanna felt there was something almost sacred about the relationship between the two objects—something so intimately woven into the threads of moonlight as it flooded through the window, it was as if time and timelessness had somehow become one. Joanna was delirious with fatigue, but she fought desperately not to close her eyes. A part of her was terrified of falling asleep. What if grandma Bessie was right? What if she got too comfortable and stayed too long, allowing whatever she didn't know she was looking for to find her instead—before she was ready—before she could run? Or even worse— what if it already had?

Chapter 6

Despite a groggy stiffness, the price of spending the night cramped up on the couch, Jo woke to a sunlight and wholesomeness she'd long ago abandoned with the innocence of her childhood. She sat up to meet the sweetness of the memory halfway. The fresh country air marbleized with early morning dew as it rose from the grass and foliage outside the opened windows. Chirping birds formed a welcoming committee in the nearby trees and for the moment, Jo even felt a little grateful for the bizarre and upsetting events that brought her to this place. She was grateful too for the fresh coffee and bagels soon to come. It was a simple, uncomplicated gladness; one that lie ever so gently upon the surface of her skin. Looking around at her modest accommodations, Jo tried not to draw a million comparisons to the luxury and comfort of her loft. She hoped that showering wouldn't wash away this tenuous sense of ease before it had a chance to sink deeper into her core. On the nearby coffee table a glint of sunlight caught the metal band of her watch that encircled the small Cheerio. Jo leaned forward and picked it up, trying not to over-analyze her sentimental attachment to the thing. After a time she got up, carried her secret possession across the room and set it down on the kitchen counter while she looked for a safe place to keep it. An empty glass jar seemed perfect. Jo unscrewed the lid and dropped the Cheerio inside. Then she replaced the top and set the jar down on one of the cabinet shelves with that silly, decorative piping running along its edge. Somehow her unexplainable affection for both these things seemed to justify their proximity. Careful not to fall back into such uncharted emotional territory, Joanna slammed the cabinet door and wandered off to the bathroom to tend to much simpler matters instead. With no idea where this new day would lead, Jo was sure it had to begin with a long, hot shower. Considering the antiquated plumbing, she hoped there would be enough hot water to loosen her muscles, if not her doubts about her decision to stay.

Having slept more soundly than she had in years, Beth showered and dressed with the unbridled enthusiasm of a child. Her husband wasn't even gone a full 24 hours and her son hadn't yet left for camp, but her own summer already felt like it had taken on a life all its own. She hesitated in front of the mirror, wondering if she looked okay. Then she wondered, okay for what—okay for whom? She checked herself from becoming any more neurotic so early in the morning. Chances were she'd have the rest of the day for that. Beth could hardly wait to get downstairs for another look at her paper bouquet. It was her only tangible proof that Joanna wasn't some imaginary playmate she'd made up in her mind.

Beth hurried downstairs, relieved to find the flowers on the piano just as she remembered placing them in the moonlight. In renewed awe of Joanna's talent, Beth studied each and every stem, leaf and petal all over again. When she was finally able to tear herself away, she set about making a fresh pot of coffee while BJ watched from his favorite patch of sunlight on the floor. As she unloaded the dishwasher, Beth wondered how Joanna had found her first night in the carriage house and what she would be like first thing in the morning. With good reason, she was almost afraid to trust that the delicate rapport they managed to strike over dinner would actually carry into the next day. Beth poured herself some coffee and checked the time. She was relieved that Steve would be arriving soon, providing not just bagels but some easy, familiar company. At the very least she knew she could count on his generous smile and easy going nature to get the day off to a pleasant start. Displaced from his own small town roots to pursue a degree in English literature at U-Mass, Steve had come to think of the Garrisons as his surrogate family. Ben's mentoring turned more nurturing than advisory and after graduation he invited the talented, struggling writer into his family's fold. Despite the young man's own turmoil over a brief and failed marriage to his high school sweetheart, Steve's loyalty to the Garrisons in the aftermath of their son's tragic death earned him a permanent place in the couple's heart. In the most thoughtful of ways he assumed the role of Adam's 'big brother', offering the boy not a cheap replacement but a sensitive presence whenever it seemed he needed one most.

At 27, it was quite obvious that Steve possessed two natural gifts—one for friendship, and the other for writing. In his relatively young life he had already learned enough about loving and losing to add a touch of complexity to his otherwise carefree disposition and simple boyish charm. But would his capacity for despair ever grow large enough to bring real depth and credibility to his work? Early on Steve had admitted to his revered professor that he feared he lacked a certain innate temperament necessary to generate a full blown case of angst—that noble state of inner turmoil he'd convinced himself was absolutely essential to the life of any great writer. Ben was amused by his student's youthful notions and tried to reassure him that given the naturally disappointing and disillusioning course of life, eventually the young man would have plenty of chances to reap the creative rewards of misery and heartache. True to form, Steve took his professor's prediction in his usual happy-go-lucky stride and decided to make the most of these light hearted years. While he waited for those dark clouds of human suffering to thicken into something worthy of his craft, Steve accepted his own easy going nature and supported his writing habit with carpentry jobs. Not surprisingly, he always whistled as he worked.

Beth heard a car pull into her driveway. Assuming it was Steve, she came out onto the porch to greet him. It was too late to take back her welcoming smile. Nick shut off the motor and got out.

"Glad you're so happy to see me. I wasn't sure how you'd feel about me dropping by unannounced this early in the morning."

Beth tried to temper her annoyance.

"I thought you were Steve."

"I'll take that beautiful smile of yours anyway I can get it, even by default."

Inhaling deeply, he gave Beth an uninvited hug.

"I don't know what smells more delicious… you or that cup of coffee you're holding."

"You can have a quick cup before you leave."

Ignoring her not so subtle message, Nick followed Beth inside and watched while she filled another mug. Taking it from her, he held his hand around hers and smiled much too intimately.

"Hmm, what more can a man ask for first thing in the morning?"

Beth's patience was wearing thin. She was unaware that Joanna was standing on the porch. Hearing their voices, Jo had deliberately stepped away from the door to eavesdrop on the conversation.

"What are you doing here Nick?"

He gulped his coffee.

"I know Ben left yesterday. I just wanted to make sure you… and Adam… were okay."

Listening intently, Jo was sure that Adam was a mere afterthought. She heard the resentment in Beth's response.

"Why wouldn't we be?"

Even Nick couldn't ignore Beth's tone.

"To be honest, Ben was uneasy about leaving you alone this summer. He asked me to check on you from time to time."

Beth became furious with her husband. When he called later, as she was sure he would, she'd give him a piece of her mind. Nick tried calming her down.

"I guess I should have called first."

"If you had, I could have saved you the trip."

Beth was fed up with being patronized and baby-sat.

"As you can see I'm perfectly fine, so you can move on. The day is young—I'm sure there's a damsel in distress out there somewhere waiting for you with more than just a second cup"

"Is *that* what you think this is all about?"

Beth raised her eyebrow.

"Isn't it? Hasn't it always been?"

Joanna had heard enough. She hesitated for another moment, hoping to hear Nick's answer, but her curiosity and the enticing aroma of fresh brewed coffee got the better of her. Jo knocked on the screen door, catching Beth off guard.

"Morning!"

Her tone sounded more like a proclamation that she was still around rather than a casual greeting befitting a new day. Feeling her body go limp and rigid at the same time, Beth worked to conceal both. Nick turned to see who was at the door. His pleasure was apparent. This was not at all how Beth wanted this new day with Joanna to begin

"Hi, come in."

Beth made an obligatory, bare bones introduction.

"Joanna Cameron...Nicholas Milos. Help yourself to some coffee. I was just walking Nick out to his car."

Beth took the mug out of Nick's hand and physically pushed him toward the door. Stubbornly resisting the weight of Beth's shove, Nick's eyes remained fixed on Joanna's every move. She had already dismissed his presence and was filling her mug.

Nick stole one last, lustful look at Joanna's statuesque torso clad in a faded, sleeveless work shirt and a pair of cut off jeans.

"Until we meet again."

Her long bronze legs led his eyes downward to a pair of sweat socks and hiking boots. With her back still to him, Jo barely managed a response.

"I'll be counting the minutes."

Beth continued to push her weight against him and didn't stop pushing until she had Nick back in his car. He was no less intrigued from a distance than he was up close.

"Who the hell was *that*... and is she married?"

Beth just shook her head.

"When did you ever let that stop you?"

Nick conveniently ignored the truth of her observation.

"Wow, what a body!"

"Trust me. It's not attached to a head you'd want to mess with. Besides, this is one you'd have to fight for. Adam was instantly smitten and Steve hasn't even met her yet."

Nick's eyes were still trained on the kitchen door.

"A shot at her would be worth dying for. Where'd she come from, anyway?"

For her own amusement, Beth answered literally.

"She came from the carriage house where she spent the night." She offered the basics, nothing more. "Look, it's a long story and I'm short on time. We met yesterday and she might be staying in the carriage house for the summer."

"So now Ben's left behind not one but two beautiful women to go off and ramble on about some obscure topic in 19th century literature."

"Believe it or not, some men actually find stimulation beyond the pages of Penthouse of Playboy."

Nick smiled—not with a smirk or suggestive innuendo, just the warm smile of a real friend. The kind he *could* be. The kind he had been when Danny died.

"Does Ben know how lucky he is?"

"He knows."

"I sure hope so."

He leaned through the opened window and squeezed her hand with real affection.

"Seriously Beth, if there's anything you need this summer, don't hesitate to ask."

She acknowledged his sincerity.

"I won't."

Nick backed his car halfway down the driveway, then stopped. Beth folded her arms and walked tentatively over to the car, afraid he'd add something inappropriate and ruin the moment.

He sounded almost shy.

"If you're going to the 4th of July concert, I thought maybe we could go together."

Beth hesitated and he understood perfectly well why.

"C'mon. What could be less intimate than you, me and a thousand other people all listening to Beethoven under the stars?"

He looked at her with sad, puppy eyes.

"I promise, I'll be on my best behavior."

Beth was glad he understood her reservations.

"Nick, you don't have to be on your 'best behavior'. You just have to be a good friend."

Embarrassed by the simple reminder, Nick's head fell with the weight of her rejection. Beth conceded.

"Alright. Pick me up at eight. I'll pack some wine and cheese."

"Beth…"

He seemed at a loss for words.

"Thanks."

"For what?"

Nick clasped the steering wheel for something to hold onto.

"I'm not sure. Maybe for seeing through the obnoxious façade of a lost and lonely man."

No matter how many times it happened, Beth was always amazed at how easy she made it for people to be vulnerable—how they willingly dropped their guard and just surrendered the truth at her feet. How wonderful it must be, she imagined, to feel that understood by someone to risk being yourself. She envied his relief.

"Your welcome Nicholas."

Beth stood there as he backed his car the rest of the way out of her drive way. For his sake, she continued to smile and wave until he drove away, much like a loving mother sending her child off to school. Wondering if people ever really outgrew their insecurities, Beth walked back toward the house where she knew she was about to face more than a few of her own.

Jo was leaning against the counter drinking her coffee. Her body language suggested she had no intention of moving until she got some answers. It was entirely irrelevant whether she had the right to any at all.

"Who's the jerk?"

Beth poured herself another cup of coffee. She'd spent so much of her life explaining people to each other. She was bored and tired of it. She certainly didn't owe Joanna an answer but she obliged her anyway, in part out of habit, in part for the sake of ready-made conversation.

"He's a colleague of Ben's at the University and a long-time friend. We used to spend a lot of family time together, until his divorce."

"Gee, why am I not surprised the guy couldn't hold a marriage together?"

Beth smiled, acknowledging Joanna's impression. She recalled Nick's vulnerability just moments ago in her driveway.

"He's not incorrigible all the time. He can actually be quite genuine. I suppose you'd really have to get to know him."

"Thanks, I'll pass."

Beth looked at the clock over the kitchen window, relieved to see that it was almost 10 o'clock.

"Steve should be here soon with those bagels. I'm sure you'll find his company a lot more pleasant."

Jo responded with indifference.

"I'm not interested in bonding this summer… with anyone."

Beth attempted a reasonably safe question.

"How was your first night? Were you comfortable?"

Joanna couldn't remember the last time she felt *comfortable* anywhere—least of all in her own skin. She kept the truth to herself.

"It was fine but I see I'm gonna' have to shower a lot faster than I'm used to."

"We've been meaning to replace the hot water tank for years."

Beth awkwardly suggested an option.

"Once Adam leaves for camp, if you'd prefer to soak in a hot luxurious bath feel free to use the tub in his bathroom anytime."

Even if her body pleaded for the soothing relief, Jo's stubborn mind would never permit it. This was not the time in her life for 'luxuriating' in anything.

"Somehow I wouldn't expect to find an abundance of bath oils and scented candles in Adam's bathroom. He strikes me more like the ring-around-the-tub, hair in the sink kind of guy."

Beth laughed

"Throw in a few wet towels on the floor and you've described the room perfectly." She hesitated. "There are plenty of both in *mine* though." Beth sipped her coffee and lowered her eyes self-consciously. "Not that I use them. Maybe this summer…"

The intimacy of Beth's confession made Joanna nervous. She needed to change the subject—and that image—fast! She looked at the refrigerator door.

"What did you do with the magnet that rolled under the table yesterday? It's not back up there with the rest of them."

Beth pretended to barely recall the incident at all.

"Who knows what I did with it?"

She hoped she sounded convincing since her explanation was far from the truth. In fact, Beth remembered precisely what she'd done with it. After picking it up and holding it against her heart, she'd brought it up to her bedroom and placed it on the night table beside her bed. For some ridiculous reason—like Joanna and that Cheerio—Beth felt compelled to have it close by. Despite her unease, Beth was intrigued with the keenness of Joanna's observation.

"Do you always notice everything?"

"Sometimes even *more* than everything."

Joanna watched as the disquieting thought slipped under the woman's skin. She rinsed out her mug and placed it in the dish drain.

"Thanks for the coffee."

Puzzled by her own behavior, Beth was relieved Jo had let the subject of the magnet go.

"There's plenty more. Just help yourself."

"Maybe later."

Once again Beth looked up at the clock. Once again the space between them started to thicken. The sharp, sudden ring of the phone interrupted their silence. Beth prayed it wasn't Steve saying he'd be late—or even worse, that he couldn't make it at all. She was counting on him for so much more than just breakfast. She was counting on him to save her life. Her voice was tentative.

"Hello."

Fortunately it was only Adam hoping to negotiate a bit more time with the newest love of his life. Beth was unyielding. There remained far too much to do before he left for camp the next day. He had to get a haircut. He had to finish packing. He had to clean his room. And most importantly, he had to give her some meaningful 'mommy time' before he left her for the arms of another woman. She insisted he stick to his promise and be home by noon. When he began to whine, she quietly and calmly hung up on him—something Beth had never done in her life. Pleased with this uncharacteristic response, a small piece of satisfaction broke off and squirmed its way passed her smiling lips.

"Gee, that felt awfully good."

Joanna had caught enough of the conversation to understand Beth's sense of triumph. For her own part, she faked despair.

"I've lost him forever, haven't I?"

"I'm afraid so. Think you'll survive?"

"I'm crushed, but I suppose I'll get over it… eventually. The hardest part will be having to give up the notion of having you as my mother-in-law."

Beth groaned.

"God, can you imagine? What would people say?"

It was as if the lighthearted remark had sparked a rebellion inside Jo's head. She had ignored 'raised eyebrows' all her life.

"Who gives a damn what people would say?"

Beth didn't know what to make of the defiance in Jo's tone. It seemed to come out of nowhere. Even BJ scrambled to his feet, not sure who or what he was supposed to be guarding. Realizing she'd startled both of them, Joanna tried to defuse her response.

"Never mind. I'm not daughter-in-law material anyway." Jo was eager to establish a greater purpose to her day than standing around conjuring up images of the absurd. Right now, 'reality' felt absurd enough. "Since I've already hung the screens, what's this Steve character coming over here to do this morning… beside feed me bagels?"

"To save me from you," Beth thought to herself. Instead of admitting that, she explained that the frame above the carriage house door needed reinforcing and several of the shingles on the roof needed re-tacking.

"Where's your ladder and tools? I'll get started on it."

Beth looked at Joanna as if she'd just suggested scaling the Empire State Building.

"I told you, I know what I'm doing."

Fearing another outburst, Beth was careful not to doubt her.

"I'm sure you do but you're not here to do repairs on my house."

Joanna wasn't quick enough to check herself.

"What the fuck *am* I here for?"

Her question caught both of them equally off guard and made both of them equally nervous for lack of an answer. At least tending to a concrete chore would provide some immediate space from each other. A shingle was far simpler a thing to nail down than that question. Beth conceded.

"You'll find everything you're looking for in the garage. Just promise me you'll be careful."

"I'll be fine just as long as *you* don't come anywhere near me with anything on wheels."

Beth's face grew flushed as Jo's eyes hinted at playful revenge.

"For whatever it's worth, I have every intention of wreaking havoc on *your* life as well."

Behind a measured smile, Beth's heart began to pound with an odd mix of excitement and fear. When the phone rang, she literally lunged for the receiver. This time it was her husband. His 'timing' both reassured and annoyed her. She hoped her voice disguised both.

"Ben, how are you?"

Not interested in hearing their conversation, Joanna turned to go. As she pushed through the door, Beth called out to her.

"Joanna, please be careful!"

She returned to her conversation.

"I'm sorry hon. How was your flight? How are your folks?"

"It was fine. They're fine. Who's Joanna?"

Ben's question was certainly reasonable and simple enough. It was the answer that felt nearly impossible to explain. As she watched Joanna disappear into the garage, Beth felt torn between wanting to tell him everything and wanting to tell him nothing at all. She knew he had every right to know, but in her heart she resented having to explain any of it, even the parts she could. Ben grew concerned by her curiously long pause.

"Beth, are you still with me?"

Drowning in conflict, the phrasing of his question seemed somehow ironic.

"Yes, I'm still with you."

He repeated the question.

"Who's Joanna?"

Beth drew a deep breath and in the simplest terms described the events, if not all the emotions, that had transpired in the short amount of time since he'd left. He listened closely to her self-conscious account, wisely not speaking until she was done with her explanation. Then, like a parent who'd decided to let his child make her own choices and learn by her own mistakes, he simply validated her decision and gave her his blessings. Fully expecting to get a lecture or advice, Beth found herself equally resentful of his patronizing approval. There was no possible way her husband could win, and none of it was really his fault. She felt badly for making him the 'bad guy' and quickly minimized the significance of the whole thing.

"It probably won't work out and she'll be long gone by the next time you call."

"Frankly I hope not. I'd feel a lot better knowing you had some company all summer."

His discomfort annoyed her.

"By the way, I didn't appreciate you asking both Adam and Nick to stand guard over me."

Ben stumbled.

"How did you know?"

"Never mind that! Just tell me if there's anyone else you have stationed on duty."

"I might have mentioned it to the head of security at the university… and, just for good measure, the National Guard."

"Please tell me you're kidding."

"I know you have reason to doubt it, but of course I'm kidding. You're entirely on your own from here… just the way you want it."

She was quick to correct him.

"It's the way I *need* it, Ben."

There was no point in challenging her.

"Whatever."

Continents apart, they were both willing to let the semantics of their life go for now. Instead, they discussed his parents' unstable health, Adam's raging hormones and the list of things that needed Steve's attention. Privately, Beth was both grateful and saddened by the safety of their bond. She'd grown accustomed to hiding there, in those kinds of conversations, even as she ached to be discovered and cast out. She shifted the receiver to the other ear and looked out through the kitchen window, over at the carriage house. Joanna was positioning the ladder up against the wall. A tool belt hung from her hips. In that moment, Beth felt completely unsure of her own existence. It was as if the familiar had become the unknown and the unknown, oddly familiar. She felt her life invaded, but from the inside, out. Her senses became jumbled and confused. She began to panic. Just when she thought nothing could save her, the sound of Steve's truck renewed her faith in miracles. Still holding the phone, she blurted out her relief.

"Thank God!"

"Beth, are you okay?"

"I'm fine."

"You just said, 'Thank God'. Thank God for what?"

Beth dismissed his concern

"Who knows? Never mind. Let me go. Steve just pulled up. I'll make sure Adam calls you before he leaves for camp tomorrow."

"Okay. You and I can talk more then."

For the sake of her husband's comfort Beth agreed, though she wasn't sure what more there was to say at this point. For now she was just eager to get off the phone.

"Send my love to your folks. I really do miss them."

"I will. Say hi to Steve for me. Remind him to keep hammering out those chapters in between hammering down those nails this summer."

"I'll tell him those are your orders."

"It's just that he's got a real gift. It shouldn't go to waste."

Deep inside, Beth felt her own heart rage, then grow still with regret. What had she done with her own gift? She forced herself to focus on the future and not the past. Ben sensed something was wrong. He hesitated before saying goodbye.

"Beth, I'm sorry about trying to protect you from a distance."

"I know."

"It's just that I love you so much."

"And don't think for a moment I don't love you back Professor Garrison."

Beth knew that was what he needed to hear to make their separation more bearable. The truth may have been more complicated than that, but it certainly wasn't a lie. She did indeed love him. Very much.

Steve came through the door in his usual high spirits. Beth was enormously relieved by his arrival. Her voice bordered on ecstatic.

"Hi sweetie. I'm sooo glad to see you!"

Steve put down the bag of bagels so he could hug her tightly with both arms. Standing well over six feet, he bent his broad, muscular frame to make it a little easier for her to return his affection. Steve was thoughtful even in that kind of way. From the very first time they'd been introduced to one another at an obligatory school function, he and 'Professor Garrison's wife' had an immediate rapport. In a room full of posturing and pretense, Steve had gravitated to Beth's natural warmth and sincerity. In an atmosphere of one too many grandiose intellectuals, she in turn was charmed by the refreshing simplicity of his conversation and by the gentle, charismatic ease of his smile. Theirs was a fondness as mutual as it was deep, and from that evening on it only grew stronger and more valuable to both of them.

"Thanks for the bagels."

"No problem. I might have picked up a carpentry job as well. The owner's thinking of expanding. He asked me for an estimate."

Beth handed him his usual black coffee in the largest mug she had.

"Well far be it from me to tell you what to do, but I just got off the phone with Ben who told me to remind you not to forsake your pen for a hammer indefinitely."

Steve took a full gulp of coffee, his mouth smiling even as it formed around the mug.

"Sometimes it feels like I should be paying that guy a salary for being my full-time conscience. The funny part is, I don't remember hiring him."

"That's because you didn't. He created the position for himself. Besides, he'd never take money for the job. He does it out of love, God bless his little heart."

Steve appreciated Ben's good—but misguided—intentions.

"Then I guess I'll just have to mail him a pink slip and relieve him of his duties."

Beth sighed.

"Good luck trying. What makes you think he trusts you to manage your life any more that he trusts me to manage mine?"

"Don't tell me he left you with instructions too?"

Beth continued slicing the bagels while they spoke.

"Are you kidding? I'm his wife. I get the Professor's royal treatment. Instructions! Expectations! Even 24 hour guards!"

Steve laughed at the remark. They both knew Ben meant well for her. It was a relief to be able to share her frustration with someone who really knew her husband and could truly appreciate his often heavy-handed show of love. She became playfully suspicious.

"Please tell me he didn't pay you to build an impenetrable fortress around me. The poor man's convinced himself I need some serious protection this summer."

"From whom or what?"

"From myself, I would imagine."

Steve picked up one of the bagels, ripped off a piece and shoved it into his mouth.

"Why? Do you pose some kind of threat to yourself?"

Beth took his question to heart.

"Sadly, no. But I can't help thinking maybe it's time I did."

Beneath his smile, Steve's eyes reflected a quiet acknowledgment of her unfinished life. He studied her seriously for a moment.

"Hmm... 'The Dangerous Beth Garrison'. Now she'd be rather intriguing, I'd bet. Yeah, I could definitely see that!"

Beth reacted awkwardly to his musings.

"You writers are all the same. I'm sure the character you're imagining in your head would be far more exciting than anything I could possibly live up to."

"I don't know about that. With a little practice I'll bet you could be quite an unpredictable and provocative woman."

Beth embellished the preposterous prediction.

"I think you're right. I might even risk experimenting with a new dish detergent… or even more daring, a new fabric softener! And if I'm feeling *really* brazen, I just might change the color of the bathroom towels!"

Steve had always appreciated Beth's ability to laugh at herself, but this time he sensed the importance of remaining serious, even if disguised in humor.

"Everybody's gotta' start somewhere. Who knows where such radical steps will lead? Today a different soap, tomorrow a different you!"

For a moment the pair looked at each other, then both burst out laughing. When their laughter subsided, Steve was quick to hold Beth to her own words.

"Maybe you're right, though. Maybe it's time you *did* become more of a threat to yourself."

Beth nervously tried stopping him with her eyes, but they betrayed her and begged him to press on. He answered their plea in the kindest way he could.

"You've always been there Beth, helping everyone else live their dreams. You deserve to have your own. Whatever they might be. Whatever they might cost."

She was enormously touched by his words—even more, by his obviously deep understanding of the underlying issue and all that remained at stake. She fought back tears to thank him.

His easy smile brought her back to safety.

"Think I should charge more for my carpentry because I can hit more than a nail on the head?"

"It certainly deserves some kind of compensation."

He kissed her affectionately on the cheek.

"Your friendship's always been compensation enough for me, Beth. I hope you know that."

She nodded.

Relieved to see her more comfortable, he chomped on what was left of the bagel and washed it down with his last slug of coffee.

"Speaking of carpentry, tell me what needs to get done and I'll get started."

Beth pointed through the window in the direction of the carriage house.

"It needs some reframing and a few minor repairs here and there."

Joanna was up on the ladder, hammering away. Even from a distance, her well-toned body made quite an impression.

"I'll be more than happy to take a closer look but from what I can see there's not a single part of her that needs work."

Beth shoved him playfully.

"Not the woman, silly. The carriage house."

"What can I say? Even us sensitive types have pathetically unevolved libidos." He continued to stare through the window. "Who is she anyway, and where'd she learn to swing a hammer like that?"

First Nick, then her husband and now Steve. Give or take a few changes in the tide, it felt like the same question kept washing up at Beth's feet. Drowning in the thought of trying to explain, her ordeal turned deliriously simple.

"Her name's Joanna. Why don't you bring her some breakfast in exchange for all the fascinating details of her life."

Reveling in the easy solution, Beth took out a plate, smeared some cream cheese on an onion bagel and fixed a fresh mug of coffee. She placed both on a tray with a paper napkin. As if sending a soldier into battle armed with only a toy water gun, she smiled slyly and handed him the tray.

"Here ya' go honey… a little breakfast for a little conversation. Good luck trying to make the trade. Oh, take this." Beth folded a red dishtowel and placed it neatly beside the plate. "Just wave it when you're ready to surrender and I'll come get you."

The odd smile on her face gave Steve concern.

"What's that supposed to mean?"

Beth reflected on the private hell of her last 24 hours.

"Let's just say she can be a little tough to get to know… maybe even a bit caustic, arrogant, defensive." Beth remembered the bouquet of flowers and realized she was being unfair. "Why don't you go out there and form your own impression?" She held open the screen door and followed him out onto the porch. Beth couldn't resist one last warning. "Be careful when you put your hand out. Sometimes she bites."

Steve sounded skeptical.

"I'll make sure to have a bagel in it then."

"Better a bagel than a finger sandwich," Beth thought to herself, finding much too much delight in the challenge he was about to face. But as she watched him cross the yard, Beth's amusement turned into something else. The closer he got to the carriage house, the more desperate she became to witness every detail of their introduction. A part of her hoped it would go well for him. Another part of her hoped he'd fail miserably. Unfortunately, the timing of Adam's return pulled Beth's away from where the eyes of her heart wanted to be. Instead, she watched her son trudge up the driveway, his reluctance and backpack in tow. Despite her love for him, at that precise moment his return felt like just another in a lifetime of distractions. As she watched her son approach, she could feel 'The Dangerous Beth Garrison' slip further and further away. Behind her welcoming smile, Adam's mother bargained with her frustrated alter ego not to abandon her completely. "He leaves for camp in just 24 hours. Please, don't give up on me."

From just a few feet away Steve watched as Joanna, unaware of his presence, deftly slipped the pliers back into its holster and pulled out the hammer hanging beside it. He waited respectfully while she used the back of its head to pry up several rusted nails from above the doorframe.

"I really admire a woman who knows her way around a tool belt like you do."

Replaying Beth's warning in his head, Steve waited tentatively for Joanna's response. In spite of her reluctance, Jo found his introduction too clever to ignore. She allowed herself to smile while she continued to pull up the next nail.

"How long have you been standing there grading me?"

"Long enough to remember something my pop used to tell me when I was a boy. Why put a ball on wheels when it already rolls by itself?"

"Meaning what?" Jo asked nonchalantly, her back still toward him.

"Meaning, I don't know why Beth called me over this morning. It's obvious you can handle anything that needs fixing yourself."

Jo twisted her body just enough to face him. Steve was holding the tray out in front of his chest like a proud boy scout, his white t-shirt as crisp as his smile. Given his unpretentious charm, Joanna was surprised how strikingly handsome he was with his dark wavy hair and soft brown eyes. His rugged LL Bean looks obviously hadn't gone to his head.

"I'm Steve McCormack. I come bearing breakfast."

Jo crossed her arms, letting her body language speak for itself.

"What's with the red towel?"

Steve wasn't sure how truthful he should be, but the honesty of his nature won out.

"Beth kinda' implied you oughta' be wearing some kind of warning label or disclaimer around your neck."

He couldn't tell whether she was amused or resentful of Beth's description.

"Did she now?"

He hoped his smile would soften the rest of it.

"Yup. She said to wave this red towel when I feared for my life and she'd race over to save me."

"She and what army?"

Steve's smile slowly faded.

"Should I just put the tray down and run while I can?"

Joanna she sat down on the top of the ladder.

"That depends. What's on the plate?"

"An onion bagel with cream cheese."

"Spill any of the coffee?"

He looked down at the mug and beamed with a foolish sense of pride.

"Not a bit."

Joanna extended a fleeting smile.

"Then I guess it's safe for you to stick around."

She climbed down from the ladder and removed the tool belt from around her waist. Steve put the tray down on the arm of the nearby Adirondack chair and extended his hand.

"Nice to meet you."

Joanna deliberately used the red towel to wipe her hands before clasping his.

"You might want to reserve your judgment about that, considering Beth's warning." She picked up her bagel, ripped off a bite and washed it down with a full gulp of coffee. In spite of herself, Jo already cared enough to put him at ease. "Relax, I don't attack before noon."

She allowed a measured smile to reassure him of at least some temporary degree of safety.

"So, what else do you do as impressively as you swing a hammer?"

Joanna remained intentionally evasive. She already found Steve much too congenial to risk sharing the specifics of her life.

"Let's just say I'm a veritable wiz at an untold number of things."

She was counting on her smugness to put him off. It didn't work

"You must spend a whole lotta' time pondering which… if any of it… matters at all."

Jo was not only amused by his response, she was intrigued with how comfortably he seemed to absorb things, not the least of which was her icy stare.

"I'll bet you're a 'veritable wiz' at pondering, too."

This time Joanna actually laughed out loud. She was surprised how good it felt to get such an uncomplicated response to such a complicated truth. She was impressed with how Steve handled her and how easily he made her laugh. However reluctant she was to admit it in that instant, the arm of her heart reached out and claimed him as a friend. But Joanna's decision was as practical as it was pure. After all, she considered the carriage house extremely dangerous territory and Beth Garrison a force to be reckoned with. If indeed she was going to be engaged in the battle of her life this summer, Joanna could certainly use a comrade, an ally, someone who obviously knew his way around behind enemy lines. When it came right down to it, Steve's friendship could mean the difference between her survival or her demise, and judging from the warmth in his eyes as he watched her finish her bagel, she figured maybe 'The Gods' were going to give her a fighting chance.

For the better part of the morning Beth fought her own distractions in order to keep her son away from his. Having gotten very little sleep the night before, Adam was dizzy with fatigue and infatuation—a deadly combination under any circumstance especially with so much left to do. Packing for camp had its own ritual. True to tradition, it was the usual battle of wills. After years of sending him off, what he did and didn't need still hadn't resolved itself. If anything, it felt like the older he got, the wider the gap became. But this year, her son was lucky. This year Beth was too tired to fight him on most of it. Or maybe, 'The Dangerous Beth Garrison' simply couldn't have cared less. She just wanted it over and done with so she could get him on that bus and move on to her own life.

"Packing went pretty easy this time, didn't it mom?"

When he got no response Adam looked up from his duffle bag. Beth was standing in front of his window, staring outside.

"What are you looking at?"

His question startled her. She felt like she'd been caught spying, which was exactly what she'd been doing and of course flatly denied.

"Nothing in particular."

Adam joined her at his window that overlooked the backyard. Steve and Joanna were working together on the carriage house. Seeing her sparked another uncomfortable question.

"How was your dinner with her last night?"

Beth's casual description bore little resemblance to the weight of the truth. She was unable to take her eyes off the pair. Even from a distance it was easy to see their comfortable exchange of tools, playful shoves and casual conversation. Beth tried to conceal her jealousy as she compared the immediate grace and ease of their rapport to the awkward maneuvering of her own. Their bodies seemed to glide about in each other's space like two choreographed dancers who'd been paired together many times. She thought of her own fractured dance on egg shells and cut glass, and how being in the same space with Joanna always felt like they were two wire hangers that somehow became impossibly tangled in a test of wills. Steve had taken off his t-shirt and tossed it onto the grass, partially covering the red towel she'd given him to wave when he needed her rescue. All at once, Beth felt foolish and discarded, angry and upset. She resented the simple freedom of his exposure—how easy everything seemed to be for him, especially when she herself had never felt more uncomfortable and repressed. None of it made any sense. Why should it matter whether he and Joanna hit it off; whether they share a hammer, a drink, or even a bed? Adam had been sizing things up too.

"They make a pretty hot couple, don't ya' think?"

Beth had tortured herself long enough. She forced herself to turn away, stubbornly avoiding both his question and the calamity of emotions pounding bitterly on the wall of her chest. At this point she had absolutely no idea what to expect of herself, but she had a very clear picture of what she expected of her son, and she was no longer counting on some stupid bet with Joanna to get it done.

"I'm going downstairs to fix some lunch. Meantime, you're going to finish cleaning your room. And don't forget, this time we're using *my* definition of clean, not *yours*. I don't want to have to do a thing in here after you're gone except maybe sit on the edge of your bed and miss you."

Surely 'The Dangerous Beth Garrison' would permit a little sentimentality from time to time.

After he'd finished, Adam begged for some time to hang out with Steve and Joanna. As reluctant as she was Beth agreed, hoping that a closer look would reveal an undercurrent of tension between them she hadn't been able to detect from the window. At the very least she was determined to cast Joanna an 'I told you so' look about how very likeable Steve was. At this point Beth was desperate to feel smug about something.

Adam's infatuation with Joanna sprang to life.

"How's it going?"

Jo concealed her amusement.

"I missed you last night, but a man's gotta' do what a man's gotta' do, right?"

Steve greeted the boy with some affectionate roughhousing while Beth stood awkwardly by holding a lunch tray. In a moment that felt as unforgiving as the midday heat, Beth sought relief under the patio table umbrella. Joanna joined her. Her arms, face and chest had turned a shimmering bronze from working in the sun. Her long black hair had been pulled back into a thick braid. As Jo used the back of her hand to wipe the beads of perspiration from her forehead, Beth tried not to notice her undeniable beauty. Except for the pouring of lemonade the two women sat in a deadlocked silence made all the more apparent compared to the animated exchange between Adam and Steve. Guessing they were comparing notes on the woman sitting opposite her, the assumption all but ruined Beth's appetite.

"I'm not very hungry. Would you care for my sandwich?"

Joanna had been wondering when Beth would finally speak to her. She couldn't remember if she had given her a reason not to.

"Steve and I are gonna' grab some lunch on the way back from a couple of estimates he's gotta' give. He wants my input on the bids. We'll probably be working together on some jobs over the next couple of weeks."

Beth tried to disguise her jealousy.

"Perhaps you'd like me to make some of those finger sandwiches for your lunch box."

Joanna knew she had Beth's remark coming but she had no intention of explaining how good it felt to be in such safe and uncomplicated company. She had no intention of describing how exhilarating it was to be straddling a ladder in an old pair of jeans instead of crossing her legs in a Donna Karan suit—to be handling rusty nails instead of shiny paper clips—to be slugging ice water from a gritty bottle instead of sipping pretentious cappuccino at an equally pretentious café. Connecting with Steve was like connecting with a part of herself—the part she long ago 'traded up' for a more sophisticated model. Granted, he was considerably younger, but his enthusiasm was refreshing. In his desire to achieve something really 'big' with his talent, Steve reminded Jo of herself in earlier years when 'big' meant something more important that a six figure salary and a corner office with a panoramic view. How many nights had she worked late trying to recall, as she watched the sun set behind the city skyline, the inner landscape of her own heart as clearly as she'd come to know the details of those buildings. But most importantly, the truth was that Steve McCormack was completely 'manageable'. Just the opposite of the woman whose roof, and spell, Jo had foolishly agreed to live under and who now awaited her response.

"The red towel was a cute touch."

Beth felt foolish.

"I was just being protective. The men in my life seem quite vulnerable around you."

Joanna finished what was left of her lemonade and smiled.

"In case you've forgotten, I was the one who got dumped recently."

"You seem to have bounced back quickly enough."

Joanna pushed out her chair and extended her long legs, as if commanding more space.

"It's what I'm good at."

Beth was tired of the battle—the one of wits and the one raging inside her own head.

"Fine. You're on your own."

"Like we agreed."

Just as the two women were settling into a tenuous truce Adam swooped up his basketball from the grass and tossed it to Joanna.

"How 'bout a game of 21? Me and you against Mom and Steve."

Beth didn't wait for Joanna to answer.

"Out of the question! Eat your lunch and then we're going to the barber's."

Jo stood up and turned to Steve.

"On that note, I'm going in to take a shower. Then we can split."

"Ready whenever you are."

With time to kill, Steve remained at the table with Beth.

"Well, the frame and shingles are as good as new."

Beth struggled not to blame him for her discomfort.

"Thanks. What do I owe you?"

"Not a thing."

Uncomfortable enough about being upset with him, she was hoping to at least pay off some of her guilt.

"I insist."

"Forget it… I'm not taking your money. Besides, Jo did all the work."

Beth tried to ignore that he'd already begun using her friendlier nickname.

He was eager to talk about their plans.

"We're gonna' be working up some estimates on a few jobs together. She's one helluva' carpenter and I could really use some help these next couple of weeks. She refuses to take any money though, so I agreed to do some modeling in exchange for her time. She wants to get back into painting and sculpting this summer. Said she hasn't done it since art school."

With a mix of envy and intrigue, Adam chomped on his sandwich.

"You mean like with no clothes on?"

Steve grabbed his t-shirt and whipped it around, playfully snapping Adam on his arm.

"Why not? The ladies tell me I've got plenty to be proud of."

As he winked at her son, Beth felt an unexplainable sense of rage encased inside her trumped up show of concern.

"How are you going to work all day, model into the night, then go home, get up and do the same thing all over again on so little sleep?"

Steve looked at her mischievously.

"Maybe if I play my cards right I won't be going home… or sleeping much… this summer."

Adam groaned with envy.

Steve waited for Beth's reaction.

"Would I have your blessing?"

Battling a mix of feelings, Beth shrugged.

"You don't need my blessing Steve. She looked down at the grass. "It's obvious you didn't need my red towel."

Anxious to move away from him and the moment, Beth began collecting the plates and glasses and haphazardly piled them back on the tray. When Joanna came out of the carriage house, she couldn't help notice how completely mesmerized both Steve and her son had become as they watched Jo approach. She'd washed her hair and was again wearing it loose. She'd changed her jeans and a soft cotton tank top accented the contour of her breasts as she strode across the lawn. Her sunglasses made it virtually impossible to read her eyes and Beth was the only one who seemed to wonder if that was entirely deliberate. When she got to the table, Jo made it clear she wasn't sitting down.

Steve got up and tussled Adam's hair.

"Have a great time this summer kid. When you get back from camp we'll compare notes."

Adam looked longingly at Joanna.

"You coming back tonight?"

"Why wouldn't I be?"

She lowered her glasses just enough to rattle him.

"No reason. Catch you later then. Maybe shoot some hoops."

"We'll see. I wouldn't want you to leave for camp feeling defeated."

Though she presumed to be talking to Adam, Jo stared directly into his mother's eyes.

"That's an awful feeling, isn't it Beth?"

Beth agonized under her carefully guarded expression.

Without so much as a glance back, Joanna opened the door and slid into the passenger side of Steve's pick-up. Along with a handful of Dunkin' Donuts napkins and a curled spiral notebook, dozens of loose business cards lay strewn across the length of the dashboard. Jo recalled the crisp weekend morning runs with her father to give estimates or visit job sites. In those days her feet barely touched the muddied floor mats of his truck, but riding beside him, 'talking shop' always made her feel ten feet tall. One Christmas he'd even presented her with her set of personalized business cards. She could still remember the thrill of running her small fingers across the black embossed letters of her name and title just below his company logo: 'Joanna Cameron, carpenter-Journeyman. All through elementary school she carried those cards in the back pocket of her jeans. She remembered how wildly her heart beat the day she handed one to the beautiful Mrs. Naughtin. Her little body actually trembled with excitement as the teacher took the card from her hand and read it. Whether genuinely impressed, or genuinely kind, the woman smiled so intently into Joanna's eyes she thought her legs would buckle out from under her. It didn't matter that what Mrs. Naughtin needed was to convert one of the rooms of her home into a nursery for the baby she and her husband were expecting. Joanna pretended not to know how babies were made and wouldn't allow herself to believe that the beautiful Mrs. Naughtin could ever let a man climb on top of her that way. Joanna convinced herself it must have happened while her beautiful teacher was asleep.

One summer vacation after another Jo worked alongside her father and by the time she graduated college, she was as skilled and knowledgeable as any foreman on his crew. When she turned 21 he made a whole-hearted offer to turn Cameron Construction into a father-daughter business, but by then, Jo had become more enamored with the idea of seeing her name engraved on a shiny plaque on an ad agency door than the side of a muddy truck. Believing that his daughter always knew what she wanted, Jo's dad didn't try to talk her out of her decision. If anything, he wished her luck and remained as supportive as ever. Still, sitting in Steve's pick-up all these years later, it took only a second for all those wonderful old feelings to come rushing back. Jo had gotten her plaque and a big impressive office to go with it, but somehow it never brought the rewards she'd expected.

Steve tossed his tools into the back of the truck and came around the side to kiss Beth goodbye. This time she barely managed to kiss him back and she did not unfold her arms so she and Steve could exchange their customary, warm hug. He felt her stiffen.

"Are you okay?"

"Why wouldn't I be?"

"I don't know. You just seem a little strained this morning."

Beth shrugged off his observation, secretly trying to understand it herself. Her jealousy made no sense. After all, wasn't this precisely what she was hoping for—that Steve would put some distance between herself and Joanna?

"I have a lot on my mind, that's all."

He leaned over and whispered in her ear.

"Or maybe 'The Dangerous Beth Garrison' is a little edgier than the woman we both know..."

Steve climbed in behind the wheel and started the engine. As the truck started to roll, he called out to her jokingly.

"Don't wait up for us mom."

Though motionless, inside Beth felt herself lunge for Steve's throat. As he drove off, she imagined throwing rocks at his truck. Beth no longer recognized herself. She was certain this was what it felt like to be possessed. Adam's passing remark didn't help.

"My bet is he nails her in less than a week!"

Behind the rigid tolerance in her eyes, 'The Dangerous Beth Garrison' was already plotting her son's demise. It would be cruel and merciless. Not unlike this day.

Steve had suggested Trudy's. Although she wasn't particularly keen on returning to the scene of the crime so soon, Jo wasn't about to let her emotions rule.

Trudy hurried over to greet them—those same ridiculous yellow earrings slapping at the sides of her head. She reached up and planted a familiar kiss on Steve's cheek.

"Hiya handsome. Can't stay away, can ya'?"

He laughed, pleading no contest. Trudy nudged Joanna.

"And hello to you too, doll! Obviously you're meetin' all the nicest people in this town. But just so ya' know the score... I've got dibs on this one."

"I'll consider myself warned."

Trudy's eyes twinkled with mischief.

"Good, 'cause if I'm ever a free woman, he's all mine!"

Jo put up her hands.

"Got it!"

Steve didn't have to pretend to be disappointed.

"You're not even gonna' fight for me?"

"What's the point? She already stood up to me yesterday in the parking lot. I know when I've met my match."

Trudy crossed her arms victoriously.

"Now that that's settled, ya' wanna' see menus or are ya' the only people in this cockamamie world who know what they want?"

Joanna felt relieved to be sure of something.

"I'll have a cheeseburger deluxe, well done and a lemon coke."

That sounded good to Steve.

"Make that two."

Trudy looked up from her pad.

"Hmmm… sounds like you got a lot in common. You just keep in mind what I said, missy."

Steve waited until Trudy pushed through the swinging doors into the kitchen.

"Quite a character, isn't she?"

"You sure she's the one you wanna' ride off into the sunset with?"

"Why, you offering me another option?" Steve challenged her obviously forgone conclusion. "We *do* seem to have an awful lot in common."

"It's opposites that attract, remember?"

Steve had already mastered her scowl.

"Far be it from me to fight the laws of nature or that look in your eyes."

Joanna appreciated his resilience and decided he deserved at least an offhanded compliment.

"Trudy's a lucky woman."

"Funny, my ex-wife didn't seem to think so."

Joanna was surprised to learn he'd been married.

"Ah, a man with a past."

"Does that make me intriguing?"

It amused Jo to think that it might, if she were living in someone else's skin. Steve was certainly one of the most physically attractive men she'd met in a long time. She liked that his toned physique was the result of his labor and not some gym membership, and that he was no more invested in the size of his biceps than the God given cut of his jaw. It struck her that everything about him seemed natural. It was the current of life that pulsed through his veins, not a regiment of vitamins, that gave him his energy and stamina. Trudy returned with their lunch order.

"By the way doll, Ruby's already workin' on that car of yours and from the looks of it, he's makin' it his own personal mission to get it back to you even better then before."

She placed Steve's platter in front of him.

"I assume you heard about the little accident Beth caused out there in the parking lot yesterday morning? Your pretty little lunch date's got herself quite a temper from what I saw. I'd try and stay on her good side if I were you."

Steve wisely intervened.

"Jo's staying at the Garrison's. That's how we met."

Trudy didn't appear the least bit shocked by the unlikely turn of events.

"See, that's just what I'm talkin' about. Whatever brings good people together."

Once Trudy moved on to serve another customer, Steve lost no time picking up where he'd left off.

"You never answered my question. Is a guy with a past more intriguing to you?"

"*Anyone* with a past is more intriguing to me."

In spite of herself, Jo *was* curious.

"Mind talking about it?"

"What would you like to know?"

"Whatever you want to tell me."

"Let's just say my high school sweetheart preferred the romantic notion of being married to an aspiring writer more than she liked the reality of it. The marriage lasted a grand total of two years or as she once put it, until the 209th page of my work in progress.

"Was the split mutual?"

"It would be more accurate to say the *disillusionment* was."

He tossed an onion ring into his mouth.

"Her version was that our real life fell apart while I was consumed with creating a fictional one."

"And *your* version?"

Steve became thoughtful.

"That sometimes art imitates life, and sadly, sometimes it destroys it." He seemed almost apologetic. "It's not that I didn't love her. But writing's always been the one thing that's made me feel whole. Sometimes wholly inadequate…

sometimes wholly insane… but whole nonetheless. She knew that when she married me, but that didn't stop her from quickly growing to resent it. So now instead of sleeping with this incredibly sexy woman, for the last few years I've been sleeping with a spiral notebook and a real cool flashlight pen." Steve's face broke into one of those wonderful smiles. "I've only had to replace the battery once!"

Jo watched him devour much of his burger in one bite. His eyes flashed with something more to add, but his manners prevented him from talking with food in his mouth. As soon as he swallowed, he continued.

"Did you know that ball point ink's a lot tougher to get out of cotton sheets than semen?"

Joanna burst out laughing at the unexpected remark.

"Occupational hazard of a struggling writer, huh?"

Steve finished his burger and wiped his mouth.

"I suppose so."

Joanna wasn't quite buying his 'lonely-hearts' account.

"Please don't ask me to believe you've been celibate since then."

Steve grinned like a child caught in a little white lie.

"Well, it *is* a college town, teeming with beautiful young coeds. So sure, I've shared a couple of extra curricular activities with a few of them. But there's never been anyone serious since my wife." Steve's face became very sincere. "That's the truth."

Jo sensed he was waiting for a response.

"Okay, that part I believe." She was eager not to have him become too invested in whatever she thought. "Does your ex live around here?"

"No. After we separated, Peg went back to our hometown in Iowa. She married a friend of mine… a local guy who flies crop dusters for a living. They already have two kids and a dog."

Joanna played with her straw.

"What about you?"

"Lets see, I've taken in one stray cat, sold two short stories and finished five more chapters of my novel. In between I've gutted and renovated six restaurants and over a dozen houses."

"Sounds like you've both moved on."

"Guess so. We exchange letters every year around Christmas. I'm glad she's happy. Peg's a really sweet girl. I was way more complicated than she ever signed on for."

Trudy came over with two fresh cups of coffee and some apple pie.

"It's on the house. I figure the longer you stay, the longer I get to keep my eyes on ya'."

Steve flashed her one of his lazy smiles and she walked off a satisfied woman. He quickly refocused on his lunch companion.

"So what about you? Ever been married, yourself?"

"What makes you think I'm not married now?"

He took a gulp of coffee.

"Writer's intuition'. It's the next best thing to a woman's intuition."

Though she admitted his instincts were right she was quick to set the record straight.

"Which is not to say I haven't been involved."

"But it hasn't been the 'real deal' yet, has it?"

"So says your crystal ball?"

"No. So says the wall around your heart. Seems more like it's there to stop someone important from gettin' in rather than to make sure someone important doesn't get away."

Steve's perception was more than Joanna had bargained for. Despite her guarded expression, he continued.

"I'm not sayin' an untimely lover's spat hasn't ever *inconvenienced* you… just that it hasn't ever *devastated* you. Kinda' like maybe a break-up ruined your weekend plans, but not your whole life."

Joanna didn't know whether to resent or applaud him. She simply pushed aside her plate along with the accuracy of his observation.

"It would be wise to remember we'll be working with power tools. I'd just hate for one of those saws to slip…"

Steve understood that meant the conversation was closed. He signaled Trudy for one last refill and the check.

"I'm sorry if I've offended you."

Joanna leaned hard against the back of the booth and crossed her arms.

"Trust me, you'll know when I'm offended."

Her eyes drifted out through the window into the parking lot, the scene of yesterday's unfathomable events. She couldn't erase the image of Adam's mother from her mind. Jo tried to convince herself that her interest was nothing more than natural curiosity and if she was going to put up with Steve's troubling insights, she sure as hell intended to get some useful information out of him in return. Joanna was careful to sound as casual as possible.

"How long have you known the Garrisons?"

"About six years now. Peg and I came east right after the wedding so I could do my post grad work at U-Mass. That's where I met Professor Garrison... Ben. He agreed to be my thesis advisor, but he turned out to be a lot more. He's a brilliant scholar. Really knows his stuff. He's a really swell guy too, with a great family. After my divorce, they took me in like a third son."

Steve hesitated, realizing that Joanna might be confused.

"Adam had an older brother, Danny. He died in a car accident a few summers back. It'll be three years the 7th of this month. The kid just graduated from high school."

Jo recalled the pain of Beth's conversation the night before. She pretended not to know a thing.

"That must have been awful."

She wanted to press Steve for a million answers but she forced herself to let the conversation unfold naturally.

"Do they know what happened?"

"Supposedly the car he was driving skidded off the road and slid down the embankment, but not before it flipped over several times. Judging from the tire tracks, the police seemed to think he lost control of the car coming around one of the curves, maybe trying to avoid hitting a deer or raccoon. He was a real responsible kid. He didn't drink and it's hard to imagine he was speeding... but who knows." Steve stared out through the window. The sadness in his eyes was very real. "By the time they got him to the hospital, he'd slipped into a coma. He never regained consciousness and died two days later. He was such a great kid. He wanted to be a concert violinist. He'd even won a scholarship to Julliard. He was an incredibly gifted musician just like his mother. Maybe she'll play the piano for you sometime. She'll blow you away."

All at once Joanna's worst fears were realized. That majestic instrument indeed belonged to Beth. Jo kept her thoughts to herself as she considered the increased threat.

"Was anybody else hurt?"

"No, he was alone, on his way home from his best friend's house. Jason was going backpacking across Europe for the summer, then off to college somewhere on the west coast. Supposedly they were saying goodbye."

Steve's heart filled with sadness.

"I guess some goodbyes are more final than others."

Joanna certainly had her share. She let him continue.

"The whole family was a wreck for a long time. They went into grief counseling, mostly for Adam's sake. Eventually he and his dad began to heal but Beth just seemed to get worse as time went on."

He thought about his good friend.

"Not that she'd ever tell you so."

Joanna sat forward, intent on learning more.

"What do you mean?"

"Beth's never been one to burden anyone with her own problems. She's a pro at brushing herself off and moving on. She hasn't though, not this time. Maybe I shouldn't say this, but I really think that losing Danny gave her the perfect excuse to just give up on her *own* life entirely. Let's face it, when a mother loses a child who could blame her, right?"

"Did she admit that to you?"

"No and she can deny it all she wants but I know I'm right."

It was obvious that Steve's perception gave him an awareness he sometimes wished he didn't have. His voice sounded heavy.

"I'm glad she decided not to go to England with Ben this summer. Maybe she's finally ready to face herself."

He smiled as if trying to lift his own spirits.

"Just this morning I kidded her about the possibility of becoming 'The Dangerous Beth Garrison'. I tried to convince her to use this summer to explore her options. You know... take some chances... run with the wolves. I'll bet behind all that domestication there's an untamed woman aching for some time off for good behavior."

He paused.

"I know you just met her, but what do *you* think?"

Joanna wasn't about to consider the possibility. She was having a hard enough time trying to contend with the 'tame Beth Garrison'. She looked at her watch. They'd been sitting there for almost two hours. Jo slid out of the booth, deliberately avoiding the answer to his question.

"Get the check from your lady-love and let's get out of here. I still need to pick up a few things in the supermarket before you drop me off."

Steve was predictably obliging.

"Okay but I never did find out more about *you*."

Joanna laughed to herself at the impossibility of his mission. He had absolutely no idea that she'd already disclosed as much about her life as she was going to—especially in one day. He knew where she grew up, where she went to school, where she lived and where she worked. She'd even agreed to go to some silly 4th of July concert. That was way more social than she intended to be with him, or *anyone,* and way more than he knew to be grateful for.

Joanna insisted that Steve let her off at the curb. There was no reason for him to pull into the Garrison's driveway. He reminded her that he'd swing by Monday morning to pick her up, guessing that their first job would take about two weeks. He watched her collect the four plastic bags.

"Sure I can't give you a hand?"

"I'm fine."

"Say hi to Adam and Beth for me, will ya'?"

Joanna wasn't looking for anymore contact with either of them. She'd already started walking up the driveway when he called out to her.

"Hey Jo..."

She turned around. He leaned out through the window, rested his head on his forearm and smiled.

"Never mind."

Whatever it was he was thinking, something told her to be grateful he left it unsaid. No sooner had Steve pulled away, Adam came bounding out from the kitchen onto the porch, offering to carry her groceries. There seemed to be no end to the men falling at her feet today. She was too tired to fight him off and handed over two of the four plastic bags. They were almost at the carriage house when Beth came looking for her son. Not expecting to see Joanna, she was caught off guard and was a lot friendlier than she wanted to be considering Jo's parting remark.

"I didn't hear Steve pull into the driveway."

Now imagining 'The Dangerous Beth Garrison', Jo was all the more reluctant to be engaged.

"I bailed out at the curb. He said hi."

Beth nodded. She wished she could have prevented BJ from tagging along as Jo and Adam made their way across the backyard. How many more times was she going to be left feeling abandoned in one day? Beth crossed her arms and called out to her son.

"I want you back here in ten minutes young man! You still have to call your father."

Joanna held the screen open and the three disappeared inside.

Adam waited while Jo put away her groceries. As she bent over to stack the lower shelves of the fridge, she knew his eyes were glued to her ass. She tossed him a can of soda.

"Great haircut. I like it."

His hair was buzzed up the sides and spiked with gel on top.

"Mom hates it."

Joanna shrugged.

"Don't sweat it. It's part of her job description. They'd throw her out of the union if she didn't give you a hard time. If you ask me, your mom seems like a pretty cool lady."

"I guess."

Joanna still had a few last licks to get in before she ran out of time.

"How's your friend Jeff, the one with that little problem last night?"

Adam began to squirm awkwardly in his chair.

"He'll be okay."

It was obvious he wanted to change the subject.

"So you and Steve are gonna' work together, huh?"

She let him think he was off the hook.

"Yeah, we are."

He cut right to the chase.

"And he's gonna' model for you totally naked?"

Jo flashed a deliberately suggestive smile.

"I don't know. Would you do it if I asked you?"

Adam became instantly flustered. He was beet red when his mother appeared at the door. Despite the tone of her voice Adam was never so happy to see her.

"Okay buster. Your ten minutes are up! Get in the house and call your father now!"

Adam gladly bolted for the door.

"Gotta' go. Thanks for the soda."

Joanna followed him outside.

"Have a nice summer kid. I'm sure Lori's gonna' love running her fingers through that hair of yours."

Adam stopped dead in his track. How did she know about Lori? He turned around and glared at his mother. Beth glared right back, by now thoroughly annoyed with the antics of both Adam and Joanna. As she followed her son back to the house, Jo called after her.

"Can I talk to you for a minute?"

Beth stopped, but stood her ground. This time she made Joanna come to her.

"What is it?"

She crossed her arms and waited for Jo to reach her. There was something about Beth when she'd been pushed to her limit—when she was tired, tense and provoked—that indeed made her dangerously appealing. Joanna fought the attraction.

"Does that offer to use the washer and dryer still stand?"

"Yes."

"Then I think I'll be taking you up on it after all."

Jo felt compelled to offer an excuse.

"Steve and I are gonna' be working together on a few jobs, so I'll probably need to do more laundry than I expected."

Beth struggled to appear indifferent.

"Whenever. Feel free."

"I'll buy my own detergent though."

"Fine."

"Do you have a problem with me using the pool?"

"Since Adam included it as a selling point, consider it a part of the accommodations."

Jo offered an appreciative smile but Beth remained intentionally expressionless.

"Anything else?"

"Yeah. Have any idea where I could buy some modeling clay around here? I'd like to do some sculpting this summer."

Beth tried her best to ignore Steve's comment about modeling for her.

"There's a place in town called 'Mats N' More'. It's a frame shop but they carry a fair amount of art supplies. If they don't stock it, I'm sure they can order whatever you want."

In spite of everything, Beth extended an offer.

"If you like, I could show you where it is."

"Steve's giving me a grand tour of the area. I'll stop by then."

Once again Beth felt like a complete and utter fool.

"Fine. I'll leave you the keys to the Jeep tomorrow."

Beth knew that under the circumstances Jo would feel uncomfortable accepting her generosity, so the gesture more than served its purpose.

Before Joanna could respond, Adam yelled from the porch.

"Hey mom, dad's on the phone. He wants to talk to you."

"Terrific," Beth thought to herself. "That's just what I need to end this day—a long-winded list of reminders from him."

"I'll be right there."

She turned to Jo.

"Is that it then?"

Joanna nodded, but that was hardly the truth. There was so much she wanted to say, but she knew she shouldn't. So much she wanted to explain, but knew she couldn't. She searched Beth's eyes, hoping they'd assure her that somehow she understood. But this time Jo saw only hurt—old hurt, new hurt, hurt still to come and somehow she felt unexplainably responsible for all of it. She watched Beth walk back to the house, the curve of her shoulders resigned to their weight. When Jo was absolutely certain Beth was far enough away, she apologized under her breath.

"Please... forgive me."

Beth lie on her back, staring up into the darkness. She was utterly exhausted and hopelessly awake. She'd been tossing and turning in bed for the last two hours, but the harder she tried to let go of the day, the more its unsettling details replayed in her head. She looked at the clock again. It was 3:30 in the morning and she had to be up in less than three hours to get Adam over to the camp bus by seven. Too restless to lay there a minute longer, Beth swung her legs over the side of the bed and sat up. Her eyes swept over all the familiar shapes and surfaces of the darkened room and came to rest on the flower magnet she'd placed on her night table the day before. Beth fought her immediate impulse to hurl the stupid thing out her window in the direction of the carriage house. Instead, she scooped it up in an angry fist, swooped downstairs into the kitchen and slammed it back onto the refrigerator door. She was almost at the landing when she abruptly turned around and marched back downstairs. She swiped the magnet off the door, walked over to the garbage, flipped open the lid and tossed it inside. It was oddly gratifying to see it sitting there mixed in with all the discarded scraps and remains of the day. Satisfied that she'd deposited her foolish sentimentality where it rightly belonged, Beth stomped back upstairs, refusing to permit herself even a glimpse of Joanna's bouquet from across the room. Determined to meet this next day head on, Beth pulled up her knees, crossed her arms and stubbornly decided to wait for the sun to rise. Then she would put her son on his bus, go home and get on with the rest of this god-forsaken summer, with no one to contend with but herself.

Among the many things 'The Dangerous Beth Garrison' was determined to prove she could live without, sleep was one of them. The illusive, infuriating Joanna Cameron was another.

Chapter 7

From all outward appearances, Adam's departure went exactly as it always had. Amid the mayhem of countless other families all doing the same thing, it was a mad flurry of overstuffed backpacks and luggage hurled from the rear of family cars and placed in an orderly fashion at the side of the bus. Children, like mischievous puppies straining to get at one another, attempted to break free of last minute hugs and parental reminders. Eventually, the fresh-faced counselors herded the last of the unruly pack onto the bus while parents gathered in friendly, supportive clusters to wave good-bye. Year after year, it never seemed to matter that the children on board had long stopped waving back as the groaning camp bus pulled away.

Many of the parents lingered in the parking lot to chat with one another. Although beckoned into several groups, Beth was feeling much too private to be drawn into small talk. It was highly unlike her to lie and say she had to be elsewhere, but that's exactly what she did. As she walked back to her car, she wondered what other changes she would undergo this summer while Adam was away. While he was off, no doubt having the time of his life, she would be struggling fiercely to reclaim her own. She wondered what kind of woman her son and husband would find when they returned and whether either of them, lost in the usual self-absorbed details of their own lives, would even notice the profound changes in hers. One way or the other Beth was determined to make sure there would be some.

Unlike the trip back from the airport just two days earlier, this time Beth didn't invent reasons not to go straight home. This times she was more than ready to face whatever—and whomever—awaited her. Back in the car, she tuned the radio to her favorite oldies station. The local weather forecast predicted an absolutely exquisite day of bright sunshine.

With the window rolled down so the whole world could hear, Beth sang along as Leslie Gore belted out "You Don't Own Me." "It's amazing," she thought to herself, "you never forget the words. It all just comes back to you." How she wished the same could be true of her dreams.

As soon as she got home, Beth put up a fresh pot of coffee, then went about her usual routine of unloading the dishwasher and taking out the kitchen trash. As she lifted the plastic bag from its bin, she spotted the small flower magnet she'd angrily discarded the night before. Feeling much more reasonable about things, she rinsed it off and placed it back on the refrigerator door, promising herself that would be the last time she'd let Joanna Cameron reduce her to such immature behavior. Nor would she let the reality of Jo living in the carriage house prevent her from enjoying a leisurely breakfast and the Sunday paper in her own backyard on such a beautiful day.

She was already on her second cup and halfway through the crossword puzzle when Joanna emerged from the carriage house with a mug in one hand and a magazine and donut in the other. Beth was grateful that Jo had chosen one of the Adirondack chairs a reasonable distance away from the patio table.

Each acknowledged the other politely. Beth tried but it was just not in her nature to leave it at that.

"Beautiful day, isn't it?"

Joanna looked around as if noticing for the first time. She ran her fingers through her hair.

"I'm not completely awake yet, but yeah, now that you mention it, it seems to be."

She took a gulp of coffee and the day gradually came into focus.

"Adam get off okay?"

Beth was surprised that Jo had even bothered to ask. She hoped not to sound as overjoyed about his leaving as she felt. If she were true to her feeling, she'd have leapt up onto the table and done a spontaneous jig, then propelled herself across the lawn in a series of double cartwheels. For a moment Beth amused herself trying to imagine the look on Joanna's face had she actually done that.

"Yes, he got off just fine."

Jo simply nodded back, hoping the less said the greater their chances for a reasonably manageable day. BJ, apparently less concerned with maintaining unspoken boundaries, pranced over to greet Joanna more warmly. After rewarding him with a few rigorous strokes, Jo settled into her magazine and Beth went back to her puzzle, relieved that this first part of the day had gone relatively smoothly.

As the morning sun climbed higher into the cloudless sky, both women kept to the safety of their reading. If neither admitted to repeated sideway glances and countless re-read lines, it would have appeared that they were managing to ignore each other's presence and were perfectly comfortable sharing each other's space. Of course the reality was something quite different and as the day wore on they each continued to work hard at avoiding the truth.

At one point Beth sat at the edge of the pool, her feet dangling in the water, while she completed an unfinished correspondence. Just a few yards away, Joanna sat cross-legged in the grass, going through a large duffle bag filled with art supplies. She made a list of what she still needed to purchase if she was really serious about being creatively productive this summer.

Except for Beth's insistence that Joanna take the keys to Ben's car—which Jo reluctantly accepted—and her polite invitation for Joanna to have a swim in the pool—which Jo respectfully declined—the two women maneuvered from one activity to the next with amazingly little exchange. Joanna tried not to appreciate how lovingly Beth tended to the painstaking task of pruning back the delicate leaves of the many potted plants arranged around the patio. Beth tried not to be impressed with Joanna's obvious skill as she worked on constructing a model's platform from a sheet of plywood and several 2x4 planks that Steve had offered from the back of his truck. Whatever notice each took of the other went intentionally unacknowledged and the morning unfolded in managed parcels and carefully dispensed smiles.

The afternoon hours passed in more of an artificial silence than an awkward one. Beth had taken the cordless phone outside, fully expecting the usual barrage of intrusive, inane calls throughout the day. But quite amazingly, none had come. Without a single outside interruption, after a while it began to feel eerily like she and Joanna were the last two people left on earth—corralled together in this totally unfamiliar and isolated place that was once her family's backyard. Suddenly, both women seemed to need the exact same thing at the exact same time—some immediate contact with the outside world, if for no reason other than to assure themselves that one was still out there. Joanna announced that she was taking a ride around the neighborhood to familiarize herself with the area. Almost simultaneously, Beth announced that she too would be going out to run some local errands and pick up some Chinese food for dinner. She offered to get something for Joanna but was careful not to imply they'd be eating together. Jo accepted her offer as carefully as it was extended and Beth went inside to get a take-out menu and a pen. Joanna circled her selections and handed it back to her with a $20 bill. Beth put both in her pocketbook and got into her car. As Joanna headed over to the Jeep, Beth called to her through her window.

"I shouldn't be more than an hour, in case you wanted to eat while the food is still reasonably hot."

"Fine. I'll be back around then myself."

Beth shrugged, implying that it didn't matter to her one way or the other.

Behind the wheel of the Jeep, Jo waited for Beth to pull out of the driveway first. Whichever direction Beth turned, Jo planned to go the opposite way.

When Beth returned home the answering machine was blinking. She pushed the button and listened to the messages while she sorted through the bag of food to separate her order from Joanna's. The first call was from her mother, to remind Beth about everything in the world she didn't care to be reminded of. Beth's mother had been a registered nurse for almost forty years. She'd spent most of her own life diligently looking after people rather than just loving them. Consequently, Beth inherited a heightened sense of responsibility to everyone around her. This summer was her first real attempt to shift her priorities. The second call was from Steve, saying that he hoped Adam that had 'shipped out' on schedule and that 'The Dangerous Beth Garrison' had herself a memorable first day. He also asked her to remind Jo that he'd be swinging by at 9:00 the next morning to pick her up. Beth was still in the process of wrestling with this new and uneasy mix of feelings towards him when she heard Jo pull into the driveway. Hoping to avoid having Jo set foot inside, she deliberately met her on the porch and handed her the bag of food along with her change. Beth relayed Steve's message flatly.

"Tell Steve that as of tomorrow the phone in the carriage house will be turned on. In the future, he can reach you directly. The number's on the receiver."

Beth started back inside.

Joanna seemed to want to engage her a bit longer.

"Nice neighborhood. Some of those Victorian houses are real knock outs."

Beth leaned against the railing.

"You do realize you're staying in one of the nicest?"

Joanna smiled at the boastful remark.

"Without a doubt! You should consider turning the place into a cozy bed and breakfast"

Beth groaned.

"Not unless I'm the one lying in bed being served the breakfast."

The image left Joanna at an uncommon loss for words. She returned a carefully guarded smile, then backed away.

Jo's changeable moods always took Beth by surprise. This time she was neither intrigued nor annoyed—just extremely hungry. She watched Joanna make her way back to the carriage house. Then she too went inside.

The sun had already begun its descent behind the distant line of trees. The two women sat alone at their separate tables, each staring out through their opened windows as the early evening sky turned a breathtaking shade of pink. A full day had passed and somehow they'd actually managed to spend most of it together, *sharing* each others space without *disturbing* it. It seemed their minimal contact and mutually polite distance was exactly what they each wanted. This was a good sign—a major accomplishment—and a most convenient lie. One they each desperately needed to believe.

Jo ate her dinner straight out of the cardboard containers and washed it down with a beer. Beth fixed herself an appetizing plate and made herself a soothing cup of tea. Ironically, they had both tuned to the same oldies radio station. Listening separately to 'Hey There Lonely Girl,' they sat in their respective isolation, reflecting on the many years that somehow brought them to this same night.

True to her nature, Joanna stubbornly refused to look at her fortune cookie. Instead she just tossed it aside. Beth eagerly broke hers open and smiled. 'Today is the first day of the rest of your life.' Nothing had ever sounded so pathetically trite—yet so profoundly true. She displayed it proudly on the refrigerator door using the flower magnet she'd rescued earlier that day. She wiped down the counter, rinsed off her plate and looked at the clock. It was only eight o'clock, but Beth decided to turn in anyway. She yawned as she climbed the steps, yawned as she washed up and yawned as she got undressed and crawled into bed. Though she hated to cut this first day of the rest of her life short, she was simply too exhausted to have it go on. She promised herself she'd just have to get an extra early start on the next one. There were two piano lessons to give, her usual volunteer work at the nursing home and her special time afterwards with her beloved Arthur.

Late night TV always made Jo hungry. She went to the fridge and dug into what was left of the take-out. With fried rice stuck in the spaces between her teeth and images of the impending summer stuck inside her head, Jo collapsed onto the sofa. For now she was just too tired to floss and too tired to formulate a plan of escape.

That night, when Joanna's resolve left its post unguarded, she dreamt of being captured—of being blindfolded with a red dishtowel—and of soft, commanding lips—insisting she give up—insisting she give in. 'The Gods' were either being kind or devilishly sly, but Jo awoke the next morning not remembering any of it.

The town's annual 4th of July concert had always drawn an enthusiastic crowd and had always been graced with an exceptionally beautiful summer's night. This year's performance was no exception. As Steve led Joanna through the seemingly endless maze of blankets and lawn chairs already staked out over the sprawling park grounds, she began to have grave misgivings about accepting his invitation. It didn't help matters that just as they'd settled onto their own small patch of grass, Steve spotted Nick and Beth off in the distance, trying to make their own way through the thickening crowd. Before Joanna could stop him, Steve flagged them over. Before Beth could likewise stop Nick, he waved back and changed course. As the two men worked to rearrange the limited space to now accommodate a second blanket, the women greeted each other awkwardly. Having managed to avoid each other for days since the Sunday in the backyard, neither was terribly thrilled with the coincidence of running into each other here. To complicate matters for Beth, she still hadn't resolved all her confusing new feelings towards Steve. Fortunately he had no idea of her discomfort. For his part, he was happy to see her, extending his usual hug and kiss. Force of habit served her well allowing her to return the gesture, if not the genuineness, of his warmth.

Not surprisingly, Nick immediately turned his attention to Joanna.

"So we meet again."

She resented being trapped by the circumstances.

"Yeah, so we do."

Conveniently thick-skinned, Nick winked at Steve.

"Look at us dirty dogs with the two most beautiful women in this town."

Joanna deliberately looked at her watch. Her expression left no doubt she was already counting the minutes left to this night.

For the next half hour, the awkward foursome exchanged food, drink and each other's woefully mismatched company. Nick persisted in pumping Joanna for the details of her life. In turn, she consistently stonewalled him. Steve tried to cajole the "Dangerous Beth Garrison'. Barely managing to be polite, Beth refused to be fully engaged. Right from the start, the whole arrangement had 'Big Mistake' written all over it and everyone but Nick seemed to notice. Instead, he refilled their glasses and proposed a toast.

"To the noble Professor Benjamin R. Garrison… who, unlike the rest of us commoners, is off on some distant shore spreading the light of the great 19th century English poets, and thus can't be with us tonight." Nick lifted his glass. "Here's to you ol' boy. Keep those literary fires burning!"

Steve chimed in lightheartedly.

"To Professor G… wherever you are!"

Joanna found herself wondering what Beth's husband was really like—what kind of man he was—what kind of a marriage they had. She found herself wondering other things too—more personal things, like what kind of intimacy they shared and what kind of sex they had. Jo studied Beth's face, watching for her reaction to Nick's toast.

Just behind a carefully guarded smile, Beth's mind wandered. The mention of Ben's name was actually the first time she'd thought of her husband in days. Beth wondered what Ben would think if he knew that. She didn't know what to make of it herself. The last time they spoke was the day after Adam left for camp. Ben had called, supposedly to find out how things went, but he kept her on the phone an uncomfortably long time. At the end of their conversation she suggested that he wait for her to call him next. Though upset, he reluctantly agreed. This time Beth wouldn't allow herself to feel guilty about what she needed. The truth was, from the moment she put Adam on the bus, she hadn't missed either of them at all. Instead, Beth had spent most of the time wandering from one hour to the next, relaxing the tightly wound coils of her designated responsibilities. She tended to everyday matters randomly, as her mood, rather than necessity, dictated. Except for honoring her weekly pre-arranged appointments, Beth basically slept when she wanted, ate what she wanted and submitted to any distraction her heart desired—with one exception. Under no circumstances would she permit Joanna Cameron to undermine her lightness of mood. It hadn't even been one full week since she was on her own. There would be plenty of time for more serious reckoning and certainly plenty of opportunities for the "Dangerous Beth Garrison' to wage mighty war inside her head.

To everyone's relief, the concert was about to begin. After a welcoming introduction by some local town officials, a fierce round of applause arose as the conductor took his place on the stage in front of the podium. He raised his baton and a respectful hush fell over the crowded lawn. Parents managed to quiet fidgeting children and teenage couples managed to live without another kiss. The evening's program included selected works of Beethoven, Chopin and Bach. While Joanna had on occasion toiled at the drawing board late into the night listening to a classical radio station, beyond those hours of solitude, she knew and cared little about any of this music. In contrast, Beth became entirely consumed from the very first note. The music seemed to hold an ethereal power that transcended any connection to her immediate surroundings. As the rhapsody unfolded and blended into the evening breeze,

Joanna was unable to distract herself from the intensity of Beth's pleasure—the way her head dropped and swayed slightly, the way her breathing deepened and the way her fingers spread, pressing against her thighs as if playing on a keyboard she had memorized in her heart. Steve noticed Joanna's intrigue. He leaned over and whispered.

"Have you heard her play yet?"

Self conscious, Jo barely shook her head. He nodded as if privileged to know some heavily guarded secret.

"When you do, you'll understand."

Joanna could have lived without the forewarning.

Beneath the vast star filled sky, enveloped in an endless sea of familiar faces, Beth suddenly felt cold, frightened and alone. She was in her heaviest sweatshirt but it hardly mattered. Her body shuddered with a sense of isolation. She ran her hands up and down her arms knowing only too well it was more than the cool night air. This was a much deeper and unbearable chill—the chill of inconsolable loss and sorrow. In a cruel gust of unfinished grief, it swept across the unguarded place, swiftly penetrating her heart and releasing a flood of images and memories of this very night. She recalled with painful detail how much Danny had loved these concerts, even as a little boy. How inspired he was by them as a young man, already on his way to becoming an accomplished violinist himself. Music had always served as a second language between mother and son. Their love of it only deepened their love for each other. Tonight, as the trees rustled against the heavens, that bond, and her sadness felt eternal. Beth made every attempt to conceal her distress, but Joanna noticed her discomfort. She instinctively reached for her denim jacket, leaned forward and draped it protectively across Beth's shoulders. Beth turned around, accepting Joanna's unexpected gesture.

"Thank you" she whispered as she adjusted the jacket slightly.

Disguising her stronger impulse to warm Beth in her arms, Jo carefully returned the woman's smile. Nick insinuated himself into the women's unspoken exchange.

"Here, take my sweater. It's much warmer."

Beth refused. Instead, she maneuvered her arms into the sleeves of Jo's jacket and pulled the sides in close to her body.

"This is perfect."

Joanna quietly gloated over his defeat, but Nick would not be disqualified quite so easily. When Beth began to rub her hands together, he immediately reached over and put them between his own.

"You're freezing."

Once again Beth pulled away, this time deliberately slipping her hands into the pockets of the jacket making them inaccessible.

Judging by Steve's disapproving glance, the two were very different breeds of men. It was obvious to Joanna he pretty much considered Nick a schmuck.

The pockets of the denim jacket were lined in soft flannel. Beth's hands warmed against it immediately. It was a warmth that quickly spread throughout her body, replacing the desolate chill of despair with a soothing reassurance. She closed her eyes and allowed the pleasure of the music to return, but with it came an unexpected sensation as well—the perverse thrill in having her hands inside such an intimate place as the pockets of a stranger. And not just *any* stranger, but the pockets of Joanna Cameron! Beth's heart pounded and her stomach plunged into a twisting free-fall. She felt deeper until her right hand came upon a set of keys buried at the bottom. For an instant she felt guilty about her discovery—like a child rifling through her parents drawer and finding something she wasn't supposed to. But under the cloak of cover, Beth's fingers grew bolder, grazing the nuances of each key like the intimate curves of a lover's body. The cold metal yielded to the warmth of her touch as she slowly and persistently traced their shape, wondering what doors they opened and into what private world they led. Beth was careful that her eyes gave nothing of her illicit trespassing away—careful not to disclose the wicked satisfaction of her unbecoming sin—all the while wanting more than anything to think that Joanna, just inches away, was watching her closely. That somehow she knew exactly what Beth was doing and was helpless to prevent her from exploring these vulnerable symbols of entry or keep her from discovering what they hid. Beth imagined an enraged Joanna finally lunging at her, forcing her down onto the blanket, wrestling her hands out of her pockets and pinning them up over her head. There, in front of hundreds of people, she would make Beth pay for invading her privacy with more than she dared to know. Beth felt her throat tighten as she let herself imagine the full weight and intention of Joanna's body against her own. As the concert culminated in a grand display of fireworks that exploded against the sky, Beth rose along with the crowd and joined in the unbridled applause. She was grateful for the timing of the finale that camouflaged the unnamed pounding in her chest.

After the last burst of color fell from the sky and the night air absorbed the final notes of orchestrated sound, the tired, satisfied crowd collected its miscellaneous belongings and gradually dispersed. As the unlikely foursome gathered up their things, Beth was relieved to see the two empty bottles of wine—desperate for *anything* that might explain her weak and trembling limbs. Her face still flushed, Beth attempted to remove the denim jacket, but Jo stopped her.

"Wear it home. You can give it back to me tomorrow."

Beth felt much too self-conscious to insist on returning it right then and there. Barely able to meet Jo's eyes, she agreed. As the crowd thinned it was hard to imagine a more awkward parting. After several stilted exchanges the two couples finally headed off in separate direction to their cars.

Though he'd suggested drinks, Beth had Nick drive her straight home. Confused and exhausted, she wanted nothing more than to be alone. As soon as he pulled up to the house she wasted no time getting out of the car, pausing only to extend a fleeting kiss on the cheek. He was still talking when Beth was already halfway up the driveway. With no hope of being invited in, Nick finally drove off. Beth felt oddly disoriented standing on the familiar porch of the place she called 'home'. When BJ greeted her on the other side of the door Beth felt relieved that there was a part of her life she could still recognize. Fortunately, there weren't any messages on the answering machine that she had to contend with. She heated some water for a cup of tea and debated what to do about Joanna's jacket. A part of her wanted to remove it immediately. Another part wanted to live in it for the rest of her life. All of it made Beth feel as close to being crazy as she ever wanted to come. As she waited for the water to boil, she could sense BJ staring at her curiously.

"Don't look at me like that" she said defensively and turned away.

Still shaky, Beth carried the steaming hot cup into the living room. She set it down on the coffee table and began to pace back and forth, hoping to walk off some of her anxiety. Eventually she collapsed onto the couch and allowed herself a few soothing sips. But the disarming heat of the liquid betrayed her and in an instant too quick to deny, Beth was reminded of the images of Joanna that still burned in her mind. Beth nervously wrestled out of the jacket and pushed it away from her. She leaned forward and covered her face in her hands.

"This is just insane! " Beth repeated at least a half dozen times, hoping the words alone had the power to change the truth. She tried to convince herself there was still no need to panic. After all, these were highly unusual times, creating highly unusual circumstances that led to highly unusual thoughts, none of which had absolutely anything to do with her otherwise most ordinary and usual life. Beth wanted all of this—whatever '*this*' was—to end in the same night. She would not allow it to carry over into the next day. She was less willing to admit that if she kept Joanna's jacket any longer she might never be able to give it up. Beth rehearsed the scene in her mind so she would be ready to act. She would wait for Jo to return home. When the woman passed the kitchen door, Beth would pop out onto the porch, lean over and hand her the jacket. All she'd have to say is 'thank you' and 'goodnight', then go back inside. It didn't have to be any more complicated than that. It was dark outside. She wouldn't even have to see Jo's eyes. That alone would keep her reasonably safe, or so Beth could only hope. In nervous anticipation, she folded and refolded the jacket several times before finally placing it on the dining room table. Emotionally exhausted, she shut all but one small lamp in the corner of the room, then returned to the sofa and stretched out across the length of it. Within the dim light her eyes drifted until they came to rest on the vase with Joanna's flowers. She recalled that first night and the unfamiliar, exquisite tension of being alone in Joanna's company. All at once Beth felt painfully alive and painfully foolish. She drew a long and conflicted breath, then closed her eyes. She was not hoping for sleep—only a dark and private space in which to hide from herself—and wait.

Steve talked Joanna into a quick cup of coffee from the local convenience store before dropping her off. Sitting in his parked truck, the steam rising from the containers in their hands, Jo saw an opportunity to get more information.

"So who's the annoying jackass Beth was with tonight?"

Steve took a gulp of his coffee and chuckled.

"Let's just say Nick's the kind of guy who gives us all a bad rep."

"What an asshole!"

"Actually, he was fairly low key tonight."

"You gotta' be kidding. There isn't a subtle bone in his body."

"Yeah, least of all the one between his legs."

Jo laughed.

"I can't believe he gets anywhere with that kind of crap."

"You'd be amazed how many women find that kind of crap flattering."

Joanna hated to think Beth could be one of them.

"What's someone like Beth see in him?"

"It's complicated. Their two families go back a lot of years. Besides, Beth sees the good in everyone."

"Even if there isn't any?"

"According to Beth there's something '*good*' in everyone... if you're willing to dig down deep enough."

"That's ridiculous. How naive can a grown woman be?"

Steve's response was slow and thoughtful.

"Ordinarily I would agree with you, but in Beth's case I'd say naiveté has its own wisdom and charm."

Steve's remark crept under Joanna's skin. It certainly had its own dangerous appeal as well. She recalled Beth's explanation of the elaborate candlelit table setting the night they'd had dinner. 'I'm celebrating my right to celebrate'. The memory of that evening made Jo uneasy. She moved to safer ground.

"She seemed really into the music tonight."

"And you seemed pretty hooked into watching her."

Joanna tried to ignore her paranoia. He took another gulp of coffee.

"When you hear her at the piano, you'll understand why. Playing it was supposed to be her life, but it didn't quite work out that way."

"If music was so important to her, why didn't she pursue it? What happened?"

Steve was surprised Jo couldn't figure it out for herself.

"First Ben happened. Then Danny happened and a few years later, Adam happened. Women like Beth never come first in their own minds. They're much more devoted to other people's lives than their own."

Steve read Joanna's body language. It was obvious that everything about Beth's choices made Jo uncomfortable.

"Let me guess, the caption under your High School yearbook photo didn't read: 'Captain of the Women's Martyr Club'—voted most likely to sacrifice her own needs."

Jo was not amused.

"You're right, it didn't. I watched my *own* mother do that. Frankly, it had very little appeal."

"So the 'selfless-female' gene skipped a generation."

She finished her coffee and deliberately crumpled the Styrofoam cup. Steve tried to fix things.

"Hey, I hope you don't think I was judging you."

"You wouldn't be the first, or the last."

"But I wasn't, honest. I'm not one of those people who think 'ambition' is a dirty word. The truth is, I admire anyone who's driven enough to go for their dreams. I hope *I* turn out to be one of them."

Jo couldn't resist teasing him.

"Just keep repeating: I'm the little flashlight pen that could! I'm the little flashlight pen that could."

Steve laughed at himself.

"So what exactly didn't your mother get to do?"

"She didn't get to live. She died of pancreatic cancer at the age of 43."

Steve's expression changed.

"Man, I'm sorry. That must have been really tough on you."

Jo shifted in her seat. She knew better than to think her discomfort was merely physical. She didn't want his pity, or for that matter, any more conversation.

"If you're done with your coffee, let's get outa' here."

She stared straight ahead as Steve pulled out of the parking lot and onto the road. The truth was he had nothing to be sorry about. Jo hadn't taken any real offense with anything he'd said. She was just extremely tired. She had more than enough to think about for one night and she always preferred to do her thinking alone. For most of the way, Steve honored her silence with his own. Just as he turned onto the Garrison's street, he slapped the steering wheel and cursed at himself.

"Damn! I just realized how hard tonight must have been for Beth. This Sunday will be three years since Danny died. These 4th of July concerts always meant so much to both of them."

Steve was distressed by his own failure.

"I shoulda' been more sensitive about it. Man, I feel awful."

"Don't beat yourself up about it. You're a good friend. None of us can be all things to all people all the time."

"None of us except Beth and your mother."

Suddenly, the significance of the upcoming anniversary loomed large in Joanna's mind. She needed some concrete plans to wedge between herself and the weight of this unwanted knowledge, something that would distract her from thinking about nothing else other than Beth's loss and how she was supposed to fit herself into such a difficult day.

"How 'bout posing for me tomorrow night after we knock off from work?"

Steve was still thinking about his friend, and still feeling guilty.

"Okay." He hesitated. "Before we get started can we order a pizza and ask Beth to join us?"

That was the last thing in the world Joanna wanted, but confidant that Beth herself would decline, she felt safe in agreeing.

Relieved, Steve drove the short distance that remained of their ride humming under his breath. Joanna marveled at how little it took to alleviate his distress. She couldn't decide if this made her like or loathe him even more.

The instant she heard Steve's truck pull up in front of the house Beth nervously sprang to her feet. Her heart pounded wildly as she listened for the sound of its door to slam and for him to pull away.

Like a teenager trying to sneak past her parents bedroom without confrontation, Joanna strode up the long driveway as quietly as she could. But just as she approached the kitchen door it swung open and Beth popped out onto the porch. She felt foolish—imagining one of those coo-coo clocks. She tried to sound casual about the planned interception.

"Thank you for letting me borrow your jacket."

Beth leaned over the railing and held it out, desperately wishing that her arm were longer to keep a safer distance between them. She'd deliberately kept the porch light off so Jo wouldn't see the likely red flush that once again spread across her face.

"I never seem to dress warmly enough for these things."

Joanna accepted her explanation easily enough.

"You didn't have to wait up just to give it back to me tonight. It's not like I sleep in it."

She tossed the jacket over her shoulder.

"Uncomfortable night all around."

Her vulnerability made it impossible for Beth not to take Joanna's remark personally.

"I'm sorry if my company ruined your date."

Joanna walked off making absolutely sure that her tone left no doubt.

"There wasn't anything to ruin. And, it wasn't a *date*. Goodnight."

Left languishing on the porch in the sloppy mess of her own emotional turmoil, Beth meekly returned Joanna's parting.

"Goodnight."

She retreated inside, secured the lock and leaned against the solid wood door.

"Thank God that's over with. Now maybe I can get on with my life as I once knew it."

Burying her face in her hands, Beth drew an exhausted but relieved breath. In the space between her fingers she caught a glimpse of BJ's all-knowing eyes staring up at her. She placed her hands on her hips and defiantly challenged his instincts.

"And what would *you* know about it anyway? You were a big clumsy puppy raised in a house that oozed convention. Convention I sacrificed dearly for! Convention that did not come easy, I might add! You could at least be grateful."

Beth needed to believe that with the return of Joanna's jacket she'd managed to put an end to all her less than conventional feelings. She prayed that tomorrow when she awoke she'd have her old life back. A life that had made, then broken, so many of its promises. But a life—and an ache—that at least Beth understood.

Ordinarily Joanna would have just tossed the jacket across the kitchen chair, but the soft haunting scent of Beth's perfume made that impossible. Replaying everything she'd learned about Beth in her mind, Jo reached into the breast pocket of the jacket for the cheap Cracker Jack toy she'd always kept there—a small plastic elephant with stiff, moveable legs. Tied to its u-shaped trunk was a string about 5 inches long with a small metal ball attached to the other end. Jo leaned forward and placed the thing on the coffee table, letting the ball hang over the side. The weight of it gradually pulled the elephant by its wobbly legs up to the table's edge where, according to some law of pulleys and levers once explained to her by her father, it stopped but didn't plunge over. Jo repeated its silly trick again and again. Each time the weight of the ball pulled the elephant to the edge and each time it stopped just shy of actually going over. It was the story of her life—the story of her greatest fear for as long as she could remember. It represented her fierce resistance to abandoning her precious balance and forsaking emotional safety. For all her outwardly brassy risk taking, for all her sexual encounters, Jo could never allow herself the only risk that really mattered. The one that meant she would have to let go completely and blindly follow her heart over the edge. For a long time Joanna stared bitterly at the toy for what *it*—and *she*—could never do.

"Coward!" she hissed under her breath as she angrily flicked the small defenseless thing off the table. She watched callously as it flew across the room, hit the wall and fell to the floor just beneath the old window frame with the heart and initials carved into its ledge. Joanna got up and looked at the small elephant lying there on its side. Like her, invisibly wounded and hopelessly tangled in its string. She would let it lie there—alone and hurting—all through the night. Perhaps it would learn a lesson from the carving just above it about what it meant to love that deeply—that indelibly—through time.

The next day after work, Steve went home to shower and change. Then true to his word, returned at six with a 6-pack and large pizza. He stopped in to ask Beth to join them for dinner but just as Jo had hoped, Beth declined claiming to have a prior commitment. In a quickly fabricated excuse she said she'd promised one of her more advanced piano students some extra time in preparation for an upcoming audition. When he asked if his company might be of some comfort to her on Sunday, Beth said she preferred being alone. Steve assured her that if she changed her mind, he'd drop everything and come over. Despite all her unresolved feeling Beth hugged him appreciatively, then suggested he not keep Joanna waiting. As he crossed the yard feeling better for at least trying, it never occurred to him that Beth might have been lying.

Unlike Steve, Jo pulled two slices from the box and wondered about the validity of Beth's excuse. Looking for anything that might distract her thoughts, Jo got up and turned on the radio. Steve took a swig of beer.

"You really like that oldies station. You listen to it all the time while we're working."

Already on edge, Joanna became defensive.

"You should have said something if it bothered you."

"It doesn't. It amuses me."

Jo never cared much for being the source of a smirk on anyone's face, even someone she cared for as much as Steve. Her tone told him so.

"And why is that?"

"'Cause you always seem so restless and anxious to lunge *ahead* of wherever you are. It's an amusing contradiction that you'd like music from the *past*." He finished his third slice and smiled. "You're turning out to be quite a complicated study."

"Just so you know… I don't appreciate being *studied*."

Steve admitted the truth.

"Trust me, it's getting harder and harder to do objectively… if you know what I mean."

Jo purposely avoided his eyes. Of course she knew what he meant. She just didn't want to deal with it. At least, not now. At least, not yet. She slapped the last slice of pizza onto his plate, tossed the empty box aside and began clearing the table even as he ate. Steve got the hint and shoved the last bite into his mouth. With the table cleared, Joanna spread out her art supplies making no apology for rushing him. Steve thought better than to force a response to his thinly veiled confession. Instead, he rinsed off his dish and dried his hands on his jeans.

"I guess I'm ready when you are."

Joanna was more than eager to move on. Or, as Steve had put it, 'lunge ahead'.

She picked up a chair and set it down on the modeling platform positioned against the wall in the space between the kitchen and living room areas. When she turned around, Steve was standing motionless—miserably uncomfortable with his choices.

"Is there a problem?"

However foolish he felt admitting it, Steve wasn't sure if she expected him to pose with his clothes *on* or *off*. Except for his earlier bragging to Adam about the prospect of 'baring all', it was never actually discussed. He dug his hands awkwardly into his pockets.

"Am I supposed to… you know… take all my clothes off?"

Joanna was momentarily surprised—then charmed—by the sheer innocence of his question. It suddenly struck her that Steve was really an old fashioned kind of guy. If there was even the slightest chance there could be something more between them, he preferred to wait and reveal himself to her in a more meaningful and intimate context. Aware that he was slowly developing real feelings for her, Jo knew this would mean trouble down the road—trouble she could certainly live without. But for the moment, she found his shy, inhibition undeniably endearing.

"Whatever you're comfortable with."

Steve sheepishly acknowledged her consideration.

"I'll keep my pants on." He poked fun at his own reluctance. "I'll take off my shoes and socks though. How's that for boldness?"

She encouraged him with a little smile. Whatever it took to finally get started. Steve played with the waistband of his jeans, took a nervous breath, then stepped up onto the platform. He really did have a magnificent body. If he ever wanted to make some *real* money, she could get him signed with one of the biggest modeling agencies in New York with just one call. He began to fidget under her scrutiny.

"Okay, what do I do?"

"It's tragically simple. Sit your ass down, find a comfortable position and don't move. You're an inanimate object until I say you're not."

"Does that mean no conversation?"

Jo smiled slyly. She'd finally found a way to stifle any more of his unwanted observations—at least for the night.

"That's exactly what it means. Don't even breathe anything that requires a response."

"I thought these sessions were gonna' be enjoyable."

"They will be… for *me*."

Steve spun the chair around, straddled the seat and folded his arms across its back.

"How's this?"

"Great… just hold that pose."

With the rules in place, Joanna sat down at the kitchen table and opened the large sketchpad to its first page. Though she'd never allow it to show, the crisp blank surface intimidated her even more than she expected it would. The truth was, 'enjoyable' was not what this night would be for either of them. She swallowed over the fear lodged in her throat and picked up a stick of the charcoal. It had been such a long time. Amazingly, the dry chalky texture still felt familiar in her hand. Behind her mask of steady, self-assurance Jo worried if it would come back to her. She had no idea whether or not the earlier gifts she'd long ago abandoned would now—in retaliation—turn their back on her as well. It would take all the courage she had to find out. She began slowly at first—unsure of the lines—unsure of herself. But from the instant Joanna touched charcoal to paper she became lost to everything except the newly awakened demands of her expression, and soon the trembling of her hand gave way to a renewed trembling deep inside her dormant soul. The next several hours slipped by unnoticed. By the time she thought to call it a night, she'd completed over a dozen studies. She turned off the radio and spread the pages out across the floor so she and Steve could view all the sketches at once. Separately and together they were a powerful and intense body of work, so much so that neither Steve nor Jo spoke a word. He was in awe of her talent. It was greater than anything he'd expected. In a way she had never known before, Joanna felt grateful for her gift and close to tears. Steve sensed that she needed to be alone with the intensely personal nature of her feelings. He dressed quickly and quietly so as not to disturb the solemn meaning of the night for her.

"Ars long—vita brevis. Art lasts—life is brief," he whispered into her ear.

She appreciated his sensitive words and thoughtful departure. For the first time, she even kissed him on the cheek. Jo stood in the doorway watching as Steve made his way across the yard and climbed into his truck. Beth's car was in the driveway and all the lights in the house were out. In the course of her feverish sketching, Jo never heard her leave or return. She closed the door and walked back over to the drawings that lay scattered at her feet. Now alone, Joanna bent down for a closer, more intimate look. It was all still there. It was all still part of her. Her eyes caressed every page. This time when they filled with tears Jo did not try to hold them back. She felt certain that tonight 'The Gods' had moved her a little closer to 'home'. What remained hauntingly unclear was whether she'd been carried another step *forward* or another step *back.*

Fixed on images of Joanna and Steve alone together in her carriage house, Beth lay restless and miserable in her darkened bedroom that felt more and more like a cage as the night wore tediously on. She'd been listening intently for hours, waiting for the sounds that assured her of Steve's leaving—the squeaky screen, the slam of his truck door, the start of the ignition and finally, finally, the gravel crunching under its wheels as the truck pulled out of her driveway. Relieved that Joanna hadn't invited him to spend the night, Beth turned onto her side. By now every inch of her body was wracked with tension. She stared vacantly at the soothing sway of the bedroom curtains, praying for sleep and your average, garden-variety nightmare from which she could simply awaken and escape.

Chapter 8

To a sympathetic heart, the magnificently clear day might have seemed cruel in its splendor—callous to the anniversary of Beth's devastating loss. 'Depraved Indifference' the law would surely have called it. But the laws of men do not apply to the often arrogant laws of nature, particularly the one that demands that life go on, insisting the sun shine, flowers bloom and birds sing, even in the face of human suffering. Gradually Beth was learning to forgive the morning sun and each new day it brought. She'd given up trying to reconcile the momentum of the world around her with the deathlike stagnation inside her heart. It had become virtually impossible to hold life back so she simply stepped aside and watched it like a passing parade. Though an occasional wave and a fake smile was enough to fool the crowd, it was never enough to fool herself.

Since Danny's death Beth had visited her son's grave on more than one occasion. The gates of the cemetery always startled her. Each time she felt as if she'd taken a horribly wrong turn somewhere and wound up there by mistake. How she wished that something as simple as a different road would lead her to a different reality. On this day Beth came to those gates recalling very little of how she got there. The actual details of her waking, her dressing and the ride itself eluded her. Before leaving the house she'd spoken with Ben and assured him that she was 'okay'. The word was general enough for her to be reasonably certain it was true. She knew he would call and though he intended his voice to be a loving reminder of his devotion on this most difficult and tragic day, it left Beth feeling even sadder for all that was lost along the way. She could no longer distinguish between the intangible losses and the tangible ones. What's more, the difference no longer mattered. As she forced herself to face one, she knew she would have to face them all. It was as if in her silence Ben had read her mind. Beth was not surprised when he tried again to convince her to join him in Europe. He in turn was not surprised when she again refused. Mutually accepting they spoke a bit longer, extending gentle and promising words, each reassuring the other that everything would be all right. Neither would admit that they had no idea what that meant. Ben was especially glad to hear that Adam had called home the night before. Beth relayed how happy she was for Adam, grateful for the resilience of his youth that somehow allowed him to absorb the gravity of his loss into the unbridled anticipation of his upcoming water skiing lesson scheduled for early the next day. Ben agreed that was indeed a blessing. With not much left to say, he offered that he'd be spending some time with his parents in the country and that they sent along their love. After hesitating, Ben asked how she was intending to pass this most difficult of days. Beth told him of her plans to visit the cemetery, then look in on Arthur at the nursing home and spend the remainder of the day quietly at home. If he had hoped for other choices, he didn't say so. Perhaps for that same reason, she accepted his need to call her again later that night. The third anniversary of their son's death was not a day for protests. It was a day to somehow just survive.

Beth proceeded past the gates and drove slowly along the winding pavement that would take her to Danny's grave. Like all the other times, she took curious note of the exacting rows of headstone that surrounded her. They seemed intent on providing a peaceful order to the otherwise chaotic nature of grief—those horribly unpredictable moments when the heart suddenly plunges and ricochets from one memory to the next, leaving the bereaved lost in a labyrinth of pain and sorrow. At least here, in a cemetery, ones descent into that dreaded abyss was thoughtfully laid out and marked by block numbers. One might visit their darkest hour and still find their way out.

The grounds seemed particularly tranquil this morning. Beth was relieved that there were no funerals going on in the immediate vicinity that would subject her to the vividly grim details of fresh death, the sight of a polished casket, the smell of an open grave with its newly turned earth, the sobs of yet another family of mourners joined forever in their loss. With time, her own suffering had become more composed and well mannered. She did not need to be stricken with such cruel reminders. Especially not today. Grateful for her privacy, Beth pulled over and turned off the ignition. She found the stillness comforting. For the moment her own eyes remained dry as she stared out across this landscape quenched by rains and an eternal stream of tears. Summer flowers dressed the earth above buried caskets; bright sunshine drenched the surfaces of etched stone. Everywhere Beth looked the forces of life seemed to penetrate the impossible boundaries of death. Hopelessly caught between trying to collect her every thought and simply trying to let them all go, Beth gathered up the things she'd brought and cradled them in her arms like she once cradled her child. She eventually coaxed herself out from the security of the car and approached her son's grave with the same soft footsteps she so often approached his crib, taking great care not to disturb the peaceful quiet of his morning nap. She recalled gently wiping the beads of perspiration from his dampened brow while he slept. With the same tenderness, Beth knelt beside the stone that bore her son's epitaph and wiped its surface, moist with the early morning dew. Still stunned and confused by what she saw, Beth let her fingers trace over the familiar letters of his name, the name she'd helped him write for the very first time, the name she'd seen in a million places—scribbled across a crayon drawing and signed on the bottom of Mother's Day cards—written on the top of homework assignments and book reports—printed on scholastic awards—featured in musical programs. The last time, it was gracefully calligraphed on his high school diploma. What was it doing chiseled into a headstone? Now, three years after his death, the reality still felt incomprehensible. As she took the bouquet of wild flowers collected from the backyard and placed it on Danny's grave, Beth accepted that a part of her would live on in a state of permanent disbelief. She stood there, barely breathing, comprehending nothing at all. Tears collected and blurred the photographs she clutched in her hand. She took a crumpled tissue from her pocket and wiped her eyes in order to see the images of her son more clearly. She kissed and caressed each and every one, speaking softly to the happy infant, the gifted child, the thriving adolescent and the sensitive young man. She felt grateful to have nurtured and known them all. For everything the two of them had shared, the edges of her grief somehow felt smoother—her pain, a little friendlier. Beth had never really examined her belief in an afterlife. She was always much too busy with what came after the shopping, the cleaning and the laundry to ever ponder what came after death. But since Danny died it was something she thought about constantly, desperate to believe that his death was not an end—that somehow, beyond explanation or proof, the connection to those we have loved still continues. Staring down at his grave, Beth recalled Danny's first day of kindergarten. He stood there on the brink of tears as she struggled to convey the concept of separation to a frightened 5 year old. He listened intently as his mother explained that although she would not be there in the same room with him, whenever he needed her all he had to do was look inside his heart and she would always be there. How many times since his death had she reached deep inside her own heart for him? Beth sat down on the grassy patch beside his grave, her eyes and heart lingering on the date of his birth. It felt like only yesterday that she sat on the lawn of their backyard, joyously watching him take his first steps towards her, then tumbling into her outstretched arms. When she closed her eyes she could still feel the weight of his small frame against her, a frame she'd hugged for a million silly and significant reasons as it matured and grew into manhood. Beth took the small pocket tape recorder from her bag and held it against her breast. In time, she pressed the 'play' button, closed her eyes and waited. Against the stillness of the air, she could hear the faint clicking of the cellophane tape advancing around the tiny mechanical spools. She knew that in a moment she would hear Danny's voice playfully announcing their duet—she on the piano, he accompanying her on his violin. By now Beth had memorized every nuance of background noise as intensely as she had their arrangement and when the music finally began, anticipation gave way to joy. Beth remembered that afternoon well. It was just a few days after he'd received his acceptance letter from Julliard. Adam was at a friend's for the weekend and Ben was away at a conference. She remembered the heavy spring showers that kept them both indoors, the scent of freshly painted shutters that drifted in from the open windows and the plate of chocolate chip cookies they giddily devoured between them. She listened and smiled as the unedited tape played on through it all—capturing the claps of thunder and the clinking of the front porch chimes against the background of every cherished note and word of their idyllic afternoon. They'd always been good together. As musicians. As mother and son. As close friends. How suddenly this frivolous souvenir would become a priceless treasure. How unexpectedly those few hours would come to preserve a lifetime. The tape came to its same abrupt end and once again Beth was left with only silence. Clutching her proof, she turned her face up to the sky and begged for answers. It offered no apology or regret for her loss. Her small, broken heart seemed insignificant compared to the largeness of its own infinite course. Whether she accepted the wisdom of the universe or cursed it bitterly was of little consequence to the powerful forces that ruled it. The choice was hers to make. Reluctantly, Beth collected her things and rose to her feet, trembling before the unknown. This was always where Ben, when he insisted on accompanying her, would predictably squeeze his wife's hand or pull her close—when he would pretend to have 'Answers' and she would pretend to believe them. For much too long this counterfeit exchange brought Beth only counterfeit relief. She was glad to be there alone this time—glad not to have to pose for his benefit or acknowledge his well-meaning advice about how best to move on. This time she looked up at the sky, leaning only on her own shaken faith. Beth knew she would have to make peace with the universe strictly on her own terms and strictly in her own time. A voice—small and faint—from somewhere deep inside promised it would guide her. As best as she could tell, it was the same voice that told her to stay home this summer. The one that encouraged her to go 'all out' with the table setting for her dinner with Joanna. The memory of that night brought a sudden wave of panic, but a soft, gentle breeze raised up to calm her and when the air grew still she could hear the voice again, telling her she must trust her fears as well. Beth took a moment to ready herself. She touched her fingers to her lips, then softly to Danny's grave. In the course of her reckoning, the dew and her tears had dried. The new day sun had blessed flesh and stone, mother and child. Both seemed at peace.

Leaving the cemetery always felt as impossible as arriving there. Once again Beth passed slowly through the conspicuous gates. This time as she gripped the steering wheel to steady herself, it struck her that this was the same car in which she drove Danny to his first day of school. She looked back in the rearview mirror. Only this time instead of graves she saw the bright red door of his kindergarten classroom. Her son was smiling his brave little boy smile as he waved goodbye to his mother.

"Don't worry mommy. You can go now," he assured her. "We'll just reach into our hearts and we'll both be fine."

Beth swallowed hard over the swell of emotion now trapped in her throat but somehow she had found the courage to return her little boy's smile.

The memory stayed with her all the way to the first intersection. When the light turned green Beth made a left and drove on. Hillcrest Manor Nursing Home was just a few miles down the road.

By all accounts, Arthur Prescott should have been dead. All the respected research studies concluded that once admitted to a nursing home facility, residents usually died within two to three years. The black humor among the Hillcrest staff was that the only way out of the place was on a gurney headed either for the E.R. or the morgue. But apparently Arthur was not about statistics. Nor was he about dying. Not only did he celebrate his ninetieth birthday five years after he'd taken up residence at the manor, but despite his set backs and permanent frailties, in less than six weeks he'd be turning one hundred. Arthur had become Hillcrest's longest and oldest resident, earning him celebrity status with everyone from the administrative office on down to the custodial staff. He held that title until a stroke at ninety-eight left him in a coma for several weeks. No one ever expected him to survive, so when he opened his eyes and bared his charming, toothless grin, Arthur Prescott instantly went from 'celebrity' to 'living legend'. But it was not just his longevity that earned him his beloved reputation. It was his sweet and generous nature. Although Arthur had never married and was himself childless, he was soon adopted by the entire staff and became everyone's great, great grandpa. Those who served his most personal needs on a daily basis did so much more out of devotion than duty.

Exactly just how Arthur Prescott came to reside at Hillcrest Manor had, unto itself, become a piece of folklore as well. On the morning of his eighty-fifth birthday, Arthur just appeared in the lobby of the nursing home. He had been helped out of a private cab and escorted inside by the driver who placed an old leather suitcase at his side, shook the old man's hand, wished him luck and drove off. In a soft-spoken, unassuming voice the well-dressed gentleman requested to meet with the director of administration. When asked if he had an appointment, he adjusted his bowtie and explained that at his age the only appointment he had was with 'Destiny'. Arthur said he was there simply because 'it was time'. The house had gotten too big, the pantry too high to reach and the mail too heavy to fetch. The receptionist was charmed by his response and he was immediately shown to the director's office. Arthur sat down, politely removed his hat and requested a cup of tea with lemon and milk. The director, a kindhearted woman with a generous smile, sat patiently by while Arthur sipped. He liked her tea. He liked the striped wallpaper in the lobby, the flowers in their garden and her lovely cameo broach. It reminded him of one his mother used to wear. Satisfied and convinced that he would be content and well cared for there, Arthur explained that except for some additional clothes and some basic toiletries to meet his personal needs, everything dear and precious to him that he wished to retain was packed in the suitcase beside him. In exchange for room and board for the rest of his days, Arthur proposed that the nursing home take everything else he owned. 'Everything else' turned out to be an estate worth well over three million dollars. Since Arthur claimed to have no other heirs and wasn't expected to live past the 2.3 years of 'normal residency', it was an offer the small, non-profit facility couldn't—and didn't—refuse. Once they looked into his affairs and established that he in fact had no living relatives to contest his unusual proposal, the attorney quickly drew up the necessary papers and Arthur was moved into a private, graciously appointed room. Much to everyone's surprise, including his own, fifteen years, two directors and five dieticians later, Arthur was still there—still taking his meals—still sipping their tea—and still enjoying the beautiful, remodeled dining room that bore a plaque with his name. It was where they would hold his hundredth birthday celebration in just a few weeks.

It was mid-morning when Beth pushed through the front doors of the Hillcrest Manor lobby. The heavy aftermath of two hundred breakfast trays still hung in the air. It wasn't a particularly pleasant odor, but it was undoubtedly the lesser of many evils generally associated with institutionalized living. After two and a half years of regular visits to the nursing home, Beth had grown accustomed to the inherent sights, sound and smells of the environment. But on this particular morning, an already queasy stomach made it harder for her to take. A large calendar hung on the lobby wall, prominently displaying the exact day, month and year in huge block letters. Seared into Beth's scorched heart, the day itself felt no less emblazoned. From the other end of the long corridor a familiar voice broke through her intense desire to simply leave. Perhaps visiting today was not such a good idea after all. Though Beth had told a select few people—Mildred Macon included—about the death of her son, she was never more specific about it than that. The woman had no idea about the significance of this particular day and Beth chose to keep it that way.

"Hey there sugar!"

Mildred's voice stretched all the way down the hall as if clearing a path for her oncoming smile. The warmth of her greeting hit its mark and Beth felt obliged to put aside her pain. It was not her style to burden anyone else.

"Morning Millie."

Beth rallied as they continued to walk toward each other. She certainly could use one of Millie's mighty hugs. Beth was holding a bouquet of flowers for the nursing station and Millie was pushing the notorious Doris Henly, Hillcrest's most ornery resident in her wheelchair, but as soon as the two women were in arms reach of one another, no obstacle could keep them apart. Millie was a short, stocky black woman in her late fifties, with enormous breasts. The only thing larger was the size of her heart. When she took you around, you knew you were pressed against the fullness of both. Beth melted into her nurturing fold and closed her eyes to hold back her tears. She was glad that Millie didn't feel her desperation, only her genuine and deepest affection. The resident in Millie's charge was clearly unmoved by the warmth of their greeting. Beth refused to let the woman's unpleasant reputation stop her from being cordial.

"Good morning Mrs. Henly. How are you today?"

"Same as yesterday and the same as the day before."

"Yes, I can see that."

Millie was quick to catch Beth's pun. Mrs. Henly stomped on the footrests of her wheelchair as if kicking the sides of a horse.

"Get a move on Mildred! I haven't got all day."

Mildred remained ever patient.

"I'm taking Mrs. Henly to the beauty shop to have her nails done."

As far as Beth was concerned 'claws' would have been the more fitting term, but the kind-hearted Millie's unflappable disposition extended way beyond even Beth's comprehension. It was obvious that even after twenty-five years of service at Hillcrest, Millie still loved her job as much as she loved life itself. Without exception, she knew the history of every resident behind every bedrail, every walker and every cane.

Beth offered Mrs. Henly a compliment.

"Your nails always look lovely."

Mrs. Henly returned Beth's kindness with an insult.

"It wouldn't hurt you to do something with those raggedy hands of yours, missy."

Millie scolded the woman as though she was talking to a child who should have known better. Unable to comprehend Mrs. Henly's sour disposition, she turned to Beth and shrugged.

"So baby, you here to entertain us with that fine piano playin' of yours?"

"No, not today. I just stopped by to visit with Arthur for a little while."

"Chances are you'll find him sleepin' like a baby. If he's up at all, he'll be plenty groggy. Poor Mr. Arthur went and caught himself a nasty cold overnight. We gave him a dose of decongestant this morning before it settled in his chest. With his hundredth birthday comin' up, we can't have the guest of honor comin' down with a case of pneumonia."

Mrs. Henly saw no reason for all the fuss and concern.

"Birthdays!" she huffed. "He should have had the good sense to drop dead before he ever came here. We *all* should have."

Millie tapped the miserable woman on her shoulder.

"I'm sorry you feel that way."

She turned back to Beth.

"'Course you'll be gettin' a special invitation. You know how much Arthur loves you. We all do."

Six months after she'd lost her son, Beth began volunteering at Hillcrest and soon became 'family'. Especially this morning she was grateful for the reminder.

"I wouldn't miss it for anything in the world."

Mrs. Henly grew more irritable. She waved her finger in Millie's face.

"Take me to my appointment right this minute you big, black ninny or I'll have you fired!"

Beth cringed at the woman's deep-seated prejudice. She searched Millie's eyes apologetically, hoping to somehow make up for the indignation she had to endure. Millie seemed to take the whole thing in stride, pretending to be shaken by the ridiculous threat.

"You heard the boss-lady. Gotta' go or I'll lose my job."

She rolled her eyes from behind the wheelchair, releasing the brake with her foot. How Millie managed to resist ramming Mrs. Henly straight into the wall was an absolute mystery to Beth. It certainly qualified her for sainthood. Millie offered a warning with her parting kiss.

"Careful roundin' that corner baby. Miguel's been waltzin' with that fancy buffin' machine of his."

Beth thanked her and proceeded down the corridor. As usual, almost every television set in almost every room was on. Also as usual, practically no one was actually watching them. Most of the residents were either napping or simply staring into space. The few that were awake and aware waved to her and invited her in for a visit. Everyone loved Beth and everyone always wanted a piece of her. It was no different than the rest of her life. But this was not the day Beth could easily afford to give those pieces away. She simply smiled, waved back and continued on.

As Millie had predicted, Beth found Arthur sound asleep, his head propped up against two pillows. She took great care to move about quietly—changing the water in his pitcher, moving the box of tissues closer and arranging the things on his night stand just the way she knew he liked it. When she was finished tidying up, she pulled the chair up beside his bed so she could sit closer to her beloved friend. For a while Beth just watched him, sentimentally recalling just how it was that they became so very attached. Except for his labored breathing and an occasional twitch, Arthur seemed to be resting comfortably. She smiled to see the small, portable tape recorder she'd given him tucked securely under one hand; the cord of the headphone wound loosely around his rail-thin arm and up under the creases of his white, stubbly chin. One of the tiny foam plugs had fallen out of Arthur's ear and was playing against his cheek on the pillow. Beth leaned closer to hear what he was listening to. Not surprisingly it was his most treasured tape—the one on which she performed all his favorite classical pieces—the same one she had played over and over for him as he lay for weeks in a coma and that later he claimed to have recognized in his sleep and called him back to her side. Beth sat back in the chair, deeply gratified that her playing brought Arthur so much comfort and joy. The doubled pillows appeared to alleviate the old man's congestion but his face was even paler than usual and almost disappeared against the institutional, white cotton pillowcase. She was tempted to stroke Arthur's hollowed cheek but didn't want to risk waking him. Instead, she got up and walked over to the window. The view looked out onto the garden. Of the many residents seated about, few seemed aware of the beauty of their surroundings. Beth couldn't help but wonder why some are cursed to outlive their appreciation of life while others must die before they get to fully explore it. For the lucky ones in between, it was indeed a most exquisite day to be alive.

Arthur began to make small, whimpering sounds. Perhaps the noises coming from the hall had seeped into his dream and troubled him. Beth quickly closed his partially opened door. Arthur seemed to sense the protectiveness of her movement. His failing vision made it all but impossible to see anything more that vague shapes and shadows. All the same, Arthur knew it was she who was there. Ever since he had miraculously awakened from his come, it was more the 'essence' of people that he recognized. Beth's in particular had become deeply familiar. His voice filled with relief.

"Mama, it's you, isn't it?"

She answered in a soft, loving tone.

"Yes sweetheart, it's me."

Never was Beth more struck with the bittersweet irony of Arthur's post coma delusion than she was on this particular day when she ached so desperately to be able to hold her *own* son's hand. Beth recalled that morning when Arthur unexpectedly regained consciousness. She was sitting at his bedside in the hospital I.C.U., just as she had been through the endless weeks he lay unchanged and motionless. She'd been stroking his arm and replaying her tape, needing to believe she was reaching him in his deep and distant sleep. She remembered how the lifeless muscles of Arthur's face seemed, as if by memory, to gradually form a smile. How his frail, once listless fingers began to tremble then slowly, instinctively fold around hers. She was just a blur against his untreated cataracts and the glare of sunlight that flooded the room but Arthur was completely sure of who she was.

"Oh mama, mama, you've come back to me" he'd whispered in a small, but joyful voice.

Beth had been extremely shaken by his first words. It seemed a cruel twist of fate to have watched her strong and healthy 18-year-old slip away, never to call out for her again—only to have this 98-year-old dying man come back to life, suddenly believing her to be his long deceased and beloved mother. In the days that followed Beth tried repeatedly to correct Arthur's perception, but even her most delicate attempts only upset him more. From the depth of his fragile state, he continued to insist on her identity. After awhile it seemed pointless to distress him further. There were so many times after Danny died she wished someone could have offered her a safe, delusional space in which to reunite. Eventually Beth relented and came to accept the role that Arthur's abandoned child-heart had assigned her. Painfully aware that he had lost his mother when he was only 12, Beth embraced his boyhood longing with a full and open heart, often assuring him that she would never leave him again. However self-serving, his delusion provided Beth with a much needed sense of purpose knowing that of all his care-givers, it was only *she* who could offer him such a powerful and deep sense of comfort. Today was no exception. She leaned over and kissed Arthur gently on the forehead. Through the parched lips of an old man came the anxious words of a worried little boy.

"I can't be sick for my birthday, Mama. Say you'll stay with me. I'll get better if you're here."

Beth reached for Arthur's hand.

"Of course I'll stay. Now try and get some more rest."

She had wanted so very much to tell him that she used the beautiful antique vase he'd given her. She knew how much it would please him. But the story of Joanna's flowers would have to wait. Once Arthur had drifted off to sleep, Beth slowly withdrew her hand and sat back in the chair. A quiet tear rolled down her cheek. It was a tear that belonged to everyone who wasn't prepared to say goodbye.

Arthur's sense of her was uncanny. Nearly blind and dulled by the dose of decongestants, he felt her sorrow even in his sleep. Without opening his eyes, he turned his head towards her.

"What is it Mama? You seem so sad today."

Beth had no intention of burdening him with the truth. Nor did she have the strength to lie. She tried to reassure him.

"Oh Arthur, my sweet precious Arthur. You needn't worry."

"But I do worry, Mama. I do. You never knew it but I watched you weep so very hard for so very long." Arthur's eyes filled with the tears of his mother's pain. "They said it was the pneumonia, but *we* know better, don't we Mama? *We* know you died of a broken heart..."

Beth could not respond. It was deeply unsettling to learn that his mother's suffering felt so much like her own. Beth struggled to maintain her composure. She rose to her feet and nervously began smoothing out the corners of his blanket. For the moment, it was all she could do to make things 'better' for the both of them. Somehow Beth managed to put aside her own discomfort to soothe his.

"I'm alright now sweetheart. You can see for yourself. I'm alright."

As always, Arthur found immediate relief in her voice. He closed his eyes, nodded and smiled.

"May I hear the music again, Mama?"

Beth was grateful to be able to grant him such a simple and comforting request.

"Of course, honey. I'll just rewind the tape."

She leaned over the frail old man and gently repositioned the tiny foam plugs against his ears. Arthur reached for his mother's long lost hand and pressed it urgently against his cheek.

"All these years… all these years… oh how much I missed your playing, Mama. Oh, how much I missed you…"

Whatever unshed tears still remained quickly collected in Beth's eyes. In that moment, who she really was—or was not—no longer mattered. The unbroken bond—the unbearable loss—she understood it all, as only a mother separated from her child could.

Beth pulled into her driveway, thoroughly exhausted. She turned off the motor and remained behind the wheel, unable to move. She looked at her watch. It was only 4:30. The realization that there were still so many hours left to this day overwhelmed her. Her impulse was to lay down across the front seat and sleep, honestly not caring if she woke the next hour, the next day or the next year. With every ounce of strength she could muster, Beth gathered up her things, dragged herself out of the car and onto the porch. As she struggled to find her house keys at the bottom of her bag, she noticed a folded sheet of paper torn from a sketchpad and left in the space between the screen and the door. She reached down and picked it up. Inside, Beth dropped everything else on the kitchen counter and immediately unfolded the mysterious page. It was a pastel study of one particular potted geranium she recalled tending to the day she and Joanna cautiously spent together in the backyard. There was a penciled inscription below.

"Your devotion is evident in your touch. I'm sure your son felt very loved.

I'm sorry for your loss on this most difficult day. Jo."

Beth was stunned by the beautiful rendering and the woman's thoughtful, sensitive words. She had no idea that Joanna was even aware of the significance of this day, let alone cared enough to do something this special. Though deeply touched, Beth was unprepared to respond. She certainly never expected to have to add Joanna Cameron to the mix of such an emotionally charged day. Beth sat down at the dining room table, staring at the drawing and rereading the lines while she played back the two messages left on the answering machine. One was from Steve, the other from her mother in Chicago. Both were calls of concern. Both asked her to call them back whenever she got in. All Beth could think about was how she was going to deal with thanking Joanna. So for now, both would have to wait. BJ stood off to the side watching as Beth paced nervously back and forth across the kitchen as if hoping to actually build up enough steam to propel her across the backyard. Finally, in a rush of adrenaline, somehow Beth found herself standing on the front step of the carriage house. The radio was on, tuned to the same oldies station that she always listened to. For a moment, the familiarity of the music helped lessen her anxiety. She knocked on the screen door and waited. When Joanna didn't answer, she peered in through the screen and called out tentatively.

"Hello..."

Beth waited another minute, then turned to leave just as Joanna came out from around the alcove. She'd obviously just showered. A thin layer of dampness still clung to her skin and she was using a towel to dry her hair.

"Hi. I thought I heard someone at the door. I wasn't sure."

"I'm sorry. I didn't mean to disturb you."

Beth stood flustered as Joanna continued to towel off her hair.

"Don't worry about it."

"I should have just called. I forgot the phone's been turned on."

"You already made the trip. Why waste the dime?"

Joanna's logic made Beth feel even more foolish than she already did.

"I'll come back at a better time. Or not. I just wanted to thank you for that beautiful drawing and note you left me." She hesitated. "I suppose Steve told you."

Joanna nodded solemnly and for the briefest moment the women held each other's eyes.

"It was very thoughtful... and very much appreciated."

Beth turned to go. Jo pushed against the screen door with her arm and held it open.

"Come on in for awhile."

Unable to think of a quick enough excuse to refuse Jo's invitation, Beth smiled awkwardly and stepped inside. The fresh scent of soap rose from Joanna's body. Her skin was tanned and radiant against the white cotton tank top. Whatever it was in Jo's life that was eating away at her certainly didn't show. By comparison, Beth felt even more drained and unattractive than she had all day. Her physical and emotional exhaustion were impossible to hide. Joanna offered her a place to start. Her eyes were cautiously tender.

"Tough day, huh?"

Incapable of putting words to any of it, Beth pushed a strand of hair off her face and looked away.

"If you don't mind, I'd rather not talk about it."

Joanna didn't ask for more. She followed Beth's eyes across the room to the studies of Steve taped to the wall over by the modeling platform. She was quickly apologized for taking liberties with Beth's property.

"I hope you don't mind. I used the kind of tape that won't damage the paint when I take them down."

Jo's apology went completely ignored as Beth was entirely taken in by the work itself. Her eyes traveled slowly form one sketch to the next.

"My God, these are incredible."

"Thanks."

Joanna folded her arms. Though it had been a few days since she'd done them, she still felt more *grateful* for her talent than *proud*. She stood quietly by as Beth crossed the room to examine the drawings more closely.

Initially Beth didn't mind that Jo was watching her. But as she studied the renderings more carefully, the torment Beth felt the night Steve modeled came racing back. How painfully jealous she had been of their time together. She became self-conscious, fearing that somehow those unsettling feelings would show. Joanna came up and stood beside her.

"He's got a magnificent body."

Though quick to agree, Beth grew increasingly uneasy. Naturally assuming it was the cumulative toll of the day, Jo groped for a way to lessen the strain. She turned off the radio, pulled out one of the kitchen chairs and motioned for Beth to sit down. She complied, more out of overwhelming fatigue than conscious choice. Staying on certainly wasn't what Beth had in mind. It was obvious Jo wasn't expecting company. Art supplies were scattered everywhere. The room felt entirely unfamiliar yet mysteriously more comfortable than it ever had before. Joanna mistook Beth's scrutiny and quickly acknowledged its disarray.

"I know the place is a mess. Don't worry, I promise it'll be spotless when I leave. You'll never even know I was here."

Beth's heart immediately sank at the prospect of Joanna's inevitable departure. The remark was a painful reminder of the strictly temporary nature of their arrangement. How could she expect Jo to know that it already felt impossible to ever forget *anything* about her being there?

Joanna couldn't help but notice that Beth's demeanor had suddenly taken a turn for the worse.

"I was just about to make myself a sandwich. When was the last time you had anything to eat?"

Beth shrugged.

"I haven't had much of an appetite today."

"No, I wouldn't think so."

As uncomfortable as she was, Beth was simply too exhausted to move.

"Maybe just a drink, if it isn't too much trouble."

Jo was glad to provide something concrete. She peered into the refrigerator.

"Mineral water, orange juice or Coke?"

"God, I can hardly drown my sorrow in any of *those*. Actually I was hoping for more of '*a drink*' drink. A glass of wine maybe?"

"There's an opened bottle, but I'm not sure it's a good idea on an empty stomach."

Beth groaned at her inability to get even the slightest relief.

"This just isn't my day, is it?"

The disarming understatement made Joanna feel ridiculous about denying the poor woman anything.

"Okay, here's the deal... you can have a glass of wine but you're eating a sandwich with it. These are your choices: ham and Swiss on rye or Swiss and ham on rye. Which will it be?"

Beth appreciated Joanna's playfulness.

"You choose for me. This is not the day to be making a monumental decision like that on my own."

Jo poured her a glass of wine and put it down on the table with a warning.

"Don't you dare touch this until I finish making us some sandwiches."

Beth looked up into Joanna's eyes and pouted pathetically. For an instant, Jo's heart went soft. She forced herself to sound much more indifferent than she actually felt.

"Fine, go ahead. If you want to end this day with a massive hangover, be my guest. It's your funeral."

The words fell out of her mouth before Jo could take them back. She was horrified by the slip.

"Shit! I didn't mean to say that. I'm really sorry."

Beth smiled forgivingly.

"Actually, I can't think of a more appropriate way to have put it." She tried to put the consequences of a hangover in perspective. "Besides, I'd say it would make a perfectly fitting end to a perfectly miserable day, wouldn't you?"

After Jo conceded, Beth took her first of several gulps. By the time Jo brought their sandwiches to the table, Beth's glass was practically empty. She reached for it again, this time raising it in the air.

"Here's to our second unlikely meal together." Beth paused and looked down at the cheap plates, the mismatched silverware and paper napkins. She was already beginning to feel giddy from the effects of the alcohol. "I set a nicer table than you."

Jo shook her head disapprovingly. Despite her best efforts, it was clear Beth was well on her way to a costly 'buzz'.

"Eat your sandwich."

Beth put down her glass. She reached over and squeezed Jo's hand. Her demeanor changed completely.

"Thank you for being concerned. Thank you for the rendering and the note. It's all incredibly sweet of you."

Joanna accepted the warmth of Beth's hand and gratitude. Although she would never admit to the full extent of her caring, Jo had intentionally stuck around all day and not left the property. This, despite the fact that they were virtually strangers and that she was probably the *least* likely person Beth would think to turn to in such a personal hour of need.

Beth took her hand away, but the connection and the question in her heart lingered.

"Did you mean what you wrote… about my devotion being evident in my touch?"

Maybe it was the day, maybe it was the look in Beth's eyes that pleaded for the truth, but whatever the reason, Joanna couldn't refuse her the honesty she was looking for.

"Yes. I meant exactly what I said."

"I had no idea you even noticed."

Jo would have left it at that, but something in Beth's eyes provoked more.

"It's impossible *not* to notice. It's there in all those snapshots that spilled out of your wallet in the luncheonette and the ridiculous amount of fruit salad you pile into a bowl. It's in the way you respond to people... to music... and a sky full of stars... the way you arrange a silly bouquet of paper flowers in a beautiful crystal vase and use Cheerios as a negotiating tool. It's in all those little marshmallows you put on top of a sweet potato casserole... and your amazing courage to get through this day." Joanna watched as Beth's eyes began to fill. "And you're right, you *do* set a nicer table, especially when you're celebrating something as insane... and important... as your right to celebrate!"

Tears streamed down Beth's cheeks. She was overwhelmed by the intimate details of Joanna's observation. She used her napkin to blot her face. Having spent so many of these recent years insecure about her identity and doubtful of her own strength, Beth felt unworthy of such a glorified and touching characterization.

"I'm not sure that what you've just described isn't just the frantic energy of an otherwise silly and absurd woman."

Joanna remembered Steve's description of Beth's unfinished dreams. She stared into Beth's eyes, searching for the fractured pieces of the woman's life. This time Beth didn't look away. Jo's was kind.

"Even if that is the case, from the little that I've seen, the world's a better place because of it."

Beth never expected to hear all she just had. Joanna never expected to admit all she just did. A vulnerable silence formed in the space between them. Looking for a distraction, Jo went to the closet for another bag of chips and Beth nervously poured herself another glass of wine. As she continued to sip, her eyes drifted back over to the studies of Steve. She noted how sensitively Jo had rendered the powerful muscles of his arms and chest. The drawings immediately conjured up a new wave of images of Joanna's body pressed against his. Suddenly, all the misery of that night returned and with it came her unfamiliar shame. Beth couldn't afford for Joanna to see anything more. Apparently she'd already seen so much. Beth stood up trying hard to ignore a sudden wave of dizziness.

"I really should go. I wouldn't want to have that hangover in front of you. I don't think I could bear the 'I told you so' I'd have coming."

Joanna moved closer fearing Beth might lose her balance.

"Will you be okay?"

"I'll be fine."

How many times had Beth promised herself she would be.

Choosing to believe her, Joanna grabbed the handle of the screen door and involuntarily flinched with pain. It was impossible for Beth not to have noticed.

"What's the matter?"

"Nothing."

"Please, I'm not nearly drunk enough to believe that."

It was clear that Beth was not leaving without an answer. Jo relented, in a round about way.

"Actually, if you've got a needle and a magnifying glass, I'd like to borrow them."

"Why? Are you planning to do your next series of studies in needlepoint?"

Joanna was again amused by Beth's resilient sense of humor. She held up her hand. The crease of Jo's palm was inflamed and swollen.

"Splinter. I though I got it out days ago."

"Obviously not. Let me see that."

Without waiting Beth took Joanna's hand and held it up for a closer look.

"Come back to the house with me. We need to clean that out before it gets any worse."

"You've had a long enough day. I'll deal with it myself."

"This is not open for discussion. We're taking care of it now. It already looks infected."

Joanna pulled her hand away. She didn't like being told what to do. Beth raised her eyebrow like a mother growing increasingly annoyed with her petulant child.

"Either you come along of your own free will or I'll drag you across this yard by that sore hand of yours."

Joanna was impressed with the woman's feisty show of bravado despite her obviously diminished capacity.

"Okay, you win."

"Good, because frankly I don't think I'm up for that kind of struggle." Beth giggled at her own confession. "Oh and grab that bottle of wine. It would be a shame to leave it almost empty."

Jo complied but as they crossed the yard, she expressed grave misgivings about the instability of Beth's step and her obvious lack of coordination.

"I'm not sure you're in any condition to be jabbing me with a needle.

"Don't be ridiculous!"

A few steps later Beth lost her footing and were it not for Joanna's quick save, she would surely have fallen. She freed herself from Jo's grip and shook herself out.

"I'm perfectly fine."

Jo looked at her skeptically and Beth became all the more annoyed.

"I think I know what I'm capable of. Shall I describe the night my whole family and I came down with the same stomach virus… how I managed to clean up my husband and both kids in between my own bouts of vomiting and diarrhea?"

Jo recoiled as Beth grew more insistent.

"Just have a little faith. Need I remind you that *trust* is the basis of any meaningful relationship?"

Hoping Joanna wouldn't ask why she said that, Beth nodded firmly at the sound of her own conviction and marched on toward the house. Jo stood there, watching the inebriated woman wobble up the porch steps and fumble at the door. When Beth finally got the thing opened, she turned around.

"Are you coming or do I have to drag you the rest of the way after all?"

As Joanna came toward her, she wasn't at all sure what she feared more—the thought of Beth poking around her throbbing palm or the threat of this utterly disarming woman poking around her brooding heart.

However lightheaded she'd been feeling up to that point, the moment Beth entered the house, she switched into a purposeful, take-charge mode. She instructed Jo to sit on the piano bench where there was a high intensity lamp. Beth went upstairs to get the supplies she needed to remove the splinter. As he followed Joanna into the living room, BJ didn't seem at all surprised that Jo did exactly as she was told. After all, he'd heard that unmistakable 'mother tone' countless times over the years and it never failed to get results.

Jo would have preferred to use the time alone to have another look around the room, but BJ seemed just as intent on getting some attention of his own. Joanna obliged his persistent nudging with some vigorous scratches behind his ears and under his chin. When Beth returned he was reciprocating with long, generous licks across Jo's hand. She shouted across the room.

"BJ, no!"

The dog's tail instantly curled between his legs at the sound of her admonishment. Beth watched him skulk off, then shook her head impatiently.

"I can't believe you'd let him lick you on that hand. Do you realize how many germs could have gotten into that wound?"

Annoyed with Jo's lack of common sense, Beth sat down on the piano bench beside her and began sifting through the first-aid box on her lap. Jo tried to apologize, then move on.

"So, do the initials 'BJ' actually stand for anything in particular?"

Beth answered without interrupting her search.

"Yes. Originally they stood for the 'Boy's Job'. With 2 small kids, the last thing in the world I needed or wanted was a puppy that wasn't housebroken. After Ben pleaded with me I finally gave in under one condition… that taking care of him would be strictly the boy's job. I guess it was silly of me to put any faith in promises. Pretty soon, like everything else, BJ became just another one of *mine*. So he went from being the 'Boy's Job' to being 'Beth's Job'. I didn't even have to change the initials, just my naïve expectations. Of course, by then he'd already stolen *my* heart as well."

Jo met BJ's eyes and his tail began to swish proudly against the floor.

"He does sorta' grow on you."

Beth had the tweezers, the needle and the book of matches she needed.

"Okay, let's have that hand."

Joanna found herself immediately obeying Beth's command. She held it out, palm up. Beth took it in her own and moved it up toward the light to have a better look. Ordinarily, the mere thought of ever sharing this kind of intimacy with Joanna would have felt altogether impossible, but the focus of her task gave Beth a familiar sense of control and safety. Over the years, it never mattered what *she* was feeling or needed at any given moment—whether it was lunch, a shower, a nap or sex. Invariably, someone *else's* needs would always separate her from her own. In this particular case, that dutiful role was a godsend. Joanna did not have the benefit of such distraction, leaving her all too aware of her own vulnerability. With Beth's eyes fixed downward, Joanna studied the woman closely. Jo marveled at the steady, confident persona Beth had assumed—not at all like the frazzled, bumbling woman who'd run her down, not once but twice, in the same hour—not at all like the woman who, just moments ago, giggled and stumbled her way across the yard. She studied the subtleties of Beth's hands while they held her own, tilting and turning it for a good look at the splinter. They were practical, sturdy hands, not particularly remarkable in any way, but hands that were honest and real, hands that had seen more than their fair share of household chores and probably not enough of the keyboard in front of her. Jo recalled how passionately those hands 'played' against Beth's thighs the night of the concert. Her touch now felt deliberate yet remarkably tender. A few age spots and everyday cuts and bruises blended into the beginnings of an early summer tan—the kind that makes all of life's blemishes a little easier to hide, at least to the eye. Beth's unpolished nails were filed to a sensible length and except for a simple gold wedding band, her hands bore no other adornment. Though not long and slender, their sensuality suggested something much more provocative. Joanna fought off other images—ones that strayed into much too dangerous territory.

Unaware that Jo's thoughts had drifted from where they had left off, Beth attempted to pick up their conversation while she continuing to maneuver Jo's hand under the light.

"How about you? Any pets?"

"Not since I was a kid. Once I moved out on my own, I didn't want to be that tied down."

"If a pet is too much responsibility, I assume you don't have any kids."

She pressed close to the infected area and Jo jerked her hand back in pain. Beth apologized and waited for Joanna's answer.

"No kids. No biological clock. No regrets."

Despite Jo's deliberately abrupt answer, Beth risked getting more personal.

"Were you always that clear about not wanting children?"

"Absolutely. I even hated *being* one. Childhood always felt like such a waste of time."

Considering the mess her life was today, Jo wondered why she was in such a big hurry to grow up.

"What is it exactly you find so objectionable?"

Joanna answered matter-of-factly.

"Primary colors. I hate them! If I had to live with all that garish red, yellow and blue I'd go out of my fucking mind! Tell me something, have you ever seen nursery furniture in chrome, marble or brushed suede?"

Beth wasn't sure if Joanna was serious.

"I haven't shopped for baby furniture in quite some time but no, I don't imagine you'd find a huge selection in those finishes."

"And all that bulbous, molded plastic! The high chair… the little step stool… the car seat. Not a damn thing is sleek or sensual."

Beth couldn't resist pointing out the obvious.

"I think they are going for safe and sturdy."

"And therein lies the problem!"

Beth was not convinced that Joanna was entirely serious. She was intrigued.

"So in other words, your decision not to have kids is based on their decorating flaws?"

"Yep! I suppose there's some other minor issues but more than anything, they'd clash with everything in my life."

Joanna didn't seem even remotely self-conscious about her reasoning and Beth wasn't sure whether to be amused or frightened.

"Those are a rather novel set of concerns."

Joanna shrugged.

"I know a lot of women who decided to *have* kids based on shabbier reasons than that."

Beth tensed. She prayed Jo wouldn't ask what those reasons were for *her*. The truth was that as the years went on, they had become less and less clear and fraught with more and more ambivalence. Although marriage and a family were things Beth always *thought* she wanted, she could no longer be sure if she actually chose it or it chose her.

Oblivious to the conflict going on in Beth's head, Jo ranted on.

"Ugh, and those God awful childproof extension gates! You have no idea how they disrupt the flow of a room. It's a visual nightmare! And all those crushed Goldfish! Do you have any idea what those thing do to the back of your car?"

Beth smiled as she recalled those early years.

"Yes, as a matter of fact I do."

"And the repetition! That alone would give me a nervous breakdown! I once made the mistake of taking a car ride with my brother and his family. I swear, if I wasn't sandwiched between my nephew's car seat and the dog, I would have opened the door and flung myself out onto the road at 70 miles an hour. It would have been the lesser of two evils compared to hearing that same fucking Sesame Street tape over and over again."

Beth certainly got her answer.

"Sounds like you've definitely made the right decision. You've pretty much described the first 7 years, except you left out the part about collapsing onto the couch after an endlessly long day only to have the point of a plastic action figure stick you in the behind."

Beth proceeded to light the match and sterilize the tip of the needle, then demanded Joanna's hand back. Jo tried to ignore what would be coming next with more small talk.

"You seem to be a natural at it... *parenting*, I mean."

Beth was not sure that was what she wanted to hear at this point in her life. Especially since deep down in her heart it certainly didn't feel that way.

"Do I?"

"Yeah, you do."

"A lot of it is just a matter of survival... yours and your family's. You either master it or you all go down in flames."

"It's that simple, huh?"

"Pretty much. But don't ever confuse simple with easy."

Beth blew out the match and ran a sterile gauze pad across the needle. She was ready to get down to business.

"Okay, I'll need you to hold still and be brave."

Joanna braced herself.

"If I am, do I get a lollipop afterwards?"

"We'll see. Maybe I'll let you watch me polish off that wine."

Beth tightened her grip around Joanna's hand to hold it steady. As the point of the needle probed for the splinter, Jo flinched with pain.

"Ouch!"

Beth grabbed her hand and pulled it back in place.

"I can't do this if you move."

"That hurt!"

Beth decided to use a little psychology while she worked to dig the splinter out.

"Since when did the thick skinned Joanna Cameron start admitting that something… or someone… hurt her?"

"What the hell's that supposed to mean?"

"That you don't strike me as being terribly comfortable when it comes to sharing your pain."

Joanna could feel her jaw tighten.

"What can I say, I guess it just slipped out."

Beth cranked up the intentionally distracting antagonism.

"I'm sure you don't let that happen often."

Since Beth's eyes were diverted downward, Jo had to settle for scowling at the top of the woman's head.

"How 'bout just sticking to whatever it is that's gotten under my skin."

Beth glanced up to calculate Joanna's expression. Her own eyes took on a satisfied grin.

"I thought that's what I was doing."

Before Joanna could respond, Beth looked back down and resumed her probing. Well aware of Jo's discomfort, she tried to sound reassuring.

"I'm almost done."

Joanna remained stoically silent as she watched Beth slowly and precisely ease the sliver of wood out from beneath her skin. The more intently Beth worked, the more Jo could feel her own annoyance melt into something else. She found herself comparing Beth's nurturing ways to Gayle's much more clinical touch. Her years of training as a physician taught Gayle to focus on *curing* people rather than simply *caring* for them. Until this moment, that distinction never even registered—much less mattered—to Joanna. She suddenly realized that not since her mother died had she felt anything even close to that kind of trust. Now, after all these years, Joanna's heart nearly broke recognizing a tenderness she had for so long lived without. As Jo struggled to reconcile what she had lost with what she had just found, Beth held up the tweezers with the sizeable splinter triumphantly in its grip.

"Got it!"

Still caught up in the private turmoil of her sudden realization, Joanna could only manage a quietly grateful nod. For Beth, it was more than enough.

"Now let's get that cleaned up and covered right away."

While Beth remained focused on applying some topical ointment and a carefully placed Band-Aid across the wound, Jo took the crucial moments she needed to recover, more from her hidden emotional ordeal than her more obvious physical one. Beth gently patted the side of Jo's hand before letting it go.

"Give it a few days. It should be completely healed."

Joanna tried moving her palm against the restrictive adhesive. It was as though Beth read Jo's mind about taking it off as soon as she got back to the carriage house.

"You'd better keep that covered or the next person to have a go at it will be an emergency room doctor, minus the T.L.C. I'll give you a tube of antiseptic and a box of Band-Aids to take back with you. I want you to use them, understand?"

"Or what, I'm grounded for the rest of the summer?"

Beth suddenly felt foolish for sounding so parental. With the immediate crisis now over, she was at an obvious loss for what to do or say next. This time it was Joanna who came to her rescue.

"What about my lollipop?

Beth smiled. It was still so early and contrary to her original plans, the idea of spending the rest of the evening alone was not at all appealing.

"I'm afraid I don't have any. Can I offer you a cup of coffee instead?" Beth could tell that Joanna sensed her desperation. "Please don't feel obliged."

"It's not that. I'm just surprised you suggested 'coffee'. I got the distinct impression you intended to polish off the wine."

Beth was embarrassed by her earlier behavior.

"The buzz seems to have worn off and something tells me I should quit while I'm ahead. I really *don't* relish the idea of a hangover."

"Wise choice. Then I'll stay and have a cup."

Suddenly the prospect of spending more time with Joanna entirely sober became a challenge Beth had not anticipated. She had absolutely no idea how things had strayed so far off course from simply thanking Jo for her note and then quickly retreating home to safety.

"I guess I'll go make that coffee then."

Joanna decided to have a little fun with their history.

"Unless you're celebrating something else, do you think this time we can use a couple of old mugs instead of your fine china?"

Beth fiddled self-consciously with the contents of the first aid box on her lap.

"Are you sure you don't mind staying?"

Jo took the box from Beth's hands and playfully shoved her off the piano bench.

"What's a girl gotta' do to get a little reward around here? First no lollipop and now you're trying to weasel out of a lousy cup of coffee."

Beth heard herself actually laugh out loud. It was something she never expected to do. Certainly not today. It felt good. Really, really good. Joanna's smile provided all the assurance Beth needed to know that it was okay for her to feel something other than sorrow. It was okay for her to go and put up that pot of coffee.

With Beth busy in the kitchen, Joanna immediately went to have another look at the old painting over the mantle. For some reason, it still intrigued her. She called out over the rumbling of the coffee grinder.

"Tell me about the painting…"

Before Joanna finished her sentence, Beth answered back from the kitchen.

"The one over the mantle?"

Joanna was unnerved. There were a half dozen pieces of art in the room.

"How'd you know which one I meant?"

Beth appeared in the doorway of the living room, wiping her hands on a towel.

"When the boys were growing up, I warned them that I had eyes in the back of my head. Maybe it's true." She joined Joanna in front of the painting. "Or maybe because it's my favorite too."

Jo wouldn't exactly have called it her *favorite*. It certainly bore no resemblance to her sleek contemporary tastes. The truth was, she was much more *drawn* to it than *attracted* to it. For the moment, the distinction didn't seem to matter.

"Where'd you get it?"

Beth gazed lovingly at the painting.

"Ben and I picked it up at one of those local auctions soon after we moved into the house. I fell in love with it the moment I saw it!"

"Know anything about the artist?"

"Very little, I'm afraid. Supposedly it's by a fairly prominent painter who lived in the area around the turn of the century."

Beth noticed Joanna studying the signature.

"You must have taken lots of art history courses. Does the name mean anything to *you*?"

"Not a thing. Then again, I slept through 90% of those slides."

Beth crossed her arms and continued to stare at the painting.

"I have no idea if the piece is actually worth anything to a collector, but it's always been priceless to me." A melancholy stillness settled in her eyes. "I can't tell you how many times over the years I've stood here alone, wondering about that woman's life often just to escape my own, I'm afraid." Beth paused. Joanna made no attempt to respond, nor did she attempt to stop her. "Something about the way she's holding those flowers... the serenity of her smile, the way the sunlight caresses her cheek. I know this sounds crazy, but there have been moments... fleeting, idyllic moments... when I've stood here and actually felt the warmth of that sunlight on my own face and inhaled the sweetness of those flowers as though I were holding them in my own arms." Tears collected in Beth's eyes. "Then the moment passes and I feel so lost... like a stranger in my own skin." Beth quickly wiped her eyes and apologized. "I'm sorry. I'm sure that's more than you wanted to know when you asked about the painting."

Jo tried to be reassuring.

"You've had an emotional day."

Certainly that was so, but deep inside her heart Beth knew it was something more than that and for some unexplainable reason she expected that Joanna would somehow understand what no one else ever could. Feeling foolish about her disclosure and her expectation, Beth tried to dismiss them both.

"I'll pour us some coffee. We can have it here if you like."

"Fine."

Once again Jo was drawn to the stately Baby Grand piano in the corner. She spotted the small index card leaning against the crystal vase in which Beth had arranged her paper flowers. She'd noticed it earlier while Beth was working on her splinter, but the card was facing away from her making it impossible to read. She picked it up and read the quote by Georgia O'Keeffe.

Beth returned to find Jo running her finger along the edge of the card. Both women were caught equally off guard. Their eyes met, then each quickly looked away. Jo replaced the card against the vase. Beth felt compelled to offer an explanation.

"It's one of my favorite quotes. Your flowers just seemed to give it all the more relevance." Before Jo could respond, Beth nervously assured her. "I hope you don't think it meant I have any expectation of us developing a friendship. I know that's not how either of us wants to spend this summer."

Even as the words came out, Beth could no longer be sure that for her that was true. For a moment, Joanna didn't respond. She crossed her arms and leaned against the side of the piano.

"*'I feel there is something unexplored about a woman that only another woman can explore.'* O'Keeffe said that too."

Beth set the server on the coffee table, sat down on the couch and proceeded to fill their mugs.

"I'd never heard that." Beth raised the mug to her lips as they formed a quiet smile. "That would certainly explain Ben's hopelessness." She had to know. "So, is there a similarly hopeless 'Mr. Cameron'?"

Joanna understood the cleverly disguised question.

"If that was your way of asking if I have a husband, the answer's no, I'm not married."

Oddly relieved, Beth tried to make light of her own inquiry.

"Let me guess, you haven't found one in the right 'finish'?"

Jo took a long slow gulp of coffee. She enjoyed this woman's sense of humor.

"Let's just say in this case it goes a little deeper than the surface of things."

Something in Joanna's tone warned Beth not to pursue the subject. Jo had no intention of lying, but she had no intention of getting into the truth just then either. It was simply easier to avoid the whole subject. Beth groped for a mutually safe place to pick up the conversation. Joanna's eyes wandered back to the piano.

"You said you'd tell me the story behind that vase you put my flowers in."

Beth turned to look back at Arthur's gift. Her expression sweetened.

"I did, didn't I? You'd probably just find it silly and boring."

Of the many things Jo had felt in Beth's company, boredom was never one of them. She crossed one leg over the other and settled back against the couch.

"Try me."

"Ben accused me of over dramatizing my connection to Arthur."

"Arthur?"

Beth's voice melted with obvious affection.

"Yes, dear sweet Arthur Prescottt. My soon-to-be one hundred year old son."

Everything in Joanna's expression questioned Beth's sanity.

"I've lost you already, haven't I?"

Joanna was not subtle.

"Sounds more like you've lost your mind."

Beth looked down at her mug.

"I don't think I can talk about this now."

"Why not?"

"Because if I go on with the story, sooner or later you're going to roll your eyes or laugh or both, and I'm going to burst into tears. I really don't think I can handle being patronized or humored about this… especially not today."

Joanna realized that for whatever reason, this Arthur person was obviously very important to Beth and that the story of their relationship held great meaning. Jo regretted her sarcasm.

"Okay. No more cheap jokes, I promise." She waited for Beth to look up. "I really *would* like to hear the story, if you still care to share it."

Beth seemed to need a little more coaxing. Jo held up her bandaged palm as a reminder.

"What was it you said earlier about *trust* being the basis of any meaningful relationship?"

Beth was embarrassed.

"Why do I get the feeling that everything I say to you eventually comes back to haunt me?"

In an unguarded moment, Jo offered Beth the truth.

"That makes us even then. I feel the same way about you." She sealed her unsolicited confession with a smile. "So what do you say, do I get to hear about Arthur and the vase or not?"

Beth glanced over at her bouquet of paper flowers, and then turned to the woman who made them.

"You do, but first I have to pee. The wine's gone right through me."

Once again Jo found herself charmed by Beth's unpretentious honesty. She had no idea how much more about Beth this story would reveal. She only knew that for the time it would take Beth to tell it, she would be treated to more of the tender, captivating warmth of this woman's company. For the rest of the night, and for the rest of the summer, Jo knew that would *have* to be enough. She knew too that it would *never* be enough.

Beth returned a few minutes later, holding a box of tissues. Her eyes were shy.

"I usually get emotional talking about this."

She curled up against the corner of the sofa, placed the tissues within arm's reach and drew a measured breath. It was nearly impossible to know where to begin.

"I assume Steve told you how my son died."

Jo nodded solemnly.

"I hope you understand, I don't think I can actually talk about that part. The details are still much too painful, especially today. Everyone tells me I've come such a long way. The truth is, I'm never more than a few precarious inches away from the devastation of that night. It's as close as my own shadow."

For several pronounced moments, Beth sat eerily still, as if searching deep inside for the lost script of her own existence. Finally, in a soft steady voice she began to describe the circumstances of her life after the sudden loss of her son.

"A year or so after Danny died I was still an emotional wreck. If I was holding it together at all, it was strictly for Adam's sake. God knows, he'd been through enough. I couldn't have him worrying that he might be losing his mother too. But behind the act, and between all the grief counseling and antidepressants, I was literally falling apart." Beth paused. "Ben had his own way of coping. He always did. As time went on he slowly began to heal. I just got worse. There were days when I knew I scared him to death. For a long time I rejected his suggestion to get involved in some kind of volunteer work, anything that might take my mind off the tragedy and give me even the smallest sense of purpose. I know he only had my best interest at heart, but I was sick of all his well-meaning advice. A part of me refused simply for spite."

Beth played with her wedding band as if to purge herself of her unintentional cruelty.

"I was so angry with the world and I took all of it out on Ben."

Jo watched as the woman's eyes grew more vulnerable—and more beautiful—the closer Beth came to the truth.

"For a long time bitterness was the only emotion I could still feel. Except for my rage, I was completely numb. I suppose I was terrified that if I let *that* go, I would feel absolutely nothing at all. I wish I could say that one day I made a conscious and courageous decision to go on living but the truth was I simply lacked the conviction to let myself die. For the longest time I lingered passively and pathetically between the two. Eventually I relented and took Ben's advice. I began volunteering at Hillcrest Manor, a local nursing home. They had a piano in the dining room. I offered to come in and play for them. I'd only confided in a couple of people, but the whole staff welcomed me with open arms."

Beth let her finger trace the rim of her cup.

"Oddly enough, it *was* therapeutic. For a few hours a week I didn't have to find a reason to live… just the right notes on a keyboard."

Her mouth turned up in an unexpected smile.

"Those first few weeks were actually quite funny when I think back on them now. I'd be sitting at the old upright piano off in the corner of the dining room, playing my heart out, only to look up and find most of the residents either sound asleep, staring off into space or bickering with one another." Beth found it amusing to think of herself in that setting. "It was okay though. Somehow the sheer absurdity of it made me feel right at home. In all honesty, I've lived most of my adult life in '*The Theater Of The Absurd*'." She paused reflectively. "I suppose that was just as true while I was growing up, but back then I was blissfully unaware that the joke was on me." Beth lifted her mug in a mock toast. "Here's to the never-ending rewards of clarity." She peered deeply into the cup in her hand, shook her head and smiled. "So you see, the absurdity of my audience at Hillcrest was no different. I grew up dreaming that one day I'd be playing on the stage of some grand concert hall, receiving thunderous applause and standing ovations for my performance. At the Manor, I honestly don't think that there were three people in that entire room who, even if they'd wanted to, could have risen to their feet on their own, much less without leaving wind."

Although Joanna couldn't help but laugh, she wondered about all the hidden disappointment buried in Beth's lighthearted description. There were so many things about Beth's life that Jo wanted to understand, so much she wanted to ask. Instead, she silently sipped her coffee and let Beth continue on her own terms. She watched as Beth turned and studied the crystal vase. Everything in her body language suggested this was where the story became more personal and more difficult to tell. Beth's voice grew softer.

"There was this one gentleman, Arthur Prescott... a dear, sweet thoroughly engaging man who, after hearing me play for the first time, actually kissed my hand and introduced himself. After that day, he would always request that he be positioned as close to the piano as the bulky frame of his wheelchair would allow. On the days I was due to return, he'd insist on wearing something befitting my beautiful playing. Millie, his aide, suggested that his bow tie and crisp white shirt was respectable enough. No matter how frail his health, Arthur never missed a single one of those sessions. Whatever I played, I could see real appreciation in his eyes. At the end of every piece, he called out 'bravo, bravo' and clapped as wildly as a 98 year old man could. In return, I would stand up beside the piano, take a bow and blow him a special kiss." Beth's eyes began to water. "I know this sounds silly, but there were times when it actually felt like we were the only two people in that room. For that one hour I seemed to have made a real difference in that sweet old man's life. I know he certainly made a difference in mine. One day I came in to find a beautiful bouquet of flowers sitting on the top of the piano, arranged in the most exquisite crystal vase I'd ever seen. It turned out they were from Arthur. He had them picked from the courtyard garden and placed in his own personal vase just for me. I was so touched that he would think to do something like that. When I admired the vase, he told me it was one of the few things he'd kept and brought with him to Hillcrest. It belonged to his mother, a gift from a dear friend who'd sent it back for her from Europe. It immediately became one of her most cherished possessions and from that day on graced her piano, always filled with fresh cut flowers from her garden. Arthur said it would bring him great joy to see it there while I played. I told him I was honored."

Jo wanted to be sure she understood.

"So in other words, he didn't actually *give* you the vase?"

Beth leaned forward and topped off her cup. Her expression grew thoughtful as she stirred in some milk.

"No, it was still very much his mother's."

Joanna studied her closely as Beth curled back up against the corner of the couch. The woman's company—and her body language—began to feel threateningly comfortable. Jo sat perfectly still, conflicted in her desire to move closer and further away.

As the early evening light quenched the room, Beth continued her story.

"As the weeks passed I became drawn to him. I would intentionally linger and we'd share a cup of tea under his favorite shade tree and talk. Arthur's an extremely private man. No one at the nursing home knew very much about his personal life but he seemed eager to confide in me. I learned that a part of the reason my visits meant so much to him was because his mother was a pianist herself. As a young child, he would spend several hours a day in her music room, listening to her play. He described those times as some of the happiest memories of his life. He was an only child and though he never actually said so, it sounded like his was a rather lonely childhood in spite of his privileged upbringing. His father was a very wealthy man, an industrialist of some sort or another. His mother came from a socially prominent family. She was much younger and more artistically inclined. From the way Arthur spoke of her, it was quite apparent he absolutely adored her. I think the older he got, the more aware he became that for her the relationship with her husband was more a marriage of convenience than anything else. His father conducted a lot of business in Europe. Arthur recalled the many trips abroad they took as a family in the early years. But as time went on, his father would go alone, often leaving them for months on end, deepening the bond between mother and son. Arthur never tired of talking about his mother. I marveled that in his childhood eyes, her beauty and talent seemed larger than life." Beth paused as if to honor his memories with silence. "And yet he often described her as being terribly sad and withdrawn much of the time. He could recall only three things that ever seemed to bring her any real joy: tending to her garden, playing the piano and visits from one particular friend… the one who'd sent her the vase. He would describe how in this friend's fiercely commanding presence, his mother would come alive. Though for much of those idyllic visits she would all but ignore him, loving her as much as he did he valued her happiness over his own. Especially since it always seemed so illusive and so fleeting."

Beth's voice began to crack. In the privacy of her own heart the description hit much too close to home. Beth managed to steady herself.

"He told me that later on in his *own* life he came to understand more about *hers*. I don't know any of the details though. He's always remained very private about that."

Jo found herself wishing Beth knew more.

"His mother sounds like a pretty complicated woman… probably way too complicated for those times."

"Or these."

The words had slipped out before Beth could check herself. She looked down quickly, hoping to conceal the depth of her own conflicts from Jo's eyes.

"Arthur must have been an extremely insightful child. I remember him telling me once that he was sure he had her *love* but never her *devotion*. Can you imagine a child being so sensitive as to realize there's actually a difference?" Beth recalled driving home that day wondering if either of her own sons had ever sensed that distinction. Haunted by that question, she forced herself to move on. "For better or for worse, his mother's torment didn't last very long. Gradually her health began to fail until eventually she could no longer leave her bed." Beth put her hand to her lips. "God, it must have been awful for him to watch her slip away like that… hour by hour, day by day." Her eyes grew teary imagining Arthur's pain. "One morning, she just never woke up. He was only twelve." Beth shuddered to think what Adam would have done had he lost her. She recalled how hard she had to fight in order to spare her own child such a tragic legacy. Her thoughts drifted back to her old friend. "All these years later, Arthur was still able to describe the lifeless pallor of his mother's cheeks in contrast to the striking intensity of the freshly cut flowers in the vase beside her pillow. Once she became confined to her bed, she had it moved from the piano onto her nightstand so that she could still delight in its splendor. Arthur described how at the same hour of each day, the sunlight would pour in through her bedroom window and catch the chiseled corners of the cut glass. On this particular morning it cast a shimmering rainbow across the fingers of her hand… the same hand that once brought beautiful music into his life and that now lay motionless at her side. He said that on the morning his mother died, her head was turned in the direction of that vase. He imagined it was the last thing her eyes rested upon before closing. He was certain of it because her expression looked more peaceful in death than he'd ever recalled seeing it in life." Beth's own eyes drifted across the room to the same vase. "What a beautiful and tragic image for a child to be left with."

Joanna poured herself another cup of coffee, surprised at how drawn in she'd become.

"Did he ever say what she actually died from?"

Beth thought about her visit with Arthur earlier in the day and recalled with vivid detail what he'd said about her broken heart.

"I died of pneumonia."

Joanna sat forward, unsure if she'd heard right.

"You just said, 'I… I died of pneumonia'."

Beth responded as if suddenly awakened from a daze.

"Did I?" Beth answered Jo's confusion with a quiet smile. "This is where the story gets more complicated and extremely emotional for me. I guess on a day like today the lines become more blurred than usual." Beth took a moment to collect herself. When she felt as ready as she thought she'd ever be, she related the highly unusual course of events as they'd unfolded. The facts were a lot easier to account for than the much more complicated truth that lived deep inside Beth's heart. She described how not long after she and Arthur had become dear friends, she got a call from the nursing home letting her know that he'd suffered a major stroke and had lapsed into a coma. Beth rushed to the hospital—the same hospital her son was taken to the night of his fatal accident. Like Danny, Arthur lay unconscious in the same intensive care unit, clinging to life. Beth's entire expression now took on the burden of those memories. "You have no idea what kind of turmoil being back in that place brought up for me. I remember thinking, this can't be happening. Why is God doing this to me? At the time, it just seemed unbearably cruel." Beth swallowed over the lump in her throat. "Given his age and condition, Arthur was never expected to pull through. Caught between rage and resignation, I felt compelled to stay at his bedside. As the days and nights passed without any change, Ben became more and more concerned about my own health. He was all too aware of what the circumstances represented and given the hopelessness of the situation, he tried everyway he could to convince me to just let go. But the more he tried reasoning with me, the more desperate I became for a miracle. I know this sounds crazy but I thought that since I wasn't able to bring my *own* child back to life, maybe… just maybe… I'd been given a chance to save someone else's."

Jo was careful not to sound belittling of Beth's perception.

"Even if that child was 98 years old?"

"You don't have children so I wouldn't expect you to understand, but when you become a mother to one, there's a part of you that becomes a mother to all." Her voice grew tender. "Each and every one of us is still just a child, really, forced by the years to pretend we're ever anything more."

A smile formed in Joanna's eyes. Grateful for it, Beth went on.

"The doctors said they can never be sure what actually gets through to someone in a coma, so anything seemed worth a try. One night I came home from the hospital, sat down at the piano and made Arthur a tape recording of all his favorite classical pieces… the same ones he loved listening to his mother play when he was a boy. It was the first time I'd really played since Danny died. I cried for him. I cried for Arthur. I cried for myself. All I could think of was how much music still connected this man to his dead mother and how much it still connected me to my dead son. The irony of it was somehow profound." Beth felt relieved that Jo didn't suggest she might be reading too much into it. "I played my heart out that night. For much of those hours I could barely read the notes on the sheet music through my tears. I never went to sleep that night. After I'd showered and changed, I went straight back to the hospital with the tape. I placed the recorder on the table beside his bed, hoping to fill the room with the sound of his most comforting memories. I kept a vigil for days and nights on end, continually playing and replaying the tape." Beth shook her head as if reliving the heartbreak of those hours. "Though he showed no signs of improvement, I kept hoping and praying that the music was somehow getting through." Relief crept into Beth's voice. "The longer I sat there the more I began to realize that whether Arthur was going to live or die, if he just followed the music he'd know he was walking in the direction of his mother's love and when he reached out to her she would be there to hold him."

Beth's expression changed. She did nothing to hide her pain. Joanna had no choice other than to remain sacredly still in the presence of it.

"Your children are not supposed to die before you. You're supposed to be there first, so you can comfort them." A tear streamed down her cheek. She wiped it against the palm of her hand and fought back the ones still forming. She wanted to finish telling the story. "It had been over a week and the doctors were certain that Arthur wasn't going to make it. At that point I was no longer hoping to be there when he awoke. I just wanted to be there when he died. Nothing Ben could say made any difference. I wasn't leaving Arthur's side." Jo watched as Beth seemed to settle into the depth of her own pain. Her voice filled with emotion. "With all the tubes and medical equipment surrounding his bed, I'd still found a way to position my chair up against the rail so that I could hold his hand. I'd sit that way for hours, the tape playing softly in the background. At some point I must have drifted off. In my dream I thought I felt his fingers close ever so slightly around mine. When I opened my eyes his eyes were still closed, but he was smiling. I was delirious with joy. My first impulse was to ring for the doctor, but I so desperately needed those few precious moments alone with him. He was, after all, *my* miracle." Beth paused again, as if to relive the sanctity of that moment. "I bent down and kissed him softly on his forehead. As I stroked his paper-thin cheek, I felt his tears. His lips began to tremble. 'Mama, mama', he whispered, 'oh mama, you've come back to me'. Those were his exact words. I'll never forget the relief in his voice but given my own loss, it almost destroyed me on the spot."

Beth seemed to need a moment before she could continue. Recalling that part of the story was still deeply unsettling.

"With all the strange and overlapping ironies of our relationship, naturally I became quite upset by Arthur's delusion. I told myself that hearing the music he'd always associated with his mother further confused his already dulled senses. I tried to clarify my identity as gently as I could without breaking his heart all over aging. 'No sweetheart', I remember saying. 'It's me, your friend Beth from the nursing home. *You're* the one who's come back, not *me*.' He became extremely quiet as I continued to explain things. I told him that he'd been very ill and understandably still quite disoriented. I tried to assure him that eventually things would become clearer to him again... that for now he just needed to rest. For the moment he seemed to be taking in what I said. Then he suddenly cried out like an abandoned child and gripped my arm. 'No mama!', he pleaded, 'It's *you*! It's *you*! It's *you*!' His urgency actually scared me. I began to panic and rang for the nurse. A team of doctors rushed in, surrounded his bed and began taking all sorts of readings. They were astonished by his recovery. I can remember standing off to the side, still dazed and traumatized by what had transpired privately just moments before. When they were through examining him I took the doctor in charge aside and told him about Arthur's delusion. He wasn't at all surprised and explained that such confusion was actually quite common in these circumstances, especially given Arthur's age and significantly diminished capacity prior to his stroke. In this case the doctor couldn't see how such a delusion would do Arthur any real harm. If anything, he felt the comfort of it might even help his recovery. Taking everything into consideration, he saw little reason to upset Arthur with the truth for whatever time he had left. He said it was my call and left the decision up to me." Beth couldn't ignore the amusing irony. "Why is it those rare times in my life when I've actually *wanted* someone to tell me what to do, I'm told that the choice is entirely mine? When I don't want anyone's opinion, everyone seems to have one."

For a few precious moments Beth found some much needed relief in the pathetically funny truth of it all. She seemed reluctant to leave that space. Jo prodded her with a question.

"So, what did you decide to do?"

Beth took a slow, deep breath as if reliving her conflict.

"In the days that followed his regaining consciousness all Arthur seemed to want was to listen to his mother's music and to hold his mother's hand, so I put aside my own discomfort about misleading him and continued to provide him with both. Despite what the doctor said, I had no idea if I was doing the right thing... for *Arthur* or for *me*. I suppose I convinced myself I was giving him something I wished someone could give me... a loved one back." At least for the moment, Beth needed to take the largeness of it all lightly. "Besides, 'reality' is such an overrated state anyway. As frail as he was, after awhile the doctors thought he was well enough to move back to Hillcrest. The staff was elated. They all missed him so much. On the day he was scheduled to be discharged, I went over to the nursing home to make sure that everything in his room was just the way he remembered it. I think somewhere in me I was hoping that being back in familiar surroundings might help him remember who I really was."

"Did it?"

"It's been almost 2 years now. It hasn't yet." Beth felt newly startled by the amount of time that had actually passed. "That morning I picked some fresh flowers from my own garden, intending to put them in the now famous vase." The memory seemed to reform in Beth's mind as her eyes drifted over to the beautiful crystal vase. "You can't imagine how strange I felt standing there arranging those flowers, imagining the woman in his memories once doing the very same thing." Beth rubbed her arms as if suddenly chilled from the inside. "There was actually a moment that felt so haunting, had I loved Arthur any less I would have run screaming from that room and never returned. But he'd already been abandoned once and as crazy as this sounds, I couldn't leave him again." Beth was afraid to look up, afraid to see the judgment in Joanna's eyes. "So I just sat there in his room, staring at the vase, waiting for them to bring him back. As they wheeled him in he seemed so happy to be 'home' and so relieved that I was there. Everyone on staff stopped in to welcome him back. Though he appreciated the fuss, all the company wore him out rather quickly. Ever the consummate gentleman, he thanked everybody for their attention before requesting his privacy. Once we were alone, Arthur asked if I would sit by his bed and play the tape until he fell asleep. With the music playing softly in the background, his head turned towards the vase across the room. I don't know how much of it he was actually able to distinguish with the little left of his vision but the most serene expression came over his face. He patted my hand and thanked me for bringing the vase. Still convinced that I was his mother, he told me to take it home, insisting that it belonged with *me*, sitting on top of my piano, just the way he remembered it. I never had any real intention of taking it. I fully expected he'd forget the whole thing and never mention it again. I stayed a while longer, until I thought he'd dozed off. Somehow, even in his sleep, Arthur must have sensed my preparing to leave. Without opening his eyes he reminded me about the vase. I hated taking it, especially under such false pretense, but I didn't seem to have much of a choice. The sad thing is that despite its beauty, I could never bring myself to use it. All I could do was keep it safe and cherish it for all that it represented. From the day I brought it home, it's been on a shelf in my china cabinet, behind glass doors." Beth wasn't sure she should say anything more. But Joanna had asked to hear the story and certainly this had become a part of it. "Special occasions have come and gone but not a single one ever felt worthy enough. Not until that night you brought me that bouquet. In a way that never made sense before, I suddenly understood that I'd been given that vase for a reason and that just like Arthur had insisted, it seemed to belong there on top of my piano together with your flowers."

Joanna was flattered by the obvious significance of her creation. In her own eyes it was just a small, spontaneous gesture. She returned an awkward but acknowledging smile. Beth was relieved that Joanna did not make fun of her decision.

"Arthur will be so pleased to know I'm finally using the vase. I haven't told him yet." Beth hoped that Joanna could now better understand. "Ben thinks that I've always read too much into the relationship but the more I thought about it, the more I realized how the convoluted nature of it fit perfectly into my already convoluted life. So, to answer your politely *unasked* question… yes, these last two years I've gone on letting Arthur believe I'm his mother. Actually, I've come to see it as a kind of blessing for *both* of us. Arthur was a child who'd lost his mother…I, a mother who'd lost my child. Serving his harmless delusion seemed to fill the void in both our lives. So when I said, '*I* died of pneumonia', I suppose it's because I've come to share his mother's life… and her *death*… as well." Just when her explanation started sounding a bit too bizarre for Jo's tastes, Beth teased her into a more comfortable space. "How many mothers do you suppose lose and 18 year old son only to find a 98 year old one, with the same love of music, no less? See what I mean when I say my life is nothing short of absurd?"

"I'll bet Mother's Day must get pretty complicated around here."

"You have no idea! Suffice it to say that coping with primary colors and bulbous, plastic furniture would be a walk in the park."

Beth caught Joanna staring at the vase. Her misgivings were hard to conceal.

"Tell me what you're thinking."

Jo was at an honest loss for words.

"Frankly, I don't know what to think."

"Yes you do. You think I'm a nut case."

Jo smiled.

"Okay, maybe just a little. But hey, most people get locked up in a padded cell for that. You walk away with a beautiful and probably very expensive crystal vase. So, I'd have to say '*crazy*' definitely works for you."

What Joanna didn't say—but what she was thinking—was that on Beth, '*crazy*' was also damn near irresistible. Beth accepted Joanna's off-handed compliment and though both women were reluctant, it seemed like the perfect note on which to end the visit. Joanna sat forward, initiating an awkward parting.

"You must be exhausted."

"Exhausted is certainly *one* of the things I'm feeling. I won't even try to describe all the rest."

Beth's weary smile exposed a vulnerability that swept across Joanna's heart, making her ache with desire to lead the poor woman upstairs and tuck her into bed. Instead, Jo picked up the coffee tray and carried it into the kitchen. She found herself deliberately stalling for more time.

"Why don't I rinse these off for you?"

Beth followed behind her.

"That's not necessary. Besides, you've already done so much."

Joanna's drawing lay on the counter, just inches away. Beth picked it up and studied it again, rereading the inscription that brought tears to her eyes.

"Thank you so much. I honestly can't imagine how I would have gotten through this day without you."

Jo moved toward the door.

"I'm glad if it made a difference."

Beth followed her out onto the porch. The cool early evening air was a relief from the intense weight of the day. The late setting sun hovered low in the sky. Despite the unbearable sadness in her chest, Beth still managed to appreciate the beauty that surrounded her.

"I love this time of day. It feels so peaceful. If nature was inclined to sigh, this would surely be the hour." Beth took a long, lingering breath, attempting to inhale not just the air but also the meaning of life itself. As she drew in the fullness of both, her heart seemed to accept the painful gift of her loss. "I suppose in the aftermath of personal tragedy, one can either live their life as if nothing will ever matter again… or as if everything matters even more than it ever had before."

Lost in the softness of Beth's eyes, Joanna felt herself wanting far too many things she knew she could not have. Struggling against her own desire, she simply nodded.

As Joanna started to back away, Beth reached out and unexpectedly hugged her. It was a sudden but unmistakably enduring embrace and before

Jo could figure out what to do with her own arms, Beth stepped back. She smiled shyly, apparently just as surprised by the spontaneity of her gesture as Jo was.

"Your company meant so much. I don't know how I can ever repay you."

Joanna held up her bandaged hand.

"Maybe there'll be other splinters."

Suddenly Beth remembered.

"You didn't take that antiseptic cream. Wait here. I'll go get it."

Beth turned and went inside. During the moments she was gone, Joanna's mind raced in circles, searching for a pretense that would grant her more time with Beth in the future. Jo was still wrestling with her better judgment when Beth returned with the tube of ointment. She reminded Jo to be sure to keep the wound covered.

"It would be a pity if your hand became so infected they had to amputate… especially since you draw so beautifully with it."

Suddenly Joanna found just the excuse she was looking for.

"Model for me! You said you didn't know how you could repay me for today. Well, that's how. You can pose for me."

Flustered by the unexpected request, Beth groped for a reasonable way to decline.

"You have Steve for that."

"He's visiting his folks next week. C'mon, what do you say?"

Just the idea of being under Joanna's scrutiny for so many hours sent shock waves through Beth's body.

"Why would you want to sketch *me*? I'm hardly an interesting subject."

"Define *interesting*."

Beth hesitated awkwardly, afraid of sounding even more foolish than she already felt.

"I don't know. Someone captivating in some way. Someone powerful, striking, intriguing, beautiful. I'm none of those things."

Joanna was surprised and curious.

"How exactly *do* you see yourself?"

Beth was not prepared to have this conversation. Especially since in these last few years she'd become practically invisible to herself. She looked down, almost shamefully.

"That's a hard question to answer."

"Then don't. Just pose for me. It's a lot easier, I promise."

Beth recalled Jo's detailed rendering of Steve's bare torso. Her voice suddenly filled with unmistakable alarm.

"You aren't expecting me to pose nude, are you?" She never let Joanna answer. "Because even if I agree, I'm not taking my clothes off!"

Though she had no such expectation, Jo couldn't resist teasing her.

"And all this time I though you were the uninhibited bohemian type."

Beth laughed nervously.

"Hardly."

She fidgeted with the collar of her blouse, now wishing that she'd buttoned it higher. Joanna hated seeing her that uncomfortable, especially at the end of such an already difficult day.

"Tell you what, if you can stand the heat you can wear a turtleneck if it'll make you feel any better."

The offer—though ridiculous—was reassuring enough for Beth to entertain the possibility more seriously.

"When would you want to do this?"

Joanna smiled triumphantly inside. She tried to sound nonchalant—as if her whole life didn't depend on that moment.

"Steve leaves on Friday. So how does Saturday night sound?"

For a fleeting, insane moment Beth felt like a young girl accepting a date. An odd mix of uncertainty and excitement swept over her.

"I suppose Saturday night is fine."

Joanna was quick to set a time before Beth changed her mind.

"That'll give you a whole week to go through your winter wardrobe."

Mirrored in Joanna's remark, Beth felt ridiculously prudish. Where was 'The Dangerous Beth Garrison' when she needed her? She tried sounding more cavalier.

"We'll see… maybe I'll just surprise you… "

Joanna's smile sent Beth into a tailspin of regret at pretending to be bolder than she really was. Now she had no choice but to live up to Jo's expectations. The sudden, piercing ring of the kitchen phone spared Beth the mental anguish of reviewing her entire wardrobe in her head. It also reminded her that she never got back to either Steve or her mother. Beth wasn't in the mood to talk to anyone else—certainly not now. She decided to let the machine answer. After its cue, Ben began leaving a message.

"It's me hon. If you're there, pick up."

It was the first time Joanna had heard the sound of Ben's voice. Suddenly Beth's husband became real in a way he hadn't been up to that point—not by scrutinizing his photographs—not even by driving his car. Jo didn't like admitting to herself just how resentful she was of his call that interrupted her time with Beth. She felt foolish for being annoyed. After all, it was perfectly reasonable that Ben should want to talk to his wife, especially considering the loss they shared on this particular day. Her jealousy felt immature and entirely unrealistic. Still, in her heart of hearts, Joanna had hoped Beth would have ignored his call.

For Beth, there was never any choice. At the sound of her husband's voice, she immediately excused herself and hurried inside to get the phone before Ben hung up.

"I'm sorry…"

Joanna pretended to be fine about letting her go.

"Of course, I understand."

Jo intentionally lingered on the porch just long enough to listen to the beginning of Beth's conversation. Her voice was warm and affectionate.

"Hi sweetie. I was just outside on the porch. It's such a lovely night."

Jo was disappointed that Beth didn't mention her company as she continued.

"Why don't I close up down here and go upstairs. We can talk from bed."

The intimacy of Beth's suggestion all but shattered Joanna's momentary triumph. As she crossed the backyard, she glanced up just as the light in the master bedroom went on. It was a bedroom with a history that this married woman shared with her husband. Jo grew even more annoyed with herself. Saturday's plans suddenly felt like a big mistake. One she couldn't afford to make. Back in the carriage house, Jo opened a beer. She chastised herself: "What the hell's the matter with me? The woman's got a fucking white picket fence around her."

Joanna brought the bottle to her lips and after a few brooding sips, she remembered the small part of Beth she still secretly possessed. She stormed the kitchen cabinet for the jar with the Cheerio, then unscrewed the lid and poured it out into her bandaged palm. The longer she stared at it the more she recalled of that first night together, then of this one. The more Joanna remembered, the less '*impossible*' seemed to matter.

With the door to the cupboard open, Joanna again fell under the spell of the pleated trim that ran along the front of the shelves. Once more she was struck by the tender, nostalgic touch that brought to mind her own mother's kitchen and her own mother's love. As one memory ushered in the next, Joanna remembered something her mother had written inside the last Valentine's Day card she would ever give her. The late Mrs. Cameron knew her daughter well.

"*The heart can never be trusted to love wisely*" she wrote. "*It can only love deeply. Be grateful for it and for all the bittersweet lessons of your desire.*"

Careful not to break it, Jo replaced the Cheerio in the jar and returned it to its shelf. For a moment she let herself consider her mother's foretelling wisdom while she ran her finger along the length of the trim. Jo shut the closet door and looked around for anything that might change things. She found nothing. Suddenly lost in the void of her own life, Joanna grew increasingly angry—angry with her mother for dying—angry with Beth's husband for calling—angry with herself for her longings. Jo turned on the radio hoping for an immediate distraction. What she got instead was Paul Anka's classic, 'You Are My Destiny'. Resigned to her own, Jo hovered close to the radio listening to the words. When the song was over, she abruptly snapped the radio off. She'd *heard* enough—*had* enough—and certainly *hurt* enough for one day.

For a while Joanna paced restlessly around the room, inching ever closer to the window with the view of Beth's bedroom. Her eyes were drawn reluctantly up to its light, then down to the heart long ago carved into the sill of the old wooden frame. Beside it was the small Cracker Jack toy she'd left there—the silly plastic elephant that always stopped safely at the edge. Joanna picked it up by its string and watched the cowardly thing, along with her own fate, dangle hopelessly in the balance. She called her impassioned resentments up from the depths of her soul and with all her might, hurled them back at Gods that brought her to this place.

"Shit! Fuck! Piss!"

Granted, they weren't the most eloquent words ever uttered but they were the only ones Joanna Cameron could think of. Loosely translated, they meant she felt helpless. Frightened. Lost.

Chapter 9

The week had flown by leaving little time or energy for Joanna to dwell on any misgivings about her upcoming plans with Beth. A grueling second week of hard physical labor and long hours left Jo thoroughly exhausted yet gratified in a way she hadn't felt in many years. Working with Steve brought back memories of the years she'd spent working alongside her father and brother. The smell of raw lumber had slowly reawakened her senses to her roots, reminding her just how much she'd left behind when she set out to conquer the boardrooms of Madison Avenue.

After packing up the last of their tools, Joanna waited off to the side while Steve talked with the elderly widow whose antiquated kitchen they'd just renovated as best her modest budget would allow.

As Mrs. Rubin clung to Steve's arm it wasn't hard to see that the poor woman was more terrified than excited by all the modern gadgetry they'd just installed. Jo marveled at Steve's reassuring kindness as he walked the woman slowly around the room, painstakingly explaining all the new appliances, yet again. He even took the time to jot down basic reminders. She seemed more appreciative of that small slip of paper than of the remodeled room. Steve sat at Mrs. Rubin's table, attentively stroking her cat while the woman hunted through the contents of several drawers for her checkbook. Steve glanced over at Joanna, fully expecting to see her impatience But this time Jo surprised him—and herself. Instead, she simply smiled back and in that unscripted moment Joanna realized how relaxed she'd become around him. She had never expected to enjoy Steve so much, intending merely to use their arrangement as a convenient distraction from her otherwise complicated life and, more crucially, from her preoccupation with Beth. But after just two short weeks, Jo's stubborn resolve turned out to be no match for the sweetness of his disposition. What had clinched his appeal was a story he'd told her over a thermos of hot coffee one morning. It was about the time he had to part with a worn out pair of work boots—ones he'd grown sentimentally attached to having started up his contracting business in them. Unable to just toss them into the trash, he decided to honor them with a proper Viking funeral. Joanna found herself thoroughly charmed as Steve described how he turned a 12" square of plywood into a miniature raft, complete with masthead and paper sail, then rolled up his pants and standing ankle deep in muck, set the old boots down on the make-shift vessel and let it go. With his head bowed and his hammer across his heart, he watched as the current carried them down river until the pair of loyal comrades drifted into obscurity.

Steve was one of those rare, natural-born storytellers with a gift for capturing all those gloriously rich details that left you wanting to hear more. His powers of observation and unusually keen insights more than compensated for the 10 year difference between them. Joanna found him to be, quite simply, *great company*. He, in turn, was equally grateful for hers. Usually surrounded by types whose conversation centered around tits, ass and whose turn it was to buy the next round of beer, Steve longed for a true sparring partner with the kind of interest she showed. Fortunately this made it even easier than Joanna had expected to keep the focus of their conversations on *his* life rather than her own. Whenever he did probe about anything personal, she became a master at saying much and telling little. Jo had wondered whether Steve realized the difference until one day he casually mentioned an old Indian saying.

"You can't push the river," his grandfather had told him on one of their fishing trips.

She suspected this was Steve's cleverly disguised way of letting her know he knew what she was doing. Though disappointed, he accepted her reluctance, for whatever reason, to share more. For as much as she'd become genuinely fond of him, it was obvious that *his* affection for her had grown far beyond that. Joanna was far and away more beautiful than anyone he'd ever seen swing a hammer, spackle a joint or scale a roof.

Jo was all too aware of Steve's eyes that much of the time followed her everywhere and that it was only a matter of time before she'd have to deal with it. But for now, the closest he'd come to proposing anything more than their reciprocal arrangement provided was to ask her to read his manuscript while he was away. To a man like Steve, Jo understood that sharing himself this way was as intimate an exchange as anything sexual. Ben was still a scholarly mentor and Beth a nurturing maternal figure. In Joanna, Steve had found a real partner—though different in temperament, equal in creative spirit, intensity and grit.

Jo was more than happy to oblige, especially since burying herself in Steve's work would help distract her from her much more dangerous interest in Beth until he returned.

Mrs. Rubin finally found her checkbook. Proud of still being in control of her own finances, she took great pains in writing the check out clearly.

"God bless you my boy. You've been a godsend."

Steve took her hands and held them in his.

"I'm glad you're pleased. I'll be out of town next week. When I get back I'll stop by and see how everything's working."

Mrs. Rubin reached for her purse.

"Please, let me give you a little something extra... you've been so wonderful."

Aware of her struggle to make ends meet on a fixed income, Steve refused.

"How 'bout some home made apple strudel from that new oven of yours?"

The elderly woman turned to Joanna.

"I'll be sure to make enough for you too, dear."

In the beginning Mrs. Rubin made little attempt to hide her misgivings about a woman being in this line of work. This certainly didn't happen in *her* day. At one point she had taken Joanna aside to remind her how important it was to always let a man feel superior. She added her impression that Steve was interested in Joanna '*that way*' and suggested if she hoped to snag him she might keep this in mind.

"It's not everyday you find a man as good in his heart as he is with his hands. He'll make a wonderful husband if you play your cards right."

Jo had smiled through clenched teeth, then quickly picked up the power hammer and spit nails into an exposed beam until the knot in her gut eased.

Steve climbed in behind the wheel of his truck, leaned back against the headrest and looked over at Joanna.

"Thanks for being so patient in there."

"Maybe your easy-going nature is rubbing off on me."

She threw in a warning.

"Don't get too used to it though. I'm sure it'll wear off before you get back."

"I guess it's just in my genes." Supposedly, my granddad was the most easy-going guy in the world. Grandma used to say, "The rain wet 'im and the wind dried 'im."

"Do you even like apple strudel?"

"Not really."

Joanna thought about what Mrs. Rubin said. While her advice may have been misguided, her observation about Steve's heart was certainly true enough.

"What time are you leaving tomorrow?"

"As early as I can drag myself out of bed. I can usually make it in a day if I drive straight through. I promised my mom I'd be there for her birthday on Sunday."

Behind a carefully guarded expression, Joanna's heart still struggled with all the years of family celebrations her own mother had missed. It was a struggle that had never gotten any easier to accept—just easier to hide. Steve interrupted his own whistling.

"Hope I can catch Beth when I drop you off. We haven't seen much of each other these last few weeks. That's unusual for us."

Jo forced herself to sound casual.

"I asked her to model for me… wanna' keep those drawing skills well honed while you're away."

Jo waited anxiously, fully expecting him to be suspicious of her motives. He wasn't.

"That's great. It'll give you guys a chance to get to know each other better."

Jo looked straight ahead in order to avoid his eyes. She'd never said anything about her previous encounters with Beth. As far as he knew this would be their first. She was curious.

"What makes you think us getting to know each other would be a good idea?"

"Not sure… writer's intuition again."

Steve didn't elaborate, leaving Joanna secretly relieved. The rest of the ride consisted of more yawns than conversation. Beth's car was not in her driveway so Steve didn't bother pulling in. For the first time since they'd met, an undeniable awkwardness fell between them. Joanna tried to make it easier.

"Enjoy your visit."

"I always do."

Steve hesitated as if to collect his courage.

"I just wish it hadn't come up just now."

He hoped Joanna would ask why. Quite intentionally, she didn't. Resigned to letting it go, Steve leaned over and hugged her warmly. Jo knew him well enough to know he was disappointed. She was equally certain that when he returned he would be intent on picking up where that embrace left off. For the time being, she reciprocated with an affectionate peck on his cheek. For him it was a kiss that made things better and worse.

"Maybe I'll call you."

"What's the matter? Afraid I'll sneak over to Mrs. Rubin's and run off with the strudel before you get back?"

Steve laughed. Encumbered by much deeper feelings, he accepted Joanna's sweetly coated boundaries.

"Okay… no calls. But you'll see, you'll miss me when I'm gone."

Jo gathered up his manuscript, opened the door and got out. She leaned in through the open window and offered him an unexpected confession.

"Don't let this go to your head, but you're *probably* right."

She felt his eyes follow her up the driveway. When she'd gotten about halfway, he called out to her.

"I expect you to be completely honest with me about my writing."

Without turning around, she called back to him.

"You can count on it."

Jo also knew that when he returned she'd have to be completely honest about some other things as well. Steve called out to her again.

"Enjoy that session with Beth. I'll be curious to know what you think of her."

Joanna could feel herself freeze in place.

"Maybe not honest about *everything*," she thought to herself.

With Jo off working all week, Beth felt safe using her own backyard—providing her chaise didn't face the carriage house. After various commitments and routine chores, she took the opportunity to do a little sunbathing a few hours each afternoon. Initially Beth felt guilty just lying around singing along to that silly 'oldies' radio station while all the other voices in her head told her she ought to be using her days more *constructively.* Days she had fought hard for. But this time guilt wasn't nearly enough to motivate her. While she'd convinced herself that when it came to a little self-indulgence she had 23 years worth of catching up to do, those loosely spent hours were hardly carefree. When the radio wasn't on, Beth found the stillness of her surroundings almost startling. Drifting along on the pool float, she closed her eyes and listened with her heart. Gone were the familiar sounds of backyard horseplay and boisterous splashing. Gone was the sizzle from the barbeque grill and the overlapping voices of her husband and kids that for so long kept her from paying any real attention to her own. Whether she preferred a hot dog or hamburger was the question that silenced all the rest that went unasked—and unanswered—leaving Beth still hungry in a place she could never reach to feed. Now, except for the distant chirping of birds and the occasional jingle of BJ's collar as he scratched behind his ear, the quiet Beth had longed for lay everywhere around her. But solitude can be as much a burden as it is a blessing. When it is born of pleasure and delight, one can actually feel their soul afloat in it. When it is formed of alienation and despair, it can become the darkness in which the soul can easily drown. It was there, in the murky nature of solitude that Joanna's question, 'How do you see yourself?' haunted Beth deeply all week. She found herself looking for answers everywhere—in front of mirrors for the obvious, in old photographs for memories, in people's eyes for their impressions and in the stillness of the night for her own truth. Every once in a while she'd catch fleeting, elusive pieces of herself—pieces she couldn't trust to be there if she turned to look again. More often than not, she saw only a faint outline, a shadowy silhouette, an empty shell. The richness of details remained blurred and largely unaccounted for, if not missing entirely. Beth was determined that by Saturday night her appearance—if not her *essence*—would be more dimensional, more vibrant, more alive. Resorting to whatever shortcuts she had available to her, she counted on the counterfeit glow of a summer tan and some new color highlights to do the trick. Her hairdresser had been suggesting it for years but she'd always rejected the idea. This week when she went in for a haircut, she'd told him she was ready. He'd asked her what it was that finally changed her mind, but she was at an honest loss to explain. Pleased and inspired by the change, Beth found herself doing some spontaneous window-shopping afterwards.

"What would 'The Dangerous Beth Garrison' model in?" she asked herself as she entered one particular store. Unsure, Beth eagerly collected armfuls of unfamiliar styles from the racks. But behind the dressing room door, one thing looked more ridiculous on than the last. She stood in front of the full-length mirror, defeated. She'd felt like a clown in absolutely everything she'd tried on.

"Why don't I just wear a pointy hat and a blinking red nose?"

Weary from the strain of trying to be someone she was not, Beth quickly redressed and hurried from the shop leaving everything she's tried on behind. She would find something in her own closet and stop this ridiculous obsessing. Of one thing, Beth was certain—a suntan, a haircut and new highlights do not a *new woman* make.

Though sporadically awakened by the glints of sunlight that filtered in past the drawn curtains, Joanna managed to sleep through most of Saturday. After a week of hard physical labor she was desperate to get some much needed rest before her sketching session later that night. Beth, on the other hand, had planned an intentionally full day for herself hoping to avoid a nervous breakdown or last minute change of heart. She'd made sure to leave only enough time to come home, shower and change into something appropriate. What Beth hadn't counted on was that choosing something '*appropriate*' turned out to be more hellish of an ordeal than anything she could have imagined. Joanna would be staring at her for hours. What kind of impression did she want to make? What did she want Joanna to see—to think—to imagine? Did she want Jo to find her attractive—appealing—maybe even provocative, in a strictly '*artistic*' way of course? With time was running out to find the right outfit, Beth tried on and tossed aside practically every article of clothing in her closet. Thoroughly drained before the night had even begun, she collapsed onto the pile of clothes strewn across her bed.

"This is insane" she thought to herself. As frustrated as she was frantic, Beth reached for the closest outfit—a pale yellow cotton tank top with matching drawstring pants—and threw it on. "Who cares what she thinks? This is light! This is comfortable! This is *me*! 'The Dangerous Beth Garrison' can just make other plans!"

A few course brush strokes to her newly highlighted hair, an impatiently applied touch of eye shadow, lipstick and blush and Beth was as ready as she'd ever be. For a moment she stared in disbelief at the disarray, then turned and hurried downstairs putting the whole mess behind her. A moment later she returned, short of breath. In the throes of her ordeal she'd forgotten her wedding band.

For the first time all week Jo bothered to close the pullout couch. Aside from that, she did little to straighten up. Short of her hopeless attraction there was nothing else Jo felt compelled to 'put away'. She'd begun sorting through a pile of art supplies on the floor when Beth knocked tentatively on the door.

"One inexperienced model reporting for duty."

Jo snuck a deep, steadying breath, then got up to greet her.

"Inexperienced but punctual."

She held the door open and Beth stepped inside. Both women worked to conceal the awkwardness that always reformed the first few moments they were in each other's company. Beth smiled shyly and extended a bottle of wine.

"I thought it was the least I could do... since I practically finished yours the other night."

Jo was glad she's listened to her mother's voice and put out some crackers and cheese.

"It wasn't necessary, but thanks."

While Jo opened the bottle, Beth sat down at the kitchen table. Joanna took two glasses from the cabinet and joined her. A smirk spread across Jo's face.

"I see you decided against the turtleneck."

Beth quickly took a sip of wine. Joanna's dreaded scrutiny had begun.

Indeed, Jo noticed everything—the tan, the haircut, the highlights. Beth looked, quite simply, stunning. Jo chose her words carefully.

"Nice look. It's all very… complementary."

Beth's heart sank.

"Ugh" she thought to herself, "what a homogenized description. New kitchen curtains can be *complementary*. The right bathroom accessories can be *complementary*." Beth offered an excuse for making such a lack-luster impression. She glanced down at what, in a moment of panic, she had chosen to wear.

"It's extremely comfortable."

The truth was, Beth looked more captivating tonight than Jo had ever seen her. So captivating that she could barely take her eyes off the woman. Beth quickly dismissed the 'token' compliment.

"Everything looks good with a tan."

Joanna couldn't afford to dwell on Beth's appearance. She pushed the plate with the cheese and crackers closer and excused the sparse offerings.

"I'm sorry I didn't get a chance to pick anything else up. Steve and I worked late every night this week."

Beth's stomach was in a knot.

"This is fine. I'm not terribly hungry anyway."

Her eyes wandered over to the wall covered with the sketches Joanna had done of Steve. He wasn't Beth's most comfortable topic of late but the drawings did offer a reasonably safe place to start a conversation. She couldn't go on avoiding her jealousy forever.

"How's your arrangement working out?"

Joanna tossed a cube of cheese into her mouth.

"Great, actually. I don't know which I've been enjoying more… all the physical labor or his company."

While Beth tried to conceal her confusing regret at having ever introduced them, Jo was uncharacteristically apologetic.

"I'm sorry I gave you such a hard time in the beginning… you know, about the finger sandwiches and all. By the way, he said to tell you he'd like to get together when he gets back."

Jo pointed to the stack of pages piled on top of the coffee table.

"He asked me to read some of his writing while he's away."

Beth tried to sound enthusiastic. In the case of Steve's talent, it wasn't hard.

"I think you'll be quite impressed."

Beth wondered if they had already slept together. Her jealousy confused her.

"I can't imagine working all day and then modeling for you nights leaves him much time for his creative pursuits."

"Are you implying that I'm monopolizing his time?"

The truth was that Beth was more upset that Steve was monopolizing all of Joanna's time, but of course she couldn't admit that. Not to herself and certainly not to Joanna.

"I'm not implying anything. I just hope he's not allowing himself to lose sight of his dream." She paused. "They can be so hard to hang on to..."

Joanna wondered how much of Beth's remark had to do with the loss of her *own,* but thought it better not to ask. At least not just then. Beth seemed tense enough. Jo reached for another cracker, this time with her bandaged hand.

Beth was glad for a chance to change the subject.

"How's that infection?"

"Almost completely healed."

Both women grew quiet. It was as if each had begun to privately recall the most vulnerable parts of that night and how they led to this one. Joanna stood up and dug her hands deep into the pockets of her jeans.

"What do you say we get started?"

"Fine." Beth rubbed her arms nervously. "Do I stand... sit...?"

From the moment she'd asked Beth to pose Joanna knew exactly what she wanted.

"I want you to hold a single pose. I'll move around and sketch you from different angles."

"Oh great," Beth thought to herself. There would be no side of her hidden from the intensity of Joanna's eyes.

When Jo placed the rocking chair on the modeling platform, Beth immediately conjured up the drab image of Whistler's Mother. By now, any hint of 'The Dangerous Beth Garrison' was all but gone.

"Why don't I put my hair in a bun and get my shawl?," she thought to herself.

As Beth moved beneath the spinning blades of the ceiling fan, Jo was treated to the irresistible nuance of her perfume. She was eager to have Beth positioned as quickly as possible, since any movement always stirred Jo's senses and with them, the molecules of desire. Beth tried to settle into the chair. Awkward and uncertain, she crossed her legs and folded her hands on her lap.

"How's this?"

Joanna pulled no punches.

"Boring as hell."

"I told you, I'm not a very interesting subject."

"Just be more natural… more yourself."

Jo had no idea how difficult a thing she was asking. Beth's body became even more rigid. Joanna struggled to help her feel more relaxed.

"How 'bout some music?"

Beth was grateful that Joanna hadn't given up on her completely.

"I suppose a bit more wine couldn't hurt either."

Jo filled her glass and handed it up to her, then turned on the radio.

"I found this really great oldies station."

Beth was thrilled to have something so simple in common.

"I know! I listen to it all the time." Her expression eased. "Those songs bring back such vivid memories… of my ponytail… my poodle skirt…"

Jo played with the volume.

"I know what you mean. They bring back memories for me too."

Beth looked at her curiously.

"Really? Aren't you a bit too young to be that familiar with that music?"

"I have an older brother who played that stuff all the time. I practically grew up with those lyrics. Those songs are in my blood." Joanna decided to risk being more revealing. "An awful lot of childhood fantasy revolved around that music."

Beth's intrigue was obvious.

"I'd spend hours perfecting my Elvis impersonation. He was my idol." Jo poured herself another glass of wine and elaborated. "Whenever my brother was out I'd sneak into his room, take a wad of his Brillcreme and slick back my hair. Then I'd go put on my favorite jeans and cowboy boots so I'd really look the part. I had this old wooden crate I used as my stage. I'd set the thing up in front of the full-length mirror on his closet door, then grab my make-shift mic… a tin can on the end of a broomstick. Pretending I was surrounded by an audience of swooning girls, I'd thrust my little 10 year old hips and croon away to a stack of Elvis records."

Beth practically squealed with delight.

"How priceless! You must have been absolutely adorable."

"I wasn't going for adorable. I was going for handsome, sexy and irresistible."

"I see…"

By any standard, Jo had certainly grown into a strikingly handsome, sexy and irresistible woman. Beth imagined that Jo knew it, too. She couldn't help but wonder what it felt like to be that sure of herself. She took another sip of wine, never expecting Jo to continue—but she did.

"I made the guitar out of corrugated cardboard and pieces of yarn from my mother's knitting bag. Each string was actually adjustable." Jo smiled, recalling the brilliance of her creation. "The best part was the strap. I'd convinced my mother to let me take it off my schoolbag and hooked it to both ends of the cardboard instrument with paperclips. God, it was brilliant!"

Beth was charmed by Joanna's childhood memory.

"Well I'm sure you and your guitar melted many hearts."

Jo laughed at herself.

"Eventually I applied my talents elsewhere.

"Like creating magnificent bouquets of paper flowers?"

"I suppose… with some award winning ad campaigns in between."

Beth couldn't resist asking.

"And your Elvis fantasy, whatever became of that?"

Joanna was playfully ambiguous.

"I'm sure if I dug down deep enough…"

By now, Jo's little diversionary tactic seemed to have worked like a charm. In the course of her story telling, Beth had become much more relaxed. Thoroughly engrossed in Joanna's childhood confession, she'd unconsciously kicked off her sandals and pulled one leg up, resting her foot on the edge of the seat. Leaning her elbow on the arm of the chair, Beth shifted her weight more comfortably onto its corner. Her other hand was extended casually, her fingers gently holding the wine glass by its rim.

"That's it!" Joanna blurted out.

Beth hadn't even realized that she'd changed positions. She seemed surprised at her new found level of comfort.

Joanna quickly gathered up some art supplies and settled herself at the table.

Beth took a deep breath and tried to block out her last minute temptation to bolt.

She tried focusing on the old Four Seasons song coming from the radio as she sat captive and powerless under Jo's scrutiny. At moments it felt so intense it was almost as if the woman was trespassing across her soul. Yet, as uncomfortable as Beth was, it was also oddly thrilling to feel that vulnerable and that exposed. Despite all she'd gone through to find something to wear, Beth felt completely naked. A slow and penetrating flush spread throughout her body just beneath the surface of her skin.

While her hand moved swiftly across the page, Joanna's eyes pinned Beth under her gaze. Within the context of her brilliant little scheme, she felt a private triumph in *capturing* Beth for an entire night.

Beth wondered what Jo was thinking as she studied her so closely but the artist's expression gave nothing away. Each time Jo looked down at her sketchpad, Beth would steal another glance, trying to imagine what the rest of this woman's life was like. Eventually, Jo stood up and repositioned her chair. As she prepared to start on her next sketch, Beth interrupted.

"Am I allowed to talk?"

Jo recalled insisting on Steve's silence.

"Sure."

Beth let her eyes wander slowly around the room while the rest of her body remained perfectly still. The interior of the carriage house had gone through several changes over the years but it never felt anything like this. The space itself seemed to breathe differently than it had with any other tenant living there. There were art supplies and artwork everywhere. Alongside boxes of pens, charcoals and pastels, paintbrushes in empty coffee cans lined the kitchen counter. A very expensive looking camera and several canisters of film sat on top of a stack of sketchpads. A large roll of canvas lay up against the wall waiting to be stretched onto various size frames. An old painting easel Jo had salvaged from a renovated attic stood in the corner beside a makeshift sculpting pedestal. On top of it sat a mound of clay under a damp cloth. Replacing the stagnant mildew of just 2 weeks ago, the smell of paint thinner and workable fixative now swirled in the air. While Joanna rummaged through her box of pastels, Beth closed her eyes and inhaled deeply. The intoxicating mix thrilled and saddened her at the same time. She was overjoyed that after all these years the carriage house was finally being used in the way she'd first imagined it—a space where the spirit was free to create. She was sad because it still wasn't *her* doing it. Beth glanced over at Joanna's duffle bag, a cruel, bittersweet reminder that all of it would soon be over. All of it would soon be gone; this summer—this woman—this intensity. Just like the dream Beth had for herself. For the first time in a long time she allowed herself to remember. It was the old, weathered carriage house out back that the recently married Beth Garrison fell most in love with when, in the Spring of 1962, she and her husband relocated from the Midwest to this quaint little town just outside of Amherst so that he could accept a faculty position in the English department of the nearby university. Surely the main house, a four bedroom turn of the century Victorian jewel with its quintessential white picket fence, was itself enough to make any young bride swoon—or so pitched the real estate broker eager for a bid. But from the moment Beth wandered off, out to the carriage house by herself and stood alone in that sun drenched room, she felt instantly drawn in by its energy, certain that within its walls she would be free to explore and express the depths of her own. There by the window, with a small heart and initials carved into its old wooden sill, is where she would place her piano—where she imagined herself playing and composing for hours on end, lost in the ivory smoothness of her own evolving dreams while Ben, in the company of fellow academians, pursued his own. Little did Beth realize how illusive *her* dreams would become. Year after year, how forbidding life would make it for her to have her solitude and the music of her own soul. She faced the carriage house everyday from the kitchen window, consumed by endless household chores. It was only 87 steps away from the back porch but it would take her more than 23 years to find herself once again in its divine light—23 years to finally cross the threshold of her own deeply rooted habits of always putting the needs of her family first. As wife and mother, Beth had mastered the deadly arts of compromise, conformity and numbing concealment. She fought through the melancholy.

"I like what you've done to the place."

Joanna naturally assumed Beth was making reference to the mess.

"Thanks. I'll give you the name of my decorator."

"No, really. The room has a wonderful energy. It feels as if a real artist lives here."

Jo took a more thoughtful look around. For the first time, she saw what Beth did.

"Yeah, I suppose it does..."

Though she quickly resumed sketching, Beth's comment had crept under her skin. Her mind wandered back to her loft in the city. She had deliberately chosen the unfinished, open space so that she could be free to create on any scale without the restrictions of a more conventional apartment. The irony was that the professional success that provided the means to afford such a space also robbed her of the raw, creative passion she had hoped to express there.

The boldly original dreams she once pursued with little more than a wild and daring heart had somehow evolved into more conventional goals pursued by calculated office politics and hard won promotions. The space she had purchased to flaunt her untamed creative spirit became a space where everything inexplicably matched. Joanna's home had become a designer's showcase rather than an artist's studio. Gradually, any evidence of raw energy was scrapped or sacrificed to the strict codes of *good design* and impeccable taste. Even the area of the loft she'd allocated as her actual 'work-space' was neat, precise and woefully confined, strictly prohibiting the sloppiness inherent in any real artistic exploration. Indeed, the very kind of mess that surrounded her here—the very kind of mess she had made in her family's attic as a wildly spirited child filled with the power and excitement of her own creativity. Without being aware of it, this odd and imperfect atmosphere allowed Joanna to once again immerse herself in the exhilarating, unruly business of self-discovery. In these last 2 weeks, she had touched more of herself than she had in years. The uncharacteristic mess that surrounded her was proof. This realization spurred by Beth's comment reassured and then frightened her.

Beth had absolutely no idea of the impact her observation had on Jo's heart. Still lost in her own newly awakened yearnings, she let herself remember out loud.

"This carriage house was supposed to be my private music room. In those early years, my piano was in here."

Joanna stopped sketching. She looked up, hoping Beth would continue.

"Why don't we take a break?"

Beth stepped down off the platform and in trance-like steps crossed over to the other side of the room. She closed her eyes as if to bring it all back.

"It was right here, in this corner." Standing beside the couch, her voice filled with a renewed sense of joy. "Have you noticed how gloriously the morning sun pours in through this particular window and how the mystery of the moonlight drenches the room?" Beth didn't wait for Joanna to answer. She turned and stared out through the window into the yard. The air seemed unusually still. For as much as her eyes could take in, not a leaf or petal moved. It was almost as though everything in the universe had stopped to listen as she gathered the courage to tell her story. "Back in the late 30's, a doctor and his wife purchased the property at auction. Apparently it hadn't been occupied for years and was pretty run down. They told us how they'd fallen in love with the place and devoted themselves to restoring the main house to its original splendor. They had this carriage house converted into living quarters for their groundskeeper. When they sold us the place, there was the most exquisite garden back here." Beth's tone became noticeably more wistful. "I wish you could have seen it. It was such a lovely view from this window. You could tell the man took such pride in caring for it. It was absolutely enchanting. Gazing out onto that garden always delighted me." Beth drew a long, regretful breath. "I don't know how I ever let them rip it all out and put in that pool. The boys were young and it just seemed like the practical thing to do."

Jo sensed the depth of Beth's regret.

"I'm sure it had its advantages on hot summer days. Kids tend to prefer splashing around in a pool than tiptoeing through the tulips."

Beth smiled reflectively.

"I suppose."

She turned away from the window and stared at the corner where her piano had been.

"When we bought the place, I was most excited about this carriage house. I pictured myself spending endless hours in here playing my heart out."

Her thoughts drifted. Jo deliberately said nothing, hoping Beth would continue on her own. She did.

"Ben and I had an understanding. He knew I didn't want to start a family so soon. It wasn't at all what I had imagined for myself back then. Those years were so filled with promise and I was so filled with dreams."

Joanna lowered the radio. Encouraged by Jo's apparent interest, Beth went on.

"I was going to be a concert pianist. It was what I prepared for all my life. It was what I lived for. It was who I was. Until I became somebody else… someone's wife and much too soon… someone's mother." Beth's voice dropped with the weight of her sacrifice. "I've always suspected that my son Daniel was conceived in this room. I'd been in the carriage house for days and nights on end, rehearsing for a final audition with the Boston Symphony. I'd completely ignored Ben for weeks in order to prepare. In those days, hard as it is to even remember them now, music was an obsession. Once I became immersed in playing, my need for anything else in life would simply fall away. I'd forget to eat, sleep and, much too casually, I'd forget my husband too." Beth sat down on the couch and stared at her own hands. "This one afternoon, Ben fixed me a lunch and brought it over. It was such a thoughtful thing to do, but the last thing in the world I wanted was to be disturbed. I thanked him and asked that he just leave the tray." Beth played with her wedding band. "All these years later, I can still remember the look in his eyes. He was so hurt… so dejected. I knew he was hoping I'd take a break and invite him to stay awhile. I could feel his loneliness… his longing… his jealousy. Though he'd never let himself admit it, Ben always saw my music as some kind of rival for my devotion. He needed to believe that he, not *it,* was the one great love of my life." Beth paused to confront the truth. "I suppose there were times when even I had wished that too, if only for his sake." Beth struggled to reconcile her past as she now relived it. "I let him make love to me that afternoon. There was a cot over on that wall. I remember telling myself that in a little while it would be over. Ben would go away feeling better and I could get back to my playing feeling a little less guilty."

She put her fingers to her lips as if to hold back the largeness of her confession. "As it turned out, I'd given up much more than that half hour. I'd given away my life's dream." For the first time, Beth looked directly into Joanna's eyes as if wanting to be held accountable for all that she had given up. "I learned I was pregnant on the same day I heard I'd been offered the position with the Symphony. Only then, of course, their concert schedule would have been much too grueling in the later months of my pregnancy… not to mention how impossible it would have been once I'd given birth. Things were very different back then. Abortion was never an option. The decision was virtually made *for* me."

The sheer pain of her recollection propelled Beth to her feet and back over to the window through which she once derived so much pleasure and inspiration. Joanna had remained discreetly silent. She watched as Beth ran her finger across the heart and initials in the old window frame.

"Have you noticed the carving here?"

Jo pushed back on her chair.

"Yeah, I have."

Beth continued to stare at the heart.

"I've often wondered about it…"

Her thoughts seemed to drift as if searching for some long forgotten memory. She turned and looked at Jo.

"Have you ever done that? Loved someone deeply enough to carve your initials into a heart with theirs."

"I once took a pocket knife and scratched my 5th grade teacher's name into my arm. Does that count?"

Beth grimaced.

"That sounds more masochistic than romantic."

"It was... especially since she had a very long name and it was definitely a case of unrequited love."

Beth could not help but smile. She tried to console Joanna's 10-year-old heart.

"I'm sure that's only because she hadn't caught your Elvis impersonation."

Jo appreciated Beth's concern for any 'deeper' scarring she might have endured.

"What about *you*?"

Beth turned her eyes back to the heart on the windowsill. Her voice grew wistful.

"I suppose I've had my share of suitors... but no, no-one worthy of carvings... or mutilations. Maybe I just got tired of hoping and settled for an embossed seal on a marriage license." She searched Joanna's eyes. "That sounds horrible, doesn't it?"

"No. Just painfully honest."

Beth was eager to distance herself from what she had just revealed.

"After I found out I was pregnant, we moved the piano into the living room. With a baby on the way, we needed the extra income that renting the carriage house to students of the university brought in."

She leaned against the wall, staring at the space her piano once filled.

"From that day on, my dream just became more and more illusive until eventually, the answer to all my silent 'what ifs?' became 'who cares?'"

It was obvious Joanna didn't know what to say. Beth walked back and joined her at the kitchen table. She poured herself another glass of wine and took a sip.

"In what I've always considered to be one of the great ironies of my life, the child I conceived that afternoon turned out to have the same passion for music that I was forced to give up in order to raise him. What was I supposed to do with that, except pour all the dreams I had for my own life into *his*. Danny was so gifted and so loveable, it was impossible to be bitter about what I'd given up." Beth's eyes filled with anguish. "When he died, I lost more than my son... more than my prodigy. It was as though I was robbed of myself all over again. Nineteen years of sacrifice had been in vain. Now, neither mother nor son would ever get to become all we were meant to be. This time, the loss was devastating. Despite the fact I still had Adam and Ben, all that was left was emptiness and with it came the deepest sense of grief and longing I'd ever known. There were days it was so great I was sure it wound consume me."

Joanna had gotten her answer and she understood it all too well. The sense of loss. The sense of longing. She needed to reassure Beth as much as she needed to reassure herself. Jo kept her voice soft.

"Seems to me you've come a long way in three years."

Beth smiled as sincerely as her heart would allow.

"Contrary to how it may seem, I'm still barely taking it one day at a time." Beth suddenly felt self-conscious. "I don't know why I'm telling you all this. You must think I've been miserable most of my life."

Joanna saw no point in being polite.

"*Have* you been?"

The straight-forward question caught Beth off guard. She was afraid to hear her own answer.

"I still have so much to be grateful for."

"That isn't what I asked."

"I know..."

Beth looked away. She was not at all surprised that Jo didn't accept her answer. The truth was, Beth was counting on it and this time she was more truthful.

"*Miserable* is such a harsh word. I think more like '*unfulfilled*'."

"What would be the difference?"

"Degree."

Joanna considered Beth's carefully measured response.

"In other words, feeling unfulfilled is the more well-mannered version of feeling downright miserable so you'd be less inclined to do anything like, let's say, spill your guts and force your family to deal with it?"

"I never looked at it quite that way, but yes, I suppose so." Beth took a moment to confront the complexity of her feelings more honestly. "The truth is I love my husband and my son completely... but it's always been with an *incomplete* heart."

Joanna was moved by the depth and courage of Beth's insight.

"It can't be easy... trying to be true to your own life without destroying everyone else's."

The toll of that compromise showed on Beth's face.

"No, more often than not it hasn't been easy at all."

"Can I ask you a personal question?"

Beth braced herself, then nodded.

"If you felt like you'd already sacrificed so much..."

Beth finished Joanna's question.

"Why did I have a second child?"

She didn't answer right away, no longer trusting her reasons for doing anything.

"My father died very suddenly. We were extremely close and I missed him terribly. Ben convinced me that bringing a new life into the world would help me heal."

"Did it?"

"It helped me stay busy. Is that the same thing?"

Preferring to be kind this time, Jo declined a straight answer. Beth understood her silence.

"No, I didn't think so either. But by then the dye was cast. I'd become a fulltime wife and mother. As time went on I just adapted to whatever those roles required." Beth's mind seemed to wander. "Sometimes I think I've adapted *too* well. Whatever I once imagined my true calling in life to be simply got lost along the way. Raising a family doesn't leave too much time to dwell on that sort of thing."

"So… the other night when I said you seemed to be a *natural* at it… the parenting thing…I guess I was way off base."

"You wouldn't have been the first to be fooled." Despite her pain, Beth became wistful. "It's a funny thing about raising kids. If you really do it right, they get you asking some rather profound questions about life. The trouble is that raising them never leaves you any time to really process all the revelations that come from it."

Joanna couldn't fathom the frustration.

"So what do you do with all those revelations you've collected along the way?"

"I don't know what other women do, but I've kept a scrapbook in my heart. I call it, '*The Beth That Might Have Been*'. Every page begins with, 'if only…'."

"Does your husband know about the scrapbook?"

Beth unconsciously began playing with her wedding band.

"Somewhere in him he's always known. It's never been one of his favorite topics, though. To be perfectly honest, it hasn't been one of mine either. Whatever conversations I've instigated over the years never seemed to resolve anything or help me reclaim what I'd let slip away. Besides, I really don't blame Ben for my lack of fulfillment. I blame myself. I was the one who compromised my own dream."

Joanna didn't say anything. Beth mistook her silence.

"I wouldn't expect you to understand. From the little you've told me, it doesn't sound like you've ever let anything come between you and your dreams."

Jo looked around the room in which she had grown so comfortable.

"That may be so of my *goals*. The truth is I lost sight of my 'dream' a long time ago."

Beth's eyes urged her to continue.

"For a long time I thought they were the same thing. By the time I realized the difference I was in too deep to make the switch. It would have meant walking away from a lucrative career and sacrificing all the material comforts that came with it. I wasn't prepared to give it all up and become a struggling artist."

"Why do you assume it would have been a struggle?"

Jo didn't have to think about it. She'd known the truth for a long time.

"Because deep in my guts I wanted it to be. I *needed* it to be. I guess I still do." She picked up a piece of charcoal and rolled it between her fingers. "What you said before about this space looking like an artist lived here… I knew what you meant and it really troubled me. The place I call home doesn't look or feel anything like this. I grew up picturing myself totally unencumbered, surrounded by the kinds of things that *served* my imagination, not *stifled* it. When you said what you said, I suddenly realized my life has become much more contrived than I ever wanted it to be."

Beth listened carefully to everything Joanna said and didn't say.

"Why do you suppose you let that happen?"

"Probably because there's always been more at stake following my heart than a trail of money. *Executing* my talents were a whole lot safer than *exploring* them. So instead of using them to make my life noble, I settled for making it credible. The truth is, I was never willing to accept the responsibility that came with my '*gift*'. I've never really known what I was meant to do with it. That kind of pursuit takes blind faith and the kind of courage I was afraid to discover I didn't have. Then one day it just became more frightening not to ever know for sure." Jo mused at the futility of her own resistance. "Trust me when I say I put off finding out for as long as I could. I had this awful hunch that standing in the light would be even more terrifying than being lost in the dark."

Beth's eyes offered more than a kind acknowledgement, one that came from first hand experience.

"Is that why you've been so reluctant to talk about your life?"

"Even if I gave you the facts, that wouldn't necessarily explain the truth."

"So skip all the facts and give me the truth."

"I've never been a big fan of doing that." Jo's expression grew mischievous. "The truth always destroys my hiding places."

Beth laughed at Jo's unexpected answer.

"Yes, the truth does have a tendency to do that."

Joanna feared that her confession sounded absurd, but absurdity was something Beth understood well.

"So what do these hiding places of yours look like?"

Joanna became playfully guarded.

"They're all brilliantly coordinated and impeccably furnished."

Beth's amusement did not blur her insight.

"I suppose you count on all that perfection and order to make you feel safe."

Beth knew that Joanna's silence was her concession. Without pushing Jo for more, she offered something from her own life.

"Sometimes the most dangerous place to be is where it feels the safest. Trust me, I've learned that the hard way. I'm afraid I've lived much too safely for much too long. It's ironic, don't you think? I had every obstacle imaginable. You've had none. Yet so far neither of us seems to feel anything even *close* to fulfilled."

Joanna was beginning to feel more than a bit uneasy. Beth was much too good at extracting more information than Jo had ever intended to share.

"Why don't we get back to sketching?"

Fearing she too had divulged too much, Beth was quick to agree. She resumed her position and Jo settled back behind her pad. With a lot to think about, both women retreated into their respective solitude. This time Beth adjusted more easily to having Joanna's eyes on her. She tried to imagine Jo as a little girl, pretending to be Elvis Presley. The notion tickled her though her expression remained unchanged. She found herself wondering what the rest of Joanna's childhood was like—her experiences with boys—her coming of age. The woman sketching her was such a mystery and contradiction in so many ways. Yet, sitting there, posing for this stranger who had come into her life in the most unusual of ways at the most unlikely of times, Beth felt oddly closer to herself that she'd ever been before. In such a short amount of time, Joanna had held up so many mirrors and asked so many important questions. She'd broken down so many walls and stirred up so many dormant emotions. For now, Beth sat there perfectly still, perfectly relaxed and perfectly content to have Joanna's eye on her for the rest of her life.

Once she'd begun sketching again Joanna felt as though she was drawing as much from memory as from the woman seated in front of her. It was almost as if the lines were already there somewhere in her heart, waiting to be transferred onto paper. It was impossible to say how much time had elapsed and were it not for the radio DJ announcing the midnight hour, neither woman would have believed how quickly the night had passed. Jo put the finishing strokes on her sketch and turned the page. She was surprised to find it the last in her pad.

"Looks like I'm out of paper."

Beth stepped down from the modeling platform.

"Guess that's our cue to call it a night."

While Beth went to the bathroom, Jo tore the sketches from her pad and taped them to the wall. The instant she emerged from the alcove, Beth froze. Mesmerized, she stared at the dozens of studies as though she'd never seem her own likeness before. Jo had captured more than the woman who was there. She'd somehow managed to capture the woman who was *not.* If Beth's sense of longing had ever been visible to the naked eye, it was there in those drawings. The validation pierced her heart. Without uttering a word, Beth crossed the room, reached out and gently placed her hand against the paper itself. Moving her fingers, she felt as if she were touching the image of her own soul. Joanna was anxious for Beth's impression.

"What do you think?"

"I don't know what I think. I haven't gotten past how I *feel.*"

Beth's eyes met the eyes Joanna had drawn. The reckoning was nearly overwhelming. She covered her mouth to hold back a gasp.

"They're portraits of my longing. The me that isn't there. How could you have captured something so intangible?"

Joanna's accomplishment defied explanation. She wondered if this was the true purpose of her gift—the purpose that had eluded and betrayed her, granting success but never fulfillment. For the first time in Joanna's adult life, she felt complete. She fought back tears and the impulse to take Beth into her arms.

"I'm glad you're pleased."

"I don't know if 'pleased' is how I'd describe it. It's not easy to see your own pain that clearly."

"I'm sorry."

"Don't be. It's actually a relief after so many years of feeling invisible."

A penetrating sense of loss swept over her. Beth's eyes looked hollow.

They came to rest on the piece of cloth Jo had draped over her makeshift sculpting pedestal. As she wandered over her mind wandered even further.

"My boys used to love playing with clay. I'd always sit with them and make something too. Of course it wasn't any good. I just liked the way it felt in my hands… so incredibly sensual." Beth grew shy. She laughed, hoping to distance herself from that last remark. "I made a wonderful ashtray though. It fetched quite a sum at our yard sale."

Jo laughed and threw the cloth aside.

"Go on, knock yourself out."

"No, really… I couldn't."

Jo ignored her. She filled a bowl with water and carried it over so Beth could moisten the clay.

"Have some fun while I clean up."

After hesitating for a moment, Beth removed her wedding band and placed it on the kitchen table. She soaked her hands and then ran her fingers across the slippery smooth surface, slowly stroking and kneading every inch. Beth closed her eyes.

"God, it's been such a long time. I'd forgotten how good this feels."

As her inhibition slowly dissolved, a deep sense of pleasure spread across Beth's face. Joanna pretended to be focused on cleaning up. With her own thoughts safely hidden in the lyrics of the oldies classic, "The Way You Look Tonight," Jo observed Beth closely. Lost in her own pleasure, Beth looked even more beautiful than ever. The song couldn't have been more fitting if 'The Gods' themselves had taken possession of the radio station. Joanna came and stood beside her. Despite being watched, Beth continued to stroke the fullness of the clay. Without permission or apology Jo came right out and asked.

"Why didn't you go with your husband this summer?"

For an instant, Beth's hands froze in place. She had no reason to lie.

"I had a lot of important things I needed to sort out. I needed time alone." She was careful not to direct her eyes away from the clay. "Why did you leave the city?"

"Pretty much for the same reason."

Beth resumed her tactilely gratifying play.

"Why Amherst?"

"I'd been sent up here on an assignment a few years back." Jo hesitated. She'd never admitted this to anyone. "Something happened to me while I was here. I don't know what it was, but after I got home, nothing in my life made sense anymore. Everything began to fall apart." That was when the disturbing dream had started, but Jo had no intention of talking about that. "Since this is where it all started to unravel, it felt like the right place to try and sort it all out."

Jo's explanation spurred a million questions. Beth asked the one least personal and most likely to be answered.

"What kind of an assignment was it?"

"The agency was shooting a commercial for a new cleaning product... one of those lame 'on-location' spots where we interviewed shoppers coming out of the supermarket." Jo suddenly realized something. "Matter of fact, it was the same mall where you and I met."

There was something about the coincidence that made Beth's heart race.

"When exactly was this?"

"I really don't remember."

"I need you to think. I *have* to know."

Beth's tone was too urgent to ignore. Without understanding, Joanna made an earnest attempt to put the pieces of that awful summer back together.

"Let's see... I guess this July would make it 3 years now. Why?"

Beth stepped back from the clay. She was obviously shaken by Jo's calculation. Joanna held out a towel for her to wipe her hands.

"Are you okay?"

"I'm not sure..."

She looked into Joanna's eyes as if seeing a ghost.

"My God, I think that was you!"

"What the hell you're talking about?"

Fearing that even the slightest emotion would surely overtake her, Beth struggled to keep her recall succinct.

"The day of Danny's funeral the traffic was diverted off the route to the cemetery... having something to do with construction. The detour put us on the road that runs past the mall you're talking about. The procession had come to a stop at the traffic light at the entrance to the parking lot. From behind the darkened window of the limousine, I noticed a camera crew of some kind. I remember watching the woman who was obviously in charge. She seemed so involved, so consumed by her work. I remember thinking how much I wished I could be a part of her life, if only for that day. How desperately I wanted to be *anyone* else... doing *anything* else... rather than having to bury my child."

Joanna stood rigid, listening intently as Beth continued to describe her memory.

"For reasons I never understood, the woman suddenly stopped what she was doing, turned and looked in the direction of my limo. I remember being stunned. I realized she couldn't possibly see me through the tinted glass... especially from so far away. It was as if somehow she had read my mind. My heart began to pound in my chest. Eventually the light changed and the traffic began to move. I don't know why, but I turned around and through the rear window I could see her standing there, straining to follow the procession as it drove off."

Beth looked deep into Joanna's eyes, pleading for confirmation.

"Was that *you*?"

Jo was too unnerved by Beth's account to answer right away. However reluctant to acknowledge her side of what Beth had so eerily described, Joanna's own memory of that day remained hauntingly vivid; the heat—the humidity—the fact that absolutely nothing had gone right with the shoot that entire morning. She remembered being in the throes of yet another argument with the cameraman when, in the midst of her frustration, a sudden indefinable sadness came over her. Something unexplainable drew her attention to the road as surely as though someone had called her name. Just outside the entrance of the parking lot, a funeral procession was stopped at the light. Her eyes became riveted to the limousine directly behind the hearse. Fighting every impulse to race over to the car, Jo could do nothing but watch and wait. When the procession began to move she recalled feeling a sense of despair unlike anything she'd ever known—a loss more profound than even the death of her own mother. Though Jo had not uttered a word, the truth was apparent on her face. Beth had her answer.

"It *was* you, wasn't it?"

Joanna felt sick. She could only nod. For a moment the two women stood there looking at each other, both equally dumbfounded. Beth struggled to contain the beginnings of a chill that threatened to spread and shake her to her core.

"My God, what are the chances we would meet again at that exact location?"

Those kinds of odds were too overwhelming for Joanna to calculate, much less comprehend. Folding her arms against her trembling body, Beth somehow found her voice.

"Jo, I need to ask you something. What made you turn around that morning?"

Joanna's eyes held none of her uncertainty back.

"I don't know."

Jo's struggle was apparent. Beth reached out and touched her arm.

"It's okay, really. I've begun to accept that there are some things that defy explanation. Like my connection to Arthur, *this* would also be one of them."

At least for the moment, Jo took refuge in Beth's philosophy. It seemed as useful and useless as anything else. Still half dazed, Beth looked back at Joanna's sketches. Though she shared nothing of what she was thinking, it struck her that their paths had crossed on two of the most emotionally traumatic days of her life—the day she had to bury her son and the day she had chosen to part with her husband. Beth wondered how much more of her life would have to fall away to finally come to know the woman in those drawings. She wondered, too, what role Joanna was destined to play in that process. Thoroughly exhausted by all that the evening had unexpectedly exposed, Beth replaced the cloth that had covered the clay. Now, without a tinted window between them and only inches apart, Joanna took a long and penetrating look at the woman in the limousine that morning. Beth smiled back at her sweetly—silently acknowledging their mysterious connection—*then* and *now*.

"I should be going."

"Thanks for posing."

"I'm flattered you asked."

Beth took one last look at the renderings.

"I don't know what to say. You're incredibly talented."

"Why don't you take them with you?"

"No. This is where I belong… here in the carriage house… with you."

Beth was immediately embarrassed by her slip.

"I meant, *they* belong here… the *drawings*."

But the drawings *were* her. Even more than she was herself. Beth was confused and exhausted.

"Please forgive me. I obviously don't know *what* I'm saying or *what* I mean. It's late. I'm very tired."

Joanna made it easy for her.

"You don't have to explain."

The two worked to negotiate a reasonably safe parting which at that point was by looking anywhere but directly into each other's eyes. Beth was within inches of the door when Jo noticed the wedding band on the table. How she wished for the power to make it, and the reality it represented, disappear. She picked it up and held it out.

"You forgot something."

Beth smiled. Instead of putting it back on, she simply slipped the ring in her pocket.

"Thank you..." her voice dropped to something almost shy, "for reminding me about so many things I'd forgotten..."

Trying hard not to read anything into the remark, Jo opened the screen door and Beth stepped out into the night. Without warning, she turned and kissed Joanna on her cheek.

"Good night."

Jo held her heart in check and accepted the platonic gesture graciously. Though it was the last thing in the world she wanted, she had no choice but to let Beth go.

"Good night."

Beth gazed up at the stars. The sky seemed as deep as it did endless. As she crossed the yard she wondered if Joanna was still watching. She wouldn't dare turn around. What if she *was*? What if she *wasn't*?

With Beth gone Joanna felt as if her whole world had come to an unbearable and crushing halt. Left floundering at the edge of her unspoken desires, she sat down at the table and stared across the room at the renderings. They were all Jo had left of the night. The hours and the woman had come and gone much too quickly and though she had learned even more than she could reconcile, it didn't feel like nearly enough. Her clever little modeling scheme now over, Jo found Beth Garrison more illusive than ever. Left behind was Beth's empty wine glass, the faint mark of her lipstick still on its rim. For a long aching moment Joanna stared at it, taunted by the impossibility of ever knowing those lips against her own. Resigned to her punishing fate, she shut the radio, turned off the lights and collapsed onto the couch. Even as a child Jo was never afraid of the dark, but lying there in the stillness, she felt herself undeniably spooked by the bizarre coincidence on the day of Danny's funeral. Stranger yet was the chance meeting at that same location just a few weeks ago. None of this was the sort of thing Joanna embraced easily. As if her deepening feelings toward Beth weren't enough, there was just one too many things about this situation that were apparently beyond her control. First thing tomorrow she would call Ruby and find out how much longer it would be before she could have her car back.

Beth entered her house feeling like a shell-shocked soldier returning from a distant war. Every part of her had been tested. Simply surviving the night left her exhilarated but no less dazed. She dragged herself upstairs and looked at all the clothing she'd left strewn across her bed. In one sweeping motion she pushed the whole pile off onto the floor. She had neither the strength nor the inclination to deal with any of it tonight. She kicked off her shoes and looked around the room. Every inch was so familiar, so ingrained. Yet sitting on the edge of her mattress in this most intimate of settings Beth felt oddly out of place. Quite by habit, her eyes traveled the same path they always took and came to rest on the same thing they always did—the wedding picture that sat atop her husband's dresser. How she wished she could remember that bride more clearly. From across the room and across the years, the young woman in that picture seemed so vague and so forgotten. Beth shifted her weight and removed her wedding ring from her pants pocket. Studying the simple gold band closely, she wondered why she hadn't immediately put it back on when Joanna handed it to her. Beth looked down at her own hand as if seeing her bare ring finger for the first time. A small amount of clay had dried in her cuticle. She smiled and closed her eyes hoping to recapture the intense sensation of *it* and Joanna standing only inches away. Beth was lost in the overpowering memory of both when the telephone on the night table suddenly rang. She dove for it instantly, unable to imagine who would be calling her past midnight unless it was bad news.

"Hello?"

Ben sounded relieved to finally get her in.

"I tried you a couple of times earlier tonight but you were out. I left two messages. Didn't you get them?"

Beth hadn't even bothered to look.

"I'm sorry. I never checked the machine."

"I didn't wake you, did I?"

For a moment, the familiar sound of her husband's voice scrambled Beth's senses. It felt like he was calling from his office on campus to let her know he was on his way home. She felt undeniably relieved that wasn't the case.

"No, I was about to turn in."

She did muse at his timing though. In a quiet act of rebellion, Beth placed her wedding band on the dresser rather than slip it back on her hand. She tried disguising her resentment for the intrusion of his call.

"You scared me."

"I'm sorry. I just needed to hear your voice." Ben maneuvered to common ground. "Have you heard from Adam?"

"Yes. I've gotten 3 postcards and an actual letter complete with orange Cheetos stains." Beth intentionally stirred a bit of sarcasm in with the facts. "That must have been some bribe you offered him before you left."

Ben chuckled and she left her insinuation at that.

"Anyway, it sounds like he's having a wonderful summer so far. He sends you his love."

"Did you read that between the stains?"

"No, he actually *wrote* it."

Ben sounded pleased to be remembered—at least by somebody.

"I just posted a letter to him the other day. He should get it soon." There was an obvious hesitation in her husband's voice. "How's the summer going for you?"

Beth answered as honestly as she could.

"I have my moments but I'm okay Ben, I really am. I needed to be here even more than I realized."

Beth sensed her husband's disappointment.

"So where were you tonight?"

Though harmless, his inquiry disturbed her. It had always been Beth's natural inclination to share everything with him. She'd spent the better part of their marriage trying to engage him in meaningful dialogue—the kind that would strengthen their relationship and deepen their understanding of each other. But this was different. This night was intensely personal. It did not belong to *them.* It belonged to *her* exclusively, like the summer belonged to *her*. Still, she saw no reason to lie.

"I spent some time with Joanna… the woman who's been staying in the carriage house."

"Right, Joanna. You haven't really said much about her. How's that arrangement going?"

The sheer mention of Jo's name made Beth's heart pound. She stood up and with the receiver pressed to her ear, pulled the extension cord over to the window that looked out onto the backyard. Staring down at the darkened carriage house, Beth lost all sense of time. When she didn't answer, Ben came to his own conclusion.

"I'll assume if you spent the whole evening together, her company must be pleasant enough."

Beth found herself privately amused by her husband's comment. Of all the words that might describe what it felt like to be in Jo's company, '*pleasant*' would never be one of them. A cool summer breeze was '*pleasant*'. Being around Joanna was like being swept up in gale-force winds. There was nothing in her life that Beth could cling to for shelter of safety. Each encounter left her more exposed and more vulnerable than the last. The difference between '*pleasant*' and Joanna was daunting, but since she had absolutely no intention of explaining any of this to Ben, she simply agreed and shifted the focus back to him.

"The arrangement is working out just fine. So tell me about you. How are your lectures going? How are your folks?"

Grateful that she asked, Ben immediately launched into a detailed narrative of his entire week. As he talked on and on, Beth shut the bedroom light and, shifting the receiver from ear to ear, managed to undress. She pulled back the bed sheet and rested her head on her pillow, letting her husband's voice and the darkness wash over her. She lay there listening patiently, with her eyes closed, her thighs partly spread and her thoughts a million miles away.

Chapter 10

With morning came the drenching rain of childhood disappointments—the kind that forced cancellation of long awaited field trips, backyard camp-outs and tie-breaking little league games. It rained hard against the shingled roofs and pouting hearts of the two grown women whose heightened intrigue now strained dismally at the soaking reality that would keep them apart. It was different for each of them. Beth knew only that she craved more of what had stirred and scared her the night before. For Joanna, the longing had a name and knowing it made it all the more impossible to ignore. Each had said goodnight secretly counting on the assurance of the next day when the sunshine and backyard would provide a casual backdrop and easy access to more of each other's company. Instead, the first storm of summer took the women entirely by surprise, robbing them of their next clandestine meeting. It never occurred to either of them that their unspoken expectations might not be met simply because of how badly both had wanted it.

Each had awakened to the claps of thunder and wrestled with her disappointment differently. Beth lay in bed staring up at the ceiling, surrendering herself to the rhythmic patter of the rain and rich fragrance of the foliage made even sweeter by the dampness. She convinced herself that such uninterrupted time was a much needed, well-deserved luxury. Beth was quite accustomed to making the best of things. Her life depended on it. Joanna's did not. She bolted from the couch and began pacing the length of the carriage house. Unlike Beth, she derived no inspiration whatsoever from the glistening lushness of her surroundings. Instead, she stared out through the screen door, blind to everything but the slate gray sky and the puddles in the grass where the earth could not drink in the steady downpour quickly enough. Resigned to their segregated fate, the women sat at their separate tables staring out into their separate space. Long ago there was a time in each of their lives when summer vacations presented a string of endless tomorrows. But now, in a summer when each of its days was precious and numbered, just a single hour lost felt like an entire lifetime wasted and unlived—an awareness that added heavily to the weight of their mugs as each nursed her morning coffee.

After a half-hearted breakfast Jo stretched several new canvases, hoping to use the staple gun to displace some of her frustration. Upstairs in her bedroom, Beth sought similar refuge in hanging all the clothing she'd left out from the night before. She took painstaking care, fussing with collars that didn't need straightening and fastening buttons ordinarily left open. She considered—then dismissed—the idea of reorganizing her dresser drawers. After all, this was the summer she'd let herself come undone, not try to make her life tidier. Eventually she decided on another luxury—a long, unhurried shower.

Standing beneath the pelting liquid massage, Beth became oddly aware of her own body. For so many years she had been consumed only by what it felt like to *survive* in her own skin. She'd all by forsaken any intimacy with her flesh itself. The sensation of her own touch awakened and frightened her. Like a virgin nervously following the unknown path of her own desire, Beth put down the soap and allow her bare hands to travel unencumbered. The tips of her fingers spread out like a band of renegades, trespassing across forbidden boundaries, deep into unmarked territory. Her body responded immediately as she had hoped and dreaded it might. She made the water hotter, relying on the steam of the shower to somehow disguise the unmistakable heat that rose from within. She wondered if the flushed body that now tingled beneath her own touch belonged to the woman whose portrait Joanna had captured—the woman whose longing Jo had excavated and exposed. For a few exquisite moments the steamy cloak served Beth's modesty well, until in her melting, she recalled the intensity of Joanna's eyes. An uncontrollable weakness swept through her body and with it came panic. Beth nervously rinsed away the remaining soap, stepped out of the tub and quickly toweled off. As the steamy fog dissipated on its surface, she purposely avoided eye contact with the mirror until she'd secured the belt of her terry robe. Even then, Beth focused strictly on the job of blow-drying her hair, not daring to confront any traces of urgency that might have remained in her eyes. She hesitated in the doorway of the bathroom fearing the intimacy of her unmade bed that threatened to seduce her into opening her robe and surrendering the weight of her blocked desire to the soft beckoning creases of its sheets. For the last two weeks Beth had slept alone in that bed. Not alone in the absence of her husband but alone in the greater absence of herself. Over the years the voice of her abandoned pleasure had become more and more obscure until finally its unanswered pleas called to her no more. But this morning its imploring whisper had returned and she ached in the place between her legs. The memory of her own passion frightened her. Despite temptation, she could not bring herself to give in. Fearing that her body would only want more of what she had taught herself to live without, Beth now clutched at the collar of her robe bringing the sides even closer together. She quickly made the bed, fussing compulsively with the ruffles of the pillow shams. Feeling only slightly less vulnerable in its finished perfection, she dressed and hurried downstairs hoping to leave this newly awakened and menacing part of herself behind.

It was never Beth's intention to go immediately to her piano, but that was where her unattended passion led her. She opened its lid, revealing the ivory path that once lead to her salvation. With her body still aching for release, Beth held nothing back. Her fingers were gentle at first, then reckless—demanding from the keys what she would not let them have of her flesh. Like the first time, she had not planned the notes she began to play. The piece, as unfinished as the woman who wrote it, was born of her mourning in the days that followed her son's death. The haunting melody had leapt up from the depths of Beth's despair; more powerful in its origin than anything she had ever composed. The notes had come to her, one after another, like familiar touchstones in an impossibly darkened room—each leading her closer to the source of a vague but healing light. Over and over she had followed those notes and over and over she would come to that same crossing. There, the inspiration would always end as abruptly as it had begun leaving her abandoned by the mystery that seemed to sustain her existence. Beth expected this time would be no different, but she was wrong. This time the path did not end where it always had. Her spirit surged as more and more notes opened up before her. She did not stop to write them down, trusting she would not forget what she had instantly memorized in her heart. She knew that these new chords were a precarious bridge she was now meant to cross. Her trembling fingers poised on the waiting keys, she trained her eyes on Arthur's vase and Joanna's flowers. In the intricate details of both, Beth found her courage and made her choice. She closed her eyes and started over from the beginning. Sensing these newest notes were somehow leading her closer to the woman in Joanna's drawings, Beth played them more passionately than anything she'd ever composed in her life. Uncertain she'd ever find more of her way, she knew only that this piece and that pilgrimage had inexplicably become one. Beth wept as she continued to worship before the sacred instrument that gave substance and glory to her otherwise unanswered prayers—purging herself—preparing herself—for all that lie ahead.

"Ellie, Ellie… I'm so sorry… so sorry…"

Joanna could feel the strain of her own voice pushing against the back of her throat until a bolt of lightening cracked open the sky, releasing her from her fitful dream. She woke in a pool of sweat, her heart pounding in her chest. Pages of Steve's manuscript lay scattered all around her. By mid afternoon, with little hope of spending any part of this day outside with Beth, Jo had decided to try and lose herself in his writing. Somewhere along the way she'd obviously dozed off. As Jo fought her way through the gripping images of her reoccurring dream, the distant sound of the piano pulled her back. Listening intently to the impassioned melody coming from the house, Jo remembered what Steve had said.

"When you hear Beth play, you'll understand."

Still shaken from the disquieting remnants of her dream, Joanna moved to the window that offered the closest exposure to the house. She leaned against the wall and closed her eyes to concentrate more fully on the music coming from Beth's living room and, most unmistakably, from the depth of the woman's soul. Though Joanna knew practically nothing about classical music the melody felt vaguely familiar—like a young child taken from the place of its first language, then returned years later, reuniting with the comforting sound of its cadence, if no longer the exact meaning of each word. The richness of the notes deepened as they moved through the dampened air. The longer she listened the more content Joanna grew with the thought of forsaking all connection to the world beyond the Garrison's backyard. Another bolt of thunder shook Jo to her senses, replacing the serenity of her seclusion with danger and fear. Suddenly panicked, she lunged for the phone on the kitchen wall. Just the sound of the dial tone was soothing enough, assuring her access to the outside world. In an instinctive act of self-preservation and for the first time since she'd left the city, Joanna made calls to her family. She deliberately kept the conversation brief, assuring them and herself of her safety and well being. Though she'd promised to keep in touch, Joanna didn't feel like talking to friends and most deliberately, she did not call Gayle. Somewhat reassured by the phone contact, Joanna again stretched out on the couch as Beth's playing continued to fill the carriage house. She stared out into space, emptying herself of everything but the solace of the each note. She had counted on the music to go on indefinitely, providing her a secret pathway to Beth's heart. Then without warning, the playing stopped and the intolerable space between them fell silent. As the day and the rain wore tediously on, the deprivation felt merciless. With so much to sort out in her own life, all Joanna could think about was the woman who looked back at her in the drawings. Jo paced like a caged animal, replaying the terms of their arrangement in her head: as soon as it became uncomfortable for either of them, she would leave—no questions asked. Since Beth was apparently taking this day in stride, there was no point in kidding herself. The attraction was purely one sided. Joanna rifled bitterly through her duffle bag for Ruby's number. Getting her car back meant getting on with her life. Convinced the sooner the better, she dialed his number.

"Come on, come on" she mumbled impatiently under her breath while the phone continued to ring.

When Ruby finally picked up, Joanna deliberately disconnected them. She refused to think about what she'd just done, or for that matter, what she was about to do. With the receiver still in her hand, Jo dialed the operator for assistance. After she scribbled the number down, she was tempted to get the number of a local shrink as well so she could have her head examined. For the next few minutes, Joanna wrestled with her better judgment. Knowing from the start it was a losing battle, she dialed the number. Jo could actually hear the phone ringing across the yard. The more times it rang, the more ridiculous she felt. She was about to hang up when Beth answered. The sound of Beth's voice brought Jo immediate relief, quickly followed by emotional chaos. She tried to sound casual .

"Hey, it's me…" Jo felt like an idiot. "Listen… about your piano playing…"

Beth assumed Jo was calling to complain about the noise.

"I'm terribly sorry. I haven't played in such a long time. I'd forgotten how much further the sound carries in the rain. I apologize if it disturbed you."

"On the contrary… I was sorry you stopped."

Beth's voice curled into something small and shy.

"I had no idea I had an audience."

"What was that you were playing anyway?"

Beth talked openly about the piece and all that it meant. She described how mysteriously it had first come to her and how impossible it had become to take any further—until today. Joanna had listened carefully.

"We're even then. I'm now in as much awe of *your* talent as you claim to be of mine."

Beth was glad Jo couldn't see her blush. Protected by the distance between them, she stared out through the kitchen window at the carriage house. Jo offered more.

"Steve was right. He said I'd understand a lot more when I heard you play. Now that I have, I don't know how you ever let yourself give it all up."

Beth didn't respond. She couldn't. It was one thing to know in her own heart just how much she'd sacrificed. It was quite another to know that someone else recognized it as well. Joanna stated the obvious.

"You certainly pour your heart out."

Beth was embarrassed by her own intensity.

"Yes well, it just seemed like a perfect day for that sort of thing. You know, purging one's soul."

"The rain certainly ruined *my* plans." Jo lied about her own expectations. "I was hoping to explore more of the area. Maybe even try some landscape painting. Don't ask me why… I've never had the urge before."

Beth's heart came alive.

"If it's inspiration you're looking for, I know the most glorious spot!"

Joanna waited, careful not to seem too eager. Just as she'd hoped, Beth offered an invitation.

"Why don't I take you there one day? You can bring your art supplies and I'll pack us a picnic lunch."

A secretly triumphant Jo was anxious to nail things down.

"Great! When?"

Beth panicked. She was not accustomed to being able to follow through on the things she most wanted for herself. *Wanting* something was one thing. Actually *getting* it was almost too terrifying a notion to fully grasp. In the space between the two Beth had learned, by necessity, to use the discarded remnants of her own desire to weave an otherwise enviable looking life. It was a heavily weighted garment laden with compromise, but it was one she'd grown quite used to wearing with quiet grace. Needing to buy herself more time to adjust to Joanna's enthusiasm, Beth over-exaggerated the demands of her schedule.

"I'll have to get back to you. As it turns out, I have a number of commitments this week."

Jo tried to conceal her disappointment.

"Fine… whenever."

Joanna had hoped Beth would suggest something more immediate, like a cup of coffee later that afternoon, but based on her own insecurity, Beth did not. Jo had no choice but to let it go—especially since she was obviously the only one doing any pining. Though their brief conversation wasn't all Jo had wanted, at least she'd heard Beth's voice and certainly a picnic with Beth was something she could now look forward to.

"Don't forget, let me know when you're free."

Beth was torn. Why not just set a date? Surely she wanted the time with Joanna as badly as Jo wanted it with her. Her fear was just too great.

"I will."

Jo groped for a way to close a conversation she didn't want to end.

"Okay then, thanks for the free concert."

"You're welcome. Consider it a 'thank you' for the portraits."

There was an awkward pause and Jo couldn't stop hoping Beth would come up with a last minute invitation. Instead, Beth simply suggested that each try to make the best of an admittedly dreary day. Nothing could have been harder for either of them.

Joanna forced herself to go back to Steve's manuscript. Beth rinsed the dishes in the sink in order to stand in front of the window that faced the carriage house. She needed time to process Jo's unexpected phone call and her own ambiguity. Her fear disappointed her. As Beth continued to stare through the rain-drenched glass, she could see a hint of her own reflection staring back. 'The Dangerous Beth Garrison' was shaking her head. She was not at all pleased.

The storm that had come and ruined Sunday passed quickly, giving way to a glorious Monday morning. It was barely daybreak when Joanna woke and decided she'd take her first swim in the Garrison's pool. The morning sun hung low, its light glinting over the tops of trees, hinting at the coming of a perfect summer's day. Ordinarily not one to be drawn in by the splendor of nature, today even Joanna lingered appreciatively on the step of the carriage house. She tossed her work shirt onto a lounge and wearing only a pair of cotton briefs, dove headfirst off the side. The water, not yet warmed by the sun or heater, stung her skin like a brazen lover biting into flesh. After several laps, Joanna stopped to catch her breath. Her nipples hardened as she stood up in the shallow water and exposed her body to the crisp morning air. She pushed her long black hair back away from her face and began her laps again.

Somewhere in the recesses of her sleep the sound of splashing water seeped into Beth's dream. Her senses scrambled to make sense of what had awakened her. As the sun poured in through the bedroom window, the realization became as stark as the rays of light. Beth lay there listening to the rhythm of the parting water, her breathing synchronized with Joanna's strokes. Unable to resist, Beth threw on a shirt and moved tentatively toward the window. Standing sheepishly off to the side, she parted the curtain just enough to glance down into her own backyard. Unaware that she was being watched,

Jo continued to swim the length of the pool, her strong body and long arms cutting gracefully through the water. It wasn't until she'd pulled herself up on the ladder at the far end that Beth realized Joanna was topless. Despite how spying made her feel, Beth found it impossible to look away. Gradually her discomfort gave way to an even more unsettling pleasure as she held the unsuspecting woman in her gaze. Jo strode back to the lounge on which she'd tossed her shirt. She used it now to towel off. As Joanna rubbed the dampened garment over her glistening body, Beth found herself mesmerized. She was grateful for the distance that made it impossible to capture Joanna's beauty in any greater detail, afraid that a closer look would only impale her deeper. Frightened by her unpredictable feelings, Beth grasped nervously for more familiar memories. Grainy 8 MM movies of her growing sons taken in that same backyard played behind her eyes as she struggled to reconcile those images with the one before her. Who was this enigmatic stranger who had replaced her family—this commanding, half naked woman who had invaded her yard? Her carriage house? Her life? Glancing up, Joanna caught Beth's movement behind the curtained window. Jo called up to her.

"Morning! Hope I didn't wake you."

Flustered, Beth called back.

"I've been up for a while. I was just opening the window wider."

If Jo was at all suspicious of Beth's excuse, she didn't let on.

"Great morning, isn't it?"

"Exquisite."

Beth was hoping to leave their exchange at that and slink away from the window, but Joanna had other ideas.

"Perfect day for that picnic! What do ya' say?"

Beth was emphatic.

"Sorry. I can't today."

She had no idea why not other than the fact that once again she'd panicked. She was not used to wanting anything so badly. It was absolutely terrifying. At the mercy of her own longing, Jo was not above pleading.

"C'mon, why not?"

"There's too many things I have to do around the house today."

Jo slung her dampened shirt over her shoulder and put her hands on her hips.

"Save it all for the next rainy day."

Beth began chewing nervously on her lip.

"I've already put them off too long."

Trying to imagine exactly what those things were, Beth couldn't think of a single one.

Joanna could not bear another day of frustration. She had absolutely no idea where she would go or what she would do, but after she showered she was dead set on getting off the Garrison's property. She tried sounding a lot less disappointed than she felt.

"Suit yourself."

Jo turned and headed for the carriage house. As impossible as it felt, Beth forced herself away from the window. She undressed and leaned her body against her bedroom wall praying that the familiar pattern of the wallpaper would brand her bare skin and remind her of her once familiar life. But suddenly all that was '*familiar*' no longer felt like enough. As frightened as Beth was to be in Joanna's company, it had become impossible to live without. She would call out to Joanna and say she'd changed her mind. Her heart pounding with anticipation, Beth pulled back the curtain and leaned out of her window. But it was too late. Jo was already gone. Brokenhearted, Beth sat at the foot of her bed trying to convince herself it was for the best.

As a result of her ridiculous excuse, Beth was forced to spend this perfectly exquisite day locked inside her house pretending to be busy while 'The Dangerous Beth Garrison' took great pleasure berating her at every turn. "Coward! Loser! Fool!" her alter ego mocked, making it nearly impossible for Beth to forgive herself. By late afternoon she was all but beaten down. When the gravel in the driveway crunched under the weight of the Jeep Beth wouldn't permit herself to hope that Joanna might stop by. "Why in the world *would* she?" Beth thought to herself as she heard the screen door to the carriage house slam shut. "I'm hopeless. Pathetically, permanently hopeless."

As the sun began to set, the wasted radiance of the day gradually thinned to a pale orange glow. By eight o'clock Beth was ready to call it an early lackluster end to a miserably lackluster day. With any luck, she'd find something boring enough on TV to lull her to sleep. She was wiping down the kitchen counter when the telephone rang. Sure it was Ben, she was less than enthusiastic. The voice on the other end jolted her.

"Hi..."

Never expecting it to be Joanna, Beth's heart began to race. She started with the safest question she could think of.

"How was your day?"

"Fine."

It was obvious from her tone that Jo wasn't interested in chatting. Beth wasn't surprised. What did she expect after robbing them of what could have been a gloriously wonderful day. Jo got right to the point. She asked if she could do her laundry.

The request caught Beth off guard. What did this mean? Was Joanna expecting to spend time together between cycles or did she intend to go back to the carriage house? Unclear which she herself would prefer, Beth didn't dare ask.

Jo sensed her hesitation.

"If it's a problem…"

"No, it's fine. Just come over."

"Thanks."

Jo hung up abruptly. Since Joanna would be on her doorstep momentarily, there was no time for Beth to prepare herself other than to practice breathing normally. At the sound of Jo's footsteps on the porch, Beth braced herself and opened the kitchen door. She was shocked by Joanna's appearance. Her skin looked pasty, her eyes bloodshot and glassy.

"My God, you look awful!"

Joanna walked past her and dropped the bag full of laundry on the floor.

"Thanks. I won't count on your vote in tonight's beauty pageant."

Beth ignored Jo's sarcasm. She was genuinely concerned.

"No, I mean it. What's wrong?"

"Don't know. Round about noon I started feeling like crap. It's been downhill from there. My head's killing me, I've got chills and everything aches."

Beth instinctively reached out and pressed her hand against Joanna's forehead.

"You've got temperature."

Joanna brushed off Beth's concern.

"I'll take a couple of aspirin. I'll be fine in the morning. Just point me in the direction of your washing machine."

Jo bent to pick up her laundry and the room began to spin. She braced herself against the wall. Beth's concern deepened.

"Are you alright?"

"Just a little dizzy. It comes and goes."

"Okay, that does it. You're too sick to be alone. The guestroom's a mess so I'll make up Adam's bed. You're spending tonight here where I can keep an eye on you. If you're not feeling better by tomorrow, I'm taking you to my doctor."

Joanna scoffed at the notion.

"No way to the first part and definitely no way to the second!"

She made an attempt to collect her laundry bag and leave.

"This was a bad idea. I'll come back some other time."

Beth blocked the door with her body.

"I'm afraid you and your laundry are both staying the night."

She spoke in the unmistakable tone of a mother who knew best. It was a tone that Joanna recognized and challenged for much of the first sixteen years of her life. It was a tone she had often missed terribly, but had learned to live without.

"Thanks, but no thanks."

"Sorry. This isn't open for debate."

"You can't keep me here against my will."

Beth folded her arms.

"Oh but I can and *will*!" Beth pointed to the hall. "I mean it Joanna! March up those steps right now!"

Joanna tried a less confrontational approach.

"You might catch whatever it is I have."

Beth pushed her towards the first step.

"Sweetie, I've survived the last twenty-one years catching the run-off of other people's lives. What makes you think your puny little virus is the one that's gonna' do me in?"

By now, Joanna was feeling much too weak to be fighting a losing battle.

"Okay, okay."

"I'll give you something to put on."

"Don't bother. I sleep in the raw."

"Not tonight with fever and chills."

"Then I'll sleep in what I'm wearing."

"Fine. If you want to sleep in clothing soaked with perspiration, be my guest. Adam's room is straight ahead. I'll go get some aspirin while you wash up. The bathroom is the third door on the right. There's a set of fresh towels on the rack."

Jo shuffled off down the hall, complaining under her breath.

Beth changed the sheets on her son's bed and opened the windows to let in some fresh air. Joanna was much too sick for the chill of an air conditioner. When she returned, Beth held out two aspirin and a glass of water.

"I'll leave the rest of the bottle on Adam's desk. It you get up in the middle of the night take two more. They'll help break the fever."

Jo swallowed the pills, then followed them up with a begrudging nod.

Beth pulled back the top sheet and motioned for Joanna to climb in.

"I want you to wake me if you need anything in the middle of the night. My room's just down the hall."

The idea of spending the night in such close proximity to Beth's bedroom only added to Jo's present misery. In one last stand, she tried to sound as threatening as she could before dropping the weight of her throbbing head onto Adam's pillow.

"You have no idea how lucky you are that I feel like shit."

"Oh, and why is that?" Beth asked casually as she pulled the sheet up under Joanna's chin.

Jo was barely capable of more than a glare.

Beth couldn't help but be amused at Joanna's stubborn fight to the finish. By force of motherly habit, she checked for a draft before turning off the light.

"Now try and get some sleep. Let's hope you feel better enough to hate me in the morning."

Beth closed the door and shook her head.

Alone in the dark, Joanna fought through her fatigue. She shot forward, tore off her clothes and threw them defiantly against the door.

"I sleep in the raw, damn it! Chills or not!"

Beth collapsed at her kitchen table and stared at the bag of laundry. With Jo finally in bed, Beth now had the rest of the evening to dwell on the consequences of her victory. In the most supreme of ironies the woman she'd consciously avoided all day was now just a few feet away from her bedroom door. What if Joanna woke in the middle of the night not feeling well? And if she slept through the night, what would the morning bring? The only way to cope with the possibility of either was to keep busy. Under the circumstance, Joanna's laundry was a reasonable place to start. Beth carried the bag down to the basement. Trying not to think about whose clothes they were, she turned the bag upside down, deliberately shoving the mass of shirts and jeans into the drum all at once. Beth felt unexplainable relief in not having to handle anything more personal in nature. She added the detergent and slammed the door. While the washer spun through its cycle, Beth retreated back upstairs and tried to distract herself with mindless chores. Eventually she curled up in a club chair, nursed a glass of iced tea and flipped through a magazine she'd already read. Beth was relieved not to hear any sounds coming from upstairs. Joanna had obviously fallen off to sleep, making her a much more manageable threat. With her eyes drifting back and forth between Joanna's flowers and the many family photographs that surrounded it, Beth found it nearly impossible to comprehend how so much of her focus had shifted in just a few short weeks. Certain that the wash was done, she returned to the basement and switched the load into the dryer. The evening was much too beautiful to wait out the next cycle indoors. She took what remained of her drink out onto the front porch and dropped into an old wicker lounge. She sank back against the soft cushions, mesmerized by the star-filled sky. Her heart formed a million questions of the night, launching them one by one into the vast galaxy that stretched out before her. At the end of a day that already felt like a thousand years long, Beth sat like a small, weary creature nestled beneath its powerful realm waiting for some profound message to drop into her lap and for yet another load of laundry in her life to dry. She was certain it would be the laundry that would come first. It always did.

Beth pulled Jo's clothing from the dryer and emptied it into the laundry basket. As she began to sort and fold each garment, she recognized the white sleeveless shirt. Overcome by the vivid memory of Jo's early morning swim and the way she used it to dry herself off, Beth clutched it against her own cheek. Its radiating warmth evoked a much deeper heat that rose from her own flesh to meet it. Beth would not let herself consider the meaning of her impulse as she nervously folded the shirt and placed it into Joanna's laundry bag. Disturbed by her behavior, Beth worked as fast as she could, removing and folding one garment after another, hoping that the momentum of her pace would get her through the rest of the woman's belongings without further incident. It did—until she came to a pair of Joanna's jeans. By the paint stain over the left knee Beth knew it was the same pair Jo had on the night she'd posed—the night Jo had exposed her intense longing that now began to reform in the stagnant basement air. Beth froze in recognition of the power Joanna had over her. Enslaved by it, she carried the woman's jeans over to the nearby ironing board. Her heart pounded wildly as she positioned the garment as if Joanna herself had mounted and straddled the board, laying her body back down against the length of it. Too ashamed to watch herself do what she was about to, Beth closed her eyes before letting her hands travel slowly up and down each leg, along the inseam and across the crotch. She felt the remaining heat from the dryer as she rubbed the palm of her hand back and forth, stroking the warm fabric from the tip of the fly to its base. Consumed by desire, Beth groped for the zipper, undid it and thrust her hand inside, her fingers ravaging every inch. She became terrified by her need to feel the places that had touched the most intimate parts of Joanna's body—terrified that doing so brought such intoxicating arousal to her own.

In those few unspeakable moments, Beth recognized absolutely nothing of herself. Never had she known such a raw and demanding lust or the kind of rapture and excitement it produced. Fearing for her life, Beth yanked her hand away and drew back as if protecting herself from the flames of a raging fire that threatened to destroy her entire world.

"What am I doing? What am I doing?"

She repeated the question over and over until the torment in her voice awakened her. Exhausted by the toll of the day, she had unknowingly dozed off. Beth frantically examined her hands, then reached for her iced tea and nervously wrapped them around the cold glass. She pressed the glass against her perspiring forehead and waited for the torrid images to recede.

"My God" she moaned under her breath.

Beth gulped the rest of her drink including what little remained of the ice cubes. With the task of actually having to retrieve Joanna's laundry still looming she hesitated at the top of the basement steps, not yet able to face the scene of her secret crime.

"It was just a dream," she tried to reassure herself as she slowly and cautiously descended.

Deliberately averting her eyes from the ironing board, Beth gathered the courage to swing open the dryer door. For an instant, the escaping heat was a stark a reminder of her shameful transgression. She reached into the machine and in one sweeping motion emptied the entire bin, nervously shoving the whole load straight into the canvas bag. Beth was not about to sort and fold any of it. She pulled the drawstring to seal off the contents, carried the bag upstairs and placed it at the far end of the hall and safely out of sight. Still trembling, Beth hurried to the small bathroom just off the kitchen to throw some cold water on her face. Barricaded behind its locked door, she tried to forgive herself for her dream and for the creamy wetness that had collected between her legs.

"Take a good look," a menacing voice commanded from deep inside her head before she could flush the sticky tissue. "Take a good look at your hunger. This is how dangerous it *can* be!"

Beth stood there unable to escape the evidence of her arousal until the sudden ring of the phone interrupted her mounting panic. Fearing the repeated ring would wake Joanna, Beth raced from the bathroom. Certainly a phone conversation—even with the devil—was the lesser of those two evils. Praying the call was not from Ben, she raised the receiver to her ear.

"Hello?"

On rare occasions, Beth's prayers were actually answered. This was one of those times when the universe knew it had given her all she could handle for the moment.

"Well hellooooo there stranger," came the unmistakably singsong voice on the other end.

Beth couldn't decide whether to laugh or cry at just whom the universe saw fit to send her instead. It was the notorious Rheeta Montgomery—formerly Reeta Gordon—Rhita Singer before that—and originally Rita Nussbaum, Beth's old college roommate. Over the course of four therapists, each more expensive than the last—three husbands, each richer than the last—and two breast implants, the second larger than the first, the only thing the woman had changed more often than the spelling of her name or the color of her hair was her religion—or as Rheeta preferred to call it, her 'spiritual persuasion'. Born of Jewish faith, she soon grew bored with her heritage the way one grows bored with an old pair of shoes. Denouncing her Judaism, she converted to Catholicism. At the center of this conversion was revenge on her parents and a holy pilgrimage to her jeweler, instructing him to melt down her solid gold star of David and remold it into a crucifix. When wearing it failed to deliver the kind of salvation Rheeta was looking for—mainly a new husband—she became understandably disgruntled with the 'Father, Son and Holy Ghost' and fired their asses—tout suite! To fill the void left by their obvious incompetence and indifference to her prayers, she decided to give her spiritual business to the Dali Lama and his crew with as much thought as she gave when switching general contractors. But inner transformation takes time—time Rheeta didn't have. Desperate for more than just an alignment of her chakrahs, she turned to an eminent plastic surgeon to complete whatever work remained on the temple of her 'soul'—that is to say, having enough liposuction done to enable her to fit into a size four gown in time for the next big society event of the season. Rheeta was one of those women whose search for a meaningful existence went only as far as her busy schedule would allow. There was a brief time, however, when she actually made an earnest attempt to squeeze in private sessions with a self-proclaimed guru between appointments with her hairdresser, aroma therapist, personal trainer and interior decorator. Mistaking a whirlwind shopping spree for a hard soul searching journey, the deeper rewards of spiritual enlightenment continued to elude her. Recently divorced and recently 'lifted', Rheeta was now more *set for life* than ever before. The only thing still missing was the slightest trace of any true happiness. This had become a real drag for Rheeta who preferred not to dwell too much on the whys and wherefores of such a depressing reality. On the upside, her reluctance to examine the incongruous subtleties of her *own* life left her with plenty of time to dabble in the lives of everyone else, and in *Beth's* case Rheeta always managed to pick the worst possible time to do it. Tonight was certainly no exception. Though ambushed and trapped was much closer to how she felt, an ever-polite Beth feigned excitement and delight at the sound of her friend's voice.

"Rheeta, hi… how are you?"

Rheeta detected an unusual shortness in Beth's breathing.

"You sound out of breath. Am I catching you at a bad time?"

"Just finishing up my exercise routine, that's all."

Beth knew that when Rheeta wasn't shopping, she was at the gym. The excuse seemed to have hit a chord.

"Oh honey, tell me about it. It's virtually impossible to keep up with the competition. Why is it that men our age are only interested in chasing twenty year old bimbos? Of course that's not your problem… being as happily married as you are."

Beth remained intentionally quiet.

"So tell me, how *is* the world's only faithful husband?"

"He's in Europe, lecturing at Cambridge this summer."

Rheeta actually gasped.

"Why you silly woman. Why in the world aren't you over there with him?"

"It's a long story."

Indeed, one with an emotional complexity Beth knew her friend would never grasp.

Rheeta didn't ask for more of an explanation and Beth didn't offer any.

"It's so good to hear your voice. When was the last time we spoke?"

"The last time you needed an ear," was what Beth wanted to say, but the sting of the truth was usually lost on Rheeta anyway.

"It's definitely been a while."

"What about Adam? With Ben out of town, I suppose the little man's been left in charge of his mother."

Beth was annoyed by Rheeta's remark, but she let that go as well.

"Actually Adam's away at camp for the summer."

"Why you little devil you. That means you have the whole summer to yourself!"

The mischievous innuendo was so far from the truth of it that Beth couldn't respond in time to thwart Rheeta's declaration.

"Well I say that calls for a reunion! My next cruise isn't until the end of August, so that leaves plenty of time this summer for a visit. The only day that doesn't work for me is August 7th. I'm meeting with my divorce attorney."

"My God Rheeta, you go through husbands like I go through gallons of ice cream."

"Well, all I can say is there's more to be gained from an empty marriage than an empty container. One fattens your waistline, the other fattens my estate. We can argue the advantages of one versus the other when we're together. Let's set a date!"

Rheeta's quick-witted comparison reminded Beth just how entertaining her friend could actually be. Perhaps an uncomplicated visit from her old college roommate wouldn't be such a bad idea. Maybe Rheeta's silly, mindless company was just what she needed to put some safe and lighthearted moments into her own life. Desperate for anything that would take her mind off Joanna, Beth agreed on Tuesday, July 30th. It was just eight days away. Rheeta would abandon the lavish surroundings of her newly renovated Boston townhouse and '*slum it*' for a few days in the quaint little town of Amherst with her oldest and dearest girlfriend. To hear Rheeta describe it, you'd think she was planning a trip to a little-known theme park called 'Beth's World', to see her favorite animated cartoon character in person.

As she circled the date on her calendar, Beth couldn't be sure if she'd made the right decision. Rheeta's idle and incessant chatter would either be her salvation or the final straw of a full-blown nervous breakdown this summer. Rheeta, on the other hand, had no such second thoughts.

"Oh Bethie, I'm so excited! I can't remember the last time we actually saw each other."

Beth answered honestly.

"It was before Danny died, so it had to be more than three years ago."

The mention of the tragedy caught Rheeta by surprise. The circumstances of other people's lives usually did.

"I remember I was in Europe when it happened. Oh honey, I was so miserable not being able to get back in time for the funeral. You know I wouldn't have missed it for the world..."

Rheeta's excuse sounded more like a conflict of interest between cruising the Mediterranean or returning to the States to attend some gala charity ball.

"I understood."

Beth always did. Even back in college, it was Beth's nature to look for and *find* whatever good there was in a person. In Rheeta's case she'd found someone who, despite her self-absorbed ways, always meant well. The fact that she never quite succeeded managed to alienate most everyone else on campus, but not her ever-forgiving roommate. The truth was, Beth had always recognized Rheeta's limitations. She simply found a way of accepting—even appreciating—Rheeta for exactly who she was. And, who she was 'inside' really hadn't changed much over time. Year after year, Beth would smile as she opened the box of long stem crimson roses that arrived without fail on every birthday since they'd graduated and gone their separate and very different ways. It never mattered that ever since Rheeta knew her, Beth's preference had been a simple bouquet of wild flowers. Rheeta loved crimson roses and always sent what she herself would have wanted to receive. The petty details of other people's tastes and preferences never seemed to register. The enclosed card would always say the same thing: "Happy Birthday to my very best friend in the whole world. Love, Love, Love, 'R'."

Rheeta basked in her friend's forgiveness.

"I honestly can't fathom how you got through that Beth. I tell everyone I meet you're the strongest woman I know."

"I'm sure whatever strength I found came from having to be there for Adam."

"Oh honey, I understand, believe me. I can't imagine what Pierre would do if something were to happen to *me*."

Pierre was Rheeta's miniature poodle. Judging them to be much too time consuming, Rheeta had wisely chosen not to have children of her own. Her marriages produced a growing portfolio, but fortunately no offspring. Beth shuddered to think of the damage Rheeta could have inflicted there. Beth decided she'd spent enough time in the 'Twilight Zone' for one night.

"So, I'll see you a week from tomorrow."

"With bells on, honey!"

"Diamond studded bells, no doubt."

"Would you recognize me in anything less?"

The idea of entertaining Rheeta suddenly felt overwhelming.

"Rhee, just promise you'll keep the sequins to a minimum. The local restaurants don't generally require full length gowns so pack 'light'... whatever that means to you."

"Don't worry honey, I always love my visits to the 'real world' every now and again. Especially when they're with you." Rheetas's voice went up a few octaves. Speaking of the *real world,* how's that hunky woodsman I met at that little Christmas thing you threw a few years back?"

Beth had absolutely no idea who Rheeta was talking about.

"What woodsman? I don't know any woodsman."

"Of course you do. He was wearing a gorgeous lumberjack shirt and tan corduroy pants. I remember he did something or other with wood."

Beth realized Rheeta was talking about Steve.

"He's not a woodsman Rheeta, he's a carpenter."

The distinction was apparently too trivial to matter.

"Now he's someone I wouldn't mind being hammered and screwed by!"

For several reasons, the least of which was dashing Rheeta's hopes, Beth chose not to mention anything about the object of his affection and her angst—Joanna Cameron.

"Yes, he's still around."

Rheeta's voice became shamelessly flirtatious.

"So you see, there *is* a reason to get dressed up."

"Rita Nussbaum, get a grip!"

Rheeta's voice dropped to a quasi-secretive whisper.

"Shhh… someone might hear you! Rita's been running from the law!"

"And all this time I though she was running from herself."

Occasionally, the 'truth' registered.

"I'm going to overlook that nasty, albeit insightful comment and count the days 'til I see you."

Beth appreciated being forgiven so easily. Especially since under the circumstances, she hardly felt in a position to judge her best friend for the inappropriateness of her attractions. Rheeta threw in a reminder.

"Don't expect me anytime before 3:00. I'm not one of those chipper 'morning people'. If it happens before noon, it happens without *me!*" Rheeta squealed with delight. "Oh, I'm so glad I called. My timing was brilliant, don't you think?"

Beth thought about what she was doing the precise moment the phone had rung.

"Yes, absolutely brilliant!"

In the uncertainty of all that remained of the night and her life, Beth attempted a letter to her son at camp. Each fabrication describing her summer thus far sounded more mundane than the last. The truth was quite another story, but nothing she dared share with another living soul—least of all her son. She started over several more times before eventually giving up. Staring at the one remaining page of the pad, a mischievous smile spread across Beth's face as she began to write.

Hi, Honey,

Hope you're having a great time at camp. Everything's just fine and dandy here, so you needn't worry about me. Whoops—sorry, I'm confusing you with dad. Speaking of your father, every time he calls (and he calls a lot more often than I'd like) he sends his love, as do I. Well, that's it for now. Don't forget, your father bribed you to do it, so make sure to write soon.

Miss you both (a little... sometimes...)

Hugs and kisses, Mom

P.S. I forgot to mention that earlier tonight I had my first ever wet dream about another woman! Yep, your friend Joanna, as a matter of fact. I'll spare you the details, but it had me quite worked up—not very motherly at all. Since you had the hots for her too, I'm sure you can understand. Nothing to be concerned about though. I'll make sure to come to my senses by the time you and your father return home.

Beth read over what she'd just written. It made her giggle out loud. Her life in utter turmoil, she was relieved that at least for the moment she could still extract the absurdity of it all. With little else to hope for, she decided to call it a night. Beth locked up and turned off the lights, but not before tearing the frivolous letter into a million pieces and shoving them deep into the garbage. "God how I'd love to mail that off," she thought to herself as she glanced back at the trash. She signaled to BJ to join her, but he appeared content to spend the night downstairs, curled up against the back of the sofa. All things considered, it seemed a safer alternative for herself as well. Brushing aside her fear, she climbed the steps and snuck past Adam's bedroom as quietly as she could. Just as she reached her own, the unmistakable sounds of someone caught in the throes of a terrible nightmare stopped Beth dead in her tracks. She tiptoed back and listened outside her son's door. Joanna's muffled pleas were fraught with torment.

"Ellie please... don't do this... I'm begging you... don't go."

The sound of Jo's suffering tore at Beth's heart. Her conflict felt impossible. The last thing in the world she wanted was to have to wake Joanna and deal with her again tonight. Concerned that a spiking fever might be the cause, Beth felt compelled to look in on her. After all, that was precisely why she'd insisted Jo spend the night. Despite her trepidation, she slowly cracked open the door just wide enough to peek inside. Bathed in moonlight Joanna lay completely naked, sprawled face down across the small single bed. The unexpected sight of the woman's body sent Beth's heart surging up into her throat, all but erasing any recollection she had of her young son ever sleeping there. Her hand froze on the knob as her eyes slowly followed the flow of the crumpled sheet that filled the spaces beneath Joanna's body and between her partially spread thighs. As Jo's nightmare loosened its grip, the splendor of her golden-tanned body drenched in the indigo moonlight continued to hold Beth against her will. She wondered how she would ever set foot in her son's room again and not be haunted by the image. Joanna would have to be on the brink of death before Beth would take another step closer to that bed, much less consider putting her hand anywhere against the woman's flesh to assess the level of her fever. Leaving Joanna to make it through the rest of the night on her own, Beth shut the door and hurried down the hall. Barricaded inside her bedroom, she felt no safer. Dispensing with her usual routine, Beth rifled through her dresser searching for the longest summer nightgown she owned. However foolish, concealing her own body felt like the only thing she could do to protect herself from the dangerous proximity of Joanna's. Beth turned off the light and dove into bed. Clutching the sheet under her chin, she stared into the darkened space trying with all her might to extinguish the burning image of Joanna from her mind. All at once the discomfort she'd felt toward Steve came into alarming focus. Spying on Joanna this morning from her bedroom window—what she'd done to Joanna's jeans in her dream—and now *this*. How many more ways did she need to be hit over the head in one day? Her odd, unexplainable resentment toward him was a simple case of old-fashioned jealousy. Well, maybe not 'simple' and certainly not 'old-fashioned', but no less undeniably true. Her awkwardness around Jo—agonizing over what to wear when she modeled—all of it suddenly made sense. Chewing mercilessly on her lip, Beth covered her eyes hoping to diminish the impact of her clarity. In the darkness she could taste the salt of blood as the sharpness of her realization pierced not just her skin but every conception she'd ever had of herself. Beth sat up and pulled her knees into her chest. She wasn't sure whether she'd need the toilet, but the moment and her stomach cramps seemed to pass. Beth lied back down and forced herself to take slow, deep breaths. After all, there was no real cause for alarm. She'd simply hide her feelings. Absolutely no one else would ever have to know. She would deal with her attraction *privately* the way she'd learned to cope with all her other unfulfilled desires—by pretending they didn't exist. This strategy had served her reasonably well for the last twenty-three years of her life. Surely it would work tomorrow as well. She would wake up, go about her usual morning routine and leave for her volunteer work at the nursing home. Praying that she would be gone before Joanna awakened, Beth would slip a casual, friendly note under her son's door. It would say merely that she was out for the morning and would be returning around one. Other than hoping that Jo was feeling better and suggesting she help herself to anything in the refrigerator, Beth would be careful not to offer anything beyond that—especially taking Joanna to that secluded hideaway for a picnic! There was no way in the world she would ever let that happen now. Steve was due back at the end of the week. Assuming he and Joanna would pick up where they'd left off—presumably in each other's arms, Jo would have little interest in spending any more time with *her*. Torn between relief and disappointment, Beth told herself that Steve's return was for the best. It would force her to face the impossibility of her attraction and focus on Rheeta's upcoming visit instead. Beth was sure that her old college roommate was just the right company at just the right time. Rheeta was simple, superficial and entirely self-absorbed. She could count on Rheeta's incessant chatter to devour her solitude and with it any 'truth' that lurked in its recesses. If Beth could just steer clear of Joanna for the rest of the week, Rheeta was definitely her best shot at survival.

With seemingly no end to this day, Beth lay perfectly still, staring up at the ceiling. She wondered what these last twenty-four hours of her life might have been like had she gone to England with her husband. With all that Beth expected she'd have to deal with in his absence, she never anticipated anything like this. Apparently 'The Dangerous Beth Garrison' was full of surprises.

Chapter 11

It was just past 10 AM when Joanna rolled over and opened her eyes. Despite her fitful night she woke feeling absolutely fine. Whatever bug she'd caught had passed as quickly as it came on. Jo sat on the edge of Adam's bed recalling the events that had landed her there. As her eyes gravitated to the clothing she'd defiantly thrown against the door, Jo noticed a sheet of paper on the floor. She bent down and picked it up. The feminine script had a soothing sweetness to it. Jo realized this was the first time she'd seen Beth's handwriting. It made her smile. Jo's eyes lingered on the strokes of Beth's pen. Her foolish heart wishing for a love letter, Jo read what Beth had actually written.

"Good morning. Hope you're feeling better. I'm volunteering at the nursing home and should be back around one. Feel free to take a long, hot shower in Adam's bathroom. There's a new bar of soap and toothbrush on the sink. I made a fresh pot of coffee and there's some bagels in the freezer. Help yourself. If you need to reach me, the number of the nursing home is on the fridge. Maybe I'll see you later—if you're around. Beth."

She had underlined the words 'maybe' and 'if'. The handwriting on the postscript appeared more erratic, almost as though written hastily by someone on the lamb.

"P.S. I did your laundry. The bag is in the hall downstairs."

Although the note didn't contain the amorous confession she'd hoped for, Jo was almost as pleased to read that Beth was gone and that she was alone in the house. She picked up her clothes and opened the door. At the click of the lock BJ appeared in the doorway of Beth's bedroom. He studied Jo curiously. Stark naked, Jo put her hands on her hips and stared right back at him.

"Don't look at me Fido… this wasn't my idea."

As long as Beth wasn't around Joanna decided to stay and take that hot shower but she had no intentions of sticking around 'til Beth got home. Feeling the rewards of her indulgence, Jo went downstairs to get some fresh clothes from her laundry bag. BJ rose, stretched out his legs and followed after her. As Jo dug through her bag for a t-shirt and pair of shorts, he wandered over to his favorite patch of sunlight and sprawled himself out on the kitchen floor. Jo went back upstairs to finish getting dressed. Much more aware of her surroundings than the night before, she noticed the room opposite Adam's. Its door was conspicuously shut. Jo was sure this had been Danny's room. She stood frozen in her knowledge that the boy was dead. She backed away respectfully and returned to Adam's room where she quickly dressed, collected her wet towel and stripped the bed. By now a clean break felt like the wiser choice than a pot of coffee. In her haste, she'd almost forgotten Beth's note. She swiped it up and read it over. Once again the ordinary message wrapped itself around Jo's heart and once again she felt herself hopelessly drawn in. The note said Beth would not be home for several hours. Just a few feet from the woman's bedroom, Jo fought with herself, knowing that to have a look would only make things worse for her. Ultimately the temptation proved too great. Jo promised herself she would not open a single drawer and look no further than what was out for her eyes to see. Accepting the limits set by her conscience, she left the rolled up sheets at the foot of the stairs and inched closer to the forbidden doorway.

In her frantic determination to leave the house before Joanna awoke, Beth had not bothered to make up the king-size bed. Joanna's sudden brush with its powerful intimacy nearly overwhelmed her. For all the countless bedrooms she had stumbled into, either stoned or drunk on lust, none had ever exposed her to such treacherous depths of desire. Amid the simplicity of the mission style furniture, muted florals and welcoming touches immediately engaged her heart. All at once, everything became both a temptation and a torment for Joanna's eyes. She could do nothing now except follow the winding path they took through the stillness of the room. As its haunting sweetness beckoned Jo deeper into Beth's most personal space, Joanna's secret longing lead her to those objects she ached most to touch—the simple, ordinary things just like Beth's note. Jo let her fingers graze the binding of the library book on the night table, across the telephone receiver and over the smooth, rounded wax of a half melted candle. Her fingers moved lightly through the delicate gold chain and locket that lay in a small pewter tray on Beth's dresser and inches away, along the top of a matching pewter frame with a photo of her two young sons. Their innocent smiles bore no clue of the tragedy to come. Since the door to Beth's closet was slightly ajar, Jo gave herself permission to have a look. She never could have imagined its disarray just a short while ago as Beth frantically searched its depths to find something to model in. Everything now hung in neatly arranged formation. A smile formed on Jo's lips. She found an odd sense of comfort in the sweetness of its order. By contrast, Ben's closet was of no interest to her. It was upsetting enough just to know it was there. A beautiful vintage atomizer caught Joanna's eye. She picked it up, held it beneath her nose and inhaled the perfume that had always weakened her. From atop Ben's chest of drawers, the couple's wedding picture tore through her intoxication with stabbing cruelty. As if in a showdown with reality, Joanna picked it up and studied it closely. The newlyweds made a perfect couple, posed in a perfect light. Beth was a beautiful young bride. Still forming in the sweetness of the young girl's eyes, Jo could see hints of the even more beautiful woman Beth would become—not just the unearned beauty of innocence but the kind that only comes once a woman had settled a score with life. Against the couple's time-frozen image Joanna could see her own face reflected in the glass. Were it someone *else's* face, and someone *else's* pain, she could have better appreciated the symbolic irony. Jo put the frame back, careful to set it down just as she'd found it. Her aching heart would have seen enough were it not for the faint scent of soap and shampoo that beckoned her into this last vestige of Beth's inner sanctum. Except for the recently used bath towel that hung haphazardly over the tub enclosure, the room appeared quietly at rest. All the usual toiletries sat poised in their places along the vanity, each one a treasure for Joanna's eyes to collect. A plastic hair clip became as precious as a piece of fine jewelry. A plain body lotion dispenser, as beautiful as any sculpted work of art. Everything that Joanna's eyes caressed held her under the unsuspecting woman's spell—a spell suddenly broken by the sight of Ben's aftershave and razor. Jo purposely avoided looking in the mirror. She did not want to see traces of her hopeless jealousy. As she turned and reentered the couple's bedroom, a slight breeze blew the curtain beside the bed as if to intentionally hold her there. It was the same window that, in the dark of night, so often drew her eye up to its small golden patch of light. She parted the curtain and gazed down into the yard. Bathed in sunlight, the vine-covered carriage house looked like something out of a dream—one from which Joanna no longer ever wished to awaken. All the gentle sounds of the universe seemed to come toward her as if to collect her silent longing and carry it back to the beginning of time. She turned away from the window and looked down at the bed. While her fingers gently traced the border of Beth's pillow, Jo's eyes drifted across the tussled sheets still creased with the memory of the woman's body. Joanna looked until she could no longer bear its painful revenge. She had gone where she never should have gone—seen what she never should have seen—and touched what she never should have touched. Now she would suffer—more than she ever thought she could. Joanna stopped to take one last forbidden look at it all, then backed slowly out of the room, her punishment as complete as her secret trespassing.

Jo grabbed the towels and sheets she'd left at the foot of the steps and raced downstairs to safety. She placed the rolled-up bedding at the basement door and wandered into the living room where she paced nervously back and forth. Once again the old weathered oil painting above the mantle caught Jo's eye. Once again she tried to make out the faded signature. Once again nothing familiar came to mind. She struggled to shrug off her curious interest in the piece, as she knew she must learn to shrug off everything else that happened to her in Beth's house since the day she arrived. The crisp ring of the telephone punctuated her resolve. Standing a few feet from the answering machine, Jo listened to the message coming in.

"Hey there Beth, Ruby here. Just callin' to say your friend's car is ready 'n waitin'..."

Joanna lunged for the receiver.

"Perfect!"

Ruby's call couldn't have come at a better time for Joanna. Reclaiming her car meant reclaiming her life, not to mention, the means to escape. Ruby offered to drop the T-Bird off around noon. In an uncharacteristic display of humility, Jo burst out onto the porch, leaned over the rail and looked up at the sky. "Yes!" she called out to 'The Gods' in a fit of joy. "Thank you! Thank you! Thank you!"

As weary as she was from the night before, Beth was intent on keeping her promise to Arthur to stay on and play a few songs privately, just for him. Beth wheeled her beloved friend close beside the piano bench, her voice as tender as her eyes.

"What would you like to hear, sweetheart?"

The fragile gentleman folded his hands politely on his lap.

"Anything at all mama... I just love to hear you play."

Beth was always touched by the tragic poignancy of Arthur's boyhood memories. She smiled back at him lovingly, grateful for whatever solace her playing could provide. Before the audience of his eager childhood heart, Beth placed her fingers on the keys. On this particular morning, his watchful quiet eyes evoked a sadness of her own—the sadness of endings—the sadness of goodbyes. Instead of his usual favorites, Beth began to play the music she'd composed at the time of her son's death—the music that had come to her so mysteriously, then stopped, until the morning of the purging rain—the morning after she'd posed for Joanna. Beth had never played the piece for him before. She had never played it for anyone other than herself. She was glad that all the doors to the dining room were closed. This time her playing was much too personal for anyone other than Arthur to hear. As she caressed and commanded the worn keys of the old upright piano, the instrument came to life as never before. She played on and on, falling deeper and deeper into the depths of the music's unknown origin. Tears had filled in both their eyes and when she was through, Arthur's trembling show of emotion surpassed any she had ever seen.

"Oh mama, mama, mama. You haven't played like that in such a long time."

Beth reached out and gently stroked the hollowness of his cheek. Her touch instantly soothed them both.

"No, You're right. I haven't..."

Arthur smiled. Even as a child he had taken great pride in knowing his mother so well.

"It' because of *her*, isn't it?"

In the course of their unusual friendship, Beth had become quite accustomed to integrating the scattered memories of Arthur's life with the actual circumstances of her own. Though she usually had no real understanding of who or what Arthur was referring to, she was never the less amazed how naturally the two sets of realities often seemed to blend. In this case, Beth thought immediately about the woman currently living in her carriage house making it easy to answer him truthfully.

"Yes sweetheart. It's because of her."

Arthur's expression grew peaceful.

"She's come back, hasn't she?"

Beth tried as best she could to understand what any of this meant in Arthur's torn and steadily decaying mind. She was always careful to question him with patience and kindness.

"What do you mean honey? *Who's* come back?"

Arthur's face became strained. This time his loss of memory brought him close to tears. His voice cracked with frustration.

"I can't remember her name mama... the artist... the one that painted such beautiful flowers for you."

So often he would confuse the past and the present in his mind. This time Beth assumed he was referring to Joanna. She had recently told him about her new friend, describing in great detail the beautiful paper flowers Jo had created for her. He'd seemed so pleased when she told him how lovely the bouquet looked arranged in his mother's crystal vase.

"Do you mean Joanna, sweetheart?"

His frail body shook with the joy of remembering.

"Yes, yes, Anne! Oh mama, will she stay this time?"

Beth had found it was easier for him if she simply allowed their conversations to flow as though they were both talking about the same thing. In that context, she thought about the terms of her tenuous arrangement with Joanna and how complicated things had already become. The future was truly uncertain.

"I really don't know, sweetie. It's hard to say."

A sudden anxiousness extinguished his joy.

"Oh mama, she makes you so happy. Beg her to stay."

Inside her heart, Beth ached from the poignant irony of his urging. On the cusp of his hundredth birthday, Arthur's eyes lightened with the innocence and excitement of a little boy.

"Will she come to my birthday party, mama?"

Beth couldn't bear to disappoint him outright.

"I'll ask honey, but I can't promise. She might be gone by then."

Her answer upset him deeply.

"No mama, you mustn't let her go! Your heart grows so heavy when she leaves."

Whatever it was Arthur was now remembering of his mother's life bore an uncanny similarity to her own on this very day. Like so many times before, Beth took the coincidence as a matter of course. Since the day he awoke from his coma, it became a part of their unusual affinity. She stroked Arthur's shoulder, careful not to raise either of their hopes.

"Let's just wait and see. Your party is still a few weeks off."

Relieved by Arthur's accepting smile, Beth's concern about Joanna now shifted to the uncertainty of a much more immediate future—the one that awaited her when she returned home. She began to feel more than a bit guilty about intentionally leaving the house this morning without knowing if Jo was feeling any better. What if, in fact, she'd gotten worse overnight? It would be just like Joanna not to call the number she'd left, even if she lay dying. Beth checked her watch. In her note she'd said she would be back around one. That didn't leave much time. She took Arthur's hands in her own.

"Honey, I'm afraid I have to be going. Joanna wasn't feeling very well last night. I should get home and make sure she's alright."

The old man acknowledged her concern.

"Yes, yes, of course mama. Go to her. She needs you so much."

Arthur watched attentively as Beth gathered up her music books and slipped them back into her case. As was their usual parting ritual, Beth wheeled her friend out to his favorite spot in the garden. He assured her it was okay for her to go and she assured him she'd visit again soon. They always sealed their promise to one another with a kiss. Haunted by Arthur's notion about Joanna's need of her, Beth hurried to her car. Unable to imagine the havoc it would unleash in her already complicated life, Beth found herself torn between wanting and not wanting those words to be true.

No matter what was going on in Beth's life, volunteering at Hillcrest always helped to calm her. Just as she had hoped, this morning was no different. Determined to keep things that way for the rest of the summer, Beth thought she'd start by picking up some fresh cold cuts at the deli. As she waited at the counter, the rack of magazines and comic books caught her eye. Recalling how she would always buy one for the boys whenever they were home sick from school, Beth picked up a Superman comic and added it to her purchases. Feeling self-conscious about her over-protectiveness the night before, she hoped the comic book would serve to keep things more playful when she got home. Back behind the wheel of her car, Beth felt pleased to be handling things so well. This was a good sign. Just a mile away from home, she turned on the radio and began singing along to one of her favorite oldies. Tapping to the beat, the sound of her wedding band clicking against the steering wheel reassured her that everything could—and would—return to normal. Once she put all her inappropriate feeling toward another woman behind her, what remained of the summer would be much more manageable. Beth felt absolutely sure of it.

Unfortunately, her certainty was short-lived—shattered into a million pieces by the sight of Joanna's gleaming Thunderbird parked at the end of her driveway. With nothing to hold Jo any longer, she could pick up and leave at any time. A part of Beth wanted to ram into the car again—anything to keep Joanna there. Another part wished she'd never hit the damn thing in the first place. The Thunderbird was back in perfect condition. Now, the only trace of their accident was hidden permanently in Beth's heart. As if the unexpected sight of the convertible wasn't enough to deal with, before she could collect her packages or her emotions Jo came striding towards her. Beaming with delight, she stood beside her prized possession and held out her hands as if to present the new improved version of both.

"Look! We're *both* all better."

Somehow Beth managed to smile, while inside her cheeks she could feel the muscles around her mouth trembling.

"So I see."

The sight of Joanna in the same pair of jeans that Beth had ravished in her dream brought an even greater sense of doom to her crumbling life. Jo came toward her.

"I woke up feeling fine. Must have been one of those twenty-four hour things. I got your note. Thanks for doing my laundry."

Beth simply nodded. Jo grabbed some of the grocery bags and followed Beth into the house, quite obviously intent on getting something off her chest.

"Now that I've got my car back..."

Beth held her breath, waiting for Joanna to announce that she would be leaving.

"What do you say we take it out a spin first thing tomorrow and go on that picnic?"

After her tour of Beth's bedroom Jo had vowed never to mention the idea again. But like all the times before, the mere sight of Beth was enough to destroy her resolve.

Beth's heart immediately leapt for joy at Joanna's proposal. A moment later, it collapsed into itself with the weight of her realization. Even if Jo were to stay on to the end of the summer, in a few short weeks she'd still be gone, leaving Beth to cope with an even greater sense of loss. The prospect terrified her. She simply couldn't afford to spend any more time in Joanna's company. It had already become too painful trying to imagine ever saying good-bye. Beth labored over rewrapping the cold cuts as long as she could. Jo brazenly grabbed a slice of ham and tossed it into her mouth.

"So, are we on?"

Beth felt hopelessly trapped by her own life. Maybe she couldn't run from herself, but she could certainly run from Joanna.

"I'm sorry, I can't tomorrow."

Joanna was clearly frustrated.

"Okay, what do I have to do? Send you a written invitation? Get down on my knees?"

Beth's amusement temporarily got the better of her fears.

"You might try that."

"Which? The invitation or the begging?"

Beth smiled to think that Joanna might actually want this day as badly as she did. She felt herself melt inside.

Joanna pressed harder.

"C'mon… how many chores can you possibly have?"

Beth hated that her life sounded so mundane. She had no choice but to lie.

"Who said anything about doing chores? It just so happens I have other plans."

"Change 'em! What could possibly be more exciting than spending the day with me?"

The truth was, Beth couldn't think of a single thing. Not in this lifetime or any other. Clutching a bagful of cold cuts that needed to be put away, all she could do was shake her head at Jo's persistence,

Jo wouldn't be deterred.

"C'mon, Steve will be back in a few days…"

Beth's stomach instantly tightened at the mention of his name. This time she did not let Joanna continue. She couldn't bear the thought that once he returned Jo would no longer have any time for *her*. She had to protect herself. Her voice turned cold, hoping that her heart would follow.

"Look, I told you I have other plans. I did have a life before you got here, you know."

Joanna's own heart could take only so much rejection.

"Fine," she snapped. "Enjoy yourself."

She turned and stormed out, the screen door slamming behind her. Beth watched through the window as Joanna stomped across the yard and disappeared into the carriage house. Seconds later Jo reemerged with a camera slung over her shoulder. She strode back across the yard, got into the T-Bird and tore out of the driveway. The sound of the car pulling away shattered all that was left of Beth's nerves. She reached into her tote, pulled out the comic book, ripped it in half and dumped it in the trash.

"Damn you, Joanna Cameron! Damn you! Damn you! Damn you!"

Beth rifled through her bag for her phone book. Drastic times called for drastic measures. She flipped through the pages until she found the number she was looking for. BJ watched her pace back and forth waiting impatiently for her call to go through.

"History Department, Professor Milos speaking."

"Nick, it's Beth."

"Hey gorgeous, how are you? Everything okay?"

Already on edge, Beth was unusually tense.

"Things are fine Nick, why wouldn't they be?"

"'Cause I don't usually hear from you out of the blue."

"I promised I'd be in touch, didn't I?"

"I just assumed you'd never really…"

She didn't let him finish, hating that he was right.

"What's your day look like tomorrow?"

Beth could feel his chest swell along with her own self loathing.

"I've got a class 'til noon but I'm free after that."

Beth could not believe what she would resort to in order to avoid Joanna Cameron.

"Pick me up when you're done. You're taking me to lunch."

Chapter 12

Beth waited for Nick out on her porch. Since Joanna had already left for the day, there was no reason to flaunt her bogus plans by making more of his arrival. As he pulled his BMW into her driveway, 'The Dangerous Beth Garrison' continued to berate her about the cowardly arrangements. It was a berating that had started the moment she'd hung up and continued straight through her sleepless night. Beth collected her bag and walked toward the car. Nick leaned over and pushed open the passenger door.

"Your chariot awaits, m'lady."

Beth waited patiently while Nick cleared the seat of loose papers and magazines.

"When was the last time you actually looked at this stuff?"

Nick sifted through the pile and pulled out an obscure French men's magazine. As he backed out of the driveway he tossed it to her.

"What's the date on that say?"

She glanced reluctantly at the explicit cover.

"May, '85."

"There's your answer."

"That's three months ago."

He smiled sheepishly.

"You know what they say… one picture's worth a thousand words. I made reservations at Café Bliss. Is that okay with you?"

Beth couldn't possibly have cared less. The name alone made for fitting enough punishment.

"That's fine." She continued to scold him about the magazine. "I hope you don't leave this kind of stuff lying around for your daughter to see."

"C'mon, give me more credit than that, will you?"

Beth opened the issue to its centerfold. Nick took his eyes off the road to leer at the seductively posed pin-up.

"Not bad, huh?"

"Not bad and not *real* either. Do you actually think that under our t-shirts and sweats, that's what average women look like?"

"Not most… but I bet you do."

Beth didn't try to hide her impatience.

"Nicholas please, don't make me regret I called."

"I was just paying you a compliment. You've got the *body*… you just don't have the attitude. Now if Good Housekeeping had a centerfold…"

Nick's observation upset her more deeply than he could have imagined. Anxious to appear less prudish, Beth continued to flip nonchalantly through the issue. Her heart nearly stopped mid-beat when she came upon a photo spread of two women making love. Ironically, the intended theme for the springtime issue was a romantic picnic. The setting, a secluded patch of grass, was complete with checkered tablecloth, wicker basket and bottle of wine. Beth could not imagine how many more ways the universe intended to make her pay for her cowardly choice of plans. Though she worked to disguise her response, Nick read her body language. He glanced over to see what had intrigued her. His eyes lingered hungrily.

"Ah… every hetero man's fantasy."

Beth became undone.

"Nick, please! Watch the road! You're going to get us killed, for God's sake!"

He obeyed but had no intention of dropping the subject.

"How about *you,* ever been with a woman?"

When she didn't answer, Nick tried the question another way.

"I mean back in college. Did you ever experiment before you met Ben?"

His question couldn't have come at a worse time in her life. She could only glare at him, praying her expression was enough to make him back off. It wasn't.

"Lots of girls *do*, ya' know."

Beth slammed the magazine shut and hurled it behind her onto the back seat.

"The issue and this conversation are officially closed."

"Don't change the subject."

"I wasn't aware we were on a subject."

"We were talking about you and another woman."

"No Nick, *we* weren't talking about it. *You* were."

Beth could hear her alter-ego chuckling as she struggled to remain composed. As usual, Nick was oblivious to her conflict.

"Beth, can I ask you something personal?"

"Would there be any point in my saying no?"

Nick laughed.

"Probably not."

"Then ask whatever you want. It doesn't mean you're getting an answer."

"Fair enough."

He looked at her earnestly.

"Have you ever been with *anyone* besides Ben?"

Beth crossed her arms.

"I'm not having this conversation with you, Nicholas!"

She caught a hint of amusement in his eyes.

"I'll take that as a 'no'."

Beth turned away and stared out of the window. Being Nick, of course he persisted.

"Don't you ever wonder what it would be like with somebody else?"

"I wonder about a lot of things. Right now I'm wondering what I was thinking when I called you."

Nick was apparently hell bent on getting an answer one way or another.

"Seriously Beth… if you knew you were going to die tomorrow, you wouldn't rather have sex with me than *lunch*?

"Positively *not*!"

"For such a damn sexy lady, you lead an awfully prudish life."

Beth flinched. Her secret attraction to Joanna cloaked in playful ambivalence, she let 'The Dangerous Beth Garrison' fire back.

"I said I wouldn't want to have sex with *you.* I didn't say I wouldn't consider having it with anyone *else*."

Nick took his hands from the wheel and began to applaud.

"Well alright then, there's hope for you yet."

His eyes flashed with curiosity.

"Anybody I know?"

Somehow the whole conversation had gotten much too close to a topic and a temptation Beth wanted desperately to avoid. Her voice filled with a fatigue well beyond her immediate frustration with him.

"Nicholas, why are we still talking about this?"

His smile was altogether genuine.

"Believe it or not, this isn't about me trying to get into your pants. It's about me trying to get inside that proper little head of yours and maybe get you to shake things up a bit."

Behind a blank expression, Beth recalled what she'd done to Joanna's jeans in her dream. She honestly couldn't imagine how much more shaken up her life could become.

Nick risked being even more sincere.

"Prude or not, I think Ben's the luckiest guy in the world."

As awkward as it was in forming, Beth thanked him with a smile. Little did he know how much more *complicated* rather than *lucky* things actually were for her husband. Nick announced that he had to make a quick stop at the post office before they went to lunch.

"Gotta' get something out registered mail. I shouldn't be more than a few minutes."

Time was of no consequence to Beth. She had already forsaken the day.

Secretly she was grateful for the unexpected moments of privacy. As soon as Nick disappeared into the building, she reached around to the back seat to retrieve the pornographic magazine. Her fingers trembled as they worked to find the page of the two women making love, her eyes devouring every detail of the steamy Sapphic acts. However staged the models, Beth was greedy for *anything* that brought her own secret desires to life. She spent the next several minutes stealing as much as she could of the lesbian imagery while constantly glancing up at the blue door of the post office. Beth prayed the line inside was unusually long. At the first sight of Nick, she instantly flung the magazine onto the back seat and tried to remain poised while he got back in.

He looked at her curiously.

"Hey, are you okay?"

"I'm fine."

"You look a little flushed."

Still burning beneath her skin, Beth dismissed his observation. Nick pulled out of the spot and started down the street. The restaurant was just on the other end of town.

"Hungry?"

Beth nodded, her heart secretly aching at his choice of words. For the next few blocks she stared out of the window in silence. It was an absolutely exquisite day—perfect for an idyllic picnic with the only person in her life that could have fed *all* her insatiable hungers.

When she'd left early that morning, Joanna had no idea where her frustrations would take her. All she knew was that she didn't want to stick around to watch whatever plans Beth had, unfold. Though she'd taken along her sketchpad and camera, it was not inspiration Jo went in search of—it was *escape*. By midday it was apparent that the distraction she'd hoped for would continue to elude her. The wasted day seemed as good as any to get her grocery shopping over with. From the moment she turned into the Campus Plaza Mall, whatever little distance she'd managed to put between herself and Beth instantly dissolved. Only this time, the impact of their earlier collision was much more internal.

Jo took a wagon and wandered aimlessly around the supermarket. Halfway down the cereal aisle, the box of Cheerios immediately brought back memories of their first dinner together and of that silly little token of Beth's courage she'd stolen and placed in a jar for safekeeping. One image stampeded over the next, trampling her already bruised heart. Tangled up in their short but hopelessly complicated history, Jo suddenly remembered her even more haunting encounter with Beth three years earlier on the morning of her production shoot and Danny's funeral. By now, everything about this location had become far too overwhelming. She made up her mind that from now on, she would get whatever groceries she needed at the local convenience store where she and Steve always stopped for coffee. For now, the only things that stood between her and a clean break were the few items in her cart. As Jo waited impatiently on the express checkout line, Trudy's unmistakable voice came from behind.

"Hey there doll, see you're returnin' to the scene of the crime."

Jo turned and caught the top of Trudy's carrot red hair. The woman looked just as much a caricature as she had the day she'd brazenly stepped in and rescued Beth from Joanna's rage. The penciled lines of Trudy's eyebrows were drawn much too long and her rouge applied much too heavily. Her signature sunshine earrings still dangled from the sides of her head. She held up a large jar of mayonnaise.

"Can't keep enough of this stuff in stock."

Trudy didn't wait for a response.

"Got plenty now to make you the best darn roast beef sandwich in town."

Joanna declined as politely as she could, but Trudy wouldn't take 'no' for an answer.

"Get your stuff checked out, toss it in that spankin' new car of yours, compliments of my Ruby, and meet me back at the luncheonette in 5 minutes." Trudy dug into her apron pocket to pay for the mayonnaise. "And mind ya', I don't take well to bein' stood up."

Jo hadn't eaten all day and could do with at least a few bites.

The lunch crowd had thinned out. Trudy motioned for Joanna to sit anywhere she liked. Jo looked at the booth she'd shared with Beth and Adam the morning of the accident, then deliberately chose a stool at the counter instead. She'd had more than her fill of memories for one day.

Trudy set a glass of water down in front of her.

"Lemme' get those folks at table five their check, then I'll fix ya' that sandwich myself."

Making the most of her few minutes of solitude, Jo sipped her water and let her eyes wander along the wall near the cash register. Several 'lucky' dollars bills were taped alongside the restaurant's business license. Two framed photographs hung nearby. One was a glossy 8x10 of Trudy standing proudly outside in front of her luncheonette. Behind her, a large banner in the window read "Grand re-opening!" The second photo was much older—a sepia toned image of a stoic looking couple standing outside an old-fashioned general store. Judging from its appearance, the picture seemed to be taken sometime around the turn of the century.

Trudy returned with Joanna's platter and a cup of coffee for herself. She came around the counter and sat down on the next stool.

"I'm pooped. Think I'll take a load off and join ya'."

Trudy watched with delight as Jo took her first bite.

"What'd I tell ya'. Best roast beef sandwich in town, huh?"

"It's great, thanks."

Trudy poked Jo in the arm.

"So, how 'bout that man of mine. Bet ya' can't believe the job he did on that car of yours."

Jo was genuinely grateful.

"Yeah, he did a fantastic job."

"He told me he dropped it off at the Garrison's the other day. Heard about your little arrangement. That Beth, she's a great gal, isn't she? Told ya' so right there on the spot when you were cussing her out." Trudy nudged Jo with her elbow. "Ya' gotta' admit, that accident turned out to be the best thing that could'a happened to ya'. Found a great place to stay and a great fella'!"

Jo put down her sandwich.

"Sorry but you're way off base on that one."

"Now don't go bein' coy with me doll. I saw the way Steve was lookin' at ya' that time ya' came in here." She nudged Jo again. "But don't think I'm gonna' give him up that easy."

"What about Ruby?"

"Now ya' see, that's a problem. I'm crazy about that guy too. How's that song go… 'torn between two lovers'?"

Trudy slapped Joanna so hard across her thigh that Jo wondered if she hadn't spiked that coffee with something stronger than just milk. It seemed absolutely useless to try and clarify things about her relationship with Steve so Joanna just let it go. She was halfway through her sandwich and wasn't planning on staying that much longer anyway.

As Trudy took another gulp of her coffee Joanna saw real signs of exhaustion on the woman's face.

"Long day?"

Trudy leaned over just enough to rest her head against Jo's shoulder for a minute.

"Tell ya' somethin' doll, in this business, they're *all* long days… some just longer than others."

Jo pointed to the photograph of Trudy on the wall.

"When was that taken?"

"Oh Jesus, that was back in June of '62. Twenty-three years ago! Feels more like a hundred and twenty-three lately. Can't seem to walk away from the place though. Guess it's in my blood. My folks ran a soda fountain in town for forty years before that. Worked there with my brother and sister the whole time we were growin' up." Trudy took another gulp of her coffee. "Met my husband workin' behind that counter. He wandered in one afternoon and ordered two hot fudge sundaes. Said he was celebratin' landin' some mechanic's job at the local gas station. Wound up ownin' the place after a while. That's my Ruby. Eventually he sold the business and opened his body shop. Earned himself quite a reputation too. Lookin' at what he did with that car of yours, guess it aint hard to see why. Times I coulda' sworn that man loved his cars more than he loved me."

Joanna thought about Ruby's obvious affection for his wife.

"Trust me, they don't even come close."

Trudy smiled contentedly.

"Listen to me ramblin' on and on about my life. Bet you're sorry ya' asked."

Surprisingly, Jo was actually enjoying the conversation.

"Not at all."

Trudy stared wistfully at the photo.

"Back in the mid fifties some developer type came in and built this mall. It was a whole lot smaller than it is today but with all the traffic passin' through, pop thought it was a better location for business, so he up and moved the soda fountain here. Said it was meant to be… like returnin' to his roots. But that's a whole 'nother story. Pop turned the business into a luncheonette, worked it a few more years and then, one day, decided flat out he'd been doin' it long enough. Gotta' tell ya', I'm startin' to know what he meant. Anyway, since nobody else in the family wanted any part of it, with Ruby's blessin' I went ahead, remodeled and renamed it. Days like this, I sometimes regret it too. Been a lot of changes around here. Seen a helluva lot of businesses come 'n go over the past thirty years, but we keep makin' the rent. Must be that homemade roast beef sandwich you're eatin'."

Joanna envied how neatly Trudy could sum up her whole life. She pointed to the second picture on the wall.

"What about that one?"

Trudy's face lit up with pride.

"That was taken back in 1880. It's my grand-daddy and grandma in front of their general store."

Trudy spun around on her stool and pointed outside through the luncheonette window.

"Stood right over there where that monster of a supermarket is today. Used to be horse and buggies loadin' up out there, not fancy cars and SUVs."

Despite her exhaustion Trudy was proud to be sharing her family's legacy.

"Back then that intersection out front was nothin' more than two dirt roads and where this strip mall is standin' was once considered the center of town. Ya' had your post office, your bank, your saloon and in the middle of it all, my family's general store. Opened back in 1875 and stood proud for the next thirty-five years 'til the fire of 1910 swept through here and burned every last one of those buildings to the ground." Trudy nodded boastfully. "We may not be the *oldest* family name in this town, but we damn sure own a piece of its history."

Joanna was intrigued.

"Mind if I have a closer look?"

"Wouldn't mind at all."

Trudy went around the counter and took the old photograph off the wall. She wiped the accumulated residue of cooking grease from the glass with the edge of her apron before handing it over.

Jo respectfully wiped her own hands before accepting it. As she studied the old photograph, she could feel her throat becoming curiously dry. For an instant it felt as if she'd actually inhaled the dust of that hot summer day into her lungs. Without taking her eyes away, she reached for her glass. After a gulp of soda, the feeling disappeared. A victim of her own exacting nature, she became fixated on extracting every last detail that the image could yield. As if looking for the smallest clues to an unsolved mystery, Joanna scrutinized every inch of the time-worn photograph which included, in addition to Trudy's grandparents on the front step of their store, a small, short haired dog, several wooden barrels and an old-fashioned bicycle leaning up against the rail of the store's porch. Wishing she could crawl deep into the cracked and faded image, she settled for letting the tips of her fingers brush gently over the glass, across the frame of the bike. With her eyes still hungry for more and her heart heavy with a reluctance she didn't understand, Joanna handed the frame back to Trudy who smiled as she gazed at the picture of her grandparents.

"Bet they'd like knowin' we're still here doin' business right here where they did. Not many families can say that." Trudy took a thoughtful look around. "Kinda' makes me sad to think I'll probably be the last generation to do it though. Nowadays, the young ones go off to college and never come back. Seems our two boys can't get *far* enough, *fast* enough. 'Grown and flown' is what Ruby calls 'em." Trudy sighed like a woman who was tired, not just from the day but from the years. "I suppose I'll hang on as long as these old bones let me. Besides, can't imagine it's gonna' be too easy to unload this place." Trudy winked at Jo. "Unless of course one of you young upstarts is ready to trade her ambition for an apron."

"You wouldn't be hinting that that *someone* might be me, would you?"

"Hell no doll. Don't take this wrong, but from what I've seen in the little time I know ya', you aint got the temperament to deal with the public. My bet is you'd run this place into the ground before that hot roast beef sandwich got cold."

Joanna laughed at Trudy's apt prediction.

"You're probably right. Guess I'll stick to what I do best."

"Is what you do *best* what you do *happiest*?"

The unexpected question hit Joanna hard. It took her a moment to decide if she should answer truthfully. Ultimately, she saw no reason to lie.

"It used to be, but it hasn't felt that way in a while."

"Well then, change it doll! The heart's shaped like an arrow 'cause it's meant to be followed."

Jo wiped her mouth.

"Thanks for the sandwich and the advice."

Trudy looked squarely into Joanna's eyes.

"In your case, I'm bettin' the second part's gonna' be a lot harder to digest."

Pretending to overlook Trudy's observation, Jo stood up and dug into her pocket.

"What do I owe you?"

"Not a thing. Both are on the house."

"Thanks, but it's really not necessary."

"You're right, it isn't. Turns out very little in this life is and that's a damn shame. Folks givin' and takin' less and less from each other, 'til one day they stumble onto somethin' that really is... somethin' they can't live without. Only by then they don't have a goddamn clue how to just be grateful and welcome it into their life." Trudy took Jo by the shoulders. "So start by accepting the free sandwich, doll. Somethin' tells me you can do with the practice."

Joanna's expression softened with the truth of Trudy's homespun wisdom.

"Okay then, thanks."

"Ya' see, that wasn't so hard, now was it?"

Trudy walked Jo outside.

"Now don't ya' forget, 'practice makes perfect'. Today a sandwich... tomorrow who knows what someone out there might offer ya'."

Jo acknowledged the reminder with a final wave. Halfway across the parking lot she found herself gravitating to the spot where Beth's car had collided with hers. There on the ground was a small piece of the T-Bird's cracked front grill. Joanna bent down and picked up the bittersweet reminder. Clutching it in her hand, she glanced around to make sure no one else was in earshot. Then, in spite of everything, she smiled at the treasure that reminded her of Beth and whispered under her breath.

"Okay, I'm grateful. Thank you."

Trudy's little sermon had opened Jo's heart. As she got into her car, she was prepared to forgive Beth Garrison for everything—even for wasting such a glorious day. Jo reached across to her glove compartment and placed the small piece of her grill safely inside. Hooked on the oldies station, Jo turned on the radio, its dial already set there. The nostalgic sound instantly put her in too good a mood to head back just yet. Maybe Trudy was right when she said the heart was shaped like an arrow. Sitting behind the wheel of her T-Bird, Joanna's seemed to point toward town.

Lunch with Nick was more pleasant than Beth expected. It felt good to be out in the world—a familiar world that bore no resemblance to the private one on her head. Nick seemed to be having a good time as well. Beth was the only woman in his otherwise empty life he couldn't reduce to a sexual object. She was also the only one truly interested in being his friend. It was as though early in Nick's life he'd been handed a misguided script of what it meant to be a man and even when it failed him miserably, he insisted on rehearsing it faithfully. Beth always managed to help him find and trust his own voice. Often it was the voice of loneliness and pain—the voice of a shy young boy pushed into a machismo manhood by the example of a boorish father and 3 older brothers. A part of her felt guilty for exposing Nick to his own vulnerability, then leaving him abruptly to deal with it alone. With no reason to rush home, she suggested a walk down the street to the corner ice cream shop. From the look on his face, Nick couldn't have been happier if she'd suggested sex in the back seat of his car. The unlikely pair strolled arm-in-arm, intermittently licking the messy run-off of each other's cones. In Nick's delight, Beth found her own and for the length of one glorious block her heart relaxed in a rare stretch of uncomplicated joy. It was a lightness that came to an abrupt end at the unexpected sight of Joanna's car stopped at the traffic light on the corner.

The instant the light turned green, the unmistakable Thunderbird sped off leaving Beth to wonder if Joanna had seen her too and if so, just how much she had misconstrued of the couple's platonic intimacy. Full-blown dread replaced Beth's short-lived joy. She pulled her arm away and checked her watch.

"I really should get back. I promised my neighbor I'd help her hang some artwork. Her husband died a few months ago and she's trying bravely to move on."

In truth, Beth really had made such a promise, but those plans had not yet been set and certainly did not necessitate her having to rush off just then.

Nick shook his head.

"Ah, Beth Garrison the sweet dependable gal next door."

Ignoring his comment, Beth hurried him back to the car. Wishing he'd drive faster, she hoped to be home and he long gone before Joanna returned. Once they'd turned onto her street Beth strained to get a look at her driveway, relieved not to see the Thunderbird. For very different reasons, Joanna came to Nick's mind as well.

"How's that knock-out who's staying in your carriage house?"

Jo was the last thing Beth wanted to talk about.

"I wouldn't know. I assume she's fine."

Hoping to avoid any more questions she leapt from the car. She leaned in through the open window and gave him a peck on his cheek

"Thanks for the lunch Nick.."

"Tell Ben to get his ass home fast. You're too damn beautiful to resist."

Beth was always saddened by just how quickly Nick went back to being Nick. But right now she had far greater concerns, namely getting inside before Joanna drove up. Beth waved and hurried toward the house. When she reached the front porch, she scooped up the mail and fumbled for her keys. Safely inside, Beth poured herself a glass of water and collapsed at the kitchen table. Sorting through the stack of mail helped get her mind off things until she came upon a letter for Joanna—c/o her. It was from Steve. Her first impulse was to rip the thing up and throw it into the garbage. Now she had to make sure to get it over to the carriage house before Joanna got back. Avoiding a run-in with the woman was paramount in Beth's mind. She bolted from the table with the letter, dashed across the backyard and wedged the thing between the frame and screen of the carriage house door. With her heart still pounding, she raced back toward the house. Just as she reached the kitchen porch Joanna pulled up beside her in the driveway. Beth struggled not to fall apart.

"I just left a letter for you."

Joanna remained cool as she collected her groceries from the trunk. Her obsession with Beth had spun way out of control. Jo had promised herself she wouldn't say a word about seeing the couple together in town. Of course when it came to Beth, Jo had broken more than one promise to herself. This time turned out to be no exception.

"I'm surprised you're back so soon. Enjoy your little cone?"

Beth didn't appreciate the smugness in Jo's voice. Resentment replaced vulnerability.

"Yes, as a matter of fact I did."

"So tell me, was that dessert or just the appetizer to your little afternoon tryst?"

"I don't know what you're alluding to but Nick and I just had a friendly lunch."

Jo tried to stop herself from sounding as if she cared. With one arm full of groceries, she used the other to slam the trunk.

"I know what I saw."

"Which means what exactly?"

"Which means the two of you strolling down the street arm-in-arm."

"Not that it's any of your business, but that wasn't what it looked like."

Jo snapped back.

"Hey, if the cone drips, lick it."

For a moment Beth didn't know whether to be insulted or overjoyed. A part of her delighted in Jo's assumption, which cast her in a decidedly edgier life than the one she actually lived. But the moment quickly passed and a sense of indignation took its place.

"Do you actually think if I were sleeping with my husband's best friend I'd be stupid enough to walk arm-in-arm with him down the center of our small town?"

"People have been known to throw caution to the wind in the name of lust."

"You are so way off base it isn't even funny."

"Look, I don't really care what you do or don't do while your husband's out of town. Like you said, you had a life before I got here."

Jo started to walk away. Beth didn't appreciate being so easily dismissed.

"You're right, I did! And I intend to have one long after you're gone!"

Just beneath the sting of her own words, Beth had absolutely no idea how that would ever be possible. Joanna kept walking, infuriating Beth even more. She was not in the habit of shouting across her yard for all her neighbors to hear, but that's exactly what she did.

"Was I supposed to drop everything just because you're bored while Steve's out of town?"

This time Joanna spun around.

"What the hell's Steve got to do with any of this?"

"Oh please, the only reason you've even given me the time of day is because he's away."

Nothing could have been further from the truth. Since it was a truth Joanna couldn't possibly share, she retaliated instead.

"Yeah, well, he does tend to be a lot less aggravating! Besides, if I recall, *you* were the one who thought we should meet in the first place."

That was something Beth certainly didn't need to be reminded of. She didn't know what else to say.

"Look, you live your life and I'll live mine. That's what we agreed on anyway, right? So let's stick to the plan."

"Fine by me!"

Before Joanna disappeared inside, Beth needed to clarify one more thing.

"And just for the record, I'm not that kind of woman."

Jo hollered back as she bent down and removed Steve's letter from the door.

"What kind would that be? Someone alive? Someone ruled by her desires?"

Beth hated Jo's implication that a life driven by passion was somehow beyond her. A shouting match ensued.

"I just love being judged by someone who doesn't know the slightest thing about sacrifice. You can't even stand the thought of anything in your life clashing with your precious environment."

"You don't know the first thing about my life!"

"You're right I don't, and do you know why? Because you're too damn self contained to let anyone inside. And don't talk to me about a life without passion… not when it's some marble countertop or a stainless steel sink that gets you all hot and bothered."

It was obvious both women had learned just enough about each other to be able to push each other's buttons. Had they been standing any closer at that moment, they might have pummeled each other to the ground—which, given their repressed desires, might well have led to something else. As it was, they were across the yard and only inches from their respective doors which they both opened and slammed simultaneously.

Fueled by the sheer force of her frustration, Jo unpacked her groceries in a matter of seconds. She opened a cold beer and stared at Steve's letter.

"Great! This is what I need now."

Jo sat down and tore open the envelope. She took another gulp of beer and unfolded the single sheet of paper. Steve's note was short and regrettably sweet.

Dear Jo,

I know I wasn't supposed to call, but you didn't say I couldn't write. The truth is, I've been missing you something fierce. When I get back we need to talk, or at least *I* need to talk, and *you* need to listen. I'll be driving straight through and expect to be home around six, Friday night. I was hoping to drop off my stuff, shower and come right over. What I have to say can't wait. Leave a message on my answering machine and let me know if that's all right.

Until our tool belts hang as one, Steve

Joanna knew she was going to have to deal with Steve's attraction sooner or later. She just couldn't imagine it coming at a worse time.

"What the hell" she mumbled to herself as she picked up the phone. "Everything might as well all blow up at once."

With little point in putting it off, she left a message agreeing to a talk. Joanna tried not to think about how difficult their conversation would be. As her restlessness began to mount, Jo refused to hide indoors for the rest of the day. The late afternoon was a perfect time for a swim. Not only would the exercise help work off some frustration, it would allow Jo to flaunt her renting privileges and that's just what she intended to do. She deliberately dove into the pool—

counting on the splash to send a defiant message to the woman inside—a message that through its rhythmic laps indeed rattled Beth to her core.

Desperate to escape, Beth reached for the phone and called her husband for the first time. After her plans with Rheeta and visiting day at camp the following Sunday, perhaps she would get on a plane and join Ben in Europe for the rest of August. As the phone continued to ring, Beth realized she had no idea what running away would accomplish. She was clearly relived when Ben didn't answer. Deep inside, Beth knew the idea was a terrible mistake that the universe had just prevented her from making. She hung up without leaving so much as a message. Momentarily rescued but no less trapped by the immediate circumstances, Beth poured herself a glass of ice tea and retreated into the soft, welcoming contour of her sofa. While she stared at the stack of House & Garden magazines arranged neatly on the coffee table, all Beth could think about was that awful magazine in Nick's car. Against the relentless sound of Joanna's splashing, Beth grabbed the fluffiest pillow within reach. As her eyes glared at the index card with the sentimental quote, she clutched the floral chintz fabric up against her face and screamed into it as loud as she could. So much for comparing a friendship with Joanna to the delicate unfolding of a flower.

Her feverish laps left Joanna drained. She angled the chaise toward the sun and collapsed onto it with the full weight of her body. As her heart rate slowed Jo could feel herself slowly drifting off. It was the most relaxed she'd been all day until once again she was swept up and carried out to the treacherous depths of her reoccurring nightmare. It began as it always had…

She's in the parking lot of the Campus Plaza Mall, shooting the commercial the agency had sent her there to do. Surrounded by winding cables and filming equipment, the heat of the day felt unforgiving. She and her crew are growing more irritable with every take. She is in the midst of another shouting match with her assistant when she begins to feel an unexplainable force penetrating the thick, tension filled air. She turns around to the road. Stopped at the traffic light at the entrance of the mall is a funeral procession. The strange energy is coming from the limousine directly behind the hearse.

It is at this point in her dream where the reality of what actually took place that morning ends and her nightmare begins.

Compelled by the mysterious force, Joanna runs out to the road. Though she is closer now, she still can see nothing through the darkened window of the limo. Just as she reaches for the handle of the door the procession starts to pull away. In desperation, Jo calls out for the car to stop. 'Ellie, Ellie… please don't go!' She is helpless as the limousine continues on, further and further into the distance. In total despair, Joanna turns back to resume her work. Only now, there is no longer anything or anyone there. It's all gone—the crew, the parking lot, the mall itself. It's all completely erased. In its place only nothingness—a void from which she hears a faint voice calling out to her. Jo spins around in circles trying frantically to distinguish where it's coming from, but the harder she tries the more the voice sounds as if it's everywhere and nowhere at the same time.

As her feeling of desperation intensified, Jo would usually awaken. But this time she slept on and her nightmare unfolded differently.

As she turns from the road to return to her crew, instead of the usual void the scene looks just as it did at the turn of the century. Set in from the dirt road is a row of buildings—a post-office, a bank, a saloon—just as Trudy had described it a few hours before. In the middle of it all is the General Store. A bicycle leans against the rail exactly as it appeared in the photo Jo had held in her hand. The same haunting voice is calling out to her. Only now, it seems to be emanating from inside the General Store. Unable to move, Jo is forced to watch from the distance as a young woman, dressed in the fashion of the day, emerges from the store. She is accompanied by Trudy's grandfather, who is assisting the young woman with her purchases. The two chat for a while. Jo watches intently as the woman eventually lifts her long dress, mounts her bicycle and rides off. Tormented, Joanna calls out to her but the woman is either oblivious or simply unable to hear Jo's cries. As the woman and her bicycle disappear into the dust and bustle of the horse and wagons moving about, Joanna's cries become more and more urgent. 'Ellie, wait! Please don't go.'

Jo pleaded from the depth of her subconscious until the heat of the sun penetrated her distress and awakened her. She sprung forward—her fingers gripping the arms of the lounge, her heart pounding in her chest. As she waited for the symptoms of anxiety to subside, Joanna tried once again to interpret the symbolism of her dream. For the longest time she had assumed that the remote voice calling to her from the void was her mother's. Certainly the emotional impact of her mother's death had never left her. Jo assumed the procession represented her mother's funeral and the person she was running toward in the limo was really herself—a grieving, devastated young child separated from an essential part of herself forever. But now, in this new version of her dream influenced by her earlier conversation with Trudy and further complicated by her having learned of the eerie coincidence involving Danny's funeral procession, Joanna could no longer be sure of anything. What had not changed, as Jo struggled to free herself from the perils of her subconscious, was the mysterious name that remained on her lips and embedded deep inside her heart.

For the next two days, the estranged women went out of their way to keep to themselves. Whenever their paths accidentally crossed, their exchange was guarded and intentionally brief. Neither could understand why the other had not insisted on ending their ridiculously strained living arrangement—but neither did. Now, on the eve of Steve's homecoming, each tried to prepare herself for the complication of his return while all that remained unspoken between them hung in the wasted hours of that sleepless last night.

Chapter 13

The early hours of Friday dragged on endlessly. By late afternoon Joanna had done all she could to prepare herself mentally for Steve's arrival. Every word of his manuscript had been carefully read, as were the unspoken words between the lines of his brief but pointed letter. Now she could do nothing but wait to deliver her response to both. The first would be easy. Steve was certainly a gifted writer. It would not be hard to tell him what she knew he was hoping to hear. His letter—and his feelings—would be considerably more complicated to address. Jo intended to remain intentionally vague, explaining that in fact there was someone she'd left behind in New York—a relationship not quite over. She would say she was being protective of him—that she feared being unable to return the kind of love he deserved. Certainly that part was true. It was no secret that she'd arrived in Amherst with considerable emotional baggage. She hoped the reasonable explanation would be enough to get through the rest of the summer without losing his friendship. In these last few weeks she had come to truly adore him and was counting on the continued rewards of his companionship and their work to help distract her from her hopeless obsession with Beth. As the hour of his anticipated arrival grew near, Jo convinced herself that misleading Steve would be a kinder alternative to rejecting him outright. Joanna's resistance was never to the truth itself, but to the burden of having to open up and share it. Beth's accusation was certainly true . Jo wasn't exactly a *gusher* when it came to baring her soul.

With the crunching of gravel, Joanna went to the screen door expecting to see Steve's truck in the driveway. Instead she saw Beth pulling away.

The timing of her departure was not at all coincidental. Steve had called from Ohio. Beth was home at the time but didn't pick up. She listened as he left his message. He said it felt like forever since they'd spent any time together and that he was hoping to at least catch her before his plans with Joanna Friday night. It was obvious Steve was entirely unaware of her jealousy and resentment. She tried not to hate him for *that* as well. To avoid him Beth made plans for that night, arranging to help that neighbor who'd recently lost her husband. The woman lived just down the street but Beth took her car anyway, hoping to give the impression she was a lot further away than she actually was. Home was the last place Beth wanted to be when the lovers reunited behind the door of her sacred carriage house—the very place of her own unsettled desires. She simply could not bear the torturous proximity to the couple's intimacy.

Joanna remained at the screen door. After the last few days of living in self-imposed exile, the women's silent heartbreak was mutual. Jo turned on the radio for some distraction, but 'The Gods' were revengeful. The Platter's classic 'Only You' crackled through the small mesh speaker. Immersed in the sentimental lyrics, Jo leaned against the wall directly across from her studies of Beth. Steve's timely arrival rescued her from both. She snapped off the radio and stepped outside to greet him. In spite of the ordeal that still lay before her, Jo was genuinely happy to see him.

Steve was ogling the Thunderbird in the driveway. He hadn't heard Joanna approach.

"Look but don't touch!" she warned mockingly from behind.

Steve spun around.

"Hey!" His smile broadened at the sight of her. He turned back to the car, his eyes caressing every inch of the pristine vehicle inside and out. "Man, I can see now why you wanted to kill Beth for hitting this baby."

Joanna folded her arms across her chest as if to instinctively protect her heart.

"Yeah well, as it turns out, that's the least of the things I'd like to kill her for."

Steve looked up from the gleaming console.

"What do you mean?"

"Never mind. How was the drive?"

Steve was quickly reminded how often Joanna stonewalled his questions and simply answered hers.

"Knowing you were on the end of it, great."

In a sudden wave of exuberance, Steve swept Joanna up into his arms and spun her around. She smelled alcohol on his breath. Apparently he was as apprehensive about disclosing his feelings as she was in hearing them.

"Good visit with your folks?"

"Always is. You'd really love 'em."

Jo ignored the implication.

"How was your mom's party?"

"Great, but she did take me aside and tell me when she made a wish it was for some grand-kids."

Steve looked at Joanna, hoping for some kind of reaction this time. She was careful not to offer any. Still, he seemed overjoyed just to have her in his view.

"Speaking of gifts, close your eyes."

Joanna reluctantly obeyed while Steve reached in behind the seat of his truck. He pulled out a brand new leather tool belt and strapped it around her waist. Jo opened her eyes and looked down. Steve had used the loop intended for the hammer to hold 3 long stem roses.

"Those are for each of the 3 jobs we've completed since we've begun working together. The date we started is hand tooled on the inside of the belt."

Joanna was truly touched. She was also relieve he hadn't presented her with an engagement ring. Privately, she didn't know which to be more thankful for.

"I don't know what to say."

Her smile delighted him.

"I figured any woman who knows her way around a tool belt the way you do deserves to be better hung than the guy who gave it to her."

Joanna laughed as she adjusted the belt around her hips. In a playfully macho gait, she sauntered up to within inches of Steve's face and planted a surprise kiss on his cheek.

"I love it, thank you."

"You're welcome."

Steve reached around and pulled her to him. The warmth of his hug was so sincere she couldn't bring herself to resist. The bulging tool-belt pressed against his groin. Joanna took advantage of the well-placed prop to break free. Pretending to be aroused, she grabbed the leather pouch jutting out in front of her crotch.

"Okay—back off! Next thing I know you'll be accusing me of sexual harassment on the job."

Steve was reminded how much he appreciated Jo's crisp sense of humor, even if it was often at the expense of the intimacy he had begun to crave.

From over his shoulder Jo's eyes lingered on the kitchen door. Even now, days after her argument with Beth, she could still hear the harshness of its slam echoing in her heart. Tonight would be long enough without dwelling on *that*. For very different reasons, Beth came to Steve's mind as well.

"Ya' know, I called and left Beth a message to say I'd be here tonight and hoped to get to see her as well. She never even got back to me. Her behavior seems out of character. If I didn't know any better, I'd swear she was avoiding me."

Joanna shrugged. Things with Beth were complicated enough. She certainly didn't need to get in the middle of their relationship.

"I'm starved. The sooner I call for a pizza, the sooner it'll get here."

Steve reached into his truck for the bottle of champagne he'd picked up on the way over. Joanna didn't need to ask why. Bracing herself for the hours ahead, she was grateful for anything that might dull the pain of it for both of them.

The instant he stepped inside, Steve noticed the sketches of Beth on the wall.

"Wow!" He crossed the room for a closer look. "Now *there's* a side of Beth I'll bet very few people have ever seen." He turned to Joanna, who'd taken off the belt and was putting the roses in some water. "That must have been one helluva session. Looks like an understatement to say you got to know her better."

Jo tried to sound nonchalant about the details of a night that had become permanently etched in her mind and heart.

"Yeah, we talked a little."

Before he asked any more questions she didn't want to answer, Jo picked up the phone. While she ordered the pizza, Steve went back to scrutinizing the portraits. He seemed impossible to distract.

"Do you think Beth is happy?"

Fighting a losing battle, Jo came over and stood beside him.

"I don't think '*happy*' is the word I'd use to describe someone who's been through what she has, do you?"

"I'm not talking about what she's *lost*. I'm talking about what she's never *had*."

Joanna pretended to know less than she actually did. She was hoping for his impression.

"Why ask *me*? She's your friend."

Steve's eyes remained fixed on the drawings.

"Because these studies of yours capture something I've always suspected… that underneath the Beth Garrison everybody loves is the Beth Garrison nobody really knows… and to a large extent that includes Beth Garrison herself."

"Meaning what?"

"That she got married, then pregnant, much too young… that her family became her mirror long before she had a chance to take a really good look at herself through her *own* eyes."

"And if she had?"

"If she had then maybe those tender, beautiful eyes of hers wouldn't look as tragically sad as they are in these drawings. If you ask me, I think her spirit's been broken one too many times."

Joanna recalled Beth's declaration celebrating her right to celebrate.

"I don't know about that. I'd say she has a pretty amazing spirit for someone who's been through what she has. I don't know too many women who'd still be decorating sweet potato casseroles with tiny marshmallows."

"That's just it. Beth shouldn't be in the kitchen baking sweet potato casseroles in the first place. She should be traveling all over the world, embellishing it with the largess of her music… not tiny marshmallows. Have you heard her play yet?"

Jo nodded solemnly.

"Then you know *exactly* what I'm talking about."

Jo thought about her own life.

"Professional success isn't everything. Concert tours end. She'd have to come home sometime."

"All the more reason to be sharing that home with the right person."

Steve's hesitated as if torn by his loyalty.

"Don't get me wrong, I think Ben's a great guy. I just never got the feeling they were particularly suited for each other. I wouldn't exactly call them *soul mates*." He turned from the drawings and looked at her with an undeniable intensity. "I didn't come over here to talk about the Garrison's marriage…"

Jo knew that he was gearing up to say what it was he had come to say. Fortunately, the pizza delivery arrived just in time to stop him. Steve came and stood behind her while she opened the box. Jo knew she had to make a move before he did. There was no sense in wasting a perfectly good pie. She quickly turned and shoved a plate in his hand.

"Here, start with this while I pop the champagne."

"I thought we'd have that a little later."

Jo knew the disappointment *later* would bring.

"Why wait?"

She joined him at the table with two glasses intentionally filled to the top.

Steve lifted his in the air.

"To the most beautiful carpenter in the world!"

While he downed almost all of it at once, Joanna tried to steer the conversation away from the inevitable as long as she could.

"I read your manuscript. It's good, *very* good."

"You're not just saying that because I got you that great looking tool belt?

"Do I strike you as being that easy to buy off?"

"Actually, no."

Jo's eyes flashed playfully.

"Now throw in a few state-of-the-art power tools and that's another story."

Steve laughed. He was relieved to know Jo respected his writing. Still nervous about the other thing, he finished off his champagne and immediately poured himself another glass. Apparently Steve wasn't going to remain sober long enough to be engaged in a meaningful dialogue about his writing. Jo thought it best to try and get as much food into him as she could to absorb at least some of the alcohol he seemed intent on consuming. She got up and walked over to the counter to get him another slice. Once again he came up behind her, only this time, his nerve bolstered by his buzz, Steve slipped his arms around her waist and pressed his lips against her ear. For a split second Jo's heart ached for both of them, so much so that she did not instantly pull away. In that moment he mistook her sadness for surrender. He pulled her hair back and began kissing her neck. Jo tried to sound as gentle as she could.

"Steve, we can't do this."

Without letting her go, he continued with his long suppressed confession.

He stroked her hair. "I've fallen in love with you Jo."

Still encircled by his arms, Joanna managed to turn around so she could actually look at him. Her affection for him was real.

"I know you have and that's exactly why I can't let you think this is possible."

"Look, I'm not stupid. It's obvious you didn't come up here for some fresh country air. You've been walking around these last few weeks like there's a bear sitting on your chest. I'd be a complete idiot not to realize there's someone you left behind. Maybe it's lousy timing and you're not quite over him yet, but we could be so good together."

"We *are* good together Steve… as *friends*."

"We could be so much more Jo."

"No, we can't."

"Deny it all you want, but we clicked right from the start. I know you felt it too."

"I'm not denying anything. You're one of the nicest surprises of this whole miserable summer."

Steve found hope in her confession. His eyes and grip eased.

"Nothing's impossible Jo. Not when two people love each other. If it's time you need, I'll wait. I'll wait for you as long as it takes."

Ordinarily Joanna would have broken free of his arms and put some distance between them. She was surprised how deeply she had come to care for him and surprised how much her own body ached *with* if not necessarily *for* his. Instead of pulling back, she actually found herself holding him closer as if to protect him from the unkindness of the truth—a truth that would leave him wanting what he could never have. How well she understood that pain.

"*Time* isn't the issue here Steve. It's the hopelessness of it."

She reached up and stroked her friend's cheek.

"Even if a fish and a bird fell madly in love, where the hell would they live?

"In a bird bath."

Joanna just shook her head. In a mix of affection and frustration, she led him over to the couch and commanded him to sit down.

"What am I going to do with you?"

"You could just love me."

"I *do* love you. Trust me, if I didn't we wouldn't be having this conversation."

"Do you have any idea how badly I want to be with you? If you're saying you have feelings for me too, why won't you give us a chance? Please don't tell me it's the age difference."

Jo tried to be patient. She knew how much he was hurting.

"It's not that Steve."

The alcohol only made things worse. His aching heart gave way to bitter frustration.

"So what then… it can't work because I'm a simple country boy and you're some sophisticated city slicker? Or because I'm dirt poor and you're filthy rich? Or how 'bout this one… it's doomed because I'm a righty and you're a lefty."

Joanna cupped his face in her hands deliberately holding him still.

"Listen to me you irresistible fool, it'll never work because you're a guy and I'm a dyke."

It took several seconds for Steve's inebriated brain to process what she'd just said. So much for her intention of keeping things vague. Steve was undeniably stunned. There was no point pretending otherwise.

"A lesbian? *You*?"

She sat down beside him.

"Please don't go and say something stupid I'll have to forgive you for because you're drunk."

"Like what?"

"Like gee, you don't *look* like a lesbian."

"Christ, give me more credit than that." He hesitated. "I might *think* it, but I'd never *say* it."

They both laughed awkwardly. Steve got up and poured himself what little remained of the champagne.

"I'd say this calls for another toast… this one, to the depths of a man's ignorance. All this time I thought you were just fighting your feelings for me."

Joanna reached for his hand. She felt responsible for his embarrassment.

"You're right about that, I have been. I never expected… or wanted… to like you as much as I do."

Steve was still obviously confused.

"What about all those times I sensed you looking at my body, and I don't just mean when I was modeling."

"I couldn't resist looking… your body's amazing. But I was *admiring* it, not desiring it. There's a difference." Jo groped for anything that would lighten the mood. "Want your tool belt back?"

He cracked a smile and shook his head.

"Nah, you can still keep it." His eyes turned serious. "Why didn't you ever tell me, Jo?"

"I should have. I'm sorry but I came up here to brood, not bond… and in case you haven't noticed, I'm not exactly an open book."

Still struggling to reconcile Joanna's bombshell, Steve looked at her earnestly.

"Jo, Can I ask a personal question?"

She knew what was coming and nodded.

"Have you ever… you know… been with a man?"

"Several."

"And…?"

"Let's just say I test drove enough cars to know which models made my heart race and which ones didn't."

Steve made the most of her analogy.

"Sure I couldn't take you out for one more spin?"

He wasn't the first who hoped to convert her.

"Quite sure."

Ashamed for even asking, Steve leaned forward and buried his face in his hands.

"I guess I'm no different than every other jerk you've come across."

Jo squeezed him affectionately.

"You're the furthest thing from a jerk there is and one day you'll find the right girl. It's just not me."

She reached under his chin and turned his face toward hers. She wanted him to see her eyes.

"I mean it Steve. You're one of the sweetest guys I've ever met."

Despite her coaxing smile, he became all the sadder.

"I'm really lonely, Jo. I don't think I realized just how much until I met you. We really connected, didn't we?"

His vulnerability caught her off guard.

"Yeah, we really have."

He was at an obvious loss.

"So now what?"

"How 'bout for starters I forgive you for ruining a perfectly good pizza and you forgive me for ruining your life?"

The combination of her news and all the alcohol had definitely begun to take its toll.

"I'll drink to that! Got any more champagne?"

"How 'bout a cup of coffee instead?"

"Nope, don't think so."

Without warning Steve leapt up onto the modeling platform and began to sing.

"It's my party and I'll cry if I want to… cry if I want to… cry if I want to…you would cry too if this happened to you."

Joanna realized she had her hands full. She'd never seen Steve drunk before. She clapped for his performance, then coaxed him down and back to the couch.

"You're having that coffee. Now just stay put."

Steve slumped against the cushion. As Jo went about measuring the cups, he rambled on from across the room.

"I don't blame you, ya' know?"

"Don't blame me for what?"

"For being a lesbian. If I were a woman I'd definitely be one too."

For her own amusement, she encouraged him to expound on his nonsensical musings.

"And why is that?"

"Because we're one big pathetic lot, us men. And as soon as science figures out how to produce sperm without us, you can do away with the whole sorry bunch of us once and for all."

Joanna lit the flame under the perk, then came and sat down beside him. She patted his hand.

"Let's not be hasty. I say we just get through the night. We can determine your fate in the morning."

"You don't know what it's like for us guys. All we hear growing up is, 'Be a man! Be a man!'. It's the only instructions we ever get. So we try to be one and whenever we screw up, the first thing we hear women say to each other is 'What do you expect, he's a man'. Half the time we don't know *what* you want us to do."

Joanna tried not to laugh, especially since there was a lot of truth in Steve's exasperation.

"Tell you what, when the Grand Council Of Vaginas convenes, I'll make sure they take your point under advisement. In the meantime mister, drink this."

Jo handed him a large mug filled with black coffee. She also handed him a compliment.

"On the upside, your manuscript's really quite good."

"So you don't think I'm crazy to want to be a writer?"

"I didn't say that. Truth is, I think you *have* to be out of your mind. Carpentry is a much more dependable craft. But hey, it's your life."

"That's okay, I can take it."

"I know… because you're a man."

Steve made a serious attempt to sound forceful.

"Right… because I'm a man!"

His eyes were already half closed. Jo knew she was loosing him.

"Okay Papa Hemingway, we'll talk more about it when you're in better shape. Now get up."

Steve stumbled to his feet.

"You're right… I should be going."

"You're out of your fucking mind if you think I'm letting you get behind a wheel. I told you to get up so I could open the couch."

Jo tossed off the cushion and pulled out the bed. She pushed him back down on the mattress.

"Lift up your arms."

He obeyed and she removed his T-shirt. Steve teased her.

"Ah ha, you want my body after-all."

"Damn right, I do. You still owe me more modeling sessions. Take your pants off."

Jo waited patiently while Steve struggled to undo his belt and unzip his fly. Once he did, she pushed him down onto the bed and yanked his jeans off by the heels. Steve could barely pull himself up onto his elbows. He grinned from ear to ear.

"How 'bout my Jockeys?"

"Suit yourself."

As soon as she went for his waistband, Steve stopped her. His level of modesty was still greater that his level of intoxication. Jo grabbed one of the pillows and stuck it behind his head.

"Now lie back and don't give me any more problems."

"Where are *you* gonna' sleep?"

"Right next to you."

Steve did what he could to sound like a scoundrel.

"How do you know I won't try anything?"

"First, because that's just not you and second, because right now you couldn't find your dick with a roadmap, much less figure out where to stick it."

Steve appreciated how well she knew him.

Jo turned out the lights. Under the fluorescent glow of the one above the kitchen sink she went about cleaning up as quietly as she could. Steve's voice carried softly across the dimly lit room.

"I'm sorry Jo…"

She turned and looked at him.

"About what?"

"That bear that's been sittin' on your chest all these weeks."

He fell back against the pillow into a dead sleep. Joanna never liked being in the company of someone who'd had too much to drink. It usually gave them an uncanny ability to see straight through to the gritty, unedited truth and in their uncensored clarity, spew it at her feet before she was able to stop them. As Steve now lay unconscious, Jo envied his blissful stupor for the immediacy of its relief. She, on the other hand, had no such escape. Left with her own solitude, Jo reached for a sketchpad and a stick of charcoal. She cared little where her inspiration would take her, hoping only to edge herself closer to the end of another long and dismal day.

It was three in the morning when Jo finally looked up. She turned and glanced over at Steve. He was still sleeping soundly. She moved quietly to the screen door and gazed out across the yard. The house was dark and Beth's car was back in the driveway. Jo looked up at the woman's bedroom window, her torment now even greater for having been inside. She continued to stare, drowning in the memory of every intimate detail, while upstairs, Beth herself tossed restlessly in the darkness, equally tortured by the thought of Steve's hands moving slowly over Joanna's body. Eventually Jo turned away from the door and let her eyes drift across the room. Steve seemed so peaceful. In these last few weeks he had become so familiar and so dear to her heart. His strong, muscular body lay sprawled out in all its masculine splendor. It had been so long since Joanna had a man in her bed. She moved closer, careful not to awaken him. With adoring eyes she collected the sweetness of his expression. Just above the curve of his upper lip, the stubble of new beard had already broken through, exposing him to all the complicated burdens of manhood that would surely come to bear upon his gentle and sensitive nature. Regretful for her own part in his undeserving pain, Joanna ran her finger over the title page of his manuscript and then slowly backed away. She wandered over to the wall covered with the work of her own soul. Absorbing Steve's disappointment into her own, Jo stood in front of her studies of Beth. She was lost in the woman's eyes when Steve's voice cut through the stillness of the hour, startling her.

"I think she's lonely too Jo, I really do. There's so many of us out there… so many lonely people…"

Joanna turned around to find him up on his elbows. She had no idea how long he had been awake or how long he'd been watching her. Unable to find the words to acknowledge the sadness is his voice, she sat down on the bed beside him. He took her hand. It was a comfort to both of them.

"Can you forgive me Jo… for falling in love with you?"

She leaned over and kissed him tenderly on his forehead.

"Buy me breakfast in the morning, promise never to stop caring and you've got a deal."

Grateful for her reassuring terms. Steve lay back against the pillow and once again drifted off to sleep. For a while, Joanna sat there looking at him. In the soft glow of moonlight, he appeared more handsome than ever. She laid down beside him, fully clothed. Considering his desire for her she thought it would unnecessarily cruel to undress. Barely on the verge of consciousness, Steve found her hand.

"Thanks for letting me stay tonight." His voice was weighted with an impossible fatigue.

"I'm so crazy about you Jo..."

Even before she could answer, he began to snore. She said it anyway—simply because it was true and because there remained so much in her own heart she would never have the chance to say.

"I'm crazy about you too Steve, I'm crazy about you too..."

Jo was already showered and dressed when Steve finally woke to the smell of fresh coffee. He rubbed his eyes.

"Wasn't exactly the way I had envisioned our first night together, but it's sure nice to see your face first thing in the morning."

Not knowing what to expect, Jo was happy he awakened without a hangover and in his usual good spirits. She fixed him a cup and brought it over to the bed. Steve lifted himself up on one elbow and took a large satisfying gulp.

"Hmm... perfect. How'd you know?"

She winked playfully.

"I haven't forgotten how men like it."

"You didn't take advantage of me last night, did you?"

"That depends on how you look at it."

Jo pointed across the room to several new sketches she'd done of him while he slept.

His tone grew serious.

"Thanks for letting me crash here last night."

"You got yourself pretty drunk. I didn't have much choice."

"Sorry about that."

"I guess my own little piece of news didn't help any."

"Still, sometimes I think the only difference between a man and a fool is an understanding woman."

"Trust me, men aren't the only ones. Fools come in all shapes, sizes and sexual orientations." As Joanna yanked the sheets out from around his legs, she was grateful he didn't know she was referring to herself. "Now get your ass into the shower. I've been up for hours and I want that breakfast you owe me."

Steve caught her arm as his eyes searched hers for the truth.

"So we're okay. I mean in spite of *everything*?"

"We're more than okay *because* of everything."

Her smile was all the assurance he needed. Steve picked up his clothes and headed for the bathroom.

Jo kicked him playfully in the rear as he passed.

"And don't use my fucking toothbrush or my razor!"

Joanna was relieved the conversation with Steve was behind her and that the truth was finally out. Why couldn't things be that simple with Beth?

Steve emerged from his shower invigorated and feeling none the worse for all the champagne he'd consumed the night before. His hair was still wet, making the color of his thick wavy locks even more gloriously rich than usual. He whispered in her ear.

"Don't tell anyone I'm wearing the same underwear."

She whispered devilishly back.

"Don't tell anyone I'm not wearing any at all."

Steve moaned.

"Thanks a lot. I really didn't need to know that. Now I need another shower."

"Forget it! You can eat your heart out while I'm eating my breakfast."

The rough stubble of his beard was considerably darker than it was just a few hours ago. He defended himself under her scrutiny.

"You said not to use your razor."

"Actually, I like it. It has a sexy, rugged appeal." She sighed wistfully. "Like they say, 'what a waste'..."

"Since it won't be the romantic breakfast in bed I was hoping for, mind if I ask Beth to join us?"

Jo was not about to describe what their last exchange was like. She was absolutely certain of Beth's answer and that Steve was probably about to have his balls served to him on a platter, minus the extra loving touch of tiny marshmallows. She lied straight to his face.

"Fine with me. Go ask her. I'll meet you at your truck in ten minutes."

"Okay."

He stepped out onto the porch and drew a long, deep breath.

Joanna watched him stride across the lawn, whistling as he went. If she didn't know any better, she'd have sworn he'd just had a night of the best sex of his life. As he neared the house she began the countdown.

"You've got less than a few minutes left to that bubble. Enjoy it while it lasts."

Steve was already peering in through the screen door of the kitchen before Beth had a chance to collect the pieces of her turmoil. She had gone out of her way to avoid him the night before. She certainly didn't want to face him the morning after his all-night tryst with Joanna.

"Hey stranger," he called to her as he opened the door.

It never even occurred to him to ask it if was all right to come in. He planted his usual affectionate kiss on her cheek. The fact that his hair was still damp gave new life to Beth's torment. Plagued with images of steamy shower sex raging in her head, it was nearly impossible for her to look him in the eye. Steve was completely oblivious to her ordeal.

"Sorry I missed you last night."

"I got your message. I had other plans."

Steve leaned himself comfortably against the counter. His ease enraged her as Beth continued to flit anxiously around the room.

"I was surprised you didn't return my call."

"Get used to it. I've been working on freeing myself up from everyone's expectations."

Though her tone was sharper than anything he'd expected, Steve was quick to be supportive of any change she was trying to make.

"Good for you. Just as long as you're not trying to avoid *me* in particular."

His remark came much too close to the truth. Beth tried distancing herself from it.

"How was your visit with your folks?"

"Great. They always ask about you and Ben."

Beth's innermost conflicts raced to the surface.

"I can't imagine what you told them."

"What's that supposed to mean?"

"Nothing. Never mind."

Beth continued to move about the room hoping Steve would take the hint that this was not a particularly good time for a visit. Sensing her irritability, he tried leading up to his invitation.

"Bet you were surprised to see my truck still here this morning..."

Beth remained silent.

"Got myself quite a homecoming last night!"

Beth assumed he was inferring something very different than Joanna's bombshell—something very intimate, the details of which were the last thing in the world she wanted to hear. She grasped for anything that would change the subject.

"Are you growing a beard?"

Steve rubbed his cheek with the back of his own hand.

"Maybe… Jo said it gave me a kind of rugged sexy appeal. What do you think?"

Beth's thinly veiled composure had finally given way.

"You know what Steve, I've got more important things to consider this summer than whether or not you look better with a beard."

Now he was absolutely *sure* something was wrong. Steve struggled to understand what it was.

"It feels like we haven't seen each other in weeks. Hear much from Adam and Ben?"

"More from Ben."

Steve tried a little humor.

"I'm sure neither of us is surprised about that."

Still refusing to look at him, Beth barely nodded.

Steve had never seen her like this—just a degree shy of rude. He began to think maybe she was waiting for some kind of an explanation or apology. He tried to offer one.

"Ya' know, this summer's been crazy. One job just keeps leading to the next. Don't get me wrong, I'm not complaining. In this line of work, you take it as it comes and you're happy as shit when it does."

He waited, hoping she would say something. She didn't. By now there was no point in beating around the bush. He reached for her arm.

"Beth, you seem unusually stressed out. Is everything okay?"

She immediately pulled away.

"Why is that always the first question everyone always asks me?"

Steve's eyes remained sincere.

"I can't speak for everyone else. You just don't seem like yourself."

Beth snapped at his well-meaning observation.

"Why is that automatically cause for concern? Can't I be more than a one dimensionally cutout figure without it being a problem for everyone else? Why am I the only one around here who has to manage everyone *else's* complexities?"

Beth began to pace in front of him. She was hardly finished.

"Wasn't it you who encouraged me to explore my alter ego? 'The Dangerous Beth Garrison', I believe you called her. So what's the matter, she too unpredictable for you?"

Steve tried to smooth things over. Something was obviously going on he wasn't aware of. Something big! There was no way he was getting to the bottom of it all at once, certainly not with Jo waiting in his truck.

"You're a hundred percent right and I'm sorry. Can you forgive me?"

Momentarily appeased by his apology, Beth extended him the courtesy of a slight nod. He took advantage of her measured show of good will.

"So, is this *her* I'm meeting… 'The Dangerous Beth Garrison'?"

Beth remained guarded.

"It might be…"

"Okay then. How would you both like to join Joanna and me for breakfast? We can make it a foursome."

Obviously Steve had no idea what was going on inside her head. He was trying to be a friend the only way he knew how. Her resentment, if not her jealousy of him, eased enough for her to be civil.

"Thanks, but I think we'll both pass."

"Can I ask why?"

"I've already had breakfast."

Steve was cautiously lighthearted.

"What about 'The Dangerous Beth Garrison'? Maybe she's hungry."

Despite the fact that her entire world was coming apart at the seams, Beth's quirky sense of humor once again sprang to life.

"From the little I know of her so far, the only thing 'The Dangerous Beth Garrison' seems intent on is eating the old me alive."

They shared a tentative smile and both chose to leave it at that. For the first time since they'd met, the long-time friends parted on more uncertain terms than their usual heartwarming embrace ensured.

Joanna was sitting in the truck when Steve climbed in, his face noticeably troubled in a way she'd never seen before. She felt guilty for sending him off without a warning.

"So, will she be joining us?"

Steve ignored her question and started up the truck.

"I just had the strangest experience in there."

Jo downplayed her understanding of what might have gone on.

"Strange in what way?"

He pulled out of the driveway in dazed silence. They were halfway up the block when he finally responded.

"In all the years I've know that woman I can honestly say I've never seen her like that. She was actually hostile in there and the thing is, I can't figure out why or what I did."

Joanna hated to see Steve struggle with all his imagined inadequacies.

"For what it's worth, I wouldn't take it personally. The truth is, I think her reaction had more to do with *me* than it did you."

"You? Why with *you*?"

Jo felt she owed him the facts—this time, sooner rather than later.

"We sort of had a disagreement a few days ago." She hesitated. "Well, not exactly a disagreement... maybe more like a shouting match. I might have said a few things she didn't appreciate, so I'm not surprised she didn't want to be in my company this morning."

Steve couldn't imagine what the two women would have to argue about.

"What exactly did you say?"

"I accused her of having an affair with Nick."

Steve scoffed at the notion.

"Beth and *that* asshole? No way!"

"I caught them together."

"In bed?"

"No, you idiot! In town. On the street. They were strolling arm in arm, sharing a fucking ice cream cone."

"I don't care what it looked like. You misread the situation."

Although he'd immediately gone to Beth's defense, Steve couldn't help wonder if in fact her strange behavior had something to do with what Joanna saw. Could it be he was in denial about just how far Beth would go to explore that other side of herself this summer? The longer he thought about it, the more certain he was of his conviction.

"I'm sorry, there's no way Beth would get involved with the likes of him. Man, she must have been pissed as hell at you."

"It wasn't pretty."

"I'll bet!" Steve stopped at the light. "How's Trudy's for breakfast?"

Jo had all she could take of that location for a while—in reality and in her dreams.

"Anywhere but there."

"Don't tell me you accused Trudy of having an affair too?"

"Don't be a smart-ass. Just take me somewhere else."

Steve continued on to the diner on the other side of town. He was still curious about the tiff between the two women.

"What made you come at her like that anyway?"

Jo shook her head and remained silent for the rest of the ride. As usual, Steve was patient. He waited until they sat down, read the menus and ordered before bringing it up again.

"You never answered my question. What made you accuse Beth of having an affair? I mean, even if you saw what you think you saw, I still don't understand what business it was of yours."

"It's a long story."

"I'll rent the booth out by the hour. Start telling it."

It was obvious that this time Steve was intent on getting more of an explanation than Jo was accustomed to giving. It was as if their own little 'heart to heart' the night before suddenly changed the playing field, granting him the kind of access to her life he never had before. Their relationship had become more intimate. Not in the way Steve had hoped, but deeper none the less. It now demanded an openness Joanna could have lived without.

"I think I liked you more before you went to Ohio."

"Before I went to Ohio I was still hoping to bed you. Now I figure I got nothin' to lose."

"Don't kid yourself. You've got plenty to lose and they're hanging between your legs!"

"Fair enough... *my* balls for *your* story. You give it up first."

Seeing no way out, Jo recounted the events as matter-of-factly as her heart would allow.

"The night Beth posed I mentioned something about wanting to do some landscape painting. She told me about this really beautiful spot she discovered years back when she and Ben first moved to the area. Said it was her favorite place in the whole world... secluded... serene. She suggested we picnic there one day and I was pretty psyched about it." Jo wondered whether she might be admitting too much. "It turns out she's not the world's worst company." Jo tried not to read anything into Steve's smile. "Anyway, every time I tried pinning her down to set a date, she found another excuse to put it off. So I thought I'd wait 'til *she* brought it up. She never did so I asked again... kind of a spur of the moment thing for the next day. When she said she had other plans, I told her to break them. She got angry and said something about having a life before I got here. I was pretty bummed out but I figured, 'fuck it', I'll do some exploring on my own. After I had lunch at Trudy's, I took a drive through town. That's when I saw her with that schmuck. I couldn't believe it. The guy's a fucking asshole and *those* were the plans too important to break! I wasn't gonna' say anything. Who gives a crap what she does with her life? When I got back, our paths crossed... one remark led to another and we sorta' got into it. Somewhere in there I accused her of having an affair. We wound up in a shouting match across the yard, doors got slammed and we haven't spoken since. That was a few days ago."

Steve sat back and crossed his arms.

"So things haven't exactly been dull around here while I was gone."

Jo took her first forkful of food since the waitress had put down their plates.

"Shit. Now my eggs are cold. You and your goddamn questions." She pushed her plate aside, stewing over a lot more than a spoiled breakfast. "I don't get it... Beth with a guy like that?"

"I'm telling you, she's not having an affair."

"Then why wouldn't she change her plans? What's the hell's so irresistible about *him*?"

"Absolutely nothing... that's just it." Steve found all of it quite obvious. "Did you ever stop and think that maybe Nick was just safer company than you are? Judging from those studies, I'd say you exposed a side of Beth very few people ever see. Maybe the sudden intensity of that scared her. In case you haven't noticed, her life isn't exactly a walk on the wild side. I'd think sharing an ice cream cone in the middle of town with someone who's mostly interested in seeing through her blouse would be a lot less threatening than going on some secluded picnic with someone who obviously sees clear through to her soul."

"I guess I never looked at it that way."

"No, you were too busy being jealous."

Jo couldn't risk having him think he was right.

"Not jealous, *annoyed*!"

At least for the moment, he didn't challenge her on that point.

"What'd she say when you told her you were a lesbian?"

Jo played with an empty sugar pack. She wasn't used to being vague about her sexuality.

"Let's just say it never came up."

Steve shook his head.

"In other words, you let her assume you were straight."

It was not one of Joanna's most prideful moments.

"I had my reasons."

"And what might they be?"

Joanna was not having much more of this.

"Funny, but I don't recall ordering an inquisition with my eggs."

"You didn't tell her because you're attracted to her, aren't you?"

He had come much too close to the truth. Jo pounced on him.

"We lesbians have a saying, 'the shortest distance between here and hell is a straight woman' and we get there even faster if she happens to be a wife and mother."

"Is that supposed to be an answer?"

"It's as close to one as you're gonna' get."

"All the same, your little saying sounds kind of shallow to me."

"You call it 'shallow'. I call it 'safe'."

"I see, so Beth isn't allowed to hide in the company of some sexist schmuck but it's okay for you to duck behind some lame Sapphic cliché?"

However true, Jo did not like being painted as a coward.

"I'm beginning to regret not letting you get behind the wheel last night."

Steve ignored her comment.

"For cryin' out loud Jo, who cares *what* she is? All I know is that in those studies I saw *who* she is, and if I know Beth, I'm damn sure she saw it too." Steve used Joanna's silence to his advantage.

"Want my advice?"

"No!"

"Ya' know that picnic you mentioned? Ask her again."

"I guess you didn't hear me. I said 'no' to the advice."

Steve put his hands up and shrugged.

"Okay, stay miserable and angry with each other for the rest of the summer."

Joanna slammed her cup down.

"Or I can just leave."

"Yep, that sounds about right. It's obvious you're on the run from you *own* life. You might as well run from *hers* as well."

Rankled by his judgment, Jo was determined to cast him in an equally unflattering light.

"Let's say you actually know what the hell you're talking about… that this so-called intensity between us is really upsetting to her. If she means so damn much to you, why would you want to see her in such a vulnerable and threatening place?"

Steve's voice mellowed with sincerity.

"Because more than anything else in this world, what Beth needs is to look into a pair of eyes that see exactly what *you* see in hers… regardless of the consequence."

Jo wasn't sure what Steve was implying.

"Let me understand something. Are you suggesting I try to seduce the revered professor's wife."

"Moral judgments aside, you don't have to *try*. You already *have*. Just take a good look at those studies. How much more evidence do you need?" Steve remained pure of heart as he continued to speculate about her recent mood. "Whatever's going on I can guarantee you one thing, Beth wasn't prepared for it. You can't just turn your back and walk away from her now." Steve looked at Jo dead on. "Unless, of course, *you're* afraid."

He knew she would ask. He was counting on it. Not surprisingly, Jo's tone was defiant.

"Afraid of what?"

"Afraid that by the very nature of seduction, the seducer becomes the seduced."

Joanna leaned threateningly closer.

"Okay, here's the deal… you drop this subject right now and I let you live. Take it or leave it."

Steve knew he'd made his point. He also knew Jo well enough to let her think this conversation over.

"I'll take it."

He finished his coffee and signaled the waitress for the check.

Steve's unannounced visit had plunged Beth into an even greater state of misery than she'd endured all night. Now the whole 'Dangerous Beth Garrison' thing added to her bitterness. She was annoyed with him for ever suggesting such a ridiculous persona and even more annoyed with herself for turning its deeply conflicted emergence into some kind of a joke. Unsure of how much she could take, Beth got out the calendar and considered her options for what remained of the summer. Each one felt like a pathetic and cowardly escape. She could join her husband in England, she could insist that Joanna leave, or she could stick things out just the way they were and pretend her whole existence was not slowly decaying in the process. Beth stared in disbelief at the date. It was July 27th. In the course of her unraveling a whole month had somehow slipped by.

In the tiny portion of her mind that still functioned clearly, Beth realized the end of the month meant paying some bills. Welcoming anything she could accomplish simply by rote, she reached for her checkbook as though reaching for her salvation. At the moment, reconciling her bank statement seemed a much more plausible undertaking that reconciling her life. Among the statements was the one for the phone in the carriage house. She slammed her pen down.

"Why does everything have to lead me back to that damn woman?"

Fueled by her frustration and the knowledge that Joanna was out having breakfast with Steve, Beth attached a small yellow post-it note to the bill and stomped her way across the tranquility of her backyard.

Now on the front step, the shield of her steely determination suddenly felt more like a child's costume than a worthy coat of armor against the savage onslaught of images that charged at her heart. Through the screen door Beth could see the leftover scene of the couple's night of lovemaking. Despite her impulse to turn and run, the cruel traces of their intimacy drew her eyes, like a moth to a flame, forcing her to relive every dreaded detail of the tormented hours she'd spent lying awake in the dark. She noticed the new charcoal sketches of Steve taped to the wall. The intricately drawn sheets wrapped loosely around his torso concealed the most intimate parts. The tenderly rendered studies revealed more than Beth could bear to see. The empty bottle of champagne and opened bed in disarray confirmed everything she had envisioned their night of passion to be. Beth glared at the three roses and the sweetness of Steve's offering. Knowing Steve, she was certain each had a special meaning. Overcome with envy, Beth hated him for being so thoughtful. Even more, she hated him for the entitlement of his manhood that gave him the privilege of vying for Joanna's heart—the privilege of taking Jo into his arms and pleasuring her body. Once again the impossible limitation of her desire left Beth aching and empty. When her heart had withstood all the pain it could endure, she surrendered the bill she still clutched in her hand. She slipped it under the door, raced back to the house and immediately retreated up to her bedroom. There, Beth hurled herself across her own neatly made bed, buried her face in her pillow and burst into tears. Whatever clarification she'd hoped this summer would bring, Beth now felt more lost than ever before. For awhile she lay there sobbing amid the remnants of her torn and shredded life. Eventually her purging led to sleep. She woke an hour later, resolved. Beth swore to herself she had cried her last tear and sacrificed the last day of her hard-won solitude to Joanna. She washed her face, combed her hair and applied just enough mascara to mask the sadness in her eyes. She'd made her decision. When Joanna returned from breakfast, she would ask her to leave. No longer could she live under these conditions—so deeply and so hopelessly in love.

Considering the risk Steve took with their conversation over breakfast and her icy silence the entire ride back, Joanna's parting kiss was more forgiving than he expected. As she trudged up the driveway, he called out through the window of his truck.

"See ya' Monday morning. We've got two more jobs we've got to bid on and a new tool belt to break in."

Beth had been waiting nervously in her kitchen. Relieved that Jo had returned alone, her plan was to step out onto the porch, say what she had to say, then quickly retreat. Given the tension between them, Beth was counting on the fact that Joanna wouldn't need more of an explanation. As Jo's footsteps grew closer, Beth's heart raced faster. She was about to make her move when the telephone rang. From thousands of miles away Ben once again managed to control his wife's life. Beth chose to answer, well aware of her own complicity in this instance. She listened patiently as the familiar voice asked all the predictable questions. Beth answered by rote while she watched Joanna cross the lawn and disappear into the carriage house. Her window of opportunity had passed. Now Beth would have to wait for her reluctant heart to once again gather the courage to carry out her decision. Certain Jo would soon be stopping by with the check for the phone bill, she would tell her then and be done with it.

Joanna bent and picked up the statement Beth had slipped under the door. She read the unsigned note: 'If you insist on paying for the phone, I'll take a check whenever it's convenient'. Holding the brittle communication in her hand, Jo searched the eyes of Beth's portraits for everything Steve was convinced they revealed. She hated to think he might be right as much as she hated the chance he might be wrong. Both possibilities presented complications Joanna could certainly live without. She slapped the bill across the palm of her hand as she continued to weigh her options. At the very least she felt she owed Beth an apology for not minding her own business. Joanna took out a pad and some markers, scolding herself for what she was about to do.

Beth was rinsing some dishes when from the window over the sink, she spotted Joanna making her way across the yard. Certain her only hope of surviving their encounter was to keep busy, she hastily collected a can of tuna, a jar of mayonnaise and a mixing bowl from the pantry. She was groping nervously in the vegetable bin for some celery and onions when Jo appeared at the kitchen door. Her demeanor was less arrogant than Beth expected.

"Hi. Can I talk to you?"

Along with her life, Beth lay all the ingredients on the counter.

"Yes. Come in."

Grateful for the much warmer welcome that BJ extended, Jo shoved the papers she was carrying into her jeans pocket so that her hands were free to encourage him. Running her fingers through his thick golden fur, she tried to break the ice.

"I brought the check for the phone."

Beth simply nodded as she proceeded to empty the can of tuna into the bowl. Gripping the side of the dish, she somehow managed to find her voice.

"There's something I need to talk to you about."

"Yeah, me too."

Beth took a measured breath, hoping and dreading that Jo had reached the same conclusion. At least she would be spared having to banish Joanna from her life. Years from then Beth hoped that would ease even the smallest portion of her regret.

"Fine. You go first."

Joanna watched the woman methodically chopping one celery stalk after another, recalling the massive amount of fruit salad Beth had cut up the day they'd met. It was hard to believe that was only a month ago. In so little time her mild amusement had deepened into something so much more. Jo couldn't help staring at the woman's hands, marked by their constant animation and the simple but glaring wedding band. With every second that passed in silence, Beth's teeth dug deeper into her bottom lip.

"I owe you an apology for the other day. Whatever's going on, it's none of my business."

An apology was the last thing Beth expected. She let her conflict mold her anger.

"You're right. It isn't any of your business. Nor will it ever be."

Jo surprised her again, this time offering her a rare glimpse of vulnerability.

"I was disappointed about the picnic. When I saw the two of you together that day, I guess I over-reacted."

The irony of Jo's resentment over her choice of companionship triggered Beth's painful jealousy toward Steve. The bittersweet reward of it hardened her voice.

"Well now that Steve is back, he can take you on all the romantic picnics your heart desires."

The humility of Joanna's apology instantly faded.

"What the hell does that mean?"

"I think it's obvious."

With her attention entirely focused on maintaining the little composure she had left, Beth reached for the jar of mayonnaise and absentmindedly spooned an excessive amount into the mixing bowl. She hated Joanna for making her spell it out.

"The fact that the two of you are sleeping together… that you're lovers!"

"You don't know what you're talking about."

"Please don't insult me! I may not lead the most sophisticated life, but I wasn't born yesterday! This morning when I left the phone bill, I saw it all… the flowers, the bottle of champagne, the sketches, the bed! I'm not an idiot Jo. Please don't treat me like one!"

Beth's groundless accusations of an affair were now ironically reversed. Joanna's resentment sprang to life.

"We're not lovers, damn it!"

Beth felt herself ready to explode. She picked up the knife and began dicing the onion with frightening precision.

"Fine! Whatever you say!"

Joanna had to stop herself from grabbing Beth by the shoulders and shaking her. Not since the day of their accident had she felt such rage.

"Don't make me wish I'd killed you the morning you rammed my car."

Her anger had reached a pitch that roused BJ from his nap. He looked up curiously as Jo continued to rant.

"I'm gonna' say this for the last time, Steve and I are not lovers! I don't sleep with men. I'm a lesbian."

For a split second, everything in Beth's life froze. It would not have surprised her if the clock on the kitchen wall had stopped ticking—waiting for her heart to recalibrate itself and begin to beat again. She couldn't be sure that it would—not *then*—not *ever*. Beth was incapable of a response. Nor, could she bring herself to look up. While her body trembled violently from within, Beth did not move a single muscle except for the hand that immediately began a slow, deliberate blending of all the ingredients she'd dumped into the bowl. Joanna waited but got no response.

"Did you hear what I just said?"

Beth convinced herself that as long as she didn't meet Joann's eyes she would be safe. With one hand gripping the bowl, the other continued to stir faster and faster.

"Yes, I heard you."

Inside her own head Beth's tiny voice sounded as if it had come from a million miles away. The pace of her hand escalated, gradually turning the chunky consistency of an ordinary tuna salad into a puree. Joanna was desperate to know what Beth was thinking.

"The other day you accused me of not sharing anything about my life. Now that I have, aren't you going to say something?"

In spite of Jo's pressure, all Beth could manage was a trance-like nod incorporated into her now fiercely accelerated churning. Without warning, Jo reached out and grabbed Beth by her wrist, forcing her to let go of the fork.

"Okay, before you make the Guinness Book Of Records as the world's fastest human blender, I need you to stop that and look at me."

Beth felt like an absolute fool. If only for a moment, Beth mustered enough courage to look directly into Joanna's eyes. With all the treacherous glances that had come before, they had never seemed more beautiful or more demanding. The instant Jo released her hand, Beth reached for the pepper mill as if were a lifeline. She knew Joanna was still waiting.

"What do you want me to say?"

"For starters, you can tell me whether or not you hate me."

"Why would I hate you?"

"Because I had lots of chances and I didn't tell you sooner."

Beth made a ridiculous attempt to sound nonchalant about Joanna's news.

"Why? What does your sexuality have to do with me?"

Inside her own mind, Beth tried frantically to answer that question for herself. It was as if suddenly her entire existence had been placed precariously on the head of a pin, in danger of toppling over from something as ordinary as her next breath. Beth groped for a new strategy. She was not prepared to give up the prohibitive boundaries that had previously defined their relationship in her mind—boundaries that while unbearably painful, had spared her from having to negotiate the impropriety of her own desire. In the absence of those boundaries, the now terrified mother and wife struggled to find her own meaning in all of this. Her life as she once knew it drained from her body. Beth was scared to death to look down at the floor—afraid that she would see nothing more than a puddle of herself, and in its reflection the innocent faces of her husband and young son. With her knees now threatening to buckle out from under her, Beth wiped her hands and sat down at the kitchen table. Joanna's original question had become buried under so many of her own.

"I don't understand. He spent the night." Beth envisioned the room. "I know what I saw."

Joanna pulled out the chair next to her.

"He stayed over because he was too drunk to go home. There was no way I was letting him get behind a wheel in his condition."

Beth looked puzzled.

"I've never known Steve to drink excessively."

"He had something he needed to get off his chest. By the time he got up the nerve he couldn't walk a straight line, much less drive."

"Steve is one of the most expressive men I know. Maybe it's none of my business but what could he possibly have found so hard to say?"

"That he'd fallen in love with me" She hesitated about admitting the rest. "I guess my own little late-breaking confession didn't help matters. It took him the rest of the bottle to get over *that* one."

"You mean in all the time you spent together these last few weeks you hadn't told him either?"

Jo shook her head shamefully.

"That should make you feel better. At least now you don't think you're the only one I haven't shared the details of my life with. As it turns out, I'm an equal opportunity withholder."

Beth's concern shifted to Steve. Now with nothing to secretly resent him for, the full measure of her affection returned. Sympathy for the pain of his unrequited love replaced weeks of apparently unwarranted jealousy. She felt awful for deliberately avoiding him all month and especially for treating him so harshly earlier that morning. She now realized what he must have meant when he said he had himself quite a homecoming—a homecoming she wouldn't let him finish describing before practically throwing him out.

"Oh, the poor guy. He must have been devastated."

Jo didn't need Beth to make her feel any worse about the consequences of her dishonesty.

"He didn't suffer much. The champagne knocked him out pretty quickly."

"What about your relationship? You really seem to have hit it off."

"We'll be fine."

Beth's concern over Steve's reaction was a temporary distraction from her own. For the moment, she found the potentially threatening news s a bit easier to discuss.

"I can't imagine *you*, of all people, being in the closet."

"I'm not. I've been out since I was eighteen years old. There isn't anyone in my life who doesn't know." Jo could hardly explain why she'd chosen to be less than forthcoming in this case. "Let's just say that all these years later I'm finding out that *cleaning* a closet can be a lot more complicated than just coming out of one." She hesitated. "There's a lot back in New York left to sort out."

Beth's smile suggested she understood the unspoken implication. Though intensely curious, she dared not push for more details. Once again, Joanna offered her an apology, this time for her secrecy.

"I'm sorry I haven't been more open. I really hadn't planned on making any meaningful connections this summer. In fact, I was hell-bent on avoiding any."

"I know just what you mean."

"I guess we can both kiss those expectations goodbye."

Beth's voice curled modestly into itself.

"Yes, I suppose..."

"If only I'd gotten out of that mall with just a bruised ankle..."

Beth lowered her eyes.

"Yes, if only you had..."

The women fell silent, each hoping the other might confess to something more. Neither did. After a few awkward seconds they both looked away, leaving all their unspoken 'if onlys' lodged in their separate hearts. Jo saw no choice but to move on.

"So what was it you wanted to talk to me about?"

The last thing Beth wanted was for Joanna to leave now. The unexpected news had changed everything. Beth knew the only thing greater than her conflict was the threat that conflict posed to her life. In her heart, she was sure of nothing, except that she needed more time to sort things out.

"It can wait."

Between last night and this morning, Jo already had more conversation than she'd been looking for. She didn't try to hide her relief.

"Then I guess I'll head back to the carriage house and crash. It was a long night and not a whole lot of it had anything to do with sleep."

Beth had no intention of admitting just how sleepless a night it had been for her too. Joanna rubbed the back of her neck.

"I'd almost forgotten how much work a man could be."

Beth laughed.

"God yes. Even the best of them."

Jo reached into her pocket for the check.

Beth was reluctant to accept it.

"Please take it."

Jo was eager to preserve at least one small part of their original bargain, especially since it was increasingly obvious that their mutual pact to stay out of each other's lives was becoming harder and harder, if not altogether impossible. Joanna wavered about the other thing she had in her back pocket.

"For whatever it's worth, I'm leaving this for you..."

Jo leaned a curious envelope up against the mixing bowl filled with the soupy tuna salad. Beth was certain of the deliberate placement.

"What is it?"

Jo replayed Steve's observation in her head.

"Proof that I must be out of my mind!"

Before she came to her senses and snatched the thing back, Joanna made a clean break to the door. As soon as it slammed, Beth hurried over to the counter. Jo had folded a sheet of paper in such a way that it became its own envelope. On the front of it she'd scribbled a note.

"You'd suggested I might try *begging* or a *written invitation*. I figured I'd do both."

Beth smiled as her fingers worked eagerly to unfold the page. On the top Jo had drawn a small cartoon figure down on one knee with its hands clasped. Centered beneath it was a handwritten invitation.

'Against my better judgment,
the pleasure of your company is cordially requested
for an old-fashioned picnic
on the day of your choosing.
Kindly RSVP... (before I change my mind).'

Through the kitchen window Beth watched Joanna make her way across the yard. She looked back down at the sweet, silly invitation. In a moment of sheer impulse, Beth burst through the screen door and out onto the porch. Joanna had just reached the front steps of the carriage house when Beth called out to her.

"I'm RSVPing! Before I change *my* mind and against my *own* better judgment, I accept!"

Joanna froze. A triumphant smile spread across her face. Preferring that Beth didn't see, she called back across the yard without turning around.

"Are you sure?"

"I've never been less sure of anything in my life!"

Joanna's smile widened.

"Fair enough. When?"

Beth threw caution to the wind while she still had the nerve.

"Tomorrow."

Safely hidden, Joanna's heart rejoiced.

"I'll be in your driveway at ten sharp."

Beth couldn't imagine being able to wait 'til then.

"Just bring your art supplies. I'll pack us a wonderful lunch."

Jo couldn't resist teasing her.

"If it's that tuna salad you just made, you'd better throw in a couple of straws."

Jo swung open the carriage house door and disappeared inside. Still clutching the invitation in her hand, Beth wandered into her living room and collapsed on the loveseat that faced the piano. She stared at Joanna's flowers and retraced the emotionally charged weeks in between. With frighteningly vivid detail, Beth recalled the night Jo brought over her laundry and the dream in which she'd done the most unspeakable things. "Oh God," Beth thought to herself, "what if she's wearing those jeans tomorrow?" A mix of thrill and terror raced around inside her head until she could no longer tell which was chasing which.

Joanna hadn't been asleep more than ten minutes when the phone rang. She stumbled across the room to answer it.

Beth sounded nervous.

"It's just me. What if it rains tomorrow?"

Jo looked at the phone in her hand.

"Is that what you woke me to ask?"

Beth's voice shrunk with embarrassment.

"Yes."

"It won't rain."

Beth couldn't imagine how she would ever live with the disappointment if it did. Her need for reassurance was almost childlike.

"How can you be sure?"

Jo was much too exhausted to resist the forces that seemed intent on playing recklessly with her life.

"Because evidently 'The Gods' have spoken." Joanna couldn't see Beth smile. Nor could she ever imagine Beth's own sense of powerlessness where it concerned their relationship. "I'll see you at ten. Now let me get some sleep."

Even after Jo had abruptly hung up, Beth continued to speak softly into the phone.

"Please, don't be a minute late...." She held the receiver against her heart. "I think I've been waiting for tomorrow all my life."

Chapter 14

After an restless night of endless tossing, the sudden sound of splashing from the pool made the threat of Joanna Cameron all the more immediate and all the more real. Dread played leapfrog with anticipation as Beth swung herself out of bed, threw on a shirt and walked tentatively over to the window. Jo had been right about the weather. It was an exquisite day—the kind that seemed to suggest that the universe approved whole-heartedly of their plans. Under an absolutely cloudless sky Beth watched as Joanna swam her laps, marveling at the woman's carefree indulgence while she herself had to struggle just to remain steady on her feet. Beth had little choice now but to dive head first into whatever lay ahead. She opened the window wide enough to lean out and struggled to sound convincingly lighthearted.

"Morning! You were right, it's a beautiful day… guess our picnic's on."

Jo reached for the ladder.

"Disappointed?"

Beth hoped that only her words, and not her apprehension, would spill forth.

"Don't be silly."

"Good, 'cause there's no way you're getting out of it."

Joanna lifted herself out of the water and sat, bare-chested, on the edge of the pool. Beth felt instantly lightheaded. She pretended to take this second unexpected exposure to Joanna's breasts in stride.

"I'm going in for a shower. See you at ten."

Beth tried not to think about why she took extra care in shaving her legs. With years of practice readying an entire family for an outing in less time than it took most people to brush their teeth, she prepared and packed every practical thing she and Joanna could possibly need for the day. Her nervous energy only added to her efficiency and now with unwanted time to spare, Beth sat anxiously at her kitchen table, her eyes darting back and forth between the clock on the wall and the cooler she'd placed at the kitchen door. BJ hovered nearby all morning. Now he lay with his snout on her lap. After years of mutual companionship, the two understood each other well. Beth smiled at his maneuvering as she stroked the top of his head.

"I'd love to take you along but I'm afraid this is something I have to do on my own."

BJ licked her hand forgivingly, shuffled off to his favorite corner and lied down. Beth rubbed the middle of her stomach and looked at the clock. If she hurried, she still had time for one last trip to the toilet while she waited for the Imodium she'd taken to kick in. Diarrhea was the last thing she needed to add to her concerns about this day.

Joanna was leaning on the porch railing when Beth came out of the bathroom.

"Ready?"

Beth forced a self-conscious smile.

"All set."

Unable to prevent Jo from coming inside to help carry things to the car, Beth prayed that the telltale odor of her bowel movement didn't make its way past the hall before she could hurry Jo back outside. But life's little hurdles always came in threes and apparently this morning was no exception. First there was Joanna's bare breasts, then diarrhea and now this: Jo was indeed wearing the same pair of jeans Beth had caressed in her laundry dream. Beth quickly put on her sunglasses, wondering how much panic the darkened lenses could hide. Jo set the heavily packed cooler down in the driveway. Beth read her mind.

"Guess I'm used to packing for an entire family."

Jo surveyed everything they were taking along. Between the cooler, Beth's overstuffed tote and her own bag of art supplies, there was no way it was all fitting into the small trunk of her car.

"Looks like we won't be taking the T-Bird."

Beth smiled shyly.

"It really is a beautiful car. Aren't you afraid to drive it?"

"I wasn't until I met you." Joanna finished her musing privately in her own head. "There were a lot of things I wasn't afraid of until I met you…"

In a day already laced with inherent dangers and uncertainties, Beth was eager for whatever elements of assurance she could find.

"Let's take Ben's Jeep. It's much more reliable than my car."

"Fine."

Jo loaded their things in the back.

Beth waited behind the wheel recalling that the last time she'd been this nervous pulling out of her own driveway was the morning she'd taken her husband to the airport. It seemed unimaginable how that day had led to this one.

The route took them through the center of town. Beth didn't say a word about the irony of now sitting at the same traffic light where Joanna had obviously spotted her and Nick the afternoon she'd gone out of her way to avoid these very plans. She turned on the radio to fill the silence. As she pulled away from the intersection, the words to the old Johnny Mathis classis, "Chances Are" thickened in the space between them. Beth gripped the wheel and began attacking her lip. Joanna turned and focused on the passing scenery through the passenger window. Now on the outskirts of town, the landscape gave way to open fields and random roadside vegetable stands. The traffic coming from the opposite direction thinned to an occasional pick-up truck, wandering dog and dusty tractor. For a fleeting moment, the contrasting congestion of city life filtered through Joanna's mind. She didn't welcome the reminder of all she'd left behind and all that waited for her return. She wanted only this day and the company of this woman sitting beside her.

"Tell me again how you found this place."

Beth welcomed any easy question—one she could answer simply and honestly, for a change.

"When we first moved to Amherst Ben and I enjoyed hiking together. We were always looking for new trails and back roads to explore. Gradually he became more involved in his work and I became more consumed by my music."

Lost in her recounting Beth no longer felt threatened by the intensity of Joanna's eyes that now rested squarely upon her. A reflective tone crept into Beth's voice.

"I remember how awkward Ben and I were at first about our drifting. We would apologize and make excuses for our priorities, but the truth was our increasingly separate pursuits seemed to serve us well… until my solitude began to threaten his."

Jo came to her own conclusion.

"Which led to that lunch tray in the carriage house."

Beth nodded quietly. She took a moment to reconcile the course of her life from that fateful day on.

"One morning in early spring I was tending to the garden in the backyard when an unbearable sadness swept over me. No matter how hard I tried, I couldn't seem to shake it. Ben was buried in his usual paperwork. I didn't want to disturb him so I went to the carriage house hoping to lose myself in my music, but that only made the sadness worse. It was such a beautiful morning… not unlike this one. I thought maybe a ride in the countryside might cheer me up.

I remember Ben barely looked up from his reading when I announced that I was going out for a while. I'd already begun pulling out of the driveway when he bolted out onto the porch and said he wanted to join me. I found it so odd. It was almost as though he was suddenly afraid to let me out of his sight. For a moment I was tempted to let him come along, but something instinctive told me I needed to be alone even though I didn't have the slightest idea where I was going. For a while, I just drove around, following the terrible weight in my heart. I don't know how I eventually wound up at a small clearing in the foothills just outside of town." Her voice mellowed. "The moment I stepped out of the car it felt like I'd entered another world… a world that seemed to welcome the sadness I'd brought with me." Beth's voice filled with longing. "Over the years, whenever that unexplainable sadness returned, I would go back and it would comfort me every time. Of course it became harder and harder to sneak away once I had the boys."

"You mean you never once brought your family?"

There was not a trace of apology in Beth's tone.

"No. To this day Ben doesn't even know this place exists."

"Why?"

"Because it's the only place in the world where I feel free to be myself. It's just too sacred… too private."

"So until today you've only been there alone?"

A playful smile spread across Beth's face.

"I said I'd never brought anyone *with* me. That doesn't mean I was there alone."

Joanna's became instantly suspicious, then jealous, of a secret rendezvous. As was much too often the case, Beth read her mind.

"It's nothing like that."

Beth turned off the state road and onto a dirt one that now wound more steeply upward through denser foliage. Eventually they came to an unmarked fork; one road led further up, the other appeared to lead back down. She steered to the left and continued their climb. This part of the road was decidedly bumpier and much less predictable. Beth maneuvered over the terrain by heart and pointed excitedly to the right.

"It's over there, just up ahead!"

Jo followed the direction of Beth's extended arm. Through the brush she could make out a clearing about a hundred feet away. The Jeep continued to buck and bounce over the irregular road before Beth brought the vehicle to a stop. She turned off the radio, then the ignition. In the sudden absence of man-made noise all the welcoming sounds of the environment came forward to greet them. For a few solemn moments neither woman spoke a word. Eventually Beth opened her door and stood alongside the Jeep. Drawing a deeply relieved breath, she gazed at the familiar landscape as if beholding the image of a long lost friend. It had been three years. She had visited once soon after Danny's death, but hadn't been back since. After such a devastating loss, it had become much too painful to come so close to herself.

Aware of the intimate connection Beth shared with the surroundings, Jo respectfully hung back in the car. She watched as Beth took it all in, occasionally rubbing her arms from the morning chill that lingered in the mountain air. Just as on the night of the outdoor concert, Jo's impulse was to warm Beth in her arms. This time she did not even have her denim jacket to offer. After a while, Joanna came and stood quietly at Beth's side. Looking out at the expanse before her, Jo could see instantly why Beth had fallen in love with this spot. She had not overstated its splendor or its tranquility. Cloistered between thick trees and brush on both sides, a lush grassy knoll about the size of a baseball diamond extended outward before them. The rich green field sloped slightly downward so that if you were child-like enough at heart you might let yourself roll forever to the far end, over the edge and off into time. A measured distance in from the drop, an imposing boulder at least eight feet in diameter and six feet high commanded the otherwise soft, open field. Patches of wildflowers grew out from around its base like delicate offerings to a great and powerful thing. Off in the distance, as far as the eye could see, was a glorious view of the surrounding valley. Clusters of small New England towns, complete with white steepled churches lay nestled in the foothills of the majestic Berkshire Mountains. The Connecticut River wound like a ribbon through the landscape below while great puffs of clouds drifted across a magnificent open sky. The entire scene might well have come from one of those stock photo images the agency would have chosen for a print ad depicting the soothing lie of the New England countryside at its quintessential best. In spite of her long-held preference for stainless steel and other man-made fineries, Jo had to admit that every once in a while Mother Nature managed to pull off a pretty impressive thing or two herself. These immediate surroundings certainly qualified as a stunning example. Beth was gratified by Joanna's reaction.

"Breathtaking, isn't it?"

Jo nodded solemnly.

"It really is."

"I thought you'd like it."

In a burst of enthusiasm, Beth hurried back to the Jeep. She flung open the hatch, collected her tote and blanket and raced across the field. She seemed to know exactly where she wanted it spread.

"C'mon. The view is best from over here."

Joanna followed with the cooler, then went back for her camera and art supplies. By the time she'd returned, Beth had already set out the blanket and was riffling around in her bag for Adam's portable radio and cassette player. Jo tossed her own things off to the side and sat down beside her. No longer distracted by the task of setting things out, the two women now sat perfectly still, painfully aware of the few conspicuous inches between them. Jo noticed the familiar weave in the old chenille throw.

"Isn't this the same blanket we shared the night of that concert?"

Beth was surprised by Joanna's recall.

"Yes, as a matter of fact it is."

"Minus one symphony orchestra, half the population of Amherst and our would-be dates, here we are again."

Beth reflected on the deeply unsettling weeks in between

"It's been a rather interesting month."

"That would be one way to describe it."

Their awkward smiles spoke volumes about Joanna's inference—an inference that neither dared discuss at any greater length. For the next few minutes, the unspoken thrill and torment of each others company swirled around them. If their plans were a mistake, it was one each of them would have made over and over again. Trapped in a tenuous mix of emotions, each turned her eyes away from the other and focused on the sweeping view that stretched out before them. Joanna leaned back on her elbows.

"It really is beautiful out here."

"This is nothing compared to the fall."

As soon as she said the words, Beth's spirits sank with the realization that by then Jo would no longer be around. She worked to conceal the shattered pieces of her heart.

"The colors of the foliage are absolutely exquisite from up here."

Jo's heart filled with its own secret regret.

"I'm sure it's amazing."

Beth could not bear the finality of their parting.

"You'll just have to come back for a visit in the fall."

Jo was careful to keep her eyes peeled on the valley.

"We'll see…"

Each was sure the other understood the futility of hoping for anything more than this summer. Beth forced herself not to dwell on the future. She still had this perfect day and there was so much she was eager to share.

"Later on I'll show you something that makes this place even more special than meets the eye."

"What is it?"

"I'm not saying… *yet.*"

"C'mon, show me *now*."

"No!"

Jo leaned toward her threateningly.

"Show me now, or else!"

In a burst of childishness, Beth responded by sticking her tongue out at Jo, then bolted up from the blanket. Joanna hid her amusement.

"You do realize that was a tactical error."

From a safe distance Beth taunted her again with the same gesture. Jo sprang to her feet. Beth giggled and took off across the open field. As Joanna chased after her in unpredictable stops and starts, Beth couldn't help but wonder what her husband and son would think to see her now. Deliriously happy, Beth didn't quite know what to think herself. The only thing she knew for sure as Joanna closed the distance between them was that she hadn't felt this alive in years. When Jo finally caught up and grabbed her arm, Beth let out a joyful squeal. The women locked limbs and in a raucous free-for-all that disguised their desire, they tumbled together onto the ground. In their spinning, Beth's entire life had become a blur. Pinning her down on her back, Jo straddled Beth and grabbed hold of her wrists. Joanna's eyes flashed menacingly.

"Are you going to show me *now*, or do I have to make you?"

For a moment Beth remained playfully defiant. Then suddenly her childlike struggle dissolved into a much more womanly surrender. Still short-winded from their chase, her heart raced from a much greater threat—one she was not sure she would survive. As their mingled laughter gradually fell away, Jo could feel the shallow rise and fall of Beth's chest as she pressed her thighs in against her prisoner's sides. A dangerous silence replaced the carefree sounds of horseplay as Beth lie there looking up, waiting nervously for Joanna to make her next move. Their eyes exchanged a thousand possibilities. Joanna feared that the rest of her life hung in the accuracy of her reading. Beth felt the flush of anticipation as Joanna took her time considering her fate.

Overcome with a mix of fear and desire, Beth could no longer endure the suspense of whether she was about to be tickled mercilessly or kissed deeply. Their eyes locked and hers pleaded with Joanna to be spared the disappointment of one and the danger of the other. Barely audible, Beth begged for her life.

"Please don't..."

"Please don't *what*?"

Pinned under Joanna's scrutiny, Beth could not bring herself to say the actual words and so began their duet of innuendo.

"Please don't make me."

"Please don't make you *what*?"

Beth's heart pounded against Jo's persistence. She answered her faintly, praying Jo would hear her deeper plea.

"Please don't make me do what I'm not ready to do."

Jo struggled to interpret Beth's words. Was she talking about her readiness to reveal her secret or was she talking about something else? Her body aching with desire, she wanted her sacrifice known.

"I *could* if I wanted to..."

Her panting only slightly receded, Beth looked deeply into Joanna's eyes.

"I know..."

Safely hidden in ambiguity, Beth had told Joanna all she needed to know to keep her from possibly making the biggest mistake of her life. Reluctantly Jo loosened her grip, releasing Beth from her fears. Though now able to free her hands, Beth did not pull them away. Instead, she kept them in Joanna's charge hoping that her gesture was understood.

"Thank you" she added in a soft, shy voice.

Still not entirely clear whether Beth had been referring to something about the place or something else that Steve swore he saw in the eyes of Beth's portrait, Joanna rolled off the woman and onto her own back. They lie that way, side by side in the soft tufts of grass, staring up into the vastness of the sky. Neither uttered a single word. As the artificial quiet settled into the space that now separated their bodies, an undeniable sense of disappointment replaced Beth's relief. It had taken so long to come this close. Feeling the need to put an innocent spin on what had almost happened between them, she blotted her dampened face with the back of her hand.

"I haven't behaved like that in years... not since the boys were young and Ben and I chased them around in the backyard."

The mention of her family was deliberate. Beth hoped that the sober reminder would last the rest if the day.

Joanna was not in the habit of containing her desire. She lied to convince them both.

"You do know I was just gonna' tickle you, right?"

All too aware of the dampness between her legs, Beth felt ridiculous thinking Jo might have intended anything else.

"Of course."

Beth had managed to sound so convincing that now it was Joanna who felt foolish. Perhaps she'd misread the moment entirely. So much for trusting Steve's intuition. Already weary of all the second-guessing, she stood up and brushed herself off.

"I think I'll do some sketching."

Beth was quick to agree to their unspoken need for some space.

"I'll finish my book."

The two women walked silently back to the blanket. Jo collected her art supplies and Beth dove into her tote for her book. For the next hour, except for some safely stolen glances, they both made sure to avoid any contact at all.

As the sun inched it's way toward the center of the sky, Beth came to the last page of her book. She looked up to find Jo off in the distance, still deeply entrenched in her sketching. Beth played with the dial of the portable radio until she found her oldies station. She sat forward, pulled her knees in close and rested her chin on her folded arms. "Hello Stranger" played in the background as she watched Joanna closely. Seeing her there beside the rock brought a confusing but undeniable sense of comfort when everything else about Joanna's presence only seemed to wreak greater and greater havoc. When the song was over and she was sure she had collected as much of the moment as her heart could hold, she called out for Jo to join her for lunch. Jo gathered up her supplies. Watching her approach, Beth could feel herself free-falling over the safety rail that guarded her life. There was so much left of their day together. If she could just manage to avoid any more wrestling matches, Beth told herself everything would be fine. Joanna tossed her sketchpad onto the blanket and sat down. Their time apart served to restore a sense of stability to their rapport. Beth was relieved.

"Do I get to see what you were doing?"

Joanna intentionally moved the pad out of Beth's reach.

"Not until you show me *your* little secret first."

"Then I guess we'll both have to wait a little longer."

Trying not to read anything into the remark, Jo watched Beth sift through the carefully packed cooler and one-by-one spread things out on the blanket.

"I don't see that tuna fish soup."

Beth did not appreciate having to relive her reaction to Joanna's confession. She offered Jo a ham and Swiss cheese sandwich instead.

"Am I ever going to live that down?"

Jo opened the bottle of wine and poured them each a glass.

"That all depends on whether you give me something even more memorable to remember you by."

Once again the reminder hit Beth hard. Jo couldn't miss the change in her expression.

"What is it?"

"Nothing."

Beth looked away, then back at Jo. This time she couldn't lie.

"I'm just beginning to get to know you and it feels like I'm already running out of time."

Joanna wasn't prepared to handle the weight of Beth's honesty. She tried to lighten things for *both* their sakes.

"There's really not all that much to tell. I was born a premie and spent a few impatient years as a kid until finally the movie stub said 'Admit One Adult'. I played spin the bottle, started using tampons and applied for a mortgage without a note from home. After some more or less illustrious years, I showed up here and you rammed into me. See, that didn't take long and look how much time we still have left."

Beth managed a reluctant smile.

"What makes me think you left out all the good parts?"

"Okay… maybe I skipped over a detail or two, but what you see is pretty much what you get."

Beth's sadness crept back, only now it felt even larger and heavier than before. She bowed her head and dropped her eyes that seemed to be on the verge of tears. Joanna realized that her cajoling resistance to sharing more about herself was only making matters worse. She lowered herself onto her elbow and snuck up under Beth's chin so that she could meet the disappointment in Beth's eyes. Beth looked away, embarrassed. Jo's voice was commanding.

"Look at me."

Beth obeyed and Jo softened.

"Okay, ask me whatever you want. I'll answer you as honestly as I can. I promise."

Beth's face lit up like a child let loose in a candy store.

"Do you really mean that?"

Jo nodded.

Beth tested the limits of Joanna's offer.

"*Anything*?"

"Anything."

Jo smiled.

"So what would you like to know?"

Beth didn't know where to begin.

"Everything!"

"I'm afraid you'll have to be a little more specific than that."

"Tell me about your family. I know you have an older brother. Any other siblings?"

"Nope, just Ray. He's forty-two."

"Are the two of you close?"

Jo didn't have to think about her answer.

"Very. Once he got over wanting to bash my ten year old head into a wall for breaking one of his Elvis records, it's been smooth sailing ever since." Jo took a bite of her sandwich and continued. "Growing up, Ray was my idol. I always wanted whatever he had… his room, his car… his girl."

Beth pretended to take the last part of Jo's statement in stride.

"I see…"

Joanna smiled slyly, as if protecting an amusing little secret. Beth insisted on knowing the details.

"Why the smirk?"

"Let's just say that the war in Vietnam had *some* redeeming value… at least for me, anyway. Ray's number came up first in the draft lottery. Can you believe that? First! During his tour of duty I got to move into his room, drive his car and sleep with his girlfriend."

This time Beth could not contain her obvious shock.

"Did he ever find out?"

"Only about his room and his car. As it turned out his girlfriend became my sister-in-law, so we decided to keep that our little secret."

Jo finished the first half of her sandwich.

"So, what else would you like to know?"

Beth tried to rein in her intense curiosity about all of Joanna's sexual escapades. She asked a much safer question.

"Tell me about your parents."

"My dad's a general contractor. He's an absolutely amazing guy… kind, generous and loyal as hell. He's one of the most emotionally honest men I've ever known. Nothing like your typical macho Sicilian."

"So you're Italian?"

"My *temper* is. My mother was Jewish. My folks met and fell in love back when marrying out of their faith was a big deal. It took a lot of balls, but they did it anyway and wound up having a wonderful marriage for the next twenty-five years." Joanna's eyes changed. "My mother hung on 'til their silver wedding anniversary. She died the very next day of stomach cancer. She told my dad it was a milestone she refused to let death cheat them out of." Jo looked out onto the horizon as if searching for something she'd only seen in a dream. "My mother believed that the only thing more permanent than death was love… that the heart never forgets, and never lets go."

Beth caressed Jo's pain with her eyes. She was afraid to do more.

"I think your mother was right." She paused. "Her passing must have been a terrible loss."

Jo was surprised at her own honesty.

"It still is. More than I think I ever let myself admit."

Over the years, Joanna rarely spoke about her mother. It simply hurt too much. She kept the sweetest of her memories locked away and swore to herself that she would never let loving someone hurt her that much again. It had been a promise she'd been able to keep until now. Joanna became quiet.

Beth didn't try to make things better for her. Long ago she had learned to stay in her own silence—a silence that was often cruel—and by staying, she'd learned to conquer that cruelty with compassion toward others left behind—those without the comfort of another heart beating nearby and whose faith had been tested one too many times. She had learned to stay and in that silence, simply be a friend.

Eventually, Joanna found her place again. The walking wounded always did.

"For the longest time, whenever I'd see a woman anywhere… on the street… in a store… the only identity she had was that she was *not* my mother."

Beth's heart came close to breaking.

"I know. I felt the very same way every time I saw a group of boys, none of whom was my son. Then one day you begin to see people for who they *are* again, instead of who they're *not*."

Beth wondered whether Joanna had a stepmother.

"Did your father ever remarry?"

"No and not for lack of women chasing him. He's had his share of girlfriends but he never wanted to build a new life with another woman. Says he'd rather stay busy and cherish the one he'd made with my mother. I can understand why. She's a tough act to follow." A light crept back into Joanna's eyes. "She was such an incredible woman and such a wonderful mother." Her voice fell as she choked on the memories. "It's hard to talk about."

Beth's eyes were tender.

"We don't have to."

Joanna had never shown her heavily guarded pain to anyone, but then she had never known anyone like Beth.

"Actually I think I'd like to..."

For a moment it seemed as if Jo didn't know where to start. There was so much she had kept locked inside for so long. She told Beth about the cards—how when her mother found out she was dying, she went out and bought a whole collection of them for all the important occasions in her daughter's life that she knew she wouldn't be around to help celebrate. Jo described how her mother wrote them out, each with a special message, and instructed her husband to give them to Jo on all those special days. There'd been one for her eighteenth, twenty-first and thirtieth birthdays—one for her high school graduation and another when she got her BFA. She was so sure of her daughter's success she even made out cards congratulating Jo on her promotions.

Joanna looked down at her own hands that all these years later bore a remarkable resemblance to those of her mother. As she recalled her mother's devotion, Jo's eyes and voice turned painfully hollow.

"The one that still gets to me the most is the card she asked my dad to give me on the day of her funeral. It was a condolence card comforting me on the loss of my mother along with a letter assuring me that she would always be there at my side."

When Joanna looked up again Beth was crying.

"What an incredibly thoughtful thing to have done. She sounds like such a caring woman."

Jo let the weight of her unearthed sorrow settle back into the corners of her heart.

"She was."

"You must miss her terribly."

"I don't think I realized how much until I opened those kitchen cabinets in the carriage house and saw that silly piping tacked to the front of the shelves."

Joanna looked into Beth's eyes.

"The truth is, I'd never known anyone else who was that kind of mother… until I met *you.* I haven't let myself think about those things… until this summer." Jo hesitated. "It feels good to be close to them again."

Beth was gentle with Joanna's trust.

"I'm flattered you see me that way but I'm not sure I'd put myself in your mother's league."

"I know what I saw between you and Adam and I know how it felt when you took out that splinter. Trust me, you *are*."

Beth thought it ironic that the very role she was trying to distance herself from this summer was one that Joanna apparently found deeply appealing. For the moment, Beth put aside her own personal conflicts and accepted Jo's compliment with a quiet smile.

"Did your mother know you were gay?"

"We never had *the* conversation. I didn't come out until a few years after she died, but somewhere in her I'm sure she knew."

Joanna leaned back on her elbows.

"I remember this one time when I was about seven. I'd taken out two of my Barbie dolls. I was bored to tears with the stupid dress-up games, so I got a pair of scissors and cut off most of the hair on the brunette one to make it look more like me. I undressed them both, rubbed them up against each other and made them kiss. That's when my mother walked in with some milk and cookies. She wanted to know what happened to little Jo-Jo's hair. I told her the doll liked it better that way… it made her look more like Elvis. She asked me what they were doing. Making each other feel good, I told her. 'I see', she said without so much as skipping a beat, and then asked me if they loved each other. A whole lot, I told her. I was sure of it. She said she was happy for them and that she thought they were very lucky to have found each other. Then she suggested I put them to sleep so I could have my milk and cookies." Joanna seemed to revel in the vividness of her memory. "My mom pulled back the covers of my bed and helped me tuck them in, just that way, naked. She saw how frustrated I got not being able to bend their stiff, plastic arms into a real hug, so she helped me position them close together, facing each other. I can still see their tiny plastic heads on my pillow. I remember how soft my mother's eyes grew when she tried to comfort me. 'They'll figure it out honey. When two people love each other, they *always* do.' Then she sat with me on the floor while I ate my milk and cookies."

Beth's eyes began to water with the tenderness of that image while Joanna took her time remembering.

"Years later, when she was dying, she found a way of casually bringing up that afternoon. In one of our late-night talks she asked me if I remembered it. She was pleased when I said I did. She told me I always had such a challenging imagination and I told her she always had such a reassuring way of dealing with it. Before she drifted off to sleep that night she took my hand and said there was something else she wanted me to always remember. She said there would be many rewards in knowing my own *mind* but that my deepest joy would come when I found someone who would help me to lose it to my *heart*."

Beth wiped the tears that now streamed down her own cheek. Her jealousy almost prevented her from asking.

"Did you… ever find that person?"

Joanna looked down so Beth couldn't see her eyes. She hesitated, wondering whether to risk it all, then answered honestly just as she'd promised.

"Yeah, I did."

Beth was too upset to hear the confession hidden in Jo's reply. She concealed her disappointment, believing Jo's heart was already taken.

"I'm happy for you."

Joanna looked up, amazed that Beth hadn't understood. Jo tried hard to convince herself that it was for the best. She resorted to another glass of wine and her usual wry sense of humor.

"So what about you, did your mother know you were straight?"

Beth laughed as she opened a container of sliced watermelon.

"Let's put it this way… unlike yours, what my mother lacked in subtle intuition she more than made up for in expressed expectation." Beth offered Jo a piece of the melon. "If she'd ever caught me doing what you did with those Barbie dolls, not only would I have been harshly reprimanded, but I'm sure she would have snuck into my room and glued each piece of those little outfits onto their tiny bodies for good measure."

They both laughed.

Jo took a bite of the melon and some juice squirted out from the corner of her mouth. Beth instinctively reached over and wiped it away with her own napkin. God, she thought to herself, what am I doing? Joanna didn't seem to mind.

"You don't sound terribly close."

Beth held out her glass and Jo filled it with some wine.

"No, we aren't. We never were. Over the years I've learned to adjust my definition of love to accommodate *hers.* That's to say, we no longer hang up on each other. By those pathetic standards, I suppose we have a working relationship. On the bright side, my highly developed tolerance for enduring great amounts of emotional pain was honed being raised by her." Beth became much more solemn. "Unlike your mother, mine never really knew me. But even sadder, she kept me from ever knowing myself."

"What about your father?"

He died suddenly of a heart attack when I was in my late twenties. When I lost him, I lost one of my dearest friends. He was such a tender and loving man. I honestly don't know what he ever saw in my mother. He was the nurturing one. My mother *tended* to things, she never *cared* for them. There's a world of difference between the two and a child always feels it."

Joanna appreciated the subtly of Beth's perceptions.

"What did your dad do for a living?"

"He was a high school music teacher and a very gifted musician himself. I'm sure whatever talent and sensitivity I possess came from *his* side of the family."

Jo finished her watermelon and Beth handed her a plastic garbage bag for the rind. She'd even thought of that. Amused, Jo dropped it in.

"Any brothers or sisters?"

"No, just little ol' me. I'm an only child. Supposedly my mother wasn't able to conceive. The universe must have known she wasn't exactly 'mother' material, but then miraculously I came along."

Beth thought about her attraction to Joanna. She kept her musings intentionally vague.

"I guess from the very beginning, my life was destined to be one surprise after another. They say you choose *where* and *how* you come into this world. I'm not sure I believe that entirely but if it's so, that was certainly the first in a series of rather questionable choices I seem to have made for myself."

"Does your mother live around here?"

Beth finished her melon and added it to the bag.

"Thank heavens no! After my father died and I became pregnant with Adam there was some talk about her moving closer, but she ultimately decided to stay in the suburb of Chicago where I grew up. She visits a few times a year and that invariably turns out to be a few times too many. Truthfully, she always liked Ben a lot more than she ever liked me. Sounds awful, doesn't it? I hope Adam never feels that way about me."

"From what I've seen of the two of you together, he couldn't possibly."

Beth smiled, grateful for the assurance. More than anything, Joanna wanted to know about Beth's romantic past. She tried to make the question sound casual.

"So is Ben your one true love or were there others?"

A mischievous twinkle formed in Beth's eyes.

"I never slept with his sister, if that's what you're wondering."

Jo laughed. She enjoyed when Beth tossed things back at her.

"How about the more conventional 'high school sweetheart'?"

"Oh sure, there was that. He was very handsome and very bright, and most importantly, a very '*acceptable*' boy. I imagine I was in love with him at the time. I'm certain he was with me."

"Did he take you to the prom and buy you the obligatory corsage?"

"Of course."

"And did you give it up by the end of the night?"

Beth playfully slapped Joanna's arm.

"Please, *my* Barbie always kept her clothes on!"

"So you were a virgin when you met your husband?"

Compared to Joanna's notorious history, Beth felt ridiculously sheltered.

"Yes and I suppose in many ways I still am…" She began to play with the crumpled napkin in her hand. "There's so much… about life… I haven't experienced."

"For example?"

Beth began to respond, then checked herself.

"Oh no, I see what's happening here. Somehow we're talking about me instead of you. *I'm* the one who's supposed to be asking the questions, remember?"

Jo smiled like a child who'd just been caught with her hand inside the cookie jar.

"Can't blame a girl for trying."

"No, but you can punish her."

Joanna toyed with Beth like she'd never been toyed with before.

"Hmm, sounds interesting. What did you have in mind?"

After a threatening brush with Jo's eyes, Beth moved nervously past the innuendo.

"I assume the rest of your family knows you're gay?"

"Yeah, I gave notice right after I graduated from college."

"How did they take it?"

"It came with its share of family drama for a while. I'm sure it would have been easier on my dad if my mother was still around to help him sort it all out. Eventually he managed to deal with it in his own way. After going into seclusion for a few days he came to me and said, 'Look, I sure as hell aint jumpin' for joy over the news, but I don't intend to go jumpin' out of any windows either.' He asked me to give him time to get used to it and pretty soon he did. It's been fine ever since. Like I said, he's a pretty amazing guy."

"What about your brother?"

"I don't think he was surprised. He'd seen my Elvis impersonations. Maybe he never put a name to it but way down deep he had his suspicions even then. My sister-in-law was great..." Jo smiled suggestively, "as it turned out, in more ways than one. She was a big help in getting him to wrap his mind around it." Jo plucked a blade of grass and played with it between her teeth. "Of course she omitted the fact that she was the first woman I'd slept with."

The notion was beyond Beth's comprehension.

"How in the world did something like that ever happen?"

Joanna mocked her bewilderment.

"Don't all kid sisters sleep with their brothers' future wives?"

"No, not typically."

Jo deliberately took her time settling into a comfortable position before feeding Beth the details.

"I guess I was around thirteen when Ray started dating this really gorgeous girl—Stacy. She was only nineteen at the time herself, but she was all woman to me. From the very first time he brought her around, I became hopelessly obsessed. I hated my brother for being the one who got to make out with her. I was so jealous there wasn't anything I wouldn't do to sabotage their dates. This one time I secretly let all the air out of his tires so he couldn't take her to the neighborhood drive-in. They stayed home instead and he brooded while Stacy taught me how to slow dance for some lame party I'd been invited to the following week. I kept pretending to get it wrong because each time I missed a step she held me closer and tighter. I was on Cloud 9 all night, but Ray was pissed as hell." Jo shifted her weight. "My brother was a real Casanova in those days and wasn't about to settle down, especially with every girl in the neighborhood throwing herself at his feet. But Stacy wasn't one to put up with that kind of shit, so their relationship was an on again-off again thing for the next two years. By then, she'd already gotten really close to my family. She and my folks really liked each other and of course, secretly I couldn't imagine ever living without her. Once Ray was drafted and shipped off to Nam, things got even rockier between them until he eventually broke it off completely. My brother might have been a fool, but *I* wasn't about to let her go. We stayed in touch and after my mom died, Stacy was absolutely amazing. That was a pretty rough time for me. For a while there, all hell broke loose. I was in a lot of pain and started acting out all over the place. More than anyone else, it was Stacy who kept me grounded and stopped me from throwing my whole life away. By then, the '*Big Sister/Little Sister*' routine felt more like just the tip of the iceberg for me. For the first time in my life I'd fallen seriously in love. She was seeing lots of guys and I remember being really bummed out over the hopelessness of it. Anyway, the summer before I left for college I finally broke down and told her how I felt. Instead of being surprised, she said she'd known for a long time but never would make the first move. Shit, you could have knocked me over with a feather. We talked for a really long time and she admitted that in between dating my brother and a few other guys, she'd done a little *experimenting* and had a few memorable bi experiences along the way."

Jo made light of the shock in Beth's eyes.

"Let's not forget we're talking about the free love generation. Anyway, since she and Ray were completely broken off and I'd just turned eighteen, she didn't see any harm in giving me a little going away present of her own. She took me away for the Labor Day week-end and bedded me."

Jo smiled, recalling the kiss that changed her life. Beth had trouble phrasing her next question.

"Were you ever… intimate… after that?"

"No. By the time I came in for Christmas, Ray had gotten out of the service and they started dating again. I guess seeing everything he saw over there brought him to his senses and he realized what a great thing he had in Stacy. A few months later he proposed, she accepted and the rest, as they say, is history. Theirs eventually came to include a mortgage, a dog and two sons."

Beth tried to imagine the complications.

"Weren't you jealous?"

"Not in the least. I'd already moved on to a girl I'd met in college. I did get to be Stacy's maid-of-honor though. We shared a slow dance at the wedding and we even managed to look harmless enough not to have Ray cut in."

Beth tried to imagine living with such an unconventional history.

"Over the years, have things ever gotten…" she struggled for the right word, "*awkward* between the two of you?"

"Not awkward as much as privately amusing at times. I remember this one Thanksgiving not long after their seventh anniversary. She and I were alone in her kitchen. Everyone else was outside playing touch football. She was standing at the sink, rinsing off some dishes and seemed kind of quiet. I asked her if everything was all right and she made some reference to the 'seven year itch'. I came up behind her, slipped my arms around her waist and whispered into her ear that if Ray wasn't paying her enough attention she could always count on *me* to return the favor of my going away present. I even teased her about my having picked up a few more tricks over the years."

"What did she say?"

"That I wasn't bad for a *beginner*, either."

Beth felt her own face begin to flush. She played with the border of the blanket. She was almost afraid to ask.

"Did she ever take you up on your offer."

"Nah. I knew she wouldn't. She handed me some internally rehearsed line about being a wife and a mother and how that part of her life, the sexually adventurous part, was over. I was never really sure if she trying to convince *me* or *herself*."

"Why do you say that?"

"Please, just dig beneath the surface of all that *Mother Earth* crap and you have a mass burial ground... the dry dust of unquenched female desire. It's such a fucking waste. I swear, guys have it all wrong. If they really want a taste of raw lady lust they'd forget those sleazy strip clubs and take a walk down the cereal aisle of any supermarket between car pool hours. Just brush up against the bare arm of some poor, suffocated woman pushing a wagon full of groceries with a whining kid in the booster seat and you'll see more hunger in her eyes than in a room full of pseudo-erotic, well-tipped lap dancers." Joanna shook her head, assessing the toll on the female psyche in the name of domestication. "I don't know how the hell you all do it... all you wives and mothers buried alive under selfless devotion day in and day out, never once sticking a yellow post-it note on the fridge that says, 'Touch me or I'll die'."

Beth felt much too exposed.

"In the future I'll be more careful about who I brush up against the next time I'm in the supermarket."

"Or whose foot you run over with your shopping cart."

Like so many times before, Beth's heart stopped, then started up again.

"Anyway, I told Stacy that the offer was open. I knew she'd never take me up on it. Not then. Not *ever*."

"Given all that sexual repression you just described, how could you have been so sure?"

"Because I knew she was reasonably happy."

Beth let her eyes settle on her favorite part of the landscape. She emptied herself of everything but it's beauty and the truth.

"I wouldn't count on that if I were you. Over time, being '*reasonably happy*' can make a woman feel more desperate than if she were downright miserable." Beth paused to absorb the weight of her own confession. "Sometimes I think the cruelest pain of all is the kind we learn to live with."

Joanna looked into Beth's eyes. Lost in their depth, she had to grip herself tightly around the knees and lock her hands together in order to stop herself from reaching out and taking Beth into her arms.

"Either way, I think it's a fucking shame that so many married women's lives don't go *wrong* as much as they just go *dead*." Jo shook her head. "Where the hell does all that smoldering passion go?"

A heavy sigh preceded Beth's attempt at an answer.

"I'm sure it's different for each of us. In your mother's case, maybe it went into that pleated piping along the pantry shelves. In your sister-in-law's case, maybe in a perfect Thanksgiving turkey that day."

Jo turned and pinned Beth with her eyes.

"And *yours*?"

Beth began to chew the inside of her lip while she worked up the courage to answer Jo honestly.

"I suppose most recently it went into the contents of this picnic cooler…"

Her confession seemed to trail off into uncharted territory. Joanna immediately reached inside and took out a box of strawberries and a can of whipped cream. She shook the can, squirted some cream onto the top of the plumpest strawberry and pressed it to Beth's lips.

"Then here, you might as well enjoy the fruits of your labor."

Beth drew back, but Jo persisted playfully.

"C'mon, open up."

Wrestling with her own repressed desires, Beth pushed Joanna's hand away as politely as she could.

"No thank you."

"Suit yourself."

She popped the fruit into her own mouth, and then slowly licked the remaining residue from around her lips.

"Hmm… delicious… sure I can't tempt you?"

Beth felt like a prisoner forced to watch a torturous act as Jo teasingly devoured several more. Beth knew she was being toyed with.

"Stop. You're embarrassing me."

"Am I?" Jo tried shifting the blame. "Your mother would say it serves you right for cavorting with the likes of an unsavory lesbian."

Beth struck a mockingly proper pose.

"Make no mistake, Margaret Gabrielle's daughter doesn't '*cavort*'! It's simply not permitted. It never was and never will be."

Jo delighted in learning Beth's maiden name. It was another little piece of her history and Jo wanted to know it all.

Beth giggled.

"Mrs. Gabrielle's daughter also isn't permitted to pee in her pants." She turned around and looked over her shoulder in the direction of some thick brush. "Oh good, there's no line."

Jo had no idea what Beth was talking about.

"No line *where*?"

Beth pointed to some shrubs behind them.

"The ladies room. I always go over there."

Beth stood up and brushed some errant crumbs from her blouse. Once again, Jo was undeniably charmed by the woman's idiosyncrasies.

"You're one very strange woman. You do know that, don't you?"

"God yes! Don't ask me how I'm not running up and down the street in my nightgown, shrieking at the top of my lungs." She leaned down and whispered into Joanna's ear. "I *do* have one in a ready position though. It's hanging on a hook right by the front door." Beth stopped short, then confessed to the rest of it. "The truth is, I've passed for being *normal* many more years than I ever thought possible."

Jo teased her. "Apparently no one was ever watching closely enough."

"Yes, that would seem so." Beth smiled shyly. "Until *you*."

She collected a handful of tissues and dashed off into the woods.

Joanna spent the time alone trying to negotiate her impossible attraction. She'd barely managed to reign in her heart when Beth returned and sat back down beside her.

"I have to ask you something..."

Joanna braced herself. She had promised Beth the truth.

"Would you really have slept with your sister-in-law?"

"I only propositioned her because it was safe. I knew I'd never have to make that call. She'd never let it come to that."

"Because she's a wife and mother?"

"Yeah. Now let me ask *you* something. How do so many of you do it… manage to live by those rules?"

Beth leaned closer and whispered playfully into Joanna's ear.

"Vitamin M!"

"What the hell's Vitamin M?"

Beth quickly covered Jo's mouth.

"Shhh, not so loud! This is highly classified information. Vitamin M is a mother's daily dose of morality. We're all required to take a pill every time we give our kids their gummy bear vitamins. We're given a lifetime supply when we leave the hospital with our firstborn." Beth smiled mischievously. "I'd be afraid to think what might happen if all of us decided en masse to stop taking them for a week." She giggled at the thought of it. "I imagine those supermarket aisles would become a breeding ground for depraved, sex-starved housewives. Can't you see it now… all of us ripping our clothes off and throwing ourselves at the nearest stock boy? Or worse yet, hurling ourselves on top of each other!"

Joanna was constantly amused by the unpredictability of Beth's imagination. She tried not to read too much into the latter scenario.

"Now that's something your mother would certainly never approve of."

"Yes well, I guess I'm not anything like her… much to her disappointment and my relief." She sighed. "Which seems like a rather moot point when you consider the dismal fate you've assigned to all of us childbearing women."

"I never said I thought it was *dismal*. I'm sure motherhood has some pretty amazing moments, but it's like, 'hello bedtime stories—goodbye bedroom fantasies'."

Beth could feel herself becoming defensive.

"You think we never have urges?"

"I'm sure you *do*… you just never do anything about them and that's a damn shame."

'The Dangerous Beth Garrison' rose to challenge Jo on the spot.

"Tell me something then, am I to assume that the aisles of the supermarkets where all you childless, professionally successful types shop are filled with nothing but sexually empowered women?" She did not give Jo a chance to respond. "Because judging from the little you've described of it, it certainly doesn't sound like the absence of a family and a white picket fence has put you and your set any closer to that illusive brass ring."

Jo tried to apologize but Beth cut her off.

"Never mind. It doesn't matter." Her anger receded into something more reflective. "Sometimes I wonder which is the greater tragedy… a life completely dictated by the compromises of devotion or a life devoid of them entirely."

Jo struggled for her own conclusion.

"Maybe it's different sides of the same tragedy."

Beth tried to deflect the remaining sadness in her heart by gazing out onto the horizon.

"Maybe it is…" She drew a long contemplative breath. "Either way, even tragedy looks so much more appealing from up here especially on such a magnificent day."

Joanna tried to redeem herself.

"I promised you it wouldn't rain."

Beth nodded silently. She recalled how nervous she'd been about making these plans and then how she'd suddenly panicked the night before, afraid that the morning might never come. Sitting beside this stunning, difficult woman who had so unexpectedly and wondrously come into her life, Beth now found herself secretly agonizing once more—this time dreading the reality that there would likely never be such a painfully perfect day in her life again. She could actually feel her heart tear apart. She needed to save herself—to break away—to distance herself from what and whom she wanted most. Fearing that Jo might see the truth, Beth quickly got up from the blanket.

"I think I'll go pick some flowers."

Hoping that her desperate act of survival sounded casual enough, she wandered barefooted over to her sacred rock. In its presence she'd always found a bittersweet sense of herself and in turn, had always felt protective of its secret—the one she had not been quite ready to share with Joanna. As she reached out and touched her palm to its reassuring surface, the renewed bond felt as old as time itself.

Watching Beth from across the open field, Jo recalled one of her earliest lessons in drawing. It was about perspective and how the farther away an object was, the smaller it would appear. Throughout her life Jo had tried applying that same principle to her problems—the larger they felt, the further away she would try to get from them. But today distance had no bearing on the size of her dilemma. Beth on the blanket posed the same inescapable problem as Beth over by the rock. With nothing in her repertoire that permitted denial, Jo lay back and closed her eyes.

Eventually Beth returned. She sat down, leaned forward and quietly examined the handful of flowers she'd collected. Joanna pretended to be napping as she secretly watched Beth study the intricate petals. She thought of the quote Beth had placed on the piano beside her paper bouquet. Jo spoke softly.

"O'Keeffe could never accuse *you* of not really seeing a flower."

Beth closed her eyes, inhaled their fragrance, then turned around.

"I thought you were asleep."

Jo unfolded her hands from behind her head and raised herself up on her elbows.

"What is it you obviously find so interesting about them?"

"Oh, I find them much more that 'interesting'. 'Interesting' is such a clinical word. I find them enthralling… enticing… inspiring."

Careful not to damage any of the heads, Beth placed the bouquet on a corner of the blanket. She selected one from the bunch, held it up and brushed its velvet petals lightly across her cheek.

"You would think it's their beauty but it's not. It's their courage."

"Their courage?"

Beth leaned her face closer to the smallest bud.

"Yes, their courage. In spite of the fact that to do so means they're destined to wither and die, they still dare to bloom. I'm convinced that when just one of us takes notice even for a moment, the petals of flowers everywhere open a little wider. In a way they're not unlike people, really. When one of us triumphs, a part of each of us comes alive. And when one of us gives up, a part of each of us dies." Beth stroked the delicate stem. "I'm sure that's why we cry in darkened movie theaters."

Jo was charmed.

"You get all that from looking at a flower?"

"That, and so much more."

Joanna found herself quietly considering Beth's words. The longer she thought about their poignancy, the more precious the woman beside her became. While Beth's eyes lingered on the details of the flower, Jo's own caressed the slope of her shoulders and the curve of her back. She reached up to remove a small twig caught in Beth's hair.

Beth panicked and instinctively pulled away. Unsure whether this was the moment she'd hoped for and dreaded, her voice tensed with the fear of both.

"What are you doing?"

"Relax. You had a twig caught in your hair. I was just trying to get it out."

Beth felt ridiculous for overreacting.

"I'm sorry."

Her apology didn't make Jo feel any better.

"You thought I was coming on to you, didn't you? I can't fucking believe it!"

Beth wasn't sure how she felt about Jo making it sound like such a farfetched idea.

"You scared me. That's all."

She prayed Joanna would leave it at that, but her prayers weren't enough.

"Would you have reacted like that if I wasn't a lesbian?"

This time Beth couldn't lie. Jo deserved that much.

"You're not going to like my answer but no, probably not."

Jo looked away from her. The truth stung. Beth felt awful about her confession.

"If it makes you feel any better, I'm as disappointed in me as you are."

Jo pretended not to care.

"I asked you for the truth and you gave it to me. Why would I be disappointed?"

"Because sometimes the truth can be hurtful."

"You're right, it *would* hurt... if it mattered."

Beth confronted the wall in Joanna's eyes. Her voice fell against their resistance.

"It matters to me..."

Jo hid behind her trumped-up indignation.

"Do you actually think I'm attracted to every woman I meet?"

"I'm not interested in whether you've been attracted to every woman you've ever met... just whether you're attracted to *me*."

Drowning in the truth, Joanna was deliberately circumspect.

"What is that, some kind of trick question you straight women like putting to us lesbians? If we say *no*, you automatically feel rejected. If we say *yes*, you automatically recoil."

Joanna's resentment sounded convincing.

"Can we just drop the whole subject? I should never have asked."

Beth began rummaging nervously through her tote. Watching her struggle, Jo regretted handling her question to poorly. She felt she owed Beth at least part of the truth—the *safer* part.

"I'm attracted to lots of things *about* you. You're amazingly talented, incredibly bright and you've got a great sense of humor."

Beth's face registered quiet disappointment.

"I'll be certain to ask if I ever need a letter of reference."

"What did you *want* to hear?"

The question was simple. Beth wondered how one so small could threaten her entire life. In that moment she realized it was not Joanna that she was afraid of, but herself. She used that great sense of humor to avoid answering more truthfully.

"Is that some kind of trick question you lesbians like putting to us straight women?"

Amused and secretly relieved, Jo offered up a forgiving smile that pulled them both back to safety.

"You still have that twig caught in your hair. Do I have permission to take it out?"

"Yes, of course."

Joanna leaned closer, removed the twig and placed it in Beth's palm.

"Now that wasn't so bad, was it?"

Beth blushed.

"Do I still get to ask you anything?"

"Sure."

"When did you first know you were a lesbian?"

Joanna buried her head in her hands and groaned.

"There it is, the most frequently asked question when interviewing a gay person."

Even as Beth's face grew even redder, Jo knew she was still hoping for an answer. She kept her promise.

"If wanting to be the prince that rescues the beautiful princess in all those God-awful fairytales was any indication, then I'd have to say that my earliest realization was around five. Then came the Barbie dolls… I already told you what I did with them."

Beth smiled.

"How could I forget?"

"About the same time, something truly wonderful happened in my private little lesbo world." Jo's eyes sparkled with the delight of her memory. "A newlywed couple moved into the house next door… Ted and Jennifer. God, she was absolutely beautiful. The first time I laid eyes on her my stomach felt so weird I thought I would throw up. I didn't know it then but it was my first case of butterflies. They didn't have any kids of their own and Jen took an immediate liking to me. I'd live for one of her hugs. Every time she pressed me to her, my face sunk into her cleavage. Those were the only times I never minded being that short." Jo shook her head recalling the innocent torment of it all. "I was so madly in love it actually hurt to have to leave her and go to school. I was so sure she felt the same way that I convinced myself the reason she wasn't having kids of her own was because that meant she would have to have sex with her husband when she only wanted to have it with me." Jo laughed at herself. "Not even sure what 'it' was, I knew I wanted to do it with *her* too."

Beth was obviously enjoying the story.

"Naturally the truth was very different. She'd found out her husband had cheated on her. Since she wasn't sure where their marriage was going, she wasn't about to start a family. Anyway, things apparently got worse, they decided to split and he left. In my head I was so sure that she'd thrown him out so that she and I could finally be together. I was only ten and still way too young to get my working papers but I figured if I cut back on candy and comic books I'd have enough to support her on what I made from my weekly paper route and allowance. I remember going around the neighborhood, lining up odd jobs. When I'd saved enough to buy her a ring from the local five and dime, I packed a suitcase, marched into our living room and announced to my folks that I'd be marrying Jen and moving out." Jo smiled as she recounted that memorable piece of family history. "I'll never forget the look on my father's face. Of course my mother *got it* right away and very discreetly snuck off to explain things to Jennifer before I just showed up on her doorstep with an engagement ring."

Beth swooned with affection for the little girl Joanna described.

"How precious. You must have won her heart."

"To this day I don't know what my mother told her but Jen was really great about the whole thing. I actually got to propose and spend the night. Unfortunately, it was in the guest room. The next morning Jen wore my ring while she made me a stack of pancakes. She knew they were my favorite. I was halfway through when she pulled her chair up real close to mine and explained that even thought she absolutely adored me, she thought it best if she moved back to Florida to be closer to her own family. I was devastated. I told her I would quit fourth grade and come with her, but she said she didn't think that would be a good idea. She promised to write often and always wear my ring."

"You must have been heartbroken."

"I was. The day Jen moved I came as close to dying as I ever want to come. I lost interest in everything... even being Elvis. I couldn't bear the sight of pancakes. My whole family had to go without them for the next three months...," Jo's smile hinted at her remarkable recovery, "until I met Betsy."

"Another newlywed?"

"No, not this time. Betsy was just two years older than me, but womanhood had already invaded her body. Her breasts weren't nearly as developed as Jen's, but what she lacked in cup size she more than made up for in tongue kissing lessons. I never got to do any of that stuff with Jen."

Beth was thoroughly amused by Joanna's childhood adventures.

"I can see I'm dealing with someone with quite an illustrative past."

Jo laughed.

"Yeah, I must have been some handful back then."

"Oh sweetie trust me, you *still* are."

"Are you saying that as a *mother* or as an *older woman*?"

The question made Beth nervous, but she somehow managed not to let it show.

"I'm saying it as a mother who also happens to be older."

They both seemed eager to let it go at that and Beth probed a little further in another direction.

"Were you ever interested in boys?"

"When I was a kid I always liked 'em. In many ways I even preferred them to girls. I just never liked kissing them. When I was older I tried convincing myself I was bi. Don't forget, my sister-in-law was and I thought it was pretty cool to sleep with anybody I wanted to."

"So you've slept with men?"

"Sure, all of whom *I* seduced. I figured if I was going to sleep with a guy, it was going to be on *my* terms, not *his*. So yeah, there were a few. And as it turned out, that was a few too many."

Beth seemed to be between questions, so Joanna slipped in one of her own.

"What about you? Do any experimenting in college?"

"Nothing like you've described! By the end of my first semester I'd already met and settled into a relationship with Ben. I had him for companionship and my music for passion." Beth had never heard herself describe those years quite that way. The sound of it was not at all pleasing. Her regret was obvious. Jo shoved her playfully.

"So no wild 'n crazy Boogie Nights for you, huh?"

"Hardly. I'm afraid the free love era eluded me completely. I was definitely a product of the fifties, not the sixties."

"What a difference a decade can make."

Beth smiled awkwardly, anticipating Jo's next question.

"So you've never been with *anyone* but your husband?"

Almost too embarrassed to admit the truth, Beth's voice was barely audible.

"No."

Joanna didn't quite know how to respond to a history so alien from her own. Beth gathered her courage.

"Do you remember the other day when I bit your head off for saying I didn't strike you as *that kind of woman*... the kind who'd ever be willing to throw caution to the wind and risk it all to follow my heart?"

"I'm sorry. I was totally out of place."

Beth was not interested in an apology.

"I overreacted because deep down inside I was afraid to believe that maybe you were right. Not that if I ever *did* consider throwing caution to the wind it would be for someone like Nick." Beth stared out at the horizon, her heart aching to leap into the unknown. "I'd hate for you to think I'd find him worthy of such a transgression."

Joanna's throat tightened, but not enough to keep her from asking.

"Have you ever met someone who would be?"

For all the wide-open space around them, suddenly the only space Joanna was aware of was the dangerously little space between them. As her question hung in the stillness of the air, Jo could not deny the answer she wanted to hear—the answer she ached to coax from Beth's lips with her own.

As if sensing danger, Beth instinctively drew her knees protectively up into her chest and wrapped her arms securely around them. Her eyes clung to anything that saved her from having to look into Joanna's.

"Let's just say it's not Nick and leave it at that."

Disappointed, this time Jo's question was considerably safer for both of them.

"So how's it feel not having your family around these last few weeks?"

"Like I've been living between the lines of my own life story."

"Is that what you expected?"

Beth opened her arms and released herself from the shelter of her self-made cocoon.

"Nothing about this summer is what I expected."

Beth wondered what Jo made of her ambiguous response. Joanna wouldn't ask.

"Have you heard from Adam lately?"

For Beth it was a joyously simple question.

"Yes, as a matter of fact he's been writing more often than usual." She smiled. "It turns out Ben bribed him to stay in closer touch this summer... something about not wanting me to feel abandoned."

Beth's marriage was a constant source of curiosity and contention for Joanna. Wherever she could, she fished for more clues.

"Then I assume Ben's been in touch a lot too."

"God yes. He calls regularly." Beth sighed more openly than she was aware of. "My husband does everything with regularity. He's by far the most predictable person I've ever known."

"Is that good or bad ?"

Beth shrugged.

"It certainly dulls any sharp edges around my life."

"There's a lot to be said for having a sense of security."

Beth's eyes drifted slowly across the open field.

"I used to think so. Lately I've begun to wonder if being *scared* to death isn't better than being *bored* to death."

Beth's musing touched off a firestorm of issues raging in Joanna's own life. She dreaded the predictable question forming in Beth's eyes.

"What about you?" Beth hesitated. She wasn't sure she wanted to hear Jo's answer. "Is there someone back home that *you* call regularly?"

Jo understood what Beth was asking. She kept her promise and answered truthfully.

"Yes, there is somebody. But no, I haven't been calling regularly."

Beth struggled quietly with her jealousy.

"Do you mind talking about her?"

Jo wasn't really sure herself. She started off slowly.

"Her name is Gayle... Gayle Kramer."

"Is she in advertising as well?"

"No, she's a doctor... a thoracic surgeon."

Beth instantly felt inadequate. By comparison to such an accomplished woman, she couldn't imagine what Joanna found worthwhile in her own lack-luster company.

"She must be brilliant."

"She is. Beauty, brains, personality... she's got it all."

Magazine pages of vibrantly stylish women flashed through Beth's mind. There was so much more she did and didn't want to know. She poured herself another glass of wine.

"How long have you been together?"

"Last Christmas was nine years."

Deep in her heart, Beth found herself pleased and disappointed in the seriousness of Joanna's commitment.

"How did the two of you meet?"

"The year I was studying abroad in Paris she'd come over for a two week vacation before starting her residency. It was her first time in the city. A mutual friend had given her my number and told her to look me up. She did and we wound up staying together until she boarded the plane back to the states."

"Sounds like you hit it off instantly."

"I guess you could say that." Jo's mind drifted to the memory of all the sex they'd had. "We wound up exploring places you wouldn't exactly find in a guide book."

"And obviously fell in love."

"Maybe. Maybe not."

"How could you be unsure of something like that?"

Jo smiled.

"Because there's this amusing little phase in every young lesbian's life that's so distorted by the grandiose power of her sexuality and the swirling illusions of desire, that in a certain light she can actually convince herself that she's madly in love with each and every woman she meets... even if only for ten minutes."

Beth's heart proceeded cautiously.

"So had we met back then, you would have fallen in love with me... if only for ten minutes?"

Jo looked directly into Beth's eyes.

"Hopelessly." She waited for her answer to sink in. "Would you have been flattered?"

With her fingers gripping the glass, Beth returned the truth.

"Hopelessly."

She quickly looked away and finished her wine.

The twig Jo had been playing with snapped in her hands. She felt her whole life perched on nothing more than the thread of innuendo. For a fleeting moment she considered her options. Unwilling to risk disaster, she decided to return to her story. She explained that Gayle went back to the states and did her residency out on the west coast. Later that year Jo came home from Paris, landed her first job and moved into the city. She and Gayle had kept in touch for a while—even flew cross country a few times, mostly for the sex—but eventually things between them dropped off. After Gayle finished her residency, she accepted a position at Mount Sinai Medical Center in New York. They ran into each other again at the Christmas party of that same mutual friend. They were both unattached and both pretty smashed. After a flirtatious walk down memory lane, the initial sparks started to fly and they went home together that night.

"Despite a mutual New Year's resolution not to get into anything serious, we've been together ever since."

Beth drew her own conclusions.

"Nine years is considerably longer than a 10 minute infatuation. I assume this time it was the *real thing*."

"We were both young, highly motivated women on the fast track of our careers. Professional success was a real turn-on back then. I think what we fell in love with was each other's ambition."

Beth could feel her heart tighten.

"And now?"

"Let's just say our ambitions paid off. The anniversary presents get more lavish each year."

Joanna struggled for an explanation that would help Beth understand. She hoped that in the telling she might actually make sense of it for herself.

"Gayle's an amazing woman... charming, funny, bright. She's also an extremely gifted and dedicated physician. It just feels like over the years we've grown more committed to the trappings of our lifestyle than to the essence of our lives." Joanna wrestled with the sadness of it all. "From the very beginning we'd always shared a love of material things and at the end of nine years, that's pretty much all we have to show for it." She smiled at the irony of it. "That's a lot of emptiness in places beautiful possessions can't fill." Joanna's eyes grew more vacant. "Up until a few weeks ago, we were still going through the motions... attending all the right parties, showing up at all the right functions. Funny thing is, in a crowd of people we still caught each other's eye but for some reason, neither one of us ever crossed the room to say so anymore."

"And when the two of you went home?"

Jo leaned back so that the curl of her body could not hide the truth.

"In the beginning we couldn't keep our hands off each other. It was pretty damn hot! We knew lots of couples who weren't sleeping together anymore and I think we were just too scared of becoming one of them. After a while we were having what I call 'Designer Sex'... going through all the appropriate moves, making all the appropriate sounds. We just couldn't break a sweat anymore. Secretly we'd both given up trying to find each other's G-spot and came away relieved if we'd just found each other's pulse."

Beth nodded quietly. Over the years her own sex life had become virtually non-existent.

"Different genitalia not withstanding, I wouldn't be too quick to judge the merits of any long term relationship based on what it's *lost*. It's a lot less disappointing if you just appreciate what still remains."

Joanna caught Beth staring down at her wedding band.

"What's remained between you and Ben?"

Beth was not prepared to answer that—not for Joanna, not for her husband and not for herself.

"I'm the one who's supposed to be asking the questions, remember?"

Jo conceded.

"I'm sure Gayle would agree with you. To me, it just feels like the only thing we have *left* together is what we've *lost* together."

Beth pictured the couple sitting miserably in an exquisitely decorated room.

"Would it be terribly insensitive of me to say that I'm sure what the two of you lack in deeper companionship you more than make up for in being perfectly coordinated to the color scheme of your home?"

Joanna laughed.

"No, it wouldn't be insensitive. But the fact is we don't live together. Gayle has her own place. She owns a brownstone on the East Side. She's always been an uptown girl. The address suits her and it's just a few blocks from her office. My loft is way downtown in the West Village."

The notion sounded alien to Beth.

"You've been in a relationship for nine years and you don't live together?"

"Not in the city. We own a beach house together in the Hamptons. For years it was the one place we could go to escape the pressure of our jobs and reconnect."

"Why didn't you go there this summer?"

"Because lately it felt like its property value was the only value it had left."

Jo fell silent as she absorbed a much greater sense of loss. In the past, the open stretch of beach just beyond the dunes had always provided a place of healing for her—a place of deep passion and a place of even deeper peace. That she would come early in the morning—before the crowds—to be a part of the sky, the ocean and the sand was of no consequence to their eternal tryst. Between all the yesterdays and tomorrows, whether anyone watched or not, their natural bond continued in a way greater and deeper than anything

Joanna's eyes alone could ever comprehend. Amid that powerful vastness she would make a small place for herself from which to study, with a humble heart, all that was before her. At times she imagined that the waves must be weary of their constant churning and the sand, resentful of its perpetual surrender. But within the struggle they still found song and beneath a solemn stretch of sky Joanna's heart applauded as their eternal dance continued. There had always been a compelling mystery to this place that had endured through time with such grace. Where once it was along the beach that Joanna had witnessed the unfolding of eternity, now it was this view of the valley—in the company of the woman at her side—that seemed to carry Jo further along that path than she had ever gone before.

Beth was tentative about her next question.

"Have the two of you split up?"

"It's more like I've split off from myself. The rest remains to be seen."

"Was it okay with Gayle that you just left for the summer?"

"Was it okay with Ben that you stayed home?"

Beth understood the unspoken complexity behind each of their decisions.

"If you don't mind me asking, what happened between the two of you?"

Jo shifted her weight. She was becoming increasingly uncomfortable in more ways than one.

"It's a long story."

"By the time we reach a certain age, *everything* is."

"It was nothing really." Jo listened to the sound of her own explanation. "I guess you could say *nothing* was the something that happened to us"

Beth seemed to understand the treachery of still waters.

"What was it that eventually led to such a painful acknowledgment."

"Some reupholstered cushions for our patio furniture came out awful."

Jo smiled.

"You don't know whether I'm kidding or not, do you?"

Beth was too afraid to answer. It sounded almost as absurd as Jo's reason for not wanting children.

Jo reassured her.

"That's okay. For a long time I couldn't believe that was it myself. I mean, nine years down the tubes over a few inches of uneven piping?"

Joanna described how at first she and Gayle stood there arguing with the manager, insisting that the workmanship was just plain unacceptable—how they left still aggravated and by the time they'd crossed the parking lot, how they had turned on one another—each blaming the other for everything that wasn't right in their lives.

"She accused me of constantly wanting to change things and I accused her of wanting things to stay the same. We sat in the car shouting at each other until the veins began popping in our necks." Jo seemed almost relieved. "The truth was, our whole fucking life was coming apart at the seams. Obsessing over some poorly stitched cushions made the irony too rich for us to ignore. It was just a place to vent our frustrations and, I guess, our worst fears. Once we calmed down and really started talking, we both realized we couldn't go on the way things were. Gayle wanted to work things out. She suggested couple's therapy. My first impulse was to run. It always is. I went for a few sessions anyway. It wasn't like I needed Freud to tell me what the problem was." It was apparent that Joanna didn't enjoy revisiting that summer or that part of herself. "For the first time in my adult life I remember being really scared. Things got even worse after that weekend I'd come up here to shoot that commercial." Joanna said nothing about her disturbing dream that unknowingly involved Danny's funeral procession. "As soon as I got home, every part of my life began to fall apart from the inside out. Suddenly it felt like there was nothing of it I could salvage. Not even a pair of fucking cushions! Nothing I'd worked so hard for seemed to matter anymore. My whole existence became a well choreographed, tastefully decorated sham." Jo's shoulders fell under the weight of the truth. "On the good days, these last three years have felt like one long, disconnected blur."

"And on the bad ones?"

"On the bad ones, everything became much too clear."

Beth was all too familiar with the pain of Joanna's description. She phrased the next question as tactfully as possible.

"Was the relationship monogamous?"

Joanna was much more blunt about it.

"You mean have I ever cheated?" She had promised Beth the truth. "Before that weekend, no. Since then, yeah, there's been others. After I came back, I felt a kind of emptiness I'd never known before. As time went by I began to feel almost haunted. It scared the hell out of me. I know it sounds like a bad cliché, but I though maybe I'd be able to lose myself in bed with someone else."

"Did you?"

"No. They always felt like the wrong woman. The strangest part is, it was never because they weren't Gayle." Jo seemed unsure of herself. "Does that make you think less of me?"

Beth was surprised by the question. She wouldn't have expected Joanna to care one way or the other what anybody thought, least of all her. For a moment Beth said nothing. Despite the sanctity of her own marriage vows and society's strict code of morality, in the quiet recesses of her heart Beth had always recognized a fundamental difference between *monogamy* and *devotion* in any couple's life. The first required each be unfailingly faithful to the other while the latter honored an essential responsibility to be faithful to oneself. To live by one set of values exclusively without sacrificing the other was impossible and that either choice required nothing less than deep and serious soul-searching. Sitting now, beside this woman who had so awakened and aroused Beth's soul, the idea of an affair had suddenly become a lot less theoretical over the last twenty-four hours than it had been over the whole twenty-four years of her marriage.

"I wouldn't presume to judge you."

"That's not what I asked."

This time Beth answered her directly.

"No, I don't think less of you. Nor would I automatically think less of anybody. That's an extremely personal decision and one way or another, the stakes are always high."

She was afraid of saying too much more.

Jo seemed relieved and Beth did not press her for details about the affairs themselves. She did, however, ask if Gayle had ever found out.

"If she did, she never confronted me."

"If you weren't happy, why didn't you just end the relationship?"

"We stayed together for the sake of the china. It was a service for eight. We couldn't see breaking up the set without doing grave emotional damage."

Beth shoved her. Reluctantly, Jo became more serious.

"And, because splitting up was the last thing in the world Gayle wanted."

"What about you?"

"It really didn't matter. Deep down inside I knew it wouldn't be any different for me with anybody else."

Beth caught the defeat in Joanna's eyes.

"How could you be so sure?"

"Because I know me. I know I wasn't capable of anything different. For the longest time, I never wanted anything different."

"Is that still the case?"

Joanna leaned across the blanket and picked one of Beth's flowers from the bunch. She held it up to her face and studied it more closely, envying Beth for her ability to still be touched so deeply by life.

"I think I'm beginning to see that ever since my mother died I've only allowed myself to love *safely*. Lately I've begun to wonder if loving that way is really loving at all. Something changed after that weekend I spent up here. My fear of feeling nothing suddenly became greater than my fear of all the terrible 'somethings' that might happen if I really let myself care."

Jo could feel tears welling up in her eyes. She instinctively reached for her sunglasses but Beth took them from her hand.

"Don't..." she urged softly.

Jo did not fight her or her own tears, which now flowed freely.

"I watched my mother suffer and die and I couldn't do a damn thing about it." Jo wiped her cheek with the back of her hand. "After that, I swore I'd never let myself feel that helpless again."

Beth had been staring deeply into Joanna's eyes, her own now watering too. In the aftermath of Jo's confession, Beth gazed over at her rock.

"Do you think the heart yearns more deeply for what it's lost or for what it hasn't yet found?"

From inside its dark, self-imposed asylum, Jo's heart awakened to the depth of its own pain. It was much too soon to trust its freedom or its own voice. She looked at Beth, then shook her head.

"Do you *ever* ask a *simple* question?"

"I've found the simple ones aren't worth thinking about."

Jo remained uncertain and quiet until Beth rescued her from both.

"It's okay. There's often a terrifying silence between our questions and our answers." She reached over and tenderly placed her hand on Jo's. "I've come to think of that silence as the Great Loneliness in us all."

In an unscripted moment born of isolation and despair, Joanna closed her own hand around Beth's. The mutual intensity of their clasp was as threatening as it was reassuring. Beth wondered how an intimacy that had come so late could still feel like it had come just in time to save them both. Joanna found it nearly impossible to withdraw her hand. When she finally did, Beth's eyes became more urgent than demanding.

"Why did you try so hard to get me to agree to the picnic?"

Joanna leaned over and peered into the cooler.

"You didn't by any chance pack those Cheerios from our first dinner?"

Beth laughed at the reference. She shook her head, leaving Jo no other choice but to answer.

"I wanted to spend time alone with you, away from an environment and all the things in it that seem to define your life."

Joanna now demanded the same truthfulness.

"Why did you try so hard to avoid it?"

"Precisely because all those things you referred to form the crux of my identity. When I'm away from them, particularly out here, I feel free to be… I don't know… somebody else."

"Maybe that 'somebody else' is who you really are."

Beth smiled the saddest of smiles.

"That's what I'm most afraid of." Beth knew her own limitations much too well. "I wouldn't know what to expect. I've never really had the chance to find out. I'm ashamed to admit it, but that kind of freedom terrifies me. I guess I've grown accustomed to living within boundaries. As much as I may resent them, they make me feel safe." Beth turned her eyes to the steep drop below. "From the very beginning, there's been something about this place that tempts me to lean the full weight of my existence dangerously close to the edge. At times, I've stood there and actually prayed for a sudden gust of wind strong enough to push me over it." Beth's face grew solemn. "Not a silly, frivolous wind mind you, but an unpredictable, irrefutable life force… one that my conscience could say was impossible to resist. I simply can't afford to lose my balance to anything less." She turned and looked directly into Joanna's eyes as if trying to convey a coded message. "Do you understand what I'm saying?"

Joanna offered a half-hearted nod.

There was an undeniable apology in Beth's eyes.

"I hope so. When I accepted your invitation, I was counting on the fact that you would."

For a few uncertain moments, Jo played with the lone flower she'd removed from the bunch. However reluctant, she finally placed it back with the others. It was her unspoken way of assuring Beth that she'd been returned to safety.

Beth felt oddly conflicted in her relief. Her smile was incomplete at best.

"Thank you."

"I'm not sure I know for what."

Beth was accustomed to shouldering her burdens alone.

"You don't have to. I'm sure enough for the both of us." This time her smile sealed things more neatly. "May I see the drawing you were working on earlier?"

Joanna reached over and handed Beth her sketchpad. Her gesture of compliance now complete, Jo went off to use the ladies room behind the bushes while Beth delighted in her work. As in the carriage house the night she'd posed, Beth found herself in awe of Joanna's talent. She poured over the pages slowly, taking her time with each and every one. Jo returned and sat back down beside her.

"These are absolutely beautiful."

As Beth continued to flip back and forth through the pages of landscapes, Jo leaned closer to have a fresh look for herself.

"You were right about this place... there's something about it."

Beth closed the pad and rested her eyes on its cover.

"I was watching you before, while you were sketching." Beth's thoughts seemed to drift. "I watch you quite often, actually."

Joanna could feel her heart pound with uncertainty.

"Since when?"

Beth found an unusual calm from somewhere deep within—a calm that came from admitting something that longed to be said. She answered in a soft, steady voice.

"Since the day we met."

Jo was no longer sure where the conversation was going. With everything riding on getting it right, she struggled to understand.

"Why?"

Beth shook her head. She was completely sincere.

"I don't know exactly. I just know that at times it feels like my whole life depends on having you in my sight."

Joanna certainly wasn't prepared to admit just how often she'd felt exactly the same way. For the moment, she was incapable of saying anything at all. Beth wondered what Jo made of her confession.

"Does that trouble you?"

"Why should I be troubled that you're stalking me? I'll get a restraining order if it comes to that."

Beth ignored Jo's awkward attempt at avoidance.

"It's troubled *me*... at times, very deeply." She paused to consider the rest of it. "But not today. Not out here. For some reason this feels more natural than anything I've ever felt in my entire life." Beth felt relieved. "I don't know why, but I needed to tell you that."

Jo remained cautiously silent and Beth took the opportunity to apologize for something else.

"I'm so sorry about my reaction before... recoiling like that when you touched me."

Joanna accepted her apology.

"Be honest, does my being a lesbian make you uncomfortable?"

"It's not what you are that makes me uncomfortable, it's that you're so damn *sure* of what you are at a time in my own life when I've never been less sure about… well… so many things. The truth is I envy you. Except for my music, I've never known that kind of certainty about anything. When I lost that, I lost a part of myself that was still becoming whomever and whatever I was *meant* to be." Beth gazed out onto the valley. "Maybe it was silly, but I was hoping to use this summer to continue the journey… maybe find the place where I'd left off all those years ago, and move forward from there."

"And have you?"

"Sometimes I actually think *yes*. Then at other times, I feel more lost and confused than ever before." Beth took a measured breath and risked sharing even more. "Both those feelings have everything to do with meeting you." She could feel herself tense, but she pushed on. "The closest I've ever come to recognizing myself is what I saw in your studies of me."

Jo thought about her breakfast conversation with Steve. Maybe he was right after all. Still, she needed to understand more.

"Is that good or bad?"

Beth answered with a rare gift of certainty.

"It's neither. It's more like exhilarating and terrifying. No one has ever seen me like that. So vulnerable. So exposed."

"What about your husband?"

"I'm afraid, least of all my husband." Beth sighed and in that unlocked breath, her heart released a lifetime of secret isolation. She smiled the most melancholy of smiles. "So here I sit before you as unfinished as that piece of music you heard me playing on that rainy afternoon."

In that moment, Joanna could not convince herself to be more careful.

"And even unfinished just as beautiful and just as compelling."

"Is that how you really see me?"

Jo nodded.

"Why, how do you see yourself?"

Beth stumbled over a mountain of insecurities.

"Mostly I don't see myself at all. Mostly I just feel invisible."

She bowed her head, troubled by the truth.

Jo was amazed. Even now in her sadness she found Beth achingly beautiful.

"Well that's got to change!"

She reached into her duffle bag for her camera, removed the lens cap, aimed at Beth and began clicking. Beth instinctively covered her face with her hands.

"Please don't."

Jo continued to coax her.

"C'mon, look at me."

"I can't."

"Sure you can."

Beth made a series of deliberately funny faces. But as Jo continued to focus and refocus, Beth grew tired of her own charade and gradually found the courage to simply be herself, allowing Joanna to capture what only Joanna could. With each click of the shutter, Beth felt more at ease. At one point she looked directly into the camera.

"How about dangerous?"

Jo continued to snap.

"What about it?"

Beth felt slightly foolish.

"I was wondering if you saw me as dangerous too?"

Amused by the question, Joanna looked out from behind the lens.

"You're the most dangerous woman I've ever met in my entire life."

Beth's heart began to race.

"Am I?"

Joanna resumed her snapping.

"Far and away, the most dangerous! We hadn't even met and you managed to crush my foot and plow into my car."

Beth's disappointment was impossible to miss. Jo lowered the camera, reached out and gently lifted Beth's chin.

"The truth is I've never been afraid of anyone like I'm afraid of you."

Jo allowed her to smile seal her confession.

At that precise moment Beth could not bear to think of an end to the thrill of Joanna's company. The days left to the summer suddenly felt precious and few. The wasteful interruption of Rheeta's visit couldn't have come at a worse time. While she couldn't have imagined two less likely dinner companions, Beth blurted out an invitation.

"My college roommate is visiting from Boston for a few days. Why don't you join us for dinner Wednesday night?"

Jo felt selfish about having to share Beth's company. Still, for more of it she would have agreed to anything.

"Sure, why not?"

Jo captured the nuances of pleasure in Beth's eyes. She clicked relentlessly while Beth remained a willing subject, neither posing for nor hiding from Joanna's camera.

Finally she'd had enough and placed her hand over the front of the lens.

"Please, no more."

Joanna granted Beth a few minutes of reprieve.

"Do you realize that in every photograph in your living room you're always surrounded by your family? There are individual portraits of everybody except you. There's not a single one of you alone."

"Yes, I know..."

"How come?"

"Maybe because that's not how I ever wanted to be seen... *alone*."

"Why?"

Beth had never admitted the depth of her alienation to anyone before.

"Because it's always terrified me that despite a wonderful, loving family, *alone* was how I really felt...," she raised her eyes to meet Joanna's, "until I met you." Beth swallowed over her fear that threatened to silence the rest of what she needed to say. "For the first time in my life, you've made me feel alive in a way I've never known before."

Joanna couldn't bring herself to admit the same.

"I'm not sure what to say."

"You don't have to say anything. It means everything just to be able to thank you."

Jo's eyes offered their own quiet gratitude and in her smile, Beth felt it was the perfect time to at last share her secret. She leapt to her feet and held out her hand.

"C'mon. I want to show you something!"

The day was already filled with too many uncertainties. Joanna needed to know more.

"What is it?"

"You'll see. It's over there by the rock."

Jo let herself be pulled up onto her feet. The warmth of Beth's clasp spread across her body and pooled in the pit of her stomach. With each step across the sloping field, the sensation of Beth's hand continued to overwhelm her. Nothing had ever felt that natural and that conspicuous at the same time. Unable to resist, Jo finally let her own fingers curl around Beth's. Up until that moment Beth had been holding her hand. Now, in the deliberateness of Jo's own grip, their connection became complete. Without saying a word or altering her step, Beth squeezed a bit tighter to let Joanna know she was aware of the difference and that she *understood.* Her heart beating wildly, she pulled Jo around to the side of the great boulder that faced out onto the view of the valley. With her free hand, Beth pointed excitedly to a specific corner.

"Over there... go ahead, pull away the brush."

Beth released her hand so Joanna could do as she instructed. She watched anxiously as Jo crouched down and parted the cluster of weeds and wild flowers that sprang up around the base of the massive, jutting rock. There, carved into the stone, slightly up from the ground was a small heart with the initials A&E scratched into the center. Beth's own heart leapt with joy at the sight of it once again.

"They're the same initials as the ones carved into the windowsill of the carriage house." Beth bent down and ran her fingers gently over the carving. Tears came to her eyes as she envisioned the lovers' rendezvous. "They were here too Jo! Can you imagine?"

Joanna was a lot more unnerved by the coincidence than she let on. There were already too many things about this summer she didn't care to dwell on. Beth, on the other hand, wanted nothing more than to bask in the notion.

"Somewhere deep inside I know they were clandestine lovers. Don't ask me how, I just feel it. I discovered the heart on the window ledge the very first time I set foot in the carriage house and I found this one the very first time I came up here. It was like they were there waiting for me in both places." Her eyes drifted lovingly across the carving. "For some reason, I think they were meant to be my company and I, theirs."

Beth turned away from the heart and looked at Joanna.

"Now that *you* know too, it feels like our lives are all connected somehow."

Jo wasn't sure she wanted to be a part of any of it. The whole thing was beyond anything she could comprehend.

"In all this open space, how the hell did you ever find something so small and well hidden?"

"It happened the very first time I came up here. After I'd picked some wild flowers I sat down against this rock to take in the view. I have no idea what made me choose that exact spot, but the weight of my body bent the grass where I was sitting. When I stood up there it was, exposed! I recognized the initials immediately. I was so stunned it was hard for me to breathe." Beth's enthusiasm was no match for Jo's reservation. "I've never shared this with another soul. I know in my heart this place was *their* secret. I'd always intended to keep it that way... until I met you."

Beth sat on the ground and pressed her back against the rock beside the precious carving. She gazed out onto the valley, then up at Jo.

"Sit with me here a while."

Joanna looked down at her. The late afternoon sun cast itself across the soft contour of Beth's face. That alone was invitation enough. Sitting beside her, Jo looked out over the steep drop only a few feet in front of them.

"We're kinda' close to the edge."

Beth had never known a more peaceful interlude.

"It's okay. I trust you won't let me fall."

Given her own reckless impulses toward Beth, it amused Jo to be cast in the unlikely role of her protector.

"I'd say your faith's a little misguided, considering the train wreck my own life has become?"

"I'm counting on you being a lot more careful with *my* life than you've been with your own." Her eyes flashed mischievously as she locked her arm around Joanna's. "But just in case, if I do go over, I'm taking you along with me!"

The playful threat wove itself into the air around them and for the next few minutes they both sat perfectly still—arm in arm—staring silently out at the valley below. Neither dared disturb the unspoken thoughts collecting in the others' heart. For Joanna, their physical contact was nearly unmanageable. She worked to do all that she could—all that she knew she must—to control the power of her yearning so that the object of her desire was spared the danger of it. Over the last several hours, the particles of that desire had spread to every part of her body and now threatened to end in conquest. With every brush of Beth's arm, the test of Jo's friendship became greater. Self-sacrifice was not Joanna's style. She knew herself well. She knew that just beneath its orderly surface, her world was a rogue and lawless one and in that largely untamed land she was accustomed to roaming free and living dangerously—her sexual impulses governed not by circumstance or moral compass but by the selfish demands of her own restless nature. She'd always taken *whomever* she wanted—*whenever* she wanted—and dealt with the consequences after the fact. But her desire for Beth was something altogether different. Beth was altogether different. Deep in her heart Jo knew that difference had the potential to destroy them both. She leaned forward intentionally breaking their physical contact. Beth instinctively crossed her arms to compensate for their sudden emptiness. With her eyes trained safely on the horizon, she found the courage to face the inevitability of a more permanent loss.

"After this summer, when you go back…"

Jo answered before Beth could finish.

"I don't know. Gayle really wants to work things out."

"Is that what *you* want too?"

"I can't have what I want." Jo couldn't let Beth ask what that was. "What about you and Ben?"

"I'm sure he's hoping for a miracle that will give him back the woman he married."

"What are *you* hoping for?"

Beth drew a thoughtful breath.

"I'm hoping to simply make peace with that woman, once and for all."

Jo turned around to study the bolder that had been supporting the weight of their bodies and the weight of their respective lives.

"I guess you could say we're both caught between a rock and a hard place."

Beth laughed.

"It does seem that way, doesn't it?"

Her smile faded much too quickly.

"I just wish the future wasn't so uncertain."

Jo was determined to rescue Beth from her despair.

"Give me your hand."

"Why?"

Joanna became impatient.

"Lady, do you ever stop asking questions? Just give me your hand."

This time Beth obeyed without another word. Jo turned it palm-side up and brought it close to her face as if making it easier to read.

Beth smiled.

"I wasn't aware you read palms."

"I have many talents you don't know about."

Beth tried not to let herself imagine the others.

"So what do you see?"

"Shhh. This kind of thing takes concentration."

Beth waited quietly, aware that her affection for Joanna was growing deeper by the minute. As she watched Jo struggle to come to her rescue with some clever, light-hearted vision of the future, Beth sensed her companion's futility.

"It's okay sweetie, it really is. I don't expect you to save my life." Her voice carried Joanna's pain. "Nor did your mother expect you to save hers."

Joanna dared to meet Beth's eyes. Their kindness penetrated Jo's anguish. Beth's son had died in her arms. She had become much too familiar with the agony of feeling helpless.

"You have to stop blaming yourself, Jo. Your loss is burden enough."

For once in her life Joanna did not try to outrun her own heart. She looked down at the hand she still held in her own—cherishing it—worshiping it for the music it played so beautifully, the marshmallows it placed so lovingly, the clay it squeezed so joyously and the splinter it removed so delicately. In the stillest of moments, she let the tips of her fingers move gently across Beth's open palm.

With her life quite literally in Joanna's hands, Beth's eyes pleaded for an explanation. Jo refused to look up and offer her one. Beth's heart began to race. Perhaps this was the irresistible force she had been praying for—the one that would end or begin her life. There would be no way of knowing until it was too late, but this time she did not pull away. This time she did not struggle against her faltering balance. Instead, Beth closed her eyes and opened herself more fully to Jo's touch—a touch that grew unmistakably more personal with every stroke. For Beth this small patch of her own flesh quickly became a conduit of heat that threatened to arc and burst into flames, burning her entire life to the ground. Unable and unwilling to save herself, she let her head fall back and rest against the sacred rock as Joanna continued to explore the contour of her opened palm—slowly, deliberately caressing every intricate fold. The space between them filled with danger. Beth could feel herself becoming more and more aroused. The pounding in her throat spread through her body to the place between her legs. She ached for Joanna to touch her *there*—to feel how wet she was—how ready.

Though Jo longed to let her tongue follow the imagined path of her fingers along the length of Beth's arm, around the slope of her neck and behind the gentle curve of her ear, she dared not let herself move beyond Beth's wrist. Still, she could not prevent the language of even her limited touch from becoming something undeniably intimate. Their lives now poised on the brink of a risk Jo was not prepared to take, she had no choice but to stop abruptly.

With Jo's sudden and clumsy withdrawal, Beth opened her eyes to find Joanna staring vacantly at her wedding band. Neither of them spoke a single word. Joanna quickly released Beth's hand, giving her back her life. Beth didn't know what to think. Jo had deliberately coaxed her out over the edge, then suddenly abandoned her halfway through her fall. Was it because she cared too much to let her get hurt or not nearly enough to deal with all the shattered and complicated pieces of Beth's life in the aftermath of their plunge? She would never know because she could never bring herself to ask. Instead, Beth tried as best she could to ignore the crushing ache in her chest and the dampness between her thighs. She sat forward, nervously avoiding the shame of both. Beth was the first to break their painful silence—one that only a lover's kiss could have eased.

"This was such a wonderful day."

Joanna offered a cautious smile.

"Yeah, it was."

She stood up and brushed herself off, hoping to erase any remaining traces of their guarded intimacy.

"We should get going."

Though it was the last thing in the world she wanted, Beth was quick to agree.

"I just need a minute before we go."

She laid down close beside the Great Rock and positioned her cheek against its surface so that her ear pressed directly upon the carving itself. Joanna looked on skeptically.

"I'm afraid to ask what you're doing."

"It's my parting ritual. I never leave without giving them a chance to tell me what it is they want me to know."

"*They*?"

"Yes, the lovers—A&E.You have to be absolutely quiet so I can hear them. Spirit voices are very faint, you know."

"Actually, I don't know."

In fact, it was safe to say that Jo's interest in all things 'ghostly' went only so far as a child's Halloween costume. Beth closed her eyes and listened intently. A smile gradually followed several quick nods. Despite the bizarre absurdity of it, Joanna's heart swelled just the same at the sight of such a touching exchange. For that moment, the temptation to kneel down and take Beth into her arms suddenly felt greater than all the reasons not to. Fearing that this time she might actually give into her impulses, Jo deliberately focused on the safer beauty of her surroundings. When she turned back, she couldn't help notice the tears in Beth's eyes as she placed her lips to the heart and bid the lovers farewell. Jo cared too much to pretend she didn't see.

"Are you okay?"

"I'll be fine." Beth stood up and wiped her eyes. "I know this sounds silly, but sometimes I actually get homesick for places I've never been and feel hopelessly lost in places completely familiar." She gave the great rock one last pat. "It always saddens me a little to leave here. It feels as if a part of me always stays behind."

Joanna took a final sweeping look around.

"Thanks for bringing me up here. You didn't have to."

"Actually, I needed very much to have you see everything."

"Even the heart?"

"*Especially* the heart."

Jo let the fullness of her gratitude show in her eyes.

"So I'm forgiven for not telling you about myself sooner?"

Beth smiled and nodded.

What she did not say was that she would spend the rest of her life trying to forgive Joanna for everything else. Especially for breaking her fall.

Each struggling with her own reluctance, the women walked back to the blanket in silence, methodically gathered up their belongings and carried them to the car. Though the day had passed much too quickly, Beth felt enormously grateful for the bittersweet gift of it.

"Do you believe some things can't be expressed in words?"

Jo nodded.

Without warning Beth reached up and threw her arms around Joanna's neck, clinging to her tightly.

"Then I hope this says that I really *do* trust you Jo… I trust you with my life."

Beth rested her cheek passively against Joanna's shoulder and waited. She waited because waiting was all she knew how to do. Joanna was the one with the experience. Beth had none. In her innocence she held herself against Joanna, hoping that each passing moment would make it harder for Joanna to ever let her go. She waited, silently praying for the great life force to stir again—for Joanna to sweep her over the edge—only this time allowing her to fall all the way, splitting open her body and releasing the flood of her desire. Joanna struggled to ignore the punishing fullness of Beth's frame against her own. She could not let herself answer Beth's plea. In the disappointing stillness, Beth could wait no more. Reluctantly accepting that the threatening winds would not return, her hunger receded graciously into gratitude.

"Thank you…," she whispered into Joanna's ear. "for not giving up on me… for pushing for this day… for sharing everything you did." Her voice floated like a prayer drifting upward toward the heavens. "Thank you… thank you… thank you…"

Jo never reacted more carefully to anything in her life. She placed her hands lightly at Beth's waist, fighting to keep the fold of her arms from becoming a full embrace, one that surely would have demanded more. But more did not come. Instead, the women remained perfectly still—each damp with desire—each breathing cautiously—each afraid to move while their bodies remained pressed together in a precarious pact. Jo didn't know how much longer she would be able to keep her desire for Beth in check. Feeling her resolve steadily weakening she gently withdrew, taking great care not to destroy the precious gift of Beth's trust. Jo groped for something—anything—that she could manage with more certainty. She settled on the pair of star-crossed lovers and pointed towards the rock.

"So what did your friends have to say?"

Beth smiled. She knew Joanna found her behavior eccentric at best.

"'E' liked you immediately."

"What about 'A'?"

"'A' is withholding judgment."

Jo pretended to be hurt.

"Don't take it personally. 'A' is just more skeptical by nature. Does that sound like anybody you know?"

Jo scowled.

Beth looked back at the rock.

"They did agree on one thing though. They both thought it would be better if you drove."

"How come?"

"They must sense my reluctance to go back...," Beth smiled shyly, "to all those things that you said define my life." She gazed longingly at the valley. "Maybe they're right. Maybe I don't want to be responsible for getting us home. Maybe I don't want to be responsible for anything ever again."

Beth dangled the car keys, then slid into the passenger seat. Her eyes followed Joanna closely as she walked around the front of the car to the driver's side. Jo adjusted the mirrors, trying to distance herself from her own fantasy of driving off with Beth and never looking back.

"Okay, so if it's not home, where do you want to go?"

Beth sighed.

"Everywhere... nowhere." She bit her lip. "God, you must think I'm crazy."

"No, actually I think you're delightful."

Touched by Joanna's unexpected flattery, Beth let her head fall dreamily against the headrest.

"I'm going to treasure those words and this glorious day for the rest of my life." As Jo put the key in the ignition, Beth reached out and stopped her. "I really mean that..."

Joanna looked down at the hand that rested on her own. She did her best to ignore the ring on Beth's finger—a harsh reminder of what could never be. Instead Jo focused on the tenderness of Beth's touch that ended much too soon.

"So will I."

She turned the key and started the car.

Grateful not to be the one in charge, Beth watched Joanna steer the vehicle along the rough, uneven road. She fell instantly under the spell of Joanna's hands, stealing glances at their strength and sensuality. It was much too easy to imagine what it would feel like to have those hands command her naked body as skillfully. Drowning in the hopelessness of her fantasy, Beth forced herself to look away. Just up ahead was the familiar fork at which Beth had always taken a right. It was the quickest way down the mountain and onto the main road that led back to town. But today Beth did not want to take the quickest way back to all the same things in her life. Her heart responded spontaneously.

"Bear left at the fork!"

Pleased with her newfound sense of adventure, Beth smiled inside as Joanna followed her directions.

"Are you sure? I could have sworn we should have taken the other road back there."

"You're right, we should have."

Beth's eyes hinted at a playful secret. Joanna shook her head.

"Let me guess. The spirits told you to go this way instead?"

Beth giggled.

"Something like that."

Joanna looked at her more skeptically. By now she wasn't entirely sure just how much of all this nonsense was real to Beth.

"Please don't tell me you actually heard voices back there."

Beth smiled.

"Just my own… from somewhere deep inside. The one I don't listen to nearly enough."

Jo didn't hide her relief.

Beth smiled inwardly, then turned away. As Jo continued to drive on Beth stared out through the passenger window, her eyes and heart delighting in the pleasure of these entirely new surroundings. She really didn't care where the road led or even if they got lost. The only thing that mattered, as the car and her spirit absorbed the joyously unfamiliar terrain, was that she had never traveled this road before. That alone was enough. After driving aimlessly for several miles, Joanna questioned Beth's change of route.

"I assume you know where we are."

Beth sounded joyfully lighthearted.

"Nope, not a clue."

"Great. So in other words, we're lost."

Beth considered their predicament and smiled.

"What a relief. Finally my inside and my outside are aligned."

Having spent the better part of the ride fighting her urge to pull over and take Beth right there, Jo saw no point in prolonging her agony.

"I'm turning around and we're taking the other way back."

Beth grabbed Jo's arm.

"No please, let's keep going… "

Against her better judgment Joanna complied.

"One more mile then I'm turning around and your inner voice is going back the way it came!"

Chapter 15

Just as the odometer clocked the mile Jo would allow, a lush patch of wildflowers caught Beth's eye. Had she not begged Joanna to stop so she could pick some Beth would likely never have noticed a small wooden sign nailed to a tree just a few feet away. Obscured by overgrown brush, the hand painted letters read, 'Antique Shop'. It's arrow pointed straight ahead. Beth hurried back to the car and climbed back in.

"There's an antique shop up ahead!"

To see her joy, Jo would have driven to the end of the earth. Half a mile down the road the lone façade came into view. Beth squeezed Jo's arm.

"Look… that must be it! Oh I'm so happy we came this way. I knew there was a reason!"

It amused Joanna to think that such a simple thing as taking a new road could mean so much. She pulled up beside the pick-up truck parked outside. Judging from the two rusted tractors that stood nearby, apparently the old single story structure was once some kind of repair shop for various farming machinery. Beth leaned out through the window and read the sign that hung across the garage door.

"'Past Lives Collectibles'."

Her voice exploded with child-like glee.

"What a perfect name for an antique shop, don't you think?"

Jo was unimpressed.

"I guess…"

"Oh I hope it's open."

She peered in but saw no one. There were no hours posted in the window. Beth tried the door anyway and much to her delight, it opened. She turned and beckoned for Joanna to join her, then quickly disappeared inside. Jo climbed out of the Jeep and reluctantly made her way to the front step. Passing under the tinkling door chimes—a sound which had always irritated Joanna more than any other in the world—she followed Beth inside. The smell of old, musty objects hung heavily in the air. A small clicking fan positioned on the counter did little other than rifle the pages of a nearby newspaper. With no sign of the shopkeeper, the room felt like an abandoned maze of old, worn out objects. Cloudy mirrors and old paintings in ornate frames hung from every inch of available wall space.

Beth was overjoyed and wanted a closer look at everything. Instantly put off by the surroundings, Jo just wanted out. As if reading Joanna's mind, a raspy woman's voice called out from behind a closed door in the rear of the room.

"Don't go. I'll be out in a minute. Have a look around."

Beth answered back for both of them.

"We will. I love the name of your shop."

"Thanks," the voice responded.

After a moment, the toilet bowl flushed. From the sound of it, they'd caught the owner at an inappropriate time. Once the pipes settled down, Beth resumed their exchange.

"Did you come up with it?"

"The name… not the phenomena."

Beth laughed and whispered to Jo.

"She's got a great sense of humor."

The toilet flushed again.

Jo rolled her eyes. She couldn't believe Beth was having a conversation with a stranger on a toilet. Beth didn't give it a second's thought.

"I thought I knew every antique shop in the county. Have you been here long?"

"Long enough," the voice called back.

Beth began to eagerly maneuver up and down the narrow aisles.

"You're certainly off the beaten path. Do you advertise in any of the local papers?"

"Nope. Those that are meant to find me always do."

Again the toilet flushed. Beth giggled discreetly while Joanna just shook her head.

The voice continued.

"If you find anything that touches you feel free to touch it back."

"Oh I will!" Beth answered as she wandered deeper into the maze of objects.

Jo couldn't imagine how anyone could possibly find wading through such an obstacle course of old junk worthwhile. Once again, the voice seemed to respond directly to her thoughts.

"I know the place is a mess. Never saw any reason to arrange things any neater. Folks always find what they're meant to. Something about diggin' through lots of stuff that doesn't suit ya' makes finding something ya' love all the sweeter."

Beth had been rummaging through a carton under one of the tables. She considered the shopkeepers words.

"That's so very true."

The voice called back.

"Haven't quite convinced the other one though, have I? There's a lot more stuff in the other room. Have yourself a look."

Jo wondered how the woman behind the door knew there was more than one customer outside since Beth was the only one who had done any talking. Perhaps she had overheard their giddy exchange after the toilet bowl flushed. Jo stumbled over an assortment of musty-smelling odds and ends and made her way over to the doorway that opened up into what was once the garage. Her sudden presence scared a large gray cat out from under an old chest of drawers. It darted past her, leapt up onto the counter, and wisely claimed the limited range of the fan.

Beth looked up from the box.

"What a beautiful cat."

The shop keeper was still having a time of it. The bowl flushed again.

"Thanks. The day I opened the place she just walked in here from outta' nowhere. Hard to say if I found her or she found me."

"Maybe you found each other. What's her name?"

"Bridey."

Beth recognized the intended connection.

"As in Bridey Murphy?"

"Yep... you got it."

Beth laughed.

"That's so clever."

Joanna had absolutely no idea what they were talking about.

"Who the hell is Bridey Murphy?"

Beth looked surprised.

"You've never heard of Bridey Murphy?"

"No."

"She's probably the most famous documented case of past life regression."

Jo rolled her eyes.

"Please... just forget I asked."

Beth noticed a long scar along Bridey's hind leg.

"What happened to her leg?" she called out to the owner.

"She must have been a dog in a previous life… chases *cars*, not *mice*. She got side-swiped a few years back."

Beth stroked the cat behind her ears, confiding in it whimsically.

"I guess there's a price to pay for being who we really are…"

"We pay an even greater price for trying to be what we're not," the voice from the bathroom added.

Beth continued to stroke the animal in thoughtful silence, assuming that this shopkeeper with finely tuned insight would take her silence as acknowledgment enough. Joanna continued to carve her way through the cramped garage until she'd breathed in all the damp musty air she could take. She made her way back into the office and whispered into Beth's ear.

"I don't know what she's been doing in there all this time but I sure as hell don't want to be around when she flings open that door."

Beth muffled her laughter with her hand.

"I won't be much longer. I promise."

"What are you looking for anyway?"

"Like she said… the thing I was meant to find."

Joanna maneuvered to the door. She glared at the tinkling chimes as she made an impatient exit and Beth went back to searching through the overcrowded room. A partially hidden crate caught her eye. She moved several other things in order to pull it forward and have a closer look inside. As she examined the miscellaneous contents, she thought about what the owner had said about the value of the exploration itself. She smiled as her fingers unearthed just such a treasure—a small, delicate Victorian frame. Though the metal was badly tarnished, its sepia image of a woman and her young son touched Beth instantly. She was not surprised. Even since Danny's death she had continued to search for their connection in mother and child images everywhere. Sometimes finding them broke her heart. Sometimes they strengthened it. Sometimes it did both. She knew immediately that this was *the something* she was meant to find. Beth's eyes wandered tenderly from the frame in her hands to the woman pacing outside waiting for her. She stood that way for a while, quietly cherishing the sight of both.

"I see you found what you've been looking for."

The familiar but faceless voice was now standing directly behind her. Clutching the frame to her heart Beth spun around wondering which of the two the perceptive shopkeeper meant. The woman's strapping masculine appearance unnerved Beth instantly. Suddenly confronted with the most blatant of lesbian stereotypes, the color instantly drained from Beth's cheeks. In the midst of her sexual confusion, Beth now stood face to face with her own worst fear. Ignoring Beth's controlled panic, the woman smiled and extended her hand.

"Adele Brody. Everyone calls me Dell."

Beth looked at the woman's large, overpowering fingers. In the friendliness of the gesture, Beth felt like a drowning victim being rescued by the very danger she had plunged into the water to escape. Her hesitation was obvious.

"It's okay," the woman with raven-black eyes assured her, "I know what you're thinking."

Beth inadvertently stepped back.

"You're wondering if I washed my hands before I came out of there."

Dell was just trying to be kind. She knew that that wasn't it at all. She never held it against anyone though, mainly because she had never held herself up for anyone's approval. Her hair, cropped and combed into a manly cut, had not grown prematurely white from ever worrying about what other people thought of her. Quite the contrary. Now in her early sixties, Dell had always been entirely at ease with who and what she was. Without apology, she lived as comfortably in her men's shirts, slacks and shoes as she lived in her own skin all her life.

Beth finally mustered the courage to shake Dell's hand. A part of Beth felt awful about her reaction while the other part felt legitimately terrified.

Dell understood all of it and she deliberately chose to ignore all of it. She caught Beth staring at the scar across her left cheek.

"Bet you're wondering if I chase cars too?"

Beth just smiled awkwardly.

"Actually, I got it chasing girls. Caught up with one that side-swiped me with her long, painted nails. But that was way back when I was a playful little kitten myself. Pretty as you are, you don't have to worry. I've been domesticated for years now."

Dell looked at the frame in Beth's hand, then out through the window at Joanna.

"She's a real beauty, isn't she?"

Trapped by the ambiguous remark, Beth stiffened. Dell made it easier.

"You've got a good eye."

Under Dell's scrutiny, Beth was afraid to let herself want anything, ever again.

"I'm really not sure about it."

"The frame or the woman?"

Unnerved, Beth immediately put down what was in her hand.

Dell acknowledged Beth's decision.

"You've changed your mind?"

"Yes."

"Now if it was only that easy to have a change of heart."

Beth was still reeling when Joanna stepped back inside. From across the room, Dell greeted her with an insider's wink. Without a single word, Jo's nod confirmed what the other lesbian sensed instantly. Beth felt painfully naïve. What had *she* missed that Dell picked up on immediately? How could she have gone all these weeks and not known about Joanna? Another question became even more troubling. Standing on the sideline and bearing witness to the women's coded exchange, Beth struggled to understand why she felt so left out of a club in which she wasn't at all sure she belonged. Her entire existence clouded with uncertainly. Where did the truth of her identity lie? Was it in the life she'd been living or the life unexplored? Was one any less a warrior when the courage in their heart had not yet met the enemy's sword? Was one any less a poet when the words in their heart had not yet filled the empty page? If the answer was 'no', then was she any less one of '*them*' simply because the fire of her own flesh had not raged against another woman's? In the midst of Beth's private anguish, the two women seemed to be enjoying their instant camaraderie. Now it was Joanna who didn't mind staying a bit longer and Beth who was anxious to leave. Dell studied her customers.

"Nice to see you two lovebirds makin' the most of such a beautiful day?"

Beth froze. Jo quickly came to her rescue.

"We're not together."

Desperate to define her life and everything that once qualified it, Beth struggled to find her own voice.

"I'm married!"

That was all she could say.

Dell nodded.

"Got it."

Beth turned to Joanna.

"I'll wait for you in the car. Please don't be long."

As if fleeing for her life, she hurried toward the door. Hoping to calm Beth's nerves, Dell called out to her reassuringly.

"You'll want to make your first left. That'll take you back to the part of town you're familiar with. From there you'll be home in no time."

Even in her haste it struck Beth odd that Dell knew where she lived. Perhaps she'd mentioned it earlier. Overwhelmed, Beth raced from the shop. In an instant, her perfume and the tinkling door chimes were all that remained of her presence. The two women introduced themselves. Jo felt the need to apologize for Beth.

"I think you scared her off."

Dell was sympathetic.

"The poor thing, she must be exhausted. Feels like she's runnin' scared from a lot more than just me. Anyhow, sorry about the assumption."

Jo drew a hard line around her own wishful thinking.

"We're just friends."

Dell wandered over to the place where Beth had been standing.

"I'll never understand why folks always do that… put the word *just* in front of the word 'friends'. Seems to me it trivializes the most important thing two people can be to one another. For what it's worth, your *friend* really loved this."

Dell held up the small Victorian frame Beth had been admiring. Joanna took the hint.

"I'll be back."

"I'm sure you will."

Jo sensed a cockiness in Dell's tone—as if she had something else Jo could possibly want.

"I mean for the frame."

Joanna slammed the door behind her and Dell crossed her arms.

"For that too."

The door chimes were still tinkling from her abrupt exit when Jo suddenly poked her head back in.

"Gimme' your card. I'll call first to make sure you're open."

Dell was stroking Bridey along the length of her back.

"Not necessary. I'll know when you're coming."

Jo looked at her skeptically.

"Oh yeah, how's that?"

"I'll feel my laxative kick in." She winked and waved Jo off. "Now go on, get outa' here. From where I'm standin', I'd say you've kept that *friend* of yours waitin' long enough."

Jo was surprised to find Beth sitting behind the wheel of the Jeep. She climbed into the passenger seat.

"I thought you wanted me to drive?"

Beth was careful not to meet Jo's eyes. She needed to be back in control—if not of her life, then at least of her car.

"I changed my mind."

Joanna handed over the keys and Beth immediately started the engine. Gone was the giddy exuberance of being lost. Jo insisted on an explanation.

"What's wrong?"

Beth's voice was as parched as the dirt lifted up by the traction of the tires.

"Nothing."

"That's a fucking lie, and you know it."

Beth turned onto the state road, thankful to be heading back in a direction she was familiar with.

"I don't want to talk about it."

While she took quiet note of the route in order to find her way back for the frame, Jo offered her own hunch.

"Are you upset because she assumed we were lovers?"

"Don't be ridiculous! From her frame of reference I'm sure she assumes any two women walking side by side are…" Beth stopped short, unable to say the word itself.

Though Beth had ardently dismissed the notion, Dell's perception scared her. If a stranger had uncovered the truth of her turmoil then surely Joanna saw it too. Jo persisted.

"So what is it then?"

Afraid to say much more, Beth didn't respond. Instead, she gripped the wheel and drove steadily closer to home.

Jo tried being less confrontational.

"Is this really how you want today to end… in icy silence? C'mon, talk to me. Something happened back there. What was it?"

Beth felt awful. She thought about her reaction to Dell. The truth was simple. At a time when her life was never more unsettled and all her new-found longings never so strong, Beth was traumatized by Dell's extreme appearance and the stigma that went with it. If she had panicked in the face of a single encounter, how could she ever trust herself to manage the entirety of the larger lifestyle? Suddenly it felt as if she no longer fit anywhere… not in her own life and certainly not in the one that Dell and Joanna so comfortably shared. Beth felt invisible and trapped in the space between two worlds, neither one of which could accommodate the complexity of her slowly emerging needs. How could she possible make Joanna understand without confessing to everything that raged inside? She struggled for a safe metaphor.

"I feel like I'm on a child's bicycle with cumbersome training wheels, furiously peddling to keep up while everyone around me zips by on sleek five-speed racers steering their lives at lightening speed."

Joanna laughed.

"Maybe so, but what you lack in gears you more that make up for when you ring that little bell on your handle bars."

"Please don't make fun of me."

"Dell made you uncomfortable, didn't she?"

Beth felt it was safe enough to admit to part of the truth.

"She wasn't what I expected. It threw me a little, that's all."

"Bull dykes usually do."

"Doesn't it bother you?"

"Doesn't what bother me?"

"Lesbians who do everything they can to make themselves look like men. I would think it reinforces every negative stereotype imaginable."

"Oh that." Jo stared out through the windshield as she revisited old attitudes. "It used to. It doesn't anymore. Back when most of us who could chose to conveniently 'pass', it felt critical that the few who were out front and center wore a pretty face. So sure, every time a lesbian who looked like Dell swaggered down the street I would cringe." Jo shook her head. "When I think about it now, that was so fucking selfish and unfair. Those who had the guts to be themselves when it was the hardest wound up catching hell from the rest of us. Once more of us came out, each of us was less invested in someone else's appearance. These days I have nothing but respect and appreciation for a lesbian like Dell. It's pretty much a 'lez and let lez' attitude."

Beth couldn't help but laugh.

"That's a rather clever way of putting it."

"Let's not forget I'm an award winning creative director." Jo couldn't resist a teasing reference to reincarnation. "At least that's what I was in my *past* life. In my current one it looks like I've become a carpenter."

Beth relaxed enough to loosen her grip on the wheel. Joanna's was glad to see Beth smile again. They traveled the rest of the way in a much more comfortable silence, each trying to imagine how to go her separate way once they arrived home. Much sooner than either of them wanted to be, they were back in Beth's driveway unloading the trunk. Their long awaited picnic now over, the two women stood awkwardly alongside the car groping for a way to delay their parting. Joanna offered to help bring things inside. BJ insisted on

Joanna's attention while Beth went about unpacking the cooler. The remains of their picnic lunch provided the perfect invitation.

"Why don't you stay and help me finish off some of these leftovers."

Jo hid her delight while she continued to wrestle with BJ.

"Will you play the piano afterwards... the piece you played that afternoon it rained?"

"If you'd like."

Quietly reveling in the extended plans, Beth gathered up the wildflowers she'd picked.

"I'd better get these in some water before we eat."

"Wait. Which one is your favorite?"

Beth pointed to the violet pansy. Jo removed it from the bunch and fed it through Beth's hair, behind her ear. Beth instantly struck a theatrical, come-hither pose that quickly receded into a much shyer smile. Inches apart, the two women stood locked in another threateningly intimate exchange. Joanna reached up and adjusted the flower.

"Beautiful."

"It is, isn't it?"

"I didn't mean the flower." Her eyes lingered. "Beautiful and so very, very dangerous..."

Before taking her hand away, Jo allowed her fingers to brush along Beth's cheek. Her skin burned in their wake. She felt dizzy and dangerously close to the edge of her life. Had the irresistible force followed her home? Had it come now to claim her life in the same uninspiring surroundings that had for so long been the place that defined it? Once again Beth felt herself melt under the intensity of Joanna's eyes. But here there was no breathtaking view of the valley offering an eternity into which she could leap—just the top of the stairs that looked down into her unfinished basement. And here there was no Great Rock with its timeless carving to close her eyes and lean upon—just a refrigerator door covered in silly magnets. Joanna hovered longer and closer than ever before. Beth panicked. She could not allow herself be kissed just then—not there in her kitchen. She was not sure how she would ever survive the ending of that kiss and if she did she knew she would never again be able to set foot in that room to resume the same mundane routines of her life without going mad in the wake of its memory. Afraid for her own sanity, Beth hastily put down the flowers and escaped into the pantry to retrieve a vase and to slow the pounding of her heart. As they always had in the past, Beth's greatest fears slowly gave way to even greater desire. When she returned to the kitchen and the thrill of Joanna's company, Beth noticed the blinking light on the answering machine. Lost in the euphoric anticipation of their evening together, she hit the button to play back the message. There was only one. Joanna was at the sink washing her hands and Beth was setting the table when the sound of Ben's voice startled them both. It was much too late and much too awkward for Beth to lunge across the counter and turn the machine off. Instead, she and Joanna looked everywhere but at each other as Ben's voice instantly consumed the space between them.

"Hi hon. Just called to say I miss you so much and I'm not giving up on the idea of you joining me here for the rest of the summer. The longer we're apart the more I realize how much I love you. Give me a call when you get in. I don't care what time it is... I just need to hear your voice."

The machine clicked off, leaving the two women standing in a silence too impossible to ignore. Ben's sobering message had all but destroyed the potentially intimate end to the day. Refusing to abandon her hopes, Beth struggled to salvage things. She nervously continued to set the table until Joanna stopped her. Pretending that Ben's message had nothing to do with her change of heart, she reached for the paper towels and dried her hands. Even before Jo said a word, Beth's heart began to sink. She knew their night was over—ruined.

"I think I'll pass on those leftovers."

Beth felt herself on the verge of tears.

"You don't have to go."

"Yes I do."

Beth followed Jo's eyes across the room to the answering machine. Nothing more needed to be said.

In the silent recognition, Beth began to blame herself for every poor choice she'd ever made. Why did she have to listen to her message? Why couldn't it have waited—like every other important thing in her life had to wait? Confined now to her latest disappointment, she could no sooner rewind her husband's words than she could rewind the entire course of her life. Helpless to undo the damage, she offered Jo the most incomplete of smiles.

"I understand...."

Whether she really did or not was of little consequence to Joanna. She was annoyed with herself for wanting what she knew she couldn't have. Beth followed her out onto the porch. The ache of their separation had already begun. Beth needed assurance that there would be a next time.

"I hope you'll still come to dinner on Wednesday."

Even now with red flags waving everywhere, Jo knew she could not stay away. At least they wouldn't be alone and tempted to make the biggest mistake of their lives.

"So what's this college roommate of yours like anyway?"

Describing Rheeta's style was never easy. Beth kept her description playfully vague.

"Let's just say she's the polar opposite of Dell."

"What's that supposed to mean?"

"Come to dinner and see for yourself."

Jo couldn't deny her. She recalled the first time she'd accepted Beth's invitation.

"Steve and I work 'til six. I won't have time to make you another paper bouquet."

Looking into Joanna's eyes, Beth didn't know how much more Arthur's vase, or her heart, could hold.

"You don't have to bring a thing. I just need to know you'll come."

Beth's heart seemed to hang in the balance. How well Joanna understood how that felt.

"I'll be there."

Though her spirits immediately lightened, still Beth was afraid.

"Promise you won't change your mind."

How well Joanna understood that too.

"I promise."

Jo now faced the more immediate challenge of having to leave.

"Good night then."

From the very first step it felt as though she was walking against the force of a punishing wind.

Beth reached out for her arm.

"Jo… wait!"

She removed the flower from her hair and gently tucked the stem into Joanna's breast pocket. Her eyes had grown sadder again.

"Something to remember our picnic by…"

Jo looked down at her pocket, then searchingly at Beth.

"It's not a day I'll ever forget."

Beneath Beth's clothes the heat began to spread.

"Nor I."

In the last hour the sun had dropped lower in the sky. 'The Gods' had granted them the perfect day. Now they would each have to repay that debt with the torment of a mercilessly empty night. Jo forced a smile.

"I hope the pictures I took do you justice."

Bathed now in the light of dusk, Beth looked more beautiful than ever. Jo knew if she didn't leave at that moment, she would never be able to leave Beth again.

The further away Jo got, the more Beth ached. She was halfway across the yard when Beth suddenly called after her.

"Jo..."

The urgency in her voice prevented Jo from taking another step. Now a reasonably safe distance away, she allowed herself to turn and look back. From the railing of the porch Beth seemed to strain against the forbidding limits of her life. The night air carried the weight of her regret.

"I'm sorry."

Even from a distance, Beth was nearly impossible to resist. Jo did not dare ask what Beth meant. She knew what she *wanted* it to mean and she knew that it would hurt as much to hear the truth as it would to be denied it. Risking everything, Joanna answered back.

"Me too."

Jo was too far away to read Beth's eyes but her hands seemed to slide slowly down the length of the porch column as if offering an unconscious caress. Joanna locked the image deep inside her heart, then turned away and kept going.

The air inside the carriage house felt heavier than usual or maybe it was just that it had gotten harder for Joanna to breath whenever Beth wasn't around. She turned on the ceiling fans, neither expecting nor getting any relief. Jo did everything she could to ignore the studies of Beth that hung on the wall but the harder she tried, the more insistent those eyes became. Unable to resist, Jo came and stood before the one most haunting. She removed the small flower Beth had placed in her pocket and cupped it gently in her hands. She poked a small hole in the rendering and fed the stem through the area just behind Beth's ear. Flooded by the heartache of their unfinished night, Joanna thought again of her rigid Barbie dolls and the torment of their impossible embrace. From over her shoulder she heard her mother's soft whisper assuring her that somehow she and Beth would 'find a way'. When two people loved each other, they always did. But tonight it was a much harsher reality that would not bend to Joanna's desire and there was nothing to figure out except how she would live without ever knowing what it felt like to lie with Beth in her arms. This was not the sort of thing Jo was looking for when she ventured back to the town where her world had begun to fall apart. But this was what 'The Gods' most deliberately made sure she found. For the first time in her life Joanna Cameron had fallen deeply and completely in love. In the hopelessness of the situation, it only made it worse to think that possibly Beth felt the same. She had asked her for this day and finally Beth had agreed. Now those sacred hours were a part of Joanna forever. Everyplace she had ever been or might ever go would blend with the view from the place Beth had shown her. She thought about Beth's special secret—the unusual coincidence of the identical hearts. Now, as the last gift of sunlight cast itself upon the initials carved into the window sill, Jo envisioned the same sunlight settling like a soft blanket upon the Great Rock that overlooked the valley. In the presence of that heart Joanna had come closer to the wounds of her own more than she had ever thought possible and tonight she sobbed like she vowed she'd never do again after the night she'd lost her mother.

Resisting her impulse to rip it's cord from the wall and stomp it to pieces, Beth stared bitterly at the answering machine. She knew that even after she had erased his message, the reality of her marriage would still be there. She hastily scooped all the leftovers she'd hoped to share with Joanna into a dish for BJ whose appetite bore little relationship to Beth's pain. After she'd put everything else away, Beth wandered about the house aimlessly until she remembered Joanna's request. Fighting back tears, she sat down at the piano. Caressing the paper bouquet with her eyes she opened the lid, exposing the keys that would expose her soul. Certain that the cool evening breeze would carry each note, Beth played the music of her heart—offering its anguish and its apology to the woman she loved.

Indeed Joanna heard it all but unlike the day of the great rain, this time she did not call Beth to tell her so. There was nothing left to say that wouldn't lead to 'more' and 'more' was the one thing that could never be.

Beth saw no point in prolonging the night. At just past eight, she carried her heavy heart up to bed. To weak to resist, she stole one last look across the yard at the carriage house then lowered the shades to shield herself from the last remnants of daylight and longing that still clutched at her heart. She climbed into bed and curled up on her side, praying for her exhaustion to spare her the misery of the long restless hours that lie ahead. But tonight the same Gods that broke Joanna and brought her to tears demanded more from Beth than the ache of separation. They wanted her discretion, her balance, her control. They had granted her this most glorious day. Tonight they would make her pay by seizing what was left of it all.

The first of her dreams begins with her husband's voice, just as it had come through on the answering machine earlier. Without warning, Ben appears in their bedroom. Overwhelmed by his sudden and overpowering presence, Beth paces nervously as he begins going through her drawers and tossing her most personal things into a suitcase along with his—all the while insisting she go back to England with him. She tries futilely to explain but when she opens her mouth to speak, no words come out. She feels helpless to make him understand. At the height of Beth's frustration, Joanna enters the bedroom. She stands passively off to the side as if there to simply observe Beth's agony, not rescue her from it. Unfazed by Jo's presence, Ben closes the suitcase as Beth begins to plead with Jo to intervene before it's too late. A stoically silent Joanna does nothing to come between Beth and her husband who had now taken Beth forcibly by the wrist and is pulling her towards the door. Desperate to remain with Joanna, Beth breaks away from Ben's grip and runs to her side. Like a cat brushing up against her mistress, Beth rubs herself against Jo's body—aching to have her affection returned—forcing Ben to see that she is no longer his. But the more Beth begs Jo to fight for her, the more indifferently Joanna responds, neither shunning her advances nor taking her into her arms. As Ben's impatience escalates, Beth becomes frantic for Jo to act. Her head now thrashing against her pillow, Beth awakened to the muffled sound of her own urgent plea. "Joanna, tell him, please… tell him what's happened! Tell him how much I love you… how much you love me. Tell him you won't let me go. Not now. Not ever."

Tears ran down Beth's cheeks as her unleashed subconscious pulled her back under. This time 'The Gods' would have the rest of her.

The scene shifts from Beth's bedroom to the grassy knoll where the two women from the pages of Nick's magazine are now engaged in their illicit rendezvous. It is the precise spot where she had spent the day fighting her desire for Joanna. The women are sprawled naked on her blanket—beside *her* rock—dangerously close to discovering the carved heart. They laugh as she stands rigidly guarding her secret. They pull her down against her will, tear off her clothes and touch her everywhere. At first Beth struggles against the undeniable pleasure of their hands and mouth, but eventually she succumbs. They make her do things—things she's never done before—things she knows she must never do again. Somewhere in her ecstasy the other two women cease to exist. In their place, she has become one and Joanna the other. Locked in the forbidden acts of her dream, Beth emerged from its grip, her body writhing, pleading for release. Unlike the morning in the shower, this time Beth could not escape the demands of her arousal. This time her aching flesh would not be denied. Her heart pounding in anticipation, she slid her hands under the covers and worked her panties down past her hips, over her ankles and kicked herself free. Her nipples hardened beneath the tented sheet as she bent her knees and opened her legs—slowly and deliberately inching along the inside of her thighs with the back of her hand, moving ever closer to the soft, damp mound that concealed the volcanic core of her desire. A low primal moan escaped from years of neglect, as Beth spread herself apart revealing her hunger to the hunger of the night. Her fingers still remembered how she liked it as they teased and stroked the long abandoned place of her ecstasy until her creaming smothered the hard, swollen piece of flesh now under their command. She heard Joanna's voice, felt Joanna's eyes—demanding her surrender.

"Oh God yes..." she cried out as if directing other hands—Joanna's hands.

Beth's breath quickened as she pulled away the sheet, exposing herself to the darkness that had almost forgotten the salty scent of her lust. Straining to get at herself, Beth drew her knees up closer to her body. Her whimpers mirrored the steady rhythm of her fingers pushing harder and faster into her flooded canal. Her hips bucked beneath the will of her hands that brought her closer and closer until she exploded against them. She came in long rolling waves, moaning and arching against her own palm while the tips of her fingers continued in small, tender circles to caress the part of herself that sill throbbed. She had forsaken it for so long. Now she would wait for the intensity of its spasms to slowly recede back into quiet hiding.

When it was over, Beth rolled onto her side. She stared at her husband's untouched pillow while all the lingering sensations of making love with Joanna filtered through her mind. She thought about what Nick had asked her—if she'd ever regretted never having been with anyone else. She hadn't answered him. Sex with her husband had always been adequate, but never complete. She was a virgin at twenty when they met. She had always appreciated Ben's tenderness but never did his touch ignite the passion and fire that now burned within. For all the times he had taken her in his arms, never once did she feel truly possessed. As one wedding anniversary blended into the next and daily routines reinforced their bond, Beth came to accept him as the person she belonged *with*, but sadly not the person she would ever belong *to*. Over the years the unspoken truth still took its toll. The death of their son had only made her gradual withdrawal, complete. She had learned to live without so much. Until now. Until Joanna. Beth was not afraid of falling in love with

Jo. She knew she already had. She was afraid of what would happen to her life now that any future without Jo was meaningless. Beth's eyes drifted over to the clock on her husband's nightstand. It would be several more hours before the hint of daybreak would filter in through her bedroom window, casting its familiar light in all the same places and making it seem as if nothing had changed. That alone brought fresh tears of pain so deep that this time even 'The Gods' cried with her.

Chapter 16

Joanna was already waiting at the curb when Steve pulled up Monday morning. He held out the usual Styrofoam cup of coffee, fixed just the way she liked it. Even the plastic lid was bent back, ready for her first sip. Steve watched her face as she took her first, satisfying sip.

"Feels like we've been doing this a lot longer than a few weeks, doesn't it?

Considering the truth of his remark, Jo felt the need to remind them both.

"Don't get used to it. The summer's half over."

As Steve pulled away from the curb the reality of her leaving cut like a rusty saw.

"What if I put your name first on the door of the truck?" His offer was as genuine as the sadness in his eyes. "I'm serious Jo… just say the word and we're in business for real."

"I have a life back in New York, remember?"

Especially after her picnic with Beth, that was a reality more painful than Jo let on.

"Yeah, I know… not that you've ever been willing to talk about it."

"It's complicated."

"Not so complicated that a first grader couldn't read between the lines. 'See Jo run. Run Jo run. See Jo run from her life'."

Steve waited, fully expecting to pay for his sarcasm with a lethal dose of hers. But on this particular morning, Joanna was unusually preoccupied. She played with the lid of her coffee container.

"I told her. When you dropped me off after breakfast Saturday morning, I went and told Beth I was a dyke."

Steve kept his eyes on the road.

"It's about time. How'd she react?"

"Unlike you she didn't proceed to get herself drunk."

"That's because she hadn't fallen in love with you."

"She was making tuna salad. After I told her she started hacking at it until it was pureed. I had to grab hold of her hand to get her to stop and look at me."

Steve considered Beth's reaction.

"Hmm, then again, maybe she has..."

Joanna knew it wasn't wise to say anything more, but she needed to talk and he was her one and only ear.

"I took your advice about that picnic she'd been avoiding."

"And?"

"She finally said yes."

Steve was careful to disguise his hunch.

"Was that *before* or *after* you told her you were a lesbian?"

"After. Why?"

"Just curious."

An undeniably smug smile spread across his face.

"So when are you guys planning to go?"

"We already went yesterday."

Steve's smirk widened into an actual grin.

"You sure work fast. I'm impressed."

This time Jo warned him with more that her eyes.

"Keep it up and you'll be getting the rest of this coffee in your lap. If I gave her too much time to think about it I knew she'd change her mind."

"What was there to think about? It's only her life she's risking."

Joanna didn't appreciate his implication. Nor, in it's aftermath, did she need to be reminded of the very real danger the day posed to her own.

"It was a fucking picnic, for Christ's sake... that's all!"

Steve knew when to back off. He waited a few minutes for Jo to calm down.

"She's pretty terrific company, isn't she?"

Jo's mind wandered to the torment of their parting. A reflective nod was as much as her heart could offer.

"So was this secret place of hers everything she'd described?"

Joanna's mind seemed a million miles away.

"Yeah it was."

Steve thought about the vulnerability in Beth's eyes—the smoldering sadness Jo's portraits revealed, exposing an emptiness that begged to be filled. He phrased his next question delicately.

"So did you make the most of the inspiration?"

"I filled a sketch pad and shot a roll of film."

Joanna had finished more than half of her coffee. There was less of it now for her to pour onto his lap.

"That wasn't what I meant."

An icy stare was the only response Joanna granted him. She realized her mistake in mentioning even the little she had. For the rest of the drive she stared out of the window and ignored him. Once they arrived at the house they were renovating she assumed the work itself would distract him. She was wrong. For the next several hours Jo spent her time ripping out nails, tearing down dry wall and fending off Steve's persistent effort to continue their conversation. He tried one more time while they gathered up their tools. Irritable from hours of fighting him and her own heart at the same time, Joanna nearly bit his head off. With the last of their equipment loaded into the truck, they climbed into the pick-up. It was obvious by Jo's stony silence that the air needed to be cleared. Steve knew the burden was his.

"Okay. You obviously don't want to talk about Beth or the picnic. Fair enough. Why don't you tell me about that bear then… that great big grizzly thing that's been sittin' on your chest since the day you got here? I think after all these weeks you owe me at least that much."

Joanna was willing to compromise, especially since she knew he was right.

"Fine. Start driving and I'll start talking."

As Jo reluctantly shared more about her life with Gayle back in New York, Steve listened thoughtfully. He knew Jo liked her life neat and orderly and it was obvious in her telling how deeply troubled she was by the whole unruly mess. For a while Steve said nothing. He seemed to be considering everything Jo had—and had not—said.

"Sounds like you've got yourselves one helluva problem."

I'm sure Gayle and I will work it out."

"I'm not talking about you and Gayle. I'm talking about you and Beth."

Joanna's voice sharpened with denial.

"How many ways do I have to say this? Beth's life has got absolutely nothing to do with mine. Our meeting was nothing more than a freak accident and once this summer's over, I'm sure we'll never see each other again."

In contrast to Joanna's agitation, Steve remained calm.

"I took lots of fishing trips with my grandpa. This one time he said, 'Son, people don't meet when the timing's *perfect*… they meet when the timing's *meant*.'"

Instead of hitting Steve with his own hammer, Jo drew a line with her eyes that warned him not to cross. With less than a mile left to their ride and another four weeks left to the summer, she just wanted to get through both anyway she could. Changing the subject seemed to offer reasonable hope.

"Have you ever met Beth's friend Rheeta?"

"Yeah, at a Christmas party at the Garrison's a few years back."

"What do you know about her?"

"Enough to know she spells her name R-h-e-e-t-a and to avoid her like the plague." Steve turned onto Beth's street. "Why the curiosity?"

"She's visiting for a few days and Beth invited me to have dinner with them Wednesday night."

Steve broke into a fit of laughter.

"That's really funny. You and Rheeta at the same table breaking bread together. Now that's something I'd pay big bucks to see."

Joanna was beginning to have her doubts about Beth's invitation.

"She's Beth's friend, how bad can she be?"

Steve pulled up along the curb in front of the Garrison's house.

"Tell you what. I'll let you answer that when I pick you up Thursday morning for work… that is if you haven't been locked up on assault charges. In which case I'll just swing by the courthouse and post your bail."

Jo couldn't help wonder what she'd gotten herself into.

"Thanks for the offer, if it comes to that."

"I'll be waiting by the phone with a cashier's check."

Jo was relieved that Beth's car was nowhere in sight. She got out of the truck and slammed the door. As Steve watched her trudge up the driveway, he thought about her predicament and called after her.

"There's gotta' be a better way for you to spend more time with Beth without subjecting yourself to the likes of Rheeta."

Joanna could feel her jaw clench but she refused to turn around.

"Ah, what we do for love" he added playfully.

This time Jo picked up a handful of gravel. Fully prepared to hurl it at Steve's truck, she spun around just in time to catch his wisecracking grin as he shifted gears and sped away. Jo checked her watch. It was only six o'clock but she was just too tired to head over to Dell's to pick up that frame. It would just have to wait one more day. Instead, she took a shower, washed down some leftover take-out with a cold beer and collapsed onto the couch. Tomorrow would be another day of tearing down more walls and reinforcing others—the kind she would need to protect her heart from everything her denial could not.

Depending upon how Beth looked at it, a visit from Rheeta couldn't have come at a better or worse time. Getting ready for her friend's arrival was an exercise in futility. Beth knew she could prepare endlessly and still fall woefully short of Rheeta's expectations. Nevertheless, after volunteering at the nursing home in the morning Beth spent the better part of Monday trying. At the very least it provided a safe distraction from her growing obsession with Joanna. Buried under the melodrama of Rheeta's self-absorbed life, Beth would be temporarily spared the burden of her own. The more she thought about it, the more convinced Beth was that the grande dame's visit was a blessing in disguise. For the next few days she would be able to take refuge in the shadows backstage while the flamboyant Rheeta stole the limelight. Beth would not allow herself to project beyond that. Once Rheeta left, the rest of the summer would demand the performance of a lifetime under a spotlight her unrehearsed heart was not accustomed to.

By days end, with preparation for Rheeta's arrival in place, Beth sat on the edge of her bed and stared at the phone. Resigned to the fact that a day or so wouldn't erase any of her conflict, Beth was determined to return her husband's untimely call. Before she dialed, Beth opened the bottle of his cologne, closed her eyes and inhaled deeply. With everything that had transpired since he'd left, it frightened her to realize how easy it had been to forget his place in her life—how vague his physical presence had become compared to the intensity of Joanna's. The last few weeks had all but obscured the last twenty-five years of her marriage. He was relieved to finally hear back from her, while she neither apologized nor explained her reason for not returning his call sooner. Beth kept the focus of the conversation on how things were going in England. When he pressed her for more news about life back home, she told him about Rheeta's upcoming visit. For the first time all summer he said he was glad to be so many miles away.

"Honestly Beth... I don't understand how you put up with someone so phony."

"I don't think of her as phony, just a bit theatrical."

"Theatrical is an understatement! I never met anyone who spent so much time posing for life rather than living it."

Beth couldn't argue with his assessment.

"Who knows? Maybe one day she'll bring home an Oscar for special effects."

"Any one of her outfits ought to do it."

"Such is life on Planet Rheeta."

"Well, all I can say is happy landing tomorrow."

Their blended laughter felt good to both of them. Gradually it fell away.

"And how's what's her name... Janis... Janet... the woman staying in the carriage house?"

Beth found the irony of Ben's guessing tragically amusing. He had lost his wife completely to someone else—someone whose name he hadn't thought enough about to remember.

"Her name is Joanna, Ben. Joanna Cameron."

Beth paused. In the silence she could hear herself tell him the rest, 'She's the most incredible woman I've ever met and I've fallen madly in love with her'. Instead, she spoke of Jo in the most general of terms, struggling to sound as casual as she could. Ben listened half-heartedly, waiting for his wife to finish.

"After Rheeta leaves, how about getting on a plane and joining me for the rest of the summer?"

Considering her obsession with Joanna, the notion sounded more absurd to Beth now than it ever had before.

"The first Sunday in August is visiting day at camp, remember?"

"So leave Monday, a week from today."

This time Beth declined without offering an excuse, leaving Ben to absorb his disappointment.

"Half the summer's over anyway. I'll be home in less than four weeks."

Beth knew her husband well enough to know he was trying to gauge her feeling about their separation. She felt manipulated. Her resentment thickened in her throat while her heart raged with conflict. She began to pace irritably around the perimeter of their bedroom, stretching the telephone cord and her nerves to their limits. Like so many times before, Beth gravitated to her window and stared out at the carriage house. She knew Joanna was inside and she ached to be there with her.

"I have to go Ben."

She used some last minute preparation for Rheeta's arrival as an excuse. Ben was reluctant to let her go and he made a point of reminding her how badly he continued to miss her. Beth was sure that a part of him meant for those words to be reassuring. But she was equally sure there was another part of him that meant those same words as punishment. In recent years, his devotion had become a double-edged sword. Each time Beth allowed herself to fall against it the blade cut deeper. Though she had always managed to hide her suffering well, tonight her pain was simply too great to contain. She longed for Joanna's arms but that was a place reserved only for her dreams. Even as she hurt, Beth ended her conversation with Ben as gently as she could. Now banished from everything in her own life that once felt familiar, Beth retreated to her piano adorned with Joanna's paper bouquet. Like a long and faithful friend, the great instrument welcomed her back unconditionally—forgiving her for the years of abandonment. Once again the long neglected keys awakened to the memory of her gifted touch. The music poured forth from her heart filling the room, the night and the woman in the carriage house who stood beside the carved windowsill listening intently to every tormented note.

At precisely three o'clock Tuesday afternoon 'Hurricane Rheeta,' as Ben had so aptly named her, blew into the town of Amherst packing gusts and gripes even greater than expected. Even before the silver Jaguar had come to a stop in the driveway, Beth was hit with it all. The traffic outside of Boston was a nightmare. The drive was tedious. The local streets were much too windy. The signs were to small to read and for the last three quarters of an hour Pierre's poor little bladder was on the verge of bursting. Without waiting for the door to open, the miniature poodle leapt from Rheeta's lap through the open window and headed straight for Beth's geranium. He lifted his leg and peed directly onto the clay pot. Beth watched the terracotta pot darken with Pierre's soaking. Without so much as the slightest apology, Rheeta's expressed concern was for her precious animal.

"Oh my poor baby."

'My poor flowers' Beth thought to herself from the porch. Rheeta's visit was off to its usual whirlwind start. Rheeta never simply got out of a car. After carefully checking her make-up in the rear view mirror, she lifted herself from the plush six-way bucket seat as though an audience of adoring fans had gathered for her arrival. Beth couldn't resist some affectionate teasing.

"Sorry there's no red carpet. I sent it out to be steam cleaned but they couldn't have it back in time."

"Excuses! Excuses!" Rheeta peered critically over her Gucci sunglasses at Beth's old beat up station wagon. "Honestly honey, how many more years are you planning to hold onto that eyesore?"

Beth took the remark in stride.

"It's wonderful to see you too."

Despite the fact that Rheeta's large rimmed straw hat made it almost impossible, the two women hugged each other joyfully. Beth already knew to be careful not to ruin the moment by smudging Rheeta's make-up. After an otherwise heartfelt embrace, Rheeta stepped back and grabbed Beth's hands.

"Let me look at you. Why you little devil, you've lost weight since I've seen you last."

'The death of a child will do that to you', Beth thought to herself.

Rheeta pulled Beth back into her arms and squeezed tightly.

"Oh honey—we have so much to catch up on!"

Beth kept her expectations in check. She understood that loosely translated, that meant Rheeta had so much to tell *her*. It wasn't until Rheeta had let Beth go that she noticed the vintage T-Bird parked in front of Beth's old jalopy.

"Hmm. I see hubby is going through the obligatory mid-life crisis."

Beth folded her arms, instinctively protecting her heart.

"It's not Ben's."

"Well it's certainly not *yours*, of that I'm sure."

'The Dangerous Beth Garrison' began to stir.

"Why do you say that?"

Rheeta waved her off dismissively.

"Honey, it's just not *you*, that's all."

"How do you know I haven't changed?"

"Nobody changes that much! Well maybe some do, but not you." Rheeta stroked her friend's cheek as if to appease her. "And that's what we love about our ever constant, ever dependable Bethie. You never change and all of us count on that." Oblivious to Beth's resentment, Rheeta gasped. "Please don't tell me so much time has passed that the car belongs to Adam."

"Adam is just thirteen years old Rheeta."

"Thank heavens the years aren't flying by that fast. I'm just healing from my last face lift." She eyed the New York license plate with growing curiosity. "So whose car is it then? I demand to know right now!"

Beth strained to extend Rheeta the benefit of her endless patience. Surviving the next few days in her friend's company depended upon it.

"It's a long story." Of course Beth had no intention of sharing anything more than the most basic of facts. "I'll tell you about it after you've settled in."

"Excellent! I can't wait to get out of these clothes."

Rheeta popped open the trunk and Beth peered inside at all the luggage.

"What makes me think you've brought more than a few changes?"

Rheeta clapped her hands and Pierre came racing out from behind the rosebush. She clapped again and he leapt up into her arms. Rheeta shifted the small nervous animal into one hand and grabbed her Louis Vuitton make-up case in the other. Carrying the two things that mattered most to her in the whole world, Rheeta beckoned for Beth to follow along.

"Be a love and grab those suitcases."

Beth shook her head and assumed her role as bellhop lightheartedly, lugging the two large suitcases up the driveway and onto the porch.

"My God Rheeta, what have you got in here?"

"It's just some play clothes and a few accessories. It's so hard to know what one wears out and about in a little town."

Beth already felt weary from more than the weight of Rheeta's luggage.

"We're keeping it low-key, remember?"

"You never know who I might run into."

"Trust me... *the woodsman*, as you refer to him, is definitely not your type."

Rheeta batted her heavily made-up eyelashes.

"Actually, I was thinking more along the lines of that handsome Greek college chum of Bens."

"Nick?"

"Precisely! Perhaps you might give him a call and let him know I'm in town for a few days. Maybe I'll let him take me to dinner so we can finish what we started at your little Christmas party a few years ago."

Beth marveled at how easy it was for people like Rheeta and Nick to just take whatever and whomever they desired. Considering how badly she wanted Joanna, it didn't seem fair.

"As it turns out, you're both divorced and available... not that something so inconsequential as your marital status would stop either of you."

"Why Beth Garrison, I've never known you to be judgmental."

Rheeta held the screen door open as Beth dragged the luggage inside. The truth was, Beth was just plain jealous. Considering the weight of both, she was glad to drop the suitcases as well as the subject. Rheeta was hesitant about putting her precious Pierre down, referring to BJ as 'that big, hairy beast'. Beth assured her that BJ was in far greater danger from her skittish little runt. Once the two dogs sniffed around and established some ground rules of their own, the foursome settled into a manageable rapport considering the dizzying mix of temperaments. Since the guest room was temporarily out of commission, Beth carried Rheeta's suitcases up to Adam's room. Anticipating a litany of complaints about the makeshift accommodations, Beth was surprised when Rheeta seemed amused. She looked around the room as if it were an instillation in a museum entitled, 'puberty'. Mixed in among the countless poster of rock stars, racing cars and sports heroes were several provocative photos of women in bikinis. Rheeta giggled.

"Can't you just feel the raging hormones in here?" She sat down at the foot of Adam's mattress and bounced up and down playfully. "I was all of fourteen when I gave up my cherry in a room just like this one. His parents were out paying a Shiva call. I guess you could say it was an afternoon devoted to stiffs."

Beth laughed. Encouraged, Rheeta continued mischievously.

"It was the first blow job I'd ever given. I didn't know what the hell I was doing. Not that it mattered. He came in less than ten seconds."

Beth smiled awkwardly, recalling her friend's reputation in college. The football team had aptly nicknamed her, 'Rita The Peter Eater'. Beth had always felt a quiet regret for her friend's misguided promiscuity. Rheeta reached for Beth's hand, her eyes and voice filled with uncommon urgency.

"Honey, can I ask you something?"

Beth was prepared to answer from the depth of her soul if it could provide something essential to her friend.

"Of course, anything."

"Do you swallow?"

Momentarily stunned, Beth could barely swallow her own saliva. So much for soul searching questions.

Rheeta tightened her grip as if trying to squeeze out a response.

"Oh c'mon, we've been friends forever... you can tell me."

Certain that Rheeta would not let up until she got an answer, Beth offered the shortest one possible.

"No."

Rheeta coaxed her for more.

"Go on!"

Beth kept her confession as brief as possible.

"Whenever I tried I would gag so Ben always pulled out right before."

"Ah that husband of yours, always the consummate gentleman. When I think of all the cum I've taken from the pricks in my life. Honestly, you're so lucky Bethie. Granted, Ben may not be the sexiest man alive but I'll bet there isn't anything in the world that guy wouldn't do for you."

"Think he'd let me run off with another woman?"

Rheeta burst out laughing at such a preposterous notion.

"That's what I love about you honey... you have such an outrageous sense of humor."

Beth felt a sudden rush of relief, then defeat that her deepest desire was not taken at all seriously. She changed the subject quickly.

"I left some fresh towels in the bathroom."

"Wonderful! If I need more I'll just call down to the front desk."

Rheeta took Beth's face into her hands, looking right past her friend's melancholy.

"Oh Bethie, I'll admit I was cursing the hell out of you in the car but I'm soooo happy to be here now."

"Me too. Once you're unpacked we'll have lunch around the pool."

Rheeta was in an unusually agreeable mood.

"Sounds perfect." Rheeta clapped her hands and Pierre came racing out from under Adam's desk. She held out her arms and the yelping ball of cotton leapt into her lap. "Ah there you are, my sweet precious love."

Beth left the slobbering couple rubbing cold, wet nose to surgically enhanced one.

Alone in the kitchen with BJ, Beth bent down and whispered into his ear.

"Forgive me for dragging you into this but I really needed the distraction. Just work with me. It's only for two days."

Beth emptied the refrigerator and began arranging an assortment of things on a large platter. Just as she'd finished Rheeta called down, naming all the foods she couldn't or wouldn't eat. Beth sighed, rewrapped half of everything she'd just set out and called up to say that she and the food would be out on the patio.

A full forty minutes later Rheeta finally emerged in a garish pink and orange cruise wear ensemble. The brim of its matching sunhat was almost as wide as the table umbrella. She carried Pierre in one hand and a gift box in the other. Both were adorned in festive bows. From behind her sunglasses Rheeta looked down at Beth and shook her head critically.

"Shame on you Beth Garrison. How can you sit in the sun like that without protection? Aren't you the least bit concerned about your skin?"

Beth shielded her own eyes with her hand.

"Let's just say that these days, my concerns run a bit deeper."

With great theatrics, Rheeta settled into the other chaise while Beth poured her some iced tea.

"Thank you honey." Rheeta raised her glass. "Here's to our blissful little reunion." As she sipped, she looked around. "What a sweet little backyard. I always forget how lovely 'cozy' can be."

"I'm sure those rambling estates you've lived in can be such a drag after a while."

"You have no idea. Give or take a marble fountain here or there, you've seen one formal garden, you've seen them all." She surveyed the platter Beth had prepared, then bravely placed a slice of pepperoni on a cracker. While not terribly thrilled with its taste, she was nonetheless genuinely thrilled to be sitting beside her best and oldest friend. Oozing with delight, she extended the gift box.

"Here Bethie… this is for you." Rheeta fidgeted as Beth untied the ribbon. "You're one of the hardest people to shop for."

"It's just that our tastes are different."

"To say the least."

Beth lifted the lid slowly. She had no idea what ostentatious thing to expect. As it turned out, she was greatly relieved and deeply touched. Inside was a small satin cushion trimmed in delicate lace and embroidered with the words 'friendship is the place the heart calls home'. Beth lifted it out and held it against her breast.

"It's just perfect Rhee. Thank you so much. I'll treasure it forever."

Beth leaned over and kissed her. Rheeta squirmed with delight.

"I got it at one of those little sidewalk craft shows. I thought it would go perfectly with your… um… décor. Everything is so, shall we say, broken in."

"I like to think of it as comfortable and homey." It wasn't hard for Beth to read her friend's mind "Not exactly your kind of place, right?"

Rheeta wrinkled her nose and shook her head unapologetically.

"Not really." She patted Beth's hand. "It certainly suits you though, honey. Nothing glamorous or showy, just warm and welcoming through and through."

Beth smiled.

"I'll take that as a compliment."

"Do! That's certainly how I meant it." Rheeta reached over and squeezed Beth's hand. "The truth is, I don't tell you nearly often enough how much your friendship means to me. No one's ever understood me the way you do." Rheeta quickly wiped a tear from her eye. She couldn't have her mascara run. "Look at me, getting all weepy and sentimental."

Beth took a tissue from her pocket and offered it to her friend. Her own eyes began to fill with emotion.

"Don't worry. Your secret's safe. No one ever has to know that under all that glitzy armor there's a soft, vulnerable heart."

Rheeta blotted her eyes.

"Please, you mustn't tell a living soul… especially my ex-husbands! I have a reputation as a cold, money-grubbing bitch to live up to."

Beth couldn't help but feel sorry for her friend who had everything and nothing.

"So truthfully Rheeta, how are you these days?"

Rheeta took a handful of grapes and sat back nonchalantly.

"It's the usual life after settlement… a new investment portfolio to consider, a new home to redecorate, the hottest new spa to visit, the latest cosmetic procedure to schedule, blah, blah, blah."

"You never did tell me why marriage number three ended."

"It was too soon after Danny's accident. I couldn't see bothering you with the petty details of my life." A rare wave of guilt swept across Rheeta's heart. She rested her hands on Beth's. "Can you ever forgive me for missing the funeral?"

It had been easier for Beth to just let it go. Now, three years later, she accepted Rheeta's belated touch.

"Don't worry about it."

"I can't imagine what it must have been like."

Beth didn't care to relive the worst days of her life for the sake of Rheeta's conscience.

"No you can't. You never will."

Rheeta nodded solemnly. Beth just wanted to move on and her friend's ever unsettled life now provided plenty of material. When she wasn't spending vast sums of her husband's money, Rheeta spent the better part of each of her marriages crying her eyes out. Now, three unhappy endings later the only thing left to dry was the ink on her latest, hefty divorce settlement. She presented Beth with the short version.

"Scott and I couldn't decide what to do for the holidays last year, cruise the Mediterranean or file for divorce. We couldn't agree on a vacation so we hung up on our travel agent and called our lawyers instead."

Despite Rheeta's cavalier attitude, Beth offered her sympathy.

"I'm sorry it didn't work out."

"Don't be. How many times can you charter a yacht or rent a villa before you go out of your mind?"

Beth let her head fall against the back of the chaise. That was the closest she'd come to a vacation in years.

"I wouldn't know. I could tell you how many times you'd have to clean a house or fold the laundry."

Both women laughed at the absurd difference in the burdens each had born over the years. Rheeta looked down at the simple gold band on Beth's finger.

"Tell me, what's it like to wear one of those things for twenty-five consecutive years?"

Beth smiled quietly. She knew Rheeta needed for her to be happy. She needed to know that somebody was. Three pre-nups later, marital bliss had certainly eluded her. Beth answered her in the simplest terms possible.

"It's not for everyone."

Naturally Rheeta assumed that Beth was referring to her, and Beth was more than happy to let her think that. Rheeta quickly buried whatever regrets she might have had in the more tangible rewards of her three fabulously failed marriages.

"Well, your grass may be greener than mine Mrs. Garrison, but I can guarantee you that my stock portfolio is greener than yours."

Beth raised her glass of iced tea.

"Well, here's to everything we've each invested our lives in."

"Viva la difference!"

For the next several minutes the women laughed themselves silly. Beth couldn't remember the last time she'd felt that lighthearted about the course of her life. Eventually Rheeta struck a sobering note.

"Now suppose you tell me what that sexy little sports car is doing in your driveway."

Beth took a guarded breath and presented only the bare-boned facts. She explained about the accident in the shopping mall and how Adam masterminded the idea of having Jo stay in the carriage house for the summer to compensate her for the damage to her car. Rheeta seemed intrigued.

"Hmm, too bad you couldn't have run into someone tall, dark and handsome. Now that could have made for an interesting summer..."

Beth looked away awkwardly. Rheeta recalled their phone conversation.

"How come you never mentioned her when we spoke."

The embarrassing memory of that night made Beth even more uncomfortable.

"I wasn't sure she'd even be staying this long."

"So where is Miss T-Bird now?"

Beth described Jo's impressive artistic and carpentry skills. She went on to explain about the arrangement Jo had worked out with Steve for the summer.

"She helps him with his contracting jobs and he models for her in their spare time."

Coming to her own selective conclusion, Rheeta was quick to applaud Joanna's cunning monopoly on the handsome carpenter's time.

"I like that woman's style!"

Beth began biting on the inside of her lip. This was the part of the conversation she was dreading.

"Trust me, that's not what's going on."

Beth was struggling with the simplest way to present the fact of Joanna's sexuality, when Jo herself suddenly appeared at the gate of the backyard. It was their first encounter since they stood together in the burning ruins of their Sunday night plans. It was too late to reach for her own sunglasses. Beth made the introduction, praying that her eyes wouldn't give her heart away. Rheeta sat forward and extended her manicured hand.

"That's spelled R-h-e-e-t-a."

"So I've heard."

Steve's account was right on the money. Rheeta was every bit the character he'd described. She took it upon herself to extend an invitation.

"Why don't you pull up a chair and join us?"

As much as Jo would have gladly lingered anywhere—even in hell—if it meant having Beth in her sight, she was anxious to shower, change and make her way back to Dell's while it was still light. Those back roads were unfamiliar enough in the daytime and Jo already felt *lost* in more ways than one.

"Thanks, but I can't."

Joanna glanced at the platter. She recognized some of the leftovers from the picnic. Holding Beth's eyes, she bent down and helped herself to a slice of ham.

"Just can't get enough of some things..."

Beth felt herself flush. Satisfied, Joanna turned to Rheeta.

Guess I'll see you tomorrow then."

Beth explained that Jo would be joining them for dinner Wednesday night. Rheeta was delighted.

"Splendid." Once again she extended her hand. "'Til then."

Joanna wasn't sure if this time she was expected to kiss Rheeta's ring. With great effort she managed to contain her amusement.

"Enjoy your evening ladies."

As soon as Jo walked off, Beth could feel her heart sink lower in her chest. Rheeta leaned over and slapped her friend's arm.

"You said she was talented and handy. You neglected to mention she was absolutely stunning!" Rheeta sipped her iced tea while she sized up her competition. "Now that's someone I'd definitely prefer not to be seated next to at a singles club."

Rheeta's remark was as close to a perfect opening as Beth could ever have hoped to get.

"Well, unless you were frequenting a gay bar, I don't think your paths or stools would likely cross."

"What do you mean?"

Beth's mouth was so dry her tongue stuck to the roof of her palate, making it practically impossible to speak.

"Joanna is a lesbian."

Rheeta's whole body shot forward. Her own mouth dropped open.

"No!"

"Yes."

"No!"

"Yes."

"Well now, I'll bet she must have shocked a few unsuspecting suitors along the way with that little bombshell!"

With the memory of her own embarrassing response still much too vivid, Beth dropped her eyes. Like a stalked animal hoping to avoid danger by blending into its environment, she sat perfectly still, barely breathing, praying that the threat of Rheeta's curiosity would pass. Unfortunately, it didn't.

"Is there a lover?"

"She had a girlfriend back in New York."

"Is it serious?"

"They've been together nine years."

Rheeta leaned in closer.

"So what's she doing all the way out here in the boonies for the summer, all by her lonesome?"

For more than one reason, Beth was reluctant to share the details of Joanna's personal life. Rheeta filled in the blanks herself.

"Let me guess… trouble in paradise?"

"Something like that."

"How much do you know?"

Beth lied outright.

"Not very much."

Rheeta sat back.

"Well it's comforting to know we heteros aren't the only ones with screwed up love lives."

Beth hoped that would be the end of it. It wasn't.

"So how's this little arrangement Adam set up working out?'

Beth lied again.

"It's serving its purpose."

"Do you come and go like ships in the night or have you spent time together?"

Beth remained intentionally vague.

"It varies."

"I see…"

Beth couldn't tell if Rheeta was staring at her, scrutinizing her responses or if she was just being paranoid. Unable to decide, she nervously offered more.

"She's incredibly talented. I posed for her one night while Steve was out of town."

"I hope you kept your clothes on!"

"Rheeta, you're impossible."

"Look honey, as much as I hate to admit it, even without a stitch of make-up, you're still one of the most gorgeous women I know." She eyed Beth up and down. "Granted, you could use a little help in the wardrobe department but if I were a lesbo, I'd have tried to get you out of your plain little outfits a long time ago."

Hiding her disappointment, Beth was able to tell the truth.

"Well, she *hasn't*."

"Good! Now you just be sure to keep it that way 'til Ben gets home."

'The Dangerous Beth Garrison' wondered how much damage she could do with a solid punch to Rheeta's reconstructed nose while the milder mannered Beth simply tried to change the subject.

"Speaking of outfits, is there anything left under the one you've got on that's still really yours?"

Rheeta beamed, unbuttoned her blouse and stuck out her newly enhanced breasts.

"What do you think? They cost a fortune."

"I think you'd better be careful then. Plastic tends to melt in the sun."

"They feel incredible! Go ahead, touch them."

"Thanks, but I think I'll defer that privilege for husband number four."

Suddenly aware that Joanna was standing behind them, Rheeta hurried to button her blouse as if guarding a national treasure.

Jo was nonchalant.

"Don't put them away on my account. Anything that pricey is worth flaunting."

Rheeta remained uncharacteristically silent.

Sensing that Beth needed the physical contact as much as she did, Joanna intentionally rested her hand on Beth's shoulder.

"See you tomorrow at seven."

In the secret relief of Jo's touch, Beth looked up into her eyes.

"Come hungry."

Jo removed her hand and replaced it with a coded message.

"I will be… I've barely touched a thing since Sunday."

The two women exchanged a fleetingly intimate glance and Jo strode off in her usual self-assured gait leaving Beth to fend for herself against the onslaught of Rheeta's suspicions.

"Okay Beth Garrison, I demand to know what that was all about."

Beth began attacking the inside of her lip.

"What are you talking about?"

"I'm talking about that look."

"What look?"

Rheeta's entire body became as rigid as her tone.

"Don't play coy with me! The two of you were staring into each other's eyes."

Beth offered her a cracker.

"Don't be ridiculous… I was squinting."

Rheeta wasn't having any of it—not the cracker, not the explanation.

"Oh… is that what it's called in these simple little towns? I suppose she was squinting too?"

"I don't know what she was doing and I don't know what you're making such a big deal over."

Unfortunately for Beth, what Rheeta lacked in general awareness she more than made up for in the subtle art of seduction and she was definitely not letting this go.

"Look honey, I know flirting when I see it and call it whatever you'd like, flirting was what I saw!"

Beth had to resist suffocating her friend with her new cushion.

"Just drop it Rheeta! I think some of that silicone has leaked into your brain." Beth laid back and deliberately closed her eyes hoping to shut Rheeta out. "I think I'll doze for a while. It's been a long day."

"I'll bet the nights around here have been even longer."

Rheeta reached into her straw bag and pulled out a trashy romance novel.

Pretending to ignore the innuendo, Beth shoved her hands under her thighs to keep herself from leaning over and strangling the life out of her oldest and dearest friend.

After a less than carefree drive trying to spare her precious T-Bird the wear and tear of the unpaved back roads, Joanna was in no mood for the irritating door chimes that announced her arrival at the antique shop. Once again the owner was nowhere in sight. Jo called out into the cluttered space.

"Anybody around?"

Much to Jo's relief, this time Dell's voice came from the adjoining garage and not the other side of the bathroom door.

"Just gimme' a minute."

Dell dusted off the old musty portfolio.

"What'd I tell you Bridey?" she whispered into the cat's ear. "Here she is now."

Pretending to be surprised, Dell came through the doorway with the portfolio under her arm.

"If it isn't the brooding artist from New York."

She propped the portfolio up against the counter. Joanna stepped back.

"How did you know where I'm from?"

"Could be my supernatural powers or it could be that your New York license plates are a dead give away. Take your pick. Either way, that's a nice set of wheels you're driving."

"And how'd you know I was an artist?"

"Pure intuition. I can smell the breed from miles away." Dell smiled. "As for the *brooding* part, based on all the ones I've known, that usually comes with the territory."

Joanna relaxed a bit.

"I came back for the frame."

"Eventually we all come back for one reason or another."

Jo reached into her pocket.

"How much do I owe you?"

"Tell ya' what, stay a while, share a beer and it's yours… no charge."

Jo looked at her watch. She still had a few hours of daylight to find her way back.

"Why not?"

Dell pulled out two wooden folding chairs from the back. She popped open two bottles and joined Joanna in the small cluttered space. Although her overpowering frame dwarfed the rickety chair, Dell seemed perfectly comfortable. She clinked her bottle against Joanna's and took a long, satisfying swig.

"So how's that *friend* of yours?"

Jo answered safely.

"She's good."

Dell took another gulp.

"Ya know, there's a few truly *happy* people out there… probably all of a dozen or so. Then there's the rest of the world, all the sad people wearing brave little smiles. Unfortunately, I think your friend is a part of that group."

Jo was still cautious.

"Maybe you're right…"

"Hers is such a beautiful smile though, isn't it?"

Jo played with the rim of her bottle. Her mind seemed to drift. Dell got up to get a bag of pretzels.

"It's a drag, isn't it… when the wrong person makes you feel all the right things?"

Jo could no longer shoulder the weight of her denial.

"Yeah, it is."

After the last several days of holding Steve at bay, it felt good to finally let her guard down and admit the truth.

"Aint much you can do in that case 'cept drop to your knees and pray for one of two things. Either ya' pray for what's left of your life to be spit back in pieces or ya' pray to be devoured and swallowed up whole." Dell shook her head. "Take it from me, I know. Been there myself. After leaving a trail of broken hearts, one day I came face to face with someone who stopped me dead in my tracks. Talk about obstacles and complications. Try being a big, white in-your-face bull dyke in the early sixties falling for a young, single black woman raising a three year old girl on her own while trying to get into law school before the civil rights movement. Now those were forces to be reckoned with." Dell swigged some more beer. "Care to hear the details?"

Jo leaned forward on her elbows.

"Sure."

"We met at a small grassroots meeting in the basement of a Baptist church. It came outa' nowhere and hit me like a ton of bricks. Soon as she stood up to speak I realized the fire in Sarah's eyes came from the fire in her belly. She wasn't only beautiful, she was brilliant. She could light up a room from the inside out. We marched together in Selma Alabama with Dr. King and we've been stridin' through life arm-in-arm ever since. Over the years the causes have shifted but the fight's always been the same. For Sarah it's always passionate, always personal and always about human dignity. Not a day's gone by that that woman hasn't taught me to be a better person than I was the day before."

"What about the kid?"

"I won't lie and say it was a walk in the park, especially in the early years. The sixties weren't like today for a family like ours, but somehow we managed to raise a precocious little girl in pigtails into a proud and independent woman who just graduated law school herself. Guess you could say some twenty years later my prayers are still being answered."

Dell nudged her arm.

"So what about you? What are you prayin' for?"

"Praying's not my style."

Dell reached for a handful of pretzels.

"Didn't think so." She paused. "So if it aint prayin', what are ya' plannin' to do?"

"Nothing. Just get through the summer, leave the same way I came and never look back."

"Bad idea. We come into this world already owning things we haven't yet found." Dell reached down to stroke Bridey. "Deny love and the senses betray life."

"Who said I was in love with her?"

"Didn't have to."

"It doesn't matter anyway. She's hardly what I'd call available."

"Maybe her family's laid claim to the wife and mother but my bet is that the woman is there for the taking." Dell gave Jo a minute to let her hunch sink in. "Your friend's obviously in unfamiliar territory. She's confused… probably scared outta' her mind. She needs *you* to make the first move."

"Well that's never gonna' happen. You're talking about a woman who's been married twenty-five years and never's been unfaithful."

Dell dug into the bag of pretzels.

"Not unfaithful to her husband maybe but unfaithful to herself the whole way through."

"Either way, I'm not about to mess with a record that spotless."

"'Spotless' is for counter tops and kitchen floors, not a woman's heart. I'd venture to say hers could do with a few deep scuffs."

Joanna found herself considering Dell's perception.

"Maybe you're right but my better judgment tells me not to find out."

"Too bad. Better judgment's been responsible for some of life's deepest regrets." Dell pretended to back off while she finished her beer. "The way I see it, all human dilemmas come down to two questions… '*what if*?'… and '*what now*?'. Guess it depends on which one you can live with not knowing the answer to."

Jo trained her eyes squarely on Dell's.

"Then suppose you answer this one... why all the interest in two lives you know nothing about?"

"Maybe I don't know the facts, but I do know the truth. They're two very different things and acknowledge it or not, the truth is always known."

"Meaning what, exactly?"

"Meaning nothing. The truth doesn't need a context. It exists solely for itself." Dell sensed Jo's burden and her resistance. "Plato believed we come into the world knowing everything we need to know. Birth itself is just a forgetting. Some think we're here to learn new lessons. I'd say it's more about remembering the old ones." She studied Jo's face. "Sometimes when it feels like we're losing our mind, we're really that much closer to finding our soul."

Dell's attempt to reassure Joanna failed miserably. That kind of talk always did. Jo looked around the room impatiently.

"This conversation's starting to get as old as all the rest of the shit in here."

Dell stretched her legs out in front of her.

"So you like things spanking new, huh?"

"Except for vintage cars, yeah."

"Watcha' got against the past?"

Jo swigged her beer.

"There's no future in it."

Dell laughed as the cat jumped up onto her lap.

"Bridey and I like your sense of humor, Cameron. It suits you... like a coat of armor."

Bridey walked across Dell's lap onto Joanna's. Jo immediately pushed her back. Dell reassured her.

"Don't worry, she's harmless."

"I'm not worried, I'm allergic."

"Would that be to dander or just the unknown?"

Joanna ignored Dell's baiting.

"Where the hell do you find all this junk anyway?"

"Mostly it finds me. I think of it as one big clearing house... like a cosmic lost and found."

Jo was quickly tiring of Dell's answers. She was close to the end of her beer and her patience. She checked her watch.

Dell knew she'd better make her move. She reached for the portfolio and pulled it towards them.

"Take this for instance... found it at an estate sale a number of years back.

Here, have a look while I go get that frame for your friend. Ironically, I picked that up at the same sale."

Dell placed the portfolio directly on Joanna's lap, then got up and went behind the counter. Jo had been largely uninterested in looking through the musty pages, but that changed instantly when she saw the first sketch. Dell watched quietly from behind the counter as Joanna's eyes burned against the watercolor image of a large bolder—unmistakable in its shape and size as the same one that jutted up from the grassy knoll where she and Beth had picnicked. Her body stiffened as she rifled through the collection of sketches, one of which depicted a woman sitting at the base of the great rock, holding a bouquet of flowers. Dell was careful not to make a sound. Obviously shaken, Joanna's voice sounded hollow.

"This is the same place we'd just come from the day we stopped into your shop."

"Aint that something."

For the next several minutes Jo said nothing as she continued to examine the renderings much more closely. Dell wandered back and peered over Jo's shoulder.

"Looks like quite a beautiful spot. Must be damn near impossible to fall in love with a place without falling in love with the person who brought ya' there."

Jo didn't respond. What was the point? She couldn't deny the truth of it anyway. Dell remained casual.

"I didn't pay a whole lot for 'em. I think I got a good deal."

Joanna remained fixed on the water colored landscapes.

"What do you know about these?"

Dell never lied unless she felt the truth would hurt even more.

"Not much really. Unfortunately none of 'em are signed or dated."

Joanna was clearly distraught in the absence of more information. Dell tried to provide some relief.

"It's kind of nice not knowing. Makes 'em feel all the more timeless, in a way."

Jo was neither soothed nor satisfied. She studied each of the renderings more closely trying to extract whatever she could from their details.

"The dress… it looks like the late 1800s."

Dell leaned closer.

"You could be right." She looked down at her own clothes. "Never paid much attention to what a woman wore… then or now."

"How much do you want for these?"

"Sorry, they're not for sale. She tried to soften Joanna's obvious disappointment. "Besides, what would Miss Spanking New want with a bunch of old, musty drawings?"

Jo ignored Dell's sarcasm as she focused on the rendering with a view of the valley. She was absolutely certain it was the same one she'd shared with Beth just a few days earlier. Watching Joanna struggle hopelessly with the coincidence, Dell offered something that might guide the suffering woman's heart.

"Our eyes take us to the horizon. Only our faith can take us beyond it."

Dell closed the portfolio and took it from Joanna's hands. She wiped the glass of the small Victorian frame and presented it in its place.

"Beautiful, isn't it? Your friend was drawn to it right away… until I scared the hell outa' her."

Joanna stared at the sepia image of a mother and her small child. Dell moved closer to have another look for herself.

"Can't tell ya' how happy it makes me when someone wanders in here and finds a piece of herself." Dell paused. "Especially that poor woman. She's lost so much of what she's loved."

"How would you know what she's lost?"

"Simplest way to put it is I've always been able to see the whole picture without having to connect the dots." Dell snuck in one more observation. "The other thing I see clear as a bell is that you've lost just as much as she has and not without good reason, you've never been more scared of anything in your life than the way you feel about her."

If there was one thing Joanna hated, it was somebody telling her how she felt—especially when they were right. She stood up, slammed the empty beer bottle on the counter and dug her hand into her pocket.

"I'll pay you for the frame."

"Put your money away. I was just holding it for her anyway." Dell followed Jo to the door. "Like I said, some things belong to us long before we find 'em."

Through the window, Dell spotted her lover's car pulling off the road. Sarah parked alongside Joanna's T-Bird.

"Ah, there's my happiness now."

An attractive black woman with a tight Afro and a strong ethnic flair to her jewelry emerged from a nondescript sedan. Her long, flowing skirt and matching blouse accentuated the smooth, graceful strides of a woman whose life was entirely balanced from the inside out. Dell's delight in her girlfriend's arrival was apparent.

"Stay and let me introduce you."

"I can't."

Dell patted her on the back.

"I understand. There's only two times in any of our lives… those times when we *can* and those times when we *can't*."

Joanna scowled at the tinkling chimes. Dell grabbed her arm.

"If you're ever in the mood for some more 'available' company, North Hampton's just a few miles away. It's not the Big Apple but it's the cradle of lesbian civilization around here. We can go for drinks. I can introduce you around. Maybe even hook you up."

Joanna yanked her arm free.

"I'm not looking for a fucking community or to get laid. I'm looking for something that once resembled my goddamn life!"

Jo stormed off towards her car, brushing rudely past Dell's girlfriend. Dell scooped Bridey into her arms.

"Aint that the truth." She sighed sympathetically into the purring cat's ear. "The question is, which one?"

Dell remained in the doorway watching adoringly as her lover came toward her. Sarah turned and looked back at Jo. Her ever-constant support of Dell's fledgling enterprise rang clear as her voice.

"You had a customer! Good for you baby."

Dell sheepishly admitted the truth.

"Not really. I tried, but she wasn't buying any of what I was selling. Not yet, anyway."

The women kissed and Dell followed her girlfriend back into the shop. Sarah was still curious about the woman who'd nearly knocked her down.

"Well, she certainly was in a big hurry to get wherever it was she was going."

"Not without kicking and screaming all the way."

"She does seem rather intense."

"She's got a lot on her mind and much of it is stuff she's not quite ready to deal with, I'm afraid. Spent so much of her life *making* things happen, she's never learned how to just *let* things happen."

Sarah understood. She always did.

They stood together and watched through the window as Joanna peeled back onto the road. Sarah rested her head dreamily against Dell's arm.

"She drives a nice car though…"

Dell took a last look as the T-Bird disappeared in a cloud of dust.

"Yeah… problem is she likes her route smooth 'n clearly marked and unfortunately, they stopped paving the road *she's* traveling down miles before the place she's gotta' go to reach home."

"Uncharted territory, huh?"

"For her, definitely."

"How can you tell?" Sarah stopped herself. "Whoops, guess that was a foolish question."

Dell smiled. She turned Sarah around and pressed her lover to her.

"Have I thanked you lately?"

Sarah threw her arms around Dell's neck.

"For what baby?"

"For going along with this crazy life of mine." Dell looked into her lover's deep, soulful eyes. "Do you remember that day?"

Sarah's voice filled with sadness.

"How can I forget? You'd read me the obituary of a young man… a promising musician with a scholarship to Julliard who died in a tragic car accident not long after his high school graduation."

The pain in Dell's heart on that day had never diminished.

"Daniel Garrison."

There were times when even Sarah was still surprised.

"That was three years ago. You still remember the boy's name?"

"I've been living with it and his mother's suffering ever since." Dell let her forehead rest against Sarah's. "I remember crawling into bed with you that night and telling you it had begun… the falling away… the unraveling of one life into another. I told you I needed to open this shop and that it had to be *here*, out in the middle of nowhere… a place where I could bring some of that fine old gentleman's things. You took me into your sweet, loving arms and instead of telling me I was crazy, you just asked, 'after you open, then what?'"

Sarah stroked Dell's face as though touching an angel.

"I remember you said, 'then I sit there and I wait'."

Dell was touched that Sarah still recalled that night so clearly. Her eyes filled with unspeakable gratitude. She took Sarah's hand and held it against her heart.

"You'll be happy to know the wait was worth every minute. I met the boy's mother the other day. She came into the shop with that woman who just left."

Sarah grew more solemn.

"I see. What was she like?"

"Just as sweet and deserving as I imagined." Dell's eyes filled with urgency and tears. "She found something Sarah… she found something she *needed* to find."

Sarah lovingly put her lips to Dell's cheek.

"Then it was good that you were here."

Dell basked in the quiet reward of her lover's kiss. Sarah smiled.

"So tell me Madame Antique Dealer, exactly how many others have come through this door since you opened?"

"Well let's see now… if you count Bridey and those six lost boy scouts that makes a grand total of seven."

Sarah shook her head.

"My poor baby. How have you managed to sit here day after day for the last three years and not go mad?"

"Some would say that I already am."

Sarah was all too aware of the blessing and burden of her lover's calling.

She looked into her beloved's eyes.

"I adore you Adeline Brody, with all my heart and soul."

Dell pressed herself against Sarah's body.

"I'll bet you say that to all the good-looking butches who come bearing gifts."

"Not one like *yours* baby, not one like *yours*."

Sarah planted a light kiss on her lover's lips.

"You ready to go sugar?"

Dell glanced at the portfolio leaning up against the counter.

"I'd say my work here is done for the day."

"Good, then I'm taking you home."

"You always do."

Sarah waited while Dell put out a fresh plate of food and water, then bid Bridey a special goodnight.

"Nice workin' with ya'."

Dell locked the door behind her as the tinkling of the chimes faded into the air. The women walked to the car hand in hand, the way they walked through life.

"So my legal eagle, how are things back in the more conventional workplaces of the world?"

"Try picking up that briefcase in the back seat and see for yourself."

Dell reached around and grabbed the handle of Sara's attaché case. She could barely lift it.

"Jesus! What the hell's in there?"

Sarah started the car.

"Paperwork my dearest… lots and lots of paperwork."

"I thought computer's were going to make paper obsolete?"

"Obviously not in *this* lifetime."

The women looked at one another, then burst out laughing. As the car pulled away from the shop, Bridey watched from behind the plate glass window still warmed by the last rays of the setting sun. Guardian of the stillness and the sacred belongings that surrounded her, she laid herself down beside the old portfolio and purred with a contentment that welcomed all the mysteries of night.

Chapter 17

On Rheeta's insistence, Beth had agreed to let her friend treat her to dinner at the most expensive restaurant in town. Though she was sure the invitation had more to do with Rheeta wanting to be seen in one of her garishly extravagant outfits, Beth accepted the gesture hoping that the frivolity of a simple night out would further distract her from deeper concerns. The reservation was made, Beth's attire was predictably critiqued, Pierre was locked safely away from 'the big hairy beast' and the two friends set out for what Rheeta called, "A big night out on the tiny town." For the next few blissful hours Beth actually managed to lose herself in one too many glasses of wine and far too many details of Rheeta's lavish and ridiculous life. By the time they returned home, Beth's mood was considerably more lighthearted. As she lay in bed, she realized she'd almost forgotten the pleasure to be found in the sound of her own laughter.

Joanna's night was not nearly as carefree. Plagued by the renderings in the old portfolio, she paced the length of the carriage house for several hours before finally falling into a wretchedly fitful sleep. At one point, she woke abruptly and reached out for the small Victorian frame she'd placed on the table nearby. The room was too dark to study the image that had drawn Beth's heart. It was enough just to know that it had.

Beth suggested a casual backyard barbeque for Wednesday night's dinner but the mere thought of eating outdoors with mosquitoes sent Rheeta into a neurotic, bug-swatting tailspin. Beth made several menu suggestions, each of which Rheeta politely wrinkled her nose at. Eventually a simple baked lasagna and salad were replaced by the chicken cordon bleu that now sizzled in the oven. Rheeta was enthused about the evening plans. Every now and then she liked the idea of a home-cooked meal, so long as somebody else was doing the cooking. As the dinner hour grew near, Rheeta's excitement peaked necessitating a little 'beauty rest'. She left Beth to set the dining room table and attend to some last minute details. After the last twenty-four hours a break from Rheeta's incessant chatter came as a relief and in a moment of quiet inspiration, Beth carried the crystal vase with Joanna's paper flowers from the piano and placed it on the table as a centerpiece. The memory of that first night washed over her. Beth checked the clock. She had less than an hour to prepare for their next encounter. That included a quick shower, a touch of eye shadow and a silent prayer that she would somehow survive the night flanked by her two mismatched dinner companions.

Beth was checking on the progress of dinner when she heard Joanna's footsteps. The sudden flush to her cheeks had nothing to do with the heat inside the oven.

Jo let herself in.

"Sorry I'm a little late."

'Only by twenty-six years', Beth thought to herself as she nervously removed her oven mitt. Jo's hair, still wet from her shower, was pulled back off her face into a long, thick ponytail. This seemed to intensify the beauty of her eyes, making it even harder for Beth to meet them. Joanna glanced at the table setting in the dining room.

Beth rolled her eyes.

"I wanted to do a barbeque. Unfortunately, Rheeta and 'simple pleasures' aren't particularly compatible." Beth lowered her voice to a safe whisper. "Even on Prozac."

Jo laughed.

"I see. Is she always so hard to please?"

Beth continued to whisper.

"Rheeta raises the perpetual state of dissatisfaction to an art form."

"So where is the guest of honor… or should I say, the guest of horror?"

"Knowing Rheeta, she's been waiting for you to arrive first so she can make a grand entrance. If you act impressed I can assure you, the rest of the night will be easier on both of us."

"Your friend sounds like quite a trip."

"More like an excursion into the absurd."

"Maybe I should cancel my reservation while I still have a chance."

"Too late. Your seat on Air Rheeta's been confirmed. Just buckle up and prepare for a bumpy ride!"

Joanna considered Beth's resilience.

"Somehow you still managed to look beautiful tonight… in spite of it all."

Beth handled the disarming compliment awkwardly.

"Thank you…"

She handed Joanna a bottle of wine along with a corkscrew.

Jo was happy for the distraction.

"So how long is Rheeta staying?"

"She leaves tomorrow afternoon. I'm sure she's got a team of handlers back in Boston waiting to pamper her poor, exhausted body."

"Sounds like by then you'll be needing the same."

"Are you offering?"

The flirtatious remark caught them both off guard and unlocked all the unfinished business between them. The cork removed, Joanna extended the bottle of wine. In the clumsiness of their exchange their hands grazed, releasing a lifetime of unanswered questions. Stumbling over her own heart, Jo asked just one.

"Have you been okay… you know… since Sunday night?"

"I have to be. I have no choice. I felt worse for you. I'm so sorry our plans had to end so… abruptly."

Drowning in a sea of ambiguity, Jo struggled to survive.

"The day was special enough."

"Still…"

The simple word, like a swaying bridge, hung in the space between them. Aching for a way to cross it, Joanna reached into her pocket for the frame. She'd wrapped it in a sheet of paper from her sketchpad. In the absence of ribbon and a real bow, she simply drew one on top.

"This is for you."

Beth seemed to delight as much in the clever wrapping as in the surprise.

"What is it?"

"Open it and see."

Jo watched as Beth worked to carefully undo the paper without ripping it. At first sight of the frame, Beth gasped and instantly held it to her heart. Tears began to flow as she reunited with the tender image she'd regretted leaving behind.

"You can't keep doing this."

"Doing what?"

Beth could not risk a more truthful answer.

"I don't know what to say."

There was every reason in the world to just leave it at that but overwhelmed with emotion, Beth's heart ignored them all. She put down the frame, reached up and threw her arms around Joanna's neck. Jo stiffened out of necessity. It had felt like an eternity since the heartbreak of their unnatural parting Sunday night.

"Hold me Jo, please..."

Beth had no idea what Joanna made of her sudden plea, but her heart offered no explanation or apology for what it needed so desperately. This time Jo didn't ask for either. She slipped her arms around Beth's waist, gradually returning the woman's urgency with her own. For one exquisite moment in time everything in their two separate worlds ceased to exist.

Midway down the steps, Rheeta looked into the kitchen and froze in horror. She cleared her throat to announce her presence. Beth instantly broke free of Joanna's arms while Rheeta continued to descend the stairs in a cacophony of clinking jewelry that dangled from her ears, neck and arms. She entered the kitchen, her expression as suspicious as her innuendo.

"Well if three's a crowd, I can always make other plans."

BJ sneezed several times from the heavy scent of Rheeta's perfume. Flustered, Beth was quick to clarify what Rheeta had just seen. She picked up the frame and nervously shoved it into her friend's hand.

"I was just thanking Jo for her gift. I saw it in an antique shop we stopped into. Isn't it beautiful?"

Rheeta was not that easy to convince.

"You never mentioned that you'd been antiquing together."

"We weren't. We just stumbled onto the shop on our way back from a picnic."

"A picnic? How cozy. Just the two of you?"

Her tone made the plans sound illicit. Beth fidgeted while Rheeta took a perfunctory look at the frame and then turned, for the first time acknowledging Jo.

"Apparently Beth didn't like my gift nearly as much as yours. All I got was a little peck on the cheek."

She handed the frame back to Beth.

Jo had remained silent, letting Beth handle her own friend. She could have easily cut Rheeta down to size but she thought better of adding to a scene already fraught with tension.

"I think we can all use a glass of wine."

Sensing that behind Jo's cordial suggestion there was a less-than-friendly warning, Rheeta wisely backed down.

"Indeed."

Jo filled each of their glasses.

Rheeta smiled demurely.

"Thank you Joanna."

"Call me Jo."

Rheeta stared critically at her denim work shirt and jeans.

"I prefer Joanna. It's much more feminine." She held up her glass. "To our hostess and the dearest friend in the whole world."

After a few minutes of sipping, Rheeta began striking a series of noticeably stilted poses. Since the women's unexpected embrace all but ruined her flamboyant entrance, she was still waiting for someone to compliment her on what she was wearing. Beth was thoughtful enough to oblige.

"That's a lovely outfit Rheeta."

"Why thank you Bethie. It's just a little something I picked up on my last trip to San Tropez."

Joanna turned her back and rolled her eyes. The 'little something' was a heavily beaded turquoise jumpsuit with a plunging neckline and a pinched waist. The three inch wide alligator belt with its garish sterling silver buckle cost more that everything in Beth's closet put together. For her kindness, Beth got something less than a compliment in return. Rheeta gave the simple cotton slacks and blouse a critical once-over.

"So is that what one wears to host a dinner party in this quaint little town?"

"I'd hardly call this a dinner party, Rheeta. It's supper with a couple of friends."

The condescending insult was the last straw for Joanna.

"The thing is Rheeta, if you were as pretty as your friend Beth, you wouldn't have to work twice as hard to look half as good."

The biting remark left Rheeta no choice but to politely agree.

"Beth always did have a quiet beauty about her."

At the center of a tense moment, Beth tried to smooth things over.

"Let's just all be ourselves and enjoy each other's company. Dinner should be ready shortly. In the meantime why don't we sit down and have our grapefruits?"

She ushered the two women into the dining room. As if strategically positioning themselves for battle the rivals took seats directly opposite each other, leaving Beth between them at the head of the table. Rheeta immediately commented on the centerpiece.

"Oh Bethie, that's an absolutely exquisite vase," she paused, "and quite an amusing bouquet."

Beth beamed with delight.

"Jo made them for me!"

"I see. How... *childlike*."

"Oh, I'd say more like how charming! How imaginative! How thoughtful! They look even more beautiful in candlelight."

Rheeta looked up from her grapefruit.

"And what might I ask was the occasion?"

Jo enjoyed her own memory of that night.

"Beth was celebrating her right to celebrate."

Such a notion was clearly beyond Rheeta's comprehension.

"Leave it to my Bethie to create her own party. Did she ever tell you how she set a formal candlelit table the time she fed each of her sons his first solid food? Is that just the silliest thing you've ever heard?"

Rheeta had succeeded in making Beth feel foolish, but Joanna was deeply touched.

"I don't think it's silly at all." She held Beth's eyes. "I think it was incredibly special."

Rheeta shrugged.

"It's obvious you two have a mutual admiration society going here, so far be it from me to say another word."

In a tenuous ceasefire, each of the women retreated into scooping out her grapefruit and for a few blissful moments all was calm. Beth stood up and collected their plates.

"Assuming I can trust you both not to start a food fight, I think I'll serve dinner now."

The evening had barely begun and Beth was already on the verge of a nervous breakdown. Much to her relief, the two women remained cordial while she brought out the food. Politely passing platters back and forth, each agreed that everything looked, smelled and tasted delicious. Beth accepted their compliments graciously and with things seemingly under control, she had reasonable hopes for the remainder of the evening. Halfway through the meal's carefully navigated small talk Rheeta held up her empty glass, implying that someone should pour her more wine. Wishing she could have mixed in a bit or arsenic, Jo obliged. Rheeta deliberately used her full name.

"Ah, thank you Joanna." She took a sip, then put down her glass. "So, Beth tells me you're an artist."

Beth couldn't contain her enthusiasm.

"Jo's incredibly talented. She did a series of…"

Rheeta rudely cut her off, her eyes locked on Joanna.

"She also tells me you're a lesbian."

Mortified, Beth froze with her fork halfway to her mouth. Jo seemed unfazed.

"Also true." Without averting her own eyes, she responded with scathing precision. "I imagine that must be quite a relief knowing there's one less woman out there competing for your next husband, especially since you apparently don't seem to have what it takes to hold on to one."

Rheeta became rigid, as if preparing for battle.

"I'd say you're hardly in a position to know what it takes to hold a man."

"Well whatever position *you* use obviously isn't working. Tell me, under all that glitz and glitter, do you actually have a flattering angle?"

Beth tried to ward off disaster.

"Ladies, please!"

Rheeta couldn't be stopped.

"I wouldn't use the term 'ladies' too loosely Bethie. I know I am but I'm not sure how I would define Joanna."

Jo smiled smugly.

"I believe the word you're searching for is *dyke*."

Somehow in just a matter of seconds the woman's fragile truce had deteriorated into all-out warfare. Beth tried in vain to salvage what she could of more polite dinner conversation, but it was obvious both of her guests were hell-bent on making this a fight to the finish. Rheeta was deliberately crude.

"You'll have to forgive me but I just don't get woman who fuck women."

Joanna dug in.

"What exactly don't you get? Maybe I can explain it to you."

By now it had become impossible for Beth to get a word in edgewise. She was as afraid to leap from the runaway train as she was to stay onboard. Paralyzed, she clung to her seat as the ride got wilder.

Rheeta took another sip of wine, dismissing Joanna with her eyes.

"Thanks for the offer but I don't believe you can do *anything* for me." She intentionally leaned forward flaunting her cleavage. "Then again maybe you could, but by the time you strapped it on I'm sure I'd have lost all interest."

Jo pretended to be wounded.

"Ouch. I just felt my dildo go limp in the drawer."

"Oh God, oh God, oh God" Beth repeated over and over in her own head.

Unfortunately, Joanna was nowhere close to being finished.

"Actually Rheeta, I'm surprised you have a such a limited view of sexual gratification, especially since most women you talk to prefer being eaten to being fucked."

Jo reached over and poured Rheeta a fresh glass of wine as if to suggest she knew what Rheeta needed. She put the bottle down and smiled.

"And just for the record... you haven't been eaten until you've felt the velvet strokes of another woman's tongue."

As Beth sat perfectly still, Joanna's words sent a sudden shiver to the place between her legs.

Rheeta remained smug.

"Do tell."

Jo made it more personal.

"Tell me you never once fantasized about it."

Rheeta became indignant.

"I don't believe my fantasy life is any of your business."

"C'mon, you can admit it. Lots of straight women do."

Rheeta turned to her friend.

"Well not these two straight women, isn't that right Bethie?"

For the first time since the women began going at one another, the room fell dead silent. For a long agonizing moment Joanna watched Beth struggle hopelessly for an answer until finally the pain of seeing her suffer became greater than Jo's need to hear the truth. She moved skillfully past Rheeta's question.

"Forget about Beth. I'm talking about you and that little satin pouch of yours. You know, the one with all your sex toys."

Rheeta was outraged by the presumption but Jo persisted in wrangling her confession.

"Don't tell me a sexually sophisticated woman like yourself doesn't have at least one well used cock-shaped vibrator tucked away in her nightstand."

Jo had set the trap and Rheeta took the bait.

"What if I do?"

As Beth held her breath, Jo moved in for the kill.

"And would those be your own lovely manicured fingers working that mighty rubber shaft in and out of your wet juicy cunt until you cum?"

Beth prayed for the power to make herself disappear.

Rendered speechless, Rheeta could only glare at Jo who returned the smuggest of smiles.

"You *can* make yourself cum, can't you? I mean you're not really the frigid uptight bitch you're being tonight?"

Sitting amid the ruins of her pleasant little dinner, Beth buried her face in her hands and moaned.

By now, Rheeta was incensed.

"Yes I cum!"

Joanna sat back and folded her arms.

"Then it sounds to me like you know a lot about being fucked by a woman... even if you're the one doing it to yourself."

Rheeta wasn't accustomed to being humiliated. She had obviously met her match and she wasn't prepared to lose such a costly round.

Beth sprang to her feet and began clearing the table. Her voice shaking almost as much as her knees, she blurted out a suggestion as ludicrous as any she'd ever made.

"Dessert anyone?"

Rheeta was more than ready to see Jo leave.

"Under the circumstances, if Joanna prefers not to stay I'm sure we'd understand, wouldn't we Beth?"

Jo wouldn't give her the satisfaction.

"On the contrary, I'd love some dessert. The more decadent the better." She smiled at Rheeta. "Wouldn't you agree?"

Rheeta prepared herself for round two. She was down, but not out. She'd always been a fighter and she had the bank accounts to prove it.

"Indeed... bring it on."

If the women intended to kill each other, Beth insisted they wait until she fled the room. Between brewing coffee, rinsing off a box of fresh strawberries and cutting up a tray of homemade brownies, Beth tried to reconcile the maddening changes in her life. As she peered back into the dining room where Jo and Rheeta now sat glaring at one another in icy silence, Beth could still envision her young family sitting around the dinner table. She could still remember their voices talking about innocent things like science fair projects, little league games and birthday party invitations. The hardest words on a spelling test were now replaced with ones like *'fuck'* and *'cunt'* and *'dyke'*. Instead of filling the boy's lunch boxes with peanut butter sandwiches and Twinkies she was now inexplicably hearing about satin pouches filled with dildos, vibrators and God only knows what else! Exactly how all these unlikely things managed to sneak past her front door and invade her life was much more than Beth could comprehend. Should she manage to survive the ill-fated night, perhaps she would one day try. For now, there was still dessert to get through.

With what little remained of her shattered nerves and motherly role, Beth set down the tray as well as her terms.

"One more snide remark out of either of you and I'm sending both of you to your rooms without dessert."

Much to her surprise, both women nodded obediently and stayed on their best behavior. As it turned out, sticky fingers and the love of chocolate proved common ground for her two miserably incompatible guests. Sharing a second bottle of wine didn't hurt to bolster their tenuous rapport either. At one point Jo folded her arms and studied the old college roommates.

"I'd say you two are probably the least likely people in the world to have ever remained friends."

Beth laughed.

"You're right. I've stuck to the same thing all my life and Rheeta's tried everything for at least fifteen minutes."

Rheeta feigned a smile at Joanna.

"Not *everything*, darling."

Apparently the effects of the wine were wearing off. Jo decided it best to call it a night before Beth had to pull them apart. She thanked her for dinner, stood up and carried her plate into the kitchen. Hoping to steal even the briefest moment alone, Beth offered to walk her out. At the very least she had hoped to apologize for her friend's behavior. Before she got the chance, Rheeta burst out onto the porch suggesting she accompany Joanna back to the carriage house to have a look at her work. Beth's delight was the only reason Jo agreed. Rheeta gave the convertible in the driveway a once-over.

"I will admit, that's a rather sweet little car you drive."

Jo couldn't resist.

"Throw on a scarf… Isadora Duncan style… and I'll be happy to take you out for a spin."

Rheeta turned to Beth.

"You see, I'm trying. That remark was totally uncalled for."

Beth scolded Joanna who reluctantly apologized.

As the unlikely pair stepped down off the porch into the soft dewy grass, Beth called after them.

"I'm warning you both… if you come to blows in there, you'd better not destroy a single inch of that carriage house."

Rheeta laughed. Beth did not.

"I'm dead serious! That place means far too much to me."

Rheeta dismissed Beth's concerns.

"Don't worry honey." She slipped her arm through Joanna's and held on tightly. "See, Joanna and I have become the best of friends."

Knowing Beth was still watching, Rheeta leaned closer and whispered into Jo's ear.

"I can't see a fucking thing in front of me and I can already feel the mosquitoes eating me up alive! If you dare let me slip in this God forsaken hell hole of a backyard, I swear on these $600 mules you won't live to tell about it."

Jo turned on the lights and Rheeta recoiled from the surroundings. The couch was open and unmade, the wet towel from Jo's shower was flung across the kitchen chair and art supplies were strewn everywhere. Rheeta was appalled. Joanna tried to handle her visitor's distain good-naturedly. She picked up the towel and folded it more neatly.

"I forgot to take the "do not disturb" sign off the door. Looks like the maid never made up the room."

Rheeta was not amused.

"Do all you *bohemians* live like slobs?"

Strictly for Beth's sake, Jo tried to remain cordial.

"I wasn't expecting company." She pulled out a kitchen chair. "Here, make yourself at home."

Rheeta made a critical sweep of the room.

"If you saw my home you'd know how incomprehensible that would be. Besides, I can assure you I won't be staying that long."

Joanna recalled initially judging the carriage house through the same critical eyes.

"I felt the same way when I first saw the place. You'd be surprised how the space grows on you."

Rheeta patted her cheeks.

"It's impossibly hot in here. Put on the air conditioner!"

Jo laughed.

"There isn't any." She turned on both ceiling fans instead. "This usually helps."

"Hardly!"

Rheeta declined Jo's offer for a cold drink, tossed back her overly done hair and made her way over to the wall covered with Joanna's artwork. She was immediately drawn to the sketches of Steve with his half-naked, exquisitely rendered torso. She stared with hungry eyes.

"So that's what that gorgeous body looks like under all that flannel and corduroy. I met him you know… a few years back at one of Beth's little Christmas gatherings. Unfortunately I had a plane to catch early the next morning, so we weren't able to get to know each other better." She studied the renderings even more closely and sighed. "I fantasized about that man's body for weeks. Not that you'd understand."

Jo recalled Steve's own memory of that meeting.

"Obviously you left quite an impression yourself. He remembers you too."

Rheeta's eyelids immediately began to flutter.

"Really? What did he say?"

For some ungodly reason, Jo took pity on the pathetically insecure woman.

"He wasn't specific." Jo's good will and hospitality were both wearing thin. "Look Rheeta, much as I'm enjoying our little girl talk I'm really beat, so why don't you cut to the chase? Say whatever it is you came back here to say and leave."

Rheeta did not like to be rushed. She much preferred rushing others. She would ignore Joanna's prodding and continue to enjoy the studies of Steve for as long as it gave her pleasure.

"How much do you want for these?"

"They're not for sale."

Jo found great satisfaction in denying Rheeta something she wanted.

"Pity. Actually I'm surprised you have an interest in the male body at all."

Joanna opened a can of beer.

"There's a lot about me that would surprise you."

Rheeta shrugged with indifference.

"Usually Beth is so easily impressed one can hardly trust her opinion, but I have to admit this time she's right. You're much more talented than I imagined."

As Rheeta moved toward the portraits of Beth, an amusing little scene formed in Joanna's head. She would give the condescending bitch more of a "private showing" than Rheeta bargained for.

"Since your tastes are obviously more discerning that Beth's, I'll take that as a compliment."

Rheeta was dismissive.

"Take it anyway you'd like."

Joanna clenched her jaw while Rheeta scrutinized her work.

"I'm relieved to see Beth kept her clothes on."

Rheetas's eyes wandered around the room to the sculpting pedestal. She was curious about the oddly shaped mound of clay sitting on top.

"I suppose that would be an example of your more abstract style?"

Jo followed her across the room.

"No, actually it's something Beth did the night she posed."

The souvenir of Beth's touch had provided too much joy for Jo to consider destroying. Rheeta mocked the childlike creation.

"And to think of all the time that woman wasted on the piano instead."

For Joanna, the memory of that night was much too precious to be trashed by Rheeta's sarcasm.

"Beth told me how she and the boys used to play with clay. I was just introducing her to a little long lost pleasure."

"I'll bet there's a *lot* of things you'd like to introduce Beth to."

Much preferring to slug Rheeta, Jo took a slug of beer instead.

"What is it about my friendship with Beth that you find so threatening?"

"Threatening?' Rheeta laughed. "I'd say pathetic is more like it. It's obvious you have a thing for her and if you think for a minute she feels the same way about you, you're sadly mistaken."

"And I assume your three failed marriages make you something of an expert on mistakes."

"Look *Jo*... as you liked to be called... I wasn't born yesterday. Beth may be a bit sheltered and naïve but *I* know exactly what I saw in that kitchen earlier tonight. So why don't you just run along, lift your leg and piss all over someone else's life?"

"Females squat."

"My point exactly."

Jo leaned against the wall and crossed her arms.

"The penis envy jokes are so old Rheeta. Don't you have anything else in your boring little repertoire?"

"How about this—stay away from Beth, or else."

"Is that some kind of threat?"

"Yes! And I trust it's straightforward enough for you." Rheeta brushed Joanna rudely aside. "Do pardon the pun."

Jo had just about all she could take. It was time to have a little fun with the pompous twat and send her on her way. Rheeta had wandered back to have another look at the portraits of Beth. She pointed to the small flower Jo had placed through the hair of one of the renderings.

"What's that about?"

Jo began setting the stage for her revenge.

"Just some stupid flower Beth picked and wanted me to have. She can be so overly sentimental. I didn't know what the hell else to do with it so I stuck it there."

"That's my baby you're talking about and I happen to think her sentimentality is one of her sweetest, most endearing qualities."

Jo finished her beer and then sauntered over, deliberately positioning herself directly behind Rheeta.

"That kind of crap is lost on me."

Joanna sounded so convincing, Rheeta was beginning to think that maybe she'd read things wrong.

"Well it's obvious from the way Beth talks, she thinks the world of *you*."

As long as Rheeta didn't seem to mind, Jo moved closer.

"Beth's okay I guess. I just prefer a little less sugar and a lot more spice."

Jo hovered closer still.

"You're way off base if you think Beth is my type." Jo lowered her voice as well as her eyes. "Fact is, I like my women much more fiery… across a dining room table and under me in bed."

Joanna's little charade was working like a charm. Rheeta began to fiddle nervously with her necklace and Jo poked fun at her shock.

"Don't pretend all that hostility and fireworks over dinner wasn't sexual tension. "I've been fighting my attraction to you all night."

Rheeta turned her head ever so slightly in Joanna's direction. She seemed to be struggling with the devil and the unexplainable pleasure she derived from Joanna's confession.

"I see…"

"Do you?"

Jo let her voice trail off as she wrapped her arms around Rheeta's waist and rubbed herself up against the woman's rear. She expected Rheeta to push her away—maybe even slap her across the face—but Rheeta's protest was surprisingly mild.

"What do you think you're doing?"

Jo prepared herself for the performance of a lifetime. Seeing Rheeta squirm was worth every minute of her own ordeal. Jo put her mouth against Rheeta's ear, letting the heat of her breath suggest even more.

"I can't possibly be the first woman to come on to you…"

Rheeta was as undeniably flattered, as she was flustered.

"As a matter of fact you are."

Her obvious conflict served Joanna well.

"Then let me show you what you've been missing."

She brushed Rheeta's hair aside and ran her tongue along the woman's exposed neck.

Rheeta froze like an animal cornered. Not knowing how else to save herself, she remained perfectly still, waiting for her predator to go for the kill or spare her and move on. She did not have to wait long. In one commanding move, Joanna turned her around and took her firmly into her arms. There was a cocky assurance in Joanna's eyes.

"All the better. I like the idea of being the first."

Rheeta suddenly felt trapped by much more than Joanna's arms. She'd never known such a mix of loathing and desire. The contradiction slowly began to betray her. She felt a rush between her legs.

Jo used the full weight of her body to push Rheeta back against the wall. The kiss was harsh and demanding. Rheeta's surrender, immediate.

Joanna gloated.

"You like it rough. I thought so."

Jo had no choice but to fondle Rheeta's breasts. Her nipples instantly stiffened and rose against the silk jumpsuit. Jo was certain she heard Rheeta moan.

A moment later Rheeta came to her senses and pulled her mouth away.

"Take your hands off me right now or I'll…"

Joanna tightened her grip.

"Or you'll what… beg me to make you cum?"

Rheeta forced herself to feel something other than aroused. She forced herself to feel outraged.

"No—I'll scratch your eyes out!"

Jo glanced at Rheeta's long fingernails. Sensing that things could go either way, she grabbed Rheeta by the wrists. Rheeta struggled against her.

"We both know why you really came back here and it wasn't to see my etchings or to warn me about Beth. If it'll make it easier to live with, you can always tell yourself you didn't want it to happen."

Rheeta swallowed over the pounding in her throat.

"You're crazy!"

Reveling in her success, Jo was secretly hoping not to have to take the amorous charade much further. She began kissing Rheeta's neck and unbuckling her belt.

"C'mon, just let it happen. I never kiss and tell."

Jo caught Rheeta eyeing the unmade bed and for a horrifying moment she was certain her wicked plan was going to backfire. 'Shit, what the hell is she waiting for?," Jo thought to herself as she pushed Rheeta down onto the rumpled sheets and reluctantly climbed on top of her. Rheeta gasped under the slow grinding rhythm of Joanna's hips. Left with little choice—in a risky make or break move—Jo put her hand between Rheeta's legs. Rheeta had soaked through the crotch.

Mortified, Rheeta panicked.

"Let me up or I swear I'll scream bloody murder!"

Secretly relieved, Joanna rolled off the visibly shaken woman. Her eyes intentionally lingered on Rheetas's crotch

"Just send me the bill for the dry cleaners."

Humiliated, Rheeta became enraged.

"Go fuck yourself!"

"Sure you wouldn't rather I fuck you?"

"I hate you more than I've ever hated anyone in my entire life!"

She pushed Joanna aside, ran to the bathroom and slammed the door. Barely able to look at herself in the mirror, Rheeta had never taken so little time to make herself presentable. Moments later, still feeling unbearably exposed, Rheeta came bolting out and hurried toward the screen door.

Jo gladly held it open for her.

"Shall I be a gentleman and walk you home?"

The intentional remark sent Rheeta fleeing for her life.

"Stay away from me, you filthy lesbian!"

Jo laughed to herself as she watched the frantic woman struggle to collect what little she could of her dignity and balance while racing across the yard. As the wobbling figure stumbled along in the dark, Jo called out to her.

"Careful there honey… things tend to get even more slippery when wet."

Chased by the taunting reminder, Rheeta quickened her pace. When she finally disappeared from view, Joanna went back inside. The heavy scent of Rheeta's perfume still hung in the air.

'Fucking asshole', Jo mumbled under her breath as she used the back of her hand to wipe away any loathsome traces of the woman's lipstick. Though basking in Rheeta's misery, Jo now felt lost and alone. She gravitated to her portrait of Beth—the one with the flower Rheeta had questioned her about. In truth Jo had never thought of herself as sentimental. She was convinced that the pain of her mother's death had permanently sealed off that softness of heart. Standing now in her empty victory, Joanna reached out and tenderly cupped the delicate petals. It was a bittersweet gift to learn she'd been wrong.

In the time it took Joanna to turn Rheeta's gilded little world into complete and utter chaos, Beth had put away the leftovers, run the dishwasher and cleaned up the kitchen. While she waited eagerly for Rheeta to return, she began a letter to her son at camp. She'd gotten as far as, "Hi sweetheart, I miss you so much," then stopped. The half of Beth's heart that honestly didn't feel that way simply sighed and went along with the half that did. It always had. As she reread the sentence over and over, the conflict felt uncomfortably familiar.

She was struggling to get down more when Rheeta burst through the kitchen door obsessing over her expensive grass-stained shoes. Beth put aside her letter, eager for Rheetas's reaction.

"Well?"

"Well what?"

"What do you think of her work…she's amazing, isn't she?"

Rheeta ignored the question.

"What did you do with the rest of the wine?"

"It's in the fridge."

Rheeta helped herself to it.

"Let me tell you, that woman's quite a piece of work herself!"

Watching Rheeta polish off a second glass, Beth grew concerned.

"Honey, maybe you should slow down."

"Stop being a mother hen. The last time I checked I was over eighteen."

"I'm sorry. It's just that you're acting a bit strange." Beth nudged her playfully. "I mean, even for *you*."

Rheeta was not amused.

"I'll be leaving tomorrow!"

"I know. You have an appointment with your lawyer. That's assuming you can still drive."

"Beth, I'm insisting you come back to Boston with me. You need to put some distance between yourself and that woman."

"First of all, don't tell me what I need. And secondly, that woman has a name."

"Yes, and more than one comes to mind." Rheeta guzzled more wine. "The change of scenery will do you good. You'll stay with me until Ben gets home."

Beth became indignant.

"I'll do no such thing! If you don't need a mother hen, what makes you think I do? I believe I'm over eighteen as well."

Now on her third glass, Rheeta was growing a little more drunk and a lot less tactful.

"Look, I've been around a lot more than you have and I'm telling you, that lesbo is not to be trusted."

"Okay Rheeta, suppose you tell me exactly what happened in there."

Rheeta would sooner be caught without make-up on than ever admit the truth.

"Nothing happened! You really must put air conditioning in that place. It's oppressive."

"Obviously something's got you all worked up and I can't believe it's the heat."

Rheeta went on the offensive.

"How could you let her talk to me like that over dinner."

"For what it's worth Rhee, you started it. I wanted to wring your neck myself. You were so crude"

"She had it coming."

"Based on what… that she neglected to wear a pearl necklace and earrings to my so-called dinner party?"

"No! Based on things you wouldn't… and *shouldn't…* know about."

"Rheeta please, you're beginning to sound eerily like Ben."

"I still say you should come back with me."

"Look, I'm not going to stand here and argue with you about this. It's absolutely out of the question! I'm not going back to Boston so you can baby-sit me until my husband picks me up and takes me home. I have no intention of leaving my own house just because you disapprove of someone else's lifestyle."

Given her recent brush with that lifestyle, the conversation was closing in on something Rheeta did not care to discuss.

"Fine, suit yourself. I'm going to bed." She grabbed the half empty bottle of wine. "And I'm taking this with me."

Beth had never known her friend to drink quite so excessively.

"Honestly Rheeta, are you sure you're okay?"

"I'm exhausted, that's all."

"You're just not used to fresh country air."

"'Fresh' might be an apt description for a *lot* of things around here."

Rheeta was halfway up the stairs, bottle in hand, when Beth called after her.

"Rhee… can I ask you something personal?"

"What is it?"

"I was just wondering…"

Rheeta prodded her impatiently.

"You were just wondering *what*?"

Beth blurted out the rest.

"Do you really have a satin pouch with a phallic shaped vibrator in it?"

"It's not satin. If you must know, it's a lovely brushed suede in a soft peach tone."

Beth tried to contain her shock.

"So you *do* have one?"

"Yes, I have one. Doesn't every woman over the age of sixteen these days?"

"I don't..."

Rheeta rolled her eyes.

"Why am I not surprised?"

"I wouldn't even know where to purchase one."

"No, of course you wouldn't. Sometimes I forget just how sheltered a creature you really are. Now if you'll excuse me, I really must exfoliate." From the top of the landing Rheeta looked down at Beth. "In case you're not familiar with that practice either, it has nothing to do with sex."

Beth suddenly felt the need to apologize for everything in her life, her innocence included.

"I'm sorry dinner was such a fiasco."

"By the time I finish what's left in this bottle the whole miserable night will be nothing more than a hellish blur, just like each of my three pathetic marriages...," she slammed the door to Adam's room, "and this ruined jumpsuit."

Beth returned to her letter only to find that trying to focus was as hopeless as she was beginning to feel the rest of her life was. She locked up, shut the lights and went upstairs. Left in the wake of Rheeta's perception, Beth felt pitifully naïve. She tried reading in bed, but all she could think about as she listened to the sound of Rheeta's endless shower was what the contents of such a satin pouch might include. Beth closed her book mid-sentence, reached over and opened the drawer of her nightstand. Instead of a bag filled with all the props and paraphernalia a more sexually enlightened woman might pleasure herself with, she stared down at a box of tissues, a roll of ant-acids, a Chapstick and a pair of old airline booties. Beth didn't know whether to laugh or cry. Undecided, she sat on the edge of her bed and for the next little while she did a fair amount of both.

Dell had been right on the money when she tagged Joanna 'a brooding artist'. Only now instead of ruminating behind the closed door of a plush executive office, Jo had gradually learned to do it outdoors where the warmth of the sun could sooth at least the surface of her troubles and the gentle sounds of the backyard could serenade her unrest. She knew that every bit of this new courtship with nature's offerings had been Beth's influence and the result of falling madly and hopelessly in love. It was simply too glorious a morning not to enjoy her coffee outdoors. Joanna's newly awakened senses had come to require at least that much of each new day.

Beth was busy unloading the dishwasher when she thought she heard the screen door of the carriage house squeak open. She peeked out through the kitchen window to find Joanna—clad in a white T-shirt and shorts—sitting on the edge of the pool. Her feet dangled in the water while she nursed a mug of coffee. Beth could no sooner control the pounding in her chest anymore than she could keep herself from going to the woman's side. She nervously secured the knot of her terry robe and poured herself a cup of coffee. With her eyes closed and her face tilted up toward the sun, Joanna was unaware of Beth's approach. The unexpected sweetness of her voice filtered gently through the mangled web of Joanna's heart.

"No work today?"

Jo opened her eyes. Everything inside her sprang to life at the sight of the woman she loved.

"The boss gave me the morning off. He had some stuff to take care of."

"Mind if I join you?"

"It's your backyard."

"Yes, but it's your solitude."

"I should warn you, my solitude can be a pretty dark place."

"I'll take my chances."

Beth maneuvered herself down beside Joanna, struggling to keep her coffee from spilling and her robe from opening. As the raft floated lazily by, she let her toes test the temperature of the water and inhaled a deep, exhilarating breath.

"What an absolutely exquisite morning!"

The color of the sky against the treetops was as vivid as any nature could render. Beth sighed.

"Do you realize that since our picnic, each day has been more perfect than the last?" She smiled. "I'd like to think that means the universe isn't having any regrets."

Recalling how painfully the day had ended, Jo risked asking.

"What about you?"

"Absolutely none."

"Me either."

"Good, then it's unanimous!" Beth playfully splashed the water with her toes. "I can actually count on one hand the number of times that's been the case. Most things in my life have been riddled with compromise, disappointment or regret." She was determined not to ruin the moment with the weight of her past. "I love my gift. Thank you so much for the frame. It was so thoughtful of you to go back."

The memory of Beth's gratitude was still fresh in Jo's mind.

"Your appreciation certainly gave Rheeta an eyeful."

Beth recalled the thrill of being in Joanna's arms.

"I know. Her timing couldn't have been worse."

'Or better' Jo thought to herself, thinking how differently that moment might have ended had they been alone.

"Knowing I was a lesbian didn't help."

Beth wasn't sure whether she had betrayed Jo's confidence.

"I hope you don't mind that I told her."

"Why should I mind? It's nothing I'm ashamed of."

"Nor should you be. Beth took a sip of coffee. "Who cares what Rheeta thinks anyway?"

"Judging from your reaction when she saw us, obviously *you* do."

Beth could feel Joanna's eyes waiting for the truth.

"It's not that I care what she thinks. I just don't care to hear about it for the rest of my life."

It was clear that Beth was more uncomfortable than she could admit. Jo decided to let it go.

"What in the world were you thinking when you put us together at the same table?"

"I suppose I was being a selfish. I couldn't bear the thought of another night alone with her." 'And another night without seeing you', Beth thought to herself. "How did your private gallery showing go?"

Counting on the fact that Rheeta was too humiliated to admit the truth, Jo wasn't sure what Beth knew.

"What did *she* say?"

"Hardly anything, which for Rheeta was strange unto itself. As you can tell, Rheeta fancies herself a connoisseur on everything." Beth shrugged. "She did return rather upset. Something about the stain on her shoes. She said they were ruined and rambled on about hating grass." Beth came to her own conclusion. "Well I didn't hear you two tearing the place apart, so I assume you managed to strike some kind of a truce."

Jo took a sip of her coffee and purposely avoided Beth's eyes.

"I guess you could call it that. Speaking of the devil, where is your highness this morning?"

"Rheeta isn't what you might call an 'early riser'. She'd much prefer to let the rest of us catch the worm and have something more lavish served to her in bed at a much later hour."

"Then shouldn't you be in the kitchen polishing the silver tray?"

Beth laughed.

"Though I'm sure there'll be hell to pay for it, I thought I'd let her fend for herself this morning."

"That's kind of risky, wouldn't you say?"

"I guess I'm just in a risk-taking mood today."

"Enough to answer that question she asked you last night?"

Beth's bravado suddenly turned to panic. She pretended to have forgotten the moment that had stopped her heart.

"What question was that?"

"The one about your fantasy life."

Beth teeth immediately dug into her lip.

"Oh, that one…"

"Yeah, *that* one."

Beth was shrewdly evasive.

"I can't afford a fantasy life. I'm much too busy trying to negotiate my real one."

Joanna resented being robbed of the truth, twice. She reached down into the water and splashed Beth's robe until it was drenched.

"Oh I'm sorry. Did I get you wet?"

'The Dangerous Beth Garrison' had been provoked. Without warning she retaliated by shoving Joanna off the edge of the pool. Standing in the waist-high water, her erect nipples showed through the soaked cotton T-shirt. Though the sight instantly left Beth weak, she continued her playful taunting.

"Look who's even *wetter*."

Joanna's eyes flashed with a mischievous revenge too sudden for Beth to escape. Before she could back away, Jo grabbed the ties of Beth's robe and used them to pull her down into the pool. The force of the impact lifted and parted the soaked garment, exposing Beth to the chill of the water and the heat of Joanna's eyes. Her nipples stiffened in response to both. Beth worked feverishly to regain her dignity and retie her robe. Joanna mocked her.

"Relax. I've seen more than my share of women's bodies."

"Well you haven't seen *mine* and I'd prefer to keep is that way."

Jo watched Beth continue to struggle with the impossibly wet knot.

"Wouldn't it just be easier to take the damn thing off?"

"Actually, it would be easier just to kill you."

Jo laughed at Beth's exasperation.

"C'mon, don't tell me you've never gone skinny dipping?"

"This may come as a shock to you but when you're raising a family, running around naked is generally not the rule."

"So try it now…liberate yourself!"

The mere suggestion triggered a lifetime of regrets that Beth was desperate to make Jo understand. Her voice cracked under the strain of trying to hold her robe and her life together.

"Do you have any idea what it's like to be that free for a moment… for a day… or if you're really lucky, maybe even a whole summer… only to be caught and put back in a cage where you're forced to survive in captivity for the rest of your life?"

As Beth continued her futile struggle with the knot, Joanna grew more sympathetic.

"Let me give you a hand with that."

Torn between her anger and her undeniable attraction, Beth recoiled from both.

"Haven't you done enough already?"

Powerless over her own desire, Jo could not leave the poor woman alone.

"Maybe I have, and maybe I haven't."

Once again her beautiful eyes flashed with mischief. She began splashing Beth mercilessly until finally, the frazzled woman began splashing back. The horseplay quickly escalated into something more demanding. As each fought to gain the upper hand, their bodies came together in a struggle for their lives. Each time their entangled contact felt more deliberate. Each time the ache of pulling back felt worse. As their hunger found less and less disguise, Beth tried to restore a sense of propriety before it was too late.

"Shhh… we'll wake Rheeta!"

Joanna couldn't have cared less. The more Beth insisted, the more spitefully rowdy Jo became. Hoping to restrain her, Beth grabbed hold of Jo's T-shirt, but Joanna was much too cunning. She bent her head, raised her arms and slipped out of the shirt altogether. The sight of Jo's breast suddenly exposed Beth to more of her own desire than she could bear. She quickly averted her eyes.

Jo took the waterlogged T-shirt and teasingly wrung it out over Beth's head. Beth wiped the water from her eyes. She had never felt so taunted by so many feelings at the same time, and she knew that the beautiful, arrogant woman standing in front of her was responsible for all of it.

"I hate you, Joanna Cameron!"

For all the same reasons, Jo bore equal frustration.

"I hate you too Beth Garrison!"

Just inches apart and reduced to a nearly impossible longing, Beth's only hope of survival was to escape. She turned and pushed through the water—away from temptation and towards the steps.

"Why did you have to come into my life?"

Jo shouted back at her.

"Why did you have to come into mine?"

As Beth neared the rail something deep inside Joanna could not bear to let her go. Fighting for her own survival she dove under the water, caught Beth around the thighs and pulled the fleeing woman backward into the pool. Through her soaked and clinging robe, Beth could feel the fullness of Joanna's breasts pressed against her back. The swell and fall of Jo's breathing was overwhelming. Fearing for her life, Beth tried to break free.

"Let go of me!"

Jo tightened her grip, pulling Beth even closer against her.

"Make me..."

Imprisoned by Joanna's arms, Beth struggled futilely against her own desire until she felt herself grow weak. Her legs ceased their useless thrashing. Her hands that had fought to pry Joanna's from around her waist now came to rest submissively upon them. Their bodies rested. The water grew still. The universe waited.

"Please Jo" she pleaded again, "let me go."

Joanna loosened her grip ever so slightly. She put her mouth against Beth's ear and repeated the only terms she could live with.

"Make me..."

Beth closed her eyes and let her head fall back against Joanna's shoulder.

"God help me. I don't know how..."

The confession would surely have led to more had Beth not opened her eyes just then and noticed Rheeta between the parted curtains of Adam's window. By the time Beth managed to pull away, her horrified friend had already disappeared from view. Beth panicked.

"Oh God, I think Rheeta was watching us this whole time."

Joanna wasn't about to relinquish the most important moment of her life to the likes of Rheeta.

"Who gives a damn? She couldn't care less about you if she tried."

"I think I know my friend a little better than you do."

"How can you call that pompous, self-absorbed bitch a friend, unless deep down inside you're really a masochist who likes being abused."

"Don't psychoanalyze me Joanna!"

"Hey, I just call it like I see it. What the hell makes you keep that miserable woman in your life anyway?"

"Gee, I don't know. Maybe my sense of loyalty. Maybe my sense of patience. Maybe my sense of compassion."

"Or maybe your sense of loneliness, insecurity and self-degradation."

Never before had anyone provoked such extreme emotion. Never before had she been so frightened by those extremes.

"I can't keep doing this!" Fearing for her sanity, Beth backed away and once again pushed toward the steps. "Rheeta was right. I need to get away from here for a while."

Joanna raged inside.

"Away from here or away from *me*?"

Beth avoided the question.

"She invited me to Boston. I'm taking her up on it."

Jo was too stubborn and too proud to let Beth see her pain.

"So go!" she shouted at the woman's back.

Had Beth not been so intent on getting herself to safety, she would have turned around and pounded her fists against Joanna's chest. Instead she kept moving forward, feverishly parting the water with her arms.

Not since her mother's death had Joanna felt such a crushing sense of abandonment. As she watched Beth inch ever closer to the steps with each stride, she lashed out.

"That's right, run away!"

"I'm not *running* away! I'm *getting* away. There's a difference."

"I know a textbook case of avoidance when I see it."

Beth turned and glared at her.

"Yes! As a self-described escapist, I imagine you would."

As Beth stepped out of the pool, Jo could feel her entire life slipping away. Resigned to losing the only woman she ever loved, Joanna pretended to release her willingly.

"Fine. Do what you want."

"I intend to!"

"Right! Just as long as it doesn't raise any eyebrows… especially the ones penciled on Rheeta's ugly face."

'The Dangerous Beth Garrison' stopped dead in her tracks. She didn't like being made to feel like a coward at a time in her life when she had fought fiercely to be the bravest she could.

"Go to hell Joanna!"

Jo flung her T-shirt onto the grass, then lifted herself out of the pool. Once again the two women stood face to face. Joanna ached for Beth's lips.

"Hell would probably have been an easier place to stay."

Beth could no longer endure the futility.

"I guess there's only one solution…"

"I guess so."

Joanna was intent on proving how little she cared.

"Tell ya' what, just to show you there's no hard feeling I'll stick around and watch BJ while you're gone. Stay in Boston as long as you like. When you get back I'll leave, so you won't have to do '*this*' anymore."

Beth clutched at her dripping robe while her heart broke just beneath it.

"I think that would be for the best."

Feeling more desperate than she'd ever felt in her life, Joanna was determined not to fall apart.

While resentment served the women's resolve, no amount of anger could dull the private anguish of their inevitable parting. Struggling to conceal their pain, they turned and went their separate ways, each leaving her coffee mug at the edge of the pool. As the raft drifted in the bittersweet reflection of their once perfect morning, the two cups sat side-by-side—now as empty as the women who shared them.

Rheeta paced back and forth in the kitchen, waiting for Beth to come through the door.

"Please tell me I didn't see what I thought I did."

Her robe soaking wet, Beth held up her hand as she stormed past Rheeta and headed for the hallway steps.

"Spare me your shock and outrage. I'm in no mood for either!"

Rheeta followed right behind.

"Beth honey, what in the world is going on with you?"

Halfway up the steps, Beth stopped and whirled around.

"I swear I'll throw you right over this railing if you don't leave it alone."

Rheeta was as persistent as she was thick-skinned. She took her chances.

"I haven't seen you this upset since Danny died."

Water now dripping onto the step from the hem of her robe, Beth laced into her friend.

"How the hell would *you* know how I was when my son died? This is the first time you've showed up since then!"

Expecting Beth's usual forgiveness, Rheeta offered a litany of excuses.

"I was living abroad... I was going through my second divorce... it was a terrible time for me... "

"It's always about *you* Rheeta. And you know what, that's okay. I accepted that a long time ago. But please don't stand here and presume to know what I was feeling back then... or now... because you can't! You never will!"

Beth had never sounded so harsh. As she continued up the stairs Rheeta followed after her.

"You're right and I'm sorry. But I demand to know what was going on in that pool."

"Demand all you want. I'm not discussing it with you."

"Beth, please calm down. I'm not passing judgment."

"Oh, since when?"

Rheeta set a lifetime record and apologized twice in one day.

"I never mean to be critical."

Beth was too raw to mince words.

"Then I suggest you go back into therapy because what you *mean* and what you *are* couldn't possibly be any further apart."

In the name of friendship, Rheeta took her lashing.

"That may be so, but it doesn't stop me from caring." Rheeta knew all too well what Joanna was capable of. "I'm worried about you honey, that's all."

Beth began to cry and tremble with uncertainty.

"I'm worried too Rhee... I'm worried too."

"Honey, you're shaking!" Daring to ruin her outfit, Rheeta took Beth into her arms. "I'm not leaving you like this. Please, I'm begging you. Come back to Boston with me for a few days and let me take care of you."

Beth pushed Rheeta away.

"I'm not a child damn it! I don't need someone to take care of me." She wiped her eyes and composed herself. "Besides, I have to be at the nursing home tomorrow morning."

Rheeta followed Beth into her bedroom.

"Tell them you can't make it."

"I have a commitment, Rheeta. A commitment! Maybe that doesn't mean anything to you but it does to *me*!"

"Fine. Do whatever you feel you have to. I'll send a limo to drive you back to Boston."

The suggestion sounded preposterous.

"You'll do no such thing. I'm perfectly capable of driving myself."

"Then have yourself on my doorstep by tomorrow afternoon."

Beth looked down at the puddle of water around her feet. Her resolve wavered.

"Maybe I will..."

Rheeta put her finger under Beth's chin.

"What do I have to do to get you to take the *maybe* out of that sentence?"

Beth expelled a weary breath.

"Promise no sermons, no badgering and no meddling."

"Deal!"

Beth had good reason to doubt her friend's word.

"I mean it Rhee... if you so much as mention Joanna's name..."

"Joanna who?"

Beth reached for a Kleenex and blew her nose. Her life felt as crumpled as the tissue in her hand.

"Okay, I'll come..."

Rheeta clapped joyously.

"Wonderful! You won't be sorry."

Beth knew that was impossible, especially since the ache of being apart from Joanna had already begun.

Sensing Beth's reluctance, Rheeta hurried her along.

"Now go take yourself a nice hot shower while I finish packing. Before I leave we'll share one of those luscious scones with some coffee."

"I've already had my cup...," 'and had my chance' Beth's heart added silently, certain she would never have another.

The painful memory brought a second wave of tears as she shuffled off to the bathroom.

Rheeta was so concerned about her friend's fragile state, she actually carried all her own luggage downstairs and out to the car. She'd just come back into the kitchen when the telephone rang. Toweling off, Beth heard it too. She called down to Rheeta.

"Let the machine answer. I don't want to talk to anyone right now."

Ignoring Beth's request, at the sound of Ben's voice Rheeta immediately picked up.

"Well hello handsome."

Ben disguised his regret.

"Hi Rheeta. Beth mentioned you'd be visiting. How are you?"

"You know me... between marriages and cosmetic surgery I'm richer and more beautiful than ever."

"Is that so?"

"To see me naked, you might wonder if you married the wrong woman."

Ben laughed. Rheeta was the complete antithesis of his wife in every way imaginable.

"I think we both know I took the only bride for me."

"Ah, the last of the true romantics."

"Yup, that's me. Where is the woman of my dreams anyway?

"I believe the lucky Mrs. Garrison is taking a shower."

Ben knew he was desperate when he relied on the likes of Rheeta's perception to serve as a barometer.

"Be honest... how does Beth seem to you?"

In her head, Rheeta replayed the unsettling scene she'd witnessed earlier.

"She's acting a bit odd. Not quite like the Beth we both know."

"What do you mean?"

As insensitive as she was, Rheeta had no intention of betraying her best friend's innermost conflict. She walked over to the kitchen window and stared loathsomely at the carriage house.

"Let's just say your wife could do with a little change of scenery. I managed to convince her to come to Boston for a few days."

"I'm glad. I just wish I could have talked her into coming to England with me."

"The summer's not over yet." Joanna had step outside. "Maybe I can get her to change her mind."

"Try really hard. I miss her terribly."

Watching Jo's every move, Rheeta became all the more resentful of her influence.

"She misses you too Ben."

"Did she actually *say* that?"

"She didn't have to, I know my Bethie."

From so far away, Ben had little choice but to count on Rheeta's power of persuasion.

"Do whatever you can to convince her."

"Honey, if it was up to me she'd be on the next flight out."

Rheeta seethed as Joanna draped her wet T-shirt and shorts over the chaise to dry. With Beth still upstairs, she knew this would be her last chance settle a score. She was eager to get off the phone.

"Gotta' go now sweetie so 'cheerio', as they say in ol' London town. I'll tell Bethie you called."

Before he could say goodbye, Rheeta hastily hung up and raced outside.

Joanna was staring hopelessly at the two mugs left at the edge of the pool when Rheeta accosted her.

"You and I need to have a little talk."

Jo was in no mood for either Rheeta's overbearing personality or her perfume.

"Just can't stay away, can you?"

Rheeta stiffened indignantly.

"Trust me, if it wasn't for the wine..."

"Look, spare me the oldest excuse in the book and just tell me what the fuck you want."

"What I want is what's best for Beth."

"Like you would know... or care."

Rheeta pursed her ruby red lips.

"Contrary to what you may think, I value that woman's friendship more deeply today that I ever have."

"Why? Isn't a 3-way mirror company enough anymore?"

Jo turned and headed back to the carriage house. She swung open the screen door and Rheeta rudely followed her inside.

Joanna glanced over her shoulder with contempt.

"I seem to recall last night got a little hot for you in here. Aren't you afraid your face might run?"

"Just for the record, I'm not the brainless bimbo you take me for."

"I hate to burst your implants, but you lost your 'bimbo' status twenty years ago."

"I happen to see a lot more than you give me credit for."

"Actually, I'm, amazed you can see anything at all past those mascara-caked eyelashes."

"Oh, you'd be surprised and whether I like the idea or not, it's quite obvious you and Beth have developed a special... shall we say... affection."

After her fight with Beth, Jo was in no mood to debate that point.

"Whatever road you're going down, do me a favor. Take a short cut, then drive yourself over a cliff."

"Regardless of what you think, Beth means the world to me."

"Gee, I can't imagine why. She's obviously not a part of your set. She's much too genuine and real."

"Well, dare I point out that 'little Sally homemaker' is certainly not a part of yours either?"

"You just wasted ten more seconds of my life."

Rheeta did not like to be hurried. She wandered spitefully over to the portraits of Beth.

"You may indeed have captured her on *paper* but over my dead body will you ever get her in *bed*." Rheeta turned to Joanna and gloated as though she'd just swiped the last cookie out of Jo's hand. "I've convinced her to come to Boston. She leaves tomorrow, right after whatever it is she does at that God awful nursing home."

Jo came within inches of Rheeta's face.

"If you really gave a damn, you'd know that what she does is plays the piano for the residents... Arthur, in particular. He happens to be one of the few people that's brought her a sense of comfort and purpose since her son died. But of course, that would presume you actually cared."

"I care enough to get her the hell away from here. In fact, I'm making it my personal mission to see to it that Beth doesn't give you a second thought." Rheeta tossed her hair back. "Not for a single, itty-bitty second."

Joanna pushed Rheeta toward the door.

"Your little visit is just about over."

Rheeta sneered.

"So's yours honey. I'm going to do whatever it takes to get Beth on a plane to England to be with her husband for the rest of the summer."

Joanna opened the screen door, grabbed Rheeta's arm and practically threw her out.

"Take your hands off me!"

"Funny, they didn't seem to bother you last night."

Rheeta pulled herself free.

"Don't flatter yourself. I assure you, that little drunken indiscretion was as forgettable as you are."

"Just for the record, what may or may not be forgettable to you was nothing short of repulsive to me! I pity your next three husbands."

"And I pity *you* because Beth happens to be very much in love with the one she has."

As she walked away, Rheeta's voice dripped with smugness.

"Nice to have met you '*Jo*'. How sad for you that's not short for Joseph. Perhaps some intensive therapy might help you work things out."

"I'm a lot more comfortable in my skin than you are in yours!"

Jo slammed the screen door so hard it almost came off its hinges. After some erratic pacing, she picked up the phone and left a message on Steve's machine.

"Where the fuck are you? How long does it take to get your damn teeth cleaned and your tires rotated?"

She slammed the receiver into its cradle, paced some more then called him back.

"Call me the minute you get in!"

She hung up, stormed over to the sculpture stand and stared at the tender reminder of Beth's hands. Wrought with emotion Jo pounded her fist into the clay, deliberately destroying the shape if not the memory her heart had sought to preserve.

Satisfied that she'd left Joanna in defeat, Rheeta returned to the house and called up to her friend.

"Honey, that was Ben on the phone. I told him you'd call him back."

Beth looked at the wet robe lying on the bathroom floor. Burdened by its memory, she called down.

"I asked you to let the machine pick up."

Rheeta stood at the foot of the stairs.

"We haven't spoken in years. What was the harm? I told him you were in the shower, we chit-chatted a bit and that was that."

Beth came down the steps looking a lot more refreshed than she felt.

"Swear to me you didn't say a word about Joanna."

"The name never crossed my lips."

Rheeta smiled and swept a strand of hair off Beth's forehead.

"I knew a shower would do you a world of good. You look much more like yourself."

"Whatever *that* is these days."

"Honey, I'm afraid I'm already running late and my attorney gets paid by the hour whether I'm holding his dick or not." Her voice filled with excitement. "But now that you're coming to Boston, we'll have the next few days to look forward to. I left directions on the pad on the counter, though I'd really prefer you let me send a car."

"The drive will do me good. Besides, I have to leave from your place early Sunday morning. It's visiting day at Adam's camp." Beth read Rheeta's mind. "And no, I won't call him and say I can't make it, so don't even suggest it."

"How early is early?"

"Around six-ish."

Beth saw the horror in Rheeta's eyes.

"Don't worry. I wouldn't think of waking you. I'll just let myself out."

Rheeta's eyes flooded with mischief.

"Or maybe we'll stay out all night and not go to sleep at all! Wouldn't that be fun?"

Beth suddenly felt overwhelmed by Rheeta's expectations.

"Rhee please... I'm absolutely drained as it is and I'm certainly not packing anything appropriate for a night on the town."

Rheeta didn't want to give Beth any reason to change her mind.

"Honey, you just come in your big fluffy slippers and let me take care of the rest. I guarantee, we'll send you off to that silly camp feeling like a brand new woman."

"I'd settle for just being able to recognize the old one..."

Were she not in such a hurry, Rheeta would have gladly stayed on to kill Joanna for ruining her best friend's life. Instead, she clapped her hands and Pierre leapt up into her arms. Beth assumed her role.

"I'll go up and get your luggage."

"Everything's already in the car. Seemed to me you were carrying a heavy enough load, so I got one of the other bell-hops to do it. Too bad though, you missed a very generous tip."

Beth appreciated the gesture, especially coming from Rheeta.

"Thank you."

She followed Rheeta out to her car.

Pierre settled into the plush leather passenger seat and Rheeta slid in behind the wheel. Before she donned her oversized sunglasses, she looked over at Beth's rusting station wagon.

"You know honey, it's an awfully long trip. I'd feel much better if you took the Jeep."

"The truth is it'll ruin your reputation if one of your snooty Beacon Hill neighbors see my jalopy parked in front of your brownstone."

"So what? I'll just change my identity and start a completely new life somewhere else. It's not like I haven't done that at least a half dozen times already."

The women giggled. Beth was relieved there was still a part of her that could laugh.

"Now *that's* the Rita Nussbaum I know and love."

Rheeta lowered her voice.

"And *that's* the Rita Nussbaum who loves you too… with all her heart."

Several incarnations later, Rheeta Montgomery put on her Gucci sunglasses and started her newest Jaguar. She squeezed her friends hand.

"Oh Bethie, I'm so glad you decided to come!"

Rheeta put the Jag in reverse.

"Now all I have to do is follow the yellow brick road back to civilization, right?"

"Just click your heels twice and you and Todo will be home in no time."

Even as Beth waved Rheeta off, that decision already felt like the worst mistake of her life.

Surrounded by crumpled tissues Beth sat at her dining room table, her head buried in her arms. She had just plucked another from the box when the phone rang. Comforted by Steve's voice, she raced to pick it up before he finished leaving a message.

"I'm here!"

Even as she said it, Beth realized that no two words were ever less true.

"It's nice to hear your voice lady. I miss the hell out of you."

"I miss you too." Beth needed reassurance. "Do you think we can get together when I get back?"

"Sure! Back from where?"

"Rheeta's invited me to spend some time in Boston. I'm leaving tomorrow."

"Jo mentioned she was visiting. Don't get me wrong, but if memory serves I'd have thought these last few days with her would have been way long enough."

"I have my reasons…"

"I see."

As Steve quietly put two and two together, things started to make sense. Jo and Rheeta must have clashed like the natural born enemies he knew they'd be. Beth had somehow been caught in the middle and faced with all her own conflict, her visit to Boston probably seemed like the lesser of two evils. If the tone of Jo's message was any indication, their impending separation had left her crazed. With all the pieces coming together in his head, Steve didn't let on to any of it.

"Listen, Jo called a little while ago. I tried to get back to her but she's obviously out." Convinced of the women's unresolved attraction to each other, Steve imagined that their parting would be anything but easy. "Will you be seeing her before you leave?"

Beth dreaded the impending ordeal.

"Yes. She's agreed to watch BJ while I'm gone. I have to talk to her about his schedule and routines."

Steve guessed that Joanna's offer gave her the perfect excuse to stay on—at least until Beth returned. He kept his suspicions to himself.

"In that case, would you tell her I'll swing by the usual time tomorrow morning and that I'm sorry I got hung up longer than I expected today."

"I'll give her the message."

"Thanks."

Steve could sense his friend was suffering. He knew sure as hell that Joanna was.

"Beth, are you alright?"

"I'm fine Steve."

"You don't sound fine. Wanna' talk about it?"

"I'm just tired honey, that's all."

Though Steve would've bet otherwise, he pretended to buy Beth's excuse.

"I'm sure entertaining Rheeta took its toll. At least in Boston *you'll* get to be the pampered guest."

At the mere thought of Rheeta's overbearing nature all Beth's reservations came racing forth.

"Steve, what am I doing?"

He answered the only way her could.

"You're doing what you need to do."

"Why doesn't it feel that way?"

"Probably because what you *need* to do and what you *want* to do are two entirely different things." That was as much as he would say—at least for now. "Either way, I'm gonna' hold you to those plans once you get back."

Beth's voice sounded unmistakably sad.

"Good. That'll give me something to look forward to."

Steve intentionally fished around for more clues.

"I would have thought there'd be a lot to look forward to. Jo mentioned you spent a really nice day together while I was gone. Sounded to me like you guys were just starting to get closer."

He waited to see what Beth would say.

"The whole thing was a terrible mistake. Sometimes I feel as if my whole life should be one big 'do-over'. I'll call you when I get back."

"If you don't, I'll hunt you down."

"Don't worry, I promise. I can use one of your hugs."

"It has been a long time."

Beth reflected on the weeks she'd intentionally and needlessly avoided him.

"That's been entirely my fault. I'm sorry."

"Apology accepted. We'll talk more about *everything*, when you get home."

Home was nowhere except in Joanna's eyes.

"Would you mind if we talked less and hugged more?"

"Whatever you need Beth." His heart ached for hers. "Is there anything I can do for you while you're in Boston?"

"Yes. You can rewrite the story of my life, starting with these last few weeks."

"I'm afraid that's way out of my range. I'll do everything in my power to see that it has a happy ending though. You have my word on that." Steve sensed her vulnerability. "Just promise me you won't let Rheeta do any major editing of her own while you're in her clutches."

"I'll do my best, though I'm quite sure she's stocking up on red pens even as we speak."

Somewhere in their coded exchange each had shared what they needed to in order to say goodbye. Beth's sadness lingered in Steve's heart as he peered into his refrigerator. After guzzling down a quart of orange juice his thirst was quenched, but not his concern.

"Jesus Christ, Jo" he mumbled under his breath, "what the hell have you done to that poor woman?" He shook his head. "And what must she be doing to you?"

Although Beth was aware of the precise moment Jo had returned, it took her over an hour to muster the courage to face her. Now, standing on the step of the carriage house, Beth knocked timidly against the frame of the screen door.

"Is this a bad time?"

At the sound of Beth's voice, Jo pushed back her charging emotions.

"It's as good as any."

As Beth let herself in, Jo purposely kept to her task. She had purchased a full length mirror, set it up beside her easel and had just begun working on a self portrait—something she hadn't attempted since she was in art school.

For a moment Beth stood silently by.

"That must be very challenging."

By not diverting her eyes from the canvas, Jo was able to avoid Beth's.

"I figured it was time to take a good, hard look at things... starting with myself."

"This certainly seems to be the summer for that sort of thing."

Joanna wasn't interested in making small talk. What she wanted was to be making love.

Beth pushed on.

"Steve called earlier. He asked me to let you know he'd be by the usual time tomorrow. He said he was sorry about how things turned out this morning." She hesitated. "For what it's worth, so am I."

Joanna stopped and looked up. She was careful to make her plea sound more like a demand.

"Then don't go!"

As soon as their eyes met, Beth had to stop herself from begging for Joanna's arms.

"I think my leaving for a few days will be good for us."

"There is no *us*! There's *me* and there's *you*!"

Beth fought back tears.

"You're right. Getting away will be good for *me*. I need a break Jo. I'm tired... tired of digging up the past... tired of delving into my subconscious... tired of looking into my soul." She walked over to the wall and gazed painfully at her portraits. "You see too much. You demand too much." She turned back to Joanna, her eyes pleading for forgiveness. "I can't do it anymore."

Jo was hurting much too much to be sympathetic.

"Enjoy Boston then. You'll be in good company. I'm sure the deepest Ms. Silicone has ever delved has been through her cosmetic case."

Rheeta's a lot brighter than you give her credit for. Aside from her real age, she'd die if anyone knew she was a member of Mensa and believe it or not, she's capable of being quite sincere."

"Yeah, sincere about casting everyone into condescending stereotypes."

"At least she does it out of hopeless insecurity. You do it for a living. All you Madison Avenue types like nothing more than to pigeon-hole the rest of us with your demeaning demographic and market research studies." Beth's anguish came pouring out. "Admit it! When you stood in that parking lot berating me you thought I was nothing but a mindless housewife."

"I was thinking a lot of things back in that parking lot."

"Like what?"

In spite of her anger at the time, Jo recalled how intensely drawn she was to Beth.

"It's not important."

"No, I guess it's not."

Beth tried collecting the remains of her own heart; the pieces she'd found and the pieces she'd lost to this infuriating, irresistible stranger. Resigned to their parting, she explained about BJ's routines—when he was accustomed to being let out and what he was to be fed. Jo listened stoically to all of it while she went about preparing her palette. Beth attempted to reassure them both.

"I won't be gone more than a few days."

"When you get back, you get back. I'll write you a check to have the place professionally cleaned and I'll be out of here in an hour."

Beth could feel the life drain from her body at the thought of Joanna's leaving. The idea of erasing the last traces of the woman's presence was beyond anything her heart could imagine. Jo repositioned the mirror as if to suggest she wanted to get back to work. Beth was unable to stop her hand from trembling as she placed the extra set of house keys along with a small slip of paper on the kitchen counter.

"In case for any reason… you need me, I'm leaving Rheeta's number."

The irony of the words drove a stake through Joanna's heart. She turned away so Beth could not see the suffering in her eyes.

"Trust me, I won't!"

Her fragile composure nearly shattered, Beth fought back tears.

"I'll let you get back to your self-portrait." Her eyes swept across the beginning brushstrokes. "I hope when it's finished you don't see in *yours* what you managed to expose in *mine*."

Joanna denied their unspoken intimacy.

"I captured your likeness. Nothing more."

Beth would not permit such a convenient lie.

"I think we both know that's not so."

She ached for Joanna's forgiveness, but dared not ask for the one thing she was unable to grant herself.

"I'm sorry our… *arrangement*… didn't work out."

"Let's face it, the whole thing was doomed from the start."

Prepared to take whatever punishment she found there, Beth forced herself to meet Joanna's eyes.

"Could we at least try not to be angry with each other."

Jo dug bitterly through her box of paints and squeezed the entire tube of yellow onto her palette.

"No problem. I'll just give myself a big round smiley face? Would that make things easier for you?"

Unsure how much more she could take Beth walked slowly to the door, silently praying for Joanna to stop her. From a place as dark as any she'd ever known came the hardest two words she'd ever spoken.

"Goodbye Jo."

Jo would not allow herself to turn around. She knew watching Beth leave would bring more torment than she could bear. Her heart lashed out as she scraped the paint with her palette knife.

"Better warn the population of Boston you're coming considering what a menace you can be behind the wheel."

Against the cruelty of Joanna's parting words, Beth let herself out.

The sound of the door slammed against Joanna's heart. The full-length mirror now served as an inescapable reminder of the truth. With her jaw clenched Jo stood rigid, holding herself in check for as long as she could. When desperation finally gave way to rage, she picked up the coffee can filled with brushes and hurled it at the wall.

Halfway across the yard Beth froze in place, immobilized by the crashing sound of Joanna's despair. For a few moments, Beth just stood there, allowing herself to cry. Then she closed off her heart, wiped her cheeks and walked on. She had spent so much of her life weeping from a place she could not reach to soothe. She could not afford to give anymore time away.

Beth packed haphazardly, giving little thought to what she should take. The most important thing to her survival was what she was leaving behind. She placed the single piece of luggage near the kitchen door as a deliberate reminder to her wavering resolve. Dinner consisted of a bowl of cereal which she ate hastily and prayed would stay down. The serenity of summer's early evening felt especially cruel. Barricaded inside, she retreated to her piano where, from her self-imposed exile, she could force Joanna to at least hear how undeniably she hurt. Each impassioned note penetrated deeper and deeper until the haunting melody became woven into every fiber of Joanna's existence. Though she fought bitterly to take back her heart, her attempt was futile. As Beth continued to play Jo continued to paint, adding layer upon suffocating layer of heartache with every stroke of her brush. As the orange streaked sky gradually darkened, the weight of night fell upon the pair with a despair greater than either woman had ever known. As the miserable hours wore on, keyboard and canvas bore the yearning of untouched flesh.

The following morning Beth arrived at the nursing home, once again managing to put aside her own pain to serve the needs of others. As always, after her playing she stayed on to spend some time alone with Arthur. On this particular morning he was feeling more tired than usual and preferred his bed to their special bench in the garden. Beth stood by as the orderly got Arthur out of his wheel chair and made him as comfortable as possible. Arthur never failed to thank whomever it was that tended to his needs and for that, everyone on the staff always reciprocated with special kindness. After the aide left, Beth pulled up a chair and sat close beside him. Despite Beth's best attempt at hiding it, Arthur had an uncanny sense of her sadness. It was a recognition imbedded deep inside his own. His parched lips moved with concern.

"What's is it momma?"

"It's nothing sweetheart, really." She stroked his hand. "I'm just a bit under the weather today."

"Don't worry momma, Anne will take care of you."

Beth was surprised he remembered Jo at all.

"Joanna honey, her name is Joanna."

"Does she know you're not well?" Arthur tensed. "You must tell her momma. You *must*!"

Beth decided to be honest in the kindest way she could. She hoped that by sharing the truth with him she might slowly begin to accept it too.

"She knows honey, but unfortunately she won't be here much longer."

Arthur grew more agitated.

"No momma! You mustn't let her go! You can't be apart! You'll get sicker and sicker until one day you'll die!" Arthur's body began to shake. "Please don't die momma, please!"

The fragile old man and the frightened little boy began to weep. Arthur clutched Beth's hand as tightly as his weakened fingers would allow. Beth anguished over his lifelong sense of abandonment. She leaned closer and stroked his cheek.

"I won't die sweetheart, I promise." Beth blotted his tears. She thought it might help to talk about happier things. "Let's not forget you have a special birthday coming up."

The gravity of his loss seemed to recede back into his past. A gentle smile took its place.

"I love parties momma. Whose birthday is it?"

Beth's heart spilled forth with joy.

"Yours honey. You're going to be one hundred years old in just a few weeks."

"Yes I am!" Arthur declared. His smile widened as if proud to be a part of his own longevity. "Everyone is going to be there."

"Yes sweetie, absolutely everyone."

Beth lovingly applied a bit of balm to Arthur's chapped lips while he lie there anticipating the happy day. Through the haze of his cataracts, she could see a childlike excitement in his eyes.

"Anne's coming too, right momma?"

Instinctively Beth protected him from the truth.

"She wouldn't miss it for the world."

Comforted by her assurance, Arthur's body seemed to relax. He grew sleepier and eventually closed his eyes. Beth knew it wouldn't be long before he lapsed into a peaceful nap. Adoring him as much as she did, Beth stayed and held his hand. Through the tenderness of her touch, the gentle old man and the sweet little boy slowly drifted off in the reassuring presence of his mother's love.

Beth walked slowly through the parking lot to her rusty station wagon. Earlier that morning, already riddled with doubt, she thought perhaps Rheeta was right in cautioning her not to trust the worthiness of her own car. Heeding her friend's advice, she'd gone so far as to toss her luggage in the back of Ben's Jeep and had slid in behind its wheel. But at the last minute 'The Dangerous Beth Garrison' had a sudden and certain change of heart. If, as Jo had accused her, she was in fact running away, Beth was determined to do it in her *own* car and on her own terms. If the vehicle broke down—like her life had broken down—she'd get out and push the damn thing the rest of the way! After all, the dented hunk of metal couldn't possibly weigh more than the ten ton block of reluctance lodged in her heart as she pointed both towards Boston.

Chapter 18

Exhausted from a drive that contrary to her insistence had not done her even the slightest bit of good, Beth now stood in the entrance foyer of Rheeta's newly renovated brownstone trapped in the fierce grip of her friend's welcoming embrace. Only Rheeta's perfume was more overwhelming.

"Oh Bethie, I can't believe you're really here!"

'Neither can I', Beth thought to herself.

Pierre yapped incessantly as his mistress led Beth into the parlor room. Rheeta struck a pose as if presenting her most impressive accomplishment to date.

"Ta da!"

Beth took a sweeping look around at the lavishly appointed surroundings. The notion that 'less was more' was a concept that had eluded Rheeta entirely. This was apparent in her wardrobe and it was twice as glaring in her home. The room looked like a garish stage set of a Venetian palace. At quick glance there seemed to be almost as many gilded clawed furniture legs as there were Baroque pillows and braided tassels. Beth did not have to pretend to be dumbstruck.

"It's definitely you."

Rheeta beamed.

"I'll save the nickel tour for later."

Beth was relieved. She'd already used whatever tact she could summon on the parlor alone. Rheeta clasped her hands with delight.

"I hope you're hungry."

"Exhausted more than anything else."

"I told you to let me send a car. I see you took that old death trap of yours after all."

"A girl's gotta' do what a girl's gotta' do."

"Well, you made it here alive. That's what counts."

Rheeta took Beth by the hand and led her through a set of French doors that opened into a formal dining room. An ornately framed oil painting of Rheeta took center stage above the gilded fireplace. A massive crystal chandelier hung from the ceiling above a Louis XIV table that sat twelve. There were more clawed furniture legs and more tassels than Beth could count. She knew Rheeta was waiting. Once again the truth served.

"I'm speechless."

"Sotheby's certainly owes me a fruit basket this Christmas." Rheeta had set out two place settings of fine china, polished silver and crystal goblets. "I had the local gourmet shop deliver a smorgasbord of delights." She motioned for Beth to sit, then disappeared through another set of doors.

Beth focused on the painting over the mantle.

"That's quite a portrait of you."

"I commissioned it after my first face lift."

"Most people would have just taken a before and after photo."

"Oh Bethie, you know I'm not *most people*."

"No, you're certainly not."

As she continued to stare at the painting, her mind drifted back to the night she'd posed for Joanna. Beth's heart sank. Rheeta reappeared with a large sterling silver tray filled with exotic looking hors-d-oeuvres and decadent pastries. Everything looked scrumptious but Beth had no appetite for any of it.

"You really didn't have to go to all this trouble."

"This is just the beginning. I've got everything all planned."

"Rhee, please. You promised."

"I heard you loud and clear honey and I've blocked off plenty of fluffy slipper time. We're in for the rest of the day and night… just you, me and the ice crusher. I even gave the housekeeper the weekend off so we can kick back and be our silly little schoolgirl selves." She winked at her oldest and dearest friend. "How's that sound?"

Beth could feel the tension across her shoulders loosen a bit. Perhaps Rheeta really *had* heard her this time. Beth extended a weary smile. She felt so small; the chair she was sitting on—and her burdens—so large.

"It sounds perfect."

Rheeta filled their glasses with expensive champagne.

"Here's to the last twenty-five years and the next thirty-six hours!"

Beth tried not to imagine what those hours would be like. The old friends toasted and took their lunch.

The full tour of the house ended in Rheeta's 'piece de resistance'—her bedroom. Over the hand carved, gold leafed headboard hung another oil painting of Grand Dame Rheeta. This one depicted her sprawled naked across a settee. Her most private part covered by a single crimson rose, the rest of her surgically enhanced body lay fully exposed.

"I had it commissioned after the lipo and boob job."

Beth struggled to form a compliment out of her disbelief.

"Both surgeon and artist certainly did you justice."

"For what they each charged, they better had!"

The ornately decorated guest room was on the top floor with its own marble bath and Jacuzzi. Beth was touched by the bouquet of bright yellow daisies that adorned the imposing dresser. In a rare gesture, Rheeta had put aside her own taste.

"They were the closest I could come to those silly wild flowers I know you love."

"Thanks Rhee. It's so sweet of you."

The women shared an emotional hug until Rheeta feared for her mascara.

"Why don't you unpack and take yourself a nice, long bubble bath."

The idea sounded wonderful.

"I think I will. Maybe I'll even take a little nap afterwards."

Rheeta patted her friend's cheek.

"Whatever that little heart of yours pleases."

The weight of Rheeta's remark exposed Beth to the impossibility of her deepest desire. Were she to do just what her heart pleased she wouldn't be in Boston, but in Joanna's arms.

With Beth and her objections tucked neatly away, Rheeta immediately set the next day's plans in motion. She called her salon and made appointments with everyone on staff. After a morning of excessive pampering they would take in an outdoor art show in the park. Then, it was on to a glorious shopping spree. Rheeta would buy her friend something sinfully expensive to wear to dinner later that night. She phoned her favorite French restaurant and reserved their best table for eight.

It was hours later when Beth woke from her much needed nap. With her hair still tousled she threw on a pair of sweats and shuffled downstairs in her fluffy slippers. Rheeta was curled up on the sofa. She put down her glass of wine and closed her book—the latest of trashy romance novels.

"Well, aren't you the picture of boudoir glamour!"

Beth looked down at her disheveled outfit, wiped her eyes and shrugged.

"I can't believe I slept so long."

"Not to worry. I wasn't going to let the party start without you." She patted the spot beside her. "Come sit down."

Beth obeyed. She leaned over to get a glimpse of what Rheeta was reading. "Anything good?"

"Nothing good ever comes from losing one's heart."

Beth kicked off her slippers and curled up her legs. She felt a quiet pity for her friend's history.

"You sound so jaded."

"Do I? Well in my experience all roads lead to heartbreak and all heartbreak leads to a divorce settlement with more money… which as it happens, is the color of jade. So I suppose I *am* a bit jaded but, I might add, quite wealthier for it." Rheeta squirmed. "Ready to party?" She leaned over and reached for a small onyx box on the coffee table. "To hell with the smoothies. I've got something far better."

Rheeta took out a book of matches, some rolling paper and a small bag of marijuana. Seeing no point in trying to discourage her, Beth leaned back against the arm of the sofa and watched her friend roll a joint. Rheeta lit up, took a long stoke and passed the joint to her best friend.

"I thought we'd get stoned instead of smashed.

"No thanks."

Rheeta became suspicious

"Why Beth Garrison, I'll bet you never got high even once!" She shook her head. "Oh c'mon honey, give it a try. For once in your life, let your hair down."

Hoping for anything that dulled her heartache, Beth took the joint and put it to her lips. After a few choking coughs, she managed to inhale a reasonably long drag. Its effect was almost immediately. Rheeta took a few more hits herself, then passed the joint back to Beth. She watched in amusement as Beth honed her technique.

"Why you straight laced little devil! You have all the makings of a full blown pothead."

Before long the old roommates were each slumped against a corner of the sofa, rambling on in giddy, incoherent thoughts. Rheeta reached down and picked up one of Beth's fluffy slippers.

"I can't believe you really own a pair of these ridiculous things."

Beth grabbed her slipper back and held in close to her as if protecting a precious child.

"And I can't believe you really own a dildo!"

Rheeta became indignant.

"Yes well, without naming names, I didn't appreciate how a certain dinner guest twisted things around like that."

"Can I see it?"

"See what?"

Beth giggled.

"Your dildo."

"Definitely not."

"Why?"

"Because it's personal, that's why!"

Beth was not above begging.

"Oh c'mon. I'll never get another chance?" She pulled at Rheeta's arm like a whining child. "Please, please, please…"

"Oh alright!" She yanked her arm away. "I need another hit first." She lit up, took another drag and stumbled dizzily across the room. "You have to know how much I love you to do this."

Beth clapped her hands.

"I do, I do. Go get it!"

Rheeta mumbled something and dragged herself up the stairs to her bedroom while Beth sat cross-legged, rocking anxiously on the couch. Gone were any traces of an endlessly patient mother.

"C'mon Rhee! What's taking so long?"

Rheeta called down to her.

"I'm peeing damn it. Hold your goddamn horses."

Beth took another hit of the joint and called back.

"I don't wanna' hold my horse—I wanna' hold your dildo."

Rheeta appeared on the steps.

"Here, for God sake." She tossed Beth the long suede pouch. "Now leave me alone. I'm getting something to eat. I've got the munchies."

Rheeta disappeared into the kitchen while Beth's fingers worked to undo the knotted drawstring. She squealed as she reached in and took out the thick rubber shaft. Holding it at its base, Beth watched the incredibly lifelike cock sway back and forth. Amazed, she called to her friend in the kitchen.

"My God Rhee! I can't believe it looks so… *real*!"

Rheeta called back.

"Like the ad says, 'We've come a long way, baby'."

Beth was thoroughly intrigued.

"Is this considered a small, medium or large?"

Rheeta answered impatiently.

"It's a fucking dildo, not a goddamn soft drink. So, inch for inch, how does Ben stack up?"

Beth giggled.

"Let's just say I think he'd be pleased."

"Well lucky you."

The size of her husband's penis was never the problem. Sadly, what *was* could not be substituted by anything stored in a drawstring pouch. Beth fondled the amazingly lifelike shaft.

"How in the world do they make these things look and feel so much like the real thing?"

"They're not all like that. Some are rigid and smooth. Others have vibrators built into them."

Beth shook her head.

"Ah, the lengths we go to…" She burst out laughing at the unintended pun. "Where on earth did you get it?"

"It was an anniversary present. Husband #2 was a pencil dick. The wad of cash in his pocket was thicker and way more gratifying. I was going out of my mind. It was this or an affair. At the time, it seemed the more sentimental choice."

Beth marveled at how casual all this was to her friend.

"Does it require any special care?"

"Well there's no male ego to deal with, if that's what you mean."

"I mean how do you clean it… afterwards?"

"Just a little soap and water. If it's been really good to me, I'll give it a spin through the rinse cycle of the dishwasher."

Beth had become suspiciously quiet. Rheeta waited for her next question, but it never came. She finished piling an assortment of hors-d-oeuvres onto a tray and returned to the living room. Beth was lying back on the couch holding the base of the dildo against her crotch. She thrust her hips and beckoned in a mockingly deeper voice.

"Hey baby… wanna' fuck?"

Rheeta set the tray down, crossed her arms and shook her head.

"Beth Garrison, I do believe you're as high as a kite!"

Beth giggled and stroked the length of her mock erection.

"Come on! Climb on and let me rock your world!"

Rheeta bent down and impatiently swiped the dildo from Beth's hands.

"Give me that thing!"

She quickly returned the sex toy to its pouch and placed it safely out of Beth's reach.

"I said let your hair down… I didn't say raise mine."

Rheeta spread some Brie on a cracker.

"Here, if you want to shove something into a hole, then shove this into the one in your face."

As she nibbled on the cracker, Beth's mind began to wander.

"Have you ever wondered what it's like… you know… to have a penis between your legs?"

Rheeta's jaw dropped.

"I'll assume that's the pot talking and pretend I didn't hear that."

"No really Rhee, don't you wonder what it feels like to be inside another woman?"

"No Beth! I most certainly do not!"

Beth let her head fall back against the sofa.

"Lately I have…"

Rheeta pushed the tray aside.

"Maybe we should have stuck to smoothies after all. Let's talk about something else. Tomorrow for instance."

Within the last twenty-four hours Beth had given in to a much more devastating compromise. Rheeta's insistence seemed insignificant by comparison.

"Fine, let's talk about tomorrow."

Rheeta launched into a description of their elaborate plans. Knowing how useless it would be to try and dissuade her from any of it, Beth simply listened. Once again overwhelmed, she excused herself for bed. She prayed for enough sleep to survive the day that lay ahead—the first of so many excruciating days of her life that would no longer include Joanna.

From the moment he picked Jo up the next morning, Steve realized that Friday would be as unproductive a workday as they came. If Joanna had never swung a hammer in her life she couldn't have been more useless. Obeying her threat not to mention Beth's name, he was left with little choice but to spend the day tiptoeing around the exposed wires of a demolished wall and the exposed nerves of his partner's heart. He realized just how defeated she was when she didn't object to resorting a tray of various size screws he'd accidentally kicked over. Every once in a while he would look over at the pathetic woman sitting on the floor, sifting through the hardware like a child trying to fit the pieces of a puzzle. This was not the arrogant, self-reliant Joanna he knew. This was the Joanna who had fallen most inconveniently in love. With little he could offer in the way of distraction, he agreed to pose for her on

Saturday night. However futile, Jo was intent on trying to erase the traces of Beth from her life and that included finally using that once precious mound of clay she'd sought to preserve. Steve dropped her at the curb and watched helplessly as she trudged up the Garrison driveway.

The absence of the old station wagon that had plowed into her stung badly. Comforted by the connection to Beth's life, Joanna brought BJ back to the carriage house for company. She picked at some leftover deli meat and fed him the rest. For the next several hours the dog lay contentedly on the opened sofa while Joanna stood beside the full-length mirror and transferred her pain from flesh to canvas. As the gut wrenching self-portrait evolved, so did the early part of the night. Eventually Jo put down her paintbrush and looked at her watch. It was after eleven and although she knew it was late, she was desperate enough to dial anyway. Her sister-in-law picked up on the second ring. Jo apologized.

"I'm sorry. I hope I didn't wake you."

"Hardly. It's the only time I can get anything done around here and there's still a mountain of paperwork between my head and my pillow. Is everything okay?"

"No, not really."

It was not like Joanna to sound so forlorn.

"What is it honey? What's wrong?"

"I need to ask you something and I need an honest answer."

"Okay."

"Are you happy?"

Without knowing why—out of the blue—she was being asked, Stacy tried to put her answer in context.

"Well, let's see… after supper tonight your brother finally finished the tile work in the downstairs bathroom he'd been promising to do for the last six months, I'm currently riding around with a bumper sticker on my car proudly announcing that my child is on the honor roll and we just found out that your oldest nephew's orthodontia work won't be quite as extensive as we thought which means there just might be a little extra money for me to splurge on a new bedspread for a bed on which I actually had some fairly decent sex once in the last three months. So to answer your question, if I don't look back or ahead any further than that, then as we speak life is good and yes, I suppose I'm happy." Stacy had a question of her own. "While it's awfully nice to know you care, why the sudden interest in my happiness?

Joanna didn't know where or how to begin.

"I'm in love, Stac. Hopelessly, madly in love."

Jo's sister-in-law had always been exceptionally quick witted.

"Honey, you' can't be carrying a torch for me this long. It's just not healthy."

With Joanna's laughter came a hint of bravado.

"You wish."

"Maybe at times…" Stacy became more serious. "What makes me think you're not talking about Gayle either?"

Joanna felt utterly lost.

"I met someone Stac… someone incredible… someone amazing."

"And let me guess… someone *attached*?"

"Not just attached. Someone with a husband, a kid, a dog and a house with a white picket fence."

"Oh dear, the fence is never a good sign."

Stacy's attempt to lift her sister-in-law's spirits failed miserably.

"I don't know what to do. I feel as though I'm going out of my fucking mind."

Stacy closed the door to the den where Joanna's brother lay asleep, then took the phone and locked herself in the bathroom. For good measure, she lowered her voice to a whisper.

"And how does she feel about you?"

"I think she feels the same way but I'm not sure." Jo began to pace. "Christ, I don't know anything anymore."

"That doesn't sound like you."

"I know. That's what scares me."

"I'm still not sure how *my* happiness factors into all this."

"I just figured your life came as close to hers as I could get."

"Why, because we both have a husband and kids?"

"Yeah."

"So in other words, you'd like to apply a 'one size fits all' assessment of our fulfillment?"

"Something like that. What do you think?"

"Well aside from being personally offended on her behalf as well as my own, I think it's a grossly oversimplified approach to a very complex issue."

There was no mistaking the change in Stacy's voice.

"Great, now *you're* angry with me too."

"Not angry, just disappointed. You're a lot smarter than that Jo. You should know better."

"Aw c'mon Stac... now you're sounding like a mother."

"I believe that's why you called."

Stacy knew her sister-in-law felt foolish. Her heart melted protectively around Jo's.

"She must be very special."

"She is."

"Have the two of you slept together?"

"We haven't even kissed."

"Now that *really* doesn't sound like you!"

Joanna's mind flooded with memories.

"We've come so close, so many times. I think we're both terrified to cross that line."

"And rightly so. It takes a certain courage for each of us to know our own heart. It takes an even greater courage for us to follow it." Stacy paused. "Tell me everything."

Jo explained all the overlapping events and emotions of the past month leading up to Beth's leaving and her desperate call tonight. Stacy listened with a concerned heart to all of it.

"Honey, I can't tell you what to do. What I can tell you for sure is that from the sound of it you're playing with fire... and I'm not talking about the kind of heat made in a bed. I'm talking about the kind of blaze that has the potential to destroy this woman's life, especially after everything she's been through."

Joanna didn't need to be reminded of all that was at stake.

"Never mind, I'll figure it out."

"No, let's talk some more."

"There's really nothing left to say. I'm sorry I bothered you."

"You weren't a bother when you were eleven and you're not a bother now." Her voice lightened with the sweetness of a summer evening long ago. "Remember that night you were so jealous that your brother was taking me to the drive-in that you punctured his tires?"

"How could I forget? You wound up staying home and teaching me how to slow dance instead."

"Yes, well I think I may have created a monster. You've been used to getting your way with women ever since. You're not eleven anymore Jo. You can't go around letting the air out of people's tires. If you want her to stay, you've got to do better than that."

"Maturity certainly cuts down my options, doesn't it?"

"I'm afraid so but the truth is ultimately a lot harder to change than a tire.

She can walk away from a flat a lot more easily than her feelings."

"Does that brother of mine realize how lucky he is?"

"He gives me every reason to believe he does."

"He'd better! Do me a favor, don't mention why I called."

"I won't."

"Stac… just for the record, it's nice to know that you're happy."

"I honestly am." Now it was Jo's happiness that remained unclear. "Will you still be coming home at the end of the summer?"

"I left a lot behind. I'll be coming *back*, but I'd hardly call it *home*."

Stacy knew enough to leave it at that.

"I'm always here if you want to talk."

"I know."

"Jo?"

"Yeah?"

"Promise me you'll be careful. From the sound of it this woman's heart is capable of many things, but I have a feeling it's never learned how to love *just a little*."

Joanna promised, then hung up. She leaned against the frame of the screen door and peered up at the star-filled sky that both separated her from and connected her to the woman she loved. In the light of a nearly full moon she could make out the two coffee mugs still sitting along the edge of the pool. Beckoned by the painful reminder, Jo reached for her denim jacket and an open bottle of wine. She would need both to endure the chill of the mountain air and the long hours between darkness and morning.

The doting staff at 'The Shangri-La Day Spa and Salon' had somehow managed to erase all but the deepest traces of Beth's heartache. From the penetrating massage to the tips of her new highlight, Beth emerged from the revolving doors certainly looking, if not *feeling,* like a new woman. Though unenthusiastic about being primped and pampered for so many hours, it was impossible to ignore the second glances from more than one stranger along the Boston streets. By the time they'd reached the art show, Rheeta had gone from feeling proud of her radiant Pygmalion to feeling downright jealous. When Beth suggested they separate for a while, Rheeta was quick to agree and the two wandered off in different directions.

As she drifted aimlessly from one booth to the next, Beth's heart searched for Joanna everywhere in the crowd much like it had searched for her son in the years following his death. At one point Beth noticed a young lesbian couple a few booths away. She found herself staring longingly as they stood with their arms around one another, looking at one particular painting. Beth hovered more closely to eavesdrop on their conversation, which centered around whether or not to splurge on the expensive piece. Eventually they agreed that the painting would make the perfect anniversary present and look great over their bed. As the couple waited for the artist to wrap their new acquisition, their jubilation spilled over into their affection. They kissed openly, indifferent to the public eye. Beth couldn't recall ever feeling so jealous. The women couldn't have been more than thirty. She'd already had two children by then. Their lives seemed open to all kinds of possibilities. Hers felt all but sealed. Struggling with her own innermost longing, the carefree ease of their intimacy nearly broke Beth's heart. Lost in her turmoil, she had no idea that Rheeta had been eyeing things too. Sizing up Beth's intense fascination with the couple, Rheeta immediately swooped in. She locked her arm in her friend's and whisked her out of danger.

"Maybe an art show wasn't a good idea after all."

Without mentioning a word about what she had just witnessed or what she suspected it had to do with Joanna, Rheeta picked up their pace.

"Let's go! Next stop... Chez Amour."

"I'm afraid to ask. What's Chez Amour?"

"It's an upscale intimate apparel boutique... much like Victoria's Secret, only a thousand times more expensive."

Buying something ultra feminine had always managed to rescue Rheeta from the more complicated perils of womanhood. Since Beth was a woman, Rheeta naturally assumed it would work for her too. Beth protested—Rheeta insisted—and the women were on their way.

As soon as Beth caught sight of Chez Amour's window display, Rheeta had to drag her through the door. Surrounded by sultry manikins dressed in provocative undergarments, Beth could not remember the last time she'd felt so insecure and out of place. She pulled Rheeta close and demanded to know what they were doing there.

"We're getting you something to wear to dinner tonight. Preferably something that doesn't make you look so... *motherly*."

"I *am* a mother! A low cut dress and push-up bra isn't going to change that!"

Rheeta was on a personal mission.

"Well for once in your life you're going to be something else! Tonight you're going to be someone sophisticated and seductive, even if it's only 'til the stroke of midnight."

Beth considered her friend's intention, then turned and headed directly for the door.

"This is ridiculous. I'm getting out of here!"

Rheeta grabbed Beth's arm and held her in place.

"Your terms were 'no lectures and no meddling'. You never said no satin and lace." She shoved Beth toward her favorite saleswoman. "Eva, meet Beth…my oldest and dearest friend in the world."

Eva, a beautiful young girl with the figure worthy of flaunting, extended her hand.

"How do you do?"

Rheeta held Beth out by the shoulders as if presenting a specimen.

"I want to transform this little cocooned caterpillar into an alluring butterfly."

Eva was confident.

"Well, you've brought her to the right place."

Beth feigned an awkward smile. Though 'Eva the perfect' was easily half Beth's age she was as seasoned a saleswoman as they came. Sensing Beth's reluctance, she reached for her virgin customer's hand.

"Come on. I'm sure we can find something that will make you and Rheeta happy."

Beth was unenthusiastic.

"It's never been done before."

Eva smiled reassuringly.

"Trust me. I've been known to work miracles."

"Good, 'cause that's what it'll take."

As Eva led Beth toward the racks of evening apparel, Rheeta followed eagerly behind. Beth turned and confronted her.

"Go away! I refuse to do this with you standing over me."

Rheeta threw up her hands and backed off.

"Fine! Just promise me you'll think 'elegant French restaurant', not 'PTA meeting'." Rheeta leaned close and whispered into Eva's ear. "Money is no object. I want everything changed! Everything that shows…," Rheeta winked, "and everything that doesn't."

Eva had her orders. Catching the resistance in Beth's eyes, she understood both the delicate nature and the largeness of her mission. Only the least scandalous and most tasteful items made it into the dressing room. One by one Eva helped Beth try them on, reminding her that a woman's body is all in her mind. In a little over an hour the mission was complete. Relieved to be back in her own clothes, Beth thanked Eva for her patience as well as her unspoken understanding. Though Rheeta was dying of curiosity, Beth spitefully refused to let her see what she'd picked out. Rheeta was none the less thrilled just to be spending large sums of money and carrying out shopping bags filled with obscenely expensive merchandise. In their co-mingled states of euphoria and fatigue, the women returned to the townhouse to rest before dinner. For Beth, the day had felt endless. Behind the closed door of the lavish guestroom she sat on the edge of the bed, her arms wrapped tightly around her own waist. Consumed by her longing for Joanna, she fought hard to compress gut-wrenching sobs into a stream of quiet tears.

Saturday was no less of an ordeal for the woman Beth left behind. Joanna awakened at the crack of dawn with the muscles of her back as sore as her heart. Confronted by the painful sight of the two mugs, the challenge of getting on with her day loomed large. Jo lifted herself out of the chaise, collected her denim jacket and empty bottle of wine and dragged herself back to the carriage house for a shower. BJ's wagging tail was Jo's only source of comfort as she shuffled toward the bathroom.

As Jo toweled off, she considered her options for this most miserable of days. Still raging from a sense of abandonment, she could get revenge by trespassing through every inch of Beth's house—exposing everything that was not hers to expose—touching everything that was not hers to touch. Such a violation of Beth's privacy was not beyond the demands of Joanna's pain. In the midst of her deprivation she knew she could convince herself that the rules of decency did not apply. Or, she could take the high road and return to the sacred place where Beth herself had so often gone to sooth her own soul. She could lean upon the great rock that had become Beth's comfort and expose herself to the same open stretch of sky, hoping that 'The Gods' might look down and—in pity—grant her even the slightest relief. As she wrestled with her choice, BJ's watchful eyes reminded Jo of her own conscience. She tended to his needs, quickly threw some art supplies in the car and drove off before she could change her mind.

Steeped in distraction, Joanna found her way back to the cloistered spot purely by heart. The setting was just as breathtaking as she'd remembered. As Jo crossed the grassy knoll in the direction of the large boulder, she recalled the portfolio of sketches Dell had placed on her lap. Still unnerved by the eerie coincidence, Jo hesitated. But the tranquility beckoned to her, offering a serenity greater than her fear. Settled against the rock she pressed the full weight of her life against its surface, confessing the secrets of her heart to the one carved into its base. In its company, Jo felt Beth's presence everywhere around her. Everyplace her eyes rested another memory unfolded, each as merciful and merciless as 'The Gods' could render.

As the two women moved separately through their day, their suffering united them in ways greater than their separation. By late afternoon as Beth was being dragged through the unlikely door of Chez Amour, Joanna sought equally uncommon refuge at Dell's. Though she had had no intention of stopping at the antique shop on her way back, that is precisely where her heart had led her. Each time she knocked on the locked door a little harder and a little more desperately. In her infinite wisdom, Dell knew when *not* to be available. This time, the shopkeeper sat perfectly still just inside the adjoining garage. Well aware of Joanna's pain, Dell cracked open the back door to let Bridey out so that she could offer whatever unspoken consolation Jo would allow. As Joanna peered in through the plate glass door, Bridey meowed and rubbed herself up against Jo's leg. Jo tried knocking one last time but Dell continued to ignore her. Discouraged and annoyed with herself for stopping in the first place, Jo kicked the door, scowled at Bridey and got back in her car.

Dell listened intently as Jo drove off. Though she knew it was safe to come out, she chose to remain in the garage surrounded by trunks filled with Arthur's belongings. She had been clutching a piece of his mother's jewelry. Dell opened her hand and revealed a gold, heart-shaped locket with initials A&E inscribed on its face. The date 6/28/1886 and the words 'forever in my heart' were inscribed on the back. What she knew about the two photographs inside moved the large, burly woman to tears.

Beth stood in the parlor of Rheeta's townhouse staring numbly out of the window. Ready for the last half hour, she'd been waiting patiently for Rheeta to make her grand entrance so they could leave for the restaurant. Beth's heart had grown even heavier for the extra time she had to think. The only interest she had in their evening plans was getting another step closer to the end of an emotionally embattled day. Early tomorrow morning she would be leaving to visit her son at camp, requiring yet another round of participation and interest she couldn't imagine mustering. Suddenly it felt as though her entire existence had come down to faking everything that was expected of her. It saddened Beth to realize what an expert she had become at it.

As she descended the staircase bejeweled and overly dressed, Rheeta announced her own entrance.

"Let the evening begin!"

Beth turned around to grant the silly woman the audience she craved, but this time Rheeta herself was struck by her friend's beauty. With Eva's help, Beth had selected an exquisitely simple ensemble. A sheer flowing kimono graced a sensual, silk V-neck camisole with the merest wisp of spaghetti straps. The matching skirt accentuated the womanly curve of Beth's hips. Her own understated gold necklace and earrings complimented the soft highlights and sheen of her hair. Unlike Rheeta's heavily applied make-up, Beth's skin glowed naturally, enhanced only by the slightest touch of lip-gloss and eye shadow. Rheeta gasped.

"My God, you're stunning! Look what I've created."

Beth already felt self conscious enough in her lacy undergarments and strapless bra. She did not need to be scrutinized further.

"Can we just go?"

Rheeta stood with her hands on her hips.

"I don't know if I want to be seen in public with you. No one will even notice *me*."

"I promise to direct all interested parties to you. Besides, I hardly think that's true."

"Have you looked at yourself at all?"

She dragged Beth over to the full-length mirror in the entrance hall. Looking from the tips of her new sandals to the flow of her newly styled hair, all Beth could see was the sadness in her own eyes. Rheeta pointed out everything else in between.

"No wonder Ben hasn't left your side since the day I introduced the two of you."

'Never left my side and never exposed my soul', Beth thought to herself as she eyed the telephone across the room. Her heart ached for Joanna's voice.

"I think I should call home, just to make sure everything is okay."

Rheeta grabbed their bags and ushered her toward the front door.

"Bad idea! Let's go."

Beth was not alone in her longing. At precisely the same hour, Joanna found herself poring over the series of photographs she'd taken of Beth the day of their picnic. She had made a special stop at the drugstore on her way back from Dell's to pick up the developed roll of film. Her eyes hungrily devoured each and every print. The day before she had angrily discarded the slip of paper on which Beth had left Rheeta's number. Now, unable to bear another moment of separation, Jo reached into the garbage and retrieved the crumpled paper. Pacing back and forth without the slightest notion of what she would say, Jo picked up the phone and dialed Rheeta's number. Just as it began to ring, Steve appeared on the doorstep with a six-pack. Joanna slammed the receiver back on its cradle, shoved the slip of paper into the pocket of her jeans and gathered up the stack of prints.

"C'mon in. I was just calling to order a pizza. The line was busy."

Steve put four of the bottles in the refrigerator and popped two open.

"No you weren't. You were calling Beth."

In a way, Jo was grateful for his smug assumption that helped seal her resolve. With her innermost conflicts now hardened into a solid block of denial, it would be his persistence to get at the truth pitted against her stubborn refusal to admit it. Up 'til now Steve had gone along with her rules, but tonight he intended to dig in like never before. Sensing his determination, Jo turned the radio up to challenge his course.

"One way or the other we're gonna' talk about this Jo."

She responded by deliberately turning the volume up even higher.

"Sorry but I can't hear you."

Le Chateau was every bit as trendy and pretentious a restaurant as Beth dreaded it would be. As the maitre d' showed the women to their table, Rheeta pretended not to mind that Beth drew considerably more stares. Beth simply would have preferred to have been invisible. The women were seated, their chairs politely pushed in and a leather-bound wine list extended. Since Beth couldn't have cared less, she was more than happy to let Rheeta make the selection. Beth fidgeted with her napkin while her friend swirled and sampled the first sip, then nodded approvingly. The waiter filled their glasses, recited the specials and bowed discretely, leaving the pair to peruse the menu. With her stomach in knots, Beth wanted nothing more than a soothing bowl of French onion soup and some bread. Ignoring Beth's preference, Rheeta ordered full dinners for each of them. Waiting for the first course to arrive, Rheeta scanned the room with the eyes of a hawk scouting for prey.

"Don't look now, but that gorgeous silver haired man at the bar is cruising you."

Beth was mortified. She could barely bring herself to look up. Rheeta tried to control her jealousy.

"Didn't I tell you that you look stunning tonight? The least you can do is acknowledge him."

Like a well-mannered child, Beth raised her eyes and returned the man's smile. As she did so she intentionally lifted the water glass with her left hand so that he would see her wedding band. The women were halfway through their appetizers when the waiter returned with a bottle of champagne. He addressed Beth directly.

"Excuse me Madame but the gentleman at the bar hopes that you will accept this as a compliment to your beauty which he has asked me to tell you has not only enhanced this room but his life."

Beth was speechless. She had expected that their polite exchange would have been the end of it. The waiter stood by politely.

"Will you accept?"

Rheeta responded for her.

"Yes, of course she'll accept."

Though the flattering gesture was not directed at her, Rheeta looked over and flirted shamelessly. Beth extended her own shy and appreciative smile. The waiter filled their glasses and left the bottle in the champagne bucket beside the table. Rheeta glanced at the label.

"Well he may have chosen the wrong broad but he certainly has impeccable taste in bubbly."

Beth leaned toward her dinner companion, pretending to be engaged in general conversation.

"I can't believe it. I'm absolutely certain he saw my wedding band."

Rheeta sipped her champagne and rolled her eyes.

"Honestly honey, it's a ring not a chastity belt. You're so painfully naïve."

"Does *everybody* just go after whomever they desire?"

"Yes! And it might surprise you to know that more often than not, they get to them."

"We're obviously living in two different worlds."

"Well, I'm living in the *real* one with everybody else while you, my dear, are living in a little time-warped bubble."

Beth looked at her wedding band.

"Are you saying I'm the only person who still believes in the sanctity of this thing?"

"I'm saying you need to lighten up. A little harmless flirting in a marriage is what 'hamburger helper' is to the same old meal."

Beth stared at her ring. She preferred not to think about all the times this summer her feelings for Joanna make her wish she wasn't wearing it. Her heart sank in the renewed conflict.

"Let's just drop it."

"Fine by me, toots. Personally I've always enjoyed wearing a rock a lot more than a ball and chain."

Apparently Rheeta was well acquainted with many who dined at Le Chateau and much of the remaining dinner conversation consisted of a rundown of who *was*—and who *had been*—sleeping with whom. Rheeta seemed to derive a certain thrill in sharing the timeline of heartbreak and betrayal, requiring little of Beth's response. Dinner was beautifully presented, exorbitantly priced and entirely wasted on her. Rheeta looked at Beth's barely touched plate.

"Honey, please don't tell me you're dieting because you certainly don't have to watch that waistline of yours."

For Rheeta, life held no other consideration than how something might affect her appearance. In a moment of sheer insanity, Beth confessed the truth.

"I hate the way I left things with Joanna…"

Rheeta rolled her eyes.

"Oh her." She dabbed her mouth with the linen napkin as if subconsciously still wiping away Joanna's kiss. "Beth, you've *got* to get that woman out of your mind."

Beth felt defeated. It wasn't as though she hadn't been trying all day.

"I just can't."

"You can and you will!" Rheeta signaled the waiter for the check. "I'm going to the little girls' room and then we're getting out of here. I know just what you need."

Beth was already regretting her honesty.

"I'm already exhausted Rhee and I have to get up early tomorrow, remember?"

Determined to save her best friend, Rheeta pushed her chair out and stood up.

"I'm sorry but desperate times call for desperate measures!"

On her way to the powder room Rheeta made a deliberate stop at the bar. She sat down on the stool beside Beth's admirer.

"Thanks for the bubbly, good lookin'."

The man finished his drink.

"Your friend is lovely."

"Yes, but altogether unavailable. Now moi, on the other hand…"

Rheeta shamelessly scribbled her own name and number on the cocktail napkin and stuck it in the pocket of his jacket. Once Rheeta descended the stairs to the restrooms, the gentleman paid his tab, got up and approached Beth's table. She was noticeably uneasy. A fleeting smile from across the room was one thing, but she certainly wasn't prepared for a more personal encounter. He was even more handsome at close range.

"Did you enjoy the champagne?"

Beth nodded shyly.

"Yes, thank you."

"I hope I didn't offend you, it's just that I couldn't help but notice that you're the most beautiful woman in this room."

"The gesture was very sweet." Beth began to chew nervously on her lip. "It's just that I'm..."

He stopped her.

"You don't have to explain. If you weren't already spoken for I'd drop to one knee on this very spot and propose to you right now." His charm was disarming. "I'll spend the rest of my life imagining how extraordinary it might have been had you said yes."

The would-be suitor reached for Beth's left hand—the one with the wedding band—and brought it to his lips.

"Your husband is a very lucky man."

Without saying another word the man left discreetly. Once Rheeta returned, Beth immediately excused herself. She needed time in the ladies room to regain her composure. Nothing like that had ever happened to her before. She thought about the irony of the stranger's compliment. Lately her husband had reason to feel many things—the least of which was '*lucky*'. Beth stood in front of the sink staring into the mirror. However superficial, the transformation was undeniable. She couldn't help but wonder what her smitten admirer would think once the clock struck midnight and Rheeta's spell of illusions and fantasy suddenly fell away.

Beth's unlikely fairy godmother was ready and waiting when she returned to the table. The roomful of eyes that had followed Beth to her table now followed her to the door. Having received far more attention than she was comfortable with, Beth was relieved to finally be outside.

After he'd been generously tipped, the young parking attendant barely had time to step out of harms way before Rheeta peeled out of the parking lot and onto the street.

"Buckle up babe... you're in for the treat of your life!"

Beth's head fell back against the seat.

"Please slow down and tell me where we're going."

Rheeta did neither.

"Don't you like surprises?"

"I've already had enough surprises this summer to last me a lifetime."

"I'm taking you to the G-Spot. It's a club, like Chippendales... with the hottest male dancers you've ever seen in your life."

Beth's head shot forward.

"Over my dead body!"

"I believe the objective is *arousal*, honey, not death. The 'G' stands for grinding groins... and lots of 'em!"

Rheeta looked at the clock on the dash and sped up.

"We've got twenty minutes. If we hurry we can still make the ten o'clock show."

"Rheeta, I demand you turn this car around right now!"

"Don't push me Beth. As it is you're the only person who knows my real age and I've let you live this long."

While Beth seethed, Rheeta defended the plans.

"Oh c'mon Bethie, live a little. You've been shut in for so long you wouldn't know what you needed if it were right there under your own roof." Rheeta caught herself. "Oops! Bad example. Trust me, that woman is definitely *not* what you need."

"And you think some guy in a jockstrap thrusting his crotch in my face is?"

"Not just one crotch honey, dozens of them! Each and every one with a basket to die for!"

The erotic, all male review wasn't just Rheeta's idea of a good time. Apparently half the female population of Boston thought so too. The line outside the club wound all the way around the block. Much to Beth's relief, she was certain they'd never get in. Naively she hadn't considered that Rheeta knew the bouncer could be easily bought. He whispered something into Rheeta's ear, she slipped something into his hand and the pair were quickly ushered past the ropes. A number of women who'd been waiting on the snaking line booed as they went through the door. While Beth would have gladly traded places with any one of them, Rheeta seemed unfazed by their lack of fortune. Once inside, after a few more exchanged whispers and slights of hand, the women were led through a crowded maze of tables and chairs and seated just inches from the footlights of the runway. With only minutes to show time the smoke-filled club pulsated with restless, rowdy women from eighteen to eighty. Rheeta was ecstatic to be one of them.

"Still drinking what you did back in college?"

Beth nodded begrudgingly. Rheeta shook her head.

"Some things never change."

Beth sighed inwardly. If only that were true for all her preferences. Rheeta motioned to the waiter.

"A whiskey sour for my old roomie and a double shot of tequila here."

Beth looked around, trying to comprehend the insanity of her surroundings. The noise level was almost intolerable. Disco music blasted from the sound system. Beth needed to know the length of her ordeal.

"How long is the show?"

Just inches apart, Rheeta couldn't hear above the noise.

"What?"

"Beth leaned closer and shouted directly into Rheeta's ear.

"I said, how long is the show?"

"Sadly, never long enough."

The waiter returned with their drinks. Just when Beth was certain the decibel level couldn't get any higher without doing permanent damage to her inner ear, it was cranked up even higher. The room shook with hundreds of women chanting and stomping to the music. At precisely ten o'clock a husky male voice broke through over the loudspeaker.

"Everyone here swear she's over eighteen?"

The crowd roared back and then came the moment every woman in the club—except for Beth—had been waiting for. The room went dark and suddenly several beams of light ignited the stage from every direction. The popular disco hit 'It's Raining Men' rose up from the floor boards and vibrated through the frame of the chairs. Not that anyone had remained in them except for Beth and one elderly woman who looked as if she would have gladly sold her anniversary pearls for the legs to stand with the rest of her chanting tribe. The excitement of the frenzied women who had come to worship at the Shrine Of The Groin escalated to a fever pitch as one after another of their saviors appeared through the parted slit in the dark velvet curtains. Like gifts from the heavens they came—each answering another prayer, each thrusting himself at the swooning mob that reached up hoping to touch the flesh of their most sacred fantasies. The thunderous reception for one rolled into the next as the stream of costumed dancers bumped and grinded their way down the runway. First the marine, followed by the cowboy, the patrolman, the biker and the construction worker—each offering his god-like body up for the worshippers collective salvation. Encased in the pandemonium, Beth retreated into her own private world—a world now entirely dominated by her inescapable desire for another woman. The more the vulture-like crowd demanded of the male strippers, the more Beth quietly ached for the woman she loved. She ached for her lips, her arms, her breasts and the exquisite burning of Joanna's eyes. Suddenly a lifetime of resentments rose to the surface and struck Beth hard. She became furious with Rheeta for dragging her to this ridiculous place and furious with herself for allowing it. Beth had had enough. She leaned over to her chanting friend.

"Is there an intermission?"

Rheeta cupped her ear, implying she couldn't hear over the noise. Beth had to repeat the question two more times before Rheeta finally responded.

"Yes" she squealed as her eyes remained fixed on the stage. "That's when half the room races to the bathroom to wipe themselves… and I don't mean after they've peed!"

"Good, because that's when I'm getting the hell out of here."

Rheeta continued clapping to the beat of the music.

"Please don't tell me this offends you."

"I would actually have to care enough to be offended. I just want to get out of here."

Rheeta began to whine.

"Can't you at least *pretend* you're having a good time?"

"I'm sick of pretending Rheeta. I'm leaving during the intermission, with or without you."

Rheeta was exasperated. She had not taken her eyes off the stage.

"Oh, all right! If you insist on going, I'll leave with you. At least for now can you please just let *me* enjoy the show? A woman can't live on batteries alone you know."

Rheeta finished her second shot of tequila and began waving a $20 bill in the air. As she watched her friend shove it into a dancer's jockstrap, Beth sat rigid—biding her time. A misfit in the audience and a misfit in her own life, she needed to believe that somehow she would survive this mistake too.

Joanna had not sculpted seriously since art school but tonight her challenge went far beyond what her innate talent could achieve. As she studied the intricate musculature of Steve's torso she struggled to stay focused on the slowly evolving figure. Her lack of concentration was impossible for Steve to ignore. Steve had hoped that the wine they'd shared with the pizza might have weakened Joanna's resistance. He cared too deeply for both women not to at least try. Looking for a place to start, he let his eyes wander around the room. The place was a mess. The mattress of the sofa, still out.

"Don't you ever make up the bed anymore?"

"Since when did you start handing out the 'Good Housekeeping Seal Of Approval'?"

"I'm just saying, the place is beginning to look like the way you've been feeling." He rubbed his neck. "How 'bout a break?"

Jo reluctantly agreed. As he stepped down off the modeling platform he caught her staring hopelessly at the studies of Beth.

"Can't get her off your mind, can you?"

Joanna remained intentionally silent while she wiped her hands on a rag. Steve stretched his legs figuring it wise to stay limber—in case she attacked. He walked over for another look at the portraits.

"I still say it's all there in her eyes."

"In case you haven't noticed, she's gone. What's that say?"

Steve poured them each more wine. He handed Jo her glass.

"It says I'm right."

The remark set her off.

"Then suppose you tell me why the hell she left!"

Like a seasoned detective working a case, Steve pieced together all the clues.

"She left because it was the only way to get you to stay. My guess is at some point things got pretty raw between the two of you, enough for you guys to need some space. Beth figured she had to come back. You *didn't*. She couldn't risk letting you be the one to go." He walked over to Joanna's self-portrait. "I'd say your eyes look every bit as empty and sad as hers."

Jo hated that he was right. She turned her anger on him.

"Wanna' know what I see when I look into *yours*? I see someone who's hungry to feel pain. Someone so fucking happy-go-lucky he can't muster any of his own so he's got to go looking for it in other people's lives."

"Is that what you really think?"

A part of her did. A part of her didn't. Either way Jo could not afford to let him get any closer to the truth.

"Yeah, it is! I think you need something really dark to validate your writing and when you look inside you keep coming up empty." She poked him resentfully in the chest. "Suffering isn't transferable. I'm sick of being your goddamn muse. You're like some freak of nature! No matter what happens you've always got a shit-ass smile on your face and some lame piece of advice from your grandpa. Let it get messy man! Let it unwind! Let it hurt!"

Joanna heard her own words. She realized that for the first time in her own life, meeting Beth had forced her to do just that. The bittersweet rewards of that pain were hard won. Jo wasn't about to let anyone, including Steve, steal it from her for the sake of inspiration. She finished what was left of her wine and slammed the glass down.

"Get your own damn heartache!"

"I let myself fall in love with you."

"Yeah you did and when I rejected you, what happened? The next morning you were singing in the damn shower."

Steve considered Jo's observation.

"Maybe you're right. I'll have to think about it, But don't try and change the subject. We're talking about you and Beth."

"How many times do I have to say this? There is no '*me and Beth*'!"

"Now who's avoiding the truth?"

"Okay, you wanna' talk about Beth? Here's what I have to say: fuck her!"

"You can be so eloquent when you're pissed."

She pushed past him.

"And you can be such a royal pain in the ass!"

"That's it, isn't it? I'll bet you'd like fuck her."

Joanna lashed back.

"Yeah, and I just bet you'd like to watch."

"What red-blooded straight guy wouldn't?" His face became serious. "But something tells me if you two were ever to get together, three would definitely be a crowd."

Joanna tried distancing herself from the notion. It simply hurt too much to think about.

"It would never work out anyway. Even if there was nothing else standing in our way, we're much too different."

"You probably don't want to hear what my grand-daddy had to say about the strength of opposites."

"You're right, I don't."

"I'll tell you anyway. 'Son', he said, 'all those cross grains pressed up against each other is what makes plywood as strong a sheet of wood as they come. If you ever want to build yourself somethin' solid, build it with *that*'."

"Then let's test his little theory. Put all that dead weight of yours back on that platform and shut the hell up."

"Fine." Steve obligingly resumed his pose. "I'll use the time to think about what we both said." Watching Joanna pound away at the clay, he risked having it hurled at him. "Wouldn't hurt if you did the same."

Unlike Steve, Rheeta was not nearly as accommodating. Instead of offering silence, she badgered Beth all the way to the car.

"Have you completely forgotten how to have a good time?"

Beth got in and slammed the door.

"A good time?," she ranted, "my whole life is coming apart at the seams and you think watching a guy in a jockstrap performing some pseudo erotic dance is the cure? What do I have to say to make you understand? I'm sick of living a simulated life! Whatever it is I've been feeling, however terrifying, at least it's real."

Beth buried her face in her hands and Rheeta started to drive.

"Okay. I finally get it Bethie, but can we at least discuss this?"

"You have whatever time it takes to get us back to the townhouse."

That was fine with Rheeta. The shorter this conversation, the better.

"Okay then, once we're home we'll curl up on the sofa and talk about something else entirely. Something uncomplicated, like the good old days."

"No we won't! I'm through paying homage to the past. I'm forty-five years old. I haven't got that luxury anymore. I'm living in the present starting right now! As soon as we get back, I'm packing my things and driving home tonight. That's all there is to it."

"That's insane! What could you possibly be thinking?"

"I'm not letting myself think. For once in my life I'm just letting myself feel."

Rheeta waited for the light to turn green. She gripped the wheel and drove on.

"It's out of the question. I won't let you do this."

"Funny, I don't recall asking your permission."

Rheeta had never seen Beth like this before.

"It's after midnight!"

"Correct! The clock has struck twelve and your well-behaved little princess has turned back into a woman on the verge of a nervous breakdown. Sorry, the fairytale doesn't end according to plan."

"But you won't get home until after two and that's if you make it home at all in that rattling deathtrap of yours. Besides, didn't you say you've got to be up at the crack of dawn to visit Adam at camp?"

Beth had made up her mind.

"Believe me, I've squeezed much less important things into much less time."

Rheeta tried to reason with her friend.

"Obviously you're going back for that woman. What are you planning to do… burst into the carriage house and wake her out of a dead sleep?"

"If Jo's feeling what I am, sleep isn't an option. She'll still be awake."

"Well I'm sorry but I still don't like the idea. It's just not safe."

"For God's sake, it's not like I've never driven at night before."

"I'm not talking about the *drive* Beth, I'm talking about what's at the end of it."

"What's at the end of it is my home."

"Maybe it used to be, but don't let that white picket fence fool you. From what I saw, that little backyard of yours has become a field of landmines.

"One I need to cross. If I'm not killed on impact I'll send you a postcard from behind enemy lines."

Rheeta pulled onto her street, parked the Jag and turned to her friend.

"Honestly, I don't know how you can joke about this."

Beth got out of the car and slammed the door.

"I've never been more serious about anything in my life. I may not be the 'bon vivant' that you are but I'm not a child. Much as you refuse to see it, I'm a big girl Rhee—I have been for quite some time."

"Yes you are and that's precisely my point. Big girls shouldn't be racing back into the arms of other big girls."

Beth's heart clung to the possibility.

"If only she'll have me…"

Once inside, Beth stepped over the yapping poodle and headed straight upstairs. Rheeta scooped up the dog and followed close behind.

"You've lost your mind, you know that don't you?"

"Not my mind. My *heart*." Now in the doorway of the guest room, Beth turned around. "After Danny died I thought I would never feel anything ever again. Whatever small part of me still clung to life just gave up. I went from day to day, dead inside." Beth's eyes filled with wonder. "Then, from out of nowhere, she came along… this impossible, infuriating, intimidating, inspiring woman who floundering in her own life, has completely awakened *mine*."

Rheeta stroked the dog in her arms nervously.

"I'm begging you, don't do this." In a moment of rare reflection, Rheeta continued to plead with her friend. "My life's never been worth much… except maybe on paper… but yours, yours is worth fighting for."

"Don't you see? That's what I'm doing Rhee… fighting for my life! Not the one I have. The one I've always *wanted*. The one I think just maybe I can have with her."

"Are you forgetting she has a girlfriend?"

"They're not happy."

"Since when has that meant anything in a couple's life?"

"Are you really *that* jaded?"

"Are you really *that* naïve?"

Beth pushed Rheeta out of the way, but that hardly silenced her.

"Think of your family. What about them?"

"For the last twenty-three years all I've been doing is thinking of them. If I ever decide to pen my memoir I'll call it 'And Then There Was Me'."

Pierre leapt from Rheeta's arms and ran off. She didn't try to stop him. Her hands were full enough trying to corral her suddenly wild-hearted friend. She positioned herself in front of the closet, deliberately blocking Beth from the door.

"You're Ben's whole life... you know that."

"Then his life is about to get a lot more complicated. Now get out of my way!"

She shoved Rheeta aside, reached for her suitcase and flung it onto the bed. Rheeta tried to dissuade her.

"What if she doesn't feel the same way?"

"That's the whole point. How am I ever going to know? Would you have me just sit here on this bed swinging my legs while I pluck the petals off these daisies, reciting 'she loves me—she loves me not'?"

Rheeta followed Beth around as she collected her few toiletries. She marveled at how remarkably little Beth had packed for her visit.

"How in the world do you travel so light?"

"It comes with years of carrying around everyone else's baggage. It tends to get quite heavy. Whenever something had to be left behind, I got used to it always being mine."

As she continued to toss her clothes into her suitcase, Beth stared at her sweatshirt and jeans.

"I should change."

For a moment she wavered. Ultimately, getting on the road remained her priority.

"Oh to hell with it. I can't remember the last time I felt comfortable in my own skin. This ridiculous push-up bra is the least of my problems."

Her mind made up, Beth slammed the suitcase shut, pulled the zipper around and grabbed its handle. Rheeta positioned herself in the doorway.

"I won't let you do this."

"I'm warning you Rhee… don't make me knock you over that gilded banister because I swear I will!"

Rheeta grew increasingly uneasy. She had prayed it wouldn't come to this.

"Look, I think there's something you should know."

Beth was nearing the end of her patience.

"What is it now?"

"That night in the carriage house…." Rheeta drew a deep breath, half convinced it might be her last. "Joanna came on to me."

The unexpected confession paralyzed Beth. Her fingers tightened around the handle of the suitcase. She wouldn't allow herself to put it down. She wouldn't allow herself to consider the implication. More than anything she wanted to believe Rheeta was not above lying, or at the very least, terribly mistaken.

"Please Rhee, for as long as I've known you you've been convinced that *everyone* you meet finds you irresistible." She felt herself tremble with a sense of rage and betrayal. "I'm sure you were just imaging it."

How Rheeta wished that were true.

"Beth, listen to me. I know you think I live in my own little fantasy world and let's face it, I've never exactly been a slave to the truth but I swear, this wasn't something I concocted in my imagination. It really happened."

Rheeta appeared deeply upset—enough to make Beth wonder if she might be telling the truth. Rheeta looked into her friend's tortured eyes.

"I know I should have said something sooner."

Beth's heart twisted with bitterness and despair.

"Why didn't you?"

Rheeta had never seen her friends expression so vacant. She reached for her hand but Beth pulled away. Her voice evoked the image of words chiseled in stone.

"I asked you a question. Why didn't you say something that night?"

Rheeta began to pace.

"I was too upset. Nothing like that ever happened to me before. I couldn't bring myself to talk about it." She buried her face in her hands. "Anyway, I just thought you should know."

This time Beth's heart dropped along with her suitcase.

"Tell me exactly what happened."

"She kissed me."

Beth leaned against the wall to keep herself from collapsing. Her breathing became shallow.

"Did you kiss her back?"

"Yes. I'm embarrassed to admit I did."

Beth's sense of despair spiraled into confusion.

"I thought you found her loathsome?"

Rheeta's voice was smaller than it had ever been.

"She is beautiful. I was curious. I honestly can't explain it beyond that."

Beth tried to steady herself, unsure she would survive Rheeta's answer to her next question.

"Did it go any further?"

"We wound up on the bed."

Beth's throat tightened. Obviously Rheeta was right. Everyone just took whomever they wanted. Apparently her feelings for Jo were all one-sided. Rheeta recognized heartbreak when she saw it. Those were the facts and had she left it at that they would surely have stopped Beth from leaving. But Rheeta also knew that in this case the facts obscured the truth and in the end, she loved her friend too much to withhold it.

"There's something else you should know."

Beth already felt like a fool. She held up her hand to shield what little was left of her heart.

"I've heard enough."

"No, actually you haven't." Rheeta sacrificed what was left of her reputation. "It was just a game to her. I'd gone back to the carriage house to demand she stay away from you. The whole seduction was a sham… nothing more than payback intended to humiliate me. The truth is, I repulsed her. When I was too blind to see that, she took great pleasure in saying so." Rheeta raised her eyes and looked directly into Beth's. "On the other hand… I'm sure her feelings for you are quite real."

Beth understood the selflessness of Rheeta's confession.

"You didn't have to admit that. You know it would have kept me from going back."

Rheeta was already sorry. Emotional honesty had never served her well in the past.

"Please don't remind me. I'm sure I'll live to regret it when I hear that your whole life is in shambles."

Beth swept her friend up into her arms.

"I love you Rhee."

For once in her life, Rheeta's first concern was not about ruining her make-up. She pressed her cheek urgently against Beth's. The flesh of one caught the tears of the other.

"Honey please, promise me you'll be careful. Not just on the road, but once you get home."

"I'm through being careful Rhee… but whatever happens, I'll be okay."

Rheeta grasped Beth's hands in her own and squeezed tightly.

"I really need to believe that. I know I come off as being awfully shallow but the truth is I see a lot more than I care to. I always have. I guess I never quite managed to convince myself I was worth the trouble of a second glance. But you've always been different Bethie. You're so incredibly special. When it comes to your life I can't bury my head in my make-up case and pretend I don't see what's real… or what matters."

Beth wiped the smudged mascara from her friend's cheek.

"I know you always mean well Rhee, as convoluted as your thinking can be at times." She smiled. "Male strippers *included*."

Rheeta did not return Beth's lighthearted smile.

"I'm just afraid she could take that wonderful heart of yours and tear it to pieces."

"You're right, she could. But that's a risk I'm willing to take."

Beth picked up her suitcase and took Rheeta's hand.

"C'mon, walk me to my car."

The night air bristled with a mixture of anticipation and danger.

Rheeta stood by as Beth tossed her luggage into the back.

"Oh Bethie, I just hope you know what you're doing."

"To be perfectly honest I haven't the slightest idea what I'm doing, but I refuse to let that stop me. When I die, if I have any regrets at all I'd rather they be for the things I've done and not the things I haven't."

Rheeta rubbed her arms. Beth's decision chilled her from the inside out.

"I just hate to think you might be throwing your whole life away."

"My life is anything but whole. Contrary to how it looked, it never was. Not until I met Joanna."

Rheeta couldn't ignore the light in Beth's eyes. Still, all of it confused her.

"At least I was right about one thing. Everyone thought you looked beautiful tonight."

"There's only one person I want to notice. Only one person I want to exist for."

The impassioned response made Rheeta nervous. She'd never felt anything that deeply.

"Well even if you trade in everything else about your life, you really should consider keeping your hair like this. It looks fabulous."

Beth smiled gratefully.

"I appreciate everything Rhee, really. I know today must have cost you a fortune."

"I'll let my accountant worry about it. Besides, even if I had to live on cat food, you'd still be worth every penny."

Beth was sure Rheeta meant that with all her heart. She took her friend's hand.

"Thank you for inviting me. You've got a magnificent home."

Rheeta stared into her friend's eyes. In them she had always found acceptance.

"What I have are rooms full of expensive possessions. What *you* have is a '*home*'. Don't think for a minute I'm not painfully aware of the difference."

All at once Beth remembered the reasons she still adored this insanely egocentric woman—the reasons others never saw, let alone understood. She reached out and hugged her old roommate fiercely. Once again, tears streamed down both their cheeks. It was Rheeta who finally pulled away and managed a brave smile.

"Go on now. Get out of here. It's late enough as it is."

She opened the car door and shoved Beth in.

"Promise you'll call when you get home and let me know you're safe."

"Sorry Rhee…no can do. '*Safe*' is the last thing I expect to be once I get home."

"You're sure you have to do this?"

Beth slipped her hand under her friend's chin.

"I'm sure."

Rheeta shook her head, not at all sure how any of this came to be.

"And to think you were once the voice of reason… the pillar of the community… the mother of all convention. Let it be known from this night forth the destruction of civilization as we know it rests forever in your hands."

Beth sighed wistfully.

"If my happiness upsets the balance of the universe, then from here on in, so be it."

She turned the key in the ignition and Rheeta stepped back from the rumbling old car. Through the opened window, Beth reached out hungrily for more than her friend's arm.

"What was it like Rhee… her lips, her kiss?"

"Intoxicating."

Each stared silently into the other's eyes—one hoping desperately to know that kiss, the other hoping desperately to forget it. As Beth pulled away from the curb, Rheeta's description echoed in her heart until the network of bustling city streets gradually gave way to an open stretch of highway. The headlights of oncoming traffic—like sudden bursts of reckoning—came, then passed. One after another they formed a chain of memories that had once defined Beth's life—each one different in its revelation—each one bringing something forth—each one carrying something away. In her unconditional surrender Beth now forgave them all for the parts of herself forever lost in their unfolding. Under the vastness of the star-filled sky her life no longer felt measurable in years but rather something that blended with time itself. Joanna Cameron had mysteriously provided a piece of eternity for Beth to touch, to trust and to carry with her along the path of her own redemption—the same path that led her home tonight. At one point Beth reached over and turned on the radio. It was still tuned to the usual oldies station. 'Going Out Of My Head' by Little Anthony & The Imperials couldn't have been a more fitting song. It had always been in the sanctuary of darkness that Beth's heart would sing—and sob—its loudest. Alone in her car tonight, she did both. By the time her tears had dried, Beth wasn't sure whether she'd been at the wheel for minutes or hours. The answer came in the once again familiar landmarks of her neighborhood. Unlike her soul, the tree-lined streets were peaceful and still. It was just past two in the morning when Beth turned back into her driveway. Miraculously, the old green tank had gotten her home. Now, in those hours before dawn, she would have to trust her inexperienced heart to take her the rest of the way.

Chapter 19

It was after two in the morning when Beth pulled into her driveway. She was encouraged to find the lights in the carriage house still on. Set in her intentions to send Steve on his way, she made sure not to block him in. As she started across the once familiar backyard, everything in her life now felt vague and unreal except for the music emanating from the carriage house. The fact that Joanna had the radio tuned to the oldies station Beth had been listening to much of the ride home provided encouragement enough to steady her gait. By the glow of the moonlight she walked toward it—the music, the carriage house, the woman who stirred her soul. It was as if every part of her being was intent on fulfilling its destiny. The closer Beth got to the front porch, the more frightened but determined she became. Tonight there would be nothing left unspoken. She had not come this far to turn back now.

Steve had been willing to stay as long as Joanna wanted to work. He would model until dawn if the distraction helped her get through the night. For the moment, each had taken a much-needed break. Jo had gone to the alcove for a new supply of clay while Steve, clad in a pair of bathing trunks, leaned against the kitchen counter, chomping on a handful of chips. He'd just taken another mouthful when Beth unexpectedly appeared at the door. Even before he could clear his throat, 'The Dangerous Beth Garrison' let herself in. He raced over to greet her.

"Didn't you say you were spending the weekend in Boston?"

Beth remained stiff within the welcoming fold of his arms.

"I changed my mind."

She offered no other explanation. Given the nature of the women's unfinished business, Steve knew that the tension of that moment would pale by comparison to what was soon to come. He tried to warn Jo about Beth's unannounced return.

"Hey, look who's back" he called out just as Jo came around the hall with a fresh brick of clay.

The sight of Beth stopped Joanna's heart mid beat. She shielded herself the only way she knew how.

"What happened, did Rheeta walk past a full-length mirror and forget all about you?"

Beth turned in the direction of Jo's voice. The sudden sway of her dress caught Steve's eye. In all the tension, he hadn't yet gotten a good look at her.

"Wow, you look sensational!" He nudged Joanna. "Doesn't she?"

Jo wouldn't permit herself even the most fleeting glance. It was as if her whole body sensed the danger of Beth's beauty. Deliberately avoiding his question, she moved past both of them and slammed the brick of clay down onto the sculpting pedestal. With Beth's eye boring down upon her back, Joanna began to rip off small chunks of clay and knead them between her fingers. She motioned for Steve to resume his pose.

Caught in the raging crosscurrent of the women's unresolved desire, Steve was afraid to move. Despite his uncertainly, he climbed back up onto the modeling platform and waited for whatever would happen next. When it became obvious that Beth had no intention of leaving, Jo took bittersweet revenge in dismissing her.

"In case it's not apparent, I'm in the middle of something."

'The Dangerous Beth Garrison' fired back.

"In case it's not apparent to *you*, my driving back here in the middle of the night brings whatever you're doing to an immediate end!"

Though he dared not move a muscle, deep inside Steve applauded Beth's defiance. Knowing it would challenge her own, Jo was less appreciative of Beth's courage. She tried stonewalling.

"I hate to disappoint you but I have nothing to say."

"Well I do and you're going to listen. You, Steve, are putting your clothes on and leaving… right now!"

"Yes ma'am!"

Wanting nothing more than to escape before things really escalated, he leaped from the platform and reached for his jeans. Joanna tried to stop him.

"Don't listen to her."

Steve hastily gathered his things.

"She's right Jo. You guys need some time alone."

Without stopping to tie the laces of his sneakers, he grabbed his T-shirt and the opened bag of chips.

Joanna gripped his arm as though clinging to the side of a lifeboat. She was desperate to prove she would survive this night.

"I'll call you later. We'll go for breakfast."

Steve had his own hunch about where the treacherous hours between then and dawn would lead, and a booth at Trudy's wasn't one of them.

Moving quickly he kissed each of the women on the cheek, then fled for his life.

The screen door slammed behind him and suddenly the music coming from the radio was the only sound left in the room. That, and the wretched pounding inside each of the women's chests. Joanna began to move about, as if to clean up.

"What was the matter? Afraid I'd let BJ starve just to get even with you?"

Beth answered quietly.

"No..."

Jo kept moving.

"Then why *are* you here?"

Beth followed Jo with her eyes

"I'm not sure, but whatever it is I'm tired of trying to figure it out by myself."

Jo hid behind a wall of indignation.

"You had no right to barge in and throw Steve out like that."

"He's a writer. One day the melodrama will serve as inspiration."

Joanna kept to a deliberate pace until finally Beth could wait no more.

"Jo, what are you doing?"

"What's it look like? I'm cleaning up."

"No... what are you doing to *me*... to my *life*?"

"I don't know what you're talking about."

"I think you do. We need to talk."

For the briefest of moments, Jo let herself meet Beth's eyes. Instantly disarmed, she quickly turned away.

"Look, I really don't need this right now."

"The timing's not exactly perfect in my life either."

Jo turned the volume up on the radio. They were playing 'Big Girls Don't Cry'. Beth shook her head.

"You'll do anything to avoid this conversation, won't you?"

Jo's pain hadn't subsided.

"I wasn't the one who ran off to Boston."

Beth's heart began to race at the memory of being pressed against Joanna's breasts.

"The other morning in the pool... I felt... so many things. You're right, I panicked and ran." She searched Jo's eyes. "I'm still scared... more than ever... but I swore to myself that if one of us runs, it's not going to be me."

Joanna's silence only hardened Beth's resolve.

"It's my house. Why should *I* be the one to leave?"

"I never said you should."

Jo brushed past her with the dirty dinner dishes.

"No, but you've certainly had a lot to say about everything else I do. You, Rheeta, Ben—even my thirteen year old son! I'm sick of being treated like a child who doesn't know what's good for herself." Beth's impatience escalated. "And talking about childish behavior, you don't want to know what I think of the antics you pulled in here with Rheeta."

Joanna shrugged.

"I'm surprised she told you. I didn't think she had the guts."

"Well she did, and she told me why as well. You should be ashamed of yourself. How manipulative can you be?"

Jo looked smugly at her own hand.

"Judging from her response, manipulative enough."

Beth was not amused.

"Well… I've had it with all of you! From now on, no one tells me how to run my life! Understood?"

"Perfectly."

Jo reached for her duffle bag.

"Then *I'll* leave. That was the plan anyway, right? As soon as you got back, I'd pack my things and split."

'The Dangerous Beth Garrison' yanked the bag from Joanna's hand.

"You're not going anywhere until we talk!"

Jo crossed her arms. Despite her guarded stance, she had never felt more vulnerable.

"Fine, let's get this over with so I can get the hell out of here."

Beth pressed in on her now throbbing temples.

"God, why do you have to make everything so hard?"

"You're the one who asked for this, not me."

"The afternoon of our picnic… what did you mean when you said you couldn't have what you wanted?"

Jo immediately resisted.

"Just leave it alone."

"I want to know."

"I'm warning you Beth, leave it alone!"

"Why won't you tell me?"

"Because there's no point, that's why."

"You have no right to decide that."

Jo deliberately turned away, desperate to preserve the illusion of indifference.

Beth was nearly defeated by it.

"Why won't you look at me?"

Joanna spun around, counting on her anger to coral her desire. Nearly drowning in Beth's eyes, Jo had never fought so hard against the her own heart. It left her exhausted and bitter.

"You can't have it both ways! I can't tell you and protect you at the same time."

"I never asked to be protected. Maybe the person you're really trying to protect is *yourself*."

"So what if I am? My whole goddamn life is unraveling!"

Jo stared through the screen door, captivated by the shimmering lights of the pool and the tranquility of Beth's backyard.

"Yours feels so wholesome… so full."

Beth couldn't help but laugh at the irony. She knew she might just have easily cried.

"God, haven't you heard *anything* I've said these last few weeks? It's not my *life* that's full, it's my *plate*… and with very little that's ever satisfied my hunger." She continued to talk to Joanna's back. "You don't see the difference because you're afraid to acknowledge there *is* a difference. You insist on reducing me to some happy little homemaker because anything more is too threatening for you to deal with." She walked over to the wall covered with the portraits Joanna had done of her. "For weeks you've hidden behind your sketch pad, your camera, your easel, studying me from every conceivable angle because studying me was a lot safer then getting close to me… or letting me get close to you." Beth turned from the portraits and faced Joanna. "Well it's not okay to expose my heart while you keep yours neatly tucked away in shadows."

Beth had come much too close to the truth.

Joanna retaliated.

"You don't know what the hell you're talking about."

Beth responded with a quiet certainty.

"Don't I? I think the problem is I know more about you than you ever wanted me to. Perhaps more than anybody ever has."

Joanna applauded mockingly.

"Well hooray for your powers of perception. What do you want me to say?"

Beth took the question to heart.

"I'm not sure. I just know I'm tired of being studied like a potted plant or any of the other inanimate objects you capture so exquisitely, then turn to a clean page and move on. I'm through posing just because it's safer for you that way." Beth's pulse began to race as she prepared to bare her soul. "I'm not a still life Joanna. I'm a woman."

In that moment Beth was ready to confess to it all—how she ached to be held and caressed, not rendered and taped to a wall. Joanna stopped her.

"Okay, I get it. Your modeling days are over. Is that what you drove all the way back here to tell me?"

Beth struggled to find her place.

"That's part of it..."

"Look, it's three o'clock in the fucking morning. Let's not drag this out, okay?"

"I need to know what you want from me."

"I don't want anything from you Beth."

"I'm afraid to let myself believe that."

"Well you'd just be kidding yourself if you didn't."

Joanna's resistance was no match for the urgency that lingered in Beth's eyes.

"Don't you understand? I can't *let* myself want anything from you."

"Tell me why not. You owe me at least that much."

"Why? Just because I'm living in your carriage house I have to play by your rules?"

"No. Because for as long as you've been living in my carriage house every rule that's ever meant something in my life no longer seems to apply." She pleaded with her eyes. "I'm afraid I'll go mad without something to take their place."

The pressure to provide an anchor for Beth's life when her own was so hopelessly adrift proved too great an irony for Joanna. She began pacing, then stopped in front of the woman who had opened her heart.

"You've got a husband and a son, both of whom need you... that's why not!"

Beth had repressed the hauntingly question too many times throughout her life. Tonight she unlocked her heart and her pain.

"What about *me*? What about what *I* need?"

Her piercing cry filled the room. Deep inside the walls long saturated with her tears, the carriage house itself recalled the stain of her sacrifices and wept for each of them. All that Beth had once forsaken there now seeped from the pores of the grieving wooden frame, filling the cupped hands of 'The Gods' who had come to collect the spilling. When they could hold no more of it they cast their arms upward, disbursing the sacred particles of Beth's soul into the stagnant night air that now awakened and swirled across the valley. The sudden gust rustled the branches of mighty trees, blew the soft tufts of wildflowers along the base of the great rock, swayed the overhead traffic light at the entrance to the strip mall and rolled an empty soda can against the tire of Steve's truck parked in front of an all night convenience store.

While he waited for the clerk to finish buttering his bagel, Steve politely stepped aside so that the only other customer—a white haired woman with a manly crew cut and shoulders broader that his own—could get a better look at the candy selection. Despite her curiously masculine appearance, Steve was careful not to stare. He'd already had more than his share of lesbian troubles for one night and this one looked as though she could easily whip his ass. In contrast to her overpowering demeanor, the woman glanced up and offered an acknowledging smile.

"Some nights feel a helluva lot longer than others, don't they?"

Steve had been wondering how things were going back at the carriage house.

"I'll say."

The woman went back to perusing the candy and Steve's eyes drifted over to the pay phone. It gave him an idea. Without looking up from the selection the woman sighed.

"Decisions, decisions, decisions. Some are so much tougher than others." Her eyes still focused on her choices, the woman interrupted her own humming. "I'd say the one *you're* wrestling with right now's a really good idea."

Steve was stunned. The woman chose a Hershey bar with almonds, stood up and dug into her pocket to pay the cashier. She turned, casually slipped a quarter into Steve's palm and closed his fingers around it. With her hand still clasping his she looked deep into his eyes, almost as if casting a spell.

"Make the call." She winked approvingly. "It's now or never."

Dazed, he collected his bagel, stumbled toward the pay phone opposite the restroom, dropped the coin into the slot and dialed. When he turned around again, the woman was gone.

Simple as that Dell had read Steve's mind, then vanished like an apparition into the night.

"Answer me Joanna." Beth pleaded again. "What about what I need?"

The urgency in her voice was indelible. Jo knew that for as long as she lived she would never forget the sound of it. From the very beginning, the demands of Beth's heart had stirred and frightened her own. Jo tried to spare them both.

"You don't need this. Haven't you had enough heartache in your life?"

"My God yes. That's precisely why I do need this… why I do need you."

They were the words Joanna had longed to hear. Her heart surged—then instantly fell.

"I can't give you what you need Beth… what you deserve."

"Can't you see? You already have."

"You asked me what I wanted from you. Why don't you tell me what you want from me?"

Unlike Jo, Beth no longer struggled against their fate.

"I'm not sure. I just know what I don't want. I don't want to waste another moment of this precious summer fighting with… or being apart from… you."

Every cell of Joanna's being longed to reach out for Beth, but every sane thought she had warned her, "Don't!" Every hurt she'd ever endured ached to be soothed by Beth, but every sane thought told her, "No!" All of her senses strained to be filled with Beth but again, every sane thought insisted, "You can't!" If she had only wanted these things from Beth, Jo would have been reassured. But the truth was, she needed them—needed them more desperately than anything she'd ever needed in her life. She was not afraid of falling in love with Beth. She knew she already had. She was afraid of what would happen if Beth loved her as much. What would happen when that love deepened and the calendar page turned? Jo's dread of the inevitable was enough to stop her.

"The summer's going to end, Beth. It's already half over."

"You don't have to remind me. I've lived with the clock ticking every day since we met."

Jo needed to remind them both.

"I can't stay. We both know that."

Beth had already made her peace with the unforgiving reality.

"I'm not asking you for a future. I'm begging you for a memory… one I can cherish for the rest of my life… one that will remind me what it felt like to truly be alive."

Jo fought against the plea in Beth's eyes.

"You don't know what you're getting yourself into."

"You're right. I don't." Beth moved closer. "But I'm willing to risk everything to find out."

"Well I'm not!"

Clinging to her resolve Jo stepped back, hoping to put a safer distance between them. Beth would not let it stand.

"Tell me something. What were you planning to do... just pack up, leave me a check for a cleaning service and never look back? Am I that easy to forget?"

Already tested beyond measure, Joanna slammed her fist on the counter.

"Easy! You think any of this has been easy for me? From the very first time we sat opposite each other in that damn coffee shop, I've been torn between wanting to kill you and kiss you."

"And now... this very moment?"

Joanna deliberately crossed her arms to prevent herself from doing either.

"Nothing changed. I still want to do both."

Joanna's confession was hard won. Beth's uncertainty had finally come to rest.

"So I'm not the only one who's been lying awake nights telling myself this can't be happening... terrified to think you weren't feeling the same... terrified to think that you were?"

Jo shook her head.

"No, you aren't the only one."

Even as she admitted the truth, Jo went about collecting her things. Her impenetrable resistance drove Beth crazy.

"Look at me Joanna! Or are you too afraid the complications might leave a telltale smudge on one of your precious stainless steel surfaces?"

Incensed Joanna turned abruptly, ramming her toe into the sculpture pedestal.

"Fuck!" The pain shot up through her leg, fueling her anger. "I'm warning you! If you say another word... "

Beth would not be silenced.

"Or is it some cardinal rule you have about never getting involved with someone...," she forced herself to face the truth, "inexperienced?"

Jo had yet to stop moving about.

"Let's not forget unavailable too!"

Beth's eyes lingered on her wedding band.

"No one's more sorry about that than I am."

In her heart Joanna knew that wasn't what was stopping her. In the past she'd slept with countless women precisely because they were unavailable. But Beth was different. Jo know she didn't want Beth for a summer of her life.

She wanted Beth for the rest of her life and she knew that *that* could never happen.

Beth pleaded again.

"Jo please. Look at me."

"I can't damn it!" She took one of the paintbrushes beside her easel and began smearing it wildly across the surface of her self-portrait.

Beth grabbed her arm.

"Don't!"

Jo broke free.

"Why not? Why the hell shouldn't it look like the rest of my goddamn life?"

She continued to mutilate the canvas until her face was completely obscured. Beth stood off to the side, horrified.

"Joanna please, you're scaring me."

Jo was out of control. She snapped the brush in half and hurled it at what little was left of her likeness.

"I'm scaring you? I'm scaring the hell out of myself! Ever since I met you I've been going out of my mind. You… this place… it's all too much! I came up here to salvage what was left of my fucking life and now even that's in ruins!"

As if the universe itself had arranged to punctuate Jo's torment, a sudden bolt of lightening split open the sky. A few seconds later, violent claps of thunder rumbled through the floorboards beneath their feet. The lights in the carriage house flickered and the radio waves became riddled with static. The women stood frozen in their arrested pain, waiting for the forces of nature to offer its cue. A moment later, power was restored to the tension-filled room and Joanna found her place within it.

"Please, just go home Beth. Go back to your house… your family… the quaint little world you came from… and leave me the hell alone."

Beth's heart raged between defiance and defeat.

"I can't. Maybe if you weren't so goddamn self absorbed you'd see that yours isn't the only life that's been turned into shambles since we met. It's not my fault that whenever you look at me all you let yourself see is somebody's mother and somebody's wife."

Joanna was deliberately crude.

"How would you like for me to see you… up from between your legs, creaming into my mouth, begging me to make you cum?"

Beth slapped Jo hard across the face. The unexpected force sent Joanna reeling backward into the sculpting pedestal, sending the unhardened statue smashing to the ground. Mortified by the consequences of her humiliation, Beth covered her mouth.

"God, I'm so sorry."

She waited for Joanna's fury, but it did not come. Instead, Jo looked down at what was left of her long hours of work and shrugged. Her voice was as hollow as her eyes.

"It doesn't matter."

"How can it not matter? You've been working on that piece all night."

Jo remained chillingly detached.

"That's the convenient thing about being... how did you put it... 'so goddamn self absorbed'. I get to decide what is and what isn't important without involving another living soul."

Beth's tenuous courage crumpled into self-degradation.

"You're right. I've done nothing but ruin your life." Her voice began to crack. "First it was your car, then your self portrait and now this. Can you ever forgive me?"

Jo bent down and collected what she could of her heart and the semi-soft pieces of clay.

"Look, I told you it doesn't matter." She slammed the remains back onto the pedestal. "Nothing matters anymore. Nothing! I just want to forget about it... all of it. Forget we ever met... forget everything we ever shared... " She closed her eyes, desperate to shut Beth out any way she could. "Please... just go and let me pack. I need to get out of here. Tonight!"

Beth could not bear to lose Jo so suddenly. With nothing else to sustain her will to live, her body went limp.

"Is that what you really want?"

Joanna deliberately avoided Beth's eyes. Too often they had broken her resolve. She reached for the screen door and held it open.

"Yes. How many times do I have to say it?"

Devastated, Beth fought for a shred of dignity. As she moved toward the door her tears betrayed her.

"You won't have to say it ever again, I promise."

Joanna remained rigid, fighting the torment of their inconceivable parting. She needed to tie things up anyway she could.

"I'll pay you for the time I was here. Just name your price."

Beth wiped her eyes.

"That would make it much neater for you, wouldn't it?" Her hurt escalated. "Well I'm sorry. I won't let you handle this like some little diversion you can just put on your Am Ex card and pay off at the end of the month… not when I've told you everything this carriage house means to me, and what it's meant to have you in it." Beth's voice began to crack. "I won't accept a single penny. You're going to leave here with that balance hanging over your head… and heart…for the rest of your life. Just as I'll have over mine. If that's the only connection that remains between us at least I'll know you're out there somewhere suffering from the same unfinished business I am."

'The Gods' watched as Beth stepped outside onto the porch. When Joanna didn't stop her, they went wild. Scornful of Jo's resistance, they struck back mercilessly, sending another roll of thunder across the valley. Once again the floor of the carriage house shook with their rage, the windowpanes rattled in their old wooden casings, the lights flickered erratically and the radio crackled with static. The frightening jolt delayed the women's parting just long enough. Caught up in their swirling turmoil, neither was sure of what she'd just heard.

"Go ahead Steve. Our lines are open. You're on the air."

As they both stared at the radio, its reception suddenly cleared. Whatever doubt either of them had turned to absolute certainty when they heard the familiar voice.

"If they're still listening, I'd like to say something to my pals Beth and Jo who are probably out there just wasting more time and about to make the biggest mistake of their lives."

Stunned, Beth took a step back inside and Joanna let the door close behind her. The women stood side by side as Steve continued to address them over the air.

"Beth, you're the bravest woman I know. You proved that tonight. Jo, don't be a fool. For once in your life, don't run. Take that incredibly beautiful woman who's come back to you in your arms and for starters, enjoy your first dance. I love you guys. Speak to you whenever you come up for air."

The women stood motionless until the disc jockey's voice broke through their dazed silence.

"Thanks Steve. That sounds like really good advice from a really good friend. So here it is, the one you asked for. It goes out to Joe and his girl Beth. The perfect song to make it a perfect night. 'It's Now Or Never' by the king himself."

As Elvis' velvet gloved voice filled the room, the radio itself became the only safe place for Joanna to look. The opening lyrics exposed her to all she had fought so hard to ignore.

"It's now or never, come hold me tight, kiss me my darlin', be mine tonight..."

For Beth, the radio announcer's assumption that 'Joe' was a man became a stark reminder of the forbidden line she was about to cross—if only Joanna would have her. She looked at the provocative figure standing before her. 'Joe' was certainly no man and this was surely something no man had ever made her feel. Though her life hung in the balance, Beth could not ignore the amusing irony of Steve's dedication. She smiled tentatively.

"Do I at least get to see your Elvis impersonation?"

Embarrassed by the confession of her childhood antics, Jo loved and hated Beth for remembering absolutely everything she'd ever told her.

"Sorry, but I didn't pack my cardboard guitar."

Beth's voice sweetened around Jo's playful but cautious excuse.

"Even without it, you still make me swoon."

Joanna dared to meet Beth's eyes that now seemed to now plead for her to make the next move. Suddenly everything impossible—everything rational—everything sane—fell away until all that was left between them was the music and the magnetic force of their desire. Certain this would be her last chance to save them both, Jo held out her palms to show they were covered with dry clay.

"I'll ruin your dress..."

Beth knew Jo meant to say 'I'll ruin your life'. Ignoring the thinly veiled warning, she came dangerously closer.

"I don't care about the dress." She reached out, took Joanna's hands and placed them around her waist. Through the delicate fabric, her body radiated heat. "I don't care about tomorrow." Against the background of another roll of thunder, Beth's eyes grew more intense. "I don't care if lightening strikes me dead as long as I die here in this carriage house... and in your arms."

In a moment that consumed all others that had ever come before it, Beth slipped her arms around Joanna's neck—aching to be shown the steps to this new and frightening dance. Her heart pounded wildly as Joanna pulled her closer, at last devouring what little space was left between their bodies and their separate lives. Encircled in Jo's arms, Beth molded herself to Joanna's body. She pressed her cheek against Jo's shoulder and Jo let her own rest against Beth's hair. For one exquisite moment they stood perfectly still—lost to everything and everyone that had ever owned them. Whether it was the world that disappeared around them or they who disappeared into it, alone together in this timeless space they remembered nothing that had ever come before and imagined nothing after it. From across the universe, word spread from spirit to imprisoned spirit that two of their own had managed to escape the boundaries of their lives and find salvation in each other's arms. Too seldom were there such triumphs to share—too few, the reasons to rejoice. More spirits ascended from the heavens to keep the pair safe. With hands joined they formed an invisible barrier around the carriage house allowing nothing in the logical world to invade this sacred space except for the intentionally chosen song that flowed through the radio.

Without daring to break their embrace, Beth stepped out of her sandals. Jo could feel the fullness of Beth's body slip lower against her own, creating an even more perfect fit. Jo ran her hands across the dampness of Beth's back as Beth closed her arms tighter around Joanna's neck. Now with one foot in each world, Beth Garrison and Joanna Cameron began their dance and as they swayed all the natural rhythms of the universe moved with them. The rain pounded the rooftop and drenched the shingles of the carriage house as the women danced closer and closer—slower and slower—until without warning, the severity of the storm once again interrupted the electrical power. The room fell instantly dark and silent. Without the accompaniment of the music, the women stood motionless in each other's arms. Inside the cocoon-like shelter, the rhythm of their shallow breathing became the only sound. There was no disguising its urgency.

Suddenly faced with her inexperience, Beth hoped that the darkness concealed the flush of her cheeks.

"So what happens now?"

"Well, we can go back to fighting if you'd like. Or we can call a truce and go back to just being friends."

"Both sound equally dismal for different reasons."

Beth ached to be possessed and forced to surrender her life completely or set free in order to preserve what was left of it. Joanna granted her the relief of neither. Instead, she ran the back of her hand along Beth's cheek.

"There is a third option."

Joanna's hand continued its gentle insinuation while she waited for Beth's decision. She didn't have to wait long.

"I think I'd like to try that one."

Joanna brushed her lips lightly against Beth's ear. The contact was electrifying.

"Would you?," she whispered, allowing the heat of her breath to spread downward.

"Yes..."

Joanna let her tongue glide slowly across the curve of Beth's chin and along the length of her neck as she coaxed again.

"Are you sure?"

Waves of immeasurable pleasure spread through Beth's body. With each one, more of her own juices collected in the space between her legs. She closed her eyes and clung to Joanna's shirt to keep herself upright.

"Yes... yes... yes."

Summoned by Beth's breathless plea, Joanna's tongue resumed its course—each time widening the path of her own desire—each time coming closer to Beth's lips, now parted and ready for hers. Beth heard herself moan.

"Kiss me... please... kiss me..."

Joanna cupped Beth's face in her hands. She swept up from beneath her chin and sealed Beth's mouth with her own. So great was their hunger for each other, their greed exploded instantly. Behind the crushingly intimate seal of their lips, their tongues swirled and circled in a frenzied exchange of unleashed desire.

Beth had never known such a consuming intimacy or felt the kind of arousal it provoked. The urgency of it made her gasp.

Having stolen all she could of Beth's surrender, Jo tugged teasingly on Beth's lower lip with her teeth. She ran her tongue lightly over the spot left bruised and swollen by Beth's habit.

"What happened to your lip?"

"I chew on it whenever I'm nervous."

"Feels as if you've been nervous a lot lately." Joanna read the confession in Beth's eyes. "So I make you nervous?"

After their kiss there seemed little left for Beth to deny.

"You obviously make me feel a lot of things...."

Embarrassed, Beth escaped Joanna's embrace and turned away. Jo came up and stood behind her. She let the back of her hand wander slowly down the length of Beth's arm.

"I'm sorry I make you nervous."

She deliberately let her touch linger until Beth was helpless to resist.

"No you're not. You're not sorry at all."

Jo slipped her arms around Beth's waist and pressed her mouth to Beth's ear.

"Am I making you nervous now?"

Beth could not protect herself against the intimacy of Jo's breath. Once again her heart began to race.

"Yes."

"Do you forgive me?"

Beth's resistance mixed with the slow burn of arousal.

"I don't think I'll ever forgive you."

Joanna felt a renewed sense of responsibility and with it came renewed doubts.

"It's not too late..."

Beth closed her eyes and let her head fall back against Jo's shoulder.

"It is for me. It's been too late from the moment we met."

When Joanna didn't respond Beth turned around, terrified to think that the kiss they'd just shared might be all she would ever know. She searched Joanna's eyes.

"But if you don't..."

Jo placed her hand over Beth's mouth to silence her. In the stillness that magnified the pounding of her heart, Beth felt the intensity of Joanna's eyes penetrating deep into her soul. When all that was there became hers alone Jo moved her hand away, once again exposing Beth's lips to her own. Beth clutched at Joanna's shirt as waves of pleasure washed over her. One after the other—cresting, falling, cresting, falling—each one pulling her deeper into the riptide of her own desire until she could do nothing to save herself but plead for Joanna's rescue. No longer was Jo's kiss enough. Beth ached for her hands. Her flesh begged for them—burned for them—everywhere. Gasping, Beth pulled her mouth away. Still hungry for contact, Joanna's lips pressed against the base of Beth's throat until sweet breathless sighs gave way to long surrendering moans.

Jo slid the camisole off Beth's shoulders and let it fall to the floor. Beth's head fell to one side as Joanna's tongue immediately lay claim to the newly exposed flesh.

"Oh God. I want everything from you Jo... everything. I want your tenderness... your rage... your brilliance... your darkness. I need your hands all over me and your mouth... I want it to steal every secret I've ever kept from myself..."

Now only the residue of clay on Joanna's hands stood in the way of Beth's salvation. She led Joanna over to the sink, turned on the faucet and placed Jo's hands under the warm, running water. Joanna studied Beth's solemn expression as she slowly worked the sudsy cleanser between Jo's fingers with her own. Under Joanna's watchful eyes Beth's breathing synchronized with the intimate, purposeful rhythm of her task. Bathed in moonlight, she performed it with a greater serenity than she had played her beloved piano and with greater tenderness than she had nursed both her infant sons. Joanna remained motionless and silent as Beth rinsed the last traces of clay from her hands. She turned off the water and in final preparation for what was to come, Beth took Jo's hands—those sacred instruments of her pleasure—wrapped them in the small terrycloth towel and gently blotted them dry. Lost to all but the hypnotic spell of the moment, the woman were unprepared for the sudden restoration of electric power. For the first time since the storm had left them without it they stood in the explicit glare of light, exposed to all that had transpired between them in the stillness and shadows. Steve's dedication long over, the Mel Carter ballad, 'Hold Me, Thrill Me, Kiss Me' now filled the room. Quiet smiles quickly gave way to something much more demanding. Under the clicking blades of the old ceiling fan, each stepped closer. As their bodies came together, the swirling pocket of air from above did little to relieve the heat that radiated through their clothes. Framed in each other's arms they closed their eyes and swayed in place, letting the lyrics and the dampness of their flesh speak their desire. Consumed by the fragrance of Beth's perfume, Joanna buried her face in the curve of her neck.

"Whatever you're wearing, it's driving me crazy."

Beth began to offer its name but Joanna stopped her. She pressed her mouth to Beth's ear.

"No! Don't tell me. I only want to know it by what it's done to me all summer... what it's doing to me right now."

Beth moaned to hear Joanna's confession—moaned with delight to know that she had not lived these last weeks of tortured longing alone. Now overcome by that longing Beth's conscience at last broke free, releasing her from every role and rule that had prevented her from crying out sooner.

"Make love to me Joanna... please, make love to me."

Jo let the words settle between them—the words she had longed to hear—the words she had longed to fulfill. She reached for the wall switch and turned off the light. Holding her with her eyes, Joanna's fingers worked to undo the zipper of Beth's dress. She moved it down slowly from between Beth's shoulder blades, along the curve of her back, to the base of her spine. She slipped the thin spaghetti straps from Beth's shoulders and the dress fell around her hips. She seemed to enjoy the lingerie's seductive details. As Jo's finger traced the delicate lace that trimmed the cup of the strapless bra Beth began to feel like a fraud, fearful of the expectations that went along with its allure. Beth's voice cracked nervously.

"This isn't really me. Rheeta dragged me into this ridiculous shop and insisted. This was actually the tamest thing I could find."

"I see..."

Joanna reached over to shut the radio.

In the stillness, Beth grew desperate to make her understand.

"I know what it must look like... and I wouldn't want you to think you were getting something you're not."

Joanna smiled and pulled her closer.

"And what might that something be?"

"I don't know." Trapped in Jo's arms, Beth struggled to find the right words. "Someone sexy... provocative...daring..."

Joanna ran her finger from the tip of Beth's chin down between her cleavage and back.

"I happen to find you all those things...," her hand moved again, "and it has nothing to do with this bra."

Even in the darkened room, Beth could feel Joanna's eyes bearing down hungrily upon her. Now faced with the fullness of those desires, Beth feared not being able to satisfy them.

"Joanna wait."

With her imagination running rampant, Beth began to tug nervously on the button of Jo's shirt. She could not bring herself to look up from its stitching.

"There's something else you should know..." Her throat tightened around the words. "Unlike Rheeta and apparently all the other sexually liberated women of the world... I don't have a pouch filled with sex toys."

Jo pretended to be disappointed.

"You don't?"

"No." Beth bit down mercilessly on her lip. "And I'm shamefully ignorant about things like vibrators and dildos..."

As the anxiety in Beth's eyes deepened, Joanna's amusement receded into something more tender. She cupped Beth's face in her hand and lifted it up to hers.

"Any more disclaimers?"

Beth lowered her eyes.

"No..."

Even before the last of Beth's confessions faded into the air, Joanna swept her up into her arms.

"Good, because there's something you should know. I'm going to kiss you now like you've never been kissed before, and this time I'm not going to be able to stop."

No longer able to resist the temptation of Beth's lips, Jo returned her own against them. Making good on her promise, Jo's tongue coaxed what was left of Beth's parched insecurities into a pool of swirling desire. Almost instantly the waves of pleasure rippled downward, flooding the already dampened space between her thighs. Beth could not conceal her arousal. Her nipples rose and pushed against the silky smooth cup of her brassiere as she molded as much of herself to Joanna as she could. The sensation nearly overwhelmed Jo's senses and with it her guarded emotions.

"God, how I've wanted you this way."

Their bodies pressed together, Beth absorbed the agony of Jo's confession into her own.

"For so long... so long..."

Across the room, the conspicuous sofa bed that had for so long defied their attempts at denial now offered itself up as a moonlit shrine for the worship of each other's flesh. The queen-size mattress lay open, its springs ready to receive the rhythm of their hips—the bed-sheet, eager for the soaking that hungry mouths could not contain. Still, Beth needed to be shown the way. Following the path of her eyes as she stared across the room, Joanna took her hand and led her there.

As the women stood at the foot of the bed, their hushed protectors gathered outside the rain-soaked window to bear silent witness to destiny's unfolding. Immune to the steady downpour, the spirits rejoiced as Joanna took Beth into her arms and kissed her. It was a kiss so imploring it released in Beth a plea that echoed through time.

"Make me forget... make me remember..."

Those were the last words uttered. Now all that was left unspoken between them was no longer in the nature of words to express. Joanna worked purposefully at removing Beth's clothes until all that remained of her cover was the cloak of her perfume. As she stood naked, flames from Joanna's spiraling caresses grew up from the clothing that lay at Beth's feet. But even engulfed, her flesh on fire, Joanna was not yet satisfied that Beth was entirely hers. Determined to have it so she took Beth's hand—the one that bore her wedding band—and brought it up to her mouth. Spreading it apart from the rest, Jo ran her lips along Beth's finger until she came to its base. There she probed the small v-shaped crevice with her tongue, intentionally insinuating where else she would soon do the same. The intensely erotic simulation sent the throbbing in Beth's neck downward to the pit of her stomach. Then further still to the place beneath it. Jo lowered her mouth around the length of her finger. Soaking this last vestige of Beth's conscience with her saliva, she slowly eased the gold band up with her teeth. After a lifetime of obeying its sacrament, the ring and her guilt now slid off easily. The darkened window mirrored back the indelible image of Beth's emancipation. In its shimmering reflection, she witnessed the destruction and resurrection of her life. Time itself seemed to stand still as she watched Joanna reach over and place the ring on the windowsill, close to—but quite deliberately outside—the sacred carving of the lover's heart. Transfixed by the image, all the once forbidden boundaries of Beth's own heart fell away. Now it was she who craved possession of the woman who so possessed her. In her urgency Beth's fingers trembled on the first of Joanna's buttons, but before she could continue Jo stopped her. She eased Beth down onto the unmade bed, gradually replacing the silent command of her eyes with the weight of her own body. The exquisite rub of Joanna's clothed frame against her bare skin intensified Beth's arousal. Clasping Beth's hands in her own, Jo raised herself up on her elbows and began a slow gently grinding with her hips. The dampness that had been concealed between Beth's legs quickly soaked the thigh of Joanna's jeans. Jo longed to touch her there—longed to slip her fingers deep into the well of Beth's desire—but her style would deny them both a little longer. As Joanna continued to work herself between Beth's legs, Beth moaned and arched her hips.

"Joanna please… I need your body."

Beth managed to free her hands. Once again she clawed at the buttons of Joanna's shirt. Once again Joanna resisted. She lifted herself up and stood at the edge of the bed. Abandoned by the cover of Joanna's body, Beth instinctively drew the bed-sheet up around her. She watched—transfixed—as Joanna began to undress herself. Jo had nothing on beneath her work clothes evoking in Beth all the raw, repressed improprieties of her own nature. As Jo kicked aside the threadbare jeans, Beth could not recall a more insatiable craving for an untamed life. For all the torturous glimpses she had caught of it in the past, Joanna's bronzed statuesque frame had never looked more magnificent or more commanding than it did now, standing over her, chiseled by the sharp beam of moonlight that struck against her body. Jo reached down and pulled away the sheet, exposing Beth to the hunger of her own eyes. Left unshielded from their greed, Beth nervously opened her arms and Joanna lowered herself into them. Nothing in either of their lives had ever prepared them for such ecstasy. As their bodies came together, a searing heat radiated between them. It came from everywhere… their eyes, their breath, the pores of their flesh. Joanna rode her gently, taking Beth further and further from all she'd ever known—until she recognized and responded to nothing except Joanna's command. A sound escaped from deep inside Beth's throat. It was a sound that transcended the nature of physical pleasure. It was the sound of her soul's rebirthing. She clung to Joanna's back, unable to bear ever being apart from her again. Jo remained in Beth's arms for as long as her own escalating desire would allow. Gradually she slid lower, sinking between the fullness of Beth's breasts. Beth closed her eyes and succumbed to the sweet savagery of Joanna's mouth that sucked and tugged on her hardened nipples. She clutched at the bed sheet as Jo slid lower still.

The clouds moved faster now, as if to keep up. Once again the exposed moon sent streaks of light through the lover's window, casting a winding network of trails that crisscrossed the undulating landscape of Beth's writhing body. They were the trails that Joanna would slowly and deliberately trace with her tongue until she found the one that led her to the intimate place of Beth's fire. Her thighs opened to Joanna's velvet probing the way flowers—and prisoners—strain toward the sun. Engulfed in the pungent aroma of Beth's arousal Joanna's finger entered her boldly, taking possession of the silken canal while her mouth lay claim to the throbbing mound just above its entrance. Beth strained against her for more, until more was no longer enough. With every stroke and caress another piece of Beth's old life burst apart, then faded from her memory until nothing was left holding her to this world except the sensation of Joanna's touch.

Jo knew exactly what she was doing. She knew by the steady rocking of Beth's hips and the trembling of her thighs as she pushed with the soles of her feet against the curve of Joanna's shoulders, raising herself upward, yielding more and more of herself to Joanna's will. She knew by the way Beth's fingers gripped the sides of her head, pressing it harder to her engorged flesh and by the arch of Beth's neck as sweet sighs gave way to courser groans the closer she came to the edge until finally Beth exploded, thrashing violently against Joanna's mouth—spasming around the thickness of her exquisitely embedded fingers. In the powerful rush of her climax, Beth called out for the lover she had forsaken—pleading for her forgiveness—her salvation—her soul.

"Joanna... Joanna... Joanna."

Long after it had faded into the stillness, Beth's cry echoed through the chambers of Jo's heart. It was as if she had never before heard the sound of her own name—never heard it uttered with such haunting urgency—such tenderness.

The sheer poignancy of it instantly erased everything she had ever known of herself up until that moment. Now having heard it on Beth's lips, Joanna would never be lost again, never doubt the reason for her existence nor the place she belonged. Nothing in the realm of her experiences had ever moved Jo so deeply. All at once her usual sense of conquest fell at the mercy of Beth's undoing. For all her sexual prowess, Joanna had never known the kind of surrender Beth had offered or the feeling of oneness it provided.

Shaken by the intensity of their union, neither woman dared move from her position. Instead they recovered separately, just as they were, their bodies resting in their petrified stillness while the words 'I love you' strained within the well-guarded gates of their hearts. Only after Beth's spasms had fully subsided did Joanna attempt to slowly withdraw her fingers. Before she could suffer the certain ache of their abandonment, Jo tended Beth's still pulsing crest with soft, sucking kisses as only another woman would know to do. Straddling the precarious line between tenderness and new temptation, Beth moaned and stroked Joanna's hair. When she imagined it possible to ever live without the ecstasy of those velvet kisses, Beth drew Joanna back up into her arms. She was embarrassed by the scent of her own juices that lingered around Joanna's mouth, and more embarrassed still by the illicit flavor of Joanna's kiss. Jo was reassuring, her smile tender.

"You taste delicious."

Beth responded modestly.

"That felt delicious… as if you couldn't tell."

Joanna smeared her fingers mercilessly across Beth's lips. Helplessly exposed to the evidence of her own lust, Beth hid behind closed eyes while she licked each of them clean. Gradually her worship turned more demanding. Her mouth now hungered for its own taste of Joanna's flesh—those intimate places she had dreamt of for so long. Beth's kisses grew ever more searching—her touch, increasingly more bold. Joanna responded with subtle reluctance. As Beth persisted, Jo's resistance became more deliberate. Beth was confused. She would have thought that Joanna would have wanted—even expected—her to reciprocate. She didn't understand. She sat forward, suddenly protective of her heart.

"Why not?"

The truth was much too threatening for Joanna to share. Making love to Beth had left her even more vulnerable than she'd ever imagined. Nearly consumed by the powerful intimacy, Jo was desperate to preserve what little she could of the ever-weakened boundaries that still stood between their lives.

"You don't have to."

Beth was hurt. It was evident in her eyes and in the way she quickly gathered the sheet up around herself. Jo tried to soften the sting of her rejection. She began by taking the sheet away and pulling Beth back down into her arms. The splendor of Jo's body was impossible to resist. Jo used soft, lethal caresses to coax Beth's surrender until it was complete.

"All I meant was, you must be exhausted. The drive back from Boston… the arguing… that orgasm. How much more do you want to do in one night?"

Relieved by Jo's explanation, Beth allowed the truth of her fatigue to rest fully in the fold of Joanna's arms.

"I suppose I am a bit spent."

Her admission was punctuated by a long, involuntary yawn, not unlike that of an exhausted child up long past her bedtime. In the presence of its endearing innocence, Jo fell even more deeply in love with the woman in her arms. She placed the errant strands of hair adoringly back behind the ledge of Beth's ear. Beth basked in the sweetness of Jo's consideration. In all the years of raising a family, rarely—if ever—did her physical or emotional fatigue have any bearing on what had been expected of her. She yawned again.

"I'm so sorry."

Jo pressed her lips gently against Beth's forehead, providing all the forgiveness Beth needed to lie contentedly on the edge of sleep. After a few minutes of uncompromised serenity, she whispered softly.

"Jo?"

Joanna too had drifted off. At the sound of Beth's voice, she instinctively pulled her closer. Beth tried to maneuver within the space of Jo's arms. It was useless. She whispered again—this time more purposefully.

"You have to let me go."

The reality of their inevitable parting broke through Joanna's sleep, immediately crushing her heart.

"I know…" Her groggy voice thickened with reluctance. "But do we have to think about it now?"

Beth instantly recognized Jo's pain.

"No silly. I mean you have to let me up so I can use the bathroom."

Beth was deliberate in not turning on the bathroom light. She did not want to be tempted to look in the mirror. At least for this precious interlude, she preferred to exist solely in the reflection of Joanna's eyes—penetrating, adoring eyes that followed Beth's naked, shimmering form back across the darkened room.

Joanna was almost afraid to trust that the woman coming toward her was not just a dream—afraid to think that her weeks of longing were not now cruelly betraying her senses. As if reading Joanna's mind, Beth sat down on the edge of the bed beside her. Without saying a word she took Jo's hand, brought it up to her own cheek and held it there until the warmth of her flesh replaced all doubt. Not until she was sure it had did Beth reach for the alarm clock. Jo watched her fiddle in the dark with its tiny knobs.

"What are you doing?"

"I'm setting the alarm."

Joanna playfully indulged the absurdity. She took the clock out of Beth's hands.

"Not necessary. Breakfast in bed is being served all day."

"God, that sounds deliriously wonderful but I can't stay." She took the clock back. If only she had a choice, Beth would gladly have spent the rest of her life in Joanna's arms. She took a long wistful breath. "I have to be up and out of here in less than three hours."

Jo shot forward.

"Okay, what am I missing?"

Beth's shoulders fell with the weight of her explanation.

"What you're missing, my dear, is a harsh dose of reality. I have to shower, change and be on the road to New Hampshire by seven. It's visiting day at Adam's camp."

This 'morning after' was definitely a first for Joanna. She couldn't have been less prepared or less able to hide her disappointment.

"Please tell me you're kidding!"

Beth was not at all surprised by Jo's reaction. She simply absorbed it into her own.

"Oh, how I wish."

Beth finished setting the alarm and placed the clock back on the table. Joanna looked for the slightest sign of compromise in Beth's eyes, but saw none. This day's plans were sealed at Adam's birth. Jo knew she didn't stand a chance of convincing Beth to change them. The sadly ironic timing of their interlude—as with all the deeply personal moments of her life—was not lost on Beth. Long accepting of the juxtaposition, she tried to lessen the cruelty of it for Joanna. She cupped a maternal hand under Jo's chin.

"Welcome to my life, sweetie. What can I say?" Beth offered the most bittersweet of smiles. "You may have managed to miss the primary colors and bulbous plastic phases but you're now officially involved with a young boy's mother."

For Joanna the recognition was suddenly much too real, but even before her rational mind could send in an army of second thoughts to save her, Beth crawled into bed—deliberately pressing her back against Joanna. She pulled Jo's arm around her, tucking her hand mercilessly between her breasts. The last remnants of Joanna's reluctance instantly dissolved into bliss. She buried her face in the tufts of Beth's hair.

"I'm not letting you get behind a wheel on just two hours sleep. If you have to go, I'll drive you."

Their bodies—if not their lives—fit perfectly. Beth snuggled even closer.

"It's sweet of you to offer, but I'll be fine, really. Besides, I don't think a day of pre-teen melodrama and color war is exactly your fare."

That part did sound absolutely miserable, but then there was something else.

"It's not just the drive. I can't bear the idea of letting you out of my sight so soon."

With her back still to Jo, Beth had the advantage of hiding the deepest of smiles.

"I definitely like the sound of that reason."

Even so, Beth wasn't convinced that having Joanna there wouldn't be too much of a distraction. She wasn't at all sure she could negotiate the demands of her role with the demands of her heart so soon and for so many hours. Sensing Beth's conflict, Jo let her hand intentionally slip between Beth's thighs. The heat was still there.

"I obviously know how to drive you crazy. Seems to me I've earned the right to drive you up and back from camp."

"I suppose it would be unfair not to make you my chauffeur as well as my lover. Just don't say I didn't warn you...," she moved against Joanna's hand, "about everything..."

Beth yawned again, this time without apology. Joanna's lips rested as indelibly upon Beth's heart as they did against the curve of her neck. Though impossibly exhausted, Beth fought to stay awake. She was not yet ready to relinquish all the glorious sensations of this moment.

"I can't believe I'm finally in your arms."

Jo whispered softly into Beth's ear.

"So, no regrets?"

Deep inside Beth's heart the question spawned a haunting melancholy. Her eyes drifted across the room to the corner where, in the early years, her piano had been. She relived the afternoon Ben had brought her lunch, then pressed her into having sex on the small foldaway cot. She thought about the consequences of that fateful concession and how the unplanned pregnancy that resulted from it ultimately sealed the course of her life. Suddenly drowning in the unlived portion of it, Beth turned inside the circle of Joanna's arms and faced her.

"I have a million regrets, my darling. A million and none at all." She looked deeply into Joanna's eyes, her voice as tender as her touch. "Has that ever happened to you before?"

"Has what ever happened to me?"

Beth knew Joanna was just pretending not to understand. She knew because asking took no less courage than answering.

"Those feelings… the ones we're both too scared to talk about… the things we're feeling right now…"

Beth rested her head against Joanna's heart and waited. Instinctively, Jo hesitated until nothing in her life mattered more than the truth. She closed her eyes and pressed Beth closer.

"No."

That was all Joanna said. That was all she needed to say. With her face safely hidden beneath the curve of Jo's chin, a private tear streamed quietly down the side of Beth's cheek. Joanna felt it drop into the crevice between her breasts. By the time it had dried the lovers had drifted off into the most peaceful sleep either had ever known.

Chapter 20

Were it not for the unfailing powers of maternal instinct, Beth might well have slept straight through the morning—her blissfully sated body enveloped in the pocket of her lover's arms. A critical twenty minutes past the hour the alarm was supposed to have gone off, Beth's eyes shot open. She bolted upright, reaching across Joanna's body to examine the malfunctioning clock. Awakened by the abrupt movement, Jo struggled to grasp the crisis at hand. She lifted herself up on her elbows, shielding her eyes from the early morning sun.

"What's wrong?"

Beth pounded the plastic casing with her hand.

"The damn thing never went off! We're late!"

Jo let her hand wander lazily across the length of Beth's bare back.

"Maybe it's the universe's way of saying it has other plans for us today."

Beth slammed the clock down onto the table.

"We can debate that on the ride up." She swung her legs over the side of the bed and looked back at Joanna. "If you're still coming. You have a choice, I don't."

After last night, Jo knew that was no longer true.

"Not only am I coming with you, I can't imagine another way I'd rather be spending this day."

Grateful for the lie, Beth leaned across the bed and brushed a strand of hair back from Jo's face.

"Spoken like a true parent. You're an amazingly quick study."

Jo smiled mischievously.

"So are you…"

Without warning, she pulled Beth down against her body and kissed her deeply.

Beth's sense of responsibility proved no match for Joanna's lips. Once Jo's hand slipped between her legs, the fire spread instantly. Beth could feel herself yield. Her flesh melted into Joanna's palm as more and more of her resolve faded dangerously away. At the last possible moment Beth forced herself to resist and begged for mercy.

"Jo please… don't do this to me now!"

Pulled in a thousand directions and struggling against her own desire, Beth leaped out of bed to safety. Torn between collecting her composure and collecting her clothes, she flitted around the room while Joanna's eyes followed her every frazzled move.

"You think I'm crazy, don't you?"

Jo lay back and folded her arms behind her head.

"Actually I was thinking about the first time you modeled for me. I wanted you terribly that night."

Unfortunately, the demands of the hour left little time for Beth to languish in the sweetness of Joanna's confession. Instead, she grabbed Jo by the arm and yanked her out of bed.

"I'll meet you in the driveway in thirty minutes! And don't try to get even by making me wait for making you wait."

Beth shoved her in the direction of the bathroom. Just before Joanna was out of view, she called after her.

"Jo… "

Joanna stopped mid-step and turned around. Beth was standing in the center of the room, sheepishly clutching her crumpled clothes to her chest.

"About last night…"

Hopeless to find the right words, Beth gave up.

"God, you must know… you were there. Now go! If you're not outside in a half hour I'm leaving without you."

Beth continued to gather the last of her things, intentionally waiting for Jo to be out of the room before discretely retrieving her wedding band from the windowsill. She could not bring herself to put it on. Instead she let the tips of her fingers linger achingly on the carved initials inside the lover's heart before bidding them—and these last sacred hours in her carriage house with Joanna—adieu. After the storm's soaking, the morning air smelled especially fragrant. Even in her haste Beth closed her eyes, tilted her head back and inhaled deeply. As she darted naked across the backyard, blades of wet grass poked between her toes. With every step, Beth's body tingled with all the impossible demands of this wildly incongruous day.

Though Beth immediately felt like a complete stranger in her own house, everything appeared to be exactly as it was before she'd left for Boston. Certain that after last night her entire world would never again be the same, everything had remained oddly unchanged. This struck her as both remarkable and unimaginable. She looked around the kitchen. Not a single object seemed to scorn her. The toaster and the coffeemaker neither snickered nor gasped at her nudity. The spoon rest and the teapot did not sneer behind her back or judge her harshly for her indiscretion. She doubted that the rest of the world would be as indifferent if ever they were to find out. Even BJ, with his uncanny sixth sense, seemed not the least bit fazed by her unusual entrance. He was one of the few things Beth was able to recognize of her old life. She clung to his fur and his familiarity for as long as she could before letting him outside. While she quickly moved around the kitchen replenishing his food and water for the day, Beth played back her messages. All five were from Ben. She was not surprised. He had phoned several times since she'd left for Boston—each call, a bit more anxious and demanding than the one before. The sheer predictability of his tone depressed her. Her night with Joanna had changed everything and nothing at all. Beth knew she would have to call him back after she returned from camp. It was not a call she was looking forward to making but there was no time to dwell on that now. She had to shower, dress and collect all the things that Adam had asked her to bring. There was also the present Ben had sent that still needed to be wrapped.

Beth bounded upstairs, then suddenly froze in the doorway of her bedroom. A wave of guilt swept over her as she looked into the room she's shared faithfully with her husband all of her married life. It was a guilt she would have to conquer quickly in order not to arrive noticeably late. As much as her son would pretend to be blasé, Beth knew how much Adam was looking forward to her visit. "He damn well better be!" she grumbled to herself as she jumped into the shower for this most supreme of sacrifices. She stood under the hot running water reluctantly rinsing away the evidence of the night from the surface of her skin, while just beneath the refreshed layer, the illicit memory of Joanna's touch remained indelible seared into her flesh. Finding something 'appropriate' to wear that would conceal the embers that smoldered within proved an even greater challenge. Beth's mastery at last minute tasks yielded remarkable results in remarkably little time. With twice as much to do, she managed to herd BJ back inside and still beat Joanna to the car. Beth's eyes darted anxiously between her watch and the carriage house until finally Joanna appeared in the doorway. Beth's heart surged instantly at the sight of her. Jo strode across the yard, turning its tranquility into a swirling tempest. Beth instinctively leaned against Ben's Jeep for stability. The symbolism did not escape her.

In contrast to the three large shopping bags splayed at Beth's feet, Joanna appeared amazingly unencumbered. With her license, credit card and sunglasses in her pocket, she carried her car keys in one hand and her camera in the other.

"I thought maybe you'd come to your senses and changed your mind."

"I was hoping maybe you'd done the same. Are you sure we have to do this?"

"I'm sure I have to."

Joanna used the weight of her body to press Beth against the door of her husband's car. The sensation was too exquisite for Beth to resist. She moaned softly.

"Don't."

"Don't what? Don't start or don't stop?"

Beth didn't answer. She reached around the back of Joanna's thighs and pulled her closer.

"Please tell me you're wearing something under these jeans."

"Why?"

"Because I don't think I can get through this day knowing otherwise."

"I'm not." Jo tossed the bags into her trunk. Her tone mocked the urgency of their departure. "We wouldn't want to keep Adam waiting, now would we?"

As Jo slid in behind the wheel, Beth recalled the morning of their accident when the enraged woman wanted nothing more than to tear her apart. She was quite sure that the emotional toll of this day would not spare her life twice. She directed Joanna to the turnpike and gathered the courage to talk about last night.

"So, do you still respect me or was my mother right after all?"

"Never mind if she was right or not, does your mother know you move like that?"

As the memory of her orgasm washed over her, Beth couldn't help but blush.

"I never knew myself." She reached into her bag, unwrapped a buttered bagel and passed it to Jo. "I know it's not breakfast in bed…"

Jo accepted the bagel as graciously as her disappointment would allow.

"What about you?"

Beth could not afford to indulge her hungers.

"There's always welcoming breakfast in the dining hall. I'll have something when we get there."

"I'm afraid to ask what you've got in all those shopping bags."

"Everything a thirteen year old boy can't possibly live without."

Jo smiled.

"You mean there's a pair of 38Ds in there?"

Beth slapped Jo's arm. She struggled to get the next part out.

"There's also a present from Ben... an autographed T-shirt of Adam's favorite British rock group."

Joanna acknowledged his devotion.

"Ben's a good dad."

"He's a good man." The truth of her own words weighed heavily on Beth's heart. "He left several messages while I was gone. I should call him as soon as we get home."

Joanna kept her eyes on the road.

"Who are you trying to convince, me or you?"

Beth wrestled with her conscience.

"He is Adam's father."

"And your husband."

Beth's voice dropped.

"Yes, that too."

Avoiding Jo's eyes, Beth reached tentatively for her hand. Much to her relief, Jo still welcomed it into her own. At least for the moment, Beth relaxed. This day had hardly begun and she was already buried under the weight of its reality. Joanna saw the undeniable exhaustion in Beth's eyes.

"Tired?"

Beth managed a weary smile.

"Among other things..."

Jo reached over and took the folded slip of paper with the directions from Beth's lap.

"Try to get some sleep. I'll wake you when we're there."

"I just need a few minutes."

Her eyes filled with immeasurable gratitude, then closed for the next two hours.

Jo reached over and tenderly stroked Beth's cheek. From a dead sleep, Beth came to attention in a mock salute.

"Beth Garrison reporting for duty!"

Jo laughed.

"At ease. According to these direction, you've got another mile and a half before we reach the front line."

Beth rotated her neck.

"Have I thanked you for being my chauffer… and my bugler?"

"Don't I get credit for the other thing?"

Beth hardly needed a reminder.

"By all means. Thank you for that too."

The memory ended all too abruptly when the camp's entrance came into view. Beth's stomach tightened into a knot.

"Pull over a minute. I need to freshen up."

Jo waited while Beth reapplied some lip gloss and ran a brush through her hair. She nervously smoothed out the front of her cotton tank top as though the wrinkles were her sins.

"How do I look?"

"You mean for a woman who's been burning the candle at both ends?"

"That's a rather respectable spin on a woman who's just had the best sex of her life." The sound of her own confession made Beth feel even more exposed. "Seriously Jo, do I look okay?"

Jo removed her sunglasses for a long honest look.

"You look better than okay. You look irresistible."

"I was going for something more… motherly."

"Then you're asking the wrong person. You erased 'motherly' hours ago! Can I drive now?"

Beth nodded and Jo shifted into gear. She slowed just before the main gate.

"You ready?"

Beth gazed across the already crowded parking lot.

"Last night made me ready for absolutely anything or absolutely nothing else, depending upon how you want to look at it." She turned to Jo. "What about you… are you ready?"

"Not even close."

"Well then, welcome to the world of parenting my dear. Ready or not, whatever it takes you just show up."

Amid the throngs of people unloading their cars, Joanna maneuvered the T-Bird into one of the few remaining spaces. At the last possible minute Beth reached into her pocketbook for her wedding band. She met Joanna's eyes in a tortured exchange.

"Adam notices everything…"

Before the women could protect their hearts, children of every age, shape and size descended upon them. They came—like a swarm of locusts—from every direction, covering the ground as far as the eye could see. Knowing that her son was somewhere among them, Beth instinctively opened her heart. Joanna instinctively clenched her jaw. As the unruly mass began swarming around them Beth whispered into Joanna's ear.

"Now smile and pretend there isn't anywhere else in the world you'd rather be."

"You mean like between your legs?"

Beth moaned helplessly under her breath as she waved her arms in the air.

"Adam honey! Over here!"

From halfway across the field, the boy recognized his mother's call. He immediately broke from the pack and cut a path through the crowd in the direction of her voice. Just before he reached her opened arms, Adam checked his enthusiasm and slowed down. Beth saw through her son's tempered response. His joy in seeing her was undeniable. Much too suddenly Beth was reminded of her importance in his life. The lover she'd become in the hours before dawn instantly dissolved into the mother she had to now be. Despite his resistance Beth swooped Adam up and smothered him with maternal kisses.

Joanna remained intentionally close to her car. Every instinct told her to get in the T-Bird, drive off and never look back. Instead, she watched jealously as Beth pressed her son to her breast—the same breast that just a few hours ago belonged to her and her alone. It would be Joanna's first reckoning with that dose of reality Beth had warned her about. Adam squirmed in his mother's arms.

"Hey c'mon. It's only been a few weeks."

Adam finally broke free of his mother's stifling embrace.

"Hey Jo! Mom never mentioned you were coming."

Joanna walked reluctantly toward them.

"It was a last minute decision."

Beth looked at the her son and her lover standing side by side. Beneath her lighthearted smile, she struggled to reconcile the impossible demands of her heart with the equally impossible demands of the day. Suddenly, the only thing greater than her need to relieve her bladder was her need to get away from the them both.

"You two get reacquainted while I run to the bathroom?"

Alone with Joanna, Adam was struck with their unfinished past.

"Listen, I know I said I'd write..."

For the intrusion of this day, Jo was determined to make him pay.

"Yeah, so what happened to that promise?"

Adam avoided her eyes.

"I'm kinda' with someone else. It just sorta' happened."

As she watched him wrestle with his conscience, it was never more apparent that Adam had his mother's eyes. Much as Jo would have preferred to deny the reality, he was indeed the child of the woman she loved. Inside her head, Jo heard herself make him an offer: 'Kid, I have more money than God. Just name your price. How much do you want for your mother?'

Adam seemed to be waiting for her forgiveness. Under the circumstances, Jo decided to be kinder than she felt.

"Don't worry about it. I'm with someone else too."

It's Steve, right?"

How badly Jo wanted to wipe the smirk off his face with the truth.

"Sorry but I never kiss and tell. Besides, it doesn't matter. I don't think it's gonna' work out."

Adam's reassurance was as innocent as his age.

"Don't worry. For a babe like you, there'll be plenty of others."

"I'm afraid it's a little more complicated than that."

She tousled his hair with a mixture of resentment and affection.

Adam was relieved.

"So we're cool?"

"Yeah, we're cool."

Back in her good graces, Adam's eyes gravitated to Jo's chest. He may have found himself a little camp sweetheart but Jo's womanly breasts were still something for the pubescent thirteen year old to behold. Joanna deliberately crossed her arms. Under the circumstances, she wasn't feeling quite benevolent enough to let him have it both ways.

Beth returned to the welcoming smile in Joanna's eyes. Oblivious to their coded exchange, Adam was much more intent on tearing through the shopping bags. Beth saved him the trouble.

"Everything you asked for is in there… including a present from dad."

"Great. I'll go through it later. Let's dump this stuff in my bunk and head over to the dining hall. If we're lucky maybe they'll still be some glazed donuts left."

"One can only hope," Jo mumbled under her breath as they trudged off through the clusters of family reunions going on all around them. Adam ran ahead to meet up with some of his friends. Left blissfully to themselves, the women stayed deliberately close so that their arms would brush as they walked. Starved for each other's flesh, the limited contact felt all the more titillating. Jo could not imagine how she would ever make it through the day.

"Can we leave yet?"

"I'm afraid not."

Joanna groaned. It wasn't as if Beth hadn't warned her.

"So what did you and Adam talk about?"

"I told him what we gave up to be here today."

Beth's eyes widened in horror.

"Relax. I just jerked his chain about dumping me for another girl. Then I admitted I'm involved with someone else too."

Beth tensed.

"I'm begging you Jo, behave yourself."

"Do I have a choice?"

"No. At least not for the next six hours." Beth leaned teasingly closer. "After that you can break all the rules..."

The large noisy dining hall was bustling with staff and visitors. Beth's popularity from previous years was instantly apparent as family after family called her name or grabbed her arm drawing her into their circle. Jo tailed along from cluster to cluster, graciously enduring the same tedious introduction followed by the same tedious small talk. When she'd had enough she whispered that she would be waiting at a table off to the side. Beth followed Joanna longingly with her eyes until eventually she lost her in the crowd.

On either end of a long banquet table piled high with assorted pastries, two overzealous campers handed out flyers describing the days events and activities. While she sat in a corner sipping numbly from her Styrofoam cup, Jo took a reluctant glance at the bright orange sheet of paper. The more she read, the more she winced. At ten sharp—in a little less than a half hour—there would be a welcome address from the camp director at the flagpole. This would be followed by a morning of color war games at various venues throughout the campgrounds. There was also an art show displaying the finest in camper creativity. At noon, a complimentary boxed lunch would be served on the ball field. She assumed the bleachers were available for 'preferred seating'. The camp's annual talent show started at three and ran for what Joanna imagined would be a miserably boring two hours. Refreshments and a farewell message followed at five, officially ending Joanna's day in hell. Family and friends were welcome to stay on for another hour until the campers were due back in the dining hall for dinner. As far as Joanna was concerned, that was not even an option. At five past the hour all she intended to be was that much closer to the Massachusetts state line. Jo crumpled the flyer into a ball, shoved it into the empty cup and tossed both into the nearest garbage can.

She looked down at her watch. Five o'clock might just as well have been twenty years away.

Not without a great deal of finesse, Beth managed to finally break away from the obligatory smiles and small talk. She found Joanna sitting alone in a remote corner of the room, sulking.

"I read the flyer. There's no way I'm ever gonna' make it."

Beth pulled over a chair and sat down beside her. Under the table, she rested her hand on Joanna's lap.

"Sure you will." She squeezed Jo's thigh ever so discreetly. "Just think about all the ways I can make it up to you once this ordeal is over."

With their fledgling intimacy lifted by the promise of things to come, the couple sat in isolated bliss. For a few precious moments the rest of the world seemed a million miles away, until Joanna spotted a familiar and particularly loathsome face in the crowd.

"Isn't that that asshole colleague of Ben's?"

Beth followed Joanna's eyes. Sure enough, Nick was predictably sweet-talking one of the more attractive women in the room. Beth's shoulders slumped in defeat. Running into him—especially today—was a complication she didn't need.

"That's him alright."

"What the hell is he doing here?"

"He's got a daughter Adam's age. They've both been going to this same camp for years."

Nick had spotted them too and was already on his way over. Now hopelessly trapped between Joanna's blatant hostility and Nick's equally blatant stupidity, Beth prepared to navigate herself through the tense encounter. Should she be lucky enough to survive these next dreadful moments, she could then look forward to the rest of this God forsaken day. Not surprisingly, Nick's eyes were fixed on Joanna.

"I see you're standing in for Ben."

Already self-conscious, the blood drained from Beth's face. What was he implying? A wave of relief came when he pointed to the leather case slung over Joanna's shoulder.

"Ben's a camera buff too." Nick took Beth around and turned her toward Joanna. "Just between you and me… don't you think this woman should be in front of a camera and not behind it?"

Beth was terrified that he would see everything that she was feeling… everything that she'd always felt whenever her eyes met Jo's. He coaxed her for a response.

"Is that centerfold material, or what?"

Beth could feel her stomach tighten as she struggled to keep the memory of Joanna's body rubbing against her own from showing on her face.

"Yes, she's beautiful."

Pretending to search for her son in the crowd, Beth immediately looked away. Nick didn't seem to notice her discomfort or, for that matter, the tightness of Joanna's jaw. Beth remained expressionless.

"I'm surprised to see you here. Doesn't Sandy usually come up for the day?"

"She's on the west coast visiting with her sister for a few weeks."

"So you're here by default."

Nick leaned closer as if sharing a well-guarded secret.

"Actually, the day has its advantages. Just beneath all the fun and games, this place is crawling with sex-starved divorcés. With a trained eye you can pick 'em out in the crowd." Nick reached into his pocket and pulled out a folded camp flyer. The back of it served as an appendix to his little black book. He was there less than an hour and he'd already logged three numbers. He refolded the sheet and slipped it back into his pocket. "Years back I actually left here with a dozen numbers."

Beth just shook her head.

"Was that after your divorce or while you were still married?"

He smiled sheepishly.

Joanna could not contain her distain.

"I'm surprised you're interested in women your own age. I'd have thought the nineteen year old counselors were more your fare."

Nick winked at her slyly.

"That's a separate list." He reached into another pocket and took out a carefully folded napkin. "Just one so far, but I'm workin' on it. Speaking of counselors, did you hear the latest camp scandal? Last week they fired two girls—the art counselor and the theater director. Rumor has it one of the campers caught them going at it pretty good in the back of the Arts & Crafts shack. The kid supposedly freaked. What a schmuck! A few years from now he'll spend his last dime to see the exact same thing."

Joanna's blood began to boil. The plea in Beth's eyes was the only thing keeping her silent.

"Anyway, the two counselors were sent packin' faster than you can say 'weenie roast'."

Nick's eyes had already begun to wander as he stalked new prey.

"Well ladies, I think I'll be movin' on. My radar says that hot little momma over there can use a little of Poppa Nick's TLC."

Beth watched him manuever through the crowd

"T.L.C. must mean thick, long, cock."

Jo turned away. She was disgusted with him for everything he'd said and disgusted with herself for everything she'd wanted to, but for Beth's sake, had not. Joanna was not accustomed to compromising herself and Beth knew it.

"Thank you."

Jo remained stone faced. It was hard for her to acknowledge that she was annoyed with Beth as well. Beth understood. She touched Jo's arm, testing her forgiveness.

"I'm sorry."

Joanna met her eyes. Her disappointment was impossible to hide. Beth felt horrible. She checked her watch. There was no time to make things better.

"It's almost ten o'clock. We should find Adam."

Joanna nodded. It was all she could do. The day hadn't even started and the uncomfortable reality of their very different lives had already begun to set in.

From years of experience, Beth knew what to expect as the two stood side by side among the crowd of visitors gathered at the flagpole. Joanna, on the other hand, did not and no sheet of paper could ever have prepared her. Immediately following the opening address it came upon them like a great tsunami—a tidal wave of non-stop activities and scheduled events that tore the secret lovers apart. Hopelessly adrift they struggled to preserve what they could of their battered intimacy, sending subtle, reassuring messages back and forth with their eyes. As the endless color war games played out, Beth succumbed to the crowd of enthusiastic, cheering parents while a resistant Joanna retreated to the sidelines, desperate to maintain her autonomy and what was left of her shattered eardrums from the constant shrill of shrieking children. Every now and again Beth would look out beyond the sea of waving arms and cast an apologetic smile in Joanna's direction. Despite Jo's nodding acceptance Beth's private reckoning deepened by the minute, wreaking greater and greater havoc within her own heart. After the games she continued to mingle as an increasingly sullen Joanna continued to withdraw. By noon, their stolen glances had become less and less frequent and less and less assuring. When their eyes did meet, the cruel reality became harder and harder to ignore until what little still survived of their conflicted and precarious intimacy felt all but destroyed.

Next on the day's scheduled events was the complimentary boxed lunch dispensed at home plate of the ball field. As the doomed lovers waited on the slow moving line their once playful brushing was now consciously restricted, almost as if each was making a deliberate attempt to wean herself off their hopeless, insatiable need of the other's flesh. Instead of sitting as close together as they could on the bleachers, the women chose to sit cautiously apart. Adam planted himself between them, unaware of the punishing symbolism. Adding insult to injury, he was eager to relate everything he'd found out about the 'lezzie counselors'. Influenced by the collective mindset, he thought that girls kissing girls was 'twisted and gross'. Ordinarily Beth would have offered a lesson in tolerance, but not today. Not wishing to prolong the subject, she sat in uncharacteristic silence. It was a silence Joanna chose once again to honor, but not without a deepening resentment. Avoiding each other's eyes altogether, the women ate what little they could while Adam devoured his sandwich and rambled on incessantly about the most inane things. Somehow Beth managed to put aside her own pain and listen attentively. Joanna instinctively tuned him out. She wondered how much of her own mother's yearnings she, as a child, had missed. Finished with his chips, Adam popped the cellophane bag. He tossed Jo the camera.

"Take a few pictures of me and mom so she can send it to my dad."

If it were possible, Adam had just worsened their ordeal. Accommodating his simple request felt nothing short of daunting. In the performance of her life, Beth and her son playfully toasted with cans of soda. As Jo reluctantly focused her lens, she understood that what she was capturing was so much more than just a fleeting pose. For Beth it was by necessity, a fundamental and lifelong priority. If that were not so she and Jo would still be in bed, lying in each other's arms. For Joanna, the image of such strong maternal devotion and the story it told was as devastating as it was undeniable. Once again in her life she felt the power of a mother's love, only to fear being abandoned and left to live without it. As Beth continued to smile for the camera, her own camouflaged expression concealed the same wrenching conclusion she saw in Joanna's eyes. What had happened between them the night before could never—must never—happen again.

After lunch there was still the afternoon talent show to endure. The small wooden folding chairs only added to the women's misery and discomfort. Act after act they partook in the obligatory rounds of applause while their inconsolable hearts lay morbidly still. When the long awaited intermission finally came, Jo freed herself from the packed, noisy room saying that she was going down to the lake to shoot some pictures. Beth didn't try to stop her. Were she in Joanna's shoes she certainly would have done the same, probably much sooner. All during the intermission talk of the lesbian counselors circulated endlessly. If anyone had a different opinion of the firing, Beth never heard it mentioned. Grateful that at least Joanna was not around to hear the small-minded comments, she sat there in silence. She had worried that this visiting day would be a rude awakening for Jo as to the sobering realities of her world. Little did Beth know how bitter a taste she would get of Joanna's world as well. Resigned to the hopeless conclusion that neither world could accommodate the other, Beth retreated into the plaguing depths of her own solitude. Yet, when the show was over, Joanna was waiting faithfully for her outside. Amid the exiting crowd, the couple's eyes locked in a quiet recognition that both celebrated and mourned their undeniable love. Both depleted, they stood shoulder to shoulder while the camp director delivered his farewell address. Afterwards, the visitors and campers shared their goodbyes. Adam flagged down Lori and her parents. He had introduced Beth and Jo to them earlier in the day. As the family approached, Beth wanted nothing more than to flee. Joanna had wanted that from the moment they'd arrived. For her son's sake Beth struggled to remain cordial, exchanging platitudes about the day she feared would never end. With one arm draped around his girlfriend, Adam nudged Joanna with the other.

"You still gonna' be around when I get back?"

Joanna tried not to blame him for his unknowing part in ruining not just this day, but the rest of her life. She answered flatly.

"No, I'll be gone by then."

Though the words crushed his mother's heart, her pain went undetected as another idea took shape in Adam's head.

"Why don't you, me and dad spend Christmas break in New York!"

Jo read the torture in Beth's eyes. She yanked the brim of Adam's baseball cap.

"Why don't we just take things one vacation at a time?"

Desperate to end their ordeal, Beth turned to Lori's parents.

"It was nice meeting you." She squeezed the woman's hand and kissed her cheek. "You have a lovely daughter."

Lori's mother took Adam around.

"And you have a very handsome and charming son."

Lori's father shook Adam's hand.

"Sorry we didn't get to meet your dad. Maybe some other time."

Lori's mother winked at Beth.

"Yes, perhaps we'll be planning a wedding in the future."

Both kids appeared increasingly anxious to break away from their ridiculous, gushing parents. Adam checked his watch.

"Gotta' go or we'll be late for supper."

Somehow finding the strength to conceal her daylong agony, Beth swept her son up into her arms and clutched him tightly. While her urgency was real, it was surely displaced.

"I love you," was all Beth could say before letting him go.

Joanna bided her time while the parents watched their kids wander off into the sunset hand in hand. How Beth secretly ached to be able to do that with Joanna. Lori's mother leaned her head against her husband's arm and sighed.

"There's nothing sweeter that young love..."

For Joanna, all the festering resentment of the day came to an angry head.

"And to think they fired those two counselors for the exact same thing."

Neither of Lori's parents knew what to make of Jo's unexpected remark—or how to respond to it. They parted quickly after that. Whether or not Beth expected one, Joanna offered no apology for what she'd said. Flanked by hordes of departing visitors, the women made their way toward the parking field. This time they walked in stoic silence, the space between them now guarded and deliberate. It was an especially miserable end to an especially miserable day.

Drowning in turmoil, Joanna sat stone faced behind the wheel. She rotated her neck in a vain attempt to loosen the tension, preparing for the long ride back. Beth felt entirely responsible.

"I'll drive home if you'd like."

"Do you know how to drive a stick?"

"No."

Jo started the engine.

"Then, you can hardly make good on the offer, can you?"

Beth couldn't help but read between the unforgiving lines of Joanna's remark.

"You must hate me." She stared at her wedding band, fighting back tears. "I could think of any number of reasons why you would. I know I should have spoken up in defense of those counselors."

Jo attempted to shrug off her very real disappointment.

"And if you had, what would you have said?"

"Exactly what you had the guts to say to Lori's parents… what you wanted to say to Nick and everyone else but didn't because of me."

Neither woman found the slightest relief in Beth's acknowledgement. She tried to excuse her cowardly silence.

"I wanted to… honestly. It's just that I was feeling…"

Jo cut her off unsympathetically.

"I knew exactly what you were feeling Beth. I could have predicted it. But unlike you, I don't have the luxury of remaining silent. It's my lifestyle, not yours, they were condemning. Let's face it, that's the least of it."

Beth could feel her heart shatter into a million pieces.

"I know… "

For the first time since they'd left the campgrounds she found the courage to actually look at Joanna.

"This was a terrible mistake, wasn't it?"

Jo kept her eyes deliberately focused on the road.

"Today or last night?"

Beth's throat tightened around the heartbreaking reality.

"Both."

Joanna gripped the wheel as if mightily trying to steer them away from the dreaded conclusion. The day had dealt its final blow. Their doomed love affair was over before it had even begun. Beth's body slumped against the door in despair. She turned and stared blankly out of the passenger window as a stream of quiet tears blurred all that passed. She wondered what it was about the juxtaposing nature of desire that once acted upon manages to both crystallize and obscure the rest of ones life at the very same time. And in the end, what did it all matter anyway? Against the backdrop of quaint country roads the two women retreated into a dismal silence. With her life frighteningly off course Beth clutched the piece of paper with the directions, speaking only to relay the necessary turns that would lead them back to the interstate. Joanna followed each of the commands without saying a word. For the next several miles the couple sat in the their self-imposed exiles, their bodies only inches apart—their lives separated by forbidding odds. Neither seemed willing or able to put words to her pain. The impenetrable reality made it damning enough. Resigned to their parting, Joanna had already decided that she would leave the very next day. There was no point in prolonging the agony. She drove steadily on until the green interstate sign loomed up ahead. For Beth, the arrow might just as well have pointed toward hell than home. Just before the entrance she grabbed Joanna's arm.

"Don't get on!"

Jo applied the brake and slowed down in time to avoid the ramp. Beth's pulse quickened.

"Turn the car around!"

"Right here?"

"Yes!"

Jo looked at the oncoming traffic.

"But it's a double yellow line."

"For God's sake Joanna, I'd say we crossed more than that in these last twenty-four hours. Just do it!"

Jo swerved and made a hairpin u-turn. She'd assumed Beth left something behind at camp and was not pleased having to drive back to get it.

"So, what'd you forget?"

Beth's heart had triumphed over all reason.

"It's what I can't forget. It's what I can't live without." For the first time all day, Beth's eyes sparkled. "I want to make gross, twisted love with you and I can't bear to wait the next few hours to do it."

"But I thought..."

Beth refused to be reminded.

"Let's not Jo! Let's not think at all. Not tonight! Not tomorrow! Not until the day you have to leave."

Joanna remained cautious.

"And then what?"

"Let's not think about that either!"

Jo had never wanted anything more in her life, but the day was a forbidding reminder. Beth persisted.

"Please, all I'm asking you for are these next three weeks." She had already made her peace. "I'll make them last a lifetime if I have to."

With good reason, Joanna was afraid to meet Beth's eyes. She knew the moment she did she would have no choice but to accept the complete madness of her terms. Jo's smile, though reluctant, was all Beth needed for her heart to come alive.

"Make a left at the next stop sign. There's a small motel about a mile down that road. With any luck they'll still have a vacancy."

"Yeah, we can pay the devil and spend the night."

Jo's warning fell on deaf ears. At the first sight of the Crow's Nest Motel, the last remnant of Beth's conscience gave way .

"This is a sports car, isn't it? Can't it go faster?"

Her reckless enthusiasm was hopelessly contagious. Jo shifted gears and floored the accelerator, sending the car and its passengers careening toward immeasurable joy and certain heartache.

The vacancy sign of the small, one story motel was as glorious as anything Beth had ever seen. She sent Jo to the office to get them a room and from the vending machine, every last piece of candy. Having not eaten much of anything all day, she was ravenously hungry. Beth waited impatiently by the car, her eyes darting anxiously between the office door and her wedding band. She was resolved that once she removed it, it would be for the next three weeks. It was midway off her finger when, much to her horror, neighbors from down the block came out of the room directly in front of Jo's car. Beth quickly slipped the ring back on as Evelyn Dreyfus raced ahead of her husband to greet her.

"Eugene, look who's here! It's Beth Garrison."

The short stocky woman enveloped Beth in an overly zealous hug. Her husband was much more reserved, sticking to a neighborly smile. Evelyn bubbled with delight at the coincidence.

"I see you and Ben decided to stay over too. It's always such a long day."

The Dreyfus' son went to the same camp. Somehow Beth had managed to avoid bumping into them all day. Now, at the most inopportune time, her luck had run out.

"Actually, Ben is abroad this summer. I drove up with a friend."

"Oh."

Beth had never read so much into so little a word. Feeling self conscious about the real reason they were taking a room, she concocted a more acceptable excuse.

"We would have driven back tonight but my friend came down with a stomach virus. I thought it best if we spent the night before heading back."

Beth's eyes shifted nervously to the office. Early on in her life she had mastered the art of hiding what she was feeling. Until Joanna, she never had any reason to hide what she was doing. Covering her tracks was a skill she knew little about. To Beth's relief, Evelyn seemed to buy the story.

"That's awful. The last time Gene caught one of those bugs he was miserable for days… vomiting, diarrhea, sometimes from both ends at the same time."

Eugene didn't seem terribly happy about his wife sharing the personal details of his ordeal. He inched away in the direction of their car. Evelyn patted Beth's hand.

"Staying over is a smart idea. The last thing the poor dear needs is to be sick like that on the road."

Beth could not stop herself from embellishing Joanna's condition.

"I know. She seemed to be getting greener and greener by the minute."

"Where's your friend now?"

"She's getting us a room."

Evelyn looked surprised.

"Why didn't you go and let her wait in the car?"

Wishing she'd have quit while she was ahead, Beth groped for a reasonable explanation.

"She needed the bathroom. She assumed there was one in the office."

Evelyn sensed her husband was anxious to get going.

"Why don't you join us for dinner while your friend rests up? You can bring her back some soup and crackers."

In the last five minutes, Beth had gotten much better at lying.

"Thanks, but I couldn't possibly leave her. She's in terrible shape."

"I understand."

Just as Beth seemed to have pulled herself out of the hole she'd dug herself into, Joanna came bounding out of the office grinning from ear to ear. She was waving a key in one hand and carrying an armful of junk food in the other.

Evelyn looked understandably confused.

"That's odd. Your friend doesn't seem at all in distress."

Beth blurted out the only thing she could think of.

"It comes in waves!"

Before Beth could regain her composure, Joanna was upon them. Beth nervously made the introduction. Jo was still puzzled.

"What comes in waves?"

"That nasty stomach virus you've been battling all day.

Jo knew instantly why Beth had lied. She would spare her reputation but not her nerves.

"Oh that. It must have been something I ate last night."

Behind the intimate recognition, Beth remained expressionless. She chastised Jo for the very purchases she'd asked her to make.

"What are you doing with all that junk food? Honestly, you're such a glutton for punishment."

"We'll see who moans first."

For more reasons than one, Beth was anxious to get inside.

"What room are we in?"

Jo checked the number on the key.

"Three."

Evelyn squeezed Beth's arm.

"I can't believe it! You're right next door to us. What were the chances we'd be staying at the same motel, let alone sharing a wall?"

Beth's smile concealed her dread.

"Yes, what were the chances?"

Joanna sensed Beth needed to be rescued. She clutched her stomach.

"Uh oh… I think I feel one of those waves coming on."

Evelyn pushed them both toward the door.

"Go!" She watched sympathetically as Jo worked the key into the lock. "You take care of her now Beth. We'll try to be as quiet as we can when we get back. If the TV's too loud, just knock on the wall. It's the only way I can hear it over Gene's snoring."

"I'm sure it won't be a problem" Beth called back to her, practically shoving Jo inside. "The louder the better," she snuck in under her breath as she slammed the door behind her. Beth fell—with the weight of her life—against it. Their clandestine hideout was a modestly furnished walnut paneled room with all the usual cheap and chipped furniture. A poorly framed landscape hung on the wall over the bed and an awful tweed industrial carpet clashed with everything else in the room. For Beth, the setting, just as it was, was paradise. She immediately turned on the air conditioner, lowered the blinds and hung the 'do not disturb' sign on the outside of the door. The Dreyfuses still hadn't pulled away. She waved to them coyly through the slightly cracked door, then clicked it shut, locking out the world and every damning thing in it. At last she and Joanna were alone. Gone were the hordes of innocent, fresh-faced campers. Gone were the annoying wholesome activities and decent, doting parents. Gone was the pretense that she was one of them when all she could think of was being in the arms of the woman who drove her to the edge of madness. Beth snuck a peak through the slats of the blinds. At least for now, even Evelyn and Eugene Dreyfus were gone too. Beth broke into a fit of deliriously giddy laughter. Joanna leaned against the dresser and crossed her arms.

"Suppose you tell me what all that was about."

Beth knew Jo was referring to her lie.

"Get yourself over here first."

Joanna sauntered toward her. Beth reached out and impatiently drew her closer.

"Kiss me," she demanded. "Kiss me before I die from waiting."

Joanna pressed her up against the nearby wall with the weight of her body. Still bitter about the torturous hours that had come between them, she came down onto Beth's mouth with a force as ruthless as it was reassuring.

"Like that?" she whispered, still close enough for Beth to feel her breath.

Beth hungered for more, but this time Jo wasn't obliging. She was waiting for an explanation.

Beth pouted, hoping to win Jo's sympathy.

"I didn't know what else to say. I guess I was projecting… my stomach's been in knots all day."

Beth might have been too beautiful to resist but Jo was hardly through making her pay.

"If your tummy aches why don't I just rub it?"

Jo slipped her hand between Beth's legs and gently messaged her. Beth moaned.

"That's not my stomach."

"But it feels better, doesn't it?"

Jo continued to rub in slow, deliberate circles.

"God yes… everything feels better."

Jo smiled, then suddenly took her hand away.

"You don't have a change of clothes. I wouldn't want you to soak through these."

Beth closed her eyes and concentrated on the lingering sensation of Jo's touch.

"I'd say it's a little late to worry about that now."

Joanna glanced around the room.

"Not exactly the most upscale accommodations, huh?"

"It's got a bed. That's all I care about."

"And a bible in the nightstand to warn us we're going to hell for the sins we're about to commit on it."

"As it turns out, I'm not much in a reading mood." Beth's eyes sparkled shamelessly. "Though I suppose it wouldn't hurt to pray that on this particular night Eugene Dreyfus snores especially loud."

Jo noticed a small pamphlet beside the phone.

"What do you think the chances are that this place has room service?"

Beth pulled her closer.

"The only thing I have a craving for is right here in my arms."

Beth's playfulness receded into something much more solemn as she removed her wedding band. She placed it into Joanna's palm and closed Jo's fingers around it.

"Keep this for me and don't give it back until the day we have to say goodbye."

Joanna understood what Beth was asking. She knew that by entrusting her with her ring, Beth was entrusting her with her life.

"Are you sure that's what you want?"

"Want would imply I have a choice." Her eyes filled with tears. "Ben is coming home on the twenty-fifth. If only 'til then, what I need more than anything I've ever needed in my life is this time with you."

Regardless of the consequences, Joanna could not deny her these next three weeks anymore that she could deny herself the same. As she watched Jo tuck the band inside her pocket, Beth wiped away her own tears and with them any allegiance she'd ever felt toward anything and anyone other than herself. She leaned her cheek against Joanna's shoulder and waited for Jo's arms to make everything right.

"Hold me Jo. Hold me and promise that no matter what happens… no matter how wonderful and painful things get… you won't leave a moment sooner than you have to."

With a desire greater than anything that forbid it, Joanna brought her lips down to Beth's. In a kiss that broke every pact she'd ever made with herself to remain safe, Jo sealed her promise to the woman she loved more than life itself. Beth wanted nothing more than to wash away every last trace of condemnation this day had inflicted upon them. Breaking free of Joanna's arms, she began peeling off her clothes.

"Shower with me!"

Complete with a dripping faucet, the small green-tiled bathroom was anything but luxurious. Inside the cramped shower stall the couple maneuvered playfully, alternately kissing, stroking, probing and sponging as the sudsy water streamed down across their bodies. They toweled each other off hastily.

Beth grabbed Jo's arm and pulled her out of the bathroom, deliberately stopping in front of the dresser mirror so she could see them together, naked. As if moving in a dream, Beth positioned herself in front of Joanna and brought Jo's hands around her waist. Pressing herself against Jo's body, she took her lover's hands and guided them along her goose-bumped flesh. Her nipples rose instantly. She spread her thighs and pushed Joanna's hands downward.

"Touch me…," she whispered breathlessly. "I want to watch."

Joanna stroked Beth's throbbing clit into a hardened knot. Monitoring Beth's expression through the mirrored reflections, she slipped her fingers deep inside. Beth moaned helplessly.

"Oh God, feel how wet I am… see what you do to me."

Were it not for Joanna's arm around her waist, Beth could not have remained standing. Jo smeared her fingers across Beth's breast, leaving a silky trail. This time, Beth pressed Joanna's hand greedily to her lips, reveling in the image of sucking it clean. Now it was her turn to make Jo feel what she did. Beth led her over to the bed. She tossed back the spread and pushed Jo down onto the crisp white sheet. But before Beth could begin, Joanna sprang forward. Positioning herself at the edge of the mattress she pulled Beth to her. Beth straddled Joanna's lap, her arms wrapped tightly around Jo's head, pressing her close. Their bodies rocked together as Jo licked the fullness of Beth's breasts. As her hunger grew, Beth used the weight of her body to once again push Joanna down onto her back. Once more she attempted to climb on top but Jo rolled her over, assuming the position of control. This time Beth would not be denied.

"You had your turn last night. Now it's mine."

For a moment Jo was amused but much too suddenly Beth managed to take alarming possession of her body. It was one thing for Jo to make Beth yield to her will. It was quite another for her to be conquered by Beth's. For Joanna, things didn't go that way. This was the last shred of her existence not yet woven into Beth's. Joanna fought fiercely for her life until her resistance became too obvious for Beth to ignore. Damp with perspiration and desire, Beth stopped—her breathing heavy, her eyes hurt.

"If it's something I'm doing wrong…"

Though it would have been easier, Jo couldn't let her think so.

"It's not you."

"What is it then? Why won't you let me make love to you?"

Without answering Joanna turned away, leaving Beth to come to an almost unimaginable conclusion.

"I'm not frigid." The irony crept into Jo's voice. "Getting off has always been the easy part for me."

Beth held Joanna's eyes until they told her everything they needed to know.

"It's the intimacy you can't handle, isn't it?"

Jo remained silent. She had often been swept away by desire but it had always been a desire she controlled. Tearing off her clothes had never meant tearing down her wall.

"I've never had to… before you."

At the sound of her own confession, Joanna's heart sank with defeat. She moved to the edge of the bed and buried her face in her hands. Beth immediately raised herself up on her knees, leaned forward from behind and enveloped Jo in her arms. The weight of her breasts pressed softly against Joanna's back was impossible for Jo to ignore. She closed her eyes, hoping to block out her misery and lose herself in the sweet, rocking embrace. Making sure to stay close, Beth shifted over to Joanna's side. She spoke to her softly.

"Jo, look at me."

Joanna's eyes remained fixed on the chair in the corner of the room. She shook her head. Her words were carved from a hopelessness that had set a long time ago.

"I can't."

The last woman Joanna completely loved had become terminally ill and died. The devastated youngster vowed that after her mother's death she would never again allow herself to need anyone that much again. Faithful to her own promise, that was the way Joanna had chosen to live her life until it became the only way she knew. Then fate introduced her to another mother—someone else's mother—Adam's mother—and all the same wonderful things about this woman reopened the seal around her heart. Jo realized that on the deepest of levels the qualities that most drew her to Beth were the very qualities that would ultimately tear them apart, leaving her abandoned and devastated yet again. And then there were the unhealed scars from the ravishes of her mother's cancer. Joanna had witnessed the worst of her mother's suffering down to the last horrific stage of her life. The torment Jo had experienced as she watched her mother's once comforting, reassuring body wither away to a frightening skeleton left such an indelible mark on her young psyche that long after Joanna had grown into adulthood the only way she could derive any sexual pleasure was to induce a punishing disconnect between her own physical and emotional life. In perhaps the cruelest of ironies, Jo could only become aroused if she remained untouched. As the years went on the heart she was guarding had become all but vacant. Her voice echoed that emptiness and isolation.

"You don't understand."

Beth drew Joanna into her arms.

"I think I do." She stroked Jo's cheek tenderly. "It wasn't you my darling… it was your mother that died. You just chose to stop living."

Jo looked up. No one had ever understood her so intuitively and so completely.

"How do you know? How do you always know?"

Beth extended a gentle smile.

"I'm a mother too, remember?"

Joanna could feel tears welling up in her eyes. Despite everything she'd done to avoid them, her childhood memories had remained all too clear.

Beth saw into the darkness of Joanna's heart.

"Tell me everything you don't want me to know."

Jo drew a long, pained breath.

"The day we buried her I buried a part of myself. I never wanted to hurt that much again."

How well Beth understood the desire to shut down.

"Unfortunately our hurting is essential to our healing. Trust me, I seem to have become an unenviable expert in the art of grieving."

Joanna's torment had not diminished with time. Her voice cracked with the rawness of her recall.

"I loved her so much, as hard as I knew how. It wasn't enough, She died anyway."

Beth brought Jo closer. She struggled to overcome the pain of her own loss in order to comfort the woman in her arms.

"I'm afraid loving doesn't give us the power to *save* each other from death. It just gives us the courage to be there for each other in the face of it."

Joanna remembered the awful feeling of powerlessness.

"I swore I'd never let myself feel that helpless again."

"That kind of resolve comes with a terrible price. Your mother gave you life, Jo. Not just for *her* sake but for your *own*. Don't be afraid to live it."

The tears that had collected now started to flow.

"She tried telling me so many things… things I never truly understood until I met you."

Remembering only brought more pain. This was not what Jo imagined she'd be doing in a motel room with the woman she had dreamt of being with all her life. But then nothing had turned out the way she'd imagined—not from the very first moment she'd met Beth. Jo struggled to pull herself together.

"I don't do this."

"You mean let someone see you cry?"

Jo tried to wipe away what remained of her tears.

"Yeah."

Beth risked being playful.

"Would you like me to get your sunglasses so I can't see your eyes?"

"Don't bother."

When it came to Beth, that once reliable tactic had proven useless from the start. Beth smiled playfully.

"See… there's signs of progress already."

For the briefest of moments even Jo found a glimmer of hope, but all too quickly it faded into the same familiar despair she'd known all her life.

"It wasn't just losing my mother. Sometimes it feels like I was born cheated by life."

Beth understood immediately. She'd been haunted by that same feeling for as long as she could remember—almost as if her entire being had been formed of emptiness. Her son's death had only made it worse. Their separate lives suddenly felt inexplicably bound by overwhelming loss. Beth reached for Joanna's hand and folded her own around it.

"The summer Danny was four we spent a weekend at the Cape. I'd packed his favorite stuffed animal… a soft, fluffy pink rabbit with big, floppy ears. We'd given it to him for his first birthday and he'd slept with it every night." Beth's eyes watered as she clung to the memory. "This one afternoon we decided to go to a nearby park. Danny insisted on taking Floppy along. When we got back to the hotel room I realized that we'd left the rabbit behind. Danny was so upset it broke my heart. We went back to the park but when the stuffed animal was nowhere to be found, Danny became inconsolable. I tried reassuring him that another child must have felt badly that Floppy was all alone and so they took him home and would love him just as much. The night we got home I dreaded putting Danny to sleep. I imagined that being back in his own bed would only intensify his sense of loss. I'd always encouraged him to talk about his feelings, so when I tucked him in I asked him how it felt not having Floppy to cuddle with. I was sure he would break down in tears. Instead, he looked up into my eyes and said he felt a little bit sad and a little bit happy. Needless to say, that wasn't what I was expecting. As I sat beside him, stroking his hair, I told Danny that I understood why he felt *sad* but I didn't know what it was about his ordeal that made him feel *happy*. Without the slightest hesitation he reached over, pulled another stuffed animal into his arms and tucked it up under his chin. In the quietest voice he said, 'I'm happy about all the things in my life I *haven't* lost'."

Joanna looked as shocked as Beth had back then.

"Those were his exact words. I'll never forget them. It wasn't until years later that I realized my son possessed an innate wisdom that had allowed him to make his peace with life." Beth wiped a lone tear from her eye. "I had no way of knowing it then but I truly believe he was teaching me how to survive losing him one day. You have no idea how many nights I've laid in bed crying myself to sleep, trying to live by those words." Beth turned and looked at

Joanna. "All these years later, I'm still trying…"

Jo could see the vulnerability in Beth's eyes. The pain seemed to make them all the more beautiful.

"I don't have your kind of courage, Beth. I couldn't add miniature marshmallows to the top of a sweet potato casserole."

Beth patted Jo's hand affectionately.

"Let's face it honey, you would never think to make a sweet potato casserole in the first place."

Jo laughed.

"That's true." A cautious smile lingered in her eyes. "Speaking of carefully placed marshmallows, your breasts felt nice on my back before."

Beth's heart filled with renewed expectation.

"Did they?" She immediately resumed the position Jo had described, this time intentionally brushing herself more sensually across Jo's back. "How do they feel now?"

"Pretty fucking wonderful."

She pressed her mouth against Joanna's ear.

"Please… don't rob me of the chance to know what I'm capable of doing… what I'm capable of making you feel…"

Without permission, Beth coaxed Joanna face down onto the mattress. Straddling her around the hips she lowered herself onto Jo's body, letting the pendulous sway of her breasts graze tauntingly over Jo's shoulder blades, down along the small of her back, into the crack of her buttocks and slowly along the length of Jo's thighs. She rolled Joanna onto her back. Their eyes locked in a lustful stand-off as Beth began touching her in ways Jo had never been touched before—kissing her in ways Jo had never been kissed before.

"Trust me," Beth whispered each time her lips swept across another part of Joanna's flesh. "Trust me…," she implored as her fingers kneaded the nipple of Joanna's breast and the other hand worked her legs apart.

Jo grabbed Beth's wrist, at first pushing her away, then pushing her deep inside so that Beth could feel the explicit evidence of her victory.

"Damn you Beth Garrison… damn you… damn you… damn you…"

Beth punished Jo's resentment with greater demands.

"I'm going to taste you Joanna… I swear I'm going to taste you if it's the last thing I do."

In a sudden and overpowering move Beth brought Joanna's hips to the edge of the mattress, then dropped to her knees on the floor at the foot of the bed. She spread Joanna's thighs apart and positioned them over each of her shoulders. Beth's heart pounded wildly at the sight of Joanna's aching, engorged flesh—at the center, its glistening pearl there for her taking. She grasped Joanna's forearms and pulled her body downward until every inch of the exposed mound was pressed fully against her mouth. Their simultaneous moans blended with the creaking bedsprings as the two remained locked together in consummated bliss. Beth would have been content to draw her last breath there, drowning in Joanna's sweet, caramelized juices, were it not for her commitment to her lover's pleasure. Without experience Beth relied on her instincts and the charged signals of Joanna's body to tell her everything she needed to know. All of Joanna's conflicts were evident in her arousal. She gripped Beth's head encouraging her to continue while she fought against the threat of being consumed. As if challenging Beth to stay with her Jo bucked violently, like a yet unbroken stallion attempting to throw its novice rider. Through it all Beth retained control—her tongue and fingers taking greater and greater charge until the part of Joanna that ached to be possessed could no longer resist. Betrayed by her own body, Jo came in fierce, purging tremors—spasming around the length of Beth's finger, spilling her poisonous history into the healing suction of Beth's mouth. Knowing that in the past Jo had used sex as an *escape* from intimacy, Beth waited cautiously, fully expecting that she would now pull away. She didn't. Instead Joanna laid passively, at last tamed yet remarkably unharmed. Until that moment Jo had never truly understood the difference and as a result had spent the whole of her life deliberately avoiding both. Her crucial sense of control was something Jo would never have chosen to give away. From the moment they had met, it was something Beth had managed to win from her. She was the first and only woman to whom Joanna felt she ever truly *belonged*. But now was not the time to tell Beth so. Now was the time to dwell privately and to cherish this unlikely savior in whose arms she had finally found her lost and lonely soul. Not quite ready to retreat from the territory she had risked everything in her life to claim, Beth rested her cheek against Joanna's thigh while she continued to stroke the soft tufts of Joanna's damp public hair. In spite of her victory, Beth had never felt such overwhelming defeat. She forced herself to hear the truth.

"How many women have you been with Jo? I want to know so I can hate them all."

Joanna closed her eyes and a sea of faceless lovers passed behind them. Beth asked again.

"Tell me. How many have touched you this way?"

Joanna pulled Beth up into her arms. There was only one truthful answer.

"None."

A stillness settled between them. It was a stillness that gave Joanna real peace, for the first time in her life. For the next few minutes Beth lay inside the fold of her lover's arms. When she looked up again she saw that Jo had fallen off to sleep. Careful not to disturb her, Beth slipped gently out of bed. She pulled the cord of the telephone around the wall into the bathroom and quietly closed the door. Since they would obviously be spending the night, BJ needed to be looked after. Mustering her courage, Beth placed the phone on her lap and dialed her friend. Steve answered on the first ring. Though his conscience told him he had done the right thing, he'd been hanging around waiting for the call that would tell him so. Sensing her discomfort, he tried putting her at ease.

"Well, if it isn't 'The Dangerous Beth Garrison'…"

She kept her voice intentionally low.

"Dangerously *crazy* is more like it."

"You call it crazy… I call it courageous."

"When my whole life implodes, the difference will hardly matter."

"On the contrary. That's when the difference will matter the most."

Beth wasn't reassured.

"I suppose that remains to be seen."

She explained where they were and what she needed him to do. Steve was happy to oblige.

"Why are you whispering?"

"Jo is asleep."

"You must be even more dangerous than I imagined."

"God, this is so awkward. I'm not sure what else to say."

"A simple 'thank you' will suffice."

For lack of something more redeeming, Beth went with Steve's suggestion.

"Okay, thank you."

"You're welcome." Beth could hear the satisfaction in his voice. "Nice touch huh… the radio dedication?"

"It *did* have its desired effect."

"What can I say? I'm just a romantic at heart."

"Well just so you know, I'm holding you responsible for my demise."

"I'd like to think of it as your *happiness*… but fair enough."

Beth couldn't help feeling terribly self-conscious.

"You don't think less of me?"

"Why would I think less of you?"

"For being unfaithful to Ben."

"I'd be more disappointed in you if you'd have been unfaithful to yourself."

Steve knew his friend well enough to sense her tears. He tried to be reassuring.

"Beth, listen to me. You couldn't be a more devoted wife and mother. You've been through so much. No one deserves a little happiness more than you. Don't worry about BJ. I'll take a ride over there now. In the meantime, is there anything else I can do?"

Beth hesitated.

"There is *one* thing."

"Name it!"

"Do you think you can write me a happy ending to these next three weeks?"

"You're a survivor Beth. Survivors get to write their own endings."

The inevitable felt almost impossible for her to bear.

"This one will be the painfully shortest of stories."

"Sometimes those are the ones we remember for a lifetime."

Beth let Steve's words settle in her heart.

"Thank you for not judging me for this. I know how much Ben means to you."

"He means a lot to *both* of us Beth and for as long as I've known you you've done nothing but honor that affection with the most amazing devotion. This summer is about what *you* need."

Beth's mind drifted back to the morning of her husband's flight.

"Somehow I don't think Ben would see it quite the same way."

"No probably not, but he'll only hear about it when… or if… *you* decide he needs to know."

Beth remained silently appreciative. Steve added one more thing.

"Now you have to promise me something… that you'll make the most of these next few weeks."

Beth's heart raced ahead of itself.

"God, I'm going to try."

"Good. Now when Jo wakes up give her a message for me. Tell her that effective midnight tonight, she's officially laid-off for the rest of the summer."

Beth understood the generosity of Steve's gesture and the sacrifice that went with it.

"But the two of you have been so busy lately and I know you can use every job you can get."

He dismissed her concern.

"I can handle whatever we started. The rest will just wait. Besides, I have an incomplete manuscript I've been ignoring way too long. Seems your courage is contagious." Steve could feel her unspoken affection. "I love you too Beth. Get home safe and call me whenever it is you guys come up for air. We'll share a pizza."

Beth agreed. With a much lighter heart she tiptoed back into the room just as Joanna was waking up. She replaced the phone on the nightstand, gathered up the stack of candy and crawled back into bed. Jo propped herself up on a pillow and Beth tossed her a Snickers bar.

"You better not have been dreaming of anyone but me."

"Rheeta, actually." They burst out laughing. "Who were you talking to?"

"I called Steve to ask him to look after BJ tonight."

"I'm sure Cupid was quite pleased with himself when you told him why."

Beth ripped open a bag of potato chips.

"It did sound as if he was intending to bronze his bow and arrows."

Beth dug into the bag.

"Oh, by the way... he fired you. As of tomorrow you're officially unemployed."

Joanna looked genuinely disappointed. Beth put aside the bag of chips.

"Don't worry sweetie, I have a feeling something else is about to open up."

She spread her legs and pressed Jo's hand there. Jo immediately began massaging Beth's already throbbing core.

"How do you know I'm qualified?"

Beth moaned with pleasure.

"Hmmm... I can tell."

Jo continued to rub the now slippery mound, showing off her undeniable skills.

"What position did you have in mind?"

The floor of Beth's stomach tightened with anticipation.

"You can start with this one..." She lay back, opened her thighs and spread herself apart. The giddiness in her voice deepened into urgency. "Make me cum, Joanna. Make me cum every way you know how."

The Dreyfuses did not return from their dinner for several hours. Wrapped in each other's arms, the lovers now lay quietly in the darkened room. As the unmistakable sound of late night TV filtered through the paper-thin wall from the room next door, Beth was reminded that this was just another ordinary night in the lives of so many ordinary couples. She rested her cheek against Joanna's heart and for the briefest of moments she let herself pretend they were one of them.

Chapter 21

Fortunately for Beth, she and Joanna managed to check out without running into the Dryfusses. The far greater burden of having to return her husband's calls still awaited Beth once she returned home.

Beside the answering machine that blinked with several more messages from Ben was a deliberately placed note from Steve reminding her to make the most of the next few weeks.

Joanna went back to the carriage house in order to give Beth some privacy. The unmade bed was just as they had left it. So too was the mutilated selfportrait. Jo reached into her pocket for Beth's wedding band, then placed it in the jar along with the lone Cheerio. As Jo studied the two small circular objects—one a reminder of their first night together, the other a reminder of their last—she feared that the sound of Ben's voice would bring Beth to her senses. Overcome with jealousy, Jo raced across the yard and burst into the house. Beth had chosen to make the call to Ben from their bedroom. Joanna bolted upstairs unannounced, stopping abruptly at the bedroom door. Beth read the uncertainty in Jo's eyes. She placed her finger to her lips, a signal for Jo to be extremely quiet, then patted the bed motioning for her to sit down. Joanna's worst fears dissolved instantly. Immediately her sense of triumph led to even greater liberties. She slid her hand under Beth's shirt and undid her bra. Testing Beth's conscience, Jo began rubbing her lover's back, then slowly moved around to her breast, taking Beth's nipples first between her fingers, then her lips. Beth did nothing to stop her. Instead, she closed her eyes and shifted the phone to her other ear giving Joanna greater access to her body. She continued to converse with her husband. By the time the conversation ended, Beth had soaked through the crotch of her panties. Unable to recall anything of what she had said to her husband other than an empty promise to keep in touch, Beth hung up and immediately began tearing off Joanna's clothes, then her own.

"I want you."

"Here?"

"Here! Right now!"

Beth shoved her husband's pillow under her hips, exposing herself more fully to Joanna's mouth.

"Punish me Jo... Punish me for needing you this way... Punish me with your tongue... your hands... your body. Brand me everywhere with your name."

Joanna did all Beth had demanded of her. When she was finished his wife's juices covered much of Ben's pillowcase. As Jo slid the soiled prop out from under her lover's hips, Beth was shocked by what she herself had been capable of—shocked at how low her heart could stoop in order that it might reach the summit of its splendor—how much it could steal from itself to fulfill itself—how cruel and unbecomingly it could behave toward one in order to share its tenderness and beauty with another—and ultimately, how deceitful and disloyal it could be in order to live honorably in the place where the truth of its duality rages on, tearing each of us apart and making each of us more than whole.

As she rested in Joanna's arms, Beth followed Jo's eyes to the wedding picture on top of Ben's dresser. Jo confessed.

"I was in here once before. The morning after I was sick... while you were at the nursing home."

"Did you find what you were looking for?"

"I'm not sure what I was looking for but I left pretty tortured."

"I see..." Beth understood the agony of wanting what she thought she could never have. "It might help to know the torture was mutual. That night you were in the throes of a nightmare. When I looked in on you, you were sprawled naked in my son's bed. God, how I wanted to go to you... to touch you..."

Joanna smiled and eased herself out of Beth's arms.

"Where are you going?"

"To give you a second chance."

Without saying anything more Jo returned to Adam's room and laid back across his bed, waiting for the pounding in her lover's heart to spread downward. As if moving in a dream Beth went to her son's room. She stood in its doorway, once again mesmerized by the sight of Joanna's body. She had lived within these walls for the last twenty-five years, but never in this space. The home she had once created for her family had become a den of lustful indulgence. Its wholesome foundation shook with the unleashed improprieties of her own desire—a desire that obliterated everything else. Once Ben's wife—once the boys' mother—Beth had become a woman possessed. She no longer existed in the world as anything but Joanna's lover. She came to her now—led by the hand of the devil himself—to do things in her son's bed that would surely condemn any God-fearing woman to hell.

Over the next several hours the women's craving for each other followed them everywhere. Their lust formed and dissolved, only to form again. Beth had decided she would spend the rest of the summer sleeping with Joanna in the carriage house. As the couple prepared for their first night, Beth stood in the doorway of the bathroom watching as Joanna brushed her teeth. Every ordinary act had become another sacred moment to memorize. She would have three weeks of these moments—and then what? Her heart refused to think about that now. Tomorrow posed its own compromise.

"Jo, would you hate me if I didn't cancel my visit to the nursing home in the morning?"

Beth handed her a towel to wipe her mouth.

"Are you assuming I can't live without you?"

"Not assuming… just hoping."

"As long as you promise to make it up to me when you get back."

"Oh, I more than promise…" Beth nibbled on her ear, hinting at more. "As long as we're bargaining, how would you feel if I invited Steve for dinner Saturday night? I think we owe him that much, don't you?"

"I'll call him first thing in the morning."

Beth's eyes lingered upon the reflection of them together in the mirror.

"It really wouldn't be our one week anniversary without him."

"Just as long as he doesn't stay long… I've got other plans for the rest of that night."

The compromise suited Beth just fine.

Night draped itself upon them like a soft summer blanket as the couple lay peacefully in one another's arms. Beth's eyes drifted to the corner of the room. Jo sensed her preoccupation.

"What are you thinking?"

"Not thinking… just remembering…" Without diverting her eyes, Beth drew Joanna closer to her body and to her memory. "I was picturing my piano over in that corner by the window the way it used to sit years ago."

Her voice trailed off. Newly opened to her deepest longings, Beth's original dream for herself felt hopelessly out of reach. Jo could feel her melancholy.

"Why don't you move it back in here?"

Beth's heart strained to absorb the largeness of her sacrifices.

"Maybe someday…"

Resigned to things as they were, she drifted off to sleep.

Still holding Beth in her arms, Jo's eyes remained fixed on the corner of the carriage house. *Someday* was closer than Beth could ever have imagined. *Someday* would be their one-week anniversary.

As soon as Steve answered the phone Joanna got right to the point.

"Just for the record, I didn't appreciate getting laid off."

Steve was glad to hear her voice.

"And how do you feel about just getting *laid*?"

"I mind that less."

"I thought you might."

Joanna became serious.

"We're in the middle of a pretty big job. Are you sure you don't need me?"

"I'd say Beth needs you more."

Joanna didn't argue.

"There's something else she needs that I can use your help with... moving her piano back into the carriage house."

Steve was painfully aware of Beth's unrealized dreams.

"So far I'm liking the sound of this."

"This Sunday's our one-week anniversary. I'm gonna' suggest we spend the day where we had our picnic. While we're gone, think you can handle the move?"

Steve considered the logistics.

"Me and a couple of buddies roll the piano out of the living-room through the French doors that open up onto the patio. That puts us about a hundred feet from the side of the carriage house. We unseal the double doors they used for the buggies... move the couch out of the way... roll in the piano... reseal the doors... and presto! One carriage house complete with its own baby grand piano... just the way it was always meant to be."

Jo wondered if, in his enthusiasm, Steve might be underestimating the task.

"Are you sure?"

"Trust me, piece of cake!"

"How much time will you need?"

"Be gone by noon and don't come back before 6."

"So where's the beautiful virtuoso now?"

"At the nursing home."

"At least you don't have to worry about losing her to anyone *there*."

"I don't know. She seems pretty crazy about this one old geezer."

"So you know about Arthur?"

"Got the whole story."

"Leave it to Beth. It's not every woman who's got one son with raging hormones and another with hardening of the arteries."

"She's also crazy enough to invite you over for dinner this Saturday night."

"I'd have thought you guys would want to spend that night alone."

"Don't worry, you won't be staying late. Only this time *I'll* be the one throwing you out. Just be here around seven."

"Great. When the moment's right you can show me exactly where you want us to put the piano."

"Thanks, this really means a lot."

Steve knew her appreciation was genuine.

"People have been known to move mountains for love. Why not a baby grand?"

He expected some flack over the 'L' word, but it never came.

"I won't forget this."

"I'd imagine there's a lot about this summer you won't forget."

Jo deliberately changed the subject.

"Where can I get a roll of film developed in an hour?"

After he told her, Jo was anxious to get there quickly.

"See ya' Saturday night. Gotta' go."

Joanna nursed a cup of coffee while she waited for the processing to be complete. One print in particular—a picture of Beth sitting at the base of the Great Rock—captured Jo's heart. She purchased a simple frame and slipped the photograph inside.

Back at the carriage house she let her fingertips graze over the image and said the words out loud.

"I love you Beth Garrison. I love you more than I thought I could ever love anyone in my life."

Struggling with her heart, Jo opened her duffle bag and hid the frame inside. Her secret plan well in place, she decided to go for a swim. Jo was midway through her eighth lap when Beth pulled into the driveway. As always, at the sight of Joanna's body her heart raced ahead of her footsteps. Beth quickly undressed and slipped naked into her lover's arms.

"Miss me?"

"Didn't even notice you were gone."

"Hmm… I'll have to work on making my absence felt."

Her kiss was deep and searching. Joanna confessed.

"Okay, maybe I missed you a little. How's Arthur?"

"Sweet as ever. The whole place is buzzing with plans for his party." Beth squeezed her hand. "Come with me Jo! I'd love for you to meet him."

"Forget it! There's no way I'm putting myself in the middle of mass incontinence."

"Shame on you. Where's your sense of humanity?"

"I guess it's not nearly as developed as my sense of smell. Thanks anyway, but I'll pass."

"Please… I know it would mean so much to him to have you there."

"The guy doesn't even know me."

"He asks about you all the time. I think he senses how much you mean to me. Won't you at least think about it?"

"I'll *think* about it… but I'm not promising."

"Maybe not yet but I have the next eleven days to work on you."

"Speaking of invitations, Steve said yes to Saturday night."

"Wonderful! Have you had lunch yet?"

"No, I waited for you."

Beth pulled Joanna closer.

"I seem to recall when we first met you said something about no finger sandwiches, so perhaps I could interest you in something a bit more… *exotic…*"

Beth lifted herself out of the water, maneuvered her hips close to the edge of the pool and spread her legs. As she moved through the waist-high water, Joanna could not take her eyes away. She gripped Beth's thighs and pressed her mouth to her lover's offering. Beth moaned with pleasure as she lowered herself down upon the surrounding blanket of grass. A burning from deep within pushed to the surface of her skin meeting the penetrating rays of the sun until it felt as if her whole being radiated with heat. Gazing up into the fiercely blue sky, Beth followed the hypnotic course of a gliding bird, matching it to the course of Joanna's tongue as it glided across the length of her swollen, aching flesh. She clutched the sides of Joanna's head and closed her eyes, convinced that heaven was no longer a place, but this incredible, exquisite sensation.

In the secluded days and nights that followed, the couple fell deeper and deeper into a space lost to time. There was no other hour—no other mark—except for the making of love and the resting from making love. They slept only when they felt exhausted and ate only when they felt hungry. They moved through a world—apart from the world—speaking to no one—missing no one—needing no one but the nearness of each other. For all the lovers Joanna had known—for all the lovers Beth had not—they were equal in their surrender and equal in their command. Certain that their rapture could be no greater than the last time, they discovered the thrill of being wrong. The cruelty of their bliss was that their happiness was what often hurt the most. Were the lovers not careful to protect their hearts, the air itself could easily have torn their delicate world apart.

It was on this well-guarded doorstep that Steve arrived at seven o'clock sharp Saturday night, with a bottle of wine and his usual warm smile. He greeted Beth first with the most reassuring of hugs.

"You look fantastic."

Beth blushed. She had never felt more ashamed or more alive.

"Are you saying infidelity becomes me?"

"I'm saying *happiness* becomes you."

Joanna worked the cork up through the neck of the bottle hoping that a glass of wine would serve to calm Beth's nerves. Steve, too, did his best to put her at ease.

"Whatever you're cooking smells delicious."

"It's just lasagna."

Unsure about everything, Beth checked on the dish she'd made a thousand times, then pointed to the couch. She was, as always, disarmingly honest.

"Can we please sit down before I collapse from anxiety?"

Steve deliberately chose the rocker so that the women could have the couch.

"I'll bet this is the first time since last week that the bed's been closed, huh?"

Joanna laughed. Beth remained still and awkward, intentionally sitting a respectable distance away from her. Steve couldn't bear the tension.

"Hey… it's *me*, remember? You can relax. Hell, you can even *touch*."

Joanna too had all she could take of their ridiculous formality. She reached out and pulled Beth into her arms. Beth instantly melted against her and for the first time since Steve had arrived, all three could finally be themselves. Steve lifted his glass.

"Here's to following your heart."

Altogether unsure of where that road would lead, the women fell silent. Steve attempted to rescue them from the moment.

"Okay, pop quiz! Jo, fill in the blank: first thing in the morning, Beth is…"

"As horny as the night before."

Beth instantly turned beet red. She shoved Joanna, then sprang up to check on dinner.

As the two continued to joke with each other, Beth struggled with a sudden wave of melancholy. How often it had felt as if she and Joanna had met already knowing everything about one another. How she ached to be able to live out her life basking in that familiarity. Determined not to spoil the evening, Beth managed to hide her sadness and for the next several hours the three enjoyed the truest and closest of friendships, all the while careful to avoid any reference to life past the summer. A little past midnight Joanna tapped her watch. Steve was quick to take the hint.

"Well ladies, I think this is where I came in... or should I say got thrown out one week ago." He stood up. "I don't imagine you'll need that radio station to run interference tonight."

Jo was quick to assure him.

"I think we can take it from here."

Detecting a subtle but undeniable sadness in Beth's eyes, Steve made sure to give her an extra strong hug while he whispered in her ear.

"Make beautiful music together."

Beth could not do more to thank him than to return the warmth of his embrace with equal affection.

"Good night honey. Get home safe."

Jo wanted to run through their strategy for the next day.

"I'll walk you to your truck."

For a moment, Beth lingered at the screen door. She smiled to see Steve with his arm around Joanna, remembering a time not so long ago when such a sight would have crushed her heart. Now she need only prepare for Joanna's return and try to forget that the romantic night ahead was also bringing them one night closer to their last.

As Jo and Steve crossed the yard, she ran down some last minute instructions. He was to leave the pictures of her family in the house.

"There's a framed photo of Beth in my duffle bag. I want nothing on the piano except for that picture, the vase, the index card and that sheet music that's open on the stand."

"I'll take care of everything. Just enjoy your picnic."

"I want everything to be perfect. She deserves it."

Steve rested his hand on her shoulder.

"She doesn't need for things to be perfect. She just needs you."

Jo didn't respond.

"You're really in love with her, aren't you?"

Unable to deny the truth, Jo nodded.

"Have you told her so?"

"No."

"What the hell are you waiting for? It's obvious she loves you too."

Joanna found herself in a place she'd never been before.

"What am I gonna' do Steve?"

"When does Ben come home?"

"His flight's scheduled for two weeks from today."

"I wish I knew what to tell you."

"You're a writer... can't you give him some tragic ending?"

"Let's not forget I actually *like* the guy."

"Some would say you have a funny way of showing it."

Steve looked over at the carriage house. He truly adored the woman inside.

"Apparently my loyalties are divided."

"Then at least get the hell out of here so I can finish what you started last Saturday night."

Her eyes grew sincere.

"That sappy radio dedication stopped me from making the biggest mistake of my life."

Steve thought back on the moments leading up to his call.

"Actually, I can't take all the credit. I probably wouldn't have done it if it weren't for this white-haired, broad-shouldered dyke with a sweet tooth. She was the one who planted that song in my head and the quarter in my hand. Next thing I knew, she was gone."

Steve didn't seem to notice Joanna's brow tighten as he described the strange encounter with a woman who sounded suspiciously like Dell.

"Don't forget, be gone by noon and don't come back before six."

After he'd driven off, Joanna stood under the deep star-filled sky, baffled by the mysterious occurrence. What would Dell be doing out in a storm at three in the morning? And what were the unlikely odds that she would cross paths with Steve—not to mention the impact their meeting had on the outcome of that night? Jo turned toward the carriage house. The soft glow of candlelight emanating from its windows was enough to quell even this most unsettling of coincidences.

Joanna stopped in the doorway and smiled. Candles were set about in almost every corner of the room. Cast in the golden yellow light, Beth was already waiting for her in bed, the sheet pulled modestly up around her waist.

"I thought you wouldn't mind if we dispensed with last week's argument and dance." Her eyes were soft and inviting. "We've already wasted so much time…"

She waited anxiously for Joanna to undress and climb in beside her. The candlelight caressed their union. Beth closed her eyes to seal in forever the memory of the way they fit.

"Happy one-week anniversary my darling."

Joanna returned the sentiment with the sweetness of her kiss. In its aftermath, Beth reflected on the night.

"Steve is such wonderful company." She giggled. "I thought he'd *never* leave."

"You're shameless. You know that, don't you?"

"I wasn't until I met you."

Jo responded by sweeping across Beth's nipple with her tongue.

"So where would you like to begin?"

"Funny you should ask." Beth reached behind her pillow and held up the jar containing her wedding band and the Cheerio. "How about with you explaining this."

Jo swiped the jar from Beth's hand.

"How'd you find that?"

"I was putting away the dishes. I moved the coffee mugs and there it was."

Embarrassed, Jo addressed only half the contents.

"You asked me to hold your wedding band. It was the safest place I could find."

"It's not the ring I'm curious about."

Jo leaned forward awkwardly.

"It's a Cheerio, okay?"

"Yes sweetie, I can see that."

There was nothing for Jo to do but admit the truth.

"Remember the first time we had dinner together… you got the insane idea that if we each tossed a Cheerio in a dish every time we didn't want to talk about something it would keep things safe between us."

Beth circled Joanna's nipple with her fingertip.

"The idea seems to have failed miserably."

Jo knew that Beth was still expecting and explanation.

"That was the one *you* tossed into the dish. I wanted a part of you, so when you left the room I swiped the only thing I thought I could ever have." Jo didn't have to admit more, but she did. "You have no idea how many hours I sat with that thing in my hand, aching for it to be more… how many nights I put it on the coffee table and fell asleep holding it in my sight."

Beth was undeniably touched.

"Come here you silly, sentimental woman." She reached over and drew Jo back into her arms. "So you wanted me from that very first night?"

"I wanted you in the goddamm parking lot when Trudy was trying to stop me from tearing your head off!"

Beth held Jo all the closer for the gift of her confession.

"I had no idea I tormented you so."

Once again Jo felt helpless to her attraction.

"You did…" Her mouth sought the fullness of Beth's breasts. "God… you still do…"

How deeply Beth understood Joanna's hunger—a hunger that felt so much older than this hour, this summer, this life. As the spirits hid in the flickering candlelight, Beth lay back to remember and receive it all.

The next morning Joanna awoke to the aroma of fresh coffee and biscuits baking in the oven. Beth appeared from the alcove. She was toweling her hair.

"I thought I'd make up for visiting day with a belated breakfast in bed."

Jo smiled. Secretly concerned about the hour, she snuck a quick look at the clock. It was closing in on ten.

"How much longer 'til they're ready?"

Beth knew it would be at least another 10 minutes. She crawled back into bed, leaned over and kissed Joanna deeply.

"What's the matter, don't things heat up fast enough for you around here?"

Before Jo could answer, Beth kissed her again. It would not be the first time that the flames of their desire sent their plans up in smoke. This morning, Joanna could not afford to let that happen.

"What I'd really like is to make love to you on a blanket next to the rock. What do you say?"

Beth had waited her whole life to be in Joanna's arms. She could wait a little longer.

"Go take your shower. The biscuits will be ready by the time you're out."

She was thrilled with their plans.

"I can't think of another place I'd rather spent this day."

"Sure you wouldn't rather take a ride up to camp and see how the color war games are going?"

Beth cast a lascivious glance at Joanna's body.

"Quite sure."

Once again they took Ben's Jeep. Beth no longer felt the least bit guilty about using her husband's car to deliver her to a place where she would make passionate love with someone else. Consumed by her desire for Joanna, Beth felt no digression was too egregious—no sin too evil—no recrimination too damning.

The view from the great rock on this most exquisite of days was more magnificent than Beth could ever remember. But as the couple stood in each other's arms gazing down at the valley, a gradual darkness eclipsed its beauty. Not wanting to spoil things for the other, the women found sufficient excuses to be briefly apart. Beth went off to pick flowers—Jo went off to sketch—all the while stealing glances of each other they knew would have to last a lifetime. When Jo could take no more of their separation she returned to Beth's side. Slipping her arms around Beth's waist, Jo put her lips against her ear.

"I want you..."

This time Beth's eyes did not plead to be spared. Joanna pressed Beth up against the great rock and unbuttoned her blouse. Cupping her breasts, she ran her tongue along the length of Beth's neck circling her nipples and down the center of her belly. Jo could feel Beth's stomach tightened with greater and greater anticipation. Beneath its unyielding surface, the majestic stone melted from the heat of Beth's flesh where the memory of her surrender already lay buried deep within its core. Beth moaned as Joanna lowered her shorts and dropped to her knees, burying her face between Beth's thighs.

Over the next several hours the women took turns preying upon their helpless, insatiable hunger for each other's body. Sometimes their passion struck suddenly—without warning—and sometimes it mounted slowly—gradually pulling them under. By late afternoon the couple lay exhausted in each other's arm. They drifted off to sleep and woke to find the sun much lower in the sky. Joanna discreetly checked her watch. It was past five and safe to think about heading back. Unlike the Sunday before at camp, this time they walked hand-in-hand back to the car. The silence that now fell between them was not formed of estrangement and heartache but of intimacy and peace. They kissed one more time and headed home—not to a quintessential Victorian masterpiece with a white picket fence and not to an ultra chic loft with a breathtaking view—but *home* to their carriage house—a small, unpretentious space in which their mismatched lives had found perfect collaboration.

When Joanna pulled into Beth's driveway she was relieved not to see any trace of Steve or his friends. She took Beth's hand and led her across the yard. Just before they reached the step of the carriage house, Joanna held Beth back.

"Wait! Close your eyes."

"Why?"

"Just close your eyes. It's a surprise."

Joanna opened the door and stepped aside to watch Beth's expression.

"Okay, open them."

Beth gasped at the sight of her piano sitting exactly as she had described it to Jo a few nights before. Her body trembled with emotion. Though Steve was forced to move some of the furniture around to accommodate the massive instrument, the room itself remained respectfully undisturbed. Signs of the women's intimacy were just as they'd been left. The bed was still unmade and all the melted candles were still set about. Now, there amid it all sat a piece of Beth's soul. Joanna knew she would never be able to thank Steve adequately. She also knew that for him, Beth's happiness was already thanks enough. Beth had a thousand questions but for now her heart would not permit a single one. She gazed at the specially framed photograph beside the crystal vase and then at the sheet music of her unfinished composition. As her fingers brushed lightly over the keys, something deep within told Beth it would not remain so very much longer. Joanna had remained quietly off to the side.

"Will you play for me later?"

Beth's eyes filled with tenderness and torment.

"I'll play for you later and for the rest of my life… through all the years of darkness that separate us and…"

Joanna pressed her fingertips to Beth's lips to silence her. Beth moved Jo's hand against her own heart.

"Promise me you'll listen… promise me you'll hear…"

Joanna pulled her close.

"I promise."

In the past, the women had only cried separately. Now, for the first time, they wept openly in each other's arms.

Chapter 22

The beginning of the couple's second week was not nearly as euphoric as their last. Their trials began 9:30 Monday morning when Nick showed up—unannounced—at the carriage house door. Joanna stepped out onto the porch to keep him at bay. She was barely civil.

"Something I can do for you?"

He seemed to enjoy catching her off guard.

"I came by to see if Beth was alright. Ben called me from England. He's concerned. She hasn't been answering the phone and hasn't returned any of his calls since last week. I offered to stop by and see if everything's okay. I tried the house. The car's in the driveway but she's not answering the door. Thought you might know where she is."

Beth came out from the alcove wrapped only in a towel. It was too late for Joanna to prepare her. Beth nervously tightened the towel. Jo immediately offered an excuse for Beth's being there in the first place—let alone naked.

"Ben asked Nick to stop by to see if you were okay. I was about to explain that you weren't getting any hot water because of that boiler problem so I offered to let you shower here until it's repaired."

Beth was grateful for Joanna's quick-thinking save, especially since Nick seemed to buy it.

"As long as I'm here, why don't I stay for a cup of coffee?"

This time Beth had no trouble answering herself.

"Sorry, but we're already running late. We're meeting Steve."

"What's he got that I don't?"

Beth embellished her lie.

"A kitchen remodeling job that needs a woman's eye."

"I knew I was in the wrong business. Well, do me a favor. Get back to your husband, will you? He's going out of his mind wondering why you haven't returned his calls."

Beth resented the order. She chose to ignore it completely.

"Sorry you went out of your way for nothing."

"It was hardly for nothing." He winked and gave her the once over through the screen. "The invitation's always open to shower at my place..."

Beth turned away.

"Goodbye Nick."

Joanna went back inside, leaving him standing there alone. Eventually he took the hint and left.

Beth buried her head in her hands.

"God that was close!"

"It could have been worse. You could have come out stark naked."

Beth groaned at the thought. Joanna was stern.

"You really do need to call Ben. You've been avoiding it for days now."

"I know... I know..."

Beth was shaken by the close call. Joanna tried to move past the near disastrous start to the day.

"Get dressed. I'm taking you to Trudy's for breakfast."

Beth remembered her promise to Steve. Determined not to be robbed of a single day, she rallied from the upsetting encounter and agreed.

Trudy was delighted to see them together.

"Well look who's here, sworn enemies turned best friends."

The breakfast crowd had thinned and the place was practically empty. For sentimental reasons, the couple took the same booth they had the morning of the accident. Trudy returned with two cups of coffee. Noticing the pristine Thunderbird parked outside, she smiled at Jo.

"Guess you figured out it was safer to have Beth in your car than anywhere around it."

"Safer in some ways. More dangerous in others."

Beth kicked Jo under the table.

"Well either way, glad to see you've kissed and made up."

The women looked down at their menus.

Trudy took their order and moved on to serve another customer, leaving the women alone to bask in each other's company. As they looked into one another's eyes, the upsetting incident with Nick faded into a distant memory until Trudy returned with their breakfast and noticed Beth's missing ring.

"Nothing's changed between you and Ben, has it?"

For the second time that morning Beth's heart nearly stopped. Trudy pointed to Beth's naked ring finger.

"Couldn't help notice you're travelin' light."

Beth had gotten much too used to not wearing it. Once again she lied.

"It's this awful humidity. My fingers have been swollen for days."

"Tell me about it honey… just wait 'til the arthritis kicks in"

Someone signaled Trudy for his check. For the second time that morning the women's 'cover' remained tenuous at best. Jo realized the issue wasn't going away.

"Maybe it would just be better if you wore the damn thing."

Beth stiffened and put down her fork.

"No! I promised myself I wouldn't put it back on until…"

She couldn't bring herself to finish the sentence. Jo tried to rescue them both.

"Okay. Anything else *swollen* that you'd care to do something about?"

Once again Beth fought back from the depths of her despair.

"Yes. Let's get out of here!"

Before they left Trudy inquired about Ben and Adam. Apparently reality was hell-bent on ruining the couple's day. Determined to sweeten it anyway she could, Beth grabbed Jo's arm, pulled her into the supermarket and headed straight for the dessert aisle. On their way back to the car an unmistakably husky voice interrupted them.

"I knew you were here."

With Steve's indelible description still burning in her mind, Jo spun around to see the "broad-shouldered, white-haired dyke with a sweet tooth" chomping on a Snickers bar.

"Whatcha' do, rub your crystal ball?"

Dell was amused.

"Actually, I spotted the T-Bird in the parking lot. It's a hard car to miss."

Regretting her earlier reaction to Dell's appearance and not understanding the harshness of Joanna's tone, Beth tried to make up for both.

"It's nice to see you again. How are you?"

Dell shifted the bag of litter and cat food in her arms.

"Couldn't be better. How 'bout you?"

Beth ignored the disturbing start to the day.

"We're having a wonderful summer."

Dell took another bite of her candy bar.

"So whatcha' been up to since I saw you last?"

Jo was deliberately vague.

"Little of this. Little of that."

Dell studied the women's faces and smiled.

"Judging from the glow comin' off ya', I'd say it's more like a *lot* of this and a *lot* of that."

Beth felt herself blush. It was obvious Dell sensed much more about the nature of their relationship than the couple admitted to. Dell finished the Snickers.

"How 'bout dinner and drinks Saturday night... just the four of us? I've told Sara all about you."

Joanna became suspicious.

"How would you know anything about us?"

Dell winked.

"I have my sources." She leaned over and whispered in Joanna's ear. "Surprise her with that gift yet?"

Jo nodded, giving Dell permission to bring it up.

"Find a special place for that sweet little frame you left behind when you bolted from the shop?"

Beth was grateful Dell had obviously forgiven her.

"It's on the mantle." She could barely contain her enthusiasm. "It's so much more than just the frame I love, it's the picture inside."

Dell smiled.

"So what do you say... dinner Saturday night?"

Perhaps as a backlash to this morning's setbacks, Beth was now more determined than ever to push ahead and broaden her experiences.

"Why not?"

Under the circumstances, Joanna was surprised at Beth's willingness to socialize in public with such an obvious lesbian couple. For her own reasons, she was less than enthusiastic about the plans.

"Don't you have Arthur's party at the nursing home this Saturday."

"It starts at noon. When the birthday boy is one hundred I doubt if the festivities will run too much beyond that."

Dell pretended to be surprised by the coincidence.

"That wouldn't be Arthur Prescott you're talking about, would it?"

Beth's face lit up.

"Why yes! Do you know Arthur?"

"Not *him* really... just part of his life. I purchased some of his belongings at an estate sale a number of years back. Matter of fact, there's a good chance that frame you love came from his home as well."

Beth held her hand to her heart.

"Do you think?"

Dell pretended not to know for sure.

"Open the back. Maybe there's an inscription on the photograph itself."

Beth squeezed Jo's arm.

"Wouldn't that be amazing?"

She offered Dell an explanation of her deeply complex bond with Arthur—how they'd met and how it evolved into the cherished friendship the two shared today.

Dell listened intently.

"It doesn't get any more special than that." She took Beth's hands—the hands that brought Arthur so much comfort and so much joy. "We lose what we're meant to lose so that we can find what we're meant to find. You're both very lucky. It should be a wonderful party." She turned to Jo. "You're going too, aren't you?"

Beth answered for her.

"She wouldn't miss it for the world."

Dell ignored Jo's reluctance.

"I can't think of anything that would make him happier."

Once again Joanna protested the absurdity of the notion.

"The old man doesn't even know me."

"It's not the old man who remembers...," Dell mused to herself, "it's the little boy." She turned to Beth. "Saturday night, eight o'clock. You pick the place."

Beth suggested Frieda's, just outside of town.

Dell seemed particularly satisfied with their plans.

"Gotta' get back and feed Bridey. She must have starved to death in a previous life 'cause she can't eat enough in this one." Her eyes pinned Joanna against her car. "Old hungers are usually the hardest to feed." Her expression softened on Beth. "Check inside that frame."

"Oh I will!"

Joanna waited until Dell was out of earshot.

"There's something about that woman that really creeps me out."

Beth was much more intrigued.

"Can you imagine the coincidence of that frame coming from Arthur's estate?"

Jo thought back to the portfolio Dell had shared with her the day she'd gone back to buy the frame. Preferring to put the eerie visit behind her, she chose not to mention it.

"If you ask me, she's a part of one too many coincidences. There's a lot more I'd like to know about that woman."

Beth was in too good a mood for such inconsequential concerns.

"Take me home! The only things I want to know are if that frame once belonged to Arthur and what you taste like smothered in this can of whipped cream!"

"I suppose that's your way of bribing me into going to Arthur's party."

Beth smiled mischievously.

"You'll see, dinner will be fun too. It'll be like a double date."

"Hardly."

"What would you call it?"

"A mistake."

"Don't be such a stick in the mud. Besides, I thought you'd enjoy being around another couple…," Beth hesitated, "like *us*."

After an already difficult morning Jo wasn't about to point out the laundry list of differences that made the two couples not at all alike.

"I still say you don't know what you're getting yourself into."

Beth moved her hand playfully along the length of Joanna's thigh.

"I didn't have a clue about a lot of things… until I met you."

"Don't say I didn't warn you."

The moment they got home Beth raced to the mantle.

"So much for the whipped cream," Joanna mumbled to herself.

Beth's heart pounded as she worked the intricate clasps that held the black velvet backing to its frame. Her fingers too unsteady, she passed it to Joanna for help. Once opened, Jo handed it back. Beth anxiously removed the cardboard beneath, exposing the back of the old sepia image. Indeed, it had been inscribed: 'last picture of momma and me taken in a corner of her music room—October 1897'. Overwhelmed, Beth pressed the image to her heart and began to cry. Jo would not allow herself to consider the odds of the coincidence. Eventually Beth reset the photograph into it's frame and carefully resealed the velvet backing. She turned to Joanna.

Jo knew what Beth was going to ask.

"Go ahead… give it to him for his birthday."

Beth's tears flowed even more steadily now.

"How can I thank you… not just for giving it to me but for letting me give it to him?"

Beth replaced the photograph on the mantle. Her eyes shifted back and forth from the painting she loved to the frame she loved. Jo sensed she needed time alone in the company of both.

"I'll be in the carriage house with that can of whipped cream. You might want to get back to Ben first. You really can't afford too many more close calls."

Beth knew Joanna was right. She reached for her lover's arm. Her eyes said all that was in her heart. Jo carried their message and the groceries back to the carriage house.

There was no easy way for Beth to make the call except to just pick up the receiver and dial. Ben answered on the second ring. It was as if he'd been sitting by the phone since the last time they'd spoken over a week ago.

"Beth, thank God! You had me worried sick."

"Yes I know. Nick dropped by earlier this morning."

"Why haven't you returned any of my calls?"

Beth tried to be as sympathetic as she could.

"I'm sorry. I've had a lot on my mind."

"Is everything okay? The last time we spoke you sounded preoccupied."

Beth's memory of her indiscretion was all too vivid. She placed the reason for it elsewhere.

"I must have still been tired from the trip. You know how exhausting visiting day can be."

"Yeah, they do pack a lot into those hours."

"How else can they justify the outrageous cost of a child's summer vacation?"

For a fleeting moment their laughter wove together. It sounded as familiar as it did unnatural. Beth stared at a snapshot on the refrigerator of them together. He was the one who had gone abroad for the summer and yet by staying home, it was she who had journeyed to a place much farther.

"It's so good to hear your voice Beth."

Her husband's vulnerability had always touched her and for a moment she felt a wave of regret—if not guilt—for her neglect.

"I'm sorry I haven't been in touch."

Ben took advantage of his wife's apology.

"There's still close to two weeks of the summer. Fly over here and spend it with me."

He reminded her that this was the last week of his professional obligations and that he was only staying on to spend some additional time with his parents.

"We can rent a cottage in the countryside… bike… go for long walks… just like the old times. C'mon, what do you say?"

Beth was grateful for a viable excuse.

"I can't. Arthur's one hundredth birthday is Saturday. I wouldn't miss it for the world."

Ben knew how much she and Arthur meant to one another. He didn't press her.

"Then I'll fly home a week ahead of schedule and go with you. I'm sure my folks will understand."

"No!" Beth panicked. She tried to temper her aversion to the idea with something that sounded reasonable. "That really wouldn't be fair to them. They're not getting any younger either and they get to see you so infrequently." She sensed his acknowledgment. "How are your folks?"

"They're just fine. We're having a wonderful time together, but I can't tell you how often they've said they wished you'd have come along."

"Please send both of them my love."

She asked him about how his lectures were going and listened patiently as he answered in great detail.

"I'm thrilled for you Ben. It sounds like it's been a truly wonderful experience."

"It has been but I'm getting terribly homesick. I keep telling myself the twenty-fifth is just around the corner."

The reminder tore through Beth's heart. She closed her eyes as if to shut out anything past the moment. Once again her silence unnerved him.

"You haven't really told me what you've been doing with yourself."

As she held the phone to her ear, Beth wandered over to the kitchen window and stared out at the carriage house. She remained vague but truthful.

"I'm trying to do what you encouraged me to do the morning you left... I'm trying to follow my heart."

Ben was conspicuously silent. Beth's eyes drifted to the corner of the living room where her piano had stood for the last 20 years. She made a conscious decision not to prepare him for that change. There had been so many since he'd left. Some he would see. Some he would feel. All of which she knew would come to bear upon their lives once he returned. Their conversation ended with both marking time. The thirteen days remaining meant very different things to each of them. This time he did not remind her to call more often. This time she did not promise she would. He said only that he loved her. She said only that she knew.

After she hung up, Beth sat down at the dining room table and rested her head in her arms. A steady stream of tears soaked through the linen placemat beneath .

This time Joanna had stayed away and given Beth her privacy. Now as Beth stood in the doorway of the carriage house, the strain of her conversation showed everywhere on her face. It was obvious she'd been crying. Jo didn't ask anything about the call and Beth didn't offer. Neither wanted to surrender another moment to the hopelessness of it all. Beth opened the refrigerator door. She stared into it blankly until Joanna came up from behind and wrapped Beth in her arms. Her rescue was perfectly timed.

"Hungry?"

Beth let her head fall back against Joanna's shoulder.

"I wasn't... until now."

Struggling against the weight of her heart, Beth reached for the can of whipped cream.

"Let's start with dessert and work our way backward."

Jo pressed her lips against Beth's ear.

"Backward to where?"

She let her tongue trace the length of Beth's neck. Beth closed her eyes.

"To the beginning of time..."

Tuesday afternoon Beth returned from the nursing home in wonderful spirits. Everyone on staff was excited about Arthur's upcoming birthday and Arthur himself seemed unusually alert and in better health than he'd been in weeks. Beth found herself humming as she collected the mail. There was a postcard from Rheeta who'd apparently set sail on yet another cruise and was happy to report that halfway around the world she'd found the next 'Mr. Right'. Beth shook her head and smiled as she sorted through the rest. Her heart froze—among the usual assortment of bills and junk mail was an envelope from the office of Dr. Gayle Kramer. The handwritten address was posted to Joanna Cameron, c/o B. Garrison. Her hands trembled as she felt the thickness of its contents, suggesting a long heartfelt letter inside. For the next several minutes Beth paced her kitchen floor. A part of her wanted simply to destroy the letter—just pretend it never arrived so she wouldn't have to pass it along. In the last several weeks Beth had found that she was capable of many unthinkable things—betrayal included—but being dishonest with Joanna was not one of them. Left with no other choice, Beth composed herself and walked as steadily as she could across the yard to the carriage house. Joanna was busy priming a new canvas when the screen door opened. Beth's eyes were noticeably troubled. Jo knew she'd just come from the nursing home.

"Is it Arthur?"

"No... this came for you in today's mail."

She handed the letter over.

Jo glanced at the familiar handwriting. When she looked up, the couple's eyes locked in a burdened silence. Though she didn't let on, Jo wasn't surprised. Her father had phoned earlier to wish his daughter a happy birthday. He'd mentioned that Gayle—whom he thought of as a daughter-in-law—had phoned to ask for Jo's address so that she could send a card. He'd felt awkward about their separation and about denying her request. Joanna didn't blame him. Nor was she surprised that Gayle had used the occasion as an excuse to contact her before the summer had ended as they'd agreed. Beth was respectful.

"I'll give you a chance to read it alone."

She now understood how Joanna felt when she left her to make that call to Ben after the night at the motel. As she moved toward the door, Beth could hardly breath. Joanna put the letter down and walked her outside. Her eyes followed Beth's every labored step back to the house. After the slam of the screen door from across the yard released Joanna from her painful watch, she went back inside and stared at the envelope on the table. Jo sat down and slid the blade of her palette knife along its edge. The letter was indeed long and heartfelt—the most emotionally vulnerable Gayle had been in years. As Jo slowly digested every word she could not ignore their undeniable history. Enclosed with the letter was an unusually romantic birthday card and two first class airline tickets to Paris for the September weekend that would be their tenth anniversary. In her outpouring, Gayle said she hoped that by returning to the place where the couple had first met they could find a place where they could begin again. She begged Joanna not to make any decisions until after she returned to the city and they had talked.

Up until that point Joanna had managed to avoid thinking about her life beyond the summer. Suddenly, a future *without* Beth felt as impossible as a future *with* her. Jo slipped the letter and the tickets back inside the envelope. Not since visiting day at camp had their love felt as hopeless. On that day it was Beth who had found the courage to defeat the odds. This time she knew Beth was waiting for *her* to do the same. Joanna went to the house and found Beth curled up in the corner of the sofa, nursing a cup of tea. The pain in her eyes said everything. Jo sat down beside her. She knew Beth needed to be held as much as she needed to hold her. She took the cup from Beth's hand, set it down on the coffee table and pulled Beth into her arms. Neither spoke a word as their hearts beat together. There still remained so much to know of each other—so much to reconcile—so much to heal. Beth couldn't help but fear that Gayle's letter would erase what little time they had left. Joanna looked deep into her eyes.

"Today's my birthday. She sent me a card."

"You told me your birthday was in December."

"I lied."

"Why?"

"I didn't want to acknowledge anything that had to do with dates. I just wanted to exist with you outside of time. I'm sorry."

Beth's disappointment turned to understanding. How many times had she herself stared at the calendar in an inevitable showdown with fate? She found it easy to forgive Joanna for her deceit but she knew there was more than just a birthday card and about *that* she needed Jo's complete honesty.

"What else was inside?"

"A pretty emotional letter… and two tickets to Paris for our anniversary in September."

"I see…"

Beth freed herself from Jo's arms and moved over to the window. Joanna immediately came and stood behind her. Beth crossed her arms protectively as she looked out at the white picket fence.

"I guess I've gotten used to it being *my* life that looms over us all the time. That seemed hard enough. The realization of *yours* was something I conveniently chose to ignore." She couldn't bring herself to look at Joanna. "I imagine Paris must be beautiful in the fall…"

Jo ran her hand along the length of Beth's arm.

"Not nearly as beautiful as the view from the rock."

"Will you go?"

Jo wrestled with her conscience.

"The relationship deserves some kind of closure."

Beth couldn't decide if Jo was being naive or just kind.

"I'd say it's more like a new beginning Gayle's hoping for."

Jo couldn't deny Beth's hunch. She slipped her arms around Beth's waist. This time she did not surrender. Instead, her heart remained guarded.

"Are you going to tell her about us?"

"I don't know. Are you going to tell Ben?"

"I don't know either."

Joanna fought her way through their ambivalent silence.

"You never told me how your conversation with him went yesterday."

"You never asked." Beth finally allowed herself to lean back against the temporary comfort of Joanna's body. "He misses me as much as Gayle apparently misses you."

The simply stated reality foretold the most damning of futures. Suddenly Joanna exploded inside making the mere existence of all lesser affections altogether intolerable. She grabbed Beth's shoulders and spun her around. The demand of her embrace was overpowering. There was no preparing Beth for the hunger of Joanna's kiss. The greed of it shattered every boundary and unspoken rule of their affair. No longer could Jo's heart remain in shrouded silence. No longer would it be denied the full expression of its misery and its joy. This time the woman in her arms would not be spared.

"I love you Beth… I've loved you from the first moment we met."

Beth closed her eyes, desperate to both preserve the moment and protect herself from it. A sense of elation, then doom, swept across her heart. She'd become a reluctant master of self-preservation. Beth shook her head and covered her ears.

"I'm begging you Joanna, don't ever say those words again… the words I've longed to hear… the words I can't imagine ever living without." Tears began to flow as Beth recalled her darkest hours. "Somehow I've managed to survive so much, but having to let you go is the one thing that surely will destroy me."

Joanna turned away, her expression etched in pain.

Beth took her lover's face and turned it back toward her own.

"Look at me. Everything we need for each other to know is right here in our eyes. It always has been. Please… please… please… let that be enough."

Whether their intimacy was born of playfulness or passion, it had always ended poignantly. Sometimes this poignancy opened their hearts beyond all expectation. Sometimes it broke their hearts beyond all repair. This was one of those times. Knowing that was a promise she couldn't make, Jo searched for a middle ground.

"Can we at least compromise?"

Beth knew that her life was at stake.

"No."

Jo persisted.

"I get to say it, but first you get to cover your ears."

Before Beth could disagree Joanna pulled her close and sealed the terms with a kiss. Beth allowed her eyes to soften.

"So, today's your birthday."

"Yeah."

"Do you realize I'm not even sure how old you are?"

"Thirty-six."

Beth buried her face in her hands and groaned.

"God help me, I've fallen in love with a younger woman."

Joanna tilted Beth's face up to hers.

"What did you just say?"

Knowing the danger, Beth looked into Joanna's eyes and repeated the words slowly.

"I said I've fallen in love with a younger woman."

Jo smiled tenderly.

"I like the sound of that. Say it again."

Beth's heart gave in.

"Only today and *only* because it's your birthday."

Risking her own life, Beth leaned closer and sealed Jo's ear with the softness of her lips.

"I love you Joanna Cameron. I love you… I love you… I love you."

Jo refused Beth's invitation to take her out for a celebratory dinner. Rejected too was an impromptu barbeque with Steve. Beth was disappointed.

"At least let me bake you a cake."

"Absolutely not. I still wish you'd never found out it was my birthday in the first place."

"But now that I have, isn't there *anyway* I can do to make it special?"

"Actually, there is. I'd like to lie in bed with a glass of wine in one hand and my sketch pad in the other while you play the piano… drenched in candlelight, wearing nothing but your perfume and that silk slip you had on the night you came back from Boston."

Beth folded her arms.

"Sounds like you've already given this quite a bit of thought."

"It might have crossed my mind once or twice… having nothing to do with my birthday."

"I see. And what am I playing in this little fantasy of yours?"

"That piece you played the morning after you posed."

Beth remembered that morning well.

Joanna brushed a hair away from Beth's eyes.

"It was the most beautiful thing I'd ever heard."

Beth felt the weight of its mysterious origin.

"I wish I could say it's further along than it was that morning."

"Just play that part over and over. Does it have a name?"

"I'm afraid up 'til now its title is as elusive as its ending. I think of it as the unfinished theme to my unfinished life. Maybe with the piano back in the carriage house…"

Jo was eager for an answer.

"So do I get my private concert?"

"The curtain goes up when the sun goes down."

Joanna pulled Beth closer.

"And let's not forget intermission… when the slip comes off."

"Who says you get more than one wish?"

"That one's *yours*."

Sheltered inside the carriage house that had become theirs together and theirs alone, Beth emerged from the small alcove in the white silk slip Joanna had asked her to wear. As Beth moved barefoot across the room, the particles of night air filled with the fragrance of her perfume. Watching from bed, Joanna lifted herself up on her elbow to capture Beth's every move. In the softness of candlelight it looked as if she were floating across the room in a dream. In Joanna's adoring gaze Beth found a portion of herself she'd long ago forsaken. She sat down at her piano—this commanding extension of her soul now lit by moonlight as it streamed in through the nearby window. For the next few moments, Beth stared solemnly at the vase with the paper flowers and then at the photograph Joanna had framed. Knowing that all she would play tonight had long been memorized by her heart, Beth placed her fingers lightly upon the keys. She closed her eyes as if poised in prayer. A moment later she began. As one classical piece led into the next, all the other sounds embedded in the universe receded into a respectful silence like the sections of a great philharmonic orchestra conducted by 'The Gods' to pay homage to this most sacred of performances. At first Joanna simply laid there listening to the music of Beth's heart. When it had completely overwhelmed her own, Jo picked up her pad and began to sketch. As the women exchanged the gifts that had captured one another's souls, the hours of the night became entwined with eternity.

Lulled by the haunting melody of Beth's unfinished composition, Joanna fell off into the deepest of sleep. When the sketchpad slipped from Jo's hands and fell to the floor, Beth stopped playing and turned around. Touched by the sight of her lover's peaceful repose, she watched from her piano bench as the flickering candlelight caressed the most intimate parts of Joanna's body. How Beth's heart ached to have all the days of her life end like this one. A portion of the bed sheet had spilled over the side casting Beth's eye downward to the sketchpad on the floor. Moving quietly, she picked it up and brought it over to the kitchen table. Slowly turning the pages, she let her eyes drift over the sensitively rendered lines, each sketch a more adoring testament than the last. Beth continued to stare lovingly at the drawings until Joanna's sleep turned more restless. Embroiled in her reoccurring nightmare, Joanna's stirring soon escalated into distress. Once again the tormented sounds lodged in Jo's throat formed the same repetitive plea Beth had heard that night she'd stood helplessly in Adam's doorway.

"Ellie please… I'm begging you… don't go… don't go…"

This time Beth moved immediately to comfort her. She knelt down at the side of the bed and gently stroked Joanna's face.

"It's alright sweetheart. It's alright… I'm here."

On the edge of consciousness, Joanna pulled Beth into her arms—their endangered intimacy evident in her clutch.

"I can't lose you… I *can't*."

Beth rocked Joanna against her breast.

"I'll always be yours… *always*… 'til the end of time."

The comfort of Beth's body only made the promise and Joanna's torment worse.

"How long will it take to forget this? How long will it take to forget how perfectly we fit?"

Raging against everything that condemned them, Jo tore away Beth's slip and pushed her down onto her back. She used her knee to force Beth's thighs apart, then prepared her fingers with her own saliva.

"I want to be inside you…. I *need* to be inside you…"

Looking deep into her lover's eyes, Beth reached down and moved Joanna's hand out from between her legs. She brought it to her lips and kissed it, then pressed it against her heart.

"Oh my poor darling, don't you know… you already are."

Chapter 23

The morning of Arthur's birthday, Jo woke to find Beth sitting at the kitchen table. She was nursing a cup of coffee and curling the ends of ribbon on the colorfully wrapped gift box. Joanna lay there quietly observing as Beth doted over the finishing touches. Reminded of the lovingly placed miniature marshmallows, she was once again struck by Beth's unfailing attention to life's lesser and greater celebrations. A single word formed in Jo's heart, then on her lips.

"Beautiful."

Beth turned around and held up the finished product.

"It is, isn't it?"

"Actually, I was referring to you."

Beth smiled.

"Oh."

She played with the springy coil of the ribbon.

"I hope Arthur likes it. I wanted it to look especially cheerful."

"You said the guy's practically blind."

Beth repeated with one of her favorite quotes.

"It is only with the heart that one can see rightly… what is essential is invisible to the eye."

She set the box down, staring at it in amazement.

"I still can't believe what's inside. The coincidence is astounding."

"That would be one way to describe it. 'Wishful thinking' might be another. I don't know what makes you so sure it's Arthur and his mother. The inscription doesn't mention any names."

Beth remained quietly convinced.

"Thank you for letting me give it back to him."

"Why don't you come back to bed and give me a taste of your gratitude."

"Something tells me it's not my *gratitude* you want a taste of." Beth poured Joanna a fresh cup of coffee instead and brought it over to her. "You'll have to settle for this and an English muffin. I promised Arthur I'd be there early to help him get dressed."

"Isn't he old enough to dress himself?"

Beth shoved her playfully.

"Really, can't someone on staff help him do that?"

"It's a special day. He wants his momma."

Joanna just shook her head. She found Beth's role in Arthur's life as endearing as it was absurd.

"So once again I miss out on breakfast in bed because of one of your sons."

"That's how it looks." She kissed Jo on the cheek. "Thank you again for coming with me today."

"I keep telling myself it can't be worse than visiting day at camp."

Beth leaned teasingly closer.

"And remember how well that ordeal ended for you."

As a reminder, Beth bit ever so lightly into the lobe of Joanna's ear, then left her hanging. Jo called after her.

"The least you could do is toast and butter my muffin."

"Sorry, you're on your own."

Jo resorted to spite.

"Who said you could wear my work shirt?"

As Beth continued toward the bathroom she deliberately let it fall to the ground.

"Who said you could stare at my ass?"

Beth pulled into the parking lot of Hillcrest Manor.

"Now don't forget how easily confused Arthur gets. No matter how little sense he makes, just go along with it. If you try correcting him he becomes agitated and I don't want him upset… especially today."

"Stop obsessing… I get it. Besides, if I were you I'd be more worried about the competition. Obviously I have a thing for older women and this place must be crawling with them."

Beth laughed.

"If not actually crawling, then certainly shuffling, limping or teetering."

Beth's gait was purposeful. As the couple approached the main entrance, Joanna took in what she could of the surroundings. The flowering shrubs and mature hedges that bordered the grounds of the Hillcrest Manor were meticulously maintained. The well-preserved two-story brick building with white shuttered windows boasted a gracious porch supported by five white columns. Several benches flanked the main entrance. What lay beyond the white-trimmed doors with beautiful, etched glass was a world entirely unknown to Joanna. Both sets of her grandparents still lived vital and independent lives, sparing her any real face-off with the harsher realities of aging. If the woman sitting on the front porch staring vacantly into space was any indication of what awaited Jo inside, she was in for an afternoon she wouldn't soon forget. Sensing her hesitation as they went through the door, Beth slipped her arm protectively through Joanna's.

"Don't worry sweetheart… old age isn't contagious," she whispered as dozens of faces instantly lit up at the sight of her.

Those who could manage to get to Beth on their own steam hurried for her embrace. Those who couldn't, waved, blew kisses or called to her from their chairs. Beth turned to Joanna.

"I'll assume you don't want to be introduced. Just give me a few minutes to say hello."

Jo stood rigidly off to the side, her hands dug deep inside her pockets. Despite Beth's assurance that old age was not contagious, Jo was careful not to make eye contract with a single soul while reluctantly assessing her surroundings. For all her arrogance, Joanna's usual bravado cowered in the face of the old and the infirm. It felt safer to focus on the lobby's decor rather than on its residents, many of whom seemed as inanimate as the furniture itself. The entrance hall of the manor reflected its prestigious history. Built in the early part of the century to serve the elder needs of North Hampton's wealthiest and most powerful families, the once privately held foundation now opened its doors to a much more diverse population whose only common denominator—as far as Jo could tell—was the misfortune of growing old.

A stone fireplace graced the far wall over which hung a richly hued landscape painting. Although the armchairs and loveseats were arranged for easy conversation, those occupying them appeared only to be talking to themselves. Noting that plastic slipcovers protected all the upholstery, Joanna preferred not to think about why. The festively decorated dining room was just off the lobby. Through its glass walls Jo could see the evidence of a staff that obviously held Arthur in the highest regard. Bouquets of fresh-cut flowers from the garden served as centerpieces on each of the tables. Helium-filled balloons kissed the ceiling everywhere, their colorful strings adding an ironic childlike quality. An oversized birthday banner spanned the length of the wall behind the old upright piano. Just off the lobby was a reception area. The conservatively dressed woman behind its desk caught Joanna's eye.

"You must be a friend of Beth's."

Jo nodded uncomfortably.

"She's such a honey... and oh-sooo talented. I would give my right arm to be able to play the piano like that." The woman giggled. "Of course, I would need my right arm, wouldn't I?"

Joanna returned a polite but impatient smile, then looked over at Beth while hoping to soon be rescued. Unfortunately, each time Beth pulled herself away from one resident three more would shuffle toward her. Jo looked elsewhere for relief. A set of French doors opened onto a garden where several residents sat alongside their aides. Here and there, bird feeders hung from the lower branches of trees, serving as riveting a source of entertainment as the deadened audience could absorb. Beneath the protected shade of a majestic oak tree, a staff member led a small group of residents in wheelchairs in a loosely choreographed series of upper body stretches. The longer Joanna watched the misshapen group, the more horrified she became.

Along the corridors that extended out on both sides of the lobby, countless residents—some in wheelchairs, others leaning on walkers or canes—lined the walls outside their rooms like individually rotting teeth. Some appeared slightly straighter or stronger than others, but at best, held themselves with the fragile dignity of a slightly slower decay. So many different lives, so many personal histories now blended into this pathetic, terrifying sameness called 'old age'. Joanna looked away as frightened as she was heartbroken. In contrast,Beth came toward her smiling.

"Are you alright sweetie? You look peaked."

"This place... these people... it's depressing as hell."

Beth looked around at the same surroundings.

"When you lose a child in the prime of his life, old age becomes a blessing one can only hope for themselves and everyone they love."

"Hi there sugar!"

Beth turned toward the familiar voice. Millie opened her arms and the two exchanged the warmest hug.

"Ready for the big day?"

"Can you believe it Millie, it's finally here!"

"Yup baby, it surely is."

Ever gracious, Millie acknowledged Joanna.

"And who've we got here?"

Beth pulled Joanna closer. Without explaining their relationship, she simply introduced her and said that she was staying with her for the summer. Millie extended her hand.

"Welcome to the Manor, Miss Jo. Well now, aren't you lucky to be here for such a special occasion?"

Though 'lucky' was hardly how Jo would have described it, she politely agreed. She could feel Beth's arm tighten around her own in subtle appreciation. Beth's concern turned to Arthur.

"How is the guest of honor this morning?"

Millie had checked on him first thing.

"He definitely knows somethin' big's going on but I wouldn't bet my last bedpan he knows what it is. Why don't you go on… I'm sure the birthday boy's gonna' feel a lot better once his momma's there.

Apparently the whole staff knew of Arthur's delusion. Beth leaned toward Joanna.

"It's best if I do this alone. Trust me when I say I'm leaving you in Hillcrest's most capable hands."

Jo was desperate for reassurance. She grabbed Beth's arm and whispered in her ear.

"Don't be long."

As the two stood side by side watching Beth make her way down the hall, Millie could see the guarded terror in Joanna's eyes.

"First time, huh baby?"

"Is it that obvious?"

"It is to *me* sugar. I know just what you're thinkin' but believe me, this here is heaven compared to some other places I've been at."

Something in Joanna's eyes told Millie she preferred to be spared those details. She gave Jo a once-over,

"Don't worry. A fine, strappin' woman like yourself still got a long ways to go." Millie had a wonderfully candid sense of humor. "One thing to keep in mind though when that time comes. Not everybody takes to havin' some overweight Jamaican woman livin' in their house tellin' them what to do and when to do it. Folks like that don't leave their families much choice but to put 'em in a place like this where they wind up surrounded by a nation of overweight Jamaican women tellin' 'em what to do and when to do it. Then just *one* don't seem so bad. Course by then it's too late… family's closed up their house and sold off their stuff. So unless you want your whole life comin' down to a little corkboard for your pictures and a cup for your teeth, you best not be puttin' up a fuss when you see one of us standin' in your kitchen peelin' ya' an orange."

For the first time since she'd set foot in the nursing home, Joanna found reason to laugh. Millie even joined her. A bit more relaxed, Jo made the mistake of glancing at the infamously unpleasant Doris Henly.

"What the hell are you lookin' at? Must think you're somethin', don't ya' missy? Well I was even prettier when I was your age. Still be if they'd get a goddamn hairdresser in here who knew what the hell she was doing."

Joanna looked stunned. Millie leaned in closer.

"Lord's gonna' have a lotta' forgiven' to do when she shows up! Fortunately they're not all like that." Millie pointed to a sweet little white-haired lady sitting in a corner of the loveseat. "That's 'Kisses'." As soon as Millie caught her eye, the woman puckered her lips and blew her a kiss. Millie blew her one back and the satisfied woman smiled and closed her eyes.

A dazed looking man sat opposite 'Kisses'. He wore a tin sheriff's badge on his breast pocket and plastic handcuffs around the loop of his pants. Jo tried not to stare as he repeatedly reached for the toy pistol tucked into his waistband. Millie explained.

"That's 'Officer Pat'... a retired police captain. Massive stroke left him paralyzed on one side. Wife's gone... kids couldn't manage so he wound up here."

Jo tried to make out his garbled words.

"What's he saying?"

"The only thing he ever says... 'Police officer... freeze!'." Millie pointed to a precisely groomed black woman in a wheelchair with five white dolls lined up on her lap. Every few seconds she'd pick one up and press it to her breast. "That's Miss Edna Brown. Used to be the nanny to one of the town's wealthiest families... practically raised all five kids. Never married or had any of her own... devoted her whole life to 'em. They loved her too... said she'd never have to worry about her future, that she'd always have a home with them. Five years ago the whole family died in a plane crash... small private thing went down off the coast of Nova Scotia. When she got the news poor thing damn near went mad. Thinks those dolls on her lap are those babies she raised. Sweet as Miss Edna is, try touchin' one of 'em and she'll scratch your eyes out."

Joanna began to think that maybe her initial impression was wrong—that old age wasn't the nondescript abyss it had first seemed. Everyone had a name. Everyone had a story.

Millie noticed one of the residents poking Mrs. Henly with her cane. Though no doubt the battle axe had it coming, Millie clapped her hands sternly.

"Manners please!"

Knowing how quickly moments like this could turn ugly, Millie excused herself to keep that from happening, especially today.

"Beth should be down any minute, sugar. If you aint run off by then, I'll see you inside."

Jo thanked Millie for the special attention. Now just minutes before noon, she watched as several other aides began systematically escorting the residents into the dining room. Except for a few minor squabbles, everyone seemed soothed by the predictable mid-day routine. Along the walls of the already crowded dining room, everyone on staff—including those who had the day off—congregated for the momentous occasion.

No one was more anxious than Joanna for Beth to return with the guest of honor. After several minutes a male aide rounded the corner of the now empty corridor. He was pushing Arthur in his wheelchair as Beth walked alongside holding the one hundred year old man's hand. In spite of everything she thought about the convoluted relationship, the poignant image touched Joanna more deeply than she ever expected. From across the length of the hall, the women's eyes locked in solemn recognition as Arthur's wheelchair moved steadily closer. Beth was well aware of the waiting crowd but like a mother protective of her child, she asked the aide to give them a little more time just to be sure Arthur was ready. He patted the old man's shoulder and joined the crowd inside the dining room.

Encouraging Jo to come closer, Beth bent down and spoke to Arthur softly.

"This is my friend Joanna, honey. Do you remember I promised she would come to your party?"

For a long time the expressionless old man dressed in a proper white shirt and red bow tie stared up at the woman before him. Jo reached out and took his rail-thin hand into her own.

"Happy birthday Arthur. It's very nice to meet you."

A peaceful smile spread across the old man's face. As Arthur closed his fingers around Joanna's hand, a lone tear ran down his cheek.

Beth leaned closer and stroked his arm reassuringly.

"It's alright sweetheart. It's a very emotional day for all of us."

Arthur was immediately comforted by Beth's touch.

"It's a happy day momma… such a happy day."

"Yes it is, honey… a *very* happy day and there are so many people who love you and came to celebrate your birthday with you."

Arthur's hand shook as he pointed to Joanna.

"Anne too."

Jo's eyes reassured Beth of her promise not to try and correct him. Millie came out to see if everything was all right. She fussed with Arthur's favorite bowtie.

"Well didn't your momma get you dressed up nice."

Arthur extended his cheek for her usual kiss. Aside from Beth, Millie was the other 'constant' in Arthur's life. In the company of them both he seemed all the more soothed. Millie took advantage of the stabilizing moment.

"Why don't we all go inside so everyone can wish you a happy birthday. Would you like that precious?"

Arthur looked up at Beth anxiously. She immediately took his hand.

"It's alright sweetheart. I'm right here."

Arthur held his other hand out to Jo. While she didn't relish being at the center of all the attention, Jo saw Beth's eyes pleading with her to take Arthur's hand. Millie positioned herself behind his wheelchair and pushed. As Arthur made his entrance, those with minds enough to understand the significance of the occasion began to sing, "For He's The Jolly Good Fellow." Those who hadn't the slightest notion of what was going on clapped along anyway.

Arthur couldn't actually make out the faces of all the people that filled the room but his heart recognized the company of those who so dearly loved him. Beth assisted in getting him settled while the crowd remained buzzing with joy. The celebratory lunch that followed included several heartwarming speeches, flashing cameras and a 'champagne toast' with carbonated apple cider. Dazed, Arthur sat good-naturedly through it all. When the tables were cleared of the lunch dishes, Beth took her position at the piano. On cue, she began playing "Happy Birthday." While everyone sang along, a beautifully decorated cake with 10 candles—one for each decade—was set before him. Arthur seemed appreciative until thunderous clapping overwhelmed him. Millie quickly hurried to his side.

"Would you like me to help you blow out your candles, precious?"

Arthur nodded. Whether or not he understood the significance of such a personal milestone or the reason for all the fuss, he looked genuinely happy to be a part of such a good time. While at the piano, Beth was easily coaxed into playing a medley of his favorite songs. Jo looked around the room. It was impossible not to feel everyone's appreciation. As she studied everybody's faces it was apparent that separately and together, 'mother and child' had captured every heart in the room—hers included. Compelled by her emotions, Joanna moved to the empty chair beside Arthur. He had closed his eyes to listen more intently to the music. She leaned closed and whispered softly.

"She plays beautifully, doesn't she?"

Arthur nodded peacefully. Without opening his eyes, he spoke to her.

"Remember Anne… it's in the suitcase."

"*What's* in the suitcase Arthur?"

He simply repeated the reminder with more urgency.

"Remember… it's in the suitcase."

Jo realized the futility of asking him to be any clearer. Instead, she patted his hand.

"I'll remember."

For whatever reason, Arthur seemed relieved. The two sat quietly side by side for the duration of Beth's performance—each loving her deeply.

A specially prepared tape of hits from the Big Band Era provided music through coffee and dessert. The residents responded instantly to the familiar sound of their generation. Those among them still able were invited to dance by several of the staff. Those who could not swayed along in their chairs, enjoying the memories the sentimental melodies of their youth brought back. Some smiled, others cried. With Beth on one side and Joanna on the other, Arthur sat contentedly, listening as one song led into the next. After the first few notes of Glenn Miller's 'Moonlight Serenade' he reached for Beth's hand and held it out to Joanna.

"Ask momma to dance."

Beth's eyes twinkled with the unexpected chance to be in Joanna's arms. It was an opportunity that Jo likewise couldn't refuse. She stood up and pulled out Beth's chair.

"May I have the pleasure?"

Arthur beamed to hear his mother accept. As the women took their place on the dance floor among all the other mismatched couples, Jo was careful not to hold Beth too close. As they moved together to the music the thrill of one another's body lay safely disguised in their seemingly casual contact. Beth kept her voice deliberately low.

"Too bad this dance can't end like our first."

"Why not? Seems to me there's a whole building of empty beds at the moment."

Beth sighed lovingly.

"I'm sorry you got caught up in that grand entrance earlier. I know you never expected to be at the center of attention this afternoon."

Jo concentrated on the fullness of Beth's breasts against hers.

"A lot's happened this summer I never expected."

Beth moved against her in acknowledgment.

"All the same, thank you for coming with me today."

"Thank you for inviting me."

"Do you really mean that?"

"Yes." She dared to hold Beth a little closer. "I know this is an important part of your life… this day especially."

For the next few moments they danced in silence. From the fold of Joanna's arms, Beth looked around at the room full of elderly people and peered deep into the future. Before she could stop them, the words came.

"Do you ever wonder what it would be like… to grow old together?"

Until that uncharted moment, both had been silently resigned to the limits of their affair. The unexpected question pierced Jo's heart. Misunderstanding Jo's discomfort, Beth immediately apologized.

"I'm sorry… that wasn't fair. I know we agreed to these three weeks… nothing more."

Joanna was still struggling for the right words when the song they'd been dancing to ended. Reluctantly she led Beth back to the table and with little choice let the subject drop.

Long past the hour of his usual mid-day nap, Arthur was showing signs of fatigue. The sympathetic director offered a brief message of thanks to everyone in attendance and the joyous celebration came to a close. As Beth stood protectively by at Arthur's side, the two were embraced by an endless stream of people as they left the dining room. With a helium balloon attached to the arm of his wheelchair, Arthur waited to be wheeled back to his room. Joanna would have preferred to remain in the lobby but Beth convinced her to come along. Once she'd seen to it that Arthur was propped up comfortably on several pillows, Millie kissed him on the forehead and thanked him for being the kindhearted gentleman he was. Then she graciously excused herself to give the women some time with him alone.

Beth had waited to give Arthur his gift. As he lay peacefully on the edge of sleep she sensed this was the moment. She removed the small gift box from her bag and brought it to his bedside.

"I have a special present for you honey."

Beth placed the box at his fingertips so that he could at least enjoy the sensation—if not the sight—of the tightly curled ribbons.

"I'll open it for you."

Beth lifted the delicate Victorian frame from the box and placed it in Arthur's waiting hands. As his arthritic fingers slowly moved across its surface, tears began to form in Arthur's eyes. The memory of its familiar shape told him all he needed to know about the image inside. His body trembled as he pressed the frame to his heart.

"Oh momma, you found it! You found it! Our last picture together before you got sick."

Reveling in the stunning coincidence, Beth reached for Jo's hand and pulled her closer.

"Actually, Joanna and I found it together. We both wanted you to have it."

Arthur sensed Joanna's presence.

"Anne, you've come back... you've come back to momma."

Beth caressed Arthur's cheek. She would say whatever it took to sooth him.

"Yes honey, she has... she's right here beside me."

Arthur's one hundred year old body shook with the pain of a twelve year old boy. The devastating loss of his mother had not yet eased.

"Oh momma, now you won't have to die."

Joanna's own heart ached for the permanence of his loss. Beth tried changing the subject.

"Do you remember my husband Ben, sweetheart? He's in Europe now but he told me to wish you a happy birthday. He promises to visit you as soon as he gets back."

Arthur became more agitated than she had ever seen him.

"No momma! No! Poppa must never come home!"

Once she'd managed to calm him, she leaned over and quietly explained things to Joanna's.

"When Arthur was a young boy his father often traveled abroad. From what I gather, it wasn't the happiest of marriages. Apparently his mother was most miserable when his father was around." Beth blamed herself for his distress. "I should have realized that the notion of a man coming back from Europe would trigger some of his worst memories."

Beth continued to stroke Arthur's face while he clutched the small frame that rested on his chest. Eventually the combination brought him relief. Joanna had seen and heard enough. She whispered to Beth that she would wait for her in the lobby, then moved to Arthur's side to say goodbye.

"I'll be going now..."

Arthur immediately began to shake.

"No Anne! No! If you go momma will die!"

His panicked plea left Jo no choice but to remain at Beth's side. She was quickly nearing the end of her patience with the old man's delusions. Arthur reached for her sleeve.

"I'm sorry Anne... I'm sorry for taking momma away."

Beth assumed he meant about her volunteering.

"It's only one morning sweetheart. I'm sure Joanna understands."

Arthur's fingers trembled around Jo's wrist.

"Do you Anne? Do you forgive me?"

Jo tried to keep her promise and her impatience in check.

"Yes Arthur... I forgive you... I forgive you."

Arthur relaxed. His head seemed to sink deeper into his pillow.

Jo rolled her eyes as Beth gently eased the frame from Arthur's hand and placed it on the table beside his bed.

She leaned closer.

"Try and get some rest now."

Arthur nodded ever so slightly.

"Will you stay with me momma?"

"Of course I will. Now close your eyes."

Joanna motioned to Beth that she would wait for her outside. Drained from the encounter, Jo leaned against the corridor wall before she made her way back to the lobby.

Beth remained at Arthur's bedside staring at the sepia image of his mother and her son. Arthur did not need to open his eyes.

"It's such a beautiful picture, isn't it momma?"

No longer surprised at how well he sensed her heart, Beth simply took his hand in hers.

"Yes sweetheart. It's a beautiful picture."

Arthur smiled contentedly while Beth stroked his cheek.

"We both have Joanna to thank for so much."

"Anne loves you momma. She loves you with all her heart."

Beth could feel the push of tears.

"I love her too."

As the familiar hopelessness set in, Beth allowed herself to cry.

"Oh God... what am I going to do... what am I going to do?"

Arthur did not respond. He had drifted off to sleep leaving Beth with no place to turn. Bravely, she wiped away her own tears. For all the birthdays Arthur had celebrated without his mother, Beth bent now and kissed him tenderly.

"Sweet dreams, my precious little boy."

Before she closed his door, Beth looked back one last time to be sure he was sleeping peacefully.

Beth found Joanna sitting outside on the bench. As they walked toward the car, Beth acknowledged Jo's strain.

"I know it's a lot to take in…"

"A lot to take in? That's an understatement! It's like being in the fucking 'twilight zone'!" Jo got into the car. "I need to lie down before I can even think about meeting up with that other nut job tonight."

Beth felt badly for having pushed Joanna into those plans as well.

"I'm sure she's listed. I'll call and cancel if you'd like."

Jo messaged her throbbing temples.

"And miss out on the chance to report back on how a one hundred year old blind man with dementia knew exactly what was in that frame? Hell no, I can't wait to relive *that* moment!"

Beth remained quiet and obviously hurt. Jo tried a teasing apology. She reached for Beth's hand, feigning one of Arthur's tremors.

"I'm sorry *momma*… I really am."

Beth shook her head but after a moment she was no longer able to keep a straight face.

"It's okay. I forgive you… *Anne*."

The couple looked at each other and burst out laughing. Even under the most trying of circumstances they were so good together.

Beth merged into the traffic and another topic.

"I'm curious, why do you think Dell's a nut job?"

"Don't know exactly. She just strikes me as someone who howls at the moon."

Beth giggled.

"There's supposed to be a full moon tonight?"

Joanna rolled her eyes.

"Perfect."

Back at the carriage house the exhausted couple peeled off their clothes and collapsed onto the open bed. For very different reasons, it was a long emotionally charged day for each of them. Beth lay on her side, inviting Jo to snuggle up behind her. As tired as Joanna was, the thrill of Beth's body was impossible to resist. She reached around and found Beth's nipple that stiffened instantly at her touch. Jo was encouraged.

"Wanna' fool around?"

"Don't hate me, but I'm much too tired."

Jo let her head fall back against her own pillow.

"God, you have no idea how relieved I am to hear you say that."

"Need more than an hour to shower and get ready?"

"No."

Beth set the alarm and lay back down. She was on the edge of sleep when Joanna's voice pulled her back.

"Beth…"

She was too groggy to open her eyes.

"What is it sweetie?"

What Jo had really wanted to talk about was their growing old together. Instead her heart settled on the terms of their compromise.

"I need to say it."

She waited as Beth moved her hands out from under her chin and covered her ears. Once it was *safe*, Joanna reached around and pulled her closer.

"I love you Beth Garrison."

Chapter 24

To save time the lovers had decided to shower together, but one thing had inevitably led to another and they arrived at the restaurant twenty minutes late. Jo spotted Dell and her girlfriend at the bar. They hurried over, maneuvering through the crowded room. Beth was apologetic.

"We're so sorry."

Dell smiled.

"We were always late in the beginning too. Never could get out of bed. Then one day we became the couple on time waiting for the newbees."

For Beth, the validation of her presumed intimacy with Joanna felt both wonderful and strange. In spite of all the years of couple-hood she'd shared with Ben, her entire identity shifted in that single acknowledgment. Almost as instantly she felt the unfamiliar burden of the public's perception as well. Still feeling sentimental, Dell gazed into Sara's eyes.

"What is it, do you suppose, that all these years later makes the remembering even sweeter?"

Sara patted her on the thigh.

"Mutual tolerance, my dear, to be sure."

The attractive vibrantly dressed black woman extended her hand.

"Hi, I'm Sara. It's so nice to meet you both. Dell's told me all about you."

Jo put Sara on the spot.

"What exactly did she say?"

"She said you'd be the one who'd want to know."

Sara's wink left no doubt in Jo's mind that she'd just been 'handled'. With that, her suspicions melted instantly into amusement.

The waitress approached from behind and tapped Dell politely on the shoulder.

"Your table is ready sir."

Drink in hand, Dell turned around on the bar stool. The flustered young girl was horrified.

"Oh my God, I'm so sorry."

Dell's eyes twinkled with forgiveness.

"15,283... that's the number of times someone has made that same mistake."

Sara patted the girl's hand for added reassurance.

"She started counting when she hit puberty. That was quite a while ago."

The couple's apparent ease and comfort in the world was astonishing to Beth. She envied them instantly.

The waitress clutched the menus to her chest and picked up her pace.

"Please follow me."

As the women were led to their table Beth noticed how Dell guided Sara with her arm the way Ben had always done with her. The restaurant was filled with couples—heterosexual couples—couples just like Beth had been a part of all her life. Overnight she had gone from being one of them to being one of 'them'. Now an outsider, Beth suddenly felt as if all eyes were upon her. She was not accustomed to such scrutiny. She imagined some stared with intrigue. Others with distain. It was hard for her to tell which drew more attention—Dell's extremely masculine appearance or Joanna's striking good looks. Sandwiched between the two, Beth could only hope that no one noticed her at all. Grateful that their table was off in a corner, she deliberately chose the chair that faced the wall. Joanna was aware of Beth's discomfort. Quite intentionally, she made no attempt to ease it. It wasn't as if she hadn't tried to warn her that the notion of an amusing little double date would not be the lighthearted night out Beth had anticipated.

Dell ordered a bottle of Chardonnay for the table. She filled everyone's glasses and made an impromptu toast.

"All that I know, I know because I love."

Those seated at the nearby tables turned around and stared. Dell acknowledged their attention.

"Leo Tolstoy," she added with a friendly smile.

Some nodded awkwardly, then went back to their meals. Beth consumed as much of the wine as she could in a single gulp. Dell understood. Without saying a word, she refilled Beth's glass. While the women perused their menus, Dell reached down at her feet for the sealed envelope she'd brought along and handed it to Jo.

"Happy belated birthday."

Joanna reared back in her chair.

"How the hell did you know it was my birthday?"

Dell shrugged.

"Just figured it had to have passed sometime in the last year."

Jo remained guarded.

"What is it?"

"Guess."

Joanna was not interested in playing games.

"I asked you what it is."

Sara kicked her lover under the table, encouraging Dell to simply answer the question.

"It's a book. Don't open it now though. Save it for tonight. It'll help pass the time."

Dell ignored the lingering confusion in Jo's eyes. She turned to Beth.

"Speaking of gifts, how was Arthur's party?"

Beth's face lit up with excitement. Dell pretended to be surprised.

"Don't tell me… ."

"He recognized the frame the moment I put it in his hands! Can you imagine?"

Dell reached over and squeezed hers.

"Guess that's what Keats meant when he said that 'touch has a memory'."

Sara seemed to know all about the strange coincidence. Joanna tried to read her eyes—eyes that neither confirmed nor denied whether she too found anything out of the ordinary about it. In fact the harder Jo tried to peg Sara as being every bit the odd ball Dell was, the more grounded she appeared to be. By the time their food had arrived, the crisscrossed conversation had begun to flow as freely as the wine. Though the four mismatched dinner companions had managed to strike up a comfortable rapport, it was a precarious dynamic that required careful navigation. Sara, a savvy diplomat by profession and by nature, took charge of that course. As the women enjoyed dinner she managed to keep the conversation interesting, lively and above all, safe—balancing the richness of details with a respect of boundaries. The only reference to Beth's marital status and her affair with Joanna came in the form of a politely disguised comment about life being a journey and that the only obligation one had was to see it through—first and foremost—for oneself. Sara also managed to discreetly impart that the difference between a need for secrecy and a desire for privacy rested in how one felt about the information they were guarding, suggesting that secrecy was about hiding the truth whereas privacy was about valuing it. Although Sara's tactful recognition went a long way in helping Beth find a level of comfort with the current circumstances of her life, her awkwardness at moments was unavoidable. Being sequestered away with

Joanna these last few weeks had been one thing… being out in the world in the company of other lesbians was quite another. As different as they were in temperament, the instant bond among the three women with a similar lifestyle was apparent.

With little to contribute, Beth sat quietly as the others shared colorful and amusing anecdotes about their histories. While Dell and Joanna had always 'known', Sara's story was very different. She told of a party she'd attended in her second year of law school during the height of the free love movement. After getting high and having sex with her boyfriend and his best friend, she passed a closed bedroom door and heard the sounds of two women making love. Her response caught her entirely by surprise. Aroused by the women's moans, she opened the door slightly and peeked in. She watched as the couple, locked in a mesmerizing 69, made each other cum. When the women realized her curiosity they invited her to join them. Without any previous 'leanings', the ménage-a-trios turned out to be the most sexually charged experience of Sara's life. A few years after conceiving a 'love child' with her on again-off again boyfriend, she met Dell. This time the most sexually gratifying experience of her life became the most emotionally gratifying one as well and so it had stayed for more than 20 years. For obvious reasons Beth wondered what it was like raising a child outside the laws of convention. Before she could ask, the conversation switched directions. While Sara was decidedly the more scholarly of the two, it turned out that Dell was no intellectual slouch herself. While attending graduate school on a fellowship, she was required to tutor several hours a week. One of her 'regulars' was the beautiful but academically challenged homecoming queen, Suzanna Pomaroy. It was not by coincidence that the same last name appeared on the bronze plaques of several buildings that graced the sprawling campus. Dell described how after the first tutoring session, the spoiled little Southern belle made it perfectly clear what she did and did not want in the way of lessons. Since the young woman had a reputation for sleeping with only thick-necked jocks, Dell was surprised when Suzanna locked the door of her room and announced that she wasn't into labels—she was into pleasure. Dell winked, then launched into the racy details.

Sara noticed that Beth was growing uncomfortable. She patted her lover's hand.

"Okay honey… we've all got the picture."

Joanna didn't agree. She'd almost forgotten how good it felt to be in the company of other lesbians.

This time Sara kicked Dell under the table. Joanna would be disappointed.

"I'll just say that daddy's rich little girl graduated 'Susie cum loud' with honors they could never bestow at a commencement ceremony."

After the laughter had waned Beth tried steering the conversation in another direction.

"What was your major?"

"Sitting in one hundred degree sun, chiseling away at the side of a remote mountain."

Sara boasted the more accurate truth.

"That's Dell's humble way of saying she holds a PhD in cultural anthropology and was quite a rising star in the field."

Dell shrugged off the accomplishment.

"I like digging up the past. It was a perfect fit."

Beth was intrigued.

"Did you ever find anything exciting on one of your digs?"

"Nothing nearly as exciting as the woman sitting across from me at a grassroots civil rights rally." Dell leaned closer to her lover. "Once I'd met Sara, the relevance of some ancient artifact suddenly felt a lot less compelling that the colorful trinkets that hung from her ears. Turned out I much preferred the mysteries of this brilliant mind to anything that lay buried beneath the surface of the earth." Dell finished her wine. "Expeditions can go on for months, even years at a time. Once we'd met I couldn't bear the thought of being apart from Sara for that long, so I walked away from the whole thing. Haven't been on a dig since."

Sara found Dell's hand.

"That's where she's wrong. Dell's whole life has been devoted to excavating. I don't know of anyone who's better at exploring the depths of the human heart than she is. I may bring home the money, but she brings home the magic."

Dell smiled appreciatively.

"Leave it to Sara to characterize the intangible contributions of a life adrift in such an endearing way."

Sara corrected her.

"It's hardly 'adrift'. We've got my feet planted on the ground and your head floating along in the clouds. I'd say together that affords us quite and extraordinary reach."

As Joanna thought about Sara's description she realized that she could never have imagined Gayle or herself qualifying their individual strengths or their relationship in such meaningful terms. She sat there quietly envying the couple's sense of satisfaction and fulfillment with their choices. When asked about her own story, her impressive climb to the top of the ad game felt much less rewarding than it sounded. Sara was never the less impressed.

"You must be very talented."

"I'm ambitious." Jo turned to Beth. "If you want to talk about a real gift you should hear her play the piano."

Beth put down her fork and smiled awkwardly. Self-conscious about not pursuing her dream, she immediately began to make excuses for herself. Sara recognized instantly how deeply Beth was suffering and reached out to relieve her.

"Don't do that. Don't condemn yourself for your sacrifices. Motherhood is not sainthood. A fair amount of regret… even resentment… comes with the territory."

Beth nodded appreciatively.

Sara held her eyes.

"We each do what we think is right at the time." She took a sip of wine. "I still don't think Dell ever realized just how close she and I came to not happening."

Beth was surprised.

"Why? You sounded so sure of your heart."

"Oh, I was that honey! But for the first few years of my daughter's life I'd already put her needs second to my own political and social crusades. I told myself that everything I was doing would ultimately make the world a better place for a child to grow up in… especially one who was female… and black. She was already being raised by a single mom who took more naturally to shouting activist slogans than singing lullabies. Then Dell came into my life. Dealing with an lesbian mother back in those days was simply too much to ask a six year old to handle. When it came down to it, I was prepared to choose her happiness over my own." She turned lovingly to Dell. "But thanks to this incredible woman, I didn't have to. When I asked Yolanda what she wanted for her birthday she said more than anything, a ride in a red convertible. At the time, I was lucky to be able to afford fare for the bus. I didn't know anyone who had a car, let alone a convertible. It broke my heart not to be able to make her wish come true. I'd never felt like such a failure as a mother. That night I called Dell, explained about the wish and told her I couldn't go on seeing her." Sara's eyes still registered all the pain of that conversation. "On the morning of Yolanda's birthday—after two of the most miserable weeks of my life—I heard someone honking a horn in front of the rooming house where we were living. I looked outside the window and there was Dell, sitting in a bright red convertible, holding a bunch of balloons. To this day I can still see the joy on my daughter's face. We spent the whole day riding around the neighborhood waving to people on the street. That night as I tucked Yolanda into bed she told me what she wanted for her next birthday was for the three of us to be a family, no matter what anyone else thought."

Sara squeezed Dell's hand as if thanking her for something she'd done just yesterday. Joanna's skepticism about Dell mixed with her curiosity.

"Whadya' do, pull a red convertible out of thin air?"

Dell laughed.

"Not out of thin air... off of Jimmy's used car lot. And, it wasn't red... or a convertible... least not yet anyway." Dell seemed to enjoy her own resourcefulness. "I had $250 to my name. That bought me a rusted-out sedan with over 200,000 miles on it. It took 3 days with a hack saw to cut my way around the top. I used duct tape to cover the jagged edge of the metal and then a gallon of red paint to make it the car of Yolanda's dreams."

Beth was enchanted.

"If that isn't love, I don't know what is."

Sara shook her head.

"Love or insanity. I'm still not entirely sure which. Either way, she managed to win both our hearts that day. The car died one week later but she's been making magic in out lives ever since." Sara turned to Beth. "Looks like you and I have something else in common besides motherhood. We both fell hard for women with convertibles."

Beth smiled in quiet acknowledgement while the waitress cleared the table, then asked if they wanted to see the dessert menu. Dell patted the bulge under her shirt.

"Does it look like I've ever said no?"

Beth needed the ladies room. She excused herself and stood up. With the restrooms located on the far side of the room, she would now pay the price for a table tucked away in the corner. Dreading the new round of scrutiny, Beth made her way through the labyrinth of tables without meeting a single eye, before pushing through the door. Relieved to have survived the crossing, Beth now leaned against the floral-papered wall while she waited to use the single, occupied stall. Within moments the toilet flushed, the metal door swung open and the patron emerged. Though her glance was only fleeting, the stranger's response was undeniable. She had obviously recognized Beth as one of 'them' and in that instant, a tension as real as anything Beth had ever felt formed between them. She quickly entered the stall and closed the door. Hoping to avoid a more prolonged confrontation, Beth remained inside while the woman washed her hands. She waited anxiously for the slam of the restroom door to tell her it was 'safe' to come out, but the much-anticipated moment never came. Instead, Beth heard only the sounds of a woman riffling through her make-up case. She flushed again praying that the extra few minutes would buy her more time. But the longer Beth procrastinated the more distinct her impression that the other woman was intentionally stalling as well. Running out of options, Beth eventually exited the security of the stall to share the small intimate space with the patron who was obviously intent upon making her miserable. Beth waited politely against the wall, hoping the woman would finish touching up her make-up and just leave. But the stranger moved over slightly granting Beth access to the sink and left her no choice but to come forward. As Beth turned on the faucet she could feel the tension between them. She intentionally focused her eyes downward while she rinsed the soapy water from her hands. As if to prolong Beth's agony, the woman took out a tube of lipstick and leaned closer to the mirror. Everything in her body language implored Beth to look up. Reluctantly, Beth did and in the mirror's reflection she bravely met the woman's eyes. Braced for scorn and disgust Beth saw something else entirely. There in the privacy of the dimly lit room, the stranger extended a tentative smile. She had indeed been stalling, but not for the reason Beth had presumed. The look was unmistakable. Beth recognized all the signs of attraction, conflict and fear that she'd experienced when she looked into Joanna's eyes for the first time. Beth returned something of her own awkward smile. The woman, an appealing 40-something blonde, was close to Beth in stature and coloring. Though more made-up, unlike Rheeta she did not appear to be trying to mask her age but simply trying to make the most of her naturally pleasing features. Her eye shadow and mascara did not scream of a distorted vanity but rather echoed a muffled cry to be something more than invisible—perhaps even desired. Through her sexual awakening, Beth had become more attuned to the language of longing in another woman. As she let her eyes linger, this newfound awareness aroused both fantasy and sadness. In the mirror Beth detected a slight tremor in the woman's hand as she applied her lipstick. She also couldn't help but notice the diamond engagement ring and wedding band that adorned the beautifully manicured fingers. Once Beth turned off the faucet, the silence became unbearable. The stranger searched for a connection.

"I like your hair. It's very becoming." She offered a measured smile. "Of course, it helps to have your eyes."

Beth read the unquestionable signals. The woman nervously blotted her lips. As she replaced the tube back in its case, it was painfully obvious that the stranger felt herself running out of time. Never had she come this close. Her voice cracked with apprehension.

"I was just wondering..."

Beth's eyes softened as she waited for the woman to gather her courage.

"Could you tell me where you get your hair done?"

Even as she answered, Beth knew that that was not at all the question lodged in the stranger's throat. It was, "How does it feel to kiss another woman?"

In the mirror's reflection the woman's eyes asked even more. They pleaded with Beth to actually show her. "Please...," they seemed to confess, "I don't know what it is I'm feeling... what it is I'm doing..."

Beth understood completely. She imagined pressing the woman up against the bathroom door—in part to feel the exchange of heat between each other's body, in part to prevent anyone else from entering and interrupting their anonymous encounter. She fantasized about brushing her lips against the stranger's—gently at first, then more searchingly until, like in the fairytale, she awakened the beautiful princess from her prolonged and death-like sleep. As Beth contemplated her options the room seemed to grow even smaller, the light even softer. She was certain that if she made the daring move the stranger would be hers, but she was also certain that such an experience would leave the poor woman in a state of utter turmoil. Knowing the consequences Beth could not be that reckless with another person's life, no matter how intoxicating the power. The stranger seemed to sense Beth's decision. With no choice but to let the moment pass she backed away shyly, all the more embarrassed by what she had invited—all the more confused by what she had asked. Beth could feel the woman's torment. She recalled all the times she had longed for—yet feared—Joanna's kiss. Knowing how conflicted the stranger was in her disappointment, Beth felt compelled to leave her with something more than the name of her hairdresser.

What she wanted to say was, "Whether I take you in my arms or let you walk out of here untouched, the reason is the same. It's because I understand." Instead, she simply reached for the stranger's hand. Just as Beth had expected, the woman did not resist. This time Beth did not use the mirror to search the woman's eyes.

"Do you know the diarist Anais Nin?"

The woman nodded tentatively.

Beth could feel the weight of the woman's heart along with her hand that rested in her own.

"She wrote that 'living never wore one out so much as the effort not to live'."

Beth held the woman's eyes with a hard-won assurance.

"All I can tell you is that's so very true."

The woman offered a quiet smile. She shyly withdrew her hand, picked up her purse and returned to her husband's table.

Alone in the bathroom, Beth felt the pounding of her own heart. The uncharted encounter had left her startled. Though madly in love with Joanna, she had come so close to kissing another woman—a total stranger—not because she had feelings for her she could not control, but simply because she could. Beth stared at herself in the mirror realizing she no longer knew what to expect of life—or herself. Had the stranger lingered a moment longer or taken a step closer, Beth might have changed her mind. A part of her had already begun to feel a sense of regret at not seizing the opportunity, if only for the experience. In its aftermath, Beth could only hope she'd told the beautiful stranger with the familiar longing in her eyes enough of what she so desperately ached to know.

Emboldened by the power bestowed upon her, this time when Beth crossed the room people's hushed whispers, whether real or imagined, no longer mattered. When she past the woman with whom she had just shared the intimate exchange, the terrified wife quickly averted her eyes and hid in the shadow of her husband's broad frame. Sympathetic, Beth likewise looked away.

Joanna was concerned.

"You were gone quite awhile. Are you okay?"

Beth pulled out her chair. Her nod disguised a much deeper satisfaction. Next time she would chose a seat that looked out into the room.

"I'm fine."

Dell smiled knowingly. Behind the laminated dessert menu Beth basked in the glory of her private encounter while considering her next set of choices. Feeling particularly wanton, she selected the most decadent item on the menu. Her dinner companions followed suit with equal abandon and the foursome settled into a relaxed sharing of gooey desserts and juicy tidbits from their vastly different lives. In her heightened state of awareness, Beth was suddenly struck by the pronounced richness woven of the women's laughter. The fullness—the energy—the power that emanated from the truth of the female experience nearly overwhelmed her. It came from of their bellies, the weight of their breasts and the legacy of intuition they each carried inside. Literally and figuratively it was a body of knowledge that no man, however sensitive, could ever internalize in quite the same way. The sheer freedom of their exchange awakened Beth to a level of womanhood she'd never before known. Never in such a public setting had she shared such an impenetrable connection. She felt like a new member of a private club that existed outside the rules for the sole purpose of feeling alive and good! Theirs was a joy that embodied all the giddiness of a pubescent slumber party seasoned with a bold sensuality only a group of mature women could own. The air itself ignited with the spark of the three commanding women with whom she shared the table. Despite her initial awkwardness, Beth had found her place within their robust and liberating company. It was a place she had fought for and a place she had earned—until Nick spotted her from across the room, making that place more tenuous and damning that any Beth had ever known. Before she could prepare herself, he was standing behind her. As he bent and kissed her, Nick sized up her companions. His phrasing was deliberate.

"Well if it isn't Mrs. Garrison enjoying a girl's night out!"

With her heart pounding in her chest Beth attempted a casual introduction.

"This is Dell..."

Dell immediately reached across the table and offered her hand. It was impossible not to notice it was larger than his own.

Beth's composure began to falter under Nick's unspoken scrutiny. Fed up, Joanna finished the introduction.

"And this is Sara...," she deliberately held his eyes, "Dell's lover. Obviously you and I have already met. Care to come on to me again?"

Nick held up his hand.

"I'll pass. Seems I'm not your type."

"You're right... for more reasons than the one that's suddenly obvious."

Once more he was deliberate in his phrasing as he introduced himself to the others.

"I'm a colleague of Beth's husband."

Though she found his motives transparent and despicable, Sara never the less acknowledged him warmly. Nick took his next shot.

"Speaking of Ben, I just got a postcard from him the other day."

He stared at Beth's ring finger just long enough to let her know he'd noticed the missing wedding band. Straining to remain composed, she put down her fork and looked directly at him.

"That's nice."

Nick nursed his martini.

"I think I'll give him a call and let him know I ran into you tonight."

Beth struggled bravely to defuse the thinly veiled threat.

"I'll be sure to mention it myself the next time we speak."

Nick was relentless.

"He'll be home soon. We should get together. If I know Ben, he's got stories that'll go on for months."

Beth dismissed the dread of her husband's return.

"I'm sure he's had a very interesting summer."

Nick took a smug look around the table.

"Not nearly as interesting as yours."

The remark, laced with menacing innuendo brought Beth's composure to the breaking point. She understood exactly what Nick was doing and why. Now that he'd caught her in a suspected affair—leading a double life behind her husband's back—she was no longer above reproach, but finally in the gutter along with the rest of the lying, cheating world. Her fall from grace gave him satisfaction. His intention now was not to be cruel but to dominate, the way a cat toys with a helpless mouse it has trapped in a corner.

Dell had taken a wait and see approach to Beth's ordeal. Though she could easily have intervened, she knew that the night was unfolding exactly as Beth was meant to experience it. While Sara's own intuition told her the same thing, Jo's did not. Dell sensed Joanna was about to take matters into her own hands and kicked Jo under the table. Despite her impulse, Joanna remained silent. The timely interruption of the maitre d' ended Nick's reign of terror.

"Sir, your table is ready. I've seated the lady. If you would follow me?"

Nick managed to sneak in a final blow.

"By the way, ever get that little boiler problem fixed?"

Feeling ridiculous, Beth responded anyway.

"Yes."

His parting words were ever so calculated.

"Then you'll be in plenty of hot water once Ben gets home."

Nick bent down and kissed her goodbye.

"Ladies..."

Despite Nicks loathsome behavior, Sara and Dell nodded politely. Nick turned to Jo.

"In case we don't meet again, I congratulate you on going where no man... except for Ben... has ever gone."

Once again Dell kicked Joanna's foot and once again Jo remained in her seat, letting Nick go with his balls still attached. Sara shook her head.

"He's quite a piece of work."

Beth didn't say a word. Her stomach in knots, she picked up her fork and attempted to finish her dessert. Hoping to move on, the others followed her lead. As they resumed their conversation Beth now felt like an unworthy imposter, certainly not the liberated woman the stranger in the bathroom assumed her to be. If anything, Nick had reminded Beth of her truer identity—a pathetically confused housewife whose life, once the summer ended and her husband returned, would revert back to the narrow picture of convention it had always been. Beth looked down at her plate. How utterly absurd to think that ordering a decadent dessert qualified her to sit in the company of three women whose earliest choices embodied their boldly authentic lives. How Beth wished she'd have kissed the vulnerable stranger in the ladies room earlier. Certainly, each of her dinner companions would have at some point in their colorful, adventurous pasts. Tonight she had her chance to prove she was one of them and she flat out blew it.

On Beth's behalf, her dinner companions made sure to linger just long enough not to give Nick the satisfaction of knowing he'd ruined her evening. When the moment was right, Dell signaled for the waitress. She and Jo stayed behind to wait for the check while Sara led Beth safely outside. As they walked toward the cars Sara locked her arm around the defeated woman.

"I thought you were incredibly brave back there."

Despite the bolstering words Beth didn't quite see it that way. Sara squeezed tighter.

"Stay true to yourself baby. The things that tear us apart are the things that ultimately make us whole."

Beth began to cry. Sara reached into her bag for a tissue. While Beth dabbed her eyes, Sara wrote down some numbers. She slipped the piece of paper into the pocket of Beth's cardigan.

"Call anytime you need to talk. You've got my number at home, my law practice and my office at the college."

Beth nodded appreciatively.

Sara gazed up into the vastness of the star-filled sky.

"There's something about a beautiful summer's night that always reminds me of one of my favorite quotes: 'There are years that ask questions and there are years that answer'." She took Beth's hand in her own. "When those answers come, don't let anything—or anyone—make you ignore them.

Understand?"“

Beth assured Sara she did.

While Dell waited for the waitress to return with her credit card, Joanna continued to glare at the back of Nick's head.

"Can't you do some kind of voodoo doll shit on that scumbag?"

Dell was tickled by Jo's childlike grasp of the paranormal.

"You mean prick the prick?"

"Yeah... put some evil spell on him that'll make the bastard impotent for the rest of his life."

Dell laughed. The same way she knew exactly what had transpired between Beth and the stranger in the ladies room, she also knew that Nick's date had a highly contagious case of genital herpes. Assuming that he was not a big fan of condoms, Dell was sure Nick would get exactly what he deserved.

"Just let it be. The universe takes care of things its own way."

Dell handed Joanna her birthday present and the women left the restaurant without further incident.

In the wake of the uncomfortable ending, the two couples exchanged warm but brief goodbyes. As Sara kissed Jo goodnight, she whispered in her ear.

"Try not to worry."

"She'll be fine."

"I'm not talking about her sugar, I'm talking about you."

Except for chivalrously opening Beth's door there was little more Dell could do for the burdened woman until 'The Gods' called upon her. Joanna started the car. Dell walked around to the driver's side and put her hand on Jo's shoulder.

"When the time comes, you know where to find me."

Joanna looked at her strangely.

Dell tapped the hood of the car and stepped back. As she and Sara watched the couple drive off, Dell could feel the weight of her lover's concern. Sara leaned her head on Dell's shoulder.

"Please tell me that that poor woman's going to be okay."

Dell put her arm lovingly around Sara's shoulder.

"That's not for me to say."

Sara hated the reality of it.

"She's suffering so much. Isn't there anything you can do?"

"You know it doesn't work like that."

"I know... I just wish it did"

"Times like this, so do I."

Before she started the car, Dell turned to her lover.

"Have I really made magic for you?"

Sara reached for Dell's hand and squeezed it in her own.

"Each and every day of my life, baby. Each and every day of my life."

Joanna and Beth rode the entire way home without speaking a single word. Jo pulled into the driveway and turned off the ignition.

"Tell me something… what did you expect when you agreed to these plans?"

"I don't know. I didn't think about it."

"Well maybe you should have."

Beth got out of the car and slammed the door.

"Believe it or not, I was actually enjoying myself… until Nick showed up. Of all the people in the world, why did I have to run into him?"

Joanna came around the car.

"Nick is the world, damn it! You don't get to test the water without getting wet."

The night air had chilled. Beth pulled the sleeves of her cardigan down and folded her arms across her chest.

"Please, spare me the metaphors. I think I've heard enough innuendos for one night."

"I can't believe you let that asshole upset you so much."

Beth began to walk away.

"That's easy for you to say. Forgive me if I find the reminder that I have a husband and a child coming home in a week a bit more upsetting than you do."

Jo followed after her, her tone unforgiving.

"No Beth, you're the one who's got it easy… not me. All you have to do is slip your goddamned wedding band back on and presto, you've got your whole life back. White picket fence and all."

"My god, is that what you think?" Beth began to shake with rage. "You don't have the slightest idea what this summer… what this night… has been like for me!"

"And you don't have any idea what it's been like for me!"

The trauma of it all had become too overwhelming for Beth to handle. She was sure that another moment of it would break her. There was no compromise or apology in her voice.

"I can't be with you tonight."

"What's that supposed to mean?"

"It means I need to be alone."

Deep inside Jo's heart, a swirling mix of emotions hardened into a single word.

"Fine!"

As Beth began to walk away, Joanna reached out and grabbed her arm.

"Just so you know, I wonder about it all the time...what it would be like to grow old together. I've wondered from the very first time we kissed."

Beth felt herself teeter on the brink of madness. Suddenly everything—and nothing—felt possible.

"Joanna please. I can't have this conversation with you... not now... not tonight."

"Then when?"

"I don't know. Don't you understand... I don't know anything anymore... anything!"

Beth broke free of Joanna's grip and bolted for the porch. After fumbling for her keys she slammed the door behind her. A moment later the door opened again. Relieved, Jo thought Beth had changed her mind about wanting to be alone. Instead Beth shoved BJ out onto the porch, then slammed the door again this time shutting them both out.

As the night wore on Dell's mysterious gift remained unopened. Desperate for a distraction, Jo opened the seal and slid the book out. It was a used copy of "The Search For Bridey Murphy" by Morey Bernstein.

Recalling the conversation about the cat's name the afternoon she and Beth had stumbled upon Dell's shop, Jo bitterly tossed the old paperback into the garbage and kicked the canvas duffle bag that lay nearby. Gayle's letter spilled out among her art supplies. For a long time Joanna stared at the envelope, reminded of the invitation and the tickets it contained. She bent down, picked it up and reread Gayle's words. The weight of the pages felt even heavier on this night, already swollen with her own heartache. No longer certain of what she was doing—or why—Joanna picked up the telephone and dialed. After the third ring, she was startled to hear Steve's voice. Though she had intended to call Gayle, her heart had made another choice.

"Hey..." was all Jo could get out.

Steve was amazed how much torment could fit into such a small word.

"What's wrong?"

"Everything."

"Is Beth with you?"

"No. She barricaded herself in the house. Said she needed to be alone tonight. Even kicked the dog out."

"What happened?"

"We had dinner with another couple."

"A lesbian couple?"

"No asshole, a couple of Martians."

"Hey, I was just asking. You never mentioned you knew any lesbians around here."

"Remember that woman who handed you a quarter that night? She and her girlfriend."

Steve considered the unlikely odds.

"That's one helluva' coincidence."

"It's nice to know I'm not the only one who thinks so."

"How'd you guys meet?"

"It's a long story."

"Sounds like we both have the time."

Jo wasn't interested in rehashing all her gnawing misgivings about Dell.

"It's not important, but we ran into her again last week. When she suggested dinner with her girlfriend, Beth thought it would be fun and agreed."

Steve recalled Dell's extremely butch appearance.

"Sounds pretty bold for someone in hiding."

"More like naive. I think Beth got a lot more than she bargained for tonight."

"So she didn't have a good time?"

Jo considered the emotional roller coaster Beth had ridden all night.

"Actually she was having a great time. I think that's part of what threw her. Then that asshole Nick showed up. Son of a bitch put the screws to her pretty good. I could have kicked him in his fucking balls."

"Shit."

Steve didn't need the details to imagine the toll of the collateral damage. Nor did he try to distance himself from the couple's suffering. Instead he allowed his silence to echo his regret and in that moment, Joanna's own heart got the better of her.

"Were you serious about us going into business together?"

"You bet! Does that mean you might be sticking around?"

Joanna backed away from anything that sounded like a decision.

"It doesn't mean anything, so don't go naming the side of your truck." 'Not yet anyway', she heard herself add inside her own head.

Steve sensed her uncertainty about everything.

"Long as you're on your own tonight, come on over and we'll share a few beers?"

Jo refused.

Steve knew that she was still hoping Beth would change her mind. He also knew her well enough to be leery of her judgment—especially tonight.

"Jo, can I give you some advice?"

"No."

"Let her have the night. If Beth asked for some space, give it to her."

"What makes you think I won't?"

"Because it's more like you to storm the house and try to rescue her."

Jo couldn't deny he was right.

"She shouldn't be alone. She's completely strung out."

"If she is, then strung out is what she needs to be. I know what I'm talking about. Long before you showed up I watched Beth handle some pretty tough shit… stuff that would have destroyed most other women. As confused as she may be right now, Beth knows herself pretty damn well. She knew enough not to go with Ben this summer and she knew to come back from Boston to face her feelings for you."

Jo couldn't argue about Beth's courage. She let him continue.

"If Beth said she wants to be alone tonight then trust me, that's what she needs."

Steve tested Joanna's intentions.

"I mean it Jo. Chain yourself to the goddamn refrigerator if you have to, but whatever you do, don't go in there and pump her for answers she doesn't have… at least not yet."

"Okay, okay… I hear you."

It was impossible for him to ignore her torment.

"Jo, I'm really sorry it hurts as much as it does."

She accepted his sincerity.

"I know."

"Is there anything I can do?"

"Yeah, spare me some useless crap your granddaddy told you."

"Don't worry. The old man didn't have a frame of reference for what you're dealing with."

Joanna's usual sarcasm was no match for her pain.

"Neither do I…"

Steve knew she wouldn't be calling back anymore tonight.

It was just past midnight when Joanna dropped into the empty bed. Now at the mercy of the night and the lingering scent on Beth's pillow, she pressed it to her cheek and waited for whatever daylight would bring.

From the corner of her sofa Beth stared blankly into the void that once was the living room of her home. The pounding of her heart had gradually subsided into almost undetectable beats, the cavity of her chest barely expanding enough to fill her lungs and pump life through her listless body. While her hands rested limply on her lap, the slight turn of her head served only to widen the scope of her vacant stupor. Like a familiar object that takes shape in a dense fog, the small painting above the mantle slowly emerged from the vagueness. Triggered by the cherished image, Beth's heart began to stir with recollection and the more it remembered, the more it hurt. Unlike the effects of the prescribed sedatives she'd taken in the past, this time her numbness came from deep within and as it thawed she knew there would be a price to pay. This was not the pain of a mercifully sharp knife as it cut precisely through her heart, but rather, a dull and rusty blade that ripped back and forth, shredding it slowly to pieces. Beth was convinced that this would be the night of her salvation or the night of her undoing. She did not yet understand that both were the same. These recent weeks had brought a hastened sweetness to her life the way a fruit is brought to artificial ripeness before its time. But in this state of accelerated bliss Beth had not yet done the work necessary to savor her own nectar. She had not yet dug down through the mangled underbrush of her resentments and regrets to collect the buried seeds that had for so long gone untended. As brazenly as she had dared to live this summer, surrendering to her desire had freed Beth of her inhibitions, not her demons and tonight they remained more damning than ever before. As she moved through her house she knew they were waiting for her everywhere—in her husband's study where the evidence of his accomplishments had long embittered her—upstairs where her unspeakable acts of betrayal and depraved indiscretions had played out, not just in her own marriage bed but in the bed of her child. Rooms once filled with affection now evoked only her insatiable hunger for another woman's flesh. Nothing of Beth's old life seemed real until she found herself standing at the door of Danny's room. All at once the devastation of his passing felt as fresh as the night tragedy had struck. Even as she placed her hand on the knob Beth knew there was no preparing for what she would be forced to endure. Clinging to her own life, she opened the door as cautiously as she could. She did not need to turn on the light to be reminded of the smallest details. Her heart had memorized everything in her son's room exactly as he had left it the night he never returned. In the past three years she had not found the courage to move a single thing. Now, all of it waited for her in the shadows. The hallway light filtered into the stillness of the space as if illuminating a quiet stage. Across the dimly lit room a gentle breeze swept through the curtain as if beckoning her in. Unable to live another day without it, Beth entered in search of redemption. Daniel's mother would break her silence—a silence that had so many times in the past come so close to breaking her. God would either condemn or forgive her, but tonight she was determined to release the confession she prayed would at last set her free. She sat down on her son's bed and clutched his violin. With the crushing weight of her loss came uncontrollable sobs.

"Oh God Danny… I loved you so much, but oh how deeply I hated you for ruining my life."

Despite the years of her devotion Beth had always felt responsible for her son's death—convinced that the unbearable tragedy was her punishment for resenting his life that had robbed her of her own. She had never admitted this to another living soul. Her guilt had become overwhelming. Her sobs grew deeper for the child conceived not from passion but from her loathsome passivity.

"I'm so sorry that being your mother was never what I wanted… that being your mother was never enough. Why Danny… tell me why you let me give you life but not the power to save it." She clenched her fists and pounded her son's violin. "You were supposed to become what I hadn't. How could you have deprived me of even that. How could you have wasted my life so completely… twice?" Beth held herself in an anguished knot. As she leaned forward a stream of tears, mucus and saliva coated her face and collected beneath her chin. There was a grotesque beauty in the aftermath of Beth's purging, like the bloody membrane that comes with the birthing of a new life—her life. "Forgive me Danny… please forgive me for surviving… for wanting to live." She wiped her face with the back of her hand. "Forgive me for needing the kind of love your father could never give me… for wanting bouquets of paper flowers… and the chance not to have to cover my ears." Once again Beth's tears flowed heavily. "Please… forgive me for wanting to forgive myself… for wanting to be happy… for daring to believe I still deserve to be, after all the terrible things I've kept in my heart."

As Beth waited for 'The Gods' to strike her dead another gentle breeze blew through the window and caressed the curtain. It was enough to give her hope of their forgiveness—maybe even Danny's too. She brought his violin up to her lips and kissed the cup where so often her son had rested his chin. When she was ready, she placed the violin in its case and closed the lid. Three full years after she'd lost her son, Beth laid his instrument—and her heart—to rest. There would be no more waiting for her life to begin—no more apologies—no more pleading—no more regrets.

It was in the early hours of morning when the embattled mother emerged from her son's bedroom. The cathartic purging had begun to take hold as she staggered up the steps that led to the attic. Though the stagnant air was almost suffocating she did not crack open its windows, determined instead to remain entombed with the dry archives of family history and the excesses of household belongings. As Beth moved about the congested space the parched wooden planks creaked beneath the weight of her steps and carefully guarded heart. She let her eyes drift slowly across the narrative landscape of personal history. The once valuable parts of herself too long in storage now represented little more than a testament to her mundane and ordinary existence. She thought about her dinner companions and the diverse richness of each of their lives. Where, she wondered, were her stories… her glory… her adventures? Certainly not in the carefully stacked boxes, the clearly marked cartons or the alphabetically organized files. A practical man, Ben had always reinforced everything with an excess of tape, ensuring that the bottoms would never fall out—not of the boxes and not of their lives. He had always preferred things secured and orderly, not just in the attic but in their marriage as well. Beth knew that the truth of her nature had always threatened his. For that reason she had always held back the restless, unpredictable part of herself—the part that craved freedom, not barriers—the part her husband couldn't handle, manage or contain. It all repulsed her now—the perfectly arranged contents of her life—the well-organized shelves stacked with the well-packed containers of their history. The price of her secret guilt had been resignation. Tonight the price of her healing would be nothing less than full retribution. Years of repression suddenly exploded in defiance. Beth raged against the bonds she had let confine her to her small and unimpressive life. Sitting in her son's room, Beth had found the courage to reach deep into her smothered soul and stoke its nearly extinguished embers. Now in this dry and combustible space, the flames she had re-ignited burst into an uncontrollable inferno that threatened to destroy everything in its path. She began with the cartons nearest her reach. Blinded with contempt, Beth ripped into their contents with her bare hands. Some she picked up and hurled whole. Others—like the set of her mother's china she'd always hated and the Christmas decorations that no one else ever took out or helped put away—she smashed piece by piece. She flung entire volumes of poetry she'd never found the time to read and shredded pages of music books she'd never gotten the chance to play. She tore savagely through shelves stacked with children's toys, sending pieces of board games and craft projects flying through the air. When she could no longer find anything left to hurl, she kicked and stomped what was too heavy to lift or impossible to break until everything that represented the years of her sacrifice—everything that shaved off even a single moment of her life—everything that governed or compromised her true nature—lay in shambles.

Through the night of her treacherous freefall Beth had risked her sanity to save her sanity. It remained to be seen what, if any of it, had survived. In the aftermath of her tirade, she curled up against the wall amid the ruins of her life. She stared up at the small window across the room, startled by the hint of daybreak. In her hysteria she had lost all sense of time. Somewhere in its distortion Beth heard Joanna's voice calling out to her from downstairs. Her calls unanswered, Jo raced upstairs hoping to find Beth in bed or in the shower. Joanna's voice was now fraught with panic. Still Beth did not answer. As Jo continued her frantic search she noticed the door to the attic was open. Beth knew it was only a matter of moments before Joanna would find her—moments, she feared, that came years too late.

At the top of the landing Joanna grabbed the banister to keep herself from reeling backward. When Beth had said she needed to be alone Jo imagined a sleepless night, maybe even an empty bottle of liquor. Nothing in her wildest dreams had prepared her for this. Beth offered no explanation. Horrified, Jo looked at the woman sitting curled up on the floor amid the dust and debris.

"My god, what the hell happened up here?"

Beth answered as if nothing at all was unusual.

"I was looking for something I seemed to have misplaced."

"Jesus… what?"

Beth sounded incomprehensibly casual.

"My life." Beth shrugged. "I never did find it."

Stunned, Jo cracked open the window to let in some badly needed fresh air.

"Have you lost your mind?"

Beth slapped her thigh as if just being reminded of something.

"Thank you… I knew I forgot something. Yes, I must have lost that too." She looked around. One last teacup of her mother's china still remained unbroken. "Wait, maybe it's in here." Beth leaned forward, picked it up and peered inside. "Nope, guess not." She opened her fingers and let the cup drop. It shattered into pieces. "Oh well, at least now it matches the rest of the set."

She giggled inappropriately. "I must remember to use it the next time mother visits."

Jo had switched from trying to comprehend the destruction to simply trying to clean some of it up. As she bent down to collect the broken items scattered at her feet, something primal and threatening sprang to life in Beth's voice.

"Don't you dare touch a thing!"

No longer sure what Beth was capable of, Jo held up her hands in concession.

"Okay. Everything stays just the way it is."

For the moment Jo's compliance seemed to have a calming effect. Beth's voice fell.

"I need to leave it just the way it is. I need for Ben to see what I've never been able to make him… or anyone else… understand."

Jo tried to be reassuring.

"I do."

Beth shook her head.

"No you don't. You never will."

For all Jo had come to know, the depth of Beth's suffering was just now beginning to sink in.

"Let me help you."

"You can't." Beth began to cry. "Nobody can."

Jo moved toward her, holding out her hand.

"Let's go downstairs and get you into a shower. I'll fix you something to eat. We can talk over breakfast."

In Beth's state of mind, Joanna's suggestion sounded as absurd as it did useless.

"No."

As Jo came closer, the threatening tone in Beth's voice returned.

"I'm not going anywhere."

Once again Joanna conceded.

"Okay then, we'll just stay here."

Jo knelt down and cleared a small place for herself on the floor. Beth remained cautiously passive until Joanna attempted to draw her into her arms. Beth did not want to be pacified. She immediately broke free.

"No! Go away! That's what you're going to do anyway, isn't it?" Beth held herself to stop from trembling. "Please, just go now. Get out of my house! Get out of my life!"

This time Joanna refused to listen. Again she attempted to take Beth into her arms.

"I'm not going anywhere."

For a moment, Beth did not resist.

"Yes, yes you are... and we both know it. We've known it all along."

New defeat set in around the already shattered pieces of Beth's life. Not knowing what else to do, Jo apologized for all the harsh things she'd said the night before. The memory only made it worse for Beth. The truth was a part of what hurt so much.

"You've no idea what it was like being out with the three of you. All I could do was sit there and pretend to know what all of you were talking about, when the truth was I didn't have the slightest clue." Beth shook her head in defeat. "I don't know any of the buzz words... any of the jokes... absolutely nothing in my background compares to any of yours."

"Why should that matter?"

Beth teetered between hopelessness and impatience.

"Because it's completely unnerving not to have even the slightest frame of reference for some of the most powerful emotions I've ever known in my life, that's why!"

Jo had never thought about it quite that way.

"I guess it must feel strange."

"It feels a lot more than strange Joanna, it's downright terrifying!"

"I understand."

Beth was quite sure she didn't.

"No, you don't! You couldn't possibly. You and Dell always knew who you were. Even Sara found out before half her life was over."

"Okay, so you registered a little late. You'll read the cliff notes and catch up."

Beth was not amused. Her tone said so.

"There is no catching up! At seven I was hosting after school tea parties with imaginary friends while you were grandiose enough to think you could play house with your next-door neighbor's wife! Dell spent days slicing off the top of a car with a hacksaw to get into a woman's pants while I spent mine with a can of spray starch trying to put the perfect crease in Ben's. Sara attended parties where she thought nothing of having sex with two women she heard moaning behind some door. I was a regular at Tupperware parties where the squeal of women's delight came from the thrill of plastic nesting containers with self-burping lids."

Joanna laughed, but Beth did not share her amusement.

"I'm glad you find this funny."

Beth continued to compare herself to Sara.

"Not to mention she managed to raise a child while spending her life on the cutting edge of every important social movement of the last thirty years. Wanna' know what being on the 'cutting edge' has meant in my life? It meant standing behind a table with a cake knife, year after year, at the school's annual bake sale."

Jo grabbed Beth's shoulders.

"Stop discounting your whole life. It's not fair."

Beth pulled away.

"I'll tell you what's not fair, that I've lived my entire life at the expense of discounting myself." Beth looked around. "I can see my epitaph now: 'She was the best at what she never wanted to be at all'."

Once again Beth's resentment began to flare. She picked up a scrapbook from the floor and began ripping out its pages, one by one.

"It's my life, damn it. I've earned the right to tear it apart."

Joanna tried to stop her.

"Not like this."

"You just don't get it, do you? How could you? You've always known where you belong. After the fiasco in the restaurant last night, I've never been less sure."

Jo reached out and pulled Beth close.

"I'll tell you where you belong… here… in my arms. It's that simple."

Joanna held her tenderly and for a moment Beth forgot. The moment ended.

"No Joanna, you're wrong! For me, it's anything but simple. At the end of this summer you have a trip to Paris waiting for you, if you want it. I have a husband and child coming home, whether I want it or not."

Suddenly overwhelmed by the reality, Beth broke from Jo's embrace.

"Damn you Joanna! Damn you for coming into my life and damn you for walking out of it."

Joanna moved toward her. Beth recoiled.

"I'm warning you, stay away from me!"

"Beth, please…" She continued to inch closer. Feeling trapped, Beth lashed out and scratched her across the face.

"No! Don't touch me! Don't ever touch me again!"

Stunned, Jo felt her cheek. Beth's attack had drawn blood. She looked for an apology in Beth's eyes but saw only unfinished rage. No longer sure what Beth would do next, Jo looked for something to restrain her. She reached for the broken table lamp and yanked the cord from its base.

"Don't make me do this."

Beth became enraged by the threat of being tied up. She'd been restrained all her life.

"Go to hell Joanna!"

Beth picked up a molded Christmas tree ornament and hurled it at her. It barely missed Jo's eye. Though Beth fought her violently, she was no match for Jo's determination to keep them both safe. After a hellish struggle, Jo managed to tie Beth's wrists together. Now straddling her, Jo felt as if she herself was going mad. Beth looked up at the woman hovering above her. It was impossible to ignore the evidence of Joanna's torment.

"Your cheek..."

With her wrists bound, Beth reached up and gently wiped the side of Joanna's face with the back of her hand. Though she did not apologize, it was the first sign of normalcy. Jo was gentle.

"I just wanted to hold you."

"I don't want to be held. I don't want to be loved." Beth's eyes became vacant, "It hurts too much."

Sorry for all of it, Jo moved to undo the knot. Beth pulled her hands away.

"Don't untie me..." It was clear she felt tortured by her own request. "Not yet..."

Jo reinforced the cord. Beth felt helpless to escape. It was exactly how she wanted to feel as Joanna's eyes now bore into her. Beth's heart began to pound with arousal and uncertainty.

"What do you want of me?"

Joanna tested her hunch.

"I don't want anything from you Beth."

"Liar!" she hissed back. "Everybody has always wanted something from me."

Beth strained against the cord. Surer now of what Beth was asking of her, Joanna bent and kissed her tenderly. She knew Beth did not want to be kissed at all. She did not want anything that evoked intimacy. She wanted something anonymous—something harsh and much more forbidding. Jo knew that this time Beth wanted not to be consoled, but to be consumed by her own anguished desires.

Beth wrenched her head, turning away from the softness of Joanna's lips.

"No!"

Certain of what the cord represented, Jo shook her violently.

"Say it."

Joanna's instincts were right. Beth felt herself rage against everything in her life that had ever tamed or silenced her needs. Her fury pushed against the walls of her shame until they could no longer contain the impropriety of her hunger.

"I want to be fucked! Fucked like the girl Dell tutored! Fucked like the women behind the door!"

Beth looked for evidence of Joanna's repulsion. She saw none. Instead, Joanna's eyes dared her to demand even more. Beth was deliberately cruel to the woman she loved more than life itself.

"I don't want to feel anything… I don't want to care about anyone. Not anyone. Do you understand?"

The depth of Beth's deprivation did not threaten or frighten her. Unlike Ben, Jo realized that more than anything Beth was afraid of dying without ever knowing what it felt like to live—only for herself—to belong only to herself.

Understanding this, Jo allowed herself to become invisible—to be nothing more than a conduit for Beth's most selfish desires. Cloaked in anonymity, Joanna yanked Beth's pants down around her ankles, forced her legs apart and quickly brought her to a state of frenzied arousal. The closer Beth came to the edge, the more distant her eyes grew as she continued to strain against the cord and every limitation that ever denied her fulfillment and release. Beth arched and pressed her hardened, throbbing flesh against the palm of Joanna's hand, the hand that teased but deliberately had not yet entered her.

"Fuck me!" Beth demanded of her otherwise worthless servant. "Fuck me!"

If Beth had owned a dildo like her friend Rheeta, she would have made Jo use it on her then. A dildo—the handle of a brush—anything to fill the gaping cavity of her hunger. Satisfied with the greed of Beth's demands Joanna used her fingers to perform this ultimate act of love disguised as the ultimate act of violation, thrusting them deep inside, filling Beth with the sensation her body craved. The cracked full-length mirror that leaned just a few feet away exposed Beth to the shattered image of her own ruthless desire. Unlike all the times they had made love, it was not now the sweet juices of surrender but rather a thick pungent anger that spilled from between Beth's legs and coated Joanna's hand. Beth bucked violently, fucking whatever it was that was fucking her. It could just as well have been the hand of the devil and still Beth would have pleaded for it to continue, to make her cum. The crime and the punishment had become the same. No longer was the price too high to pay—

no longer was her soul worth saving. The most ruthless of acts had become the most sacred—the most vulgar of pleas had become the prayer.

"Fuck me!" Beth cried out over and over again, until the freedom to feel nothing allowed her to at last feel everything. In that state of frenzied emancipation Beth came around Joanna's fingers with furious might, expelling from her heart every compromise—every sacrifice—every concern she had ever felt toward anyone but herself. She had never trusted anyone to serve her this way—so completely, so shamelessly. Even now as she once again searched Joanna's eyes, Beth recognized only her own craving for this woman, not the woman herself.

Joanna was remarkably accepting. She understood instinctively what Ben had never been able to—that the gift of one's heart meant nothing without the choice to withhold it. With him, there were no sharp edges for Beth to cut herself on -no unseen cliffs from which she might suddenly plunge—nothing unsavory lurking in the shadows to fear. With him Beth had always felt protected from life. With Joanna she felt exposed to the exhilarating danger of it. Jo untied Beth's hands and the two sank into each other's arms. Beth had never been more selfish in her loving, and Jo, more selfless. In the exchange they had each been transformed, joined as perfectly as anything in nature. Neither spoke a word. As they lie in stillness, Beth felt something oddly familiar. She touched herself where Jo's fingers had been. When she took her hand away, it was covered in blood. Assuming her force had done some terrible harm, Joanna became alarmed. Beth knew better.

"I'm perfectly fine." Beth looked at the blood in amazement. "It's my period."

"You told me it stopped after Danny died."

"It had." Beth sighed within the fold of Joanna's arms. "Thanks to you it looks like all the juices of life are flowing again."

As she lay in her lover's arms, Beth confided in Joanna about the time she spent in Danny's room the night before. Joanna listened quietly to the description of her lover's pain.

"I love you" Jo whispered, but only after covering Beth's ears with her own hands. Beth looked solemnly into Joanna's eyes, then reached up and took them away. Jo understood the risk Beth was taking for her. She pulled her close and pressed her lips against Beth's ear.

"I love you," she repeated tenderly.

Beth closed her eyes and gathered her courage.

"Again."

"I love you... I love you... I love you."

Beth let her head fall indebted against Jo's shoulder.

"I love you too."

In the ransacked attic that sheltered and parted them from all other life, Joanna sensed that the woman in her arms had begun to weep quietly. Holding back tears of her own, Jo tried to console them both.

"It's okay."

Beth's voice was small.

"No it's not. Without you, nothing in my life will ever be okay again."

Joanna put her lips to Beth's disheveled hair. With a gentle kiss, Beth's tears began to flow more heavily.

"Tell me Jo, because I need to know... how does my heart go on beating after this summer ends and you're no longer here to feel it?"

In need of comfort herself, Joanna begged the silence—a silence that echoed the possibility of all other sounds—to answer for her. In that silence, Jo could only press her lover against her own heart and the precious little time they still had left.

Somewhere in the chaotic, cathartic events of the night Beth had heard the distant ring of the telephone. She had assumed that on an immediate tip from Nick, Ben was already calling to badger her with his suspicions. It was not until after the lovers showered and went downstairs that Beth played back the message and learned that she was wrong. The call had come from the director of the nursing home, informing her that sometime in the early hours of the morning her beloved Arthur had passed away. This time Beth's despair did not erupt into havoc, but turned instead into quiet tears that quenched the memory of her cherished friend. After Jo helped her collect the broken pieces of her heart, Beth called back for more information. The nurse on duty had found the sweet old man with the frame Beth had given him pressed to his heart. A Mylar birthday balloon still dangled from the rail of his bed. Beth's instinct told her that Arthur had waited until she was happy. Believing that she had finally been reunited with her 'Anne', he slipped away peacefully, reassured. Such was the life-long devotion of the little boy who had so deeply internalized his mother's sacrifice and heartbreak. Now free of concern for his life, Beth would at last be able to live her own. Overwhelmed with emotion, she wept in Joanna's arms for all that had transpired in the hours before dawn.

Arthur Prescott was a kind and gentle man who would be missed dearly by everyone who knew him. Now, all that remained of his life was the old leather suitcase he'd kept on the shelf in the closet of his room. According to his repeated wishes, the suitcase and its contents were to go to Beth. While the simple service was to be open to all who wished to pay their respects, Arthur had made it clear—as late as the evening before he died—that he wanted only his momma and her companion to accompany his casket to its final resting place in the Prescott family plot. It was well known to everyone at Hillcrest that his 'momma' meant Beth and she in turn knew that her 'companion' meant Joanna. His only other requests were to be buried in the red bow tie and proper white shirt he'd always worn on the days of Beth's visits and that the small portable tape recorder with the music she had recorded for him be turned on just before the casket was closed.

On the morning of the heavily attended service, with Joanna standing at her side, Beth leaned over the open casket and kissed her precious Arthur one last time. With all the tenderness of an adoring mother she granted his request, making sure that the small foam plugs rested securely in his ears. The music would play to the end of the tape. The memory of their devotion, to the end of time.

Chapter 25

Following the heavily attended service, the ride to the cemetery was a solemn one. Given her state of mind and the heavy rain Beth didn't object to Joanna's offer to drive. Between the rhythmic swipes of the windshield wiper blades, she stared at the backlights as Jo followed close behind the slow-moving vehicle that carried Arthur's body. She thought it profound that on the very night she'd finally made peace with the death of one son—in a manner of speaking—she'd lost another. From the very beginning the two had been inexorably linked, for had she not lost Danny and sought healing by volunteering at Hillcrest, she would never had met Arthur.

Dating back centuries, Clairmont was one of the oldest cemeteries in the township. The hearse came to a stop in front of the massive oak that dominated the Prescott family plot. The ground had been opened in preparation for Arthur's burial. Other than the mound of displaced earth there was nothing that suggested the ceremonial rituals associated with the death of such a well-loved man. It would be the simple, private burial Arthur had repeatedly requested.

Beneath the steady downpour the women stood huddled arm-in-arm under a large umbrella while the driver and his assistants brought Arthur's casket to rest on the set of retractable straps that spanned the opened grave. They extended their sympathies and left the women to bid the deceased a private farewell. Several gravediggers in hooded yellow slickers waited a respectful distance away.

Just as she'd always done on the mornings she visited, Beth brought flowers from her garden today as well. Now, instead of placing them in a vase by Arthur's bed, she laid the bouquet on top of his casket. Joanna stood protectively by. Considering all that Beth had been through in these last forty-eight traumatic hours, the emotional toll seemed unimaginable. As Beth bent and put her lips to the curved lid of the coffin, she listened for the softness of music coming from inside. Whether the sound was imagined or not, the comfort was by necessity just as real. Still, she was not yet ready to leave. Locking her arm through Joanna's for stability, Beth maneuvered them around the displaced earth to have a closer look at the family plot. The grave to the left of Arthur's was that of his father. The inscription read: 'Frederick Stanton Prescott—Born November 5, 1849, Died January 22, 1921'. Though stained and pitted by the element of time, the commanding monument was a testament to the little Beth knew of him. He had obviously made notable use of his 72 years, becoming a man of great wealth if not one of generous heart On the other side of Arthur's grave was an equally ornate but somewhat smaller monument bearing the inscription of Arthur's beloved mother, 'Elizabeth Margaret Prescott—Born April 10, 1860, Died October 5, 1897. Joanna immediately stiffened.

"You never mentioned that his mother's name was so close to yours?"

Beth too was stunned.

"I didn't know. Arthur always referred to her as 'momma'. I never thought to ask." She continued to stare at the headstone. "Jo..." Beth's voice trailed off as if following an unmarked path. "Arthur's mother died on the same day as my birthday."

What little relief Beth found clutching Joanna's arm was quickly shattered when she noticed the smaller headstone to the right of Arthur's mothers. Chiseled into its otherwise unadorned surface was the name: Anne Wyatt. As in the first inexplicable coincidence, the day of Anne's death was the same as Joanna's birthday.

The disturbing discovery, coupled with Arthur's insistence on their identities, was impossible to comprehend. Suddenly Jo remembered the almost indistinguishable signature 'A. Wyatt' in the corner of the painting that hung over Beth's mantle. Almost simultaneously, the same recognition came to Beth. She covered her mouth to contain a gasp. Joanna's became defiant, as if determined to get to the bottom of some depraved practical joke.

"What the fuck's going on?"

Beth wrestled with the unimaginable. Her breathing became measured as if trying to sustain something greater than just her own existence. The possibility felt overwhelming.

"God, I've just come to terms with one life..."

Joanna was insistent.

"You're out of your mind. Those two women have nothing to do with us!"

Beth looked down at Anne Wyatt's grave as the torrential rain ran down the side of the stone.

"No matter how many times I tried to correct him, Arthur would always call you Anne..."

There was no way Joanna was going down that path.

"The guy's brain had more fucking holes in it than a block of Swiss cheese."

Beth remained silent. It was a silence Joanna would not let her dwell in.

"For Christ's sake, he thought you were his dead mother!"

Beth could feel her heart begin to open.

"Exactly…"

Joanna had heard enough. She knew Beth hadn't slept in days. Her judgment was understandably impaired.

"Let's go. I'm taking you home."

Back in the car Jo would have speed off quickly, but Beth asked her to wait. Through the rain-streaked windshield the woman watched in burdened silence as the team of gravediggers came forward to complete the work of Arthur's burial. Although the couple made every attempt to focus on the somber work of the men's shovels, neither could take their minds off the two women buried side by side beneath the rain-soaked earth.

Back at the carriage house Joanna looked for normalcy wherever she could find it. Boiling some water seemed like a place to start.

"Why don't you get out of those wet clothes while I make you a cup of tea?"

When Beth didn't answer, Jo turned around to find her staring at Arthur's suitcase. She had placed it on the floor beside the piano. Suddenly, everything took on an eeriness it never had before. Beth looked incapable of handling much more. Jo shut the whistling teapot, then came and stood reassuringly behind her.

"Are you okay?"

"Not really…"

Her voice was as weak as Jo had ever heard it. She rubbed the length of Beth's arms that by now were covered in goose bumps.

"What are you thinking?"

"Thinking is too rational a term for what's going on in my head right now."

Jo followed Beth's eyes over to Arthur's suitcase.

"You don't have to do this now, you know."

Despite her growing apprehension, Beth disagreed. Somehow, she found the courage to move toward the suddenly ominous piece of luggage. Along with its contents, the fear of the unknown now weighed heavily in Beth's hand as she lifted the old scuffed suitcase up onto the bed. She sat down beside it and let her fingers trace over Arthur's embossed initials. Beth told herself that nothing that belonged to her dear friend could ever hurt her. Once Jo realized that Beth had made up her mind to look inside, she reluctantly came and sat down beside her. With her heart pounding in her chest, Beth placed her thumbs on the set of tarnished latches and pushed. The sudden jolt of the spring was enough to send the grown women reeling backwards like two children spooked by a scene in a horror movie. Joanna hovered over Beth's shoulder as her trembling hands slowly lifted open the top. Fueled by their childhood imaginations, they were half expecting the ghosts of the two dead women to jump out at them. Relieved that was not the case, Beth opened the lid all the way. The contents did not appear nearly as threatening as the couple had imagined. With their worst fears behind them, they peered into the small, neatly packed suitcase. On top was a carefully folded shawl. Beth immediately recognized it as the one around Elizabeth Prescott's shoulders in the last photo she had taken with her young son—the photo Beth had found in Dell's shop—the one she'd given back to Arthur for his birthday—the one he was still holding to his heart when he died. Beth lifted the sacred garment, spread it out across her lap and ran her hands gently along the fabric. After a few minutes of reflection she refolded it and placed it off to the side. Beneath his mother's shawl Arthur had packed a small Victorian box with a hand-carved ivory lid. Among an assortment of hair combs, an embroidered handkerchief and other small personal affects was an unframed photograph with frayed, flaking edges. The sepia tinted image was of Elizabeth Prescott seated at her piano. On top of the instrument was a crystal vase filled with a glorious array of flowers. Both women looked across the room at the same time. The vase in the photograph was unmistakably the same one that now sat atop Beth's piano, holding Joanna's paper bouquet. Jo began pacing. Beth didn't find this particular coincidence nearly as upsetting.

"I told you that the vase belonged to his mother."

"Yeah, but of all places for it to wind up—on top of your piano—c'mon, don't you find that just a little freaky?"

Recalling Arthur's insistence that she have it back Beth said nothing.

Quietly considering the irony, her curiosity lay with what still remained in the suitcase. She lifted a cumbersome cardboard sleeve and removed an oversized, handsomely bound leather book. Embossed into the rich golden-brown cover was its title: 'Landscapes Of The Heart—The Complete Works Of Anne Wyatt'. Just beneath it were the words: Edited by Arthur Prescott. The women remained guarded as Beth placed the heavy volume on her lap and opened its cover. With great care, she turned the first few pages until she came to the dedication. Like a quiet whisper uttered in an open space, the small understated print lay in the center of the yellowing page: 'In loving memory of my mother, Elizabeth Margaret Prescott'. A few pages beyond was the introduction written by her son. With her fingers and voice trembling, Beth read Arthur's words aloud.

"The oldest child of a blacksmith and his wife, Annabelle Wyatt was born on December 18, 1862. The family, though not impoverished, lived modestly on the outskirts of the burgeoning New York City metropolis. When Annabelle was just 16 her mother died of tuberculosis, leaving her to care for her 3 younger brothers. It was a role that the brooding young woman with greater ambitions resented bitterly. Soon after, her father remarried and for the next several years the spirited young woman who had come to insist on the less puritanical name 'Anne' clashed regularly with her stepmother's archetypical rule. Drawn to the vitality of the nearby city, the increasingly rebellious Anne would often run away in search of the kind of freedom and opportunity more readily available to young men her age. In the summer of 1880, fearing for his daughter's reputation, Anne's father sent her off to live with her aunt in Amherst, Massachusetts. Though it was a thriving town in its own right, he had hoped that the quieter surroundings would keep his daughter out of harm's way and the greater dangers of her own impetuous nature. Though instantly bored with her new surroundings, the restless young woman was not miserable for long. Just days after her arrival, Anne met the beautiful and captivating Elizabeth Osborne—the woman who would become my mother. Elizabeth was the only child of Henry and Emma Osborne, at the time one of North Hampton's most prominent families. A member of one of the earliest graduating classes of the prestigious Smith College for Women, Elizabeth was not only a brilliant scholar but also a gifted pianist. The two instantly became inseparable. Inspired by the intensity of their friendship, Anne—who had never had any formal training—began to paint. The prolific body of work that emerged from those impassioned years would later earn her the reputation as one of the foremost American landscape artists of the 19th century.

In the spring of 1883, after a reticent courtship with one of her father's most promising associates, Elizabeth was persuaded into marriage with Frederick Stanton Prescott. Soon after, I—their only child—was born. During this time, Anne and my mother struggled by way of all to infrequent liaisons to maintain their deep and often tumultuous relationship. Unlike my mother, Anne had refused to yield to the conventions of the day, neither marrying nor bearing children of her own. In the winter of 1888 at the age of 26, Anne left Amherst abruptly and moved to Paris.

Long estranged from her own family and determined to leave her broken heart behind, Anne instantly claimed the city itself as her mistress. Taking up residence on the infamously bohemian left bank, she sought both refuge and inspiration in the cafes, salons and boudoirs of countless like-minded women, many of whom would come to be known as some of the most provocative and progressive artists, writers and poets of their day. I would later learn that over the 9 years of separation that preceded my mother's decline and untimely death at 37, she and Anne maintained a secret and tortured correspondence. The news of my mother's death in 1897 plunged Anne into despair. Devastated by the loss, her life spiraled out of control. She had been living aimlessly for 5 years when I contacted her in the winter of 1922. Upon my father's death the preceding year, I had occasion to go through my parent's estate. Hidden among my mother's most personal belongings I found a collection of letters representing years of their impassioned correspondence. I wrote to inquire what Anne wished me to do with the collection now in my possession. She was most appreciative of my offer to return them all to her. Though understandably reluctant, upon my invitation Anne eventually agreed to return to the states for a visit. I was further successful in convincing her to be a guest in my home just outside of Amherst, not far from where I'd spent most of my boyhood.

Our rapport was instant and disarming, making our difficult reunion much less uncomfortable than either of us would have imagined. After her brief and emotional stay, Anne returned to Paris whereupon we remained in close touch. Sensing her loneliness and isolation, I persuaded her to move back to Amherst permanently and live with me until she settled into a place of her own. Through the intimate details of the letters I had read and our subsequently honest conversation, I came to learn about the significance of the abandoned carriage house that had sheltered the women's secret and most intimate interludes both prior to and after my mother's marriage."

At Arthur's mention of an abandoned carriage house, Beth froze. It was as if all at once her mysterious connection to it had come into unbearable focus. Her heart began to pound against the walls of her chest.

"I can't...."

She handed the volume over to Joanna, her eyes imploring her to read the rest. Though reluctant, Jo continued where Beth could not.

"Once Anne had agreed to return permanently I immediately arranged to purchase the abandoned property on which the carriage house stood, hoping that it would serve to preserve the memories she and my mother had made there. Anne was deeply touched by my gesture. While she wanted nothing to do with the main house and preferred it remained boarded up, she immediately set about the necessary improvements that would make the carriage house suitable for living. In the fall of 1924 Anne officially moved in with her old easel and what few belongings still held any meaning. The carriage house became both studio and home where, in the shadow of my mother's companionship, Anne resumed painting and lived out her years. As time went on we had taken to sharing each other's company quite regularly and over the course of the next 12 years we came to think of one another as family. On the afternoon of August 12th, 1937 Anne and I were to have tea in the carriage house. When I arrived with my customary bouquet of fresh-cut flowers I found her sitting in a chair in front of her favorite painting entitled 'Ellie At Our Carriage House'." Joanna felt her throat tighten. "How often I had caught her eyes lingering there. This time would be her last. She had passed away quietly—the scattered pages of my mother's letters resting upon her lap. Though Anne had survived my mother by some 40 years I am convinced that each, longing for the other, had died of a broken heart."

Joanna fought to read Arthur's words to the end.

"After Anne's death my intension was to refurbish and live in the main house. It was my heartfelt desire to turn the carriage house into a gallery that would permanently display the works from Anne's private collection. Regrettably, financial loses sustained during the depression forced me to sell the property. Over the next 3 years I endeavored instead to publish this anthology as a loving tribute to both the artist and her beloved 'Ellie'—the woman who would forever traverse the landscape of Anne Wyatt's heart.

Arthur Prescott

N. Hampton, Massachusetts, 1940

Joanna leapt to her feet and began to pace around the room. Beth fell into a surrendering stillness.

"Ellie is the name you call out in your sleep. I've heard you say it so many times: 'I'm begging you Ellie, don't go… I'm so sorry Ellie… Please Ellie, please forgive me'."

"Shut up Beth! Just shut up!"

The last thing Jo needed at that moment was to be reminded of her reoccurring nightmare—the one that began immediately after she'd returned from her assignment in Amherst—the one that incorporated the limousine in which Beth rode past the mall where she was filming—the same mall where, three years later, they would actually meet. Nor did she need to be reminded of the mysterious switch from present day surroundings to those of an earlier century. Joanna's resistance erupted into something close to terror. Feeling a shortness of breath, she burst out onto the porch. Her heartbeat raced almost as fast as her mind. She would not allow herself to doubt whose skin now glistened in the pouring rain.

Inside the carriage house Beth's reaction had taken a more somber turn. With the volume still on her lap, she opened to the page book-marked with a folded letter. Her cry brought Joanna back to her side. The plate Arthur had referred to in his introduction—'Ellie At Our Carriage House—was the very painting that hung over Beth's mantle. Slowly Beth began to absorb the profound legacy of the artwork in her possession. The painting was of Elizabeth Prescott and the weathered structure depicted behind her was the same carriage house where she and Joanna, at last reunited, had resumed their unfinished love affair. Uncertain whether she would make it there before collapsing, Beth stood up and moved to the window with the carved heart. Standing before the now recognizable initials A&E, she broke down in gut-wrenching sobs. Jo raced to Beth's side and supported the trembling woman in her arms. The two stood together in front of the rain-soaked window, their eyes riveted upon the etched sill.

Fearing Beth might faint, Jo led her back to the bed. She placed a wet washcloth to the back of her neck while Beth sat forward with her head between her knees. Somewhat stabilized, Beth held out the folded letter she'd found tucked inside the anthology.

"Read this to me."

Joanna refused to be drawn any further into Beth's preposterous conclusion.

"Wherever you're going with all this, just leave me the hell out of it."

Beth pleaded.

"Please… I can't do this alone."

Reluctantly, Jo took the letter and unfolded it. As Joanna began to read, Beth sat quietly staring at the woman she was now convinced had twice captured her heart.

October 4, 1925

"My Dear Arthur,

I am writing to you on the eve of what would have been your mother's 65th birthday, still not knowing how or why I have survived all these years without her. It was so long ago that you—an innocent child of three, and I—your mother's secret lover—had last seen one another. On that dismal winter's day I could never have imagined that thirty-four years later I would receive such a poignant letter from the kind, thoughtful man you have apparently become.

It was a letter that, much like meeting your beautiful mother, changed the course and deepened the meaning of my life. In light of what you have come to understand about the nature of our relationship, I can only thank you for your compassionate discretion and for your desire to include me in your life. Your devotion that so sacredly embodies my connection to your mother has sustained me beyond words. As I sit here in the carriage house you so thoughtfully purchased on my behalf, so many years of bitterness and resentment toward you for being the child she would not abandon in order to come away with me have been erased by the kindness you have extended to me in these recent and most melancholy of years. I can only hope you know how very much your visits and friendship mean. Every time I have looked into your eyes—every time you have thoughtfully taken this lonely woman's hand—I am reminded of the sweetness of your mother's nature and in the warmth of each of our embraces, I am blessed and cursed to remember hers. I have begun to paint again, but only that I might feel closer to her beauty and grace.

You continue to ask whether there's anything else you might do that would help diminish this terrible ache and endless suffering and I have come to believe there is something that would bring me much solace. Assuming that you will survive me—which, given the difference in our ages, I certainly hope will be the case—I shall ask you to see to it that I be buried beside your mother, my beloved Ellie, so that we may be together through eternity as we could not be through this life. By the gift of your promise I will spend whatever time I have left within these sacred walls so filled with her memory, in greater peace and impatience.

Yours, Ever Gratefully, Anne"

The gravesite was evidence of Arthur's promise. All of it now rendered the women speechless. Beth slowly began combing through the volume to examine its haunting contents more thoroughly. Unwilling to see more, Joanna got up and stood a safe distance away. As Beth poured through page after page, the beautifully rendered landscapes rekindled a vague sense of familiarity that pulled her into an ever-deepening silence. Three quarters through the volume Beth broke down in sobs. Jo raced to her side.

"What is it?"

Unable to speak, Beth turned the book around. The plate entitled 'Picnic With Ellie 1882' depicted a woman on a blanket spread out upon a grassy knoll. In the background was a large boulder with clusters of wild flowers bordering its base. The setting was unmistakably where Beth and Joanna had picnicked and the great rock was undeniably the one on which Beth had discovered the initialed heart. Beth once again began to feel faint. Jo slammed the book shut. At this point the only thing preserving her own sanity was her stubborn refusal to believe what Beth had already begun to accept about their unimaginable history. Beth's trembling now escalated into a full-blown anxiety attack. Joanna did what little she could to calm her. This time, Beth knew she needed something more. She gave short, controlled directions.

"Go into the house. Upstairs in the medicine cabinet there's a bottle of sedatives. Bring them to me."

Joanna retrieved the pills and ran back to the carriage house. Beth was already lying down with a washcloth across her forehead. The tranquilizers were over three years old. Praying that they would still be effective, Beth sat forward and swallowed two at one time.

"They were prescribed to get me through one son's death..."

Trying to ignore the remark, Jo helped her lie back. Beth saw the growing strain on Jo's face.

"Take one yourself."

Jo refused. Now more than ever she needed to remain in control. Beth knew that if the pills were going to work at all it would be a while before they gave her any relief. In the meantime, she needed the comfort only Joanna's arms could provide.

"Hold me."

Despite being cautious, Jo leaned over and took Beth into her arms.

Still, Beth's panic could not be contained.

"Jo, why is all this happening to us?"

Joanna deliberately focused on what little she knew to be so.

"Look, it's been a really emotional day... Arthur's funeral..."

"I don't just mean today. I mean all of it... this whole summer... everything that brought us together... Ben's going abroad... my staying behind... you coming back here... the accident in the parking lot. Dell said there was no such thing as accidents in life."

Joanna was now determined to confront the woman who'd already been a part of one too many coincidences. She grabbed the keys to the Jeep. Beth raised herself up on her elbows.

"Where are you going?"

"Up to that fucking antique shop."

"Why?"

"For some answers!"

Beth couldn't understand what Dell had to do with any of this.

"Jo please, you shouldn't be driving a car in your state of mind."

"You're right. Why don't I take the family time machine?" Jo would not be stopped. "I'll be back."

The sedatives had begun to kick in. Beth was getting groggier by the minute.

"Please promise me, in this lifetime…"

Jo slammed the door leaving her heavily sedated lover curled up in a fetal position inside Ellie and Anne's carriage house.

Joanna was never one who had to dig deep to access her rage. It was always right there, just beneath the surface. Standing outside in the pouring rain, she beat her fist against the locked door of Dell's shop. Though the sign said 'Closed', Joanna could see a faint light coming from the back room. She knew Dell was inside. What Jo didn't know was that Dell had been waiting for her all morning. She'd set candles throughout the garage space and had spent the last several hours in quiet meditation, preparing herself for Joanna's arrival. Dell knew Joanna had come for answers—answers Jo would not want to hear. Jo continued to pound on the door.

"I know you're in there. Open this fucking door!"

"This isn't going to be pretty," Dell warned Bridey, lifting the cat from her lap. As she walked through the cluttered shop Dell glanced around, unsure of what would still be left of its contents once they'd had their little chat.

The irritating door chimes were the least of Joanna's concerns as she stormed inside. She was much too upset to notice that Dell had locked the door behind her. Dell treated Joanna's blatant hostility with irreverence.

"You really didn't have to drive all the way out here in the rain just to thank me for the book.?"

"I threw the fucking thing in the trash. The goddamn book wasn't even new."

"Neither are our lives," Dell mumbled under her breath. She knew Joanna had not come for quick-witted banter. "I'm sorry about Arthur. How's Beth holding up?"

Jo spun around.

"How'd you know he died?"

Dell thought it best to ease into things slowly.

"Word gets around. It's a small town."

Bridey made the mistake of brushing against Jo's leg. Dell quickly scooped the cat up into her arms. Jo glared at both of them.

"Keep that animal away from me or I'll kick that fucker into her next life!"

Dell knew they were close to the end of their small talk. She decided to test just how close.

"Sara enjoyed meeting you the other night."

Joanna erupted, swiping everything off the nearest shelf. The sound of objects crashing to the floor sent Bridey flying from Dell's arms to safer cover. Joanna's defiance had not nearly peaked. She was ready to tear the place apart if she had to.

"Suppose you tell me what the fuck is going on!"

"Why don't I fix you a cup of tea—it's very soothing."

Jo picked up a pewter candlestick and hurled it against the wall.

"I didn't come here for a lousy cup of tea! I came for answers! Understand? Answers! This is my goddamn life you're fucking with here!"

Dell knew exactly what was inside Arthur's suitcase.

"Well actually it isn't just your life, is it now? It would be Anne Wyatt's too."

Joanna was stunned into momentary silence.

"What do you know about Anne Wyatt?"

"Enough to answer your questions." Dell prepared to assume the role 'The Gods' had assigned her. "You've heard the term 'clairvoyant', haven't you?"

"You mean like a fortune teller?"

Dell knew better than to laugh.

"Not like from Central Casting, with a crystal ball, long red nails and a turban but yeah, close enough. Mystics, shamans, healers, psychics, spiritual advisors… call it what you like. That kind of thing runs in my family… has for generations.

"Like those people with three eyes?"

This time Dell laughed.

"It's called a '3rd eye'." She opened two wooden folding chairs. "Why don't we sit down and I'll try to connect the dots for you as simply as possible?"

"No fucking way! I'm standing right here with both my feet planted on the ground when you start handing me your Age of Aquarius mumbo-jumbo."

Dell knew that she had her work cut out for her. She reached behind the counter for the portfolio she'd shown Joanna on her earlier visit.

"Remember this?"

Joanna glanced at the disturbingly familiar portfolio.

"What about it?"

"Take it. It's yours."

“I’m not interested in any more of your fucking ‘gifts’.”

Dell continued to hold the portfolio out.

“No, I mean it’s *yours*, as in, you drew what’s inside.”

Joanna reared back. Dell set the record straight.

“I lied when I said I didn’t know who’d done them. They’re the work of Anne Wyatt. Bought ’em from a local art dealer several years ago. I was just holding ’em for you. I knew you’d be back… sooner or later.”

“You’re out of your fucking mind!”

Dell ignored Jo’s defiance.

“You know the painting of the carriage house over Beth’s mantle?”

Jo could feel beads of perspiration collecting across her brow.

“How the hell do you know what’s hanging over Beth’s mantle?”

Dell remained patient.

“You have to stop asking me that. The answer’s always gonna’ to be the same and it’s obviously one you’re not comfortable with.” Dell continued while she had the chance. “Why do you think it’s always intrigued you so much? You painted the damn thing yourself.”

Dell’s explanation was enough to send Joanna into a tirade. She took an entire row of old books and sent them flying from their shelf. Dell made no attempt to stop her.

“Go ahead, break everything. The truth survives anything you can destroy.”

“Fuck you!”

Jo took a second row of books and did the same. Still Dell did nothing. Only when Jo picked up a bronze bookend and hurled it at her head did Dell decide it was time to reel Joanna back in.

“Time to take a few deep breaths.” Dell shoved Joanna into the chair. “Now sit the hell down or someone’s gonna’ get hurt.”

Jo sprang back up. Dell pushed her down more forcefully.

“Look sister, there’s a reason ‘The Gods’ made me this big. I’d hate to have to throw this weight around, but if that’s what it’s gonna’ take…” Dell put the portfolio to the side for safekeeping, then sat down in the chair beside Jo. “Ya’ know, there’s a lotta’ people out there who find it comforting to think they get more than one shot at getting’ it right.”

Joanna remained adamant.

“Well I’m not one of them and whatever the hell this Wyatt chick did or didn’t do in her life has nothing to do with me and mine. Got that? Nothing!”

If Jo was going to be convinced otherwise, Dell realized she’d have to pass along the truth through another door. Shrewdly she shifted the focus.

"Ya' know, I didn't ask for these so-called 'credentials'… I was just kinda' handed 'em at birth and every now and again I get called upon to use 'em. Believe me, it's not like I'm always thrilled about the assignment. Sara and I were planning to spend July and August abroad. Instead, I wind up here in this dusty, out of the way place with nothin' to do but twiddle my thumbs and wait for you and Beth to show up. Not exactly my idea of a romantic getaway with the woman I love. Lucky for me, Sara's used to it. It's not the first time and neither of us expect it'll be the last."

Jo struggled with her repulsion.

"So Sara knows about your… 'credentials'?"

"Of course she knows. I've been living with the woman for nearly twenty-five years. It's not exactly the kind of thing you can hide."

"How could it not freak her out?"

"Not everybody has the same aversion to the paranormal as you do. I'd say the fact that I never remember to take the tissues out of my pockets before I throw my clothes into the laundry bothers her more. This other stuff just comes with the territory. Whenever it interrupts our life, all she needs to know is if it's necessary. If I feel it is, she goes with it. Whatever I have to do, I do. She's never complained." Dell winked. "Maybe 'cause I still drive her crazy in the bed."

She nudged Joanna and for a fleeting moment their interaction felt almost normal. Jo caught herself and the moment was over.

"Wait a minute! How'd you know Beth and I would show up? We found this damn place by accident."

"Nothing's an accident Jo. Nothing. As for this shop, the whole place is just a prop… me and Bridey included."

Joanna instantly shot up.

"What the fuck are you trying to say?"

Dell turned the question back to Joanna.

"Let me ask you something. Besides your attraction to Beth, what made you decide to stay in the carriage house? Let's face it, it's not exactly the kind of place you'd ever be comfortable in. It was the yellow pleated shelf piping, just like the kind your mother had in her kitchen, wasn't it?"

Joanna took a step backward.

"How'd you know about that?"

"You have to stop asking me that question. Don't you see, the piping was a prop too. Everything in life is. It was meant to open your heart to something you still longed for. Longing is longing… it's transferable from one life to another. It was enough to keep you in a place where otherwise you never would have agreed to stay." Dell ignored Joanna's mounting agitation. "Think about how many times Beth tried to take the piping down. How many times her own heart had prevented her from actually doing it. Our inner voice speaks to us all the time. Sometimes we ignore it, sometimes we don't. It all plays out just the way it's meant to. It all leads us to exactly where we're meant to be… to exactly what we're meant to find… this shop included.

The inside of Joanna's mouth was as dry as a bone. She could barely form the words.

"So this isn't a real antique shop?"

"It's as real as Beth needed it to be." Dell pointed out the obvious. "You tell me. If I were in this business to make a profit, would I have chosen such a remote location? I'm here because this is where I was supposed to be. This is where Beth needed me to be when she followed her heart and decided to take an unfamiliar way back from the place you picnicked that day… a place, by the way, which was also no accident she'd found years earlier when she went off on her own. Beth was looking for something her life with Ben Garrison or Fredrick Prescott could never provide. She was looking for her beloved Anne. She was looking for you."

Joanna broke out into a cold sweat.

"Shut the fuck up!"

She stormed toward the door. When she found it was locked, Jo reached up and ripped the chimes from its hook.

"Unlock this freakin' door or I swear I'll put my foot through the glass."

Dell ignored Jo's threat.

"I know this isn't easy for you." Dell came toward her cautiously. "I also know what you found in Arthur's suitcase. That's why you're here, right? For answers."

Joanna clenched her fists.

"Maybe I changed my mind. Maybe I'm here to bash your fuckin' head in!"

Dell accepted the possibility.

"Let's cut a deal. Just hear me out. Then if you still want a go at it, I'll let you throw the first punch."

Joanna's glare became more threatening.

"Talk fast!"

Dell made the most of the tenuous opening.

"Even I don't get all the pieces at once. The difference between you and me is that I pay attention and follow the signs as they come. You've spent your whole life ignoring 'em. Here's what I can tell you though... I felt something 23 years ago... the first time Beth opened the door and set foot in that carriage house... the day she and Ben looked at the property. I felt it the first time she stood at that window and ran her fingers over that heart. I felt it the afternoon she gave into Ben and conceived the child she didn't want. After that the signals became much more sporadic, like the voice of Beth's soul she'd slowly let die. Then one day a few years later I felt something again when I read that the estate of a local elder, Arthur Prescott, was being auctioned off. Something told me to bid on as much of his possessions as I could afford. At the time I had no idea what the connection was between them, but I did it anyway. I put everything I'd bought in storage and waited until I felt something again." Dell's eyes filled with sadness. "That something came on a stormy July night back in '82, the night of Daniel Garrison's fatal car accident." Dell seemed to wince at the memory of Beth's grief. "The minute I read the obituary, I could feel more of the pieces coming together. I just didn't know exactly how they all fit. Things were quiet again for about a year, until Beth began volunteering at the nursing home. The first time Arthur heard her play the piano the signals started up again. I felt the intensity of their bond but I still had no idea what the connection was. It wasn't until Arthur had a stroke and lapsed into a coma that I came to understand what he had been 'shown' in those moments he was pronounced dead—that the two, Beth and Arthur, were once mother and son." Dell paused as if reliving the profound moment. "Ironic that I got one of the biggest pieces of the puzzle from what everyone else around him dismissed as an old man's delusions. Truth was after Arthur's crossed over and came back, he saw things more clearly than anyone could ever have imagined." Dell let her heart wander. "The most beautiful thing about it was that Beth accepted the role out of the kindness of a mother's heart...the one she could never offer him when he was a child because of her love for Anne. All Arthur ever wanted was to see his mother happy. When he saw you both together at his birthday party, he'd finally gotten his wish and was able to let go. His was the most peaceful death any of us could ever hope for."

Although Jo hadn't stopped pacing, she hadn't interrupted her either. Dell continued as cautiously as the disquieting events that followed would allow.

"The morning of your so-called 'accident' with Beth in the parking lot, I witnessed the whole thing from my booth at Trudy's. Soon as I saw you both together I knew the time was drawing near. I understood about Arthur's stuff and why this shop had to be here between the Great Rock and the carriage house, both of which bore the same carved symbol of your love. It was a bond each of you felt but neither understood… just like on the day of Danny' funeral when that traffic detour brought the two of you close enough to be stirred by the other. Once the procession moved on, what remained was the same mysterious ache in both of you. For Beth the remembering came through the music she began to compose. For you, it was the reoccurring dream you began to have." Dell held Joanna's eyes. "I heard it the first time you called out for Ellie in your sleep and I've heard it every time since. I felt it the first time you stepped foot inside the carriage house and every time Beth came too close… every time your body ached for hers… every time you fought against your own desire to avoid being abandoned again." Dell read the pain in Joanna's heart. "I'm sorry that you had to lose your mother… twice."

Joanna no longer bothered to ask how she knew. Dell continued.

"As devastating as it was, even that was part of the plan. The loss served to jumpstart your longing, not just for her but for someone else's mother… Arthur Prescott's mother." Dell sensed something shift deep inside Joanna. "You know that stubborn, determined streak of yours? It springs from a spirit hell-bent on reclaiming something it had been robbed of. Trouble is, you just spent a lot of years looking in the wrong places for the wrong things. That's why all those material luxuries never gave you the joy or peace you felt inside the walls of that carriage house. All summer you'd both worked so hard and came so close that when Beth drove back from Boston that night, I had to make sure you didn't blow it. I couldn't very well show up at the carriage house so I used your friend Steve. 'Round about two I woke up with this feeling that told me to go to that convenience store. I didn't know why… just told Sara I had to go out, got dressed and headed over there. Soon as that guy walked through the door, I understood who he was and what I needed him to do. Even the people who seem to be on the sidelines of our lives are exactly where they're meant to be. Hell, he could've just gone straight home after Beth threw him out but once again destiny, this time in the form of a buttered bagel, brought the two of us together. The radio dedication was just another part of the cosmic plan to keep you from packing up and leaving behind your soul-mate for a second time. Unless of course you take Gayle up on that invitation and run off to Paris… again."

Whatever Dell knew about Beth's life was one thing, but her knowledge of Gayle and the contents of her letter put Joanna close to the edge. Dell tried to sweeten a truth that cut both ways.

"It's kinda' beautiful. The day of Danny's funeral you met his mother who, in a fraction of a second, awakened and stirred your soul. Now, on the day of

Arthur's funeral, you've come to realize that his mother did exactly the same thing over a hundred years ago."

Instead of finding comfort in Dell's observation, Jo went ballistic. After an initial display of defiance that included the hurling of several more objects, a much deeper vulnerability set in. It was not like Jo to ever show signs of weakness, but this was like nothing she had ever known and no amount of bravado could protect her against such a lethal dose of it.

Dell felt awful about the toll this was taking on Joanna, but this was what she had been called upon to do and as always, she was committed to seeing it through. She convinced Jo to sit down and brought her a glass of water. Joanna sat with her face buried in her hands. Dell waited patiently, then handed her an old leather journal.

"What's this?"

"It's Ellie's diary."

Joanna's eyes burned upon the cover. Dell stood close by.

"Do you remember the date you drove up to Amherst at the beginning of this summer?"

"Yeah... June 28th."

"Look at the first entry."

Jo opened to the first page dated June 28, 1880. She looked up at Dell who simply nodded, encouraging her to read what Elizabeth Prescott had written.

"It had been the most usual of morning until, mounting my bicycle outside the general store, I was stung on my cheek by a wasp. Stunned and in the most terrible pain, I lost my balance and fell directly into a poor unsuspecting woman, knocking her to the ground. Though the extent of her injuries was not severe, she was none-the-less quite vexed and flew into the most unladylike of rages. I was most apologetic. Eventually she calmed down enough for me to risk looking into her most penetrating green eyes, which caused in me a sensation I had never known before that moment. Even now as I write, I can still feel the tingling deep within. It provides such a lovely distraction from the pain and swelling of the sting. I nervously introduced myself and awkwardly imparted where I lived. Though she gave no indication that either mattered, I sensed she made a special note of it in her head. At least, I hope so since I feel as if my very soul has been set on fire and will remain so until she finds me again."

Dell waited until Joanna had finished reading.

"I saw you studying the old photograph over Trudy's cash register that afternoon you sat at the counter. I was in the corner booth."

Joanna looked up from the diary in her hands. Dell stared straight into those same penetrating green eyes.

"I can understand your fascination with the image. It's the same general store Ellie referred to in that entry you just read. Just like Trudy said, it stood pretty much where her luncheonette stands today."

Joanna felt sick to her stomach. She dropped the diary, pushed Dell aside and bolted for the bathroom. Dell listened sympathetically as Joanna heaved and flushed several times. Dell called to her through the door.

"There's some mouthwash in the medicine cabinet."

Jo didn't answer. When she finally emerged, Dell was waiting for her with a bottle of ginger ale to calm her stomach if not her nerves. Though the entry had put an end to Jo's denial, she had not yet arrived at a place of acceptance. It was impossible to imagine she ever would.

For now, Dell needed to pass along one last thing. She handed Jo an envelope containing a letter and a gold Victorian ring. Inscribed inside its filigreed heart shape were the initials 'A&E'. Dell explained about both. The ring was Ellie's. She'd given it to Anne the last time they'd met in the carriage house before Anne left for Paris. The correspondence was the first of countless letters Anne had written to her during their long and painful years of separation. Joanna looked pathetically lost.

"Why don't you stick around while I straighten up a bit."

Joanna hung her head.

Dell rested her hand on Jo's shoulder.

"Why don't you read what you wrote? Maybe it'll make you feel better to know the woman you longed for in that letter is waiting for you back at the carriage house."

Joanna placed the ring deep inside her pocket and unfolded the aged, yellowed page dated April 15, 1888.

"My darling Ellie,

I have arrived in Paris, this beautiful city punishing in its splendor that cannot be shared with you, and from this self-imposed exile I go on loving you in all the ways you have ever dared let yourself imagine.

From the very beginning you have been my heart's undoing. Since time has shown there is no resisting you, there remained no other choice but to honor yours with a distance safe enough to prevent my lustful failings. In the cruelty of my sudden departure know that my never-ending desire for you is most consuming not in its spilling forth from my flesh onto yours but rather in this desperate attempt to absorb its demands back into my own bosom that you might be spared the dangerous fire that burns there for you, threatening to destroy that which I cherish and adore most in this world.

As our devotion hides itself in shadows, the secret of our love will be forever protected by the tragedy and triumph of its own depth. My passion for you stirs in silence. My longing has no path except where it meets yours and in that place, punishment and salvation lie together in the memory of every kiss. You will never again be taken without comparing it to our hunger and I will never again surrender so completely except to your lips that have both rescued and ruined me forever. Answer each of my letters with your guilt at having chosen not to leave your husband and child to come away with me. Answer all of our pain with excuses prepared to meet the test of my bitterness that cannot forgive you for betraying your own heart. In the space between my letters, I will drop pieces of myself into idle conversations while aching for the sound of your voice. I will accept other bodies against my own that will never be free of wanting your flesh. I will take lesser companions and satisfy lesser desires until their cravings sicken me and I cast them aside to be alone, that I may at last cry out from the pain of missing you and the blissful seclusion of our carriage house.

In warning and in plea, do not dream of ever letting go of my hand that faithfully wears your ring. Along with the many, keep this first letter close to your heart—proof that beyond this dreadful separation, beyond time itself, there will be our love. My soul remains yours and yours alone. Care for it tenderly and forgive all the rest.

Anne

Dell had just finished sweeping up the last of the shattered objects. Suddenly feeling faint, she leaned against the counter to catch herself from falling. Jo raced to Dell's aid.

"What's the matter?"

Dell held her spinning head.

"I'll be fine." She closed her eyes. "Take everything I gave you and go—now!"

Joanna panicked.

"It's Beth, isn't it? What's wrong?"

Still unstable, Dell described what she felt.

"She's just discovered something that has the potential to destroy or heal her depending on how you react to it. Get me a glass of water, take your portfolio and Ellie's diary and go!"

"Will you be okay?"

"Don't worry about me. Just get back to the carriage house."

Joanna hastily collected the things Dell meant for her to have. A roll of thunder clapped across the slate-gray sky. Even as Dell struggled with her own distress, she was concerned about the lovers.

"It sounds miserable out there. Drive carefully. I can't guarantee 'The Gods' will be gracious enough to give you a third chance."

Just as Joanna reached the door, Dell remembered she'd locked her in.

"Wait."

She reached into her pocket and tossed Jo the key. Jo used it, then tossed the key back. The instant Dell caught it, both women knew it would be the last time they would meet. Despite that, neither said goodbye. Joanna tried as best she could to protect the items in her arms from getting soaked as she dashed to the car. Just before she peeled away, Jo looked through the rearview mirror. She saw Dell taping a sign across the plate glass window. In large, bold letters it read: 'OUT OF BUSINESS.'

Spurred on by Dell's urging, Joanna drove through the pouring rain. Still sick to her stomach, she had been forced to stop several times to throw open the door and retch into the pockets of muddy road. Joanna swerved into Beth's driveway and raced across the yard clutching the diary and portfolio to her chest. In the vagueness of Dell's description, Jo had no idea what she would find as she burst through the door. There was a surreal quality to the air surrounding the woman at the piano, Elizabeth Prescott's shawl draped around her shoulders. It was not the dampness that had chilled Beth to the bone. She was in tears. When she looked up, Joanna saw something in Beth's eyes—something that demanded complete stillness of her and the universe. Without a word, Beth placed her fingers on the keyboard. Reading from the music in front of her, she began to play. Joanna stood motionless, enraptured by the haunting, unfinished melody she'd first heard during an earlier rain. But unlike all the times Beth had played it since, this time she did not stop at the place where her inspiration lay incomplete. This time Beth turned the page and played on to its heart-wrenching end. Joanna went to Beth's side and swept her into her arms, relieved that what Dell had apparently felt was the exhilarating culmination of Beth's unfinished composition. Jo ignored her own ordeal.

Beth began to cry. Joanna held her closer.

"It's beautiful. I knew one day you'd finish it."

Joanna had not understood. Beth's tears came steadier now.

"That wasn't my piece." Beth guarded the words she feared would destroy Joanna's sanity. "It was Ellie's."

Unable to sleep, Beth had noticed an envelope in Arthur's suitcase. She would have waited for Jo to return before opening it were it not for its compelling label: 'Momma's Music'. Inside she found a folder containing several pages of sheet music. Across the top, Elizabeth Prescott had written its title: 'Anne's Song'. As Beth began to sight-read she'd been stunned to discover that, except for the distinctive marking of a quill pen, note for note the piece was identical to her own. It was in that moment, Dell heard Beth's piercing cry and 'saw' Beth collapse onto the floor. Slowly Beth began to process the unimaginable—that the piece she had written was never hers alone—nor was the depth of suffering that had inspired it. Both had belonged to Elizabeth Prescott as well. Apparently, the devastating loss of her son Danny had served to reawaken the grieving portion of Beth's unhealed soul—a soul she shared with the tortured woman who still grieved the loss of her forsaken love. Arthur's recognition had been right all along—he was her son after all and she, his mother. Beyond anything else Beth was meant to find in Arthur's suitcase, this left no doubt of that. Amid the scattered evidence of her past Beth's eyes had drifted to the crystal vase that held Joanna's flowers. This time the striking irony overwhelmed her. The woman Arthur had repeatedly called Anne—the lover who had sent his mother the vase from Paris—was in fact Joanna. Beth now understood his immeasurable joy at seeing the women reunited. Curled on the floor of her carriage house, her present life took on a clarity she had never known. One revelation seemed to open onto another. She had met a man whom she didn't love—whom she couldn't possibly love—not like the way her heart remembered loving—but whom she married anyway because her life with him would bring her back to Amherst where she would once again find her sacred carriage house and later, the Great Rock—both mysteriously inscribed with the same initialed heart. There, within the carriage house walls that already held so much of her tortured history, Beth would conceive a child she did not want but whose untimely death would lead her to Arthur who, in the gift of his carefully chosen possessions, would leave her with the truth that would at last complete his mother's soul. That which she had sacrificed for him in one life, Arthur had returned to her in another. In the wake of such a staggering conclusion, Beth's mind now raced to embrace what had previously eluded her. She thought about the morning of Danny's funeral—about the detour en route to the cemetery that took the procession past the parking lot of the mall where she and Joanna had unknowingly and fleetingly crossed paths. She thought about the lingering unrest that had disrupted each of their lives until years later when they both unknowingly returned to the same location at the same time for the chance to meet again. She thought about the morning of their fateful collision and how close they'd come to parting afterwards were it not for how hard Adam fought for Jo to stay at the carriage house. It had been a child of Ellie's that had once torn the lovers apart and it was a child of Beth's that had ultimately brought the lovers back into each other's arms. Beth had slowly managed to pull herself up from the floor. She had unfolded the shawl and adjusted it just as Ellie wore it in the last picture she'd taken with her young son. Instantly Beth's shoulders had remembered its weight as she colleted the pages of music written in Elizabeth Prescott's hand and placed them beside her own on the piano. Accompanied by claps of thunder Beth had played, at long last, the music of her fractured soul through to its end. She remained there at her piano waiting for Anne to return. And so it was there that Joanna, now paralyzed by Beth's confession, had found her.

Beth sealed the unimaginable truth.

"What I was just playing was composed in 1888...," she held Joanna's eyes, "by Arthur's mother."

She pointed to the two compositions she'd now set side by side on the music stand. The one in her own hand was still hopelessly incomplete. Still reeling from what she learned from Dell, Joanna ripped them from the stand. Though she couldn't actually read music, her visually trained eye worked frantically to compare the pattern of notes between them. There was no denying that the two pieces of music were in fact identical. As if casting a burning object from her hand, Joanna's fingers shot open and released the indisputable evidence. The co-mingled sheets fell to the floor around her feet. Not nearly recovered from her own sickening ordeal at Dell's, Jo immediately sank into the closest chair. She leaned forward and opened her legs, uncertain whether the suffocating terror lodged in the back of her throat would come up—or go down. Beth reached for the glass of water Jo had left by the bed. She held it up under Joanna's lips and began lightly rubbing the back of Jo's neck and shoulders. Suddenly repulsed, Joanna pulled away.

"Don't touch me!" She lunged forward, knocking the glass from Beth's hand and sending it crashing to the floor. "You're a fucking freak!" Jo looked down at the shattered pieces of glass, like the now shattered pieces of her life. "We're both fucking freaks!"

Her mind unraveling, Joanna sprang to the center of the room and turned, with fists clenched, in dizzying circles. Her eyes hunted fiercely for every shred of evidence that threatened to destroy her if she did not destroy it first. Beth came toward her.

"Jo, please..." She extended her arms. "We need each other... now more than ever."

Joanna's eyes turned even more lethal.

"No!"

Backing away, Jo stumbled over Arthur's suitcase. The sudden loss of footing intensified her vulnerability. Now threatened by everything around her—including the woman she loved—Jo looked for anything that might protect her from all of it. She picked up a pair of scissors and held it out as a warning. Beth backed off, granting Jo the smallest of relief. She stooped to save the scattered sheet music that lay near the water splattered floor. Scared to death of what it and everything else in the room represented, Joanna didn't want any of it preserved. With the scissors clutched in her hand, she took a threatening step forward.

"Leave it right there!"

Fearing that Arthur's few possessions were all she had left, Beth risked her own life to save what little remained of Ellie's. The few dampened pages were Beth's only shield as she dared again to approach the frenzied woman. Joanna warned her to keep back but Beth took a cautious step closer. In desperation Jo picked up Ellie's diary and hurled the volume at the piano, barely missing the crystal vase.

"Damn you! Damn everything you've ever written!"

With the lines of their existence blurred with uncertainty, Joanna was no longer sure whom she believed she was yelling at—a woman named Beth Garrison or a woman named Elizabeth Prescott. With her every movement now distorted by terror, Jo knocked over everything that stood between herself and the window. Using the point of the scissors she began scraping the blade back and forth across the initialed heart in a frantic attempt to eradicate what had been carved there. Before she could succeed Beth was upon her, fighting fiercely to protect the enduring symbol that had come to mean so much. As the women struggled, Joanna's fury erupted into violence. She threw Beth up against the wall and raised the point of the scissors just inches from her chest. Joanna's eyes had become frighteningly vacant.

"I swear to God, I'll kill you!"

Jo's hand shook as she held the weapon in the air, its blade pointed at Beth's heart. Beth's breathing slowed as she looked into her lover's tormented eyes.

"Go ahead. Do it here, in the carriage house. It's where our love destroyed me once. Maybe its meant to destroy me again." Tears dissolved Beth's fears. "Just promise to hold me afterwards. This time let me at least die in your arms."

Joanna had returned to Amherst hoping to put an end to her nightmare. As Beth's plea resonated in her heart, she now found herself living another. Shamed by the extent of her cruelty, Joanna turned the weapon on herself. Beth cried out.

"I'm begging you… don't! I can't be in this world without you." She waited for Joanna's eyes to once again find hers. Beth held out her hand. "Let me have them."

Jo relinquished the scissors and with it, her life. She turned away from the woman who had already forgiven her for what she had threatened to do. Repulsed by the darkness that had consumed her heart, Jo stared numbly at the collection of Anne's sketches—like Ellie's music, the tortured expression of her own splintered soul. Trapped inside with the suffocating evidence of both, Jo grabbed the musty portfolio and burst outside. As the rains came down, she stood in the center of the yard tearing at the string that held the two sides together until it broke apart and the folder fell open. A bolt of lightening pierced the darkened sky. Joanna dropped to her knees as the greedy winds swept the inherited pages up into the gusting air casting them everywhere—between the swaying limbs of trees—under the pieces of patio furniture—and into the pelted water of the pool. Several of the pages blew against the side of the carriage house where Beth stood helplessly by on the porch. She did not need Joanna to tell her what she already suspected about the beautiful images, many already bleeding into the rain soaked paper. Her impulse was to race around the yard saving what she could of her beloved Anne's renderings. It was Dell's words that stopped her: 'We lose what we are meant to lose so that we may find what we are meant to find'. Beth knew that what was sacred of their history could never be destroyed. Had not this summer and everything else leading up to it proven that? Amid the swirling pages and the story they told, Beth ran across the yard to her fallen lover. She sank down beside her and held Ellie's rain soaked shawl protectively over their heads. Beneath its shelter the women searched each other's eyes. In each of their solitudes there had always been this destiny waiting—there had always been the one crying out for the other through time. Their stories had become woven—like their lives had been woven—without edges and without seams. It was not just that the lovers had once again found each other, but that in each other they had at last found the lost portion of themselves. In this solemn unspoken exchange, their surrender was complete. Now, all that remained unfinished between them waited to be claimed. Joanna reached into her pocket and removed the Victorian ring inscribed with the familiar initials.

"Dell said it belonged to Ellie. She gave it to Anne the last time they made love in the carriage house, before Anne left for Paris. Ellie made her promise never to take it off." The voice of Joanna's soul spoke the rest. She reached for Beth's hand and slowly slid the ring onto her finger. "I'm returning your heart... and, if you'll have it, my own."

Beth fought back tears. The memory of its fit reawakened the memory of Anne's touch. She was afraid to believe that both were once again hers.

"Does this mean what I think it does?"

Jo tenderly brushed a section of Beth's soaking-wet hair away from her face.

"It means I won't be going to Paris this fall... or anytime soon... unless it's with you." Joanna had already made up her mind. Presuming Beth would divorce, she would sell her loft, leave her job and move up to Amherst. There, she would live with the only woman she had ever truly loved and partner with Steve to work at the only thing she'd ever really enjoyed. She erased all of Beth's doubt. "It means that I don't want to call out for you in my sleep anymore. I want to wake up beside you... not just for the rest of this summer, but every morning for the rest of my life. It means I want to be with you when the first leaf changes color in autumn... when the first snow falls in the winter... when the first buds form in spring... and I want to see it all through the window of our carriage house and the view from our rock. Do you understand what I'm saying?"

Beth was almost too afraid to trust that she did.

"You would give up everything for me?"

Beth's heart leapt at the possibility of a future together, then just as quickly plunged into a more foreshadowing reality.

"I can't ask that. I know what it's like to sacrifice everything in your life for someone else and I know one day you'll grow to hate me for it."

"I can't sacrifice something that has no meaning." She pulled Beth close. "Don't you know I have no life without you?"

Beth began to cry. She wasn't sure Joanna fully understood what she would be getting into. She intended to fight hard for custody of her son. It would not be fair to let Jo base their life together on false illusions. As Beth looked into Joanna's eyes, tears and rain ran together down along her cheek.

"Do you realize it also means more visiting days at camp, school concerts and class plays?"

"I know."

Beth continued to whittle away at what she presumed to be Joanna's fantasy.

"It means weekday schedules built around carpooling and weekends built around soccer practice and trips to the mall. It means endless arguments over schoolwork, curfews and wet towels left on the floor…"

"Are you trying to scare me off?"

"No. I'm trying to make sure you have a realistic picture of what life will be like if the courts grant me custody of my son." Though her eyes were adoring, Beth was brutally honest. "You've been terribly spoiled sweetie. You've had me all to yourself all summer. It won't be like that when Adam's around. Much of my life revolves around him. At best you'd be sharing me."

"He can have your days as long as I have your nights."

"I'm serious Joanna."

Jo understood that Beth's concerns were very real.

"Then let's not forget about taking out the garbage at night and emptying the dishwasher in the morning… cleaning the leaves out of the gutters and the lint out of the dryer…"

With her heart no match for her reservation, Beth threw her arms around Joanna's neck.

"No, let's not forget that."

As she clutched her lover tightly Beth also knew it would mean that more than a few people were going to hurt badly and, at least in the beginning, each of them would have to adjust to an awful lot. But this was not 1885. It was 1985. Though the world would not always be kind or forgiving, this time she had no intension of sacrificing her own heart.

"We'll be a real family!"

Joanna smiled reassuringly.

"According to Adam we're 'gross and twisted', so as 'real' families go, we're already halfway there."

Beth did something she'd never expected to do again. She giggled lightheartedly.

By now the women were both drenched to the bone. Joanna stood up and reached out for Beth's hand. Beneath the rolling claps of thunder through which 'The Gods' spoke, Ellie extended hers and Anne pulled her to her feet. Exhausted, the reunited lovers stumbled back inside the carriage house. The sacred shelter that stood between two lifetimes would keep them one more night.

Chapter 26

Beth could not tell how long she'd been standing at her bedroom window looking out at the carriage house in which Joanna still lay asleep. In the aftermath of the staggering discovery the element of time—like the soaked and scattered pages of Anne's sketches—were now indistinguishably blurred. As the early morning sun cast its ethereal light upon the still dampened shingles of the carriage house, Beth found it nearly impossible to comprehend what had taken place there the day—and lifetime—before. The stack of letters in Arthur's suitcase still remained unread. As the heavy rains continued through the night the lovers would wake trembling, each comforted only by the reassuring arms of the other.

When morning came Beth chose not to disturb the woman with whom she was sure she would spend the rest of her life. Though the path that led to their future still remained unclear and filled with predictable heartache, it was a path Beth was determined to take. The rains had given way to a glorious day—perfect for their plans to return to the great rock to read the love letters Ellie and Anne had once exchanged. Yet with all that 'The Gods' had managed to provide, not a single dry towel was at hand for a shower. Beth would have to get some from the linen closet in the house. As she moved about, Elizabeth Prescott's diary caught her eye. Beth stuck it under her arm and let herself out. Now, as she sat on the edge of the bed she'd shared with her husband for the last 23 years, Beth opened the volume that would take her back to a time long before that.

Even before reading a single word, Beth wept at the sight of the flourished script that seemed to lift from the page and become reabsorbed into the heart from which it had once flowed. Beth began with Ellie's first entry. Like Jo, she too became physically ill to read the strikingly similar date and circumstances of Ellie and Anne's first meeting. She raced to the bathroom to douse her face with cold water. For all the impossible mornings Beth had stood at that sink she'd never been more reluctant to look into the mirror. For the first time since she'd opened Arthur's suitcase, Beth Garrison peered deep into her own eyes, now sure that the tears that had collected there had never been hers alone. Beth returned to the diary of the woman and examined it more closely. While the old leather volume spanned over a decade, it had rarely been used two days in a row. In some cases there were weeks—even months—between entries suggesting that Arthur's mother had not used the journal as a daily accounting of her life but rather as a place where, whenever consumed by her emotions, she would pour forth her heart. This, for Beth, made the diary in her hands all the more compelling. Her finger eagerly scanned the pages hoping to find an entry that corresponded to this particular day—August 21st. Indeed, there was one written in 1887—less that one year, according to Arthur's introduction, before Anne left for Paris. Her heart pounded with anticipation as she began to read what was in Elizabeth's on this very day, 98 years ago.

August 21, 1887

My life only makes sense in Anne's arms. It is a sacred place, a place that says nothing else matters as long as there is this. It is a place that absorbs the flood of our hearts, mixing with the dampness of our bodies and our tears that do not make less of our words but more of our silence. When I am denied that place in our carriage house I am lost, defeated, temporarily insane. I belong nowhere in this world and in the vastness I am like a corpse abandoned by it's spirit with no place to rest. I am dead inside to everything around me. Even my child, my poor sweet Arthur, is deprived of my heart because as I hold him in my arms, I ache to be in hers. I cannot think. I cannot care. I can only suffer as I wander through these rooms that were never meant to be my home and go through the lies that were never meant to be my life. Like a ghost, I hover and wait for Anne's arms to again open that I may re-enter my own body by the familiar way it fits against hers, to once again be a part of each other's flesh as we are a part of each other's soul.

Realizing she could have written those same words on this very day, Beth turned to Ellie's final entry written a little over 10 years later.

September 25, 1897

I am not at all certain I will survive the coming of another winter. In Anne's continued absence there is only a brutal and barren darkness that seems never to end. Every time Anne writes to say she has attracted another patron or attended another party I ache to be there—to watch her fill the room with her magnificent presence that only deepens my adoration and quiet sense of privilege that the story of her life is so woven into mine… and mine into hers. Every time she tells of another adventure, laughs aloud with abandon or weeps private tears I want to stop all other sounds and movement in the universe that I may hear my beloved's voice and see my beloved's eyes whose memory even now brings such torment and comfort all at once. There are the remaining moments of my life—the fading unheralded passing of my empty existence—and then there are my memories—the coded intimate memories that live in a space so still they seem to exist outside of time itself. Those are the moments I have shared with my precious Anne. Even now, as I lay frail and slowly dying, I have never stopped collecting them, I have never stopped clinging to them, and in their grace I have never stopped thanking God. If I am to die without ever seeing my beloved again, I will search through the dark of my eternal sleep for as long as it takes for her to be there when I awake.

Knowing that Elizabeth Prescott died a few weeks later from a broken heart at the age of 37, Beth clutched the journal to her chest and lay back against her pillow. For now, it was all she could bear to read of the woman's tragic life. She held her hand out in front of her and stared at the ring Joanna had placed on her finger while the heavens had wept down upon their reunited souls. Beyond the rules of convention—beyond the scope of reason—the immortality of their love had miraculously endured. Beth was imagining their future when she heard the kitchen door slam. Anticipating their next kiss, she called down to her long-lost lover from inside her closet.

"I'm upstairs sweetheart."

The creak of the climbing footsteps sounded unlike what Beth expected. Yet they were disturbingly familiar. When she turned around, Ben was standing in the doorway of their bedroom. The couple's eyes locked in a stark, emotional standoff. Were it not for the fresh clothes Beth clutched against her chest, her heart might well have burst through it.

"What are you doing here?"

"I live here, remember?"

"It's only the 21st. You weren't due back until the 25th."

"You sound disappointed."

Beth struggled to conceal her dread.

"I'm surprised, that's all."

"I left you a half dozen messages in the last 24 hours. Didn't you get any of them?"

All Beth offered was a simple 'no'.

Though he certainly wanted to know why, Ben had a more immediate question.

"What's going on Beth… where's your piano?"

"It's in the carriage house where I've always wanted it." Old resentments crept into her tone. "Don't pretend you don't know that."

"Why now?"

"Because that's what this summer was all about, remember…following my heart."

Insecure about what bearing that had on their marriage, Ben's eyes gravitated to his wife's hand.

"That's not your wedding band." He came closer and grabbed his wife's wrist. "What the hell is this?"

She offered the truth.

"It's from an old friend."

"Rheeta?"

"No, a much older friend than that." She pulled away. "Ben, we need to talk…"

Her tone intimated something her husband was not prepared to hear.

"Is it from Arthur?"

At least for the moment, Beth honored her husband's reluctance.

"Yes, in a manner of speaking, I suppose it is." Her voice dropped. "He died two days ago."

Ben knew how devoted the two had become. He took his wife into his arms.

"Oh Beth, I'm so sorry…"

Pressed against her husband's body Beth had almost forgotten the feel of him—this man with whom she'd spent the last 23 years of her life. It would have been cruel to refuse the sincerity of his sympathy. For all that he still meant to her, Beth allowed herself to receive his affection. This was much more the reception he had hoped for. He pulled her even closer.

"God, I've missed you so much."

Even if Ben had suspected the worst, he now pretended otherwise. He tried to kiss her. He'd always done this whenever things between them became too threatening. He'd always retreated into a denial that until now Beth had allowed. This time she would not. She owed him the truth whether he wanted to hear it or not. It was a truth that was a lot easier to state than to explain. She pulled away.

"There's someone else Ben. There's always been someone else."

His face became chiseled in pain. She tried reassuring him.

"It's not what you think... until this summer I'd never been unfaithful to you." Beth looked deep into her husband's eyes. "But I've never belonged to you either. If I've betrayed you at all, it was that deep inside I've always known it... even on the day we married... and for that, I'm so, so sorry."

Ben's hurt turned to disgust.

"So Nick was right. I was a fool not to believe him."

Beth was not surprised that her husband chose to ignore the much more devastating nature of her confession, focusing instead on her infidelity.

"He told me you're having an affair with that woman Joan."

"Her name isn't Joan..." Her eyes drifted to the diary she'd placed on the dresser. "It's Anne... Anne Wyatt."

"I don't care what her goddamn name is!"

He went to the window and glared down at the carriage house as if the structure itself had somehow robbed him of his life. Now it was time to take it back. He turned away from the source of his misery.

"Okay, so you had an affair. It's over. She leaves today and we forget the whole thing."

Within her own turmoil Beth managed to find compassion for his.

"No Ben, I can't. I wont. I've met someone... someone I'd been searching for all my life." She tried to make him understand. "That person is *me* Ben, and that person can no longer be your wife."

Her heartfelt confession was dismissed.

"Listen to me Beth, our marriage has survived a lot worse than some ridiculous flirtation you obviously needed to get out of your system. You'll see, we'll get past this too."

This is what he'd always done—treated life like something to be managed, smoothed over and gotten on with.

"No Ben, not this time." Her resolve stunned him and she knew it. "I'm tired of just surviving. I want to *thrive*." She was uncompromisingly clear. "I can't do that in this marriage. I can't do that with you."

"And you can with her?"

Beth nodded. Her husband's laugh was tinged with contempt.

"You don't seriously think you have a future with that woman, do you?"

Beth looked down at the ring on her finger.

"A future... and a past."

"What the hell's that supposed to mean?"

Beth had no intention of ever offering the incomprehensible history she shared with Joanna. Nor could she ignore his suffering. She ached for both of them.

"When did our relationship go from what it could provide to what it could endure?"

As the hopelessness between them set in, Ben became desperate to have his wife any way he could. He pushed her down onto their bed and forced himself on her.

"I'm still your husband damn it!" His eyes burned with resentment. "I have needs too and I've gone without long enough!"

Beth had worn only Joanna's work shirt back to the house. Groping her crudely, Ben thrust his finger deep inside.

"Is this how you like being fucked now?"

His breath was hot against her neck. It was the same stifling, repulsive heat she'd submitted to that afternoon in the carriage house. Years of suppressed rage now provided force enough to push him off and propel herself upright.

"You think you're the only one who's gone without all these years?" She would show him the toll of her own deprivation. She would show him the evidence of her own despair. "You want to know what it's been like for me? C'mon, I'll show you!" Beth shoved her husband toward the attic door. "It's all up there… everything you stored away… everything that didn't fit your illusion of a happy marriage and a perfect life."

Beth continued to push him the rest of the way. Overwhelmed by the destruction, Ben didn't yet understand it was at his wife's hand.

"My God, it looks like a bomb went off in here!"

"It did… one night… inside of me. This is where I exploded."

He turned to his wife in disbelief.

"What are you trying to say?"

"What I could never get you to hear, Ben. This is what it's felt like inside me. This is what I could never get you to understand."

Her answer, like the damage, was beyond anything he could comprehend. Lost among the shattered pieces of their lives, now it was he who had to fight for his sanity. Ben began picking things up from the floor. For all the times Beth had been suffocated into silence, a part of her delighted in his anguish.

"You can't pretend we're not broken Ben. I won't let you. Not anymore."

He looked up at her, this woman he no longer knew.

"Did you have to ruin our lives to make your point?"

"I just ransacked our attic, Ben. Our lives were already in ruins, whether you wanted to face it or not."

He would concede to anything.

"Just tell me what you want and it's yours… a second honeymoon… a housekeeper… more therapy."

"I want the carriage house Ben, that's what I want. That's all I've ever wanted. Not the one in our backyard... the one in the painting over the mantle."

Ben looked at her blankly but it no longer mattered that he didn't understand. It was her needs that came first now.

"I want the years back. I want my passion back. Can you give that to me?"

"I can forgive you for this madness... this havoc."

In that moment Beth despised and pitied the man who'd returned looking for his wife.

"I don't want forgiveness Ben. I want a divorce."

In the hollow stillness that fell between them Beth heard the sound of gravel crunching beneath the weight of tires. Deep inside her soul she felt Joanna pulling away. Sometime during the course of the couple's dispute, Jo had come to the house looking for her. She'd seen Ben's suitcases on the porch and heard them arguing. Her impulse had been to race upstairs to make sure Beth was all right but Jo knew that would only have led to an ugly scene for all of them. She knew too that ultimately this was something Beth would have to handle with her husband alone. Their years together demanded it just as her own relationship with Gayle would once she returned to the city. In the 24 hours since Arthur's funeral, the women had reconstructed and reconciled the unfathomable nature of their past. Sealing their future together would, by necessity, take much longer than that. Joanna knew that the terms of their separation would be unbearable under any circumstance. She did it the only way Ben's unexpected return allowed. She left immediately without saying good-bye.

As the stinging certainty of her lover's departure set in, Beth's heart ached as deeply as Ellie's heart had ached when Anne left for Paris. Without a word, the tortured woman abandoned her husband and raced downstairs. Just as she'd dreaded, the turquoise Thunderbird was gone. Choking back tears, Beth ran across the yard to the carriage house and threw open the door. All of it was still there—down to the smallest detail. Jo knew Beth would need for it to be that way—a place where she could escape all doubt that they had come together again—a place suspended in time, just like their love. Joanna had left behind all of her own belongings. Her toiletries, her clothes, her art supplies were just as they had been. There wasn't anything she couldn't replace or live without, except for one thing. Beth went to the pantry and opened the door. There, inside the small glass jar, only her wedding band remained. She was certain the lone Cheerio now rested in the pocket over Joanna's heart. Beth fought hard not to find misery in all Jo had intended as comfort. She stopped herself from clutching Joanna's pillow in order to preserve the impression where she had last laid her head. How Beth regretted that they had been too exhausted to make love one last time. She rubbed her cheek against the denim jacket—the one Jo had placed around her shoulders the night of the July 4th concert. A folded piece of paper leaned against the vase Anne had sent from Paris and Joanna had filled with paper flowers. Beth took the note to the kitchen table. Her eyes caressed the stroke of Joanna's pen as her heart opened to receive her lover's words:

We seem destined to meet and be torn apart with unforgiving abruptness. As punishing as our separation will (once again) be, it's obvious we each need time with others—time to address what needs to be addressed—time to heal what needs to be healed. In the absence of any contact between us, take the letters that Anne sent to Ellie and read them over and over. They will tell you how impossible my life is without you and in her words you will know that beyond forever, I am yours. Come often to our carriage house and play Ellie's music. I will hear each note and know that beyond forever—you are mine. On this same morning one year from now, meet me at the Great Rock to continue where we left off—in our last night and in our last life. Every time I close my eyes I will see you and tell myself that I cannot miss what I am never without. Until then, my heart waits to once again beat against yours.

Jo

Beth barely had a moment to recover from Joanna's letter when her husband appeared in the doorway. His tone demanding, he held out the journal she'd left on the dresser.

"What's this?"

Beth ripped it from his hands.

"It's a diary."

"I can see that. Whose is it?"

Beth gazed at the volume as she considered her answer.

"It belonged to Arthur's mother."

Ben was too distracted to ask anything more about it. Everywhere he looked he saw evidence of the women's intimacy—the unmade bed—the nude renderings of his wife

"Where is she?" he demanded, eager for a confrontation.

"She's gone." Beth could see the satisfaction creep into his eyes. She gave him little time to enjoy it. "It's not over Ben, I can assure you."

Desperate for reassurance that the clandestine lovers had endured a separation far greater than the dreaded year ahead, Beth went to the window for salvation. As she once again beheld the indelible symbol of their love, her eyes filled with tears. There, inside the heart, Jo had carved their initials just below Ellie's and Anne's. Overcome by the tender embellishment, Beth burst into sobs. Still clutching Elizabeth Prescott's diary, she sank down along the wall and curled up on the floor beneath the sill. Torn between regretting and reveling in his wife's suffering, Ben came toward her. His presence in this most sacred of places only made things worse for her.

"Please" she begged, her eyes more vacant than he'd ever seen, "go away… leave me alone."

Ben wouldn't listen. Still hoping for a reconciliation, he crouched down beside her and took hold of his wife's arms.

"It's okay… it's okay."

The thickness of his voice—the weight of his touch—repulsed her. Beth fought him off, thrashing violently. Ben persisted, each time shaking his wife a little harder until he got through to her.

"Honey, wake up!"

Disoriented, Beth opened her eyes to find herself in bed, her husband leaning over her. Not understanding the devastation in his wife's eyes, he wiped beads of perspiration from her forehead.

"It's okay honey. It was just a dream."

The pounding in Beth's chest grew worse as the words meant to soothe shattered her heart into a thousand pieces. She shut her eyes tight, this time not to dream but hoping to die so that she would be spared the excruciating pain of a life without Joanna. Distraught and unable to bear her husband's hovering, Beth turned away from him. She rolled onto her side and waited for the anguish in her heart to find its voice. Once it did, the sound itself bled with her suffering.

"Oh God… Oh God… Oh God…"

The depth of her despair was immeasurable. It surpassed anything she had ever endured including the death of her son, for in a way this loss was even more profound—her grief, more excruciating. Alarmed, Ben drew her into his arms.

"What is it honey? Talk to me."

Beth instantly recoiled. She threw her legs over the bed to distance herself from him and the sickening reality that despite all she had lived through in her dream, everything in her waking life was still exactly the same. Beth sat at the edge of the bed, gripping herself around the waist as waves of devastation crashed to the floor of her stomach. Rocking in place, she stared across the room. There beside the door were her husband's suitcases exactly as he'd placed them the night before in preparation for this morning's departure. Haunted by its vivid detail, Beth's eyes were drawn to the place on her dresser where, in her dream, she had left Elizabeth Prescott's diary. Every word of the nonexistent volume still felt as real as the burdened entries she had read in her sleep. Beth looked down at her hand. Instead of the gold, heart-shaped ring, her finger bore the same wedding band she had worn for the last 23 years. Beth did not have to open the drawer of her night table to know she would not find the card Sara had given her in case she needed to talk. The spasmodic movement of her shoulders told Ben that his wife was crying.

He reached across their bed to comfort her.

"Beth… it was only a dream…"

Years of resentment became embroiled with her sense of defeat. Nothing her husband might have said could have made Beth feel worse. He had always been 'reasonable', always conveniently oblivious to the nature of her suffering. She tore away from him to get to the window. Her eyes bore hungrily down across the yard that showed no trace of Anne's scattered, rain-soaked renderings.

With it partially obscured by the early morning fog, Beth could no longer be sure if the carriage house itself was real or just another part of her imagination. Ben looked at the clock. His midmorning flight didn't allow for much time to calm his wife down. His concerns deepened as she quickly dressed and headed for the door.

"Beth, where are you going?"

His question enraged her. It became part of all the others he had asked over the last 23 years and never listened to when she tried to answer from her heart. This time Beth ignored him completely and stormed out of the room. Desperate to believe there had to be a way to reenter her dream, Beth frantically climbed the steps to the attic—the place she had torn apart in order to save her soul. At the top of the landing all she found was what had always been there—the neatly arranged storage of her life. For all her spent rage, not a single thing was disturbed. Deprived of the evidence of her purging, Beth's sense of defeat was now crushing. She began to sob uncontrollably, wishing simply to give up and die—as Ellie had—rather than face one more day without her beloved. The sound of her husband's encroaching footsteps deepened her contempt for him. When Ben reached the top of the stairs he found his wife curled on the floor in the corner, the same corner where, in her dream, Joanna had possessed her in the cruelest and most exalted of ways. The full-length mirror, ironically still very much intact, reflected nothing of Beth's shattered heart. The source of her misery was undetectable to the naked eye, especially to Ben's as he now stood impatiently over her.

"Am I not getting something?"

She glared back at him.

"You haven't gotten something our entire married life…mainly me"

"For God's sake Beth, pull yourself together. It was only a dream."

She couldn't bear to hear him say those words again. She lunged at him, pounding on his chest.

"Shut up! Shut up! Shut up!"

Something deep inside refused to accept it. It's clarity offered hope that her husband was wrong. If her dream had exposed Beth to anything, it was the possibility of things considered 'impossible'. Now it was only there she could look for her salvation. Despite logic she would have to rely on those things embedded in her physical world to connect her with a previous one. Fighting for her life, Beth pushed Ben aside and raced downstairs. The white baby grand piano still sat in the corner of the living room. Unlike in her dream, Joanna had not yet moved it into the carriage house on the occasion of their one-week anniversary. Beth hurried to the breakfront in the dining room. There behind the glass sat Arthur Prescott's vase, just as it had been from the very first day Beth brought it home. Having awakened from a coma and believing Beth to be his mother, he had insisted the vase was hers and that she should have it. As recently as a few days ago Arthur was still very much alive, still enjoying her music and still looking forward to celebrating his one hundredth birthday later that summer. A sudden chill swept across Beth's heart as she recalled seeing a small suitcase on the shelf of Arthur's closet the morning she'd gone back to his room to get his cardigan. It was the same suitcase she'd been left in her dream—the same suitcase that contained the most profound pieces of her identity and the connection to the woman who shared her mysterious longing.

With an even greater reverence for its history, Beth removed the delicate crystal vase from the breakfront and placed it on top of her piano, preparing for Joanna's paper bouquet. Ben had followed his wife downstairs. Now aware of its origin and meaning, Beth stood in front of the painting over the mantle examining every cherished detail of the artist's brushstroke. The piece had hung there for years. Her sudden scrutiny made no sense to him.

"What are you looking at?"

Beth's eyes remained fixed on the image.

"Me… I'm looking at me."

Ignoring Ben's dumbfounded look, Beth ran her finger lovingly across the small signature in the corner. For all that her dream had told her about the artist known only as 'A. Wyatt', it had also provided Beth with another name—a full name and with it, the city in which the woman lived. She could only pray it would be enough. Ben followed his wife into the kitchen as she reached for the phone.

"It's six in the morning! Who in God's name are you calling at this hour?"

"The woman in my dream."

Ben slapped his hands against his thighs.

"Great… this is what I need the morning I'm leaving for Europe."

Beth held for the operator as her husband paced back and forth in front of her. Finally the line opened up.

"What listing please?"

At the jolt of the operator's voice, Beth turned away from the distraction of Ben's movement. She spoke as quickly as her heart raced.

"I'd like the number for a Joanna Cameron in New York City." Beth could hardly breathe. "I think it's somewhere in the West Village. I don't have the exact address…"

Though Beth was quite sure of the panic in her own voice, the operator offered the most ordinary response.

"I'll need you to spell that for me."

Staring out through the window at the carriage house, Beth obliged as if her life hung on each letter of Joanna Cameron's name. Once again the operator responded routinely.

"Please hold."

With her stomach in knots, Beth waited anxiously. Pleading under her breath for some kind of divine intervention, she began knocking the front of her head against the frame of the door. Over the years Beth had done many things Ben thought odd—even bizarre—but this morning she'd crossed the line. He'd seen enough.

"That's it, I'm changing my reservations."

If, as her dream suggested, there was some cosmic plan to all this, then it was imperative to stay on course. Her husband's departure had to be today, the 28th of June. She was emphatic.

"No! You have to leave this morning!" Beth couldn't imagine what was taking the operator so long. She had to move Ben along. "Please, go get ready."

"Fine, but I'm calling Steve to drive me to the airport. I don't know what the hell's going on with you but I don't want you behind the wheel."

"No! I have to take you! It has to be me!" She continued to ramble on under her breath. "On the way home I have to stop at the supermarket... I have to pick up the roast beef and the miniature marshmallows for the sweet potato casserole... I have to find her car... a turquoise Thunderbird... it has to be there. I have to get stung... have to be in reverse, then step on the accelerator..."

Ben grabbed his wife's arm.

"Beth, you're not making any sense."

The knot in her stomach growing tighter, she switched the receiver to the other ear.

"God, what could be taking so long?"

Just when Beth was sure the anticipation would drive her out of her mind, the operator returned.

"I'm sorry to keep you waiting."

Beth closed her eyes and held her breath.

"I don't show any listing for a Joanna Cameron anywhere in New York City."

The operator relayed this as matter-of-factly as if she were telling Beth that she didn't have a particular pair of shoes in her size. Beth had to struggle to draw her next breath. Her head dropped with the weight of her despair. She was about to hang up when the monotone voice continued.

"I do show a listing for J. Cameron on Hudson Street."

Beth had absolutely no idea where Hudson Street was but she would have taken the number down if the address had been on Mars. She was so elated to be given *anything* that would sustain her hope she forgot to respond. The operator prompted her.

"Ma'am, would you like that number?"

"Yes! Yes, please!"

Her hand barely able to hold a pen steadily enough to write, Beth copied the number. She thanked the operator for the priceless information and hung up. Beth held up the paper as if to prove she wasn't entirely crazy.

"You see! You see! There is a J. Cameron!"

Ben walked out of the room—in part to get away from her, in part to calm his own nerves.

As she continued to stare at the number, Beth could feel the blood from her heart coursing into her neck. She looked up at the clock above the sink. It was just past 6 in the morning. She tried to imagine what she would say to the person she would almost certainly be waking out of a dead sleep: 'Excuse me, I'm sorry to disturb you at this hour but could you tell me what kind of a car you drive… do you hate primary colors… does the name Ellie mean anything to you?'. Risking much more than her embarrassment, Beth found the courage to dial. The phone rang three times. The space between each ring felt to her like an eternity but then, she reminded herself, that's what the call was all about. She rehearsed the questions over and over in her head, but she would never get to ask them of the person listed only as J. Cameron. On the fifth ring an answering machine relayed a recorded message. It was a message that, while brief, nevertheless fueled Beth's hope. The voice was that of a woman who said she would be out of town for the summer and didn't care to be reached. Something intuitive told her that she had indeed found the Joanna Cameron in her dream. Beth hung up and called back twice more just to hear the miraculous sound of her lover's voice. As she clasped the precious piece of paper with Joanna's number against her heart, Beth's relief quickly dissolved to a crushing realization—the woman who left town for the summer had no way of finding her. Joanna Cameron could be on her way to anywhere in the world. Once again Beth relied on what she had been shown in her dream—that after their mysterious and fleeting encounter the morning of Danny's funeral, ultimately it was the haunting melody Beth had begun to compose that somehow seeped into Joanna's own dream and drew her back to Amherst. Beth raced to her piano. The yet incomplete piece that had slowly and painfully emerged from Elizabeth Prescott's soul now leaned against Beth Garrison's music stand. She placed her fingers on the keys and stared longingly at the still empty vase. As Beth began to play, the impassioned notes broke the quiet of the early morning hour and sent Ben racing in from his study.

"Beth, it's 6:00 in the morning! What are you trying to do, wake the dead?"

She closed her eyes to block everything else out.

"God I can only hope that's what I'm doing."

Ignoring both the hour and her husband's reprimand, Beth continued to pound at the keys. It remained to be seen if her playing roused Joanna Cameron's soul, but it certainly was enough to wake Beth's young son. From halfway down the landing, Adam called down to his father who was pacing at the bottom of the steps.

"What the hell's goin' on?"

"Your mother's acting a little strange this morning."

"What else is new?"

Adam had already started back up the steps when his father called up to him.

"Don't go back to sleep. We're leaving for the airport in a little more than an hour."

"Like I can sleep with mom banging away on the damn piano."

By now Ben was nearing his own breaking point.

"Just get yourself ready."

"Fine. Just make her stop!"

The disgruntled 13 year old slammed the door to his room, nearly catching BJ's tail.

Beth closed her eyes and played on, oblivious to anyone and anything that threatened to silence her before she was ready to hand her fate over to 'The Gods'. Only when she had emptied herself of every note did her fingers come to rest quietly on the keys. For the next several moments Beth sat perfectly still, allowing all the natural sounds of this otherwise glorious summer morning to penetrate the prayer deep inside her heart. What was left to trust of her dream was the most sacred element of them all. Ben stopped her at the kitchen door.

"Where are you going now?"

"To the carriage house."

"Why?"

"I left something there."

"What?"

She was completely honest.

"My heart. My soul." She looked into her husband's eyes. "Please let go of my arm."

Ben's expression never looked more pained. He nevertheless released her. She ached for the man whose only failing was that he was not someone else. This was not how she had wanted to send him off. He deserved better. Despite her own suffering, she tried to provide reassurance.

"I know we have to leave in an hour. I'll be ready, I promise." Beth searched her husband's eyes. "If I've ever given you a reason to love me at all, you won't follow me."

Ben nodded solemnly. He stood at the kitchen window and watched as his wife ran barefooted across the yard. He had watched her through that same window—crossing that same yard—thousands of times before. He had always found something deeply comforting in the way Beth tended to the most ordinary things in that yard. But as the door of the carriage house closed behind her, something in his heart told him that when his wife emerged he would never see that same woman again.

The air inside its walls smelled as thick and musty as it always had when the carriage house was closed up and no one was living there. The doorframe still awaited repair and none of the window screens had yet been hung. Beth recalled the morning in her dream when she watched Joanna, up on a ladder, fixing both. She recalled the jealousy that she felt, but did not yet understand, at the sight of Steve's instant rapport with the beautiful stranger. Beyond her wildest imagination, her dream had exposed Beth to so much of what she hadn't understood. Though her rational mind had warned her not to expect any of it, Beth's eyes and heart groped for signs of Joanna's presence. She found nothing of the way the carriage house looked in her dream—nothing of the changes that had awakened her soul. The room was just as it had been left after her mother's last visit, sealed off from life like the tomb it had become to her. Leaning against the wall, Beth had to remind herself to breathe, if only to stay alive for Joanna. Her eyes traveled slowly around the emotionally charged room. Everything that now surrounded her lay like a gauze shroud over the glorious details of her dream—the walls covered with sketches—the modeling stand and easel—the piano and vase—the unmade bed. Beth choked on the stillness of the old radio through which had come Steve's dedication that led her into Joanna's arms and the unforgettable thrill of their first kiss. The memory of its static and claps of thunder was as real as the sunlight that now drenched the same room in which she stood achingly alone. Beth remembered the glass jar in which Jo had placed her wedding band and lone Cheerio. She opened the cabinet door and stared into the pantry. There on the shelf along with the silly skirt piping that had first captured Joanna's heart was the jar—painfully empty—just like Beth's life. She had promised her husband that she wouldn't be late. She turned to check the time on the small alarm clock by the side of the sofa—the same alarm clock that failed to go off the morning of visiting day. A morning that had passed—or a morning yet to come? No longer could Beth tell one from the other. No longer could she distinguish the future from the past. Clutching the back of the kitchen chair, Beth looked over at the window. She had always sensed that the truth of her life never truly emanated from her birth, but from a mysteriously demanding hour that now refused to slip by unclaimed like so many glimmers that had come and gone before it, orphaned off without a name, as uncertain of their powerful origin as she once was of her destiny and purpose. Beth crossed the room, no longer unsure. She looked down through the blur of her tears. There it was—not just as it appeared in her dream but as it had always been—the heart with the initials 'A&E' carved into the old wooden sill. It was as real as the one she'd found at the base of the Great Rock the afternoon she'd wandered off alone. It was no longer she but Anne's beloved Ellie who now stood at the window of their carriage house weeping, the tips of her fingers caressing the enduring symbol carved into her soul a lifetime ago.

"Oh God" she sobbed, consumed by the agony of not knowing if she had awakened a moment too soon or a moment too late. "Oh God." Beth fell to her knees. "I'm here Joanna... I'm here... please, please find me..."

In the quiet of the morning, Adeline Brody heard the anguish of Beth Garrison's cry. Pressing Elizabeth Prescott's diary to her bosom, Dell uttered words of reassurance.

"Breathe dear sweet Ellie, just breathe. Soon all will be well."

Sara opened her eyes to find her lover staring out of their bedroom window. Dell was rubbing her tension filled neck.

C'mon back to bed and let me work out that knot."

Dell turned around.

"There's nothing I'd love more, but I'm gonna' have to take a rain check."

Sara raised herself up on her elbows.

"Got a better offer?"

Dell smiled adoringly.

"I need to be at Trudy's this morning."

"Why... her blueberry pancakes calling to you?"

"Not the pancakes."

Sara had lived with her long enough to recognize the look in Dell's eyes. She threw off the bed sheet and went to her lover's side. Dell was holding the familiar journal in her hand. It was all Sara needed to understand.

"Today's the day?"

Dell nodded solemnly. She opened the diary to the page dated June 28th, 1880 and handed it to her. Sara read the entry. She let Elizabeth Prescott's words settle in her heart, then closed the volume and handed it back to Dell.

"It's been 105 years."

Dell met her lover's eyes.

"To the day."

"That's a mighty long time to wait."

Dell looked up into the crisp morning sky.

"It's been said that loving is the only glimpse we're permitted of eternity."

"I believe that baby." Sara leaned her head against Dell's shoulder. "I guess this means our summer abroad is gonna' have to wait too."

This was always the hard part for Dell.

"I'm so sorry."

Sara had always been amazingly resilient.

"I'll call the travel agent later." She sealed her concession with a kiss. "You'll just have to make it up to me in our next life."

Dell remained in Sara's arms for as long as time permitted, then left for Trudy's to wait in the place 'The Gods' had assigned her.

The woman in 12B had spent the sleepless night pacing her West Village loft, waiting for the first sign of daybreak. As the sun began to crest over the jagged teeth of the lower Manhattan skyline—a breathtaking view for which she paid dearly—the woman unlocked her front door and tossed the two duffel bags out into the hallway. The once unencumbered bohemian had struggled for hours with their contents. Having grown resentfully reliant on the pampered luxuries of her surroundings, she had chosen to take only the things essential to her life while sadly unable to recall with any certainty what those things once were. The sudden ring of the telephone pierced the stillness of the stylishly appointed space designed to delight her senses if not her soul. Deliberately, she did not answer. On the next ring the answering machine picked up. A knot of regrets tightened around her heart at the sound of the familiar voice.

"It's me... I need to talk to you. If you're there, please pick up." There was a pause as the caller waited. The voice fell. "I guess you've already left." There was another pause and another excruciating moment of heartache. Finally, the caller hung up.

The woman who had chosen not to answer stared across the room at the small blinking red light that now synchronized with the beat of her own heart. No longer able to erase or ignore one without the other, she let the message remain as part of all she was leaving behind. Like the final curtain of a long-running play in which she had performed, the striking brunette stood in the wings and took a last sentimental look around. Then she turned, left the stage and locked the door. Inside the loft her phone rang again. She listened with her ear to the door but this time the caller left no message. A moment later came another call, then another. She assumed it was her girlfriend checking to make sure she'd really left. Who else would be calling at this hour of the morning? As she tucked her keys into the pocket of her jeans, a frisky wire-haired terrier pup dashed out of the elevator ahead of his owner and came running toward her. The groggy, unshaven young man juggled a container of coffee in one hand and a donut in the other.

"Hey, you're up kinda' early for someone who's not trying to housebreak a new puppy."

'Sounds a lot easier than trying to break in a new life', she thought to herself.

"Tryin' to get a jump on the traffic. Hold that elevator for me, will ya'?"

The young man leaned himself against the door and gulped down some coffee while he waited for his attractive neighbor to make her way down the hall with her bags.

"Need help with those?"

"I got 'em. Thanks."

The two had been friendly for a long time—at least by transient, cosmopolitan standards. Once she'd reached the elevator he was in no hurry to let her go.

"So how's the world of the hidden persuaders?"

Hardly in the mood for small talk, she didn't want to be rude.

"Well enough to pay the obscene maintenance charges on this place."

He laughed.

"What more can ya' ask for, right?"

Often, of late, she had come to wonder. She stepped into the elevator, hoping he'd let her go. Unfortunately, he preferred to linger while the playful pup ran up and down the hall, gnawing on the end of its leash. He sized up her bags.

"Headin' out to the beach house for the holiday weekend?"

She was intentionally vague.

"No, not this time."

For the briefest of moments, the burdened woman found herself delighting in the glazed donut topped with brightly colored sprinkles. At a time in her life when everything felt so complicated, she envied the childlike quality of her neighbor's indulgence that brought such simple gratification. He misread the longing in her eyes.

"Wanna' bite?"

"No thanks."

It was not the sugar she craved but the taste of an ever-elusive feeling of contentment.

"Sure?"

"Positive."

"The young man finished what was left of the donut and smacked his lips.

"Guess that's how you keep that killer bod, huh?"

She might have smiled. She couldn't be sure. The truth was, she'd been sick to her stomach for days. She pointed to the puppy who'd lifted it's leg and was now peeing on the wall.

The owner winced.

"Oh shit!"

"That's probably next."

As her neighbor moved to scoop the animal up into his arms, she pressed the elevator button. Just before the door closed he called out to her.

"Wherever you're goin', it's a fantastic morning for a drive."

She didn't bother to answer him. Instead, she leaned the full weight of her misery against the elevator wall as it traveled down to the lobby. Her legs felt as unsteady as her heart as she walked around the corner to the parking garage. The short mustachioed attendant jumped up from the old swivel chair where he'd spent the night.

"Ah, buenos dias! Has the beautiful senorita come for her magnificent pajaro?"

"Si senor."

The two had shared the same warm exchange ever since she began garaging her prized possession there. He quickly jockeyed several other vehicles before removing the canvas cover that protected the pristine turquoise Thunderbird. Taking great care, he pulled it up to the curb and got out leaving the motor running and the driver's door open.

"Here she is senorita. Ready to fly you to the clouds!"

She managed an acknowledging smile, tossed her bags into the trunk and slid in behind the wheel. As always he closed the door for her and tipped his Yankee baseball cap. She, in turn, never failed to appreciate his old-fashioned, gentlemanly ways. This morning was no exception.

"Muchos gracias Carlos."

As she looked back through the rear view mirror, she struggled to find encouragement in the image of the good-natured man cheerfully waving her off. At the corner she let her eyes drift up along the avenue. So early was the hour that the automated streetlights had not yet turned themselves off. The bustling downtown neighborhood was unusually still. The expressionless masses had not yet awakened and packed themselves together tightly beneath the mostly unnoticed sky. The city itself had not yet risen to its fevered pitch—the clamoring drone that had always made it impossible, even for those standing shoulder to shoulder, to distinguish the faint whisper of each other's soul. A deep and mysterious urging told Joanna Cameron this was the morning she must leave before it did.

Epilogue

Who is Beth Garrison? She is the embodiment of all the unfinished women who live invisibly among us and she is the unfinished woman who lives secretly within us.

And the carriage house? It is that elusive place we have all raced by a thousand times on our blurred and hurried way to somewhere else and it is that quiet space buried deep inside that calls each of us back, time and time again, to the mysterious origin of our deepest longings.

June 28th, 1985 is simply a marker this author has placed along an otherwise seamless path that has no beginning and offers no end. It is an interlude prepared for the stillness and the stirring; a provocative whisper beckoning us closer to ourselves and to each other—the women of big cities and the women of small towns—the overachievers and the undervalued—those living in luxury and others on shoestring budgets—too many suffering in silence, too often numb to their own pain.

You have seen her and she has seen you. She is the woman on the corner waiting for the bus. She is the woman in bed waiting to be held. She is every woman who has ever waited for everyone and everything that *couldn't* or *wouldn't* wait and she is every woman who has waited until she could wait no more. She is bitter and resentful. She is loving and kind. She has been frozen and forgiving with her body. She has been frozen and forgiving in her heart. She is your mother, your daughter, your sister, your best friend. She is your closest confidante and your fiercest competitor—the woman you have envied, the woman you have pitied, the woman you have feared. She is the woman you have known all your life until one day—without warning—she becomes the woman you never knew at all.

We stand in front of each other on checkout lines. We sit behind each other at school plays. We maneuver beside each other in fitting rooms—careful not to meet the other's eyes—fearful that in them we will see the haunting reflection of our own unfinished lives.

But we needn't feel exposed and we mustn't be ashamed. Sooner or later every woman stands naked in her denial. Sooner or later there is no place left for her to hide. However different the hour, however distinct the need, she will emerge from her prolonged sleep and wake to her own truth. She will roll over onto her side and turn away from everything familiar—no longer the woman she was—not yet the woman she yearns to be. Whether she sleeps alone or shares her bed, there is no safety in her passage nor security in promises. She will likely die a thousand deaths to be born along the way.

We must be there for her awakening—the unfinished women who are dearest to us and the unfinished women who are strangers to us. Every morning we must rise from our own beds and throw open our windows to cast the wisdom we ourselves have borrowed and pledge our hearts to another struggling to become. We must remind her to breathe. We must reassure her—in all that is forsaken, all will be well. We alone are each other's comfort. We together are each other's proof that somewhere out there one among us sits at her piano in the window of her carriage house, the music of her soul providing accompaniment for our own.

To those who would argue that Beth Garrison's story requires a far too extraordinary leap of faith, my only response is a quiet smile. I've not yet met a woman who'd say that her own unflinching journey inward had ever demanded anything less.

Michelle Horwitz

Printed in the United States
143833LV00003B/3/P

9 781606 104965